ASHES
A WORLD'S FAIR SAGA

TIMOTHY LYON

PEAK PUBLISHING

PENNSYLVANIA

Please direct all mailed inquiries to:
Timothy Lyon Jr
PO Box 221
Pittsfield PA 16340
www.timothylyonjr.com

ISBN: 978-0-9970907-6-5 (hardcover)
ISBN: 978-0-9970907-5-8 (paperback)
ISBN: 978-0-9970907-4-1 (ebook)

My books may be purchased in bulk for promotional, educational, or business use. Please contact author@timothylyonjr.com for more information.
Cover designed by Timothy Lyon Jr.
Map designed by Kesara Bandara J.M
Edited by Alyssa Matesic (developmental editing), Lisa Gilliam (line/copyediting), and Rachel Sappie (proofreading).

This book shows that despite having big dreams,
we're not too little to find them.

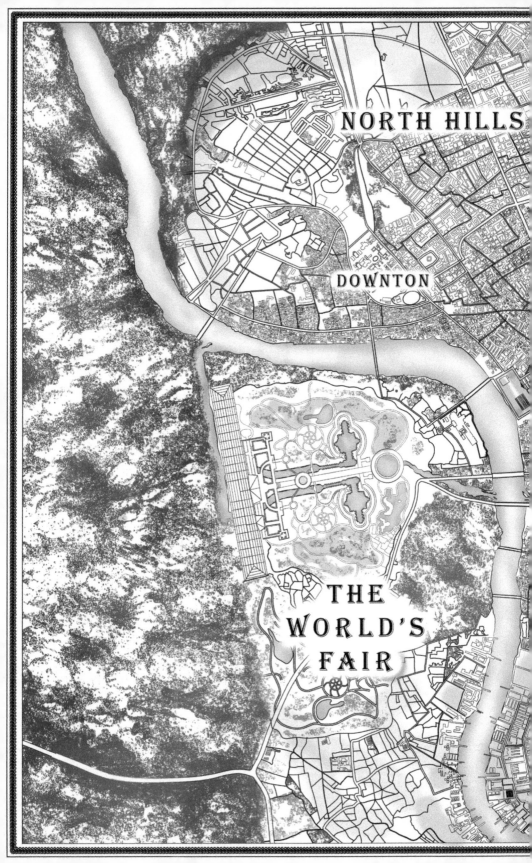

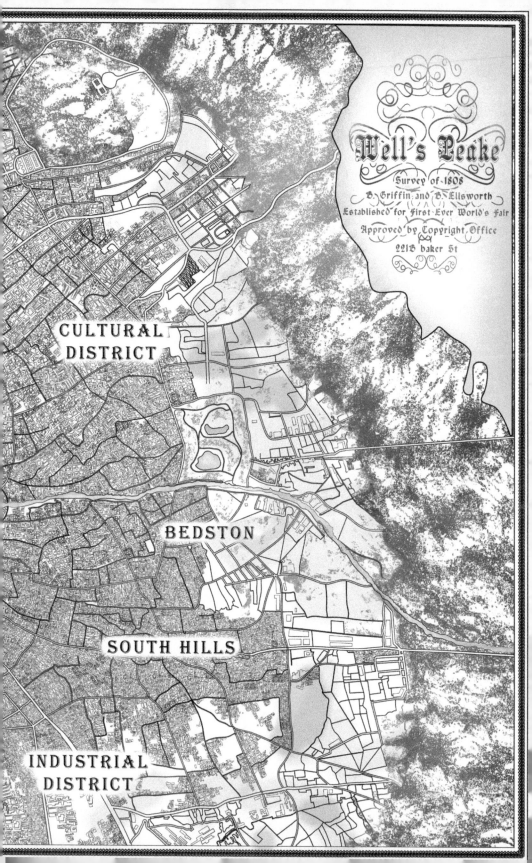

ASHES

A WORLD'S FAIR SAGA

PROLOGUE

Day and Night Pass, 1797

Someday, you'll follow your own dreams."

A girl ran through the forest snow, as high as her knees, yet it did not slow her pace. A plop came from behind, and with a pearly smile and red cheeks, she turned to a boy who raised his head from under the snowstorm, shaking his face clear with a smudged grin.

She chuckled and skipped to him as the moonlight danced through branches of pine needles. She brushed his hat off and peered into his hazel eyes, looking like a kid who got caught in the pantry.

"Are you sure we should be outside this late?" she asked.

"Yes! We are almost ten," he said. "Believe me, your best friend. You'll want to see this."

She held out her hand and helped him to his feet. They played through the frigid forest, passing the iced tips of branches and pine cones, the moon's halo lighting their way. They slowed to a walk as they passed the tree line, where meadows of unharvested wheat stood still, covered in white bliss.

"Aren't you scared?" she asked.

"Of course, but that can't stop us." The boy tightened his scarf, sniffling in the chill.

She looked at him, her toes tingling.

On a normal evening, she would be asleep, stuffed under a thick blanket, dreaming of books. The boy was not one to sneak out, especially in the frost season, but whatever it was must be important, judging by the grin on his face.

"Now, can you tell me?" she asked.

"Not yet. I want to surprise you."

"And it's about my dream?"

He glanced at her, his eyes catching the moonlight. "You'll see."

The boy grabbed the girl's hand, and they walked through the thicket and pushed wheat from their path down the rolling hill, the forest wrapping around the field. Ice snapped off the grain, showering the children as flakes danced from the clouds.

At the foot of the valley rested a blue magician's tent with white stripes, oil lamps illuminating the fabric, and a cobblestone road that led into the countryside.

The girl tugged on his jacket, stumbling in place. "What is this?"

The boy straightened his hat. "Mum and Dad took me to a magic show. The magician, she did a trick with this thing."

"What thing?"

"An invention. The one you're always talking about."

"From my book?"

"Yeah, and they said they were leaving tomorrow. I didn't want you to miss it."

The girl gasped and wrapped her arms around him. He blushed, and she strutted down the hill without him.

He shook his head, sprinting after her. She slipped, laughing as she picked herself up, the boy at her heels as they rushed to the road.

They patted their feet against the cobblestone, snow falling off their coats. As they walked towards the tent, the girl stopped, yanking the boy back by the collar.

"What's wrong?" he asked, loosening his scarf around his neck.

"It's different now that we're up close. Maybe we shouldn't be doing this."

"It's okay. We're just looking, right?"

"Yeah, but—"

"But what?"

"Like, is this what you want?"

"No, but this is what you do." The boy looked to the tent.

The wind blew, and the tarp whipped against wooden beams, the fire lighting the tent's entrance.

A heaviness filled her stomach, and she grabbed the bottom of her jacket with reddened fingertips. Closing her eyes, her hand warmed as the boy clutched hers. She nodded with a smile, and they entered the tent.

Never had she seen something so elegant. The stripes were in line with the velvet chairs, and the carpets lined each row, stretching to the center stage. Silk curtains swooned in the slight breeze from slits in the canvas.

The kids rushed down the aisle with a few dim oil lamps lighting their way, the shadows dancing behind them.

The girl twirled, gaping at stripes that circled above her, like a toy spinner her sister had given her. She slowed to a stop, pulling on her cheeks and giggling, the room still spinning around her.

The boy rubbed his hand along the fresh-cut birch, and the fragrance of rose petals lingered from the stage.

"Look at this," she said.

The boy turned, and she picked up a hat off the floor. It had a rounded crown and a hardtop, crafted with black felt. She brushed the dust off the brim, the fabric smooth under her fingertips. She set it on her head, posing as it slid over her face. "What do you think?"

The boy gulped and pulled on his scarf. "Wow, it's beautiful. Won't someone wonder where it is?"

"It was on the floor. They must have forgotten it."

The boy walked to her and rubbed the rim of the hat. "I've never seen one like it."

"Well, you can't have it. I saw it first."

"Indeed." He smiled, admiring the piece.

The girl pulled the hat off and tugged it over his head, over his soft cap. "But you can wear it for now. It's too big for me." She brushed it.

3

The boy shrugged, pushing it high enough to see. "Everyone needs a good hat."

The girl pointed at him and punched his shoulder. "So, where is this thing you have to show me?"

"Over here." The boy hopped up, holding out his hand.

She bit her lip. "Aren't you scared?"

"Yeah, you?" The boy lifted her on stage.

"Yes."

They stepped to the red drape and peeked behind the curtain.

A machine rested center stage, with a heavy blanket over the top.

"You should look," the boy said.

"Me?"

"Yes. It's your dream. Mum says it only takes one moment to make a difference. This is yours."

The girl giggled and stepped towards the cloaked apparatus, the wood creaking under her step. Her stomach tingled, and her hands felt light. Could it be what she always wanted? To see a picture in a book was one thing, but to see what she never thought could be...

"Wait, no." She stopped.

"Why?"

"Tell me first."

"Tell you what?"

"What's your dream? If my dream is to invent and change the future, and this is where it comes true, you can't follow it anymore. I don't want you to not have one. You can't follow my dream forever, you know?"

"I can try." The boy shrugged and gazed around the stage. He ran his hand across the brim of the hat. "I don't—"

"There has to be something." She grabbed his hands, shaking them.

"I... *want* to have a dream like yours. An idea that will change the world."

The girl leaned in and kissed him on the cheek. "That's a start."

The boy leaned back with an open mouth, blushing.

She turned around. "I want us both to enjoy this."

He nodded and walked over, grabbing the blanket with her. In one swift pull, they whipped it off, and it fell to the hardwood.

A blue glow glistened in the girl's eyes, and she lost herself to the machine.

Its essence was peaceful, calmer than anything she had ever experienced. Like wrapping herself in a blanket by the fireplace after a day's walk in the forest.

She kneeled, and the boy stared, lost in his trance until she touched his hand, and he joined her, never looking away from the blue aura spinning inside the middle of a circular machine.

They sat in silence as the night settled.

"I want to invent," she said. "To fix the lands from the Black Harvest, to make a machine that will change the world, in every way possible."

The boy slipped his fingers between hers. "I promise to get you there."

She rested, her pale blue eyes drifting to him. "Alek…"

He shifted to her, breathing easy and calm.

"Always remember that promise for me, please." A tear slid down her cheek.

Alek nodded, catching the hat before it slid off his head.

The two turned to the machine, holding hands as the blue aura and hum cascaded over them.

Water surged through pipes of hand-blown glass held together with copper braces and couplings. A machine hummed loudly, stretching across the room where polished couplings fused into a man's flesh, like tree roots over a rock in the forest.

Raymond thrashed as water rampaged into his stripped body, shaking, shivering as far as the restraints allowed, tightening as the overspray soaked into the leather binding.

A strangled gurgle escaped from his trembling lips, and his eyes, faded and desolate, glistened like hollowed emeralds. Veins bulged out of his skin, and his feet twisted above the floor. He clenched the armrests, his fingernails digging into the wood grain until his body went limp.

The clank of a closed valve echoed in his ears. The roar of the machine grew soft, and a wet musk lingered in the air, the fluid sloshing in waves within the tubes.

Raymond's tongue was raw as if someone had rubbed a file in his mouth, leaving behind a metallic aftertaste. Water streamed down his cheeks as his vision refocused, his muscles burned, and his head hung back towards the white oak ceiling, unflinching, unable to breathe.

After what felt like an eternity, Raymond breathed in shallow gasps, shivering from either the terror or the chill. He was unsure.

Droplets dripped down his bruised body, battered past his young age, his hands and feet white from the restraints.

He gathered some strength to lift his gaze long enough to stare at the blur before him, holding the lever.

A masked man stood with an empty stare and perfect posture. The mask narrowed like a slender face, designed with blue-and-silver beads, resembling rain on a window at night, and ripples like waves under the moonlight.

The man walked with precise steps, his chest out, a dark jacket snug to his body, opening down to a vest with thin gold lacing, watching in silence.

Raymond leaned forward, his heart throbbing against his rib cage. "Please... stop. I've done nothing."

The masked man glared, unmoving in an unsettling still.

Raymond could sense the emptiness, the void behind the mask. It unnerved him, made him want to bite his lip or rub his hands, but the fatigue and restraints held him. He wanted peace.

Memories flooded his thoughts, ones of happiness and comfort, anything to ease the suffering he endured.

Raymond convulsed, coughing, his lungs pounding, the pain returning as blood and water dripped onto his chest.

"Why?" he gasped, trying to catch his breath. "You can have the research. Just stop. Please!" Raymond sobbed, but it was hard to tell where the water ended and his tears began.

The masked man glanced over his shoulder, a gasp muffled behind the mask. "This moment was inevitable. We can guide the world, but you have misled it."

The masked man paused in a chilling silence, turning to the table with a pencil and paper. He jotted several notes and stepped to the far side of the room. With a firm pull on a hidden lever, sections of paneling dropped into the floor.

Raymond opened his eyes, looking to blocks of ice with frosted corners. Shadows of objects rested within, some human and others mechanical. Raymond swallowed hard, peering to his torturer.

"Do you know who *you* were meant to be?" The man tapped on the ice. "It's something most, if not all, struggle to understand. The need for belonging in a world that sees us as nothing more than a leaf in the wind. Each leaf has a purpose, and on occasion, those leaves fall before the harvest, shaken from the branch."

The masked man walked to the desk's edge, looking at Raymond.

"They do not deserve to fall onto the forest floor so soon before the world can see them on the old oak. You are someone who would have shaken not leaves but branches from the tree."

The masked man strode over, picked up a chair, and carried it with the utmost posture, ensuring not to scuff the carpet. He set it across from Raymond with elegance. He grabbed a handkerchief and wiped away a tear, maybe just water, off Raymond's cheek.

Raymond sat there, staring into the empty slits of the mask, unable to see the man's eyes or hear any breathing.

Raymond's head grew heavy, his breath fading thin.

"I apologize. I thought I gave you a quick death." The masked man rose. "I won't make that mistake again."

The man's words were elegant and serene, but a distortion rested within, sounding as if he was something more than human.

Raymond's eyes widened, and he tensed his neck, the leather strap clenching his skin. "There's no need to do this. I don't—"

"It's okay. It's not your fault or my fault. It'll be over soon, and you will find yourself floating, like a leaf in the harvest wind."

Raymond's eyes, once green, were gray, and his face sagged with bruises.

His jaw shivered as hope fled his thoughts. He tried to speak, but no words came, his body broken and soul crushed.

"I wish there had been a different choice." The masked man reached for the water valve and waited. "But they must know the dark side of nature."

Raymond found the strength to glance once more, his head fatigued.

Raymond sobbed in silence, shaking.

The masked man yanked the valve, clanging it against the metal.

No!

Icy water erupted in the pipes and surged into Raymond's body, battering within. Water spouted from the corners of his eyes, and his hands thrashed, the restraints cutting deep into his wrists, blood dripping down the chair.

After a moment of agony, the masked man shut off the valve and paused, holding his hand high. Raymond sat lifeless in his chair. No sobs, no breath.

Just silence.

He walked forward, pulling the cloth from his pocket, lifting Raymond's head from the backrest, and wiping his cheeks dry of tears and water.

The masked man stared at the floor, pausing while a tear dropped from below the mask.

"I'm sorry."

CHAPTER ONE

Well's Peake, 1810

Excuse me, pardon me!"

Aleksandar whipped through the crowd of the World's Fair, gardens lining the path, the wind catching his hat. He snatched it out of the air and tugged it tight, carrying a bag of couplings and seals on his back. His jacket flapped in the wind, and the breeze brushed against his reddened cheeks.

"Pardon me!" Aleksandar squeezed between two patrons, one raising his arms.

"Watch yourself!" he said, steadying himself on the white gravel.

"Indeed, sir. My apologies!" Aleksandar rounded an oak tree and a marble fountain by the river flowing from the hills to the center of the city and found himself at the grand entrance of the World's Palace. He slid to a stop as the gravel shifted under his shoes. He adjusted his jacket and checked his watch.

Five minutes.

Aleksandar pulled off his hat and pushed his acorn hair back as it waved in the cool breeze of the harvest season. His hazel eyes shined in the light, looking to the palace's tinted green glass.

The Heron Forest rose behind the World's Palace on the same hills that surrounded the great city, nearly engulfing it and spreading for a hundred kilometers in each direction before finding another city as grand as the Peake. It held the city in its valleys and hills, a center point for trade and the harvest it produced on the eastern side.

Aleksandar pulled his hat tight and sprinted off, slowing only as thousands of fairgoers flooded into the hall's grand doors. The floors, pristine with fresh-cut stone, glimmered as Aleksandar watched his steps, making sure not to trip on a random foot.

He forced himself through the crowd, knocking his knee on a hat stand. He sighed and bent down, rubbing it as the ache dulled, and lifted his head, his lips parting as he noticed the collection of hats.

Aleksandar leaned forward and rubbed his hand on the rim of a new flat cap; the felt underneath his fingertips soft and fresh. He closed his eyes and lowered his head.

Aleksandar patted the hat and walked across the aisle into his corner booth, hanging his hat on a coat rack and pulling out his pocket watch.

Exhibits, dressed in red-and-orange curtains pulled apart in the middle by golden ropes, lined the hallway as far as the eye could see.

Two minutes.

Aleksandar hummed like a tuned instrument and pulled the couplings from his bag, setting them on his workbench and locking the remaining hoses into the base of his newest invention.

The Red Breath.

He attached hoses that spiraled into refurbished valves and three speared nozzles. He checked to make sure he assembled his invention well, knowing the judges would be close enough to see the glory, to see the danger.

Aleksandar peered to the World's Fair as he did the future, with promise and ambition. His presentation had to be flawless. He snagged the perfect slot with the most potential from the afternoon crowd, knowing most people would arrive then. From his pinstriped button-up to his jet-black tie, his attire was to captivate not only the spectators but the judges, who held his future in the palm of their hands.

Aleksandar secured the last nozzle and stood with his first sense of calm since that morning.

A cough came from behind him, and he turned, eyes wide.

Five judges stood there, the middle man with a golden band sewn into the brim of his hat, and stared with arms crossed.

"Um, my apologies." Aleksandar rubbed his thumbs on the tips of his fingers. A photographer attempted several photographs as the middle judge waved his hand, silencing the crowd behind them.

"I believe it's now or never," one judge said, checking her watch.

"I'm all set." Aleksandar stood tall, rubbing his pant leg. "Thank you for your patience. I didn't realize there was a change to the required couplings."

"Be sure to check the regulations. This is your only exception, Mr. Scott."

"Indeed."

The middle judge straightened his long teal jacket, the same material all the judges modeled. The women had their hair pulled back while the men sported hats, from flattops to porkpies. A woman with a rose-handled cane watched with a bowler hat.

The middle judge stepped forward and pulled out a distinguished notepad and a pencil. He caught the dull tip and pulled it back and forth on the pencil sharpener at the end of the board.

Aleksandar took a breath.

"Mr. Scott, thank you for performing here today at the World's Fair," the judge said. "We are excited and privileged that you have entered this month's exhibition. My colleagues and I are most curious about your practice with the elements. Would you be kind enough to explain the principles for those unfamiliar?"

"Indeed," Aleksandar said. "Elemental study has three definitive principles: creation, control, and manipulation. The first is misleading in the sense that we cannot actually create the elements. Creation is the process in which we attract the element to an apparatus, like water on the top of a glass, sticking as it goes over the rim. The second principle is control. We define control as a state of stabilization. It's a challenge, whether it be fire, water, or air."

"What about earth?" a judge asked. "I was under the impression there were four essential elements."

"Only a few inventors study the elements. From personal experience, earth has proven to be the most difficult because of its diversity. I've heard of little success and found none myself with that element."

Aleksandar paused as the crowd looked with examining eyes. He gulped and moved his hands in ways he thought helped. "The third principle is manipulation. After we take control of the element, we try to manipulate it into what we want it to do."

"If you have control, is that element not already manipulated?" the chief judge asked.

"To have control means we've stabilized an element. Manipulation takes a device—what we call a controller—to affect the element to our will. An example is if we could use a device to lift water into the air, guiding it around with our machine."

Aleksandar's smile never wavered, despite his chest tightening with every question. He turned a few knobs and aligned several valves on his device. Meter-long, funnel-shaped pipes and hoses connected to the nozzle, leading to the mixed oil and solution canister.

Aleksandar held a match he'd concealed in his sleeve, revealing it like a magician. He picked up an igniter strip and lit it, the tip bursting with life, and guided it to the end of the device. A small flame caught above the nozzle. He turned around and rested his palm on a lever.

The one judge stepped forward. "Is this the flamethrower that people are mentioning?"

Aleksandar smiled. "I give to you… the Red Breath."

He yanked the lever, and the machine hissed. Fuel spiraled out of the nozzle, and fire ignited behind his display. He held his hand over his brow as fire danced in his amber eyes.

The judges watched and gasped as fire roared into the air, shadows dancing behind them from its brightness, drawing the fair's attention.

A spark flashed from a nozzle, and a piece of metal clanked on the floor. Aleksandar cleared his throat as his stomach grew heavy. He watched as small amounts of fluid dripped to the floor, then spewed out in a steady stream.

Oh.

Pulling up his sleeves, he rushed and slid under his device as the fire surged above him, the heat battering from above. He looked at the piece, realizing a pressure valve had broken.

Not good.

Aleksandar caught the judges' glance and hurried. He grabbed a mallet and wrench off the workbench and shifted under his device, the heat bearing down on him. He latched the wrench on the underside and smacked the end with the mallet. The machine hissed, and the flame grew, singeing the bottom of the red curtain hanging on the display.

Sweat dripped off Aleksandar's brow, and he closed another valve on the broken nozzle, hitting the end of the wrench again.

He jumped to his feet, the flames growing in the other nozzles, and rushed to the main lever, closing it with force. The fire dwindled and sputtered out, the metal creaking as it cooled. Aleksandar wiped his forehead and turned to the judges, who watched with wide eyes.

The chief judge let out a chuckle with a slow smile. "Well, that was close."

Aleksandar rolled his shoulders, his shirt sticking to the sweat on his arms. "And that is why you have secondary shut-off valves."

The judges gawked at each other, and one stepped back.

Aleksandar stood, breathless, glancing at the Red Breath and feeling the heat in his cheeks. He wanted to rub his pant legs or pull on the edge of his vest but waited aimlessly.

The chief judge held a smirk, jotting down notes in his notepad. He finished his sentence with a hard mark and looked at Aleksandar. "Mr. Scott, what was your reasoning behind creating the Red Breath?"

Aleksandar cocked his head, batting his gaze to the other judges, who looked as stunned as him.

"I created the Red Breath because of the Black Harvest. The fields took years to rest before they could be traveled and even longer for the farmers to till again. While fields outside the city are now safe, those in remote areas could still be tainted. The only way to ensure the fields are safe is to burn them to the roots and wait for them to grow on their own."

"Don't you think that's a little extreme?"

"It's no different than a forest fire. If the fields don't recover on their own, then they need to be burned again, making sure the black is gone. With my invention, farmers can be given cleansed fields and till again, bringing Well's Peake back to the agricultural titan it was. My flamethrower can do just that. This could be a no-contact means of burning the fields and preventing further spread."

"And how long could your machine last? Whoever would use it will be in the field."

"On a single tank, it can last for an hour with a constant stream. My fuel source is inexpensive to make and very effective."

The chief judge wrote a few more lines.

Aleksandar's gut was restless and seemed hollow as he took in the smell of heated oil and warm steel. His heartbeat was so strong; he felt his pulse in his fingertips.

The primary judge stepped forward, extending his hand. Aleksandar shook it with a light grip.

"You performed well, Mr. Scott," the judge declared. "While not flawless, you were quick on your feet and prepared. I can appreciate that."

"Thank you. This was a great privilege. The others don't seem as open to the situation as you."

The judge leaned in. "And that is why *I'm* lead judge."

Aleksandar let out a shy laugh, finding his smile.

"You performed well. Keep your head up."

"Thank you."

The judge tipped his hat and walked away with the remaining judges, their conversation muffled in the crowd.

Aleksandar gnawed his jaw and stretched his neck. He wandered to his invention, double-checking to see that everything was still in place. He glanced over his shoulder, catching the judges huddled in a circle, one glancing at Aleksandar with a stern brow.

What a disaster… Who would invest now?

Aleksandar soaked in his doubt, his hands on his hips and head down.

What went wrong? Yes, the couplings changed last moment, but that shouldn't have altered the machine's performance. The scaled-down version had no issues, and there was no sign of structural weakness—

"That was quite the display, my dear fellow," a man said with a booming voice.

Aleksandar snapped from his thoughts and turned to the man, over two meters high and twice his mass, towering over him. His trimmed beard reached to his boulder-like chest. With a shaved head and eyes as rich as whiskey, light caressed over his shoulders.

"Thank you," Aleksandar said. "Are you... Bernard Griffin?"

"I am," Bernard said with a husky and aged voice. "And you're Aleksandar Scott, the young inventor."

The man extended his burly hand, a bronze bracelet on his wrist, and Aleksandar took it in disbelief. Bernard's grip was firm but smooth and uncalloused for a man who looked like he could pull carriages on his back.

"I can't believe it. You're always on the front page, changing the city like it's simple. I can't express what an honor this is." Aleksandar let go, realizing he'd shaken the man's hand far too long, and let out a nervous laugh.

Wrinkles stretched from the corners of Bernard's eyes. He sported a burgundy jacket lined with two rows of buttons down the front and a chain hung from his pocket, a watch most likely on the inside.

"There is no need to flatter me, Mr. Scott. I'm simply enjoying myself."

"Yes, but what you observe today might be your greatest investment tomorrow."

Bernard chuckled. "I like that. Please allow me to use it in the future." Bernard turned to the Red Breath. "I caught your performance. That was rather impressive."

Aleksandar rubbed the back of his neck. "Um, I'm not sure it left much of an impression."

Bernard bent down, looking at the Red Breath. "Maybe to some, but we all see life differently, do we not?"

"I suppose so."

"You believe your mishap to be a hindrance when in reality it enhanced your performance. There's a certain beauty found in recovery, something Well's Peake endures well." Bernard leaned closer to Aleksandar's invention, running his fingers through the end of his beard. "I found it rather exciting. It could use some refinement, but the concept is there."

Aleksandar stared with unblinking eyes and a dry throat. What could Well's Peake's most influential man find so curious in his work? In an inventor who couldn't seem to follow or find basic regulations? In someone who struggled to understand his own passion?

"Mr. Griffin, I hope this doesn't come off rude, but you are, well, Bernard Griffin. I didn't expect to capture the attention of someone so influential."

"I guess this is rather unusual to just show up. To be honest, Mr. Scott, I'm interested in knowing why you do what you do. I've heard of your potential, and I'm a rather curious fella. What do you wish to achieve at the World's Fair? What motivates you?"

Aleksandar held his breath for a moment and walked to Bernard's side, both looking to the Red Breath. "Um, I want to offer the world something meaningful. I believe a few never received their chance to give the world what they have. When I have an idea, I feel obligated to share it."

"That's a grand gesture. An elegant dream, but dreams of that size do not come without intimate victories. What would you personally like to do? What inspires you to create every day?"

Aleksandar paused as he tried to find an answer to Bernard's question, trapped in his indecision and meandering thoughts.

Bernard eyed the young inventor without turning his head. "It's okay. I put you on the spot, and I apologize for that. I know it is not a simple question."

"Yeah, I'm not sure."

"That's all right, Mr. Scott. Everyone has their reasons."

"I just want to do my part in helping."

"Now that I can understand. Thank you for indulging my curiosity." Bernard turned with a slight bow. "To know how people work and understand their motivations helps me in my own endeavors. I feel we all have ambition; whether we act on it, that drives us to leave something behind that people will embrace."

Aleksandar nodded and turned to the glory of the World's Fair. Inventors from the Eastern Mountains to the Western Hills showcased inventions from their cultures. Some wore cloaks embroidered with images of lotuses, cherry blossoms, and fish, more natural in designs. Several from the Western Hills were more rigid but just as elegant in their clothing. They focused on the button-ups, high collars, and vests.

Each of their inventions had a unique look, some smooth in fashion, others rough-cornered but sturdy.

Aleksandar glanced at Bernard. "Do you think my invention could make a difference?"

"I think you can best answer your question."

"I'd like to think so because I *need* to win this exhibition if I wish to continue inventing. With the sponsorship, I could fund my workshop and ideas."

"We shall see this afternoon. Are you going to Mr. O'Connell's presentation?"

"I didn't plan on it."

"You should."

Aleksandar looked down the hallway at the stage in the center hall, the crowd growing with fairgoers.

A few patrons gawked in his direction. They nodded, and a few covered their mouths. A mom pointed her child in Aleksandar's direction.

"They are looking to you, right?" Aleksandar asked.

"You've been talking, as you say, to the most influential man in Well's Peake. People grow curious about those who speak with me."

"Why would you give your attention to me? People talk about you or Mr. O'Connell."

"I don't think people are talking about just me, Mr. Scott. Not anymore."

Aleksandar cracked a smile, his dimples catching the sunlight. His heartbeat quickened, and he felt a weight taken off his chest. Aleksandar noticed a strange shadow in the corner of his eye, moving behind his invention. He watched, thinking it was just someone in the crowd, but the shadow hovered behind his machine.

"Pardon me."

Aleksandar rounded the workbench and found a stout man crouched, about his age, tinkering with the Red Breath. He condensed the hose and pushed it together as if he expected it to get shorter. A worn-out cap covered his eyes, and he reached—

"What are you doing?" Aleksandar swatted the man's hand away from the pipe.

The man tried to stand but stumbled to the floor, a coupling clanging on the marble. He landed hard on his rump and pulled his collar up, like a child caught stealing his mother's chocolates.

Bernard walked around the bench, towering over both men.

Aleksandar checked his invention, ensuring his work wasn't compromised, and there was no chance of another incident. "You can't be messing with this. What were you doing?"

The young man's face went pale under his untamed beard, swallowing quiet words. His forest-green eyes shifted back and forth. "I'm sorry. I have, uh... I shouldn't have." The man crawled back.

"Do you know what could have happened?"

"The valve broke because of the slack in the hosing. It wasn't taut, and the extra hosing left too much room to move."

"That's not—what?" Aleksandar said, exhaling hard.

Aleksandar watched as the man paused, his hands shaking and head down. The man's jacket and hat, split at the seams, were two sizes too small.

"Are you an inventor?" Aleksandar held out his hand.

"I know only what I've seen," the young man said.

Aleksandar lifted the young man to his feet.

With one arm crossed against his chest, Bernard stroked his beard.

"Mr. Griffin," Aleksandar said, "I'm sorry to ignore you."

"It's all right, Mr. Scott." Bernard tilted his head. "What is your name?"

"Hugh. Hugh Evans." He looked between the two.

"Well, Mr. Evans, there's an exhibition Mr. Scott and I must attend, and we would be delighted if you accompanied us."

"You want *me* to join you?" Hugh rubbed his forehead.

Aleksandar looked to Bernard with lifted eyebrows, his face as blank as a new canvas. His mind raced with questions, but no answers came. Moments ago, he'd sprinted through the fair, hoping to make it to his exhibition before it was too late. Now he stood by a man that Well's Peake held high, and another who seemed overlooked from South Hills, and all Aleksandar could do was gawk, pulling on his collar.

"Don't you agree, Mr. Scott?" Bernard asked with a grin.

Aleksandar looked to Hugh, his thoughts like leaves in the wind. "Um, yes. Yes, indeed."

CHAPTER TWO

Natalia's footsteps clicked as she walked across the wood stage. Her satin vest was flawless and tailored with floral embroidery reminiscent of the finest gardens.

Sapphires reflected off her cuff links as she pulled them straight in the afternoon's sunlight, and her blue tie was snug tight under her popped collar, matching her eyes.

She stomped her boot twice and raised her hands in showmanship. "Ladies and gentlemen, welcome... to the World's Fair!"

The crowd of hundreds roared with applause as Natalia took a bow. With an enticed grin and a gleam in her eye, she guided their attention to her invention.

Cheers echoed down the marble hallways of the World's Palace. It stood two hundred and fifty feet tall at its center, crafted high with stone supports shaped like tall oaks, reaching for the heavens. The stone branches held the glass ceiling as light cascaded to the exhibitions, reflecting off specks of silver and salt in the marble floor.

A photographer captured the event, and Natalia nodded, palms steady and her head tilted back. She looked to the crowd, most clapping, but many men and women were missing a hand or an arm, while children had limp limbs, so they stomped or patted their sides.

Natalia caught the eyes of several dashing men and women and could not help but smirk with a perfected smile as they watched her as if she were a rare tulip.

"Mesdames, Mesdemoiselles, and my dear gentlemen. Thank you for your appreciation and for making the journey to Well's Peake for the first-ever World's Fair. I now *give* you the Steamrail."

Natalia flipped a switch on a control panel, and the Steamrail roared to life.

Steam burst from the engine's exhaust, the gears turned as pistons pulled, and the engine glimmered as it erupted with velocity and power.

The crowd stepped back, several picking up their children.

The Steamrail was held in place on beams while six wheels spun, three on each side, as pistons lifted and lowered in a balanced mechanical dance, steam searing out of the flue. A siren whistled, drawing every eye in the audience, and the arms circled the wheel like clockwork, the metal speeding up.

Natalia rubbed her chin, hiding part of her smile. She caressed her chestnut hair, ensuring it was still waving against her shoulders. She watched the crowd with pale moonlight eyes, biting the edge of her lip.

An older lady with a rose gold cane and a bowler hat limped to the golden ropes on the stage, pausing before the red-and-orange curtains, covering her mouth in awe.

Natalia flicked off the engine, and the steam simmered into the air. The wheels slowed to a stop, and the pistons hissed as they depressurized. The crowd applauded again, some keeping quiet. She stepped to the lip of the stage.

"If anyone has questions, I will gladly answer them," she said.

The older woman kept her head down, struggling to stay straight as her knee gave out. "How did you discover such a device?"

"It was about ten years ago. I was traveling through the Heron Province," Natalia said. "I was staying in Oakvale when a fire broke out below the water tower. The inn where I stayed was evacuated, and on the way out, I noticed a hissing noise, seeing steam escaping through the top."

Natalia paused, eyeing the dwindling crowd. "The cap launched hundreds of feet into the air, lost to the forest. This was when I realized steam builds pressure. Pressure creates energy, and with that energy, possibilities are endless. You have seen the Steam Engine run our machines and propel our boats, but now you will see them power our carriages across the lands."

Natalia paced across the stage. "I believed I could create a machine to redirect that energy, using it to propel carriages across the lands, without the need of horses, and with this idea, an engine was born: the Steamrail."

Natalia looked up to see the crowd dissipate, most moving to the fair's other exhibits, some preoccupied with kids, and a few stuck in their spot until the rest moved along the way.

Dread came over her, and her feet felt heavy as she held her arm. She waited for more questions that never came. Her smile dimmed, and her eyes wandered for anyone who wanted to greet her. After several long moments, she exhaled and lowered her gaze. She walked to her table, covered the switches, and secured a locking brace.

Reaching into her jacket, she pulled out a small journal and wrote about her invention's performance.

"So, why does an esteemed inventor showcase older inventions?" a man asked. "Why not something new?"

Natalia turned to a reporter walking up the stairs of the stage, his posture relaxed and hands in his pockets. He had a clean-cut face and ginger hair folded back with a thick balm, pressed at a high collar covering his taut neck.

He extended his cuffs and pulled out a pencil and notepad from the inside of his gray jacket.

Natalia forced a hard smile. "Because, Mr. Hawthorne, while the Steam Engine is not new, the Steamrail is. For some reason, many do not see the potential in a motorized carriage carrying them at the speed of horses across the Northern Regions."

"Ah." Mr. Hawthorne tilted his head.

Natalia watched as he avoided eye contact, jotting a note in his notebook.

"I'm not interested, Abel, but thank you," she said.

He paused and lifted his gaze. "You don't even know what I'm reporting."

Natalia pocketed her journal. "A few years ago, I would've considered an interview from the prestigious reporter who wrote *The Vine in the Valley* or *The Touch of Midnight Eve*, but I know the stories you write now."

"My stories are all based on truth."

"An article based on truth, and remaining true, are not related." Natalia grabbed her jacket off the rack and slipped it on, rubbing the underside of her cheek, catching a whiff of her berry perfume.

"My stories are of greatness and failure." Abel stepped forward. "Do not worry. I'm not keen on covering the Steam Engine that has been on display for how many years now? In the first-ever World's Fair, where people travel thousands of kilometers to see the cultures of the world, you present this?"

"It will be essential in the upcoming seasons. Imagine how quick they could have got here if the rail connected the cities of Belagrad and Redwood."

"With recent disappearances of well-known innovators and the inventors' forced reputation for being responsible for the Black Harvest, I think you have bigger things to worry about than traveling from one city to the next." Abel wandered to the engine and put his hand on his chest. "I would like to believe in your progress and that you still matter to the world."

"I'm surprised you haven't made that your headline."

"Even my editor has limits, and being the reason for mass panic during the World's Fair is not the legacy I wish to leave; unless needed."

"Abel, are you leading to something; or trying to scare me and tell me how old I am?"

"I'm lead reporter of the fair, and you're aware of what I could do for the inventress of steam power, who is now at the end of her prime?" Abel looked over his shoulder and smiled. "My editor covered you at your exhibitions, and I'm sure she'd love to see another story on you. We could help each other."

"I'm not interested."

Abel ran his hand on a piston, yanking it away from the hot metal. "Why do you insist on presenting this hunk of tin? Well's Peake is flourishing and craves the unfamiliar. You have what they want."

Natalia stepped to Abel's side and looked to the Steam Engine. "This was a favor for a friend. It is untapped potential and will soon revolutionize the transportation trade."

"Maybe, but more efficient ways of power are coming. Look at Giovanni or the mad electrician in Belagrad. This invention is half a decade old."

"They are still perfecting their methods. The Steam Engine is more capable than you give it credit."

"Your wood box on metal wheels does not impress me. All I've seen of it is from the wave of your hand."

"We do not complete a project of its size overnight."

"Who is *we?*" Abel leaned in and walked behind the Steamrail.

Natalia glanced into the distance. Bystanders watched with wide eyes and raised brows. A couple argued about how terrifying her machine was, cursing from behind her hand.

Natalia turned back to Abel, who inspected her engine with a crooked smile.

"It's being integrated as we speak," she said.

Natalia could feel Abel's lingering gaze. She brushed a few specks off her sleeve and pulled on the bottom of her vest.

Abel circled the invention, dragging his pencil along the workbench, scratching the varnish.

"Abel." Natalia tapped her fingers on the back of her hand, eyeing the scuff he left.

The reporter stood straight and chuckled. "Why haven't you shifted back into the Elemental Race?"

"I no longer enjoy elemental technology. You should search the World's Fair. There are plenty of inventors who have the story you crave."

"Yes, but you offer us promise most can't. Why not the Lunarwheel? It has more potential than this pressurized can of metal." Abel looked through the gears of the invention, making brief eye contact.

Natalia tucked her hands into her pockets, her gaze never flinching.

"It's a shame because your legacy was spotless until its presentation."

"No inventor has a perfect career, but that shouldn't stop us from trying."

"According to my editor, at its reveal, it shattered into a thousand glass shards and flooded the nearby park. A failure like that casts long shadows. And why glass of all things?"

"First off, metal corrodes inside the Lunarwheel. Also, you're fishing, Abel, and you are *not* a smart fisherman. I wish you'd return to form."

Abel put his hands on his hips. "You were so close. Why quit?"

Natalia paused. "Because I had—I had greater aspirations."

A slight burn rose in Natalia's throat. It spread like wildfire in her chest, but she held her gaze with a gentle smile. Her mind wandered to find a hold on Abel's words, but her own vanished.

She walked to the Steamrail and secured more braces that held her invention in place. She pulled out her journal and wrote something quickly, tucking it away. Abel's gaze was there, she knew it, but she could not give him the satisfaction.

Abel stepped close and lowered his voice. "And that is why I haven't forgotten you. What do you write in that journal? Do you stare into the distance because the rumors of your memory are true?"

Natalia looked over her shoulder. "You create memories with your articles, and you take them for granted. You should keep that in mind when you are basing stories off truth."

Abel closed his flipbook with a sigh. "The World's Fair is here for only a few months, ending with the Harvest Festival. Do you think without your name in my headline, you'll be remembered after this? A new age is coming, Natalia, and you hold in your hand the invention to rewrite history. This could welcome a new renaissance, one of which we've never seen. Yet, you keep to yourself when you are ahead of the best. The trophies and recognition could be vast. We could restore your legacy."

Natalia faced Abel. "Trophies mean little in what we could achieve, and recognition is only good when you're not marked as detrimental to society. The Elemental Age is in its infancy. If you're right, then it will occur after my influence has passed."

"How about we stop playing and be honest with each other. Why don't you want this opportunity? The younger generation is here, thanks to the Black Harvest, but your influence doesn't have to fade amongst them. You only need to secure your legacy. I can make that happen."

Natalia paused, looking Abel in the eyes. "Some memories are best left in the past. Some shouldn't be changed."

Abel's eyebrows lowered. "That's a shame because you have so much potential. Look at Aleksandar Scott. He alone has made tremendous advances in a short period, and I'm certain we'll remember him long after he's gone. Wouldn't you like the same?"

"Mr. Scott is young and has much to learn," Natalia said. "He has potential, but his progress is slow."

"Mr. Scott will revolutionize Well's Peake if you don't. He'll captivate audiences that once belonged to you."

"Thank you for the consideration, but I will handle my legacy from here." Natalia held her palm out, directing him off the stage.

Abel blew air out his nostrils and walked to the edge. "If you change your mind—"

"I know where to find you."

Abel nodded and walked down the steps, joining the crowd.

Natalia stared, watching until her vision of the fair blurred, and her thoughts made no sense. Her mental grasp was cloudy, like fog in the sunrise. Abel's words were provocative with no substance, and she would not give him the reaction he wished.

Sweat ran down her back, and she rolled her shoulders to ease the tension. His words were significant, but she could hardly remember them. She pulled out her journal, reading her notes, fragments coming back. Natalia wrote what words of his remained, but they withered quickly. Just pieces of a lost legacy and how she was nearing the end of her career.

Her pale blue eyes widened as clarity returned. Moments ago, she had a crowd of hundreds lingering on her every word within the World's Palace, but now nothing. Not a single eye batted a glance, nor a single cheer.

Natalia rubbed her cheek and gazed beyond the glass ceiling of the fair to the sun caressing the edge of the hills in the afternoon's fog.

CHAPTER THREE

Aleksandar covered his invention with a heavy blanket, strapping the ends to the table corners. He clapped his hands once with a lingering thought, turning from the afternoon light reflecting off his invention.

"All set, Mr. Scott?" Bernard asked.

"Indeed."

"Excellent." Bernard took the lead and headed off.

Aleksandar pulled his jacket tight, and Hugh tried to keep pace with the young inventor, slowed by his shorter legs.

Aleksandar glanced at Hugh. His weathered face carried random divots and dips. A thin layer of grease-covered his forehead under his ragged hat, and Hugh wiped it clean with the cuff of his frayed shirt.

Aleksandar followed Bernard as they entered the growing mass. Bumping hips and "excuse me" became a ritual for several minutes.

Hugh leaned in, speaking over the crowd. "I'm sorry. I didn't mean to forget my place."

"No need to worry, Mr. Evans," Aleksandar said. "However, you should've told me what you thought instead of tinkering away. Most would have been more confrontational."

Hugh looked forward at nothing in particular. "That I know."

Aleksandar paused, questioning Hugh's last words. Bernard seemed intrigued with Hugh, and he might have an interesting story to tell. To learn what Hugh knew required some training.

"If you'd like, I'd be willing to teach you instead of you having to sneak around. Unless someone else is?" Aleksandar bumped his way through the crowd.

Hugh turned to Aleksandar with hopeful eyes. His unkempt beard did little to hide his reddened cheeks. "You would teach me?"

"If you're interested. I enjoy teaching, and I could use the practice myself."

"Yes. It would mean a lot." Hugh exhaled as his eyes opened.

"Well then, how about midday tomorrow? At my exhibit?"

"Okay."

Aleksandar and Hugh found their way between Bernard and a family who looked to the large stage with bright smiles, most of them missing their left arms. The youngest of the five children had both, but Aleksandar noticed the left was immobile as the one-armed daughter hugged her mother with no concern of her own.

Aleksandar turned to study the presentation area, which had orange curtains glistening in the sunlight. Three thick blankets covered a machine, with a glimmer of metal showing below the fabric, too low to see anything. With a crowd composed of people from around the world, the judges stood at a podium.

Aleksandar crossed his arms and pushed his tongue to the inside of his cheek, looking to Bernard. "They reserved this stage for the award ceremony and other major announcements. They still allow it for public displays, but it's booked months in advance. I don't know how Owen landed it for his presentation."

"I believe Chief Constable Dekker was going to speak on behalf of the city. Perhaps something more urgent took him away."

Aleksandar looked to the stage, Owen standing at the base of the stairs, chatting with a constable. The constable held up her arms, facing the crowd, and Owen checked something on her back, something Aleksandar could not see through the horde.

Owen picked up a cane and limped onto the stage with his amber tailcoat; one hand held high to the audience. The crowd broke out into applause.

Owen pulled on his thick, groomed mustache and caressed his clean-shaven chin, giving him great stature. He wasn't from the finest cloth in the city, but he knew how to look second best.

Homing in on Owen's wave to the crowd, Aleksandar swallowed hard and clapped with the rest.

"How did he do it?" Hugh asked.

"What do you mean?" Aleksandar looked his way.

"He made a future for himself. He has what he wants and everything he needs."

"I'm sure he doesn't have everything. There's always another ledge to climb."

"He doesn't seem like he's reaching for anything. How does he get by?"

"When you win the Innovator's Challenge two years straight and create a prosthetic leg that bends for those who lost theirs in the Black Harvest, it can set you up well. He also has a way of inspiring as much as he annoys. You see that after sharing the same stage for many years."

Bernard stepped behind them as the crowd stopped clapping. "Owen is like the rest of us. He struggles, he fails, and he prevails."

Hugh looked to Bernard and let out a deep breath, his eyebrow furrowed.

Aleksandar looked to both of them, letting his mind wander as Owen dropped from the stage, a few people greeting him with firm handshakes and pats on the shoulder. Owen limped on his cane through the crowd as they separated in his presence.

Aleksandar dropped his arms as Owen walked up to him.

"Mr. O'Connell." Bernard nodded.

"Mr. Griffin." Owen raised an eyebrow to Aleksandar. "And Aleksandar. Hello. This is a new pairing."

"Owen," Aleksandar said.

"We met only a moment ago, to be honest," Bernard said. "An ambitious young man like yourself. You two are the same age, yes?"

"I'm twenty-six." Owen rested on his cane. "Aleksandar is two years younger than I."

Bernard turned to Hugh, who no longer was there, lifting his eyebrows.

"Mr. Griffin?" Owen tilted his head.

"We had another in our company, but he seems to have slipped away. Another day, perhaps."

Aleksandar caught Owen's cologne, and that too was elegant, like baked cinnamon on apple cobbler.

"I'm surprised you're here," Aleksandar said with a dry throat. "I thought you were presenting."

"Soon, but it seems the judges are preoccupied. You must have given them something good to discuss. I noticed Mr. Griffin as well and wanted to say hello."

Aleksandar nodded. "Perhaps. I had a slight hiccup, so it didn't go as planned."

Aleksandar and Owen stared as the silence grew between them.

Bernard eyed the two inventors. "What are you presenting?"

"You'll see soon enough," Owen said. "Maybe you could help persuade Aleksandar to make the leap into the Industrial Revolution."

"I'm not sure that's for me," Aleksandar said. "It has some appeal, but elemental technology seems like something I need to do."

"I'm not sure. It seems like you'd do well in an established field without the risk and lack of the elements. We struggle enough with an inventor's reputation, let alone working in a new field."

"I think what I'm doing has potential."

"Potential that will be realized?"

"Yes, maybe my inventions will rival those of yours someday."

Owen snickered and glanced at the stage. "You shouldn't waste effort on something you're not sure about."

"You have no uncertainties?" Aleksandar sucked in his cheeks as an intense thirst kicked in.

"I calculate the risks. I know what inventions are harmful, not ones that could be."

"You can't know that. That's like getting all the thread and needle for a jacket, then not stitching it because you think it won't be good enough."

"When you know the jacket won't fit, there's no sense in making it."

Bernard held his hands out. "All right, that may be enough constructive criticism for one gathering. Mr. O'Connell, I believe the judges are ready."

Owen looked over his shoulder as the judges took their seats on the stage. "I agree. Another day, Alek."

"Indeed." Aleksandar glared with squinted brows.

Owen tipped his hat and walked to the stage, the crowd still watching him.

Aleksandar bit his lip and looked at the floor. No one could crawl under his skin like Owen. His snobby passiveness, smooth and tuned, like his ability to create and woo the masses. The investors, clothes, respect—all accommodations Aleksandar wished for, but Owen had.

"That didn't seem hostile." Bernard grinned.

Aleksandar chuckled.

Bernard searched the surrounding people. "Whatever happened to Mr. Evans?"

"Here." Hugh shifted his way through the crowd.

"What were you doing back there? I was afraid we lost you. Good, we shouldn't miss what's to come."

Aleksandar, with crossed arms, watched Owen limp onto the stage, lifting his cane as he took center stage. He raised his arms, and the crowd applauded. Owen carried his fine mustache well, accented by deep-set eyes. His hair was receded and somewhat messy, along with his loose tie, but it did not diminish his relaxed professionalism.

"Welcome, and thank you for attending on this lovely afternoon," he said. "My name is Owen O'Connell. I'd like to thank the panel of judges for being here today."

"Our pleasure." The chief judge lifted his hand. "In light of everything you do for Well's Peake."

"Yes, and today I plan to do more." Owen walked back and forth, raising his cane with grandeur, catching the light.

Aleksandar noticed Owen's limp worsen as he tried to hold himself tall.

"Three decades ago, Well's Peake, along with several others, experienced one of the darkest moments in history," Owen said. "The harvest that took away our fathers, our mothers, and our children. Today, many still experience the effects on our own bodies. So many struggle to walk and pick up their own children because of immobile limbs."

Owen stood still, looking at the crowd.

"We see those who now carry the black in their genes. However, today is the day we can give back to those who have suffered from the previous generation's mistakes. We can't take away the nightmares; we can't take away the loss or the humiliation from cruel people, but what I can do is give you hope. The promise of being able to walk and the hope of living a normal life. The hope of wanting to live again."

Owen tapped his cane off the stage. With the ferrule of his cane, Owen hooked the wool blanket and swooped it off, the light glimmering off his machine.

"I give you... the Limbs of Life." Owen posed.

The blanket fell to the floor, and Aleksandar's jaw dropped with it. The machine rested on a mannequin and had eight metal limbs, all connecting to a center brass piece, crafted like the human back. It was elegant and gleamed, the arms hunched together like a cradled spider.

Aleksandar lowered his arms and stepped forward.

Owen waved his cane, facing the crowd who looked on with unspoken questions and gaping awe. He stuck out his leg, lifting the pant leg to a metal brace adhered to his skin and on his knee in a bulb-shaped socket.

"When I was a young boy, I stumbled into a field of wheat contaminated by the Black Harvest," Owen said. "My right leg was infected, but luck was on my side. Due to the brave research of many, a treatment existed by then to ensure my leg could remain intact. I faced hardships for many years and know many have endured worse. With the Limbs of Life and the support of generous investors, I will give back to the victims of the Black Harvest. I will give them the ability to walk and move as they once did, or never have."

Owen turned a dial on the podium, and the arms sprang to life, all eight in simultaneous rhythm. Owen walked forward in prowess and bowed in a moment of applause, the crowd erupting.

Aleksandar became lightheaded, and his eyes grew dry from his lack of blinking.

Owen waved his hand, and a constable walked up from the crowd, the Limbs of Life strapped to her back. Aleksandar's lips parted as he noticed an additional brace on her neck that did not connect to the invention.

"This is Lydia May, renowned constable of the Peakeland Yard," Owen said. "She has been testing the Limbs of Life, and they have helped her in the line of duty. She suffers from a spinal infection, a symptom of the Black Harvest that her mother experienced firsthand. Watch as she shows you the possibilities of a new reality."

Lydia took a hard stance, hands at her sides, as a metal exoskeleton ran along her forearms and palms. Metal rings lined her knuckles, connected to the metal mechanism composed of gears, springs, and guide wires. She rolled her shoulders, lifting her head to the glass above.

She extended her fingers, and the metal arms matched her movements. Lydia took two steps forward, and with each, the brace glimmered at her ankles. Lydia opened her hands, and the bottom four limbs bent to the floor, lifting her into the air. She towered higher than anyone in the crowd, even Bernard.

Lydia waved her arm, and the machine mirrored her every movement.

Aleksandar pushed his way through the crowd, stopping only a few feet from the stage.

Owen walked underneath her. "We no longer need to suffer. While the Limbs of Life is a pinnacle example of what we can achieve, we can now design artificial limbs for those in need. I aim to create a new movement, one that will finally bring hope to our people, so we can leave the Black Harvest in the past. This is a change we can finally embrace."

The audience erupted into deafening applause. Owen raised his cane with a generous grin and held his palm against his chest.

Aleksandar's fingertips were cold as chills ran down his arms. Owen had done it again. He created something that would surpass Aleksandar's most promising dreams and work. The world would surround him, helping him onto his pedestal.

Bernard and Hugh found their way to Aleksandar's side as the applause softened.

"Mr. Scott?" Hugh leaned in.

"I'm sorry, what did you ask?" Aleksandar never turned away.

"What does this mean for you?"

The question should have hurt, but it had already crossed Aleksandar's thoughts. He wanted to answer, but he couldn't accept the possibility of losing. He'd put so much effort into the Red Breath. The reality of not making the next step…

A heavy weight filled his chest.

"Was that not an incredible demonstration?" Bernard asked with much gusto.

"It was." Aleksandar nodded. "Owen always leaves an impression."

"That he does. He's asking for revitalization, and he will have it."

Hugh looked at Bernard with raised eyebrows. "You say that like fairness is everywhere. People in the South Hills will never see it."

"Mr. Evans." Aleksandar raised his voice.

"It's all right, Mr. Scott." Bernard folded his hands behind his back, looking at Hugh with a relaxed posture.

"It's just the truth. Nothing against Mr. Griffin." Hugh stood as tall as he could to Bernard, compared to his usual slouching.

"It saddens me, but it's the truth," Bernard said. "No city is perfect, Mr. Evans, but we must stay optimistic. If we can continue to improve ourselves, others will do the same. Less would suffer in the South Hills, and the city will grow more harmonious."

"But people starve on the streets, looking for warmth in the frost season next to trash in the alleyways."

Bernard paused and rubbed his beard. "What if, Mr. Evans, I were to address the situation first thing in the morning? I would personally go to assess the conditions. Anywhere in particular?"

Hugh's mouth gaped open. "I, ugh… Oak Lane."

"I will make arrangements for first light."

Aleksandar eyed them both, Bernard holding a sincere smile. Hugh batted his eyes, letting out a deep breath.

Aleksandar put his hand on Hugh's shoulder. "Tomorrow is a new day. Come back then, and we'll begin your training. Maybe we can find a way to help a few people."

Hugh found a smile. "Thank you. I'll be here, promise."

Aleksandar nodded, and Hugh scurried into the crowd who waited for the judge's decision.

"That was well handled, Mr. Scott." Bernard held his hands behind his back. "Without you, I don't think he would've taken what I said to heart. I'm at a disadvantage when trying to help those who don't eat at the same table I do."

"I'm not sure I did anything," Aleksandar said, watching the judges gather on stage.

The head judge walked to the end of the stage and raised his hands, quieting the crowd.

"Today, we have seen some of the most elegant, powerful, and meaningful inventions of our era." The judge paused, tilting his golden-ribboned hat. "We have seen today the bond that inventors share with their creations, and as we enter the greatest age of scientific expansion, I've never been more excited. It wasn't until today I realized making a decision would be so difficult."

Aleksandar stood, realizing he had not let himself breathe. His passions and hopes rose in his chest with a headache of excitement.

"We designed this exhibition to recognize an inventor who has shown the most promise and potential in bringing new wonders to our great city—someone who could push Well's Peake to be as grand as Belagrad. The winner will receive a year's worth of funding, all thanks to the city's prominent families. It has been an honor to watch all of you present, and we have made a decision."

The judge grabbed a silver-cast award from the podium and walked to the stage's end.

Aleksandar took a deep breath, his shoulders tense, his eyes not blinking.

"The winner of the World's Most Promising Exhibition is…" The head judge lifted the award. "Owen O'Connell."

The crowd erupted into a chaos of cheers, and hands clapped like thunder, echoing throughout the halls of the World's Fair. The curtains waved, and the sunlight caught Owen's grin.

Owen walked to the center stage, taking his place next to the judge.

Aleksandar looked on as his heart dropped into his stomach. He looked at the hands clapping next to him and the mouths chanting.

His senses dulled, and he felt nothing as a haze overcame him. Aleksandar could only focus on the harsh ringing in his ears, the possibility of no future as an inventor, and the afternoon light that shined on his defeat.

CHAPTER FOUR

Aleksandar stood amongst the crowd, his chest tightening like an unscrewed cork. His eyes fixated on the floor, staring at the sunlight's gleam on the black-and-white stones in the marble.

The icy sensation of dreams faded away and left his stomach in knots.

He clapped, hesitation between each beat of his hand. He didn't care to answer the question of whether Owen deserved his praise or the fact he wasn't good enough.

Owen held the medal high for the cheering crowd, letting it flicker in the luscious light, and bowed with a broad grin.

The applause slowed, and Aleksandar forced a weak smile, turning and moving through the crowd to his own display as a dull ring remained in his ears.

"Mr. Scott!" Bernard twisted around and followed in a graceful pursuit.

Aleksandar paced to his exhibition and pulled out a box from under the table, filled with brackets and locking mechanisms.

Bernard eased next to the desk as Aleksandar fitted the braces onto his invention and bolted them, letting out a small gasp.

"Mr. Scott, what are you doing?" Bernard asked.

"I'm securing the Red Breath," Aleksandar said. "They mandate—"

"I meant, what are you doing here? I thought you'd want to

congratulate Mr. O'Connell."

"Owen probably wouldn't notice. I'll be heading home for the night." Without a grunt or frown, Aleksandar tightened another bolt.

"Mr. Scott, I understand this may not be easy. I don't know what you're feeling, but I hope you see this is only one of many exhibitions to come. You will have your day. I believe you have great potential."

Aleksandar paused, resting the wrench on the table. "I know I will be better tomorrow." Aleksandar finished securing his device and wiped the counters clean of scraps. He kept his head high and his posture straight, looking to Bernard, worried his eyes would build up with water.

"To lose to another is not a failure if you have succeeded, as well," Bernard said.

The last thing Aleksandar wanted was to snivel in front of Well's Peake's most influential aristocrat. "You asked me what I wanted to do earlier."

"Yes." Bernard folded his arms and stroked his beard.

"I honestly don't know anymore. Perhaps I do but can't see the path. Maybe we all pretend until we find our way, but what happens when you have no means of moving forward?"

Aleksandar leaned back and closed his eyes. He could picture the Red Breath next to him. The musk of heated metal still lingering in the exhibit. The metal, smooth to the touch, polished twice with a vanilla bean cream. So much work for so little reward.

Bernard stepped forward and paused. "I don't make it a habit to reveal my plans, Mr. Scott, but I've been putting much thought into the future of Well's Peake. Something I'd be willing to share with you, hoping it will boost your spirits."

Aleksandar raised his eyebrows and removed the handle from the Red Breath. "What might that be?"

"Over the past few years, scientific growth has aggressively expanded. We entered the Industrial Revolution, not realizing it would change the world. It's not the first or the last movement to change history. We create inventions every day, and I believe they need to be watched with more care by those who care for the future."

Aleksandar paused, hanging on to every word.

"The Black Harvest has destroyed our past," Bernard said. "What we need is honest and skilled inventors who will put humanity and the next generation above their own needs. That is why I am creating a foundation known as the World's League. To build a council with those who have the city's interests at heart, a bridge everyone can cross together."

Aleksandar pulled out his chair and sat. "I'm not sure I fit your criteria."

"I'm not looking solely for skill and status, but for character to be molded. People who are still open to ideas outside their own," Bernard said. "You have the potential to be part of a league that will help guide not only Well's Peake but the province, even the Northern Regions. When the future becomes the present, Well's Peake will need guidance."

Aleksandar ran his hand along his hair, the strands soft between his fingers. He held his head low as Bernard stood beside him, kicking his heel into the floor.

"You have what it takes, Mr. Scott, to be as great as Owen O'Connell. To become as esteemed as the experienced Natalia Arlen. It'll take effort, but the Harvest Fair Exhibition is only a few months away. When better to reveal your potential than the end of the World's Fair?"

"I entered this exhibition to give the people what I thought would help them; to give something significant to humanity. Maybe Owen's right to stick to a more established field."

"At the next exhibition, make an everlasting impression and show them what you can do in your field. Be a teacher for those to come. Give them the wisdom and guidance they need for their ideas and dreams."

Bernard grabbed the handle and put it back on Aleksandar's Red Breath, looking to the young inventor. Aleksandar nodded, and Bernard opened the valve, flames erupting into the air. Aleksandar and Bernard looked to the bright fire, lost in its heat and brightness.

Bernard shut off the valve, and the flame died away. He removed the handle and set it back on the desk.

Aleksandar wanted to say something, anything, to a stranger who tried to give him hope, but the desire to be optimistic was little, and the sting of his defeat lingered.

"It's just been a long day," Aleksandar said. "I know tomorrow can be a fresh start."

"That's all right. How about this? I will leave it alone and hold off my tediousness if you meet a family friend of mine. Her name is Miss Harvey, and she's quite the inspirational young lady."

Aleksandar held up his hand. "I don't think it—"

"Mr. Scott, I could stay here and preach until your ears ring, or you can talk to a lovely young lady tomorrow after some peace tonight."

Aleksandar rubbed his forehead and looked at Bernard with tightened brows. "What's her name again?"

"Miss Harvey. Greet her at the winged fountain at two tomorrow."

Aleksandar nodded, and Bernard rested his hand on his shoulder. "Remember, Mr. Scott, as the next generation is to come, we must be the change we want it to be."

Bernard left with an enormous smile and walked into the crowd, towering over everyone.

Aleksandar patted his hands together and bit the corner of his lip. He stood, pulled on his jacket, and walked through the World's Palace as marbled trees towered and fairgoers crowded him through the arched entrance of the World's Fair.

Remnants of light from the afternoon dimmed against the cedar walls, a fragrant scent lingering in the air as Aleksandar looked out the window to the northern forest behind his house, aged and peaceful.

He stacked his workshop with bookcases and shelves full of gears, springs, and fabricated metal. A desk rested against a wall, covered with drawings and Aleksandar's schematics, and a cubby with a sofa and a coffee table rested behind him.

Aleksandar spun in his chair and lifted a hat mount with a half-shaped top hat, the brim missing on the bottom.

He stitched an elegant vine of leaves into the base, a needle stuck in the other side, threaded on the tip. Aleksandar pulled it out and continued the pattern. It was peaceful and brought a smile to his face.

The simplicity of something he loved and the smell of the lavender oil he dabbed on the hat calmed him after a long day.

Aleksandar hummed a heavenly tune in the night air and picked up a brim, wrapping it snugly around the bottom and securing it in place with a tight wrap. He pressed his hands together and set his fingertips against his lips.

Oh, it's beautiful.

A curtain shimmered, and Aleksandar paused, setting his hat to the side. He stood and crouched down, looking across the workbench.

"You're not that sneaky, Shae."

An owl leaped from behind the curtain, her wings spread wide, tilting her head, her large sunset eyes glistening in the lantern's light. Her feathers were brown like old oak, with a spot of white in the center of her chest, mirroring the pattern on her face.

"What do you think you're doing?" Aleksandar stood straight.

She cocked her head with a tiny, flat beak and leaped into the air. She grabbed a stick with her beak and flew across the room, landing next to a stone fireplace where a fire burned under a kettle of water.

Shae dropped the stick into the fireplace and hooted, bobbing back and forth. Aleksandar smiled and walked to her side, petting her with the back of his hand. Shae hooted, her chirp like echoes in a mountain valley.

He plopped into his chair to listen to the kettle creak as it grew hot and swung to and from, resting his eyes.

The kettle whistled, and Shae flew to the desk, grabbing a cup and dropping it into Aleksandar's lap.

"Thank you, baby girl."

Aleksandar opened a tin next to his chair and pulled out a bag of loose tea leaves. He dropped it in the cup and removed the kettle from the fire with an oven mitt, then poured the steaming water into his cup, letting the fragrance of Kyoto berry tea fill his nostrils.

Aleksandar lifted his cup and took a careful sip as Shae stared into the fire, bobbing her head left to right like a child.

Aleksandar took a sip, savoring the warm and smooth liquid, fighting the pressure in his chest as his mind lingered to a childhood friend, remembering their night in the forest, remembering the first moment they met. He looked up.

"I wonder if you ever asked what the point was? You would've left them in awe." Aleksandar sighed with his eyes shut.

"I wish I could find *my* opportunity. I thought I had this one. I did… I promise I'm not giving up."

Aleksandar leaned forward to Shae on the desk, listening. Aleksandar laid his head on his propped arm, reaching to pet her. She stepped back.

"Why won't you just let me pet you?"

Shae turned her head.

The bags under his eyes were dark, his dimples like anxiety marks instead of part of his enticing smile.

Aleksandar rolled his head and pulled over three octagonal pieces of paper with starred points on the edges. Inspirations and scattered ideas covered the papers. The third had a thin layer of dust on it, free of words and showing no purpose in its folded design.

Aleksandar paused and raised an eyebrow, looking at the handle from his invention with a sudden revelation.

His eyes darted to the wall next to the staircase, and he tapped the blank trinket, sending dust into the air.

Aleksandar walked over and rubbed his fingertips along the textured wall, smooth to the touch. His tips caught the cracks in the paneling, a slight breeze coming from inside. He grabbed the panel and lifted it up on a hinge, the section clicking into place. He folded several boards over each other like an origami star.

Shae hopped onto the desk and let out a hoot.

Aleksandar spun the wood as tumblers clicked into place. The wall opened into a room where a machine with a thick wool blanket rested in the middle, light flicking from the lanterns in the main workshop.

"Shae… I'm not done yet."

CHAPTER FIVE

The sunset glowed like the hayfields on a windy day, glistening off the windowsills and machinery resting on the workbenches in Natalia's workshop.

With a cup of tea in one hand and the other holding an open journal, Natalia walked through the shadows and sun rays with a graceful stride. She swung around a workbench laced with maple wood and steel.

She set her tea on a wood coaster where a faded stain aged itself into the grain and placed the book on a stand, pulling two slim bars from the side and pinning the book's pages open. The sweet musk of tea filled her nostrils with berries and herbs as the reminiscence of home and comfort spread throughout the workshop.

Natalia sipped her tea as she flipped a page in the book. She picked up a wrench and secured a pipe to a glass machine resting on the workbench, shaped like a large stretched cube with handles. Filled with water and covered in a frosted tint, it was a half meter wide, with silver braces securing its translucent form, the top arching like a carved stone on the bend of a river.

The Lunarwheel was her single greatest failure. It was an engine meant to change the world, outpower the steam revolution, surpass electricity, and stand as the building block of the energy movement to come.

Natalia set the wrench down and slipped her fingers behind the pipes, pivoting a bracket in place. Sweat dripped down her temple, and she wiped it off with her shoulder.

The chance of failing was familiar. Natalia rebuilt her machine on several occasions during her career. With each failed experiment, her desire of fixing her legacy grew, and she could not resist the temptation. After a second of wondering doubt, she grabbed a handle in the floor and lifted a hidden blast door with a slit of glass at eye level.

Natalia grabbed a control panel, set it on the stand behind the door, connected a wire into the glass machine, and plugged it into the panel. She stood by the barrier and flipped the switch.

The machine flared in a dim light, and the auger rotated once and stopped. Natalia flipped the switch off and on, hoping it would start.

The machine flared but dimmed just as quickly. She glanced at the book, turned the page, ran her finger down the journal, and walked back to the machine, flipping a few valves.

Natalia smacked her lips. "I *don't* know."

She twisted off a seal with a pop and realigned several rods and pistons, securing one with another brace.

Natalia closed the machine and moved behind the door, flipping the switch. The machinery started and dimmed out. Natalia flicked several buttons and flipped the switch on, and off, and—

The pipe blew off the back, water spurting against the wall. Glass flung against the door, and without a flinch, Natalia leaned against the steel, eyes locked on her invention.

The water inside the tank exploded into a violent whirlwind, bashing back and forth inside its prison. It gushed through the shifting tubes, spraying out the back. The water emitted its own luminance, the blue glow glaring through the orange sunset. A hundred metal objects glimmered in the workshop, like stars on a clear night.

Natalia wiped her forehead and hands with a nearby rag, never looking from the elegance and chaos.

"Come on… come on. Stabilize."

With muffled ears and glimmering eyes, her mouth dried out. If water could burn, she tasted it in the air.

The gears at the end rotated rapidly. They flinched and stalled.

Natalia chuckled with a thin smile.

The gears locked tight, and a brace shattered. Natalia placed her fists on the glass with rasping breaths, her knuckles white.

The metal braces creaked and moaned, and the room grew silent as Natalia held her breath.

The machine exploded, and the workshop echoed with a violent eruption. Glass clattered off metal, breaking on contact if it had not already. Couplings flew across the floor and pierced the walls. Water struck everything in its path, soaking papers and sizzling on metal as it rested on the floor.

Natalia leaned against the shield, crouched, and listened to the water dripping on the floor.

If it had been once or twice, she might have accepted her failure, but the never-ending struggle weighed on her shoulders.

Natalia rubbed her jaw with her fingers and sniffled, water puddling around her shoes. She stood and looked at a metal brace jarred through the peephole, dangling on the other side. The teacup on the desk was broken, dribbling over the counter and pattering on the wood floor.

Water rested at the soles of her shoes as Natalia looked out the window and saw the sun dip behind the forest, light fading from the workshop as the shadows grew long and dark.

Her invention now split down the middle, resting in two.

Natalia walked to the wall and lifted a lever. A soft click came from beneath the floor, and small drains opened in the room's corners. The water drained, and she grabbed a broom off the wall, sweeping glass across the floor.

Another night of failed proportions, but Natalia hummed and bobbed her head, smacking her lips again.

Her hands slowed to a stop, and her eyes opened wide, unflinching. Her expression was blank, and she looked on as if she did not know where she was. She set the broom on the wall and walked with a quivering lip, swallowing hard, letting out a shaky breath.

She felt like a lost soul.

The workshop seemed different from before as if her purpose was less important. She rubbed her hand down the side of the workbench, the rich maple catching her eye. On the cabinet, there was a photograph of her standing next to her husband, smiling with their elbows locked at a bar. Natalia eased into a smile, and a tear rolled down her cheek, dripping off to the floor.

I'll never forget you.

She looked back to her invention and pulled a blue journal from her vest pocket, reading through the first few pages. She had the urge to sob, but no tears came.

Natalia grabbed the photo, stuck it in the book, and walked out of the workshop.

Blackberry candles replaced the musk of singed water, wax dripping down the candles as the wisps of the flames broke the silence. Wooden floors complemented the borders of redwood paneling that rose to the lower third of every wall, where blue wallpaper with gold lacing reached the ceiling.

Natalia entered her study to the musk of aged books. They filled the bookshelves that lined the room, ceiling to floor, with a loft filled with more. A desk rested towards the back of the room with a lit fireplace.

Natalia pulled out her book, flipping through the pages, the book filled to the last. She pulled one identical to it from a shelf and rubbed her finger on the spine, feeling the tight threads of the cover. Natalia replaced the empty spot with her old one and stuffed the new journal in her pocket. She sat in her chair, looking at the fire, and rubbed her hand across her forehead, her hands clammy.

After a moment of peace, Natalia swiveled to the desk and unlocked a drawer. She pulled out a journal, resting it on the desk. It was leather-bound, engraved with rippling designs of the finest craftsmanship. Two pins, encased in a ribbon, held the book shut. She grabbed the ribbon and unwrapped it from the side lock. The leather book opened to a spot in the middle.

Natalia dipped the pen in ink, and held her hand above the paper in.

I don't understand how one could invent something in the past but be unable to recreate it in the present.

Natalia paused, rubbed the back of her neck, and leaned over the desk, her eyes going blank again. She shook her head and focused on the tip of the pen.

Seeing no fruition, yet again, makes me believe things are to be different. I have put myself on a path that was meant to bring change. Why else would inventing be such a struggle at my age?

Natalia dipped her pen in ink.

Tonight reminds me of a day long ago when I first came to the Northern Regions. I walked the street in the evening when a child tugged on my jacket. She asked me if I was the magic lady. At this point, the public didn't know me, but she did.

Her parents were not far behind and pardoned her eagerness, but there was no reason. They were lovely and asked about an apprenticeship for their daughter, after seeing me perform earlier that evening.

I had never considered teaching another with my abilities as they were, but I couldn't refuse. The little girl was enthusiastic. She begged me to make something before I left, almost ripping the back of my jacket.

I pulled out a small device I had created the year before, thanks to an electrical scientist in Belagrad.

We called my invention the Spark. It had a bronze handle with grooved curves, smooth to the touch. Two prongs rested at the end that were elegant and mesmerizing, and when activated, it spun on top, and a small light emitted from the center.

Never had I seen such a delighted smile when she ignited it. I used to spend hours lost in its beauty. My greatest ideas came to me then, and I hoped it would do the same for her.

Natalia took a deep breath, wiping a tear off her cheek. Her legs tingled, and she leaned into the chair.

The night before, my husband told me something similar, a mere hour after I thought of the Lunarwheel. Why would so many coincidences occur if I was not meant to create it? Have I grown enough to accomplish great things?

Natalia set her pen down, infused in the past, caressing the underside of her chin. She turned to her jacket on a nearby coat rack and reached into the pocket, pulling out the Spark.

It was in immaculate condition. Natalia pressed the button, and a spark surged at the end. Lost in her device, a thin smile grew across her face.

Perhaps I can no longer do this on my own. Without my husband's support, I need motivation from another, maybe someone younger with fresh ambition. I have a genuine eagerness to teach again. It might be possible they could carry on what memories I have through their work.

Together, we might finish the Lunarwheel or create an invention that will transform the world. I could finally leave a completed legacy and move on from what lingered for so long.

Perhaps I will move on with my life and settle like we always wanted.

Natalia held on to the pen and turned to the window, looking to the moon that kissed the horizon, its glow glistening off the cascading waterfall.

CHAPTER SIX

The moon rested behind full clouds in the night's cool hours. Dew covered the forest, leaving a wet musk of the approaching dawn. The few birds that remained chirped in the chill night, the rustling leaves glistening in the pale moonlight.

In his gray jacket and burgundy shirt, the masked man stomped across the grass, trampling it flat, the dew soaking into his pant legs. Flicking the water off his boots, the man snuck across the yard, slipping between shadows before resting behind the roots of aged trees.

He crept alongside a house with gentle steps, peering into the windows where dark ashes rested in the fireplace.

The masked man stepped forward but paused, staring at the ground. His head wandered. Lost in the sky, he watched the clouds hovering across the moon.

He rounded the house to the backyard, pressing between the thick trees, and pulled on several windows until one slid open without a creak. The intruder pulled himself inside.

The masked man closed the window and searched the house. With little light and thick shadows, he struggled to see.

He pulled a thin lantern from under his jacket and lit it with a match near a candle, and light shined against the mask. The mask curved like ocean ripples and the moon's crest, blue with silver beads, like rain on a window.

The masked man moved through the house and walked upstairs without a whisper. A dim light glowed from a bedroom, accenting several picture frames in the hallway.

The masked man set the lantern down and eased into the bedroom where a young man slept. A small owl watched with protruding eyes, hooting as she stared at the masked man.

Hello to you too, Shae.

The man moved around the bed and gazed at Aleksandar sleeping peacefully in the night.

Shae watched closely and inched across her post towards her master, talons breaking the silence as they etched into the wood. The man reached into his jacket and searched around for a frayed burlap sack.

Shae perched and spread her wings, her hissing growing in volume. The man moved closer, and Shae turned towards Aleksandar.

The masked man paused as Aleksandar rolled, his hand still in his pocket. He stepped back, and Shae lowered her wings.

No. Not yet.

The masked man backed up with silent steps and pulled his hand from his jacket, hands raised in peace.

Shae eyed him as he slipped out of the room, taking the light with him. He made his way into the basement, the lantern guiding him as the house rested in shadows.

The basement wasn't musky but was filled with the spice of cocobolo wood. The masked man searched the room, inspecting every machine on the workbench. He picked up a cube and sighed, setting it down exactly how he found it.

The intruder moved to the desk and skimmed the gears and inventions. There was a book with a thick cover, and next to its spine, three pieces of octagonal-shaped papers surrounded by small stacks of metal and folders.

The man observed them, finding no purpose for them. He held the lantern over the desk, metal flashing like lightning against the walls. With a still posture, he shook his head.

I don't see it.

The man walked through the workbenches towards the door when a small beaker of water caught his eye. He stopped and turned. A cylindrical staff rested near the edge.

The man glanced over his shoulder to a cracking noise behind him, hand in his jacket, waiting for any sign of Shae or Aleksandar. After a moment, he gazed at the staff and picked it up, pressing the button. The battery hummed next to the invention as the man raised the rod.

The water shimmered on the tray's edges, pulling away, floating towards the end shaft. As the man lifted the staff higher, the water followed his movements. The man's eyes peered from the darkness of the mask, wide and unblinking.

"It's impossible," he said.

The water glimmered in the lantern's light, hovering in the air. The masked man waved the handle, and the water continued to rise.

No, no, this isn't right.

The man turned off the device. The water splashed back into the tray, and he set the staff down. His face itched, his fingers grew numb, and his eyes flinched in the lantern light.

With a nod, the intruder fled up the stairs and out the back door, the crisp air rushing under his mask, his breath visible in the moonlight, and disappeared into the shadows of the forest.

CHAPTER SEVEN

Vida sat in the waiting room, gazing at the curtain that separated the cot from the examination hall. She rubbed the backside of her white gloves that reached her elbows and pulled them tight, ensuring there were no wrinkles.

Lanterns hung above, but there was no need, as the morning sun was low and shined through the windows, glowing through the curtains. The door against the hall creaked, and a stout man with round glasses and a thick mustache that roughly covered his bottom lip walked in with a binder in hand. He smelled of crisp cinnamon as if he'd been baking all morning.

"Good morning, Miss Harvey," he said.

"Hello, Arthur." Vida stood, grabbing her handbag, and walked to the doctor.

"What's it like being on the opposite side?"

"It's strange when you're used to working on the patients."

The two stepped through the curtain and into a hallway lined with carved wood with stone floor tiles. Windows reached from the ceiling to the stone, and nurses and patients walked down the hall between the morning rays.

Vida's thick brown hair bounced on her shoulders, pulled back, so it didn't fall on the front of her purple-laced dress or hide her brown eyes.

"I agree," the doctor said. "If only we could diagnose ourselves, maybe we would feel a bit more comfortable."

Arthur waved his palm, and Vida followed him down another corridor. Her steps were precise, hands folded behind her, and her purple dress was radiant in the sun, swirls sewn with glossy thread reflecting in the window.

"Well, I'm proud of you for coming in. I know this isn't easy," he said.

"I would rather help others."

Arthur chuckled. "Don't sell yourself short, Miss Harvey. Everyone needs a checkup."

The doctor led Vida into a large room. Two cots lined the walls with wood cabinets mounted against the back. A curtain draped over the window, blocking the bright morning rays.

"I see you have a pep in your step as well," she said.

"It's marvelous how the World's Fair has brought much notoriety to our hospital, being so close to the fair. To see people taking an interest in the field of medicine and coming to our exhibits is exciting. A welcome change compared to the days after the Black Harvest."

Vida sat on the bench, her back prim and straight, pulling her hair tight to the right.

"The Doyle Hall is filled with medical history and discoveries. Gives me goosebumps just thinking of it." Arthur patted his hands together.

"Do I sense some bashfulness, Doctor? Your name deserves to be on that hall." Vida smirked.

Arthur blushed and set his folder on the desk. "Don't get an old man all chipper about himself. I can't promise I'd stop talking, and you younger folk seem to grow tired of my stories."

"That's never stopped you before." Vida held a sweet smile.

They laughed together, and Arthur sat across from her.

"How's the detective novel?" she asked.

Arthur tilted his head and waved his hand with a broad grin. "That's a story for another day."

Vida took a deep breath, shaking her head and pulling on the end of her gloves.

"Why so nervous?" Arthur smiled and pulled himself closer to her. "It's a simple checkup, I promise."

"I'm not nervous." Vida pulled her hands apart and put the left on her knee.

"Would you like—"

"Yes—" Vida held her hand straight, looking away.

Arthur grabbed the glove and rolled it down her arm, removing it. He cradled her hand, softer than anyone had in a long while, the warmth of his touch on hers. Rubbing his fingers across her palm, he traced a scar extending from the center, around her thumb, and up her wrist. He pressed the hand in several spots. Vida flinched between her thumb, looking at the scar herself.

"Hold your hand out for me, please," he said. "Still doing favors for Mr. Griffin?"

Vida held her hand steady, without a flinch. "Yes, he asked me to meet with a young inventor this afternoon. He thinks with the right push; this inventor could have great potential for his league."

"Oh, perhaps a potential love interest—" Arthur looked to Vida's hardened gaze and smiled. "Oh, I'm just teasing. It would be nice to see you with an ambitious young man instead of spending all hours of the day assisting me. How about that doctor I referred to you? Are you still going to your sessions?"

"No. I'm not sure the whole mental doctor is for me. How does he understand my mind when I don't?"

Arthur raised his eyebrows. "Every so often, it's not the scars we see that affect us the most. The field of psychology is young, but it grows larger by the day. You, of all people, understand how talking can set a mind straight."

"I understand talking about the present, but the past?"

"It has helped many in light of the Black Harvest. It's becoming a serious subject in some circles."

Arthur shifted in his seat and pulled on her fingers, and Vida flinched. "I'm not sure if you've heard, but there's a new doctor in-house who can perform your surgery."

Vida looked at him without a word, and Arthur nodded.

"I've considered him as my understudy for the following term. He might be a fantastic replacement. I must make room for the next generation. It's amusing to think I survived the Black Harvest, but I turn over because I got too old."

Vida smacked Arthur's hand. "Don't talk like that. You'll always be my first choice, even if you let that mustache go."

Arthur smiled, his cheeks rosy. He held Vida's hand up high and lowered it.

Arthur grabbed a scope and looked into Vida's eyes.

Vida flinched. "How does checking my eyes relate to my hand again?"

Arthur looked on with a coy smile. "Your mother never enjoyed this part of it either."

Vida's throat grew dry, and a small pit found its way into her stomach, growing uneasy. A tear ran down her cheek, held high on her cheekbones. "I was afraid of bright lights long before."

Arthur paused and dabbed the tear with a handkerchief, Vida nodding with pursed lips.

"She was always so kind," he said.

"A kindness that's hard to find."

"This is true. Do you still write to her?"

Vida nodded, and Arthur leaned back, slapping his knees.

"Well, you appear to be in good health, which I didn't doubt," he said. "You still have a slight twitch in the hand between your thumb and index finger, but you seem to use it well. Minor compared to past examinations."

Vida held her head high, ensuring her cheek was dry. "I have my doubts the panel would acknowledge the continuing improvement."

Arthur wrote in his binder and set it on his lap. "You're well aware of the progress we are making, and there are doctors who *can* help with your scar, Miss Harvey. Removing it would make following your dream of being a physician easier. We all know you have the wit."

"But there's no guarantee. In the last medical journal, they said some side effect—"

"I know. I've read them. No, not every case is one hundred percent, but results are promising compared to the risk. You should consider it."

"It's all up here." Vida pointed to her head, slipping her glove back on. "When needed, I'm steady."

Arthur leaned in and tilted his head. "That's what I am afraid of. I know it's up here, and I think that's why you won't go through with the procedure. One of these days, you might not have the chance to focus, and when you don't, what happens when you slip?"

Vida stood and walked to the window, peering out to the hospital gardens. "Is it true if they hit a nerve, it might never recover?"

Arthur stood, his hands slipping into his pockets. "It is possible, yes."

"Then it isn't worth the risk."

"Miss Harvey, I know you mean well and have your heart set on being a physician, but you could endanger the welfare of those looking at your hands to save them."

"We live in a world of scars. We've grown to accommodate them, right?"

"To a degree, but this is a delicate matter."

Vida rubbed her hand. Fairgoers walked past the hedges and into Doyle Hall. Kids, some with missing arms, others with limp legs, played in the yard with no attention to their afflictions. The day was young, and they danced and smiled. Vida envied them. To be of tender age, to where the world was still large and dreams guided her passions. The ability to see past her own scars.

Arthur stepped beside her, hands holding the inside of his jacket. "I have new exercises that will continue to strengthen your hand."

"Thank you." Vida dropped her arms, looking at Arthur.

Arthur took a deep breath, smacked his lips, and grabbed a clipboard, writing on the paper.

Vida turned around, folded her hands in front, her shoulders pulled back. She knew what he wanted to hear, but she couldn't say it. He was logical and just as insightful, and she did not want to disappoint him. He clearly understood what happened, but the words he wanted did not come.

"I turned in that application," she said.

"Did you?" Arthur pulled off his glasses. "So you changed your mind about Blackwell?"

"Yes. If I'm going to study, I should do it at the most prestigious academy." Vida smiled.

"And you understand they haven't accepted a woman in the doctoring program since the harvest? That they accept three percent of applications in the Northern Regions?"

"I do, and I figured I could try. Maybe I stand a chance."

"There's word of a new academy scheduled to open across the river, and it's to be a progressive change in our field and to be quite luxurious."

"I don't know if I can wait that long. I'll be twenty-six next year, and no one gets admitted at twenty-seven."

Arthur nodded. "Would you be ready? After the last admission interview, after the way the last board talked to you? For being... you know—a woman. Even with my recommendation, I'm afraid for your reputation with this persistence. It could be a turnoff to certain academies."

Vida stood there, her chin still high.

"Not that it would stop you." Arthur laughed. "Well, know I have no plans to deter you like the rest, but you must promise me something. If you want certified, you need to remove that scar. The gloves are not stylish enough to hide it in surgery. Consider this, and I will keep my recommendation intact."

"Wouldn't there be another scar if they removed mine?" she asked.

"Not like you have now. Some cases reported no scarring at all."

Vida fidgeted and glanced to the window. "And the recovery?"

"As little as twelve weeks."

"As much as?"

"Six months."

Vida held her scarred hand and rubbed her finger. The smoothness of the glove grew bumpy as she felt the inside of her thumb. She sighed and shook her head. "I promise, I'll consider it."

Arthur patted her on the shoulder, and they walked through the door.

"Miss Harvey."

Vida paused. "Yes?"

Arthur sighed, setting his glasses back on his nose, and grabbed her glove.

"I need to hear you say that you understand what you're doing. That your desire to hold on to that scar will not interfere with your passion and opportunity of saving lives." Arthur straightened her glove and held it with tenderness.

"I understand," she said.

Arthur nodded. "Well then, I expect outstanding works from you."

"Thank you. Now I have a favor to ask."

"It's yours."

Vida pulled out an envelope and handed it to Arthur, his initials written on the seal.

"My recommendation?" Arthur's voice raised.

"Yes. I hope you're not mad, but I couldn't send it in. Our friendship and your reputation are too important to me, and while I have you as a reference, I can't risk causing harm to your influence."

Arthur patted the envelope in his palm. "You need not waste a favor." Arthur smiled and handed it back.

"I can't," she said.

"You don't have to send it in, but keep it and one day read it. It won't be valid for a panel after that, but it could be for you. And when you find your chance, make it worth it."

Vida hugged him, and Arthur smiled, his arms stunned in place until he returned the gesture.

"Pardon me," he said, looking to a nurse waving him down.

Vida stepped away and walked through the sunlight in the wooded hallways, placing the letter in her handbag and finding herself a bashful grin.

CHAPTER EIGHT

Nicoli tossed the handcuffs, and Mrs. Ellington caught them, looking with pursed lips. She slipped her hands in, and he walked over, securing them with a click around her wrists. He took her by the arm and escorted her to the front door, where she stopped in the afternoon light outside her estate.

Nicoli looked back at her husband, dead on the couch, blood sprayed across the cookies on the coffee table.

"I thought you were coming peacefully?" he asked.

"Would you be so kind as to grab my coat? The harvest is here, and the bitterness falls on the hills."

Nicoli glanced at the hook and grabbed her coat with a fur collar, placing it over her shoulders. The peppermint perfume on the jacket lingered, and she wiped the blood from her hand on the pelt. They walked out of the house, a stone wall circling the front of the estate. A cobblestone road led to an open iron gate, where a carriage and driver waited next to the pillar. Nicoli opened the door and guided Mrs. Ellington inside to a red seat surrounded by a cage.

Mrs. Ellington gazed at him with a frown. "You're disappointed, Mr. Lucas. Were you hoping I was another?"

"Are you capable of knowing how one thinks outside of your own twisted ways?" Nicoli tilted his head.

"Yes. I am empathetic, and that has always been my greatest strength. I see you search for more."

"Tell me. Do you even feel guilty about murdering your husband?"

"Of course I do. My only regret is being caught. He only died because of you. You would've exposed me and left my husband a joke to the aristocrats. This is your fault, Mr. Lucas."

With little remorse, no emotion, Nicoli could see through her facade. She rehearsed her words as if she thought of this moment for months. She may have loved her husband, but she enjoyed the kill more. The truth was in her eyes.

He glanced at the seat, and she sighed, stepping in for Nicoli to lock her in and secure the lock bolt, not giving her a second glance. He pulled out an envelope and handed it to the man above.

"Give this to the chief. He'll handle her."

"Yes, sir," the chauffeur said, pointing behind Nicoli. "Someone is waiting for you."

Nicoli turned to a constable in a blue parka, gold buttons stitched in the front, and two batons on his belt. Nicoli nodded to the driver, who snapped the reins and headed down the road.

The constable approached Nicoli with his chin high and hands in his pockets. "Mr. Lucas?"

Nicoli buttoned his jacket. "You're quite the way from home."

The man handed Nicoli an envelope. "Yes. I've been given orders from Chief Dekker to summon you to the Peake."

"It's a long ride from Redwood. I should consider myself honored. Did he say why?" Nicoli opened the letter, reading the request.

"He said he needs the man who catches killers."

Nicoli's stomach had settled, but his thoughts rampaged. The city within the rolling woods, where happiness called for him. It had been years since his last visit, and he longed to be there again, knowing he could only go when invited.

The constable handed him a folder. "You'll need this."

With a tug of his jacket and fingers through his hair, Nicoli nodded, pulling out the crime report and a photo of a dead man in the woods. "This report date is three days ago. Well's Peake is a week away on a good horse."

"I traveled by the Red Express, as we will. We will arrive at a new station every eight hours, swap horses and drivers. You can sleep through the nights."

"Must be serious if we get such accommodation. I'll go, on one condition. When we hit the Peake, I want my usual driver."

"Done. Let's be on our way."

Nicoli held up the photo again, looking at the name.

Raymond O'Connell.

~

Three Days Later…

Nicoli lowered the photograph of the dead man to the bottom of a tree and rocks where the body was discovered. He peered up to the horizon of Well's Peake, standing on the outskirts of the city, taking in the woodsy aroma.

The World's Fair was visible in the valley, glowing in the sunlight, where thousands of people enjoyed themselves, unbeknownst to his arrival.

Nicoli turned back to the scene and eyed the forest floor, knowing the rain from a night ago would've ruined most, if not all, evidence. The ground was hard on the green hillside, the trees high, and the canopies full of leaves changing in the harvest season.

The driver dismounted the carriage, and Nicoli held up his hand.

"One moment, Winston."

Nicoli lowered his hands and dropped his gaze, focusing on the scene, envisioning the murdered man on the ground. How he was laid, the injuries on his body. It was as if the victim was there, as vivid as the leaves landing in the grass.

The man was extremely bruised, his skin tight, and his eyes were closed, looking into the dirt. Someone placed him there carefully and in a place overlooking the city. The body was meant to be found, discovered not far off a popular hiking path for the city's elite.

His fingers shook, and he ran his palm through his hair, clenching his jaw, so his teeth did not chatter as the details of the scene grew fuzzy.

A hand patted his shoulder, and Nicoli pulled himself from his trance. He turned, Winston standing over him.

"I see your mind still slips into madness."

Nicoli stood and rubbed his bottom lip. "You catch a killer by doing so."

"That insight of yours will take you back to when you went mad, sir."

Nicoli glanced to Well's Peake. "Let me worry about that."

"As you wish."

"Winston, tell me. I've heard rumors, but what do they say in the city? About the inventors and these murders."

Winston removed his hat. "Well, inventors still have their stigma, thanks to the Black Harvest. Many know they are going missing and turning up dead. Industrial, Elemental, Medicine, innovators of all fields are being murdered. However, the city is keeping a tight lid on it. No major headlines in the press. No public confirmation."

"Surprising for Well's Peake. Redwood is known for that, but not the Peake."

"Many believe it's avoiding panic amongst the World's Fair."

Nicoli looked aimlessly around the scene. "Anything else?"

"Other than the social unrest between those of influence and those who do not? No."

"Well, there's nothing to be found here. Best we head into the city."

Winston nodded and headed for the carriage, pausing when Nicoli did not follow.

"Sir? Are you all right?"

Nicoli pushed his tongue into his cheek. "It's been a while since I've been here. I wonder if things have changed."

Winston walked to his side. "She will be excited to see you."

"You think? I haven't written to her in a month or so. Haven't seen her in years. When I realized I wasn't committing to my promise, I tried to not get her hopes up."

"How long has it been?"

"Once after the Ellsworth case. Maybe four years ago."

"Well, be sure to make amends, eh?"

Winston patted Nicoli on the back and headed for the carriage.

Nicoli smirked and looked back to Well's Peake, thinking about what was coming, knowing it had been too long.

CHAPTER NINE

Bernard looked out the hallway window, pulling his beard to a rounded edge across his chest. He rubbed his bald head and cleaned his glasses, lifting his gaze back to the streets of Well's Peake with a relaxed smile.

Carriages rattled on the cobblestone, and kids ran in and out of the road, their parents scolding them and waving them to the sidewalk. Constables patrolled the city circle, friendly with the fairgoers who flooded the city and swamped merchandise vendors.

The overcast dimmed in the afternoon, and Bernard took in the sun's warmth, knowing the frost was soon to come.

He walked down the hallway, the windows towering ten meters high. Pillars held the building, carved to resemble hay in harvest fields, and artwork lined the inside walls, each showcasing a moment from history.

Bernard admired the paintings, pausing on the last, blushing. He glanced at his pocket watch and back to the oil painting of the city, the forest in the distance, painted from a balcony high in Well's Peake.

He brushed the little dust off the frame. "You deserved better."

The door creaked behind him, and a young woman with a braid that reached her green blouse and black corset stood with a straight posture and a calm gaze.

"Mr. Griffin?" she asked with her hands at her side.

"That would be me."

"My name is Miss Fritz, but I prefer a little informality, so please call me Ellie. I apologize for my brothers. They wanted me to tell you they have arrived."

"That's all right. The world is a busy place."

"I'm glad to hear." Ellie walked next to Bernard, eyeing the canvas with him. "Quite the forgiving attitude for an aristocrat."

Bernard smiled at the young lady, his eyebrow raised. "They were kind enough to meet me at my request, so I am thankful."

Ellie gazed at the painting. "I see you like the painting. Do you know the artist?"

"I can't remember her name, but I know her face. She illustrated this from the balcony of my home when I was young. My mother donated it after my father's passing."

"I'm sorry to hear. Why did she do that?"

"He left the decision to me, and I asked her to donate it. I was obsessed with looking over the balcony, to the point I would fall asleep on the banister. My parents would watch with me, probably to ensure I didn't fall off." Bernard laughed with gusto.

Ellie giggled and covered her smile.

"There were some nights my mother would hold me close and tell me stories of how she and Father guided the city... what I wouldn't do to relive such days. Look at it now. Hung on the wall collecting dust."

Bernard took a small breath.

"My mother told me this was the vision my father held for the city. So she hired a painter to capture its essence, a reminder of what my father strived for. She hung it in my room and said, 'Bernie, this is the city our family loves and swore to uphold. If ever comes the day you look over that balcony, and it's not like the painting, know the potential is still there, it just needs your guidance.'"

Ellie looked to the canvas, leaning in. "Do you still see Well's Peake as you did?"

Bernard rubbed his palms together. "I did. That's why I donated the painting, to remind those who walked these halls of how important it is to keep the city together. It reminds me there is potential I need to discover. You seem like a very insightful young lady. May I ask you something?"

"By all means," she said.

"Do you think Well's Peake is still beautiful as in this painting?"

"I wish I could give you an answer, but I've only been back a few months. My childhood didn't have me look at the city as you did. I'm keen on the forest and the lakes over the cobblestone and brick."

Bernard nodded and turned to the painting, losing himself in a trance. It was as if he looked into his childhood. He could feel the hillside breeze wisp at the bottom of his jacket. Lavender filled his nostrils from the plants of his mother's garden. The candle wicks danced in the evening breeze, and the smooth touch of the banister was comforting on his arms, his head propped on his elbow.

"London Jean-Leon Giradi," Ellie said.

"Excuse me?"

"That's the woman who painted this picture. She was a traveler like me, and I had tea with her on the road. She was fond of harvest paintings and even captured one for me as I ran through the fields."

Bernard smiled, feeling the warmth from his childhood.

Ellie nodded and walked away, peeking inside the door. "They are ready for you, Mr. Griffin."

Bernard pulled his coat tight and walked into the World's Grand Hall, exhaling deeply.

Windows stood thirty meters high, and light bounced off two round tables as wide as the windows were tall. The hall was enormous, and chandeliers of polished crystals encased the ceiling in a glistening glow. Red banners hung low, wall to wall, woven from thick silk and cotton threads, and the smell of plaster and wood oak lingered in the air.

Bernard made his way to the inner table, his steps echoing through the hall to a pair of men who stood behind the table and a third who walked to Bernard, hand extended.

"Mr. Griffin, it's good to see you again," he said. "I apologize for the delay. We were across the city, and the World's Fair has left traffic undesirable."

"That's quite all right. I suppose I shouldn't call you Mr. Fritz since all three of you are in the room."

The men laughed. "No, Jonah will do. You remember my brothers, of course. Theodore and Dennis."

They both stepped forward and shook Bernard's hand. Jonah sported a jacket, sharp in its design, mirroring his strong jaw and seductive stare. Dennis flipped his shag hair, yanking his cuffs tight, and Theodore held his palms together, prim and proper as if he was studying Bernard from behind his oval glasses.

"Could have used a bigger hall, huh?" Theodore chuckled.

Bernard grinned. "I chose this hall for a reason. They finished it just last week, and I could not think of a better place to conduct our business."

Jonah waved his hand, and everyone took a seat around the center table.

Ellie walked to the corner and stood with her hands behind her back. Bernard batted her an eye and returned to the brothers.

"Is this hall enormous on purpose?" Dennis gazed at the chandeliers.

"Yes." Bernard turned his hand, looking for approval.

"Please." Theodore pushed his oval glasses tight on his face.

Bernard stood and pushed in his chair. He held his shoulders high and his hands broad. "Imagine a world before our own, but one on a different path. This world would've grown towards a future we did not experience. We stand now in the World's Hall, where that potential may flourish."

Bernard's voice projected throughout the hall.

"Are you referencing the days before the Black Harvest?" Theodore asked.

"Exactly. When the Industrial Revolution was in its adolescence, before the Black Harvest, the Northern Regions were in a state of unguided growth. A growth that led to destruction, a shadow of war that still affects many today. It may seem like a generation, but the Black Harvest was only thirty years ago."

Bernard stepped around the table. "We are entering another age of unguided growth and potential. To avoid repeating the past, we need guidance. We need to create a foundation composed of those with the insight and the heart of Well's Peake in mind."

Jonah's chair creaked as he rested back, and Dennis leaned forward, his hair dropping across his brow. Theodore nodded to Ellie, and she walked to a stand not far away, picked up a tray of glasses and water, and brought them to the table.

"What do you propose?" Jonah said.

"I'm looking to build a league of extraordinary people who can help guide the next revolution. Humanity will exceed its grasp, but with the right people, we can guide our ambitions, making sure we are not on the path to another Black Harvest."

Ellie poured a glass of water and set it beside Bernard.

"So we compose this league of people who *guide* inventors on how to use their inventions?" Jonah asked. "Are we talking about inventors?"

"Yes. I understand your hesitation, especially with the disdain many holds towards them, but the league will have no formal control or mandate one's free will. The league is to *guide* inventors and provide support to those pushing humanity in the right direction. To ensure technology does not revolutionize into chaos."

"And the inventors who choose not to follow the league, or whose inventions are unsafe? What happens then?" Theodore asked.

"Then they will not have the league's support, but that does not mean they can't continue with their work," Bernard said. "Men and women have made great strides, pushing humanity in ways others consider unworthy. We do not wish to stint that phenomenon, but we cannot endorse inventions that risk innocent lives. We could persuade and influence positive growth."

Jonah undid his vest button and opened a folder, looking through Bernard's proposal.

"What do you think, Miss Fritz?" Bernard asked.

Ellie tilted her head, eyeing her brothers with a stunned stare. Dennis glared, and Theodore observed them both.

"She has no stake in these decisions." Dennis set his glass down hard.

Ellie held her chin high, glaring at her brothers. "No, but I am part of this family, and I believe you asked me to partake in family matters, correct?" Ellie set the pitcher down, water spilling out the top.

Jonah flipped through the papers without a glance, and Theodore stood to avoid the running water.

"Her opinion is as important as any," Bernard said. "Whether or not she is part of your company, all people should feel they can express their opinions, and that's what I want to encourage for the league. People shouldn't fear what we are trying to accomplish. I know there is divide in the social classes, and I would like to build a bridge."

"While true, she does not hold the right of citizenship in Well's Peake." Theodore walked around the table and stood next to his sister with his hands behind his back. "I love her, but she has roamed the woodlands for many years. She revoked her right as a citizen of Well's Peake and has yet to establish her residency. Her travels may have skewered her opinion."

Ellie faked a smile with pressed eyebrows. "You know, Brother, maybe Mr. Griffin is right. Perhaps we do need some guidance because Well's Peake has yet to change since I left. This city needs help from those who have its interests at heart, not their own."

Ellie strode off, her steps echoing throughout the hall until she closed the door behind her.

Bernard exhaled, turning back to the Fritz brothers.

"My apology for our sister's behavior," Theodore said.

"There's no need. I'm afraid I might have influenced that moment." Bernard grabbed his glass. "She was honest, something I encourage."

Jonah flipped the folder shut and put one leg over the other, his eyes gentle and kind. "I'm concerned with what involvement you ask. Many could consider this a purity project, and that tends to be a never-ending money pit."

"That is not my intention," Bernard said, holding his drink, the glass chill to the touch. "This could be an establishment, a summit for inventors to create marvels. We secured the bid for the World's Fair from Redwood, even Belagrad—two cities that would have built circles around our fair with their resources, but we prevailed. Why not prevail again?"

"Redwood could not cut their own trees for decades. Hardly a force to be reckoned with, but Belagrad was quite difficult to overcome. I foresee many questioning this because many hold you in high favor. More than some aristocrats, and some might see you looking to take power."

"I don't have that mindset with the matter. Whether or not you do makes no difference to me. I know my intentions, and so do my peers. I have no desire to take the chair."

Bernard took a sip, and Dennis examined the folder, Theodore standing behind him.

"Say we are to fund this project." Dennis flipped his shaggy hair. "How do you know the council would support this World's League?"

"I've been developing this concept for many seasons. It can't belong to one man because it could flip on a coin, but to have a league of equals brings the point of debate to an equal playing field. The council is interested because of this approach."

"And who are your supporters?" Dennis asked.

"They are not ready to go public, I'm afraid."

"Shocking." Dennis patted the table with vigor.

"And you will be its grand architect?" Jonah asked.

Bernard paused, looking with focused eyes. "I will not take charge after its creation, and I will not take a seat at the table. The Creation Office would protect the rights of inventors, and those who rise together will guide the league."

"Have you submitted a claim for public acknowledgment?" Theodore asked, his glasses sliding down his nose.

"Yes, but it's minor compared to what we need now."

Dennis leaned forward. "How do you intend on choosing the inventors?"

"It is important the people elect the inventors and accept them into the community by trial of their skill and ethics."

"Ethics?" Jonah asked.

"These inventors need more than talent and influence. We'll fill the league with skilled men and women, yes, but those who have yet to be praised publicly as well. Unifying the two together will build a bridge that could lead to exponential technological expansion and a more united city. A future many dream of today."

Bernard convinced himself that the potential was in his hands from the day he dreamed of the World's League. It wasn't until that moment in front of the Fritz brothers did his unrelenting conviction shake.

"Is there anyone else invested?" Jonah asked.

"Yes, some have pledged their support while others are contemplating, but I have been working my way up. I'm aiming for the sky, Mr. Fritz. *We* need to shape the new age, with a renaissance of inventors who think on their feet and can train the next generation."

Bernard let out a sigh and rubbed his palms together. Dennis shook his head while Jonah and Theodore pointed out something on the paper.

"And where is your wealth in this grand image?" Dennis asked. "We fund your dream with no concrete promise, little to no returns, and you look to be in for less than half?"

"I believe that would lead to the most success in the league. One man cannot fund this, for it will falter within. As the voice of this project, if my funds are higher than any others, people might not see the validity of the league when it belongs to them."

"What about being credited for our investment?"

"You will each receive public honors, but the amount is to remain anonymous," Bernard said.

"Even those who put in a pound when we put in a hundredfold?" Dennis screeched his chair across the floor as he stood.

"Yes, otherwise, it defeats the purpose of the league."

"I agree with my brother." Theodore straightened his glasses, looking over the rim. "You would need to give more, or we would need something in return, Mr. Griffin."

"I can't. People will know it's an incentive. I have stripped myself of the honors."

Jonah stood and buttoned his jacket. "Mr. Griffin, I admire your vision and your prowess, but you preach something that no one will want to be part of and to those who have nothing to gain. You are thinking beyond us."

"That is why we need it. It is thinking beyond to protect from what is coming."

"Well, you have yet to convince me we are on the path to another Black Harvest. We're focused on the now." Jonah stood with Dennis.

"And I." Dennis grabbed onto his jacket.

Theodore remained quiet, flipping through the pages. His brothers looked at him, and he didn't bat a glance.

It only took one to entertain the idea, to convince the others of its potential. Bernard could see the light in Theodore's eyes, feeling as if he had yet to deny it in whole.

Bernard remained tall, folding his hands, waiting for promise.

"Brother..." Dennis gawked.

Theodore shushed him with his hand, closed the folder, and removed his glasses. "I assume you have come to us because the Royal Exchange has denied you funding. They are not the only ones, I presume. Your proposal is all risk with limited return, financially speaking."

Theodore rose and picked up the proposal. Dennis and Jonah stepped away while Theodore walked to Bernard and shook his hand.

"Please reconsider," Bernard asked. "Terms are negotiable. I assume Kenneth Forbes has invited you to his gala. Talk to the aristocrats, for many favor the league. They don't want another Black Harvest either."

"You speak as if they were all noble, Mr. Griffin." Theodore leaned in. "Why do you think the lower classes despise us so? Because of the few rotten apples."

"There are still good people up here."

"I know of at least one." Theodore pocketed his glasses and walked out with his brothers.

The door echoed and reverberated in the hall.

Bernard closed his eyes and took a deep breath. He could sense the emptiness of the room but also the potential for success. He only needed his saving grace, the one piece of the puzzle, to start what would be the greatest creation of Well's Peake. Not physical or artistic, but an ideal made real by the collection of inventors who wanted to protect the future.

He opened his eyes, and the chandeliers glistened like the heavens on the most beautiful day. The goosebumps on his arms faded, and his thoughts were still.

A cough came next to him, Ellie leaning forward with a boxed package.

"It didn't sound so promising in here, did it?" Bernard lowered his voice.

"They are just working you to judge your persistence. There is still hope." Ellie held out the box.

Bernard grabbed the gift and rubbed his hand against the package, the aroma of lilac lingering. "What is it?"

"Hope."

Bernard held the gift under his arm. "I will have to admit; this is my first failure regarding the World's League."

"It's a good thing you can try again."

Bernard laughed and held his belly as he did. "There are few people I don't know in this city, and I wasn't aware there was a Fritz sister."

"I'm not as social as my brothers."

"Would you kindly ask them to consider the matter?"

"Isn't that what I've already done?" Ellie smiled and walked to the hallway. "Good day, Mr. Griffin."

Bernard chuckled and set the gift on the table, rubbing his hand along the wrap. He untied it and pulled the package apart, careful not to rip the paper. As he lifted the lid off the box, his shoulders lowered, and a smile shined through his beard.

Bernard ran his fingers against the edge of the smooth canvas and lifted the painting into the chandelier's light, looking to the balcony from his childhood.

CHAPTER TEN

Aleksandar and Hugh stepped into the Grand Hall, sunlight beaming through the glass ceiling, reflecting off the marble floors. Chefs from all corners of the world filled the hallways with authentic cuisine.

Exhibits of new culinary dishes lined the way, judges filling themselves to the brim, searching for recipes for the most luxurious restaurants. From the sweet and tangy spices of the South to the berries and rich game of the North, chefs cooked with dramatized effort, their knives ringing off the cutting tables.

Aleksandar's mouth watered from the savories and dinners, butter melting to the sizzling herbs layered over grilled food.

A man in a beige apron opened a metal lid, beef grilling on a wood frame with garlic and onion bubbling on top. His apprentice held out a sample, and Aleksandar took it, taking a bite. The meat exploded with flavor, butter blended with fresh basil, overwhelming his taste buds.

The apprentice held the tray to Hugh, who pointed to his chest in hesitation. He held it out, careful not to drip onto his torn jacket. His slicked hair smelled floral but was heavy with pomade, and his beard was scraggly and untamed. He bit into the beef, his eyes widening.

"Where are we headed?" Hugh asked.

"The World's Workshop. The architects designed it for those interested in the fundamentals of industrial design. It seems to be the perfect place to start. You'd think they would be creative and name something without putting *World's* in front of it."

Aleksandar laughed as they rounded the corner to a banner hanging between the pillars.

Cultural District.

Coats, dresses, vests, and accessories for every occasion rested on racks, with merchants ready to sell and models sporting the newest fashions.

Aleksandar paused at a hat-making booth, admiring the craftsmanship of the stitching. A tailor trimmed off the edge of a brim, securing a wood brace to ensure the curve remained intact. Aleksandar lifted a hat, the sunlight catching the fibers in his hands.

The tailor smiled, the wrinkles from the rim of his eyes doing nothing to dim his enthusiasm. "Interested, my boy?"

"Am I," Aleksandar said. "Where did you study to shape hats?"

"Just years of practice and a never-ending desire to learn the craft. Would an apprenticeship strike your fancy?"

Aleksandar admired the hat and rested it on his head. To create something so simple but desired by all was a dream he carried for many seasons—a simple pleasure.

"If only I weren't so busy."

"The name's James Locke." James stepped from behind the cart. "If you ever change your mind, you can find me at my shop. We also sell coffee, chocolate, and tobacco if those things strike your fancy."

Aleksandar shook the tailor's hand. "Thank you. I'm Mr. Scott."

"Pleasure to meet you. Have a splendid day." The tailor tipped his head as if he had a hat.

Aleksandar turned around to find Hugh nowhere in sight. Unable to see him through the frenzy of bobbing heads, Aleksandar paced through the vendors, making his way into the Invention Hall, searching for Hugh.

Hundreds of inventors waved their hands in their displays or tinkered with newfound wonders. Custom banners stood high, and fairgoers watched with intrigue.

Inventors showcased their earlier work, while others sat on display for fairgoers to gawk with awe. Aleksandar worked his way through the crowd and paused, spotting Hugh across the aisle. Hugh sat with a pulley in hand, looking it over, his jacket hanging on the bench.

The workbench was short, with many others working on their own inventions. Hundreds if not thousands of little mechanisms from boilers to pocket watches rested on shelves between each row of benches. Orange-and-red curtains waved against the glass and tree pillars, light dancing around the shade.

Aleksandar stepped to Hugh's side and pulled on the rope, the fibers rough in his hand. The wheels, connected to the pulleys, spun in a circular rhythm, lifting and lowering the weight attached to the other end, moving at the pace of Aleksandar's arm. Hugh watched with pressed eyes.

"Seems rather simple, doesn't it?" Aleksandar said. "It's basic but teaches the fundamentals."

Aleksandar watched as Hugh remained silent, experimenting with the rope. It was like watching a child see their shadow or experience their first snow. Hugh wasn't much younger than Aleksandar, but he couldn't help but wonder if Hugh had experienced little in his childhood.

"I don't understand how inventors create, though," Hugh said, staring at the pulley. "How does an inventor design based only on an idea? Do you know what to look for?"

Aleksandar rubbed the back of his collar. "Um, it's trial and error. You develop an idea and test it. Alternative theories come out every day, and when one makes more sense to our world, it replaces the old. It's less frequent these days, but the world can still change in a season."

"I never could think of my own ideas." Hugh hunched over, tampering with the pulleys. He unscrewed the centers, removed two of the four, and assembled the lift.

Aleksandar couldn't help but hold back a smile at Hugh's quick ingenuity. "Do you know conservation of energy? One law of science."

Hugh shook his head.

"Don't worry; we'll get there."

Hugh pulled the rope, looking to the crowd.

"Is something wrong?" Aleksandar asked.

"I don't know. It just seems like I don't have the skills needed," Hugh said.

"If you don't mind me asking, what are you looking to do? I assume you want to be an inventor, but I'm not entirely sure."

"I'd like to be an inventor."

"Is there something specific you enjoy most?"

"I like changing things. I think most things could be better."

Aleksandar stood and eyed the hat stand. "So let me ask, how did you understand the Red Breath? You took it apart like you knew what you were doing."

"My luck, I guess." Hugh rolled up his sleeve. "You get used to fixing old things where I come from."

"Well, this is unexpected," someone said with a coy tone.

Aleksandar and Hugh turned to Owen, leaning on his cane.

"If it isn't Mr. Evans," Owen said.

Hugh lowered his arm and looked at the bench.

"Owen, always a pleasure." Aleksandar lifted his shoulders, hoping he didn't stick his chest too far out.

The pit in his stomach grew, and his back tightened. Aleksandar stretched his jaw, realizing he pursed his lips, trying to relax. Aleksandar found his gaze on Owen, words still drying on his tongue. Aleksandar let out a hoarse cough. "Congratulations on yesterday's exhibition." Aleksandar tried to keep the awkwardness out of his voice.

"Thank you. It's the least I could do. Hoping to change some lives," Owen said.

"I'm sure you will."

"Yes. I attended your presentation yesterday as well. The elements, I see, are difficult to work with."

Aleksandar cleared his throat. "They are, but once we determine how to manipulate them, we'll be able to use them in ways we've never seen."

Hugh eyed the two inventors, Aleksandar thankful for something to turn to other than Owen and his self-righteousness.

"That may be true, but until you learn to harness that potential, the elemental movement is a fashion statement." Owen leaned both hands on his cane, looking over Hugh's shoulder.

"I don't understand your tone," Aleksandar said.

Owen cocked his head. "Please, Aleksandar, you're not naïve. You *surely* do not believe the elements have a future, do you? We may figure out how to control them, but we'll never learn to manipulate them, let alone use them beneficially."

"Like all inventions, we start at the beginning."

"Like your Red Breath? You're blowing air and fuel through fire, causing it to shine brighter."

Aleksandar turned to Owen. "Elemental technology is coming around, and it will meet the need soon enough. It has its place."

"Your Red Breath is a risk to those who use it. A momentous idea, but a flawed one."

"Well, I still have hope." Aleksandar turned and crossed his arms. He wanted to insult Owen, but his machines were years ahead and already seen as a positive change in the community.

Owen let out a sigh and tapped his cane. "Why waste your breath on pointless endeavors? Move into the Industrial Revolution. You could be part of a movement that is more than superficial glamor. Don't leave a mark not worth leaving, and don't teach Mr. Evans about unnecessary technology. The last I heard, he's not even an inventor."

Aleksandar turned with a forced smirk. "He may not be yet, but he can change things. I've seen it. His mind gives him insight into what we and our inventions could be, not what they are."

Hugh cleared his throat, breaking the attention between the inventors before him. They paused, waiting for him to speak.

"No. I can do it," Hugh said.

Aleksandar shook his head, grinding his teeth.

"You should be a little more careful, Aleksandar," Owen said. "You can't teach when you have not been taught yourself."

"We all start somewhere," Aleksandar said. "Even the greats stood on the cobblestone we do now."

"I assume so," Owen said.

Owen rested on his cane, looking at Aleksandar and Hugh.

"I know you're a busy man, Owen. Was there something else you needed?" Aleksandar put his hands in his pockets.

Owen couldn't just leave, could he? He always had to illiterate his standing on things, making sure people knew his opinion.

Owen shook his head. "I'm curious, Aleksandar. Do you know who this man is?"

Aleksandar turned to Hugh.

"I thought I had an idea," Aleksandar said. "Seems like you will tell me."

"Some would say Mr. Evans is known as the inventor's shadow." Owen sat, pulling his weak leg on top of the other.

"What does that mean to me?" Aleksandar waved a hand.

Owen set his cane on his lap. "How did you meet Mr. Evans?"

Aleksandar paused, looking from the corner of his eye. "I found him tinkering with my invention."

"Exactly my point." Owen bobbed his cane. "He has an unhealthy habit of tampering with inventions, which aren't his."

Aleksandar tipped his head to the side, looking at Hugh. "Is that true, Mr. Evans? Do you have this habit?"

Hugh looked to the floor, breathing heavily through his nose. "I never meant to cause trouble. Your device had a weak valve. Too much pressure, and it would rupture. I never had the opportunity either, and no one would teach me."

Aleksandar let a few seconds pass and rocked in his spot. "Is that it?"

Owen's lips parted under his thick mustache, and he pushed one side straight with the tips of his fingers.

"It might surprise you what someone is capable of when they know you believe in them," Aleksandar said.

"Maybe I should leave," Hugh said.

"No, Mr. Evans, stay." Owen held his hand to Hugh. "Hold on,

Aleksandar; I have an idea. You seem to have a lot of faith in Mr. Evans. Why not let him build something? Give him a shot and see what he can do."

Aleksandar and Owen looked at Hugh.

He stood. "I… can do it."

"Excellent." Owen stood and glanced over the workbenches with raised eyebrows. He hooked his cane on the edge of the bench and limped across the walkway. He lifted a wooden machine from another table and walked back, setting a collection of parts down.

"What is it?" Hugh asked.

Aleksandar moved to the side of the bench, his arms crossed, one hand rubbing his jaw.

"What better way to celebrate the absolution of the printing press than with some healthy competition," Owen said.

Aleksandar looked at the bench. Punches, letter matrices, and several brackets of the printing press lay on the table.

"Have you ever assembled one of these?" Owen asked.

"No," Hugh said, grabbing a punch.

"Good. Simple if you know how everything works, but not so much if you've never handled it."

"I can't take it apart first?" Hugh held two parts together.

"That's reverse engineering, and I won't give you a schematic. I believe if you have natural ingenuity, you could figure it out. Now we will see. How's twenty minutes sound?"

Hugh rolled his other sleeve and pulled up a chair. He looked to Owen, who held his palm to the pieces.

Hugh took a deep breath and closed his eyes.

Aleksandar felt his jaw tense as Hugh sat there and did nothing. He wasn't sure what could be running through Hugh's mind, let alone his own.

Aleksandar reached, but Hugh opened his eyes and prodded, piece by piece, through the machinery. He held each part to each other, trying to assemble them. He attached a lever to a mounting bracket, pulled, and it pushed the tray against an empty box.

Aleksandar's hand grew sweaty, and Owen checked his watch. How fast the moment went eluded him, but he felt it passing, and Hugh was struggling.

Hugh joined the pieces of the printing press and put his hand on the lever, pulling it down. It clicked but did not budge. Hugh looked under the carriage and reached in, rotating two brackets.

Aleksandar eyed several parts on the bench, wondering if Owen put in extras to confuse Hugh.

Hugh pulled the lever again, and the machine rotated. His eyes lit up, and Aleksandar leaned in, but the machine ground to a stop. Hugh released the lever, but the press didn't turn back. He pushed with both of his arms, but the machine refused to move. He pulled again, glancing over his shoulder as beads of sweat dripped down his neck.

After a few yanks, Hugh let out an exhausted breath, his cheeks red.

"Twenty minutes have passed." Owen stepped forward and, with the end of his cane, pushed on a bolt. The punches fell onto the table, clanking off the bench and onto the floor.

Hugh's head lowered to the bolt on the bench. He picked it up and clenched it in his hand; his eyes shut tight.

"Well, you don't lack determination." Owen tilted his head. "However, we aren't always meant for certain things. I'm all for making sure, but..."

"There's a reason some don't follow their passions," Hugh said. "Because aristocrats like you ruin it."

Owen turned to Aleksandar without hesitation. "We must be careful who we hand the hammer to, for once we lay the road; there's no return."

Aleksandar stood in Owen's face. "You think you're the Maker's gift to the world, don't you? I *will* take him as my apprentice, and he will prove to you otherwise."

Owen stepped back, pushing his tongue against his cheek. "No, I am not the Maker's gift. You may not like how I go about my day, but I'm looking to humanity's future. We have let too many meddle with things they don't understand. Look at the Black Harvest. What we hope for isn't always what was given."

Owen looked to his leg, and Aleksandar inhaled deeply.

"It's not what you look at; it's what you see," Hugh said, holding the bolt from the printing press.

Owen exhaled and looked at the bottom of his cane. "How often have you failed, Mr. Evans?"

Hugh swallowed hard. "I don't know."

"How often have you tried?"

Hugh shrugged a shoulder.

"I'm assuming the same amount." Owen stepped back from Aleksandar. "I'm not sorry for who I am, but I hope you can empathize with my view. To be proven otherwise would be surprising, but we have to make the hard choices to protect the future."

Aleksandar stood as Owen walked away. He could feel the pulse in his thumbs and the tightness in his jaw. He would make sure Hugh could beat him someday to show Owen he could prepare an apprentice and thrive in the elements.

Hugh looked to the printing press, rubbing his hand along the punches, and set the bolt down.

"Are you all right?" Aleksandar asked.

"Yeah." Hugh rolled his sleeves down and slid on his jacket. "If it's all right, I'd like to leave."

"Of course."

Hugh slid his hands into his pockets and wallowed to the edge of the crowd. Aleksandar could sense his sadness, knowing what it was like to feel as if the world didn't care for you.

Aleksandar tossed the bolt to Hugh, and he caught it in his hand, almost dropping it on the floor. "I'll see you tomorrow, yes?"

Hugh lifted his head, his eyes catching the sun. "You still want to teach me?"

Aleksandar nodded. "I think Owen needs knocked down a peg."

Hugh found a smile and walked into the crowd.

Aleksandar looked over the vendors and the workbenches, peering down the hallway. The hat stand was closed. He patted his hands together and sighed. He took a dramatic step and made his way into the crowd.

Aleksandar walked through the World's Halls, admiring the food and clothing exhibits, his feet slow to move towards his booth. The shadows grew long as the sun dipped in the sky, the marble gleaming like the architects intended in the sunlight. Aleksandar enjoyed himself as the afternoon grew late.

The Red Breath rested on his bench, but a woman with chestnut hair sat next to it, facing the other way. Aleksandar walked into his exhibit, removing his hands from his pockets.

"May I help you?" Aleksandar asked.

She turned, standing in an elegant grace, pulling her jacket straight. "Hello, my name is Natalia Arlen. You are Aleksandar Scott, the young inventor, correct?"

"I am." Aleksandar nodded. "I know you. You're one of the greatest inventors of our age."

Natalia laughed, her smile lines catching the light. "Thank you, but I believe you mean of my age."

Aleksandar chuckled, raising his hands, not knowing what to do with them. "I apologize; I have had an eventful afternoon. I hope my excitement was genuine."

Aleksandar shook her hand, his cheeks filling with warmth.

"I understand those days," she said. "You wouldn't have a moment to talk, would you?"

"Yes, of course." Aleksandar turned his head, his voice trailing off. "What could Natalia Arlen want with a rookie like me?"

Natalia held up a finger and stepped to the bench. Aleksandar raised an eyebrow as Natalia pulled out a small device and set it on the bench. It had a bronze handle with grooved curves, sleek and glossy. Two prongs rested at the end that were elegant and exquisitely curved.

Aleksandar lifted his gaze to Natalia, who watched him with intent eyes.

"I have a proposition you may not want to miss."

CHAPTER ELEVEN

Aleksandar held the mechanism in his palm, unable to find words. He rubbed his fingers down the device, the craftsmanship immaculate, and when the afternoon sun hit the surface, it shined like gold.

"It's incredible, don't you agree?" Natalia asked.

Aleksandar looked at her inviting blue eyes, smirking. "It's beautiful. I don't even know what it is."

Natalia stood with poise, looking back at her fellow inventor with a grin. She held back the sides of her embroidered blue coat.

"May I?" Aleksandar asked.

"Please do," she said.

Aleksandar held the button on the side, and the prongs rotated to create a sparkling sphere, the light glinting in Aleksandar's pupils. He jerked his hands and chuckled; the top of his hand tingled and grew warm. He smelled a faint metal aroma and the hint of copper in his mouth from the vapors.

The Spark glistened and hummed low, Aleksandar's smile widened between his dimples.

"I call that little device the Spark," Natalia said. "Whenever I become stumped or need another idea, I turn it on, and as you can see, it does the rest."

"Is it creating… electricity?"

"It is."

Aleksandar let go of the button, and his shoulders dropped. "This is impossible. Even in Belagrad they use machines two stories high to meddle with this technology."

"You're not wrong. While Tesla and Alva terrify the masses in the North, I had the pleasure of meeting them. I had an idea, Tesla guided me, and the Spark was the result."

Aleksandar pressed the button again, licking his lips. He had never held something as natural as lightning in the palm of his hand.

Aleksandar set it on the table, shaking his head in excitement. "Are you hoping I come up with an idea?"

"I was hoping we would."

Aleksandar paused, sensing an unwanted presence. He looked to the side to a reporter who stared back with a devious smirk.

"I cannot believe it," he said. "Aleksandar Scott, the young inventor, and Natalia Arlen, together at the World's Fair. I never would've guessed someone so distinguished would take an interest in Mr. Scott."

Natalia smacked her lips.

"The name's Abel Hawthorne." He shook Aleksandar's hand. "Lead reporter of the *Well's Peake Commons*. If it's not too much, I'd love to interview both of you."

Aleksandar shook the man's hand with a timid stare, glancing at Natalia. "Hello."

"Miss Arlen, always a pleasure," Abel said.

"Mr. Hawthorne," Natalia said. "If I were the suspicious type, I'd point out how you've been watching me the past few days."

"Thankfully, you're not the suspicious type." Abel flashed a forced smile and pulled out his notebook and pen.

Abel glanced at Natalia, but she held herself tall and calm. If Abel was annoying her, she did little to show it. Aleksandar stepped forward, but Abel forced himself between the two.

"I beg you, just one question," Abel said.

"You may ask me, but Mr. Scott is off-limits."

Abel ignored Natalia and turned to Aleksandar. "Mr. Scott, how does it feel, despite your rise in your field, to lose the exhibition yesterday?"

Aleksandar's chest and hands stiffened as the reporter stepped closer, leaving little room.

"I—it was not what I expected," Aleksandar said with a dry throat.

"I assume not. You seemed so confident in your display, despite the—"

"Abel, don't start." Natalia lowered her brow.

"Don't worry, Miss Arlen. I was just looking for insight on the event." Abel turned to Aleksandar. "Mr. Scott, a wise man once told me that to move further, you must know where you stand. Do you know where you stand?"

"I think that is enough." Natalia grabbed Abel's notepad and tossed it to the floor.

Abel dropped his hands and let out a sharp laugh, not fazed in the least. "Miss Arlen, that was not ladylike."

"And you're not being gentlemanlike."

Abel raised his eyebrows and kneeled to his notebook. Natalia put her foot on it as he pulled. Abel sighed and stood, Natalia never breaking their stare.

"We're not making a spectacle out of this, are we?" Abel asked.

"That depends on you. Walk away now, leave your book, or see what happens. There are some fairgoers behind you who think it amusing."

Aleksandar could not help but gawk, knowing he did not exist to either of them at the moment. Abel was relentless, but he was water to stone against Natalia's never-flinching posture. She carried a confidence he could sense against Abel's amused stare.

Abel turned around, several fairgoers grinning at him. He waved to them and turned back, clicking his tongue. "You are quite clever, Miss Arlen. I wonder what you would do without *your* notebook?"

Natalia furrowed her brow at him. "Have a pleasant day, Abel."

Abel tipped his hat with an amused smile and walked away, pulling another notebook from his pocket.

Aleksandar collected himself, a burst of energy waiting to lift off his chest. His heart raced, and his cheeks hurt from his smile.

Natalia picked up the notepad and pencil, opening the pages to scribbles of notes and a few poorly drawn figures. She closed it and set it on the table.

Aleksandar pushed his hand in his hair, blushing. "Thank you. I think he might've pulled one over me."

"He intended to. Mr. Hawthorne's ways are questionable, but his writing and methods are formidable. Mr. Scott, I come to you seeking help. I would like to collaborate on an invention. A grand reputation is rumored to follow you, and you might possess the skill needed to help my vision."

Aleksandar raised his eyebrows, rubbing his shirt cuff. "I'm flattered, but I don't understand why you're offering this to me. There are inventors far more experienced than me."

"Some, yes, but after many years in the field, we inventors develop our own style and rules. Tunnel vision sets in, and all we can look at is furthering our inventions. Despite all our experience, we become what we started, beginners and apprentices."

Aleksandar rubbed his neck, the stray hairs slipping through his fingers. "So you're looking for an open mind? A young one, perhaps, but Owen O'Connell has made greater strides."

"Owen O'Connell does not dabble in the elements. I saw your presentation, and you're on the right track. You understand elemental creation and are working on how to control it. Together, we could create something marvelous."

"And you think I have the potential you need?"

"Yes," Natalia said, sounding sure of herself.

"This is just unexpected." Aleksandar grinned and looked to the fair, pulling his shoulders back. "I never dreamed that someone as seasoned as you would think my work had potential. You said inventors develop tunnel vision. Do you find yourself looking down that tunnel?"

Natalia smirked and chuckled, brushing the side of her cheek. "Yes." She walked to the Red Breath.

Never in his life did Aleksandar dream of working with someone so esteemed, to help himself into a position where he could display his invention to the world. Everything he ever strived for was at his fingertips.

"If I may ask another question, was it true you were working on a water engine?" Aleksandar asked.

Natalia gave a short, hesitant sigh. "I still am. I reach to you because I see an opportunity for both of us. We start fresh with an invention, so we have equal ground to stand on at its revelation."

"At the Harvest Exhibition?"

"Yes. We both have much to gain in influence."

Natalia's eyes drifted off to the curtains of the World's Palace. Aleksandar eyed her as she reached into her pocket and pulled out a small journal, losing her focus. She opened it to the ribbon that held its place, and she read through it. She wrote a note and put it back in her jacket, returning her gaze to Aleksandar.

"My apologies, Mr. Scott." Natalia looked down, biting the end of her lip. "I have *moments* where I'm flooded with ideas, and I must write them down. You might see these on occasion, and I hope it doesn't frighten you if you were to accept my offer."

Aleksandar gestured with his hand. "No, no, that's all right. I apologize if I stared. So just like that? We invent?"

"Just like that." Natalia nodded.

"Natalia Arlen, esteemed inventor, teaming up with Aleksandar Scott, the amateur."

"You wouldn't be the young inventor for long after."

The weight of his own words bore on Aleksandar. Several moments ago, he'd had little going for him, and now he carried the offer he dreamed of. Years of planning and working through sweat and tears could finally pay off.

He lifted the Spark and turned it on, the light steady and wisping, drawing a young girl's attention in the crowd. She looked on in awe and ran away with vigor. Natalia watched, her eyes mirroring the light.

Aleksandar turned off the device and passed it to Natalia. She rolled it around in one hand before returning her attention to Aleksandar.

"Am I able to expect great things, Mr. Scott?" Natalia asked.

A smile spread across Aleksandar's face, and he nodded. "Yes."

"Fabulous." Natalia returned a radiant smile, her face seeming to shine in the light. She held the Spark out to Aleksandar, who took the device with a hesitant hand.

"What are you doing?" Aleksandar asked.

"I want you to hold on to this until the end of our collaboration. I have an idea I would like for us to entertain, but I'm optimistic this will help you as well."

Aleksandar nodded as he looked at the device. "Are you to be my mentor as well?"

"I can help if you wish, but I know we will teach each other to an equal degree."

Aleksandar shook his head and batted his eyes to the clock on the pillar, realizing he would be late.

"Goodness, I apologize. I am to meet someone soon. I don't mean to cut you short."

"That's all right." Natalia pulled out a note and handed it to Aleksandar. "My address with a date for when we can start. I hope you will be there."

"I will." Aleksandar grabbed his jacket from the rack. "Thank you. You don't understand how much this means."

"I might. Oh, I have one condition I'd like you to consider."

"What might that be?" Aleksandar pulled on his jacket, buttoning the middle.

"Could we pursue something water-related?"

Aleksandar put the Spark in his pocket, standing before the esteemed Natalia Arlen, pleased with the prospect of what he and her future might bring.

"Indeed."

CHAPTER TWELVE

C arriage wheels rattled against the cobblestone on the outer city road, rocking back and forth as the sun gleamed through the amber leaves of the forest, glowing in the morning light.

Nicoli pulled the curtain back, looking to the city of Well's Peake as homes and brick buildings replaced the forest's trees as the carriage entered the city. He flipped down his window, the cool air rushing into the carriage and blowing his scarf to the side. He ran his hand through his long, brown hair, pushing it behind his shoulders with his eyes closed.

"Mr. Lucas, we will arrive soon," Winston said from outside the carriage. "Would you prefer Baker Street or Edinburgh Lane as our entrance?"

"Baker will be fine, Winston, thank you." Nicoli put his hands on his lap, twiddling his thumbs.

"Yes, sir."

Winston snapped the reins, and the carriage sped up as the city surrounded them.

The blue curtains danced with each bump in the road, Mr. Lucas holding still in place against the padded red cushion. He watched as kids played next to an alleyway. One pushed the other, and another slapped him back. A young girl handed out flowers on the next corner, her mother standing behind her, chatting with another man.

The horse pulled the carriage to a brick building seven stories high with white trim separating each floor. A dull orange accented the windows while lampposts riddled the siding. Winston dismounted the carriage, and the horses neighed as he opened the door with proper form.

"Peakeland Yard, Mr. Lucas," he said.

Nicoli stepped out in a tweed jacket with a slender stature, his jacket as gray as ash and collar high and tight. He scratched his beard stubble and set his flat cap on his head. He sighed, looking to the building.

"Sir?"

"I'm all right, Winston. It might be a while. How about you treat yourself to the Wellsboro Cafe." Nicoli placed some coin in Winston's gloved palm.

"You're too kind. Would you like anything, sir?"

"If you could stop at Patti's when you return, kindly pick me up a scone with clotted cream and jam. Strawberry, please. None of that other stuff. If they ask, Cornwall for my scone."

"It will be my pleasure."

Winston climbed back onto the carriage seat, and Nicoli walked into the building.

Constables sat at the front desk and nodded to Nicoli as he walked by, returning the gestures. Wood paneling lined the walls, hand-carved with antique molding running across the top, and paintings of Well's Peake and the forest-lined the hallway. He opened a dual door into an enormous suite lined with constables seated at their desks. Offices lined the back, and several stopped and stared at Mr. Lucas as he walked by.

It had been many seasons since he visited Well's Peake, let alone the Peakeland Yard. His presence startled a few, but it did not matter to him. Their opinion was their own, and Mr. Lucas preferred it that way.

Nicoli looked through an office window to see the chief writing at his desk. He tapped the glass with the back of his hand, and the chief looked with a forced stare, waving him in.

"Chief Constable Dekker."

Dekker stood and shook his hand. "Nicoli, I wondered if you would accept my invitation. The World's Fair has brought many things past my comfortability. Please take a seat."

Nicoli walked to the wood chair. "That's okay; I've been sitting—"

"Please, take a seat, for my sake." The chief sat in his chair, forearms on the table, his eyes low, carrying himself like an older man despite being in his mid-twenties.

Nicoli nodded and sat, pushing his coat back. The chief lit a cigar, his hair shaggy as if a child cut the ends and he had just rolled out of bed. The look was natural, and he could pull it off. Anyone else would not have gotten away with it in Dekker's position.

"Tea?" the chief asked, holding his hand to a teapot.

"Please." Nicoli set his hands in his lap.

The chief topped off his cup and grabbed another from the cabinet, handing it to Nicoli. Orange and lemon lingered from the cup as he poured the liquid. The cup was smooth to the touch, and the warmth of the tea spread through Nicoli's hands.

Dekker rested back into his chair and let out a heavy sigh, leaning on the desk. "Nicoli, after all the years my father served on the Peake—"

"Thirty-Two. Although I only helped for a few."

Dekker smirked. "Yeah, out of thirty-two years on the force, he never once brought his work home. Mum would ask, and never a peep. Not until you took the oath. I never heard your name until I walked onto the Peake, but I would overhear him. He wasn't afraid of you, but when you needed to be involved, he was scared of someone. I thought you a fable, straight from the Old Book."

Nicoli straightened up and took a sip, the tea's warm, citrus flavors both sweet and sour on his tastebuds. "No fable. Just a detective sipping tea at the edge of your desk."

Dekker looked past Nicoli and waved to a constable. Nicoli sipped his tea.

Dekker wrote a note and tossed the pen on the table. "My father was so worried when you were involved, but I'm relieved you're here."

"I hope I didn't stress him into early retirement." Nicoli set the teacup on the saucer, the glass tinging.

"Oh, I doubt that. When his mind's there, he's still as sharp as a tack, but when it's not…"

"The Black Harvest?"

"Yes." Dekker nodded. "They confirmed it a few months ago. It surprised them it laid dormant for so long since he had direct contact. In most cases, offspring are the ones to show dormancy flare-ups."

"I'm sorry, your father was a good man."

"Thank you. Many his age did not make it this long, so I consider the family blessed. It didn't pass to us that we are aware of, so I'm going to take that in strides." Dekker looked up. "I need your help, Nicoli."

Nicoli removed his hat and adjusted his hair. "I'm afraid with the World's Fair that your situation will escalate. I'm sure there are bodies we have yet to discover, and with so many inventors in town, it's a hunting ground."

Dekker grabbed his cigar and took a puff. "We deal with murder on the daily, but they never prepared us for this. When I told my father, he said he encountered it twice before, and they were that of nightmares. His memory slipped on the bad days, but when he remembered what I told him, I knew this was something my men and I were not prepared for."

"No one is."

"Did you read the file?"

"Yes, but it lacked some info."

Dekker grabbed a folder and tossed it across the desk. "I didn't want to risk all the info on the road. Does the name Owen O'Connell ring a bell in Redwood?"

"An inventor. He has become popular over the past few years if I'm not mistaken. Is he related to the victim?"

"The latest victim is Owen's cousin."

"Have you spoken with him?"

"He was here this morning. They were not on speaking terms, but it disturbs Owen with the unpleasant nature of the murder. He'll offer his insight on the situation since these murders seemed to be executed with elemental technology. I wouldn't mind you on the case considering the severity."

"I'm surprised you don't bring in that other fella with the hat and pipe.

He has the aptitude for it."

Dekker batted his eye. "You didn't hear?"

"No."

Dekker pulled off his glasses and rubbed his eyes. "Not that we know of. He has been missing for several months. Rumor has it he met someone as clever and mad as him. They threw each other off a balcony and into a waterfall. The chance he could have survived the fall is slim, but we never found a body. Until we do, he's considered missing. Maybe something you could look into later."

"I'm sorry. He was—"

"An asshole. A brilliant, stubborn asshole. We do miss him."

Nicoli took a sip, shaking his head. He opened the file to the image of Raymond strapped to a chair, his body bruised beyond identification. Nicoli did not flinch. He wanted to, but he couldn't show that weakness to Dekker. People looked to him for hard cases, and if it unnerved him, they would be too.

"Does that not disturb you?" Dekker asked, a shiver in his voice.

"It does. Any ideas on why Raymond was targeted?"

"Yes. Turn to Owen's statement."

Nicoli turned a few pages, and his eyes batted up. "Is that so?"

"Owen said Raymond worked closely with Owen's father until his passing, and was unaware of Raymond's involvement until after his father's death. I understand murders, but this, there's no logic to it. It makes no sense."

"Anyone involved with Owen's father is always a target. I'll see what I can do. We need to dive deeper into Raymond's work and determine what he was doing and if he had accomplices."

"I have someone on it. We can let you know what we discover, but I'm sure you'll do your own digging."

Nicoli nodded, closing the file.

"I want a tight lid on this, Nicoli," Dekker said. "You report to me and no one else. The last thing we need is citywide panic. If someone like Abel Hawthorne caught wind of anything, the World's Fair will become a dangerous place. Well's Peake is not equipped for that level of hysteria, even with extra forces from other Yards."

"Understood. I assume I have your permission for other matters."

Dekker tapped his fingers and let out a heavy breath through his nose. He pulled an envelope from the top drawer of his desk and set it in front of him. "I figured you'd bring that up, and I had your papers approved. You'll have access to our private vendors for what you need, but my situation is your primary focus. We have five bodies on the table, and Mr. O'Connell's is not even dry."

"Thank you."

The chief closed a drawer, never breaking eye contact with the inspector. "I need to understand what is happening in my city, Nicoli. I'm losing sleep over this, and I need to know if I should stay awake."

Nicoli craved to run his hand through his hair, but he restrained himself. "I'll handle it. That's why you brought me in."

"Not without resistance. Redwood may tolerate you after your dive into madness, but Well's Peake isn't as accommodating. I was able to approve two months of unsanctioned work, and it doesn't come without favors." Dekker stood, taking his cigar with him to the window and blowing the smoke against the glass.

Murderers on the streets were expected, but not to this magnitude of violence and severity.

Dekker looked over his shoulder. "I've heard of this ghost of yours. My dad believed in it, but I have yet to be convinced."

"I'm here to stop *your* serial killer."

"You and your fancy classification. You make it difficult to hand over those papers. I understand you want this, but we all have that one that got away."

Nicoli looked up with open eyes. "He didn't slip away. I just haven't caught him."

"Or proved he exists." The chief walked to the desk and rested on the edge. "I don't question your passion, but your obsession concerns me. Nicoli, I need to hear you say this will stay under wraps."

Nicoli stood. "You have my word."

"If I feel any pressure from the aristocrats, I'll deport you."

"I'll catch your killer." Nicoli took the paper and stuffed it in his pocket.

"Maybe when this is done, you can help me with another case. We have an alarming number of reports of missing people, reported around the World's Hotel. Perhaps you could look into it."

Nicoli walked to the door, standing in the frame. "Thirty-three."

"What?" The chief raised his brow.

"Your father wanted to make it to thirty-three years. He liked things in threes."

Dekker nodded, and Nicoli walked out of the office. Several constables looked at him, others paying little attention to his presence. Nicoli tipped his hat and walked down the side of the suite full of wood desks, dark wallpaper, and cluttered corners of files.

He was ready to leave the Peakeland Yard. His papers were signed, and Dekker's case should not be much of an issue for him, giving him the freedom to investigate his killer. Nicoli's stomach felt light.

Nicoli rounded the corner and bumped into a constable with a neck brace. "Lydia."

"So, you *are* here. I didn't believe it." Lydia wrapped her arms around him, and Nicoli embraced her. Her hugs were still tender and soothing.

"I was coming to see you," he said.

"Why haven't you written me lately?" Lydia let him go, still holding his hands. She kissed him on the cheek, and he blushed.

"I didn't want to upset you. I heard you've been busy."

"Nonsense. Come on. Let's go to Patti's."

"I'd be delighted."

～

Nicoli and Lydia walked down the street, Lydia with her arms behind her back and Nicoli with his hands in his pockets. People filled the pathways in the bustling lunch hour, looking to stores and restaurants in the Cultural District.

The wind blew Nicoli's scarf, the smooth cotton dancing around his collar.

"Did the chief give you much grief?" Lydia asked.

"No, not like his dad. Rather peachy in comparison."

"Does the lack of suspects concern you?"

"I'm not sure from glancing at the file. I was once told by that missing detective of yours to never make assumptions until I've collected all the evidence because if you do, you can become biased."

Lydia grinned, and they walked in silence.

"I brought you something." Nicoli pulled out a white box from the inside of his jacket and handed it to her. They shifted to a bench in front of Patti's Pub.

Lydia opened the gift to find a single white rose. Her cheeks flushed red, and she picked it up, the thorns clipped.

"Are they still your favorite?" Nicoli asked.

Lydia nodded and set her hand on his knee. "Of course."

"You're most welcome. How's Monty?"

Lydia smacked her lips and chattered her teeth. "Monty is well, and she is an excellent housekeeper. She's also very protective of Rosaline. The two get along very well."

Nicoli titled his head, and his throat went dry. He rubbed his knees.

"You can see her if you like?" Lydia said.

"No, I don't—"

"I'm sorry, I shouldn't have asked. How's Redwood?" Lydia cleared her throat and nodded.

"The trees are tall, wide, and red. They have renamed a few streets, but it's still as you'd remember."

Lydia looked away, pulling in her lip. "What assignment does the—"

Nicoli couldn't help his thoughts that battered inside his head. Lydia's words faded away, and the pit in his stomach turned to cramps. His back tensed to where he had to roll his shoulders back, letting out a rough sigh.

"I think he's here."

Lydia's froze, and she looked to the flower in her lap. "Don't."

"I think the Peake's problem is our problem. I couldn't tell the chief that."

Nicoli put his hand on her arm, and she swiped it away and walked to the edge of the street.

"No. This is no longer our issue," Lydia said. "I can't go back there, so don't bring it here." Lydia waved her palm, calming her breathing.

Nicoli stood and guided her into the alleyway, the fair's traffic walking by without a glance.

Nicoli reached for her hand. "Lydia—"

"No, Nicoli, let this go."

"He is here. He's the same person."

"Stop it."

"I *can't* let it go. You know that."

Lydia eyed Nicoli, her stare firm and piercing, her finger in his face.

Nicoli stepped back and removed his hat. Holding it against his chest, he looked away, waiting for the calm to return. The fragrance of coconut lingered from his flat cap, and his thoughts drifted to his late wife, to her gentle touch at the end of every night.

"I'm sorry, Nicoli. I can't chase him. It took me years to fall asleep without seeing that mask. I don't want to start that nightmare again."

Nicoli ran his hands through his hair again, a few strands caught between his fingers.

Lydia put her hand on his shoulder. She rubbed it and leaned against him. "You can't be certain he's here."

"I suspect he is while others may not. I have proof." Nicoli pulled a piece of paper from his jacket, holding it in the air.

"What is that?"

"I believe it to be his writing, found at a crime scene here in Well's Peake. The indents and penmanship, exact. I now have two samples."

"Those could belong to anyone. I'm not getting into this." Lydia shook her head.

"Lydia, I know this is hard. Mallory—"

She pushed Nicoli against the wall. "Don't. Let her rest."

Lydia removed her hand, and Nicoli rubbed his cheek.

"She didn't deserve what happened to her." Nicoli rubbed the ring around his finger, looking to the clouded sky.

Lydia pulled Nicoli close and hugged him. "I would do anything to bring her back to you. You understand that, right? But we know that's not possible. I know you want to bring her justice, but she wouldn't want you to poison the rest of your life chasing that monster."

"When I thought he might be here, I didn't think you were safe." Nicoli's voice shook with each word. "It wasn't smart to contact you before I arrived, in case he's watching."

"If he was coming for me, he would've done it by now. He must know I have no interest in him."

"I wasn't willing to take that chance. What happens if he finds you in the wrong alley, in the dark, in the night."

Lydia grabbed Nicoli's face in her palms, holding back her sobs. "Nicoli… I can't lose you too. You're all that's left of her, so *please* stop this. You were a kind and tender man before her passing. Remember what happened that harvest? Tell me this obsession is worth it?"

Nicoli crossed his arms, biting his bottom lip. He stepped back from the building's shadow. "I know, I know I got too close. It won't happen again."

Lydia put her hands on her hips. "I had plans, Nicoli. I wanted to settle down, and I hoped you would've been that person. We can't do that if you're dead. We were lucky to find each other after her death, and I want us together again."

Lydia hid it well, but Nicoli knew she was fighting the tears, the urge to tell him what a fool he was. She wasn't wrong. He slipped his fingers in hers, putting their foreheads together, lavender perfume brushing against his nose.

"You are on the line of obsession," she said. "It doesn't matter what his goal is. He is no longer *our* problem. We don't always catch the killer, but we are alive, and that's enough. We can still find happiness. I beg you, don't make the mistake of not letting this go."

Lydia put the rose case back in his pocket, the flower in hand.

"Do you still believe he exists?"

She held the rose in front of him, waving it in his face. "It's not worth it if he does." She threw the rose at his chest, the petals breaking off and drifting to the cobblestone. "All I hoped was to go to Patti's. Not to fall into this nightmare."

Lydia walked to the street, Nicoli reaching to hold her back, but she slipped from his grip.

Nicoli picked up the stem of the rose, with a single petal on the end. "Why can't I let it go?"

Lydia paused, looking over her shoulder, her cheeks flushed white.

Nicoli stepped out of the alleyway, carrying the broken rose, and held it out to Lydia, and she took it in her hand.

Lydia clenched Nicoli's hand, the warmth from her fingers lingering against his. "Let me show you how."

CHAPTER THIRTEEN

Vida held the envelope in her hand, tight enough to make sure it didn't blow it away but gentle enough not to crumple the contents of the package. The sun shone above the water fountain, glinting against the ripples as the wind breezed across the top.

Slivers of stone shimmered in the water, glistening against her cheek as she strolled about, rounding the fountain. Chestnut trees rose tall and wide, shading the flower gardens with their ageless beauty, squirrels running up the trunks, the leaves rustling beneath them.

Vida passed through the shadows of leaves and branches to the benches between the fountain gardens and the World's Palace. The sunlight illuminated off the glass, radiating into the gardens.

She pulled her white shirt tight, which blended into a purple dress, with her gloved hand to keep the chill out, her skirt waving at her shoes as they clicked on the path. She sat on the bench next to the fountain, crossing her legs and holding the envelope in her lap.

Vida took a deep breath, looking to the fountain's water, as clear as sapphires, with a statue towering in the middle. Fairgoers passed by, some nodding, others talking with their partners or children.

She lifted the envelope, broke the white wax seal, and unfolded the letter.

To Miss Harvey,

Thank you for your recent application to attend Blackwell Academy. We have reviewed it amongst the panel and the headmaster of our academy. While your resume and references are impressive, after heavy debate, we have determined women are not proper for the role of physicians. The hours and surgeries are considerable, and the procedures are tedious and complex for the feeble of heart.

We regret—

Vida refolded the letter with a sneer and slid it back into the envelope. Her complexion reddened, and she wiped a tear before it rolled down her cheek, eyeing the surrounding patrons, thankful no one seemed to notice. With a deep breath and a slow exhale, she forced a weak smile.

Another day, another rejection. There was comfort in it, having grown used to the disappointment to where she would not know what to expect if they accepted her. After struggling for seasons, and when it was all she ever accomplished, what would it feel like to overcome such a hurdle?

Vida pulled on her glove and rubbed the back of her hand, struggling to find the scar but content that she did not. The mist from the fountain brushed against her, and she turned to the statue of the angel looking at her with eyes that shined like frosted pearls.

~

Aleksandar looked at Natalia's note with her address written inside, struggling to keep his cheeks from hurting from his eager smile. He slid the paper into his jacket and rushed through the fairgoers to the fountain near the gardens.

The crowd of people did not thin in the late afternoon hour.

Aleksandar aimed for the arch at the entrance when a man behind him yelled loud and sharp. It was distant and unrecognizable, but his words grew clear.

"Mr. Scott! Mr. Scott, a minute, please!" The man scurried through the crowd.

Aleksandar turned and stretched his neck to an odd man in his early thirties racing up to him. He wore a Broadway hat with glasses on the brim that did little to make Aleksandar think otherwise. His jacket billowed like a cape to his boots, a crimson vest with black lacing accenting the red stitching at the seams. He sported a gentleman's cane, more for appeal than purpose.

Dark brown, straight textured hair fell to his angled shoulders like calm rain. The gentleman's mustache covered his top lip, blending into a trimmed beard that accented his sharp jaw.

Aleksandar thought the man looked odd if not for his crimson vest made of the finest silk that belonged only to those in the highest society of Well's Peake.

"Mr. Scott, can you spare a moment?" the man asked, waving his hand in the air.

Aleksandar paused, waiting for the man to catch up, glancing at the clock above the front arch.

"Mr. Scott, it's such an honor to meet you. If you were heading out, do not let me delay you. I simply wish to accompany you."

"I suppose." Aleksandar eyed the man from the corner of his eyes, who didn't seem out of breath from his quick sprint.

He waved Aleksandar to the door, and they strolled to the arch. Aleksandar noticed there were many curious glances from the crowd gawking in his direction.

"Apologies for the delay in introductions," he said. "My name is Kenneth Forbes."

"That name sounds familiar," Aleksandar said, slipping through the fairgoers to the brick pathways outside the World's Palace, the gardens blooming around them.

"I'd be offended if you didn't. I *am* the man on the hill."

"The man on the hill?" Aleksandar glanced.

"Yes, the man on the hill, the man of culture, but despite my names, I enjoy Kenneth Forbes most of all."

Aleksandar stopped and looked at Kenneth, who had his hand extended. Aleksandar shook the aristocrat's hand, finding Kenneth's handshake stern but tender. His smile and eyes looked gentle, as he stood proper and bold.

"Well, it's a pleasure to meet you, Mr. Forbes. What can I do for you?" Aleksandar asked.

"I was fortunate enough to hear about your demonstration yesterday." Kenneth lifted his cane and hands in the air, moving them with his words. "The elegance, the delicacy of what you showcased, was the most exquisite piece of art in that exhibition."

Aleksandar eyed Kenneth, thrown off by his excited nature. "Why, thank you. I suppose I wasn't aiming for beauty, but I'm glad you enjoyed it. Mr. Forbes, I don't mean to be rude, but—"

"Whether you strive for something alluring or purposeful, the visual appeal of the Red Breath was astonishing."

"Once again, thank you, but—"

Aleksandar wanted to say something, but words did not come.

Kenneth chuckled and wrapped his arm around Aleksandar's shoulder. "I see you are unfamiliar with the attention that comes with being as unique as you, Mr. Scott. I am a humble admirer." Kenneth pushed his cane against Aleksandar's chest.

"Perhaps not. Pardon me if I came off rude." Aleksandar tried to pull away, but Kenneth held him tight, like a proud father.

"Of course not. We must all grasp the towering heights of prominence." Kenneth let Aleksandar go, patting him on the back.

"You seem to have found yours." Aleksandar straightened his jacket with an embarrassed smile.

"Yes, indeed. I'm hoping to help you be just as successful." Kenneth walked to the marble pillar, tapping the bottom with his cane, leaving a scuff.

"You want to take me to fame?"

"Yes, and you should let me. I'd be astonished if you have not received several offers over the past few days."

Aleksandar walked off with Kenneth at his side. "Then you might be surprised."

"Well, then I see no reason you should deny my offer. So we have an accord?" Kenneth said, his smile perfect in every way.

Aleksandar stepped back to the fountain with an angel in the center, water flowing through its wings. "I beg your pardon, but I might have missed the offer."

Kenneth grinned at Aleksandar and walked along the rim of the fountain, running his cane through the water.

"Aleksandar, you realize who I am, correct?" Kenneth asked.

"Yes, I believe so."

"You recognize one of my many names?"

"Yes?"

"Then whatever could I want with an elemental inventor?"

"You want my *invention*?"

Kenneth clapped his hands together in a dramatic fashion. "Bravo. I sensed your intelligence and insight." The aristocrat walked towards Aleksandar with a pep in his step, batting his eyebrows.

"I'm sorry, but I can't hand over the Red Breath. It has flaws," Aleksandar said.

"No, no. I don't wish you to hand it over. I prefer you to expand upon it. Inflate the size and allow it to dance around my manor as the spectacle it should be."

Kenneth's accented words, along with his self-assurance, caused Aleksandar to pause. The man's words flowed with finesse, as if he'd been a public speaker all his life.

"What would you need it for?"

"Mr. Scott, I want it for the allure."

"To show off?" Aleksandar glanced away, swallowing hard.

Kenneth snapped his fingers. "Exactly. I *am* the man on the hill. Everyone knows my influence. Now I crave them to see it for the art that it is. With the Red Breath, its charm will surpass those of any class. You and I will bring the people of Well's Peake a moment of beautiful silence, of awe and quintessence."

"But that's not why I designed the device."

Kenneth's radiant smile dimmed into a forced one. He cleared his throat and pulled off his hat, holding it in his arm with profound sincerity.

"It helps me, Mr. Scott. I have a reputation to uphold, and it must continue to grow. Inventions serve more than a single purpose. Whether it be for the common good or the artistic world, it has earned its place. Inventions will transform the world into something marvelous and bring attention to culture and beauty, a direction they have yet to embrace."

Aleksandar looked across the fountain, looking for Miss Harvey, his collar rubbing against his neck. "I may have missed the point, but I created it for other reasons. I made it to help others, not idolize them."

Aleksandar tried to be kind, but he was already late. Kenneth's demeanor was hard to escape, and his persistence was exhausting. Kenneth sat on the edge of the fountain, hands on the helm of his cane.

"Surely there is room for compromise. We could drop the quantity of devices around the manor, and the pay would be most generous. I recognize the importance of coin to an inventor's beginnings, and I am sure you understand what I figure."

Aleksandar looked to the side and spotted several people walking through the hedges, enjoying the afternoon. After everyone he'd run into, he wished he could be one of them, at peace, without the interruptions of life and influential men. He lost himself in his daydream until Kenneth clicked his cane.

"So, Mr. Scott, do we have a deal?" Kenneth rose to his feet.

Aleksandar looked at Kenneth's extended hand and rambunctious smile, ready to secure the young inventor's fate. Aleksandar bit his lip and shook his head.

"I'm sorry, but that's not the attention it needs."

"Mr. Scott, you *must* reconsider." Kenneth stepped to him. "This is an opportunity—"

"I already found my opportunity. I don't know what the future holds, and maybe down the road there's the possibility of collaboration, but at this point my hands are full."

"Mr. Scott, you must accept this offer," Kenneth said, his voice stern but elegant. "The others can wait. Your failure at the last exhibition was insulting. That award was rightfully yours, and you have every right to claim your prize. It is what you deserve, and through me, they will see how they should not have undermined you."

"It was not mine. My loss was fair," Aleksandar said.

"It was—"

"Mr. Forbes, I appreciate your offer, but I have already accepted another, and I just can't manage them all. I have a previous engagement, and I must be going. Forgive me."

Kenneth sighed, tapping his fingers on the brim of his hat. Looking to the fountain with his tongue in cheek, he lifted his eyebrows. "I'm sorry I kept you. That was not kind of me. Good day, Mr. Scott, and I hope that future is closer than we know."

Kenneth placed his hat over his head and walked away, his eccentric and lively demeanor lost in his casual stroll.

Aleksandar then took a deep breath, hoping the stress would lessen for a moment. He planted himself on the edge of the fountain and let the sun warm his skin. The smell of water filled the air with cool comfort, misting against his cheek.

Aleksandar whispered a prayer under his breath, keeping his eyes closed and letting the noise of the World's Fair fade, like a waterfall as it neared the bottom of the stream. The sun's warmth spread throughout his veins, bringing a sense of warm relief he craved.

With a glance to his watch, he stood and made his way to the late appointment with Miss Harvey.

∼

Aleksandar paced through the gardens and out to another fountain in the middle. He eyed around, looking for the right person, the fair in full swing.

"Mr. Scott?" someone said.

Aleksandar opened his eyes to a woman in a white shirt, a purple dress, white gloves, and a subtle smile, sitting on a bench.

"Good afternoon, Mr. Scott," she said.

Aleksandar stepped towards her. "I am so sorry. You must be Miss Harvey. I'm late and—"

"That is all right. I'm sure the fair has slowed you down."

Aleksandar lifted his chin. "Yes, I don't know if you've ever met Kenneth Forbes, but he is an interesting man."

Miss Harvey chuckled. "If the rumors are true, he can be quite the personality to mingle with."

Aleksandar nodded. "I had heard of him, but I didn't realize he was so…"

"Eccentric?"

"Yes, I believe that's the word I'm looking for." Aleksandar chuckled.

"Well, regardless, Mr. Scott, it's nice to meet you." Vida smiled, and as they sat on the bench, Vida showed off her perfect composure, placing her right hand over her left.

"To you as well. I'll be honest; I didn't understand why Mr. Griffin asked me to speak with you. Did I miss something?"

Vida smiled and looked to the gardens. "Most likely not. Mr. Griffin likes to send people of potential to me, so I may persuade you of your capability."

Aleksandar listened with a wrinkled brow. "Persuade me? *What* do you do for a living?"

"Think of me as a teacher, one who inspires others to see their potential and strive to be their best. I know it might sound unorthodox, but Mr. Griffin understands that if one believes in themselves, they can do anything they put their mind to. You must have attracted his attention for one of his many great projects."

"So you're like a mentor?" Aleksandar held his hands on the underside of the bench, leaning forward. "It's just so strange. One moment I was performing for the judges, and the next, Bernard Griffin is trying to understand me."

Vida crossed her legs. "Bernard searches for talented men and women. Inventors, architects, physicians, anyone who could bring his newest visions to life. He has a persistent nature that draws people in. He has few hours of the day to persuade them all, so he hands that responsibility over to me."

"And he wants me?"

"He at least thinks you have potential."

"Huh. Has he told you anything about me?"

"A little. I'm given a name, a place, and when to meet you. A quick summary. Sounds kind of terrifying when I put it that way, but he's a family friend, so I trust him." Vida let out a small laugh, looking at him with a sincere smile.

Aleksandar leaned back and crossed his arms, the cool bars of the bench resonating through his jacket. The pit in his stomach loosened, and his suspicion of Vida grew less. Her words were soft but full, and her presence was calming compared to Kenneth Forbes.

"Whatever does Mr. Griffin expect from all this, from me?" Aleksandar asked.

"He hopes I will feed your motivation and watch you bloom into the potential he wishes to see out of you."

"Well, that is *quite* the grand dream."

Vida laughed, fixing the bottom of her dress.

"What about you, Miss Harvey? Does he follow your wisdom as well?"

"Mr. Griffin enjoys an uplifting conversation, but he is usually in high spirits. He stands where he does because he has a natural insight into people. Do you think you have this ability he sees in you?"

"I don't know." Aleksandar crossed his arms. "I haven't always been good at inventing. Some smaller success when I moved here, but I've had little."

"Most don't until they discover more."

"True. I just, I'm not sure how to keep a peaceful mindset. After yesterday's loss, how can someone not think about how they might not make it?"

Vida turned in her seat to look at Aleksandar. "As a child, my mother used to tell me we reach low points not because we are weak but because we need a reality check," she said. "Our lives become cluttered with life, and it blinds us. At these low points, we see what is important and refocus on that, whether it be our dreams, passions, or choices. Try to remember that in our darkest moments, we've always come about."

Aleksandar looked to Vida with calm eyes and reddened cheeks. A smile spread across his face, and he leaned into the bench.

"I'm seeing why Mr. Griffin believes in you," he said.

Vida waved her hands and laughed. "It is one of my talents."

"Am I allowed to ask about you?"

"Now, Mr. Scott, I don't believe it proper to ask about another's matters." Vida smirked, and Aleksandar chuckled, looking to the gardens.

Vida patted her hand and tilted her head. "If you don't mind me asking, how was it meeting the city's most endeared man?"

"Mr. Forbes? Well, he wanted to use my invention to glorify himself. I sense he doesn't take rejection well," Aleksandar said.

"He may be disappointed, but you deserve to have your choices respected."

"I feel... conflicted. This could've been a great opportunity. My inventions might have received the attention they deserved with his support."

"As true as that is, there's no point in doing something if it's done for the wrong reasons. Sounds like a bittersweet ending, but it might be for the best."

Aleksandar pulled on the brim of his hat, taking a deep breath. "Indeed, it was."

Vida rubbed her hands together, leaning back and staring into the gardens. Aleksandar craved more of her attention, her words peaceful.

He felt an unusual sense of initiative to go do something. His gaze drifted, her gloves grabbing his attention. She shifted her hands to the other knee, and Aleksandar glanced away, hoping not to have offended her.

"Find your peace, Mr. Scott," she said. "People will not lend it to you. You give it to yourself every day, a reason to put one foot in front of the other."

"Thank you, Miss Harvey. Your mother sounds like a marvelous woman."

"Yes, she is," Vida said, her voice softer than before. "It's been many seasons since I have heard those words spoken out loud. Perhaps I needed to hear them myself."

Aleksandar could see Vida had lost herself to her own thoughts and words, something he was all too familiar with.

Aleksandar rose and arched his back forward from his slouched posture, and Vida stood with him, batting a smirk.

"I appreciate the kind words, Miss Harvey, and I'm happy Mr. Griffin took an interest in me," Aleksandar said. "I'm not entirely sure which way I should go, but I know I'm going someplace. So do you give Mr. Griffin a report, saying I can be part of his league or something?"

"For now, keep pushing yourself as an inventor. Make your mark, and if I know Bernard, he will be sure to let you know."

"Okay... Um, was there somewhere I could escort you?"

"Thank you, Mr. Scott, for the offer and the compliment, but I think I will enjoy the fountain and gardens a bit longer. If it's up to Mr. Griffin, I think our paths will cross again."

"Indeed. Good day, Miss Harvey."

"To you as well."

Aleksandar tilted his head, walked down the white stone path, and wandered through the gardens, the chestnut trees surrounding him. He glanced back to Vida, and she nodded.

Vida sat on the bench and pulled out the envelope once again. She lifted the flap but stopped before removing the letter. She then closed it and tossed the parchment into the fountain. The paper darkened in the water, and it crumbled around the edges. Vida watched the letter dissolve in the afternoon light as she ran her hand through the water, her glove growing heavy.

Vida let out a deep breath, a small smile, and held her scarred hand in the other. "Thank you, Mother. For everything."

CHAPTER FOURTEEN

A little girl ran between the berry bushes with a smile and a stick in her hand, wailing it as if trying to knock something out of the air. She peeked over blueberries and lilacs to a beige house, no one in sight, sweet and fruity aromas filling her nose.

She held her palm to the afternoon sun peeking over the hills behind the house. A dog rushed around the corner with its tongue waving out of its mouth.

Yelp! The girl took off into the yard with the dog barking at her heels and its tongue waving out. She waved the stick in one fist, her other arm limp at her side, but it did not hinder her speed or diminish her smile.

"Come on, Elton, fetch, good boy!"

She ran to the edge of the garden, and the dog leaped into the air, its mouth open and eyes wide. The girl pulled the stick away and ran into the bushes. A man jumped from the flowers and lifted her off her feet.

"I got you!" Owen said.

"Da!" She giggled as he hugged her in his arms.

"Did you think you could outrun us both, Wilona?" Owen smooched her on the cheek.

The little girl laughed, pushing against her father's embrace. Wilona hugged as tight as she could and tossed the stick over his shoulder,

Elton snagging it out of the air.

Wilona was a ray of sunshine in Owen's life. Her smile and happiness were contagious, and he couldn't have been more proud. He looked at her with a gleam in his eye, knowing they would create great things if she followed in his path.

Owen set her on the grass and kissed her forehead. Wilona took off to the porch that wrapped around the two-story house, beige with white trim accenting the wood pillars. Wilona panted in exhaustion as she ran for the dog, who perked up and took off with the stick. She laughed in pursuit, skipping across the yard as the dog outran her. She jumped alongside the bush, but a branch caught her foot, and she tumbled across the grass.

Owen rushed to her, tending to his bad leg. "Wilona, are you all right?"

Wilona pushed herself up, her eyes filling with tears.

"Oh, it's okay, my love. Just a tumble." Owen hugged her close, and she wept against his chest.

"It's not fair." Her words muffled against his jacket.

Owen ran his hand through her hair. "Honey—"

"How can the other kids run around all they want, and I can't?" Wilona leaned backed and dried her cheeks with the back of her shirt. "Why don't they get tired?"

Owen wiped the last tear from her cheek and sat beside her, tucking her under his arm. "Hey, they do. You tire easier now, but you will build the endurance. You may have to work longer, but there's nothing wrong with you. We all have our own pace, and that's why we play with the dog each day."

"But why me, Da, why me? Why is it *my* arm that doesn't work?"

Owen pressed his lips together and lowered his head. He felt her trying not to sob under his arm, her shoulders shaking. "Because we made a mistake, little one, but nothing else will happen to you. I promise."

Owen took out a handkerchief from his pocket and wiped her face dry.

Wilona stood and hugged him, her small arm too short to wrap around him. Owen stood and lifted her from the ground, walking to the porch.

"How about this," he said. "Let's visit the markets this afternoon and find another toy for Elton?"

"You mean it?" Wilona's eyes widened, red from rubbing them with her hand.

"I do."

"Okay." Wilona looked past Owen's shoulder to the stone walkway alongside the house. "Da, Bernie is here."

Owen turned, and Bernard waved from behind the metal fence which encircled the back lawn, trees growing over the top, their branches hanging into the yard.

"Mr. Griffin, I wasn't expecting you," Owen said.

"No, no, I'm here unannounced."

"Please, come in."

"Thank you." Bernard opened the gate and walked into the yard.

Elton stared at Bernard with playful eyes, hunched to the ground, his tail wagging against the grass. Bernard reached for the stick, but the dog took off.

Wilona ran up to Bernard. "Bernie!"

"Why hello, little one, look how much you've grown." Bernard kneeled. "How big are you now? How old are you?"

"Tall enough." Owen put his hands in his pocket.

"I'm this big!" Wilona held her hand at the top of her head. "Am I almost as tall as you? I'm almost six!"

"Oh no, I wouldn't wish that upon you." Bernard bopped her nose. "I'm always the first to know when it rains. It's not as exciting as one might think."

Wilona giggled and put her palms on her knees.

"Honey, how about you go play in your room while we talk," Owen said.

"Okay, bye, Bernie." Wilona waved to Bernard and raced up the steps into the house, the dog following her with the stick in his mouth.

"Behave, little one." Bernard waved and chuckled. "She is quite the peach."

"I would have to agree. Would you like to come inside?" Owen waved his palm at the house.

"Thank you, kindly."

The two walked into the house, Bernard ducking under the door frame to avoid hitting his head.

They stepped into a study with only a single bookshelf. Light bounced off the amber wallpaper, against shelves of swords, from ancient to modern pieces, fresh with oil. It was narrow with two cloth chairs, a hand-stitched couch, and a workbench with finished and unfinished canes.

Owen sat in his chair, hanging his cane on the armrest.

"She is getting so big." Bernard eased his way onto the couch.

"She is. Are you okay?"

"Oh, I'm fine. I sat in a chair today, and let's just say it was one that could not handle a man of my *stature*." Bernard let out a deep laugh, and Owen couldn't help but grin.

"What can I do for you? Perhaps some scones?"

"No thank you." Bernard waved his hand. "Owen, the moment is upon us. I have finally set my vision in motion, and I wanted to bring this to you, as the first potential candidate for the World's League. I feel you'd be instrumental in its development."

"Why?"

Bernard unbuttoned his jacket and stroked the end of his beard. "Why as in you, or why as in the league?"

"As in the league."

"We've been through this."

"I know, but I need to hear it again."

"Well's Peake does not recognize the dangers yet to come. Inventors, or should I say innovators, are led astray by their ambition, while others do not understand the potential in their hands. These factors contributed to the Black Harvest, something I know you wouldn't like to happen again."

Owen looked to the engraved ceiling and loosened his tie. How two words could induce such a headache was beyond him. He held an unkind smile as his nerves tensed in his leg. It was nothing that Bernard was trying to accomplish, but to mention the Black Harvest made his jaw ache.

"If I remember your vision, we are to govern, correct?" Owen asked.

"We are to guide, not dictate." Bernard leaned back, the couch squeaking beneath him. "We have no true authority over anyone, but we have a voice for guidance. A loud one at that."

Owen lifted his bad leg over the other with his hands. "We can't expect others to listen without resistance. You could very well push radicals further into the dark, and what comes from the shadows could be much worse."

"We could protect people from themselves and others," Bernard said.

Owen slid his hands across his lap and chattered his teeth. "Have you approached anyone besides me?"

"No. You are the first to be offered a seat on the council."

"And who else do you intend to recruit?"

"I have a few. Natalia Arlen, Adrian Collis, and I've considered Aleksandar Scott, among many others."

Owen looked up, Bernard looking at him with a careful stare. "You might think I don't like him, but Aleksandar and I were on the same stage for years. He has potential, I don't doubt that, but his reasoning, and where he is heading, is my concern. New directions created the Black Harvest. This is why I'm concerned with the Elemental Race."

"That's why I want you in the league. Your insight would be most valuable to its formation. You may not like Aleksandar's direction, but we don't know where he is going. He may take us to where we need, or he might need us to guide him in dangerous situations. That applies to everyone."

"That's a risk I'm not willing to take."

"Many inventors have that capability. I believe you want this to succeed; you just have your concerns."

Owen rested his arms on the armrests and glanced into the hallway, spotting Wilona peeking through the banisters. He waved at her, and she rushed up the steps.

Owen turned back to Bernard. "What about investors?"

Bernard leaned back in his chair, hands on his lap. "There are some businesses and esteemed families who are interested. I'm working on our largest sponsor now, Fritz and Co."

"I'm surprised the brothers entertained the idea."

"They didn't, but they have a sister who I'd like to think will persuade them. Owen, this is more than some council in local parliament. We will have no direct affiliation with aristocrats. A private, self-funded, highly regarded entity. I already have a tentative application from the creation office for public announcement."

Owen stood. "What happens when investors bring an agenda forward? What if they disapprove of our actions?"

Bernard rubbed his beard. "We will set expectations before they can invest. They'll have no say in official matters, and they may elect out yearly. So those without the proper intentions will not burden us."

"And what happens when the sponsors choose not to invest?" Owen lowered his leg. "I'm sorry, Bernard, but I can't take part in those types of visions. I can only afford to be cautious, and I have no intention of repeating past mistakes."

"Mistakes that were not yours," Bernard said firmly.

Bernard was right, the mistakes were not Owen's, but that did not absolve him from the guilt, the resentment. Thoughts of the Black Harvest lingered in Owen's mind, and his leg throbbed. Owen remembered the days before his father's passing were a burden to him, the weight of an entire generation on his conscience.

Owen rubbed his leg through his pants and brace. "Whether or not they are mine, it's my responsibility not to make them again."

"You are always seeking to guide others. This is that opportunity." Bernard waved his hand.

"I don't know if my guidance is any better. I could be wrong."

"You can't keep going back to your father's mistakes. This is very odd for you. You are usually optimistic. What is wrong?"

Grabbing his cane, Owen glanced at Bernard.

"Owen," Bernard said.

Owen walked to the window, looking at his garden. Leaves fell from the trees in the gentle wind, which hummed against the glass. Clouds rolled over the treetops, graying as the harvest season began and the frost season neared.

"Owen?" Bernard rose and walked alongside Owen.

"I don't..." Owen took a deep breath. "I don't think my father's work was as finished as I hoped."

"What do you mean?"

Owen tapped the glass. "There was a murder, Bernard. My cousin

Raymond was killed just a few nights ago. Growing up, he was the older brother I never had. He was always looking out for us and helped me become the man I am today. I remember, whenever I passed primary and secondary, or when I won my first competition, it was him who stood in the crowd. After my mother, my wife, and my father, he was there. When my father passed, I discovered a journal of his work on the Black Harvest. He was trying to recreate it with Raymond's help. I severed ties after that."

Owen's leg throbbed harder, and he felt as if his heart was shrinking. Rubbing his hands against the cotton of his pants, Owen dried them off and leaned on his cane.

"In that journal, Raymond's name was everywhere. After everything he taught me, he of all people helped my father recreate what killed a hundred thousand people."

Bernard looked out the window. "You may have your doubts, but your father was a great man, a good man."

"He created the Black Harvest. There's nothing good about that."

"He was also the one who helped end it. Was there anywhere in the book where he explained his reasoning to rekindle his research?" Bernard crossed his arms and rubbed his beard.

"No. It was all research and theories. The chief constable believes it may have had something to do with Raymond's death. Someone may have killed him because they discovered what he had done or was doing. Maybe he was still working on it. You see, Bernard, the position you are asking me to fill is the same one asked of my father. To be part of something to help guide and protect people, but you need to ask, can we protect people from themselves?"

Bernard went to the window and sighed, the window fogging where his breath touched the glass.

Owen could feel his pulse rushing through his body, his leg more sensitive than ever.

What if my cousin was still working on the Black Harvest? Why was he killed? Who killed him?

Discovering that truth was all that mattered, and it ate away at him since he was informed of his cousin's murder.

"People will always need protection from their inner selves," Bernard said. "Owen, if you don't stand up, then who will? I'm not asking you to do what your father did, but to guide this generation forward in positive ways."

Owen stood there, putting his weight on his cane, the polished brass cool against his palm. He said nothing. There was nothing left to say.

Bernard rubbed his hands together and turned away. "My condolences on your cousin."

"Thank you." Owen tapped his cane with his fingers.

Bernard walked to the hallway and paused. "Your father made up for his mistakes. They put him in a difficult position in a difficult moment. He never intended to end up where he did, but he made a choice. He believed he did wrong in hindsight, and redeemed himself. I don't know how things are for you, but I hope you find your answers."

Owen nodded, and Bernard returned the gesture, leaving down the corridor with gentle steps.

Owen stood there looking at the empty room, exhaling hard.

Just let it go… don't—

"Wait." Owen walked into the hallway, Bernard standing next to the staircase towards the front door.

"Yes?" he said.

"Why is this so important to you? What makes you think a storm is on the horizon?"

"My father believed hardships will come and go," Bernard said. "The Black Harvest, a war, a technological expansion like we've never seen. I don't know, but it is coming, and we must prepare before it arrives. Society is still fractured from the harvest, and this leads to unrest."

Owen stared at Bernard, who stood as tall as the door was high, the light resting along his shoulders.

"This league must be honest and immaculate in its structure." Owen walked to the door. "There can be no secret agenda, or it will fail."

A smile slipped onto Bernard's face. "You have my word. We will prevent another Black Harvest."

Owen stood in the doorway and nodded. "When you have the financial backing, come see me. I'll at least entertain the idea."

Bernard let out a short laugh and buttoned his jacket.

"What's funny?" Owen asked.

"I have dreamed of this opportunity for many seasons. How a minute of decision could lead to the most important moment of our lives. A single droplet of water in a river that flows into the ocean. Good day, Owen."

Bernard patted Owen on the shoulder and walked out the door onto the white gravel path.

Owen closed the door and slid his cane into the umbrella holder next to the coat rack. He took a step, noticing Wilona on the staircase.

"Honey, why are you hiding there?" Owen asked.

She fiddled with her fingers together. "Was it me?"

"What do you mean?" Owen stepped forward.

"Were you two fighting about me? I heard you talking about the harvest."

Owen lowered his shoulders and let out a small gasp. He limped up the steps and sat next to her, cuddling her under his arm. "Absolutely not."

"You sounded like you were fighting."

"No, we were discussing other matters, nothing about you. If we were, nothing but good things could be said." Owen touched her nose, and she giggled.

"Okay. I thought you were. Everybody does."

"You are much more than you know, my dearest. Someday you'll realize that. You may need reminding, but I'll be there for you."

Owen squeezed her tight and rested his cheek on her head. She was everything he needed, and if he could protect her as if she was under his arm for the rest of her life, then he could live with that. Whatever the cost.

CHAPTER FIFTEEN

A young girl walked down the dirt road, the tall trees caressing her path in the afternoon light. She held a book tight against her chest.

She skipped here and there, smiling whenever a chipmunk or squirrel ran beside her, up the bark of the oaks in the Day and Night Pass. The wind blew gently in the thick forest, making branches sway above her and the woodsy aroma linger.

She rounded the corner to a tree with three spiral trunks that split into separate canopies, overlooking a white house with blue shutters. A group of boys and girls stood around a table, where a young Aleksandar stitched and sewed.

As she walked closer, their voices became clear.

"Come on, Lawrence, leave me alone." Aleksandar pushed another boy's hand off his shoulder.

"It's bad enough you're not in the fields, but you won't even tell me what you're doing?"

"I don't know. I'm trying to figure it out."

Lawrence glanced at the small group and laughed. "Mr. Scott must be so proud of his son. Lazy and stupid."

"You got me. Can you go now?"

The girl walked closer, no one paying any attention to her.

Lawrence looked over Aleksandar's shoulder and nodded, pretending he was thinking and helping. "Looks like... rubbish."

"Go away."

Lawrence swatted the fabric off the table, and Aleksandar sat there and sighed. The group laughed and shuffled off down the road, heading into the hillside. The girl stood there until Aleksandar looked her way.

"Who are you?" he asked.

"I just moved here. Up the hill." She pointed.

"In the blue house?"

"Yes." The girl stepped forward, setting her book on the table and picking up his stuff. "They don't seem very nice."

"They never hurt me, but they like to annoy me."

She set his material down. "They aren't your friends, are they?"

"No. Never. They live up the road is all. They are on their way to the festival, I think."

"That's where I was going."

Aleksandar looked to her book with a faded cover, and the creased spine was heavily worn. "What is that?"

The girl picked the book up and held it tight. "Just my story."

"Oh, okay." He rubbed his arm. "I guess I'll go inside now." Aleksandar picked up his supplies.

"No, wait, what's your name?"

"Alek."

She glanced away. "Well, maybe we can be friends? I don't have anyone to go with to the festival."

Aleksandar's eyes widened. "You want me to be your friend?"

"Yeah, why not? If you come, I'll show you my book."

Aleksandar looked to the hillside and back to his house. The girl smiled and held up her book, showing it off.

Aleksandar grinned, set his stuff down, and walked to her side. "Okay."

The girl and the boy headed off down the hill, and she let him hold her most prized possession.

Aleksandar pinned a schematic on the wall of his workshop, holding metal pins in his mouth, papers skewed around his wooden workbench. He paused, admiring the design as he whipped his pencil across it, thinking back to his childhood friend.

He drew across the paper in the lantern's light, connecting the drawing of tubes to that of the Lunarwheel. Piece by piece, he layered several designs overtop of the last, each layer adding a new level of information, from assembly to operation.

Shae sat on the edge of the workbench in the shades of the dim shop with her head cocked sideways. She hooted and bobbed back and forth.

"Good idea," Aleksandar said.

Aleksandar shuffled to his desk and paused, looking at an unfinished hat on a stand. He eyed it with a grin and tugged on the bottom, pinning a ribbon to the base of the felt hat.

"That's better," he said.

Aleksandar walked to the drawing board and whipped the pencil across the top layer, drawing a stream of water projecting in an arc from the machine.

He rubbed his forehead and stepped back, petting Shae's head. She stretched into his hand, her brown feathers flowing through his fingers.

"What do you think?" Aleksandar glanced to Shae, who no longer was there. "Shae?"

Hoot!

Aleksandar walked through the workshop, candles lit across the wood beams, and into his hidden room. Shae rested on the wool blanket, covering a machine that glimmered at the bottom from where the blanket did not reach. He sat on a cushioned chair and batted her a smile.

"I don't know, Shae, but I think we might have something."

Slam!

Aleksandar jerked awake. He turned to Shae, who soared into the air, flying straight over his head and out of the bedroom. Dullness surged through his temples as he squinted, trying to focus in the dark. He whipped the blankets off, standing in his nightgown, his leg barely supporting him since it was asleep.

Slam!

The splintering of wood rang throughout the house. Aleksandar ran out the door, bursting into a sprint as he soared down the hallway to the top of the steps, where a small balcony gave him a view of the living room.

Shae was nowhere in sight, and the living room was empty, untouched. Aleksandar covered his mouth, trying to keep calm.

"Shae? Shae, where are you?" he whispered.

Aleksandar paused, listening to the silence with nothing to direct him. He could only focus on the scuffling below and gears clanking.

Slam!

"No!" Aleksandar ran down the stairs as fast as he could, stumbling at the end. His ankle rolled, and he reached out to catch himself on the railing. It splintered as he grabbed it, but he pushed himself up and ran to the stairwell to his workshop, a cut on his arm.

Aleksandar grabbed a copper pipe from against the wall, oblivious to the weight of his steps. With the pipe ready in hand, he stepped onto the staircase.

The coarse wood was cold on his feet, and the shivers stemmed up his spine, his heart pounding in his chest. Workbenches lay on the floor, flipped and broken into small pieces. Paper and machinery lay scattered across the floor, barely visible in the dark. The darkness cast long shadows, hiding the true damage, and the scent of split wood lingered in the air.

Aleksandar lowered the bar and took a step forward with wide eyes, but he did not feel his foot touch the hardwood. The pipe rang off the floor, not feeling it slip from his grip, and everything went blurry. The back of his head throbbed, the taste of blood filling his mouth.

No more noise, no more feelings. Only empty black silence.

CHAPTER SIXTEEN

Bruised and throbbing, Aleksandar rested his head against the wood wall, his vision blurry in the morning rays that beamed through the windows of his ransacked workshop.

Split workbenches lay on the floor, and papers and machinery from the night before were missing. The room lay barren amongst the carnage, a plant and its roots lying at the baseboard, the pot busted near the window.

Aleksandar squinted as the light danced through the branches outside, blowing in the harvest wind. He swallowed hard, the taste of blood lingering in his mouth.

A doctor patted Aleksandar's head with a warm, bloodied cloth, running his hand through Aleksandar's clotted hair.

Constables searched the workshop, took notes, and chatted with one another, but Aleksandar could not comprehend their words from the internal throbbing in his skull.

Constable Lydia May picked up a folded piece of paper and set it on the desk, which was still upright.

The doctor stood and walked to a man in a gray coat, like coals in a dead fire.

Aleksandar looked around the room, his eyelids heavy with bags underneath. Between chunks of timber and scrap metal, scattered puddles of water collected on the aged floor with only a few bolts and gears. His bookshelf lay over one of his workbenches, none of the books in sight. The smell of torn paper and splintered wood filled his nostrils, and every sound the constables made rang in his ears.

He gripped his trousers with shaking hands, gnawed his teeth, and exhaled hard.

What happened?

One moment he was standing in the night, and then he awoke on the floor, his face and hair in a small puddle of his own blood. It was still dark, and he was alone, Shae curled under his arm.

The man in the gray coat walked to Aleksandar and sat on the doctor's stool. Aleksandar looked from the corner of his eyes, leaving his head against the wall.

"Hello, Mr. Scott," he said. "I know you're in a delicate state, but the doctor tells me I could ask you a few questions. Would that be all right?"

Aleksandar sat up, straightening his posture. "What if I said no?"

"Then we risk the chance of you forgetting important details, which would make it less likely for us to catch whoever did this."

"Okay, then."

"Thank you."

Aleksandar's focus drifted to Constable May, her neck brace capturing his attention like before.

"Mr. Scott, I told you my name when I first arrived, do you remember?" he asked.

"Detective Nicoli Lucas," Aleksandar said.

"Good. Do you remember being found?"

"No. How *did* you?"

"A passing merchant heard the noise this morning and reported it to the Peake. They found you on the floor and feared you were no longer with us. Can you tell me what happened?"

Aleksandar opened his eyes, attempting to ease the headache. He swallowed hard. "No. I was standing in the workshop, and then I wasn't. I woke in the night, but I don't remember for how long. There was shuffling, and that's when I knew someone was here."

Nicoli wrote in his notebook. "How much of your property is missing?"

Aleksandar closed his eyes, not wanting to admit the truth. His inventions, his money... He exhaled and stood, using the wall to prop himself up. Nicoli rose, holding his hand out.

"Doctor, should he be on his feet?" Nicoli asked.

"It won't hurt him any more than he is now, but if you get lightheaded, Mr. Scott, you need to sit. I recommend plenty of rest for the next few days, simple tasks only." The doctor put his instruments in his medical bag, clasping it shut.

As Aleksandar gripped onto the workbench with one hand, it shook from being unbalanced. Aleksandar wandered to the opposite end of the workshop, his mouth dry. Someone ripped his schematics off the wall, the pins holding back small pieces of torn paper.

"There was a book on my desk, an invention log. Did you see it?" Aleksandar asked.

"We found nothing of the sort, sir," Constable May said.

Aleksandar lowered his head. The pressure behind his eyes filled, and he clenched his fists.

It's gone... it's all gone.

The doctor nodded to Nicoli, who returned the gesture, and left up the stairs.

Constable May circled the room and ran her hand across the walls, and Aleksandar paused, watching. Her fingers lingered against the wall, between the stone and wood paneling. Aleksandar rubbed his neck and cleared his throat.

Nicoli stepped to Aleksandar's side. "We don't mean to intrude, but we'll need a detailed list of what may have been stolen. Specifically, any elemental inventions."

Aleksandar looked up, just enough to where his eyes met Nicoli's gaze.

Why the elements?

Aleksandar's voice came out broken and fatigued. "Most of my inventions were rough concepts. The Red Breath was the only one semi-completed. The first prototype was here, but my finished invention is at the World's Fair."

"Are you certain?" Nicoli asked.

Aleksandar pondered, raising his posture. "Yes… Is there something I need to know?"

Constable May looked to Nicoli, shaking her head no, and Nicoli turned back with his head tilted.

"What is it?" Aleksandar folded his arms.

"I don't know if I'm at liberty to say," Nicoli said.

"I was honest with you. I think I deserve the same." Aleksandar sat, nausea building in his gut.

Nicoli looked at Aleksandar with a blank stare, lifted his hat, and ran his hand through his hair. "Does the name Raymond O'Connell mean anything to you?"

"Yes, um, I think he's related to Owen O'Connell."

"Mr. O'Connell was found dead several days ago. He drowned, but not in the usual sense. Someone strapped him to a machine that pumped water throughout his body. Executed with some sort of water invention."

Aleksandar lifted his head, the sound of his heartbeat thrashing in his ears, his legs going weak. *A mad inventor?*

"I assume someone with elemental knowledge murdered him." Nicoli closed his notebook.

"You think?"

"Mr. O'Connell went missing along with a colleague of his, Mr. Patterson," Nicoli said. "However, Mr. Patterson has yet to turn up. Before them, a man had the ends of his fingers, head, and legs blown out, as if someone pumped him full of air and waited for him to explode. Before that, another crushed by rocks. Landslides are common in the area, but once examined, they found sand throughout the insides of his body. All had two things in common: they were killed by the elements, and they were all inventors."

Aleksandar's face turned pale. His fingers tingled, and he looked with a stern gaze. "You think your killer attacked me last night?"

"He's let no one go before, so why are you the first?"

"These murders haven't been in the news press or anything?" Aleksandar put his hands on his knees, noticing his shifting stature.

"For good reason. The World's Fair has brought many things, including rampant crime and murders. Do you know what would happen if the city was thrown into chaos at its current capacity? Even those at the presses understand the danger."

"There are hundreds, if not thousands, of inventors in Well's Peake. We deserve to know that we are in danger." Aleksandar stood, gripping the bench for support.

Nicoli let out a sigh. "I understand, but even I must follow the orders from the table."

Aleksandar looked out the window, squinting into the light, unsure of what to expect.

They could have killed him. What if no one heard the commotion, and he bled out? Maybe the killer was hoping for it.

"Mr. Scott, I need to know if your invention, if used by this man, puts more lives at risk," Nicoli said, breaking the silence.

"The Red Breath is the only invention you should worry about."

"Mr. Scott. What is this?" Constable May asked.

Aleksandar's heart skipped as Constable May revealed a hidden door within the wood paneling. Light from cracks in the wood above glimmered off the buttons on her navy jacket. A secured ladder rested against the wall, and she looked to the top. She pulled on a rope, and the hatch above opened, revealing the living room ceiling.

Aleksandar crossed his arms, and his gown ripped under his palms. "That's a chute for bringing supplies into the workshop."

Constable May closed the hatch and shut the door.

"What happens now?" Aleksandar asked, looking to Nicoli.

No one answered, and a creak from the stairwell caught his attention.

Firm steps came from the staircase, Natalia walking down with a blue hat in hand. Everyone turned to her.

"Miss Arlen? What are you doing here?" Aleksandar asked.

"I'm sorry to barge in. A colleague of mine informed me about your predicament, and the constable upstairs said I was allowed in. I felt obligated to check on you, to make sure you didn't need help." Natalia touched the splintered wood.

Nicoli stepped forward. "Miss, while kind of you to stop in, this workshop, along with the residence, is off-limits to outsiders."

"Is that why Mr. Hawthorne's upstairs peeking through Mr. Scott's belongings?" Natalia asked. "I alerted one of your men, and he is keeping watch over him now."

"Of course he is. Well, I suppose we have what we need. One of us will return for that list of inventions, unless you wish to drop it off, Mr. Scott. It is also your decision who may stay and enter." Nicoli looked at Constable May.

"If you could escort Mr. Hawthorne out," Aleksandar said.

"Constable May, help the reporter, please."

Nicoli nodded to Constable May, and they made their way out of the workshop, all the constables following.

Aleksandar listened to their footsteps above until they faded into a muffled argument, most likely with Mr. Hawthorne.

Natalia walked to the center and took a deep breath, putting her hands on her hips. "My condolences, Mr. Scott, on what could be an inventor's darkest day."

Aleksandar rubbed his arm. "Suppose I should be grateful after what they told me. I'm not dead, which could've been a darker day."

"The darkest day would still show light in the morning. Death would have brought none."

Aleksandar pulled up a tilted stool and sat on top, trying to rest from his overbearing headache.

Natalia looked at him with kind eyes. "Are you all right?"

"As much as anyone could be. The doctor says I'm still in shock and to prepare for once it fades away." Aleksandar rubbed his temples.

Natalia walked around the workshop, glancing over the bare shelves and empty benches. Aleksandar couldn't help but notice her somber suit.

Her sapphire vest accented her blue eyes. The black jacket displayed her usual style, sharp and elegant, while he was still in his nightgown, the top of his collar stained with blood.

Natalia pushed splintered boards and gears aside and picked up a piece of paper, tearing at the seams from the table. She looked it over in her palm.

"Why now? Why me?" Aleksandar asked.

"The most unfortunate things happen to us all," Natalia said. "You have been broken, but you will recover."

"Will I? Have others recovered from this? I've put so much effort into those inventions." Aleksandar leaned back against the wall, his shoulders hunched against a wooden beam.

"Yes, you will. How far along were you?"

Aleksandar let out a sob, holding the tears back. "Not far, but work had begun. They were the foundations for everything I had planned."

"Can you rebuild?"

"I could try, but the details that took several months to figure out were in my schematic book. I don't have the coin to sustain myself until I piece it together." Aleksandar's voice grew thin.

"Opportunities and unexpected people show up when turmoil occurs. People will come to your aid. If someone offers you the resources you need to rebuild, take it."

Aleksandar thought back to the previous day. Everything was in his hands and led to great opportunity. Now, everything was ruined, and he had no means to recover.

Natalia walked across the room and held the trinket to Aleksandar with a soft smile, her blackberry perfume lingering off her.

Aleksandar stumbled to his feet and took it in his hand. "I call it a trinket. There were a few others, but I assume whoever did this took them. I wrote all my ideas on these pieces of paper to think of new concepts."

Aleksandar folded the edges of the blank trinket and then set it on the desk.

"I would fold the paper on itself," he said, "until two ideas touched, and I thought of an idea. Kind of like—"

Aleksandar glanced at Natalia.

Natalia smiled and rubbed the bottom of her cheek. "Mr. Scott, no need to worry."

"I never meant—"

"It is not your fault."

"I'm so sorry. I never meant to lose the Spark."

Aleksandar shook his head, the throbbing pain in his temples, the tightness in his neck. Natalia placed her hands on his shoulder.

"Do not worry. We'll find it when they catch your thief," Natalia said. "Until then, create something new to help you through this ordeal."

Aleksandar nodded, letting his panic fade away. Natalia patted him on the shoulder and walked away.

"What all did they steal?" Natalia asked.

"Several elemental prototypes," Aleksandar said.

"Any water-related?"

"Yes. The schematics for our project were on that wall."

Natalia walked to the board and rubbed her fingertips on the ripped paper under a pin. "A shame. I was rather excited to see them."

Aleksandar walked beside her and pulled out a pin. "Miss Arlen, I don't think I can."

"Can what?"

"The Harvest Exhibition. I'm not sure how to support myself until then."

Natalia gazed at him. "What do you mean?"

Aleksandar paused, choking for a moment as he cleared his thoughts. "Yesterday, my life was in a different place when I accepted your offer. I was ready to learn, to create, but there's nothing left. I have nothing."

Natalia stepped forward. "In light of everything, it might be wise to take a few days for yourself. If you are open to an offer, I could support you financially so we may continue our work. Enough for food, boarding, and supplies."

Aleksandar took a hard look around, crossing his arms and focusing on his breath.

Natalia bit her lower lip. "Aleksandar, think for a few days. Be sure you are not giving up an opportunity you desire. When all appears lost, we still rebuild. It may not be easy, but it's possible. I can give you the means."

"I don't want to give up, but I need to set everything aside. Our invention... I think we need to put that on hold. I can't help you if I can't help myself."

"I respect that and understand the delay, but know we risk not completing an invention for the Harvest Exhibition. A few months is not long for what we have planned. Maybe inventing will keep you from falling into a dangerous state of mind."

Aleksandar looked away, shaking his head.

"Are you sure you don't want to put some effort into our invention?" Natalia asked. "Perhaps think it over for a few days."

Aleksandar let out a deep sigh, feeling the strain behind his eyes. "Not at the moment. I need to slow down so I can figure out where I am. I don't want to lose this opportunity, so I hope you will have me when I'm ready."

She nodded, rubbing the side of her cheek. "Of course. Once again, my condolences, Mr. Scott. A better day to you, and if you need anything, you know where to find me."

Natalia lifted her hat and placed it on her head, smiling as she walked up the stairs.

The door shut, and the workshop was quiet, with only Shae's fluttering in her cage upstairs breaking the silence.

Aleksandar looked at the windows and stared at the bare wall. He walked over and pressed his head against the wood paneling, the grain thick against his skin. Tears filled his tired eyes as he attempted to calm himself, feeling as if he might pass out.

The wall shifted as he slid to his feet, an outward breeze creeping from the cracks of the hidden room.

Thank you.

～

Natalia walked out of the house and looked down the street, rubbing her cheek, her fingertips lingering longer than usual.

Lydia and Nicoli stood at the corner of the intersection, conversing with other constables. They inspected Aleksandar's flat, pointing to something Natalia could not see, nor interested in. The cloudy day was soft on her eyes, the forest air blowing with the wind as the leaves changed and the harvest season took hold of Well's Peake.

Natalia headed off, looking inward to hide—

Snap!

A flash blinded her. She rubbed her eyes and found herself next to Abel, who smiled towards his photographer. Natalia looked up at another bright light.

Snap!

Nathalia took a step back.

"If I did not know better, I'd say that last photo was perfect, Miss Arlen," Abel said.

"Abel, I see you insist on making a nuisance of yourself." Natalia tried to refocus her vision by rubbing her eyes.

"I am covering, as you say, an inventor's darkest day."

Natalia paused and glared at Abel, his smile thin across his face.

"Good day, Miss Arlen."

He walked down the street, and Natalia put her hands into her pockets. She blew air out her nose, nodding to the alerted constables with a forced smile. Natalia made her way home, hopeful the young inventor would reconsider the opportunities at hand.

Aleksandar, staring aimlessly at his fireplace from his couch, let the back cushion sink around him. The sun set through the windows, and the gray-and-white clouds covered the sky's orange lush.

Shae rested on top of the armrest, looking with a tilted stare. She hopped into his lap, and he grabbed a pillow, placing it under her talons. She rubbed her head against his chest, Aleksandar petting the side of her cheek.

He stood slowly, grabbing a small leather guard, and placed it on his shoulder. Shae flew to it and landed, arching over in support.

Aleksandar walked to the staircase and headed downstairs to his workshop, still overturned in the night shadows. Aleksandar looked at the wall across from his desk.

Aleksandar tried to remember the combination, glancing at the trinket on the bench. He folded a panel to the corner and pressed others back in puzzling ways. He rotated a few pieces until the wall resembled the shape of his trinket.

The young inventor pushed on the wall, and it sank with several clicks. It spun in a circle, and he turned it until a locking clank echoed throughout the room. With a push, the room opened, air blowing out of the sanctuary.

Light reflected off the metal object in the room, hidden in shadows, and onto Aleksandar's face.

It's still here.

He found a slow smile, and he felt a weight lift from his shoulders. *Whoever* had attacked him hadn't taken everything. There was still hope, something left of his dream.

Aleksandar glanced to the floor; his smile vanished, and his face went pale.

At his feet, an envelope rested on the floor with a red wax seal.

An envelope in a room that no one should know was there.

Aleksandar swallowed hard and bent down, lifting the letter. His breathing intensified, and sweat dripped down his temple.

The outside of the envelope was blank, without a scrape or smudge. He opened it with trembling hands, breaking the wax, and his eyes burrowed into every word.

Mr. Scott,

The amount of questions you have has amplified upon opening this letter, I am sure of it, but do not let them cloud your mind with the events to occur. I have no direction for you yet, but understand things are not how they appear. The truth is hidden from the public, but it has spread amongst those who have a part in its matters. Madness has come to Well's Peake, and you must exercise caution. Inventors are at risk.

For now, be careful and mind your back. Well's Peake is in danger, and it will need our protection.

Aleksandar stared at the letter with a dry throat, stricken with dread.

CHAPTER SEVENTEEN

Abel threw papers about the desk and pinned news covers to a corkboard, with photos of the World's Fair hanging between the headlines. He sorted through them with a coy smile, clipping notes to images with a pin in his mouth.

Abel pulled out a fresh piece of paper, dipped a pen in ink, and wrote with confident enthusiasm. The words flowed seamlessly from his thoughts, and he never looked to the clock, the day fading into night as the lanterns lit the office. The pressure of the pen against the paper, the grain of the wood underneath, was comforting in his grip.

Leaning back and shaking his hand out, he hummed to the latest symphony he'd attended the night before. He grabbed some yarn, connected the pins, and pieced together his elaborate puzzle. Photo after photo, he eyed pictures of inventors, constables, and the World's Fair. He smiled at a photo of a director waving his baton above musicians at a full crescendo.

The door creaked, and he turned to his editor in the door frame. She stepped alongside his cluttered desk as he created his journalistic symphony.

"Well, if this isn't a mess," she said, straightening her suspenders.

"Now, now, Ferdie, this is art. A soon-to-be masterpiece." Abel held his hands out in grandeur.

Ferdie leaned in, pulling her auburn hair back with green eyes focused on Abel's photographs.

"Look it over. Tell me what you see." Abel rested his shoulder on the board, watching her every gaze.

To create an article that swooned the masses was riveting, but Abel could think of no better enjoyment than his editor's first look at a new story. Her persistent stare, her judgmental nods, her hesitant sighs, he welcomed them. To know he would take her from denying his column to putting it on the front of the *Well's Peake Commons* was an experience he greatly enjoyed.

Ferdie pulled out her spectacles and set them on the tip of her nose, observing the board as she crossed her arms against her striped shirt. Abel savored the quiet in the room, the rattling of carriages passing from the street below.

Ferdie picked up papers from Abel's desk, reading them in silence.

They looked at each other, Abel unable to resist a smile.

Ferdie put her hands on her hips. "You're annoyingly pretentious."

"I aim to please." Abel walked across his office and plopped on the worn sofa against the window, the cushion thumping against the glass.

"Well, I can't say you aren't passionate," she said, eyeing a photo of the World's Fair.

"But—"

"I'm more than willing to entertain your outlandish stories, but this is too much for Well's Peake with the World's Fair going on."

"All the more reason this story will fly off the stands to thousands of fairgoers. There's no greater moment in history to be the boldest leading press. You asked for it, and I have given."

Ferdie looked at the board again. "We have strict guidelines on what we can publish about the murders. You piecing the robbery of an elemental inventor together is that of pure speculation. If we ran this, you would need to take out the *investigative* liberties."

Abel slapped his knee. "I can't do that. That's where the spice comes in."

"It's speculation."

"It's educated journalism. We are using the facts and evidence we have at our disposal to compose the story."

"It's you inflating an article to your benefit without all the evidence. I want concrete facts, not your educated journalism if we were to disobey the Peake. We can survive the story if it's true, but if not, we lose everything. This is too dangerous a story, and I won't let you take civil liberties with it."

Ferdie ripped a paper off the wall and crumbled it, tossing it into the overflowing trash bin.

"What did you do that for?" Abel stood and walked to the bin, Ferdie blocking his way.

"Also, that penny dreadful stays out of the press until the World's Fair is over as well. You know, the one you tried to sneak into printing?"

"Nervous?" Abel leaned in with a smirk.

Ferdie put a finger on his chest and pushed him away. "About a mass murderer who preys on fairgoers and attempts to transform them into the living dead... for what reason would I be worried?"

Ferdie stepped to the door.

"Okay, okay, hold on. I understand your caution with civil liberties; that makes sense, but you have to admit this is not typical. This robbery wasn't about money or jewelry. Someone wanted elemental inventions, and there so happens to be an elemental killer on the streets. Think, Ferdie, about what is happening in this city as we speak."

Ferdie rolled her eyes and head back. "I must have misheard, because it sounds like you're still entertaining this. And if you keep pushing your contact at the Peake, they will eventually get caught, and you'll be spending some days behind iron."

Abel glared at her, and she lifted her eyebrows.

Ferdie pointed to a photo of Natalia and Abel side by side in front of Aleksandar's house. "And finally, you can't keep dragging her in whenever you want."

"Why not? Miss Arlen is and always will be a popular segment. Even you told me she was your hero, so I wished to impress you. Whether or not she is related to the case, it's something I can explore. Her popping in was the cherry on top. I'd be more suspicious of her arriving so quickly if I had not found out before her."

Ferdie put her fingers to her mouth and eyed Abel out of the corner of her eyes. He looked away, and she put her hands on her hips.

"Did you tip her off?" she asked, her brow furrowed.

"No." Abel scratched his cheek.

"Abel, so help me."

"I didn't tip her off, I swear. I tipped off an *associate* of hers, someone who I knew would bring it up to her, and what do you know, she showed up like clockwork."

"Oh, so now you're directly fabricating situations to your advantage?"

Abel rubbed his forehead.

"Dammit, Abel, you're smarter than this," she said. "You aren't writing fluff anymore. This is a little more serious. What if we cause mass panic? Then what? What happens when some vigilante takes action on someone innocent?"

Abel waved his hand. "Lives are already in danger, evidently, so what harm could we do? Well's Peake is distracted, and no commoner is going to go hunt for some forgotten inventor. You're overthinking this."

Ferdie chattered her teeth and waved Abel to follow as she walked into the corridor.

"I'd rather not?" He sighed.

"Now!"

Abel tossed his pen onto his desk, pondering out the window. He rolled his eyes and jogged to catch up with her. Glass windows filled the hallway leading to offices of other journalists and editors. Most were dark, with a few cleaning their desks or hanging photos with little light in their rooms. A woman set up a miniature printing press and stamped out a business card.

"You see these people, Abel? They know when to quit, when to go home to their family, their pets, or whatever lovely things they have in life. They know when to enjoy themselves and not go overboard or irritate me like a child. You have a dog who you surprisingly don't have in your office right now. Go play fetch or something."

"When have you ever been home by midnight?"

Ferdie did not reply. She stuffed her hands into her pockets and turned the corner of the brown-and-orange offices.

"Aren't you the one that told us journalism requires a never-ending study into the unknown?" Abel smiled, waiting for her to glare or scold him.

"You weren't supposed to take that literally," she said. "Keep an impartial eye, but still live your life. How long has it been since you went out for a night or spent the weekend at the club? I'm sure the card tables are cold in your absence."

Ferdie walked into her office and pointed to the couch. Abel sat in the middle as she opened a cabinet, pulling out two glasses by her fingertips. They tinged as she set them on a credenza and filled them with bourbon from the decanter. She held a glass to Abel, and he took it, holding it in his lap, the glass cool to the touch.

Abel swirled the drink, butterscotch filling his nostrils. "This stuff tastes like the back end—"

Ferdie opened her eyes, and Abel froze.

"Do not finish that sentence." She grabbed her drink from the desk. "Sit there and listen for once. Listen without giving me any comments, opinions, facts, or whatever clever remarks you consider necessary to let loose from those never-ending lips."

There it is—the blowout.

Abel tried his drink and cringed, holding back a cough. Ferdie smiled as she took a sip, as if she enjoyed his suffering.

"Abel, I love your articles. They're wonderful stories, but you've taken too much pressure from the director. You now have this lust, this never-ending desire to create the perfect story and put your name in history. I can see the appeal with the World's Fair in town and our distribution rates higher than ever, but you are no longer the city's most trusted man. People don't take your word at face value. There's doubt, and they do question."

Abel opened his mouth, but Ferdie held her hand up, Abel letting out a hard sigh.

"If I let you write the article on this elemental killer, I want it done right."

Abel tilted his head and looked at her. "Am I doing something wrong?"

"Ah! What did I tell you? Listen. You don't have to be coy with everything you do." Ferdie took a breath. "This story, I fear, could interrupt people's lives in ways I don't consider necessary. I could not care less if this were a mob boss or criminal, but you are playing loose on specifics during an event bigger than Well's Peake has ever seen. On occasion, we need to ask whether or not to publish the article."

"It's not like I haven't before."

"But this isn't like before." Ferdie held her hand out. "This a very provocative story, and we need to exercise caution. You're not wrong, it's a story worth the headlines, but not all press is good press."

"I'm here because I'm good, damn good. The story is out there. It just needs help." Abel waved his palm, almost spilling his drink.

"Let it go." Ferdie pointed her finger. "Let the elemental article go, and I'll consider your other story, the one you love to annoy me with, and if you spill that drink on my sofa, you're dead."

Abel stopped swirling his drink, sighed, and took another sip. "You would consider my theory on the Black Harvest?"

"*Consider* is the keyword." Ferdie held her glass with her fingertips, rocking it in front of her face. "*Well's Peake Commons* is building an immaculate reputation, all thanks to the World's Fair. We need to consider that. Is the story worth it? Was it brought together by someone who isn't obsessed with creating a desired lie, and is it an authentic story?"

"Every honest story has some speculation. People enjoy facts, but it's the mystery, the intrigue that keeps them attached." Abel lifted his leg and set it on the other.

"Abel, my dear, think. Is it worth it? You won't find the praise you wish for if you write stories like this. They aren't the intellectual and cultural stories you used to write. I understand why you switched directions and are fond of these conspiracy theories after what happened in Redwood, but aristocrats don't want that attention and commoners don't want to relive the past."

"Those theories have more facts than some pieces others publish."

Abel gulped his drink, the butterscotch tasting worse with every sip, and sank into the couch, eyeing the ceiling.

Ferdie stood, then sat next to Abel.

The liquor was rough and not smooth, like sandpaper if it inspired its own drink. Abel tapped the glass, thinking beyond, a drop falling onto the sofa.

Abel held his gaze, Ferdie glaring at him with piercing eyes. He rubbed the drop with his thin sleeve, and she turned away, her cheeks as red as her hair.

Ferdie cracked her neck. "I've seen writers of all kinds, and they're always chasing the story that sets them on that bloody pedestal. I've watched more people chase a dream rather than appreciate their own lives. It's not worth it, Abel. Enjoy yourself, have some fun before the fair leaves."

She wasn't wrong. On occasion, he missed teaching music, playing poker, and dining at the finer restaurants, but the pen and paper were his life and joy. The allure of something greater was captivating. Why would he want to sacrifice his desire?

"But if I have a chance for my story, it's now, while the World's Fair is at its peak," he said.

"Don't you want to be known as a writer instead of a smut journalist?"

"They were all smuts."

"I wasn't, and I don't remember ever writing a bad article if that at all persuades you."

"I know, yet you gave it all up to be an editor."

"Yes, and I don't regret it. Stomping the pavement made my feet hurt." Ferdie sipped on her drink, looking through the glass. "Do you know what makes a compelling story?"

Abel looked at her as she stared out the window. "The characters?"

"Yes, but dig deeper. What's the most important part?"

"I suppose you're going to tell me?"

"Perception, you ninny. Perception is the basis of every article in the paper. That is the strength of the journalist. Your perception and the readers. We must handle them with care because we have the power to influence an election or persuade panic in the streets."

"And I care?"

Ferdie's face went blank, and she waved her hand. She finished her drink and walked to her desk, grabbing two folders off the counter. She held them with her arm straight out and dropped them to the floor.

Abel eyed them as Ferdie sat at her desk without a glance. His fingers tingled, and his chest tightened. He wished he could take back what he said. Ferdie's glare was not normal, and his antics did not persuade her when he was so sure she would cave like usual. This was his one chance at greatness, and she was holding him hostage.

"Are those for me?" he asked.

"Those are the most prolific articles of the past thirty years. Read them, study them. You might notice a structure or find inspiration. You *won't* find much speculation in those."

"Oh, please. And who sorted through these?"

"I did."

"Is this coming from you as a friend or my editor?"

Ferdie pounded the desk with her fist and pointed. "Abel, listen, you have bent or broken almost all the golden rules, but I'm done with this. I'm shutting you down unless you read those tonight. Your story will not run, I promise you. Put in an article about the robbery, I don't care, but your conspiracy of an elemental killer stays out until you can shed all doubt from my perception. Whether this is because of my vanity or the morality of a writer, you can decide."

"Ferd—"

"Stop." Ferdie stood.

"I have the story." Abel stepped close, his palms out.

"A story with an unprecedented risk."

"This could mark me for life."

Ferdie put her hands on the desk, holding herself up. "Yes, but whether in a positive light or negative is my concern when it should be yours."

Why was she being like this? There was no reason. I had done nothing different from the ordinary except put a few pieces together that wouldn't have on their own.

Abel leaned in and poured his drink into her glass. "So now what?"

"Find a different perception."

Abel picked up the thick folders from the wood floor and walked to the exit, standing in the frame. "No legendary writer becomes such without risk."

"That is why I'm the editor, and you're the writer."

Abel glared away and closed the door with a thud, walking down the corridor. His elevated pulse throbbed in his hands, and his vision was clouded. He closed his eyes and thought to the hallway, how the greatest headlines were framed for him to look at every morning he stepped into work. His story was admirable and deserved its place—elemental killers... killing inventors. Well's Peake has not experienced such an event, and the power from his words would captivate the masses.

Abel opened his eyes to the nearby room where the cylindrical printing press churned papers out in high volumes, the musk of ink filling the air. He leaned against the beam, pushing the inside of his cheek out with his tongue, the nasty aftertaste of butterscotch lingering on his breath.

Abel glanced towards Ferdie's office and sighed, biting the end of his lip. He stuffed his hands in his pockets and made his way to his office, with the stories of the greatest in his grasp.

CHAPTER EIGHTEEN

Graying clouds spread across the sky in slivers of dark shades, illuminating over Well's Peake and its fairgoers. A soft rain fell onto the glass roof of the World's Palace, pattering above.

Aleksandar sat in his chair, resting beside the Red Breath, silent and calm. The smell of heated metal from his invention filled the air, and the savor of burned fuel lingered on his tongue. He took several deep breaths, aimlessly looking into the crowds and inventions.

What am I doing here?

Being away from the fair for a few days seemed longer as he confined himself to his house, thinking in his barren workshop. The urge to build was there, but he had no tools, no material, and no coin to buy them.

Aleksandar looked to the people with a pit in his stomach. They shifted through the halls, laughing, conversing, and observing, few paying attention to Aleksandar, one batting him a glance. He bit his lower lip until it turned raw. With the taste of blood in his mouth, he rubbed his right arm, looking for comfort.

He knew he should not have returned so soon, growing restless in his chair, but realized staying home would have driven him into a deeper conflicted state. To try was his only option.

Aleksandar stood to his invention and pulled the lever, fire surging into the roped-off display behind the workbench. The flames reflecting in his eyes as he barely blinked. Fairgoers jumped as Aleksandar stared into the light, the warmth of the flare against his cheeks. He turned off the Red Breath, and the blaze died away.

He dragged his fingernails across the wooden bench, the grain of the wood rubbing against the tips, lucky enough not to catch a splinter. Aleksandar yanked the lever again, and the Red Breath surged to life.

Someone walked up behind him. "I give you my deepest condolences, Mr. Scott. Your situation appears to have shifted for the worse."

Aleksandar shut off the machine and turned to Kenneth with his cane in hand, his hair flowing onto his shoulders, and a newspaper under his arm.

Aleksandar let out a deep breath. "Mr. Forbes, good morning. Thank you."

"To you as well. I have missed your presence at the World's Fair the past few days. I've attended many demonstrations in your absence, and all have been lackluster in comparison."

"I'm sorry to disappoint. I was indisposed." Aleksandar walked to his chair and sat, resting his arm on the workbench, the cold steel causing the hair on his forearms to stand.

"As I mentioned before, my deepest sympathy." Kenneth stepped towards the Red Breath, Aleksandar watching him from the corner of his eye.

"Don't be. It was out of your hands."

"Doesn't make the situation less unfortunate."

Aleksandar nodded in agreement and pulled the invention's locking brace, pinning the device shut.

"Is that all that's left?" Kenneth asked.

Aleksandar nodded again. "Yes. If it wasn't at the World's Fair, it might have been lost."

Kenneth lifted the newspaper in his hand for a moment, wanting to draw Aleksandar's attention, and set it on the bench corner. An image of Natalia and Abel stood in front of his house, though the fold hid the headline.

"Have you read it?" Kenneth asked.

"No."

"The article was vague and ill-prepared for my taste. Focused more on the disdain for inventors than on the robbery itself. So instead, I thought I'd come to your aid with better intentions than Mr. Hawthorne."

Aleksandar looked to Kenneth with raised eyebrows, still slumped in his seat. He rubbed his hand against his pants, the tweed gentle against his palm.

"I return, Mr. Scott, to re-propose my offer with a significant rise in coin." Kenneth waved his cane and paced, the tails of his ruby jacket kissing the floor. "I presume your financial status has diminished, along with your means of daily living, so I wish—"

"I'll do it."

Kenneth paused. His cane still in the air and mouth open with unfinished words. "I apologize. I misheard?"

"You didn't. Your offer, I accept."

Kenneth lowered his head, a thin grin slipping between his cheeks. "Just like that?"

Nodding, Aleksandar turned his attention to Kenneth, whose face shone like the morning sun. Slick and enticing, Kenneth's scarlet eyes lit up with excitement, his smile broad.

"You are not fooling around, are you, Mr. Scott? I don't know if I could handle such disappointment."

Aleksandar stood, pulling his sleeves to his wrists. "Someone told me I needed to do what is best for me. I knew then I needed this opportunity. She gave me an offer, but it didn't feel right to accept it in my situation."

Aleksandar tried to swallow his words, but they came out. He had to invent. He had to earn the coin required to create the invention that would make all his effort and sweat worthwhile. To prove himself to Natalia instead of mooching off of her. Kenneth was his last option, but now his only.

Kenneth smiled wide, putting his palm across his chest, fingers spread. He tossed his cane from one hand to another and slid two fingers along the brim of his hat.

"Mr. Scott, you cannot fathom how delighted I am," Kenneth said. "I realize your participation stems from need rather than want, but know you will enjoy the outcome of your work. This… I deserve it in its entirety, and it would be impossible without you. Thank you from the deepest part of my heart."

Aleksandar nodded and swallowed hard. "I can only hope."

Kenneth, oblivious in his excitement, ignored Aleksandar as he looked at the crowd, his chin raised in the air. He whipped out a velvet case and flipped it open on the table. He lifted a pen and dipped it into an inkwell, writing his address in a quick but flawless form.

Aleksandar gawked at the man's finesse. Kenneth was too excited for his own good, but he never seemed whimsical or childish. Every wave of his hand, the flick of his jacket, tap of his cane was a performance, and he had perfected it.

Kenneth held out the paper and gleamed at Aleksandar, his cedar cologne caressing Aleksandar's nostrils in a divine aroma.

Aleksandar grabbed the paper. "Why me?"

Kenneth lowered his arms. "You may not believe it, and while you and the many assume your work to be young, your inventions are the birthplace of what's to come. You are bringing forth an age of art, of culture. As a society, we lack in creative pursuits and true artistry, all because of the fallout of the Black Harvest. I have the vision to recollect the past, Mr. Scott, and you are part of it. While I may want your invention for flare, it is also to be a beacon of trust that we can build with inventors once again. We will enter this age together, into a renaissance I see on the horizon."

Aleksandar tapped his foot and pulled on his lower lip.

"That is my current residence." Kenneth handed him a piece of paper. "The man on the hill is easy to find. Can you begin in two days? Say nine-ish? It would endear me for an earlier date, but my manor is under stupendous renovations."

"Indeed."

"Splendid." Kenneth put his hand on Aleksandar's shoulder. "I will see you then." He tipped his hat. "Again, my condolences." He nodded in farewell and took off into the World's Palace, holding his cane high and his chin up.

Aleksandar stared at the crowd, Kenneth no longer in sight, just the swarm of fairgoers moving past him, none paying him any attention. He clenched his arm against his eyes as pressure built inside his temples, the dull ache of his injury growing. His taut cheeks flexed in frustration, and he searched for a moment's relief. He heard a shuffle from the crowds, but Aleksandar ignored it, his head heavy like a rock at the bottom of a river.

The tapping of a cane against the floor stuck out to him, and he knew Owen was near, wishing he had not noticed.

Aleksandar opened his eyes to Owen, holding Hugh by the collar, his face flushed red.

"Your apprentice, Mr. Scott, once again was tampering with my invention. As his mentor, I feel you are somewhat responsible for his actions. Don't you agree?"

Owen pushed Hugh away, who straightened his collar and glanced at the two inventors.

"The seal is too weak on the limb casing," Hugh said. "Your machine could tear and blow out. I was only trying to fix it."

"As an inventor and a natural problem solver, if I wanted assistance with my work, I would've asked for it. I will not have it tampered with behind my back." Owen waved his hand.

Aleksandar looked to Hugh, who pulled his collar higher to where his eyes met the rim.

"It won't happen again." Hugh looked away from them both.

Owen shook his head, leaning on his cane. He took a deep breath and turned to Aleksandar. "Alek, I'm sad to learn about your predicament."

Aleksandar stood there, silent and rubbing his hands against his cotton shirt. "Thank you. I'm sorry to hear about your cousin."

Owen straightened his back to where the cane lifted off the floor. "Where did you hear that?"

"From the detective at my robbery. He mentioned my intruder might have been his murderer."

Owen pressed his lips together, his mustache hanging over the bottom. "I see, but enough about that. I've heard disturbing remarks about your recent collaborations."

"With Miss Arlen?"

"No, Kenneth Forbes."

"I..." Aleksandar looked over his shoulder, looking for Kenneth. "That's impossible. He left not more than five minutes ago."

"Oh, Mr. Forbes is not one for secrecy. You will soon realize you are his show monkey in the circus he calls a lifestyle. He calls himself the man on the hill, but he is a glorified aristocrat who spends his days flaunting art galleries and throwing events with no meaning."

"Well, I don't see how that's any of your business."

"I have to ask, did you put much, if any, thought into that decision?" Owen passed Hugh and leaned against the workbench.

Aleksandar rubbed the end of his nose. "I'm doing this because it can put me back on track. To help reestablish myself."

Owen looked away and smacked his lips. "There was one thing I could never figure out, Aleksandar. It's not what you do, but why you do it. What drives you to invent when you obviously have little interest in the craft?"

Aleksandar crossed his arms, and his shirt stuck to his sweaty skin. His mouth dried, and he had a horrible thirst. Owen and Hugh were no longer his concern, only her, and how she was his motivation for inventing. His childhood friend was all that lingered in his thoughts; her passion, the warmth of her hand from the frost night so long ago. It was tender but still warm as the snow fell around them in the forested pines.

The tap of Owen's cane pulled Aleksandar back to the World's Fair, and his lip curled.

"Aleksandar," Owen said. "How many people will you hinder because your motivation is elsewhere?"

"What do you suggest, Owen? Huh? Give up? Inventions are all I've ever known. I'll push back harder because that's what I do. We share that same passion, in case you think any less of me."

Aleksandar stepped forward, hoping his stance would prove his point. Owen leaned off the desk and stood next to the aisle of fairgoers. His passive-aggressive tone was gone, replaced with a deep sigh.

A moment of silence.

Owen looked at his leg. "I'm sorry. I suppose I'm on edge with everything that has happened. Forgive me. I will leave, but do mentor your apprentice before he does something not only foolish but dangerous."

Aleksandar looked away, arms crossed, the moment weighing on him. Hugh watched with his hands in his pockets, his head low as he batted glances between the two inventors. Aleksandar's patience was running thin, and he grew frustrated with the situation, wishing none of it had ever happened.

Owen tightened his grip on his cane and stepped towards Aleksandar, placing his hand on the young inventor's shoulder. "You have the potential to be a positive influence in Well's Peake. Don't waste it."

Owen turned and shuffled towards the crowd, glancing at Hugh. "Mr. Evans. I expect you to stay out of my exhibit. Is that understood?"

Hugh nodded.

Owen walked away, Aleksandar looking to Hugh, arms still crossed. Hugh shifted around and took a seat next to the Red Breath, rubbing his hands.

Aleksandar looked off into the distance, his thoughts nowhere, anywhere but at the World's Fair.

"Um, maybe if you taught me, it could take your mind off things?" Hugh said with a cautious smile.

Aleksandar turned to Hugh, massaging his forehead. "Mr. Evans, I might have to postpone your training for a few weeks."

Hugh stood, his hands slipping to his side. "Why would we do that?"

Aleksandar looked at his apprentice, rubbing the bridge of his nose. "I don't know what to think, and I don't feel I could tutor you the way you deserve. You may not have heard, but I was robbed and have been left with nothing."

"But you sound like you know what you're doing."

"I'm sorry, but I don't have a clue right now. I don't know if I can be the teacher you need me to be."

A frown covered Hugh's face, and his shoulders dropped with a quick exhale. "Mr. Scott, you've only begun to show me what I need to know. How am I to learn more? No one will teach me."

Aleksandar looked to the fair. "We can follow up soon, I promise, but I'm no help to you at the moment."

Aleksandar could see it in Hugh's eyes, hope shattering like glass.

Hugh choked on his breath and walked around the workbench. "If you didn't want to help me, you could've said so." Hugh gave Kenneth's forgotten newspaper a childish shove to the floor and walked away, out of sight.

Aleksandar stood there, no thoughts coming to mind. No words to stop Hugh; none could explain the burden he felt after the robbery or how nothing made sense. Aleksandar could only describe himself as rocking in the carriage to every cobblestone in the road.

Aleksandar bent over and picked up the newspaper, the unfolded paper thick in his hands. Natalia and Abel stood in front of his house, posing for the camera.

The headline: *Penniless Robbery.*

Slowly sitting in the chair within his exhibition, Aleksandar lowered his head, reminded of how broken he was.

CHAPTER NINETEEN

Natalia unlocked a window in her workshop and opened it to the waterfall outside. The moonlight was peering through and reflecting off the Lunarwheel.

She pulled three tubes from the engine and laid them on the windowsill, hooking a rope around the ends. Lowering them alongside the house and tree trunks, she dropped them into the river at the bottom of the falls.

With a smile and her hair pulled back, she admired the moon as it glistened in her eyes. She looked at the waterfall, the wind brushing her hair with the water's mist in the cool harvest breeze.

The night was young, and her ambition was high. She slipped on her gloves and reached under the Lunarwheel, pushing rods into the machine and pinning them in place. The engine reminded her of a sapphire, radiant with luster and translucent like ice. She flipped the main brace over the top and secured it.

Natalia grabbed the machine and tried to shake it.

Hopefully, that's not going anywhere.

She pulled off her wool gloves and placed them next to her tea. Chai filled her nostrils as she lifted the cup to her lips, taking a warm sip, the vanilla smooth and comforting.

Let's see what I can discover.

Natalia set the tea down and walked behind the shielded door. With a deep breath, she grabbed the handle above her. The room stood still, her breathing and the roar of the waterfall outside the only noises disturbing her concentration.

She yanked the lever.

The Lunarwheel roared to life, light rippling through the workshop. Water surged through the tubes alongside the house, and the invention glowed. Natalia held goggles to her face as specks flung about, and a smile burst across her face.

Stabilize, my dear.

Natalia watched through the peephole as the engine shook despite the braces. The pipes rattled as a pin dropped onto the wood floor. The workbench, weighted at the base, shifted to the side. Natalia pressed her face against the glass, her eyes straining in the light.

A low hum replaced the roar, and her shaking breath broke the silence. Natalia's shoulders dropped, not knowing what happened. She lowered her spectacles and peeked around the shield. The engine's hum died away, water sloshing inside the machine.

Natalia felt warm inside, her pulse rising, but was confused with the device's fluctuation. A tightness filled her chest as the machine grew softer, the needle on the pressure gauge dropping. She rubbed the bridge of her nose, hoping the stress faded.

The glow dimmed across the shelves and benches, and Natalia stood as shadows filled the workshop. She rubbed her hands together, pressed her lips, and stepped forward, but the hum grew loud again. Pipes surged above her, and she shifted behind the safeguard.

The engine roared into a high winding as Natalia covered her ears. Light glimmered, and glass exploded through a clamp, spraying across the workshop.

The Lunarwheel died, and the water rested in the grain of the floorboards, pooling towards the drains. A single cracked piece of glass rested on top.

Natalia stood, eyes batting back and forth with a broad smile, her heart pounding in her chest.

If only for a second, it worked.

Natalia rushed for a pen off the desk and checked her vest, her journal nowhere to be found. She patted her pockets and searched around, looking at her jacket on the wall.

No, no, where are you?

Natalia found the journal in her inner pocket, opened it on the counter, and tried to write, but the pen was dry. She grabbed another from the workbench, wrote one word, and paused. Her grip loosening on the pen, her gaze drifting off.

The silence was stale, and Natalia stood, her mind empty. Everything that happened faded from her memory, leaving her in a state of amnesia. She looked to the pen and her book, reading the scribble she wrote before her eyes refocused, not remembering what it was about. Her eyelids fluttered, and she came to.

No, no, no.

Natalia flipped through the earlier pages and looked into the messy workshop, her fingers clammy against the linen paper. She sighed, and a tear ran down her cheek. She wiped it away with a handkerchief and stared at the room.

Once again, she stood in the shadows with no recollection, no memory of achievement or discovery.

Closing the journal, she put it in her jacket and tossed the pen on the counter. She stuck her hands in her pockets, walked to her desk, and sat, looking at the water draining through the floor.

It wasn't fair; every step she took, only to go backward. Some details lingered, but her mind was not cohesive. The cruelty of it, the irony, was almost comedic.

Natalia's gaze wandered until she stared at a photo on the corner of her tidied desk, faded and dimly exposed. Her husband sat at a bar with his arm around her. She stood with it in her grasp and took it out of the frame. She pulled her jacket on and slipped the picture into her pocket.

Natalia walked to the dome glass that overlooked the forest and blew out the only lit lantern, wandering out of the workshop of moonlight and shadows.

～

Natalia strolled the lively street, the wind nicking at her neck as the air grew crisp and thin in the harvest season. She pushed her hair behind her shoulders and turned the corner into the Cultural District of Well's Peake.

Bustling pubs and outlets lined the curved avenue with a large fountain in the middle, stores looping the opposite side of the street. The roadway was lit with gaslights, and fairgoers swarmed the circle, many dining outside the restaurants, conversing, and swooning. Maple trees bordered the curb, their leaves dancing in the wind and across the awnings and cobblestone in shades of orange and red.

Natalia walked through the crowd, sure to glide by, never bumping into anyone, not even as much as nicking the shoulders of their jackets. She turned to the Bedelia Bistro and entered through the swiveling oak door.

Violas and cellos filled her ears with the tapping of forks and knives between conversations. Orange-and-red flowers lined the wall with a hint of lemon, and a man with a thick mustache stood at the host's podium with the most polite smile.

A young woman, no older than fourteen, approached Natalia, her arm raised. "May I take your coat, Mademoiselle?"

"Certainly." Natalia pulled out the photo and handed her jacket to the coat maid.

Natalia stepped forward, and the host grinned with sharp cheeks that accented his slender vest. "Welcome to Bedelia's. What is the name on your reservation?"

"My apologies, I don't have one. I was hoping a table might be available."

"With the World's Fair, we are booked full, but something could open soon. You are more than welcome to indulge in the pub while you wait."

"Thank you. Arlen is the last name."

The host wrote in his agenda and waved his hand. "Follow me."

He guided her past the dining room, filled with suited men and women in dresses. It was lit by enormous chandeliers, candles glowing between crystals and sapphires.

Natalia glanced at the photo, looking for something that resembled the background in the image. She kept her palms behind her back, and her posture elegant as the host waved her to several chairs unused at the end of the lounge.

"Simeon will be with you soon," the host said.

"Thank you kindly."

Natalia waited for the host to walk away and pulled the picture from her vest and to the bar, everything lining up. She eyed the pub to see if anyone was looking at her, then strolled to the corner and sat on the edge of the cushioned stool.

The bar was rich like amber, the side paneling blue and unscathed. Glass dividers separated the lounge from the dining room. The ceiling was layered with varnished squares, and polished brass lined the walls with no smudges. Everything was as in the picture; no changes since the photo was taken.

Simeon strolled through the bar doors and looked to Natalia, his hair suave and his skin rich like caramel. Natalia put the photo face down, eyeing the bartender as he walked to her.

"Good evening." Natalia batted him a smile.

"To you as well. Would you enjoy the usual?"

Natalia tilted her head and rubbed her cheek. "The usual?"

"Yes—" Simeon paused, a wineglass in hand, the light catching his brown eyes.

Natalia tapped her fingers. "What do I usually order?"

"Chianti, of course."

Natalia froze, trying to remember. She knew she was in the photo at that pub, but his handsome face was not familiar. "I, um?"

"Oh, I see." Simeon popped a cork from a bottle of Chianti with a curious grin. "You don't recognize me? Not even a little?"

"Not to sound rude, but I don't."

Simeon nodded. "Well, I remember you. You come here more often when you don't remember. Two, I have one of the best memories in the city. I have never forgotten a customer's name, order, or face. I take my profession with the utmost pride, like you do, as an inventor. You are working on the Lunarwheel, yes? The water engine?"

Simeon poured Natalia a glass of wine and set it in front of her. He put his fingers on the base, swirled the glass, and waved for her to take it.

Natalia nodded and lifted the refreshment, putting her nose to the brim. Earthy with a hint of blueberries and strawberries. "I can only assume you are aware of my memory."

"I am," Simeon said, wiping the counter from the bottle he opened. "And I know you don't enjoy acknowledging it. Understandable, and not to discourage you, but I know you look to your husband in that photo. Which I still find odd, considering no one I've ever met has a photograph, let alone the means to have one taken." Simeon flipped the photo over and pushed it towards her. "Only the aristocrats could afford such things."

Natalia lifted it with wide eyes, glancing at the bartender. "What do I ask next?"

Simeon overlooked the rest of the bar, his eyes batting to each patron, and he shifted back to her. He straightened his apron, checking that his buttoned collar was straight. "You suggest that fellow in the photo's corner is me."

"I sense you don't give me the answer I wish?"

"No. I agree, it looks like my vest in that photo, but I do not recognize him and did not serve your husband. When I work the pub, I recall it all, and I've never seen him before."

"But you remember me?"

"You are here more often than you think. I remember you have different types of moments. Ones where you recall everything, several where you forget things in the short term, and on occasion, you have difficulty remembering long term."

Natalia smelled the wine again, relaxed her shoulders, and spun the glass in her hand.

Natalia could sense Simeon's kind stare. There was something else, and she didn't know if she wanted to hear what he knew. A dull ache filled her chest, but she maintained her composure, letting out her quivering breath so her hands did not shake.

"What do you want to tell me?" Natalia took a sip of wine, the sweet savor lingering on her lips.

Simeon set down a polishing rag, checking the bar once again. "Well, there is one thing that's contradicting with your visits, and that is the answer to this next question."

"What do I ask?"

"This question belongs to me, not you."

Natalia peered up, resting her glass on the side.

Simeon swallowed hard and held his fingers together. "Do you remember what happened to your husband?"

Natalia let out a rushed breath, trying to stay calm, but the pressure built behind her temples, and her fingertips tingled. "Yes. I know I lost him when I revealed the Lunarwheel."

Simeon glanced away, and Natalia studied the photo, her husband carrying the same kind eyes Simeon did. His hair was brown, and she remembered his trimmed beard being so soft, smelling of cedar. Some nights she remembered little of what happened to him, but his face, she never forgot.

"My apologies," Simeon said.

"No, that's all right. If there's one thing I remember, whether or not I always give you the answer, it's him. Even when I drift, more often than not, my mind focuses on him."

When all fades, he remains in her thoughts: the pain, the disappointment, the guilt. Natalia took a deep breath and pointed to the image's edge, to a woman's arm.

"And her?" Natalia said, pointing down.

"Sadly, there isn't enough of her to recognize. The arm is a bit lacking in features for even the best memories."

Another bartender walked from the back room, and Simeon waved her over. She worked her way down the line. Simeon nodded, and Natalia followed his lead, leaving her wine on the counter and slipping the photo into her vest. They sat at a small round table in the pub's corner, the chandelier's light dim compared to the single candle on the dinner table.

Natalia crossed her legs and put her hands on her lap, rubbing the condensation from the wineglass between her fingers. Simeon stretched his neck, resting one hand on the table lined with an orange tablecloth.

"You know, when you started coming here, you hoped that photo would jog my memory," he said. "But it's your mind you can't place. I'm sorry I cannot do more for you, and I hope your memory returns in full one day. You deserve it."

"I can't remember him like I used to. His face stays the same, but what he did for me, what we did together, grows more distant each season."

Simeon slid his hand in front of her, and she looked around. She lifted her hand, holding it in the air, then placed her fingers in his.

"Sincerely, I pray you find the answers you crave. I know I would."

His touch was tender and delicate, something she had not felt for many moons. He set his other hand on hers and patted it in support.

Natalia's eyes shot to his, embracing his touch, unsure of what she should think. "Did something happen with us?"

Simeon smiled. "As I said, I take my profession to a great degree. However, I appreciate the compliment."

Natalia smirked and nodded. "Do you think we forget our memories for some unknown reason or purpose?"

Simeon sat back, taking his hand with him. "I don't know if I'm the best to answer that because my memory is vivid compared to most. My sister used to say memories are a lie because we only remember things how we last remembered them. Stories change as we tell them. The good become great, and the bad become horrid, but why would splendid memories fade in your case?"

"Maybe it's my memory altogether."

"Perhaps." Simeon sat tall. "Can I ask you something?"

"Of course."

"Is it scary? To not remember?"

"I don't know. I can't say what I don't recall."

Natalia looked to the table, the bright orange vivid next to the candle. She didn't know what to think. Simeon talked to her as if he had always been there, but she couldn't remember his kindness. She hadn't written about him in her journals, and there was no notion they were more than kind strangers.

Simeon let out a chuckle and stood. "It was a pleasure, Miss Arlen. In case you have forgotten, *this* part of the conversation was a first. I do have one last question. What is my name?"

Natalia thought, her mind fuzzy in places, clear in others. She rubbed her cheek, and she found a faint smile. "Simeon."

"Perhaps you remember more than you think. Maybe put that blue book of yours away, and it might surprise you what happens."

Natalia nodded.

Simeon stepped behind the bar and grabbed her glass. "Some nights, we need to reminisce. That way, we can see our future with clarity." He turned with his smirk and attended to another patron.

Natalia's cheeks warmed and reddened, and she strolled to the entrance, her hands behind her.

"Miss Arlen, leaving so soon?" the host said. "I hope nothing was out of place and our service was satisfactory."

"It was splendid. Forgive me if I held anyone up. I must be going."

"Of course. Let me grab your coat. The maid is indisposed at the minute."

Natalia gave the man her ticket, and he handed her jacket to her from the stuffed closet. He helped her slide it on, and she walked out into the busy street, pulling the jacket tight.

Natalia pulled the photo from her vest, looked at it with a smile, and slipped it back into her pocket, pausing. She pushed her hand deeper into the coat, but it was empty. She checked her other pockets and exhaled, and her mind raced in the harvest night.

Her journal was missing.

Natalia walked to the window, peeking in to see that the coat maid was nowhere in sight. She paced the sidewalk to the alleyway behind the bistro, peering into the shadows, a lantern dancing in someone's hands. Natalia made her way down the alley and saw the coat maid reading her journal in the dim light.

Natalia walked to her side, her arms folded behind her, and coughed.

The young girl jerked back, holding her chest as she let out a nervous laugh. "Oh, you frightened me."

"My apologies," Natalia said. "Why are you reading in the shadows? The lantern can't be bright enough."

The young lady waved the book, her red hair and pale skin glistening in the light. "Aw, this old thing? My mother's old diary."

"Let's not be simple. We both know that belongs to me."

The coat maid stepped to Natalia and eyed her, her age or height not hindering her stance. She slipped the journal into her pocket, and her frightened stare turned to a sly smile. "You remember me?"

Natalia eyed the young lady, her memory blank. "Should I?"

The girl's eye twitched ever so slightly, and she skipped back with the lantern. "You seemed to recognize Simeon. Why not me?"

"If you'd be so kind as to hand me my journal, I'll leave it at that."

"I've been picking your pockets for months, miss, and you only noticed now? Never have you left this book in your jacket, though. Are you writing a story?"

Natalia walked forward, and the coat maid pulled out a knife.

"Come closer, please." The young lady smirked, holding the blade still and true.

"I wouldn't," Natalia said.

"I have."

The girl thrust, and Natalia grabbed her wrist, stopping her in her tracks.

The girl stood still, her eyes shuddering in the lantern's light. Natalia looked at her with a saddened gaze and hammered her fist down on the girl's arm. The knife fell to the cobblestone, and the young woman dropped to her knees, the lantern cracking off the stone.

"Ugh, my arm, you broke my arm!" The girl cradled her arm and curled over on the cobblestone.

Natalia lifted the coat maid to her feet by the collar and shook her, their gazes meeting each other. She pulled the journal from the girl's pocket and placed it inside her jacket. She pulled out some coin and stuffed them in the girl's pocket.

"It's not broken, and it will heal. Here is what will happen. You will go to your employer with your resignation papers tonight. Here is some coin to use as your arm heals over the next few days before you find employment elsewhere. Perhaps you'll learn a little humility so you grow into the woman your mother would have wanted. I hear there's work at the mills. Thieves do not belong in bistros such as this."

Natalia let go of the girl, straightening the young woman's collar. She stood, her stare blank and pressed. She rushed away towards the bustling street, whipping out of the alleyway. Natalia pushed the wrinkles from her jacket, rubbing the inside of her pocket, the journal back where it belonged.

She turned the lantern upright and carried it to the end of the alleyway, setting it on the corner.

The breeze of the cool harvest air caressed her cheeks, and she stepped into the street with cold sweats, hoping to forget how close she came to losing her memories.

CHAPTER TWENTY

Wheels of handcrafted wood with metal braces rattled down the brick road in South Hills. Two black horses with black hair towed the maroon carriage through Well's Peake in the early evening.

The horses trotted at a steady pace under the leather reins and the driver's firm grip, nipping at each other around every corner. A scarred cheek on the mare, with a new tender nip, pulled against the reins as the other horse snickered. Despite the nips and neighing, they held their speed, their hooves clopping on the leaf-covered road.

The buildings, radiant and sophisticated in their designs, captured the essence and intelligence of Well's Peake.

The town was full of inventors in a city built for aristocrats.

The carriage made its way through the district as the streets grew less maintained, more decayed, and ill-mannered. Smoke billowed out of the factories on the horizon, and workers, covered in coal and metal flake, wandered the streets.

A pair of eyes peeked from behind the bland curtains, keeping their face hidden. The driver snapped the reins, and the mares came to a stop on the street corner in a circular market of food and retail vendors. The driver dismounted from his seat and hooked the reins to a post, ensuring the horses' curiosities didn't distract them.

He walked with the utmost poise to the carriage door and opened it with rectitude. Kenneth stepped out, bringing a broad hat to his head, his shining hair waving against his shoulders. Kenneth looked up and shot a grin at his driver, Frederick, sliding his finger along the felt rim.

"Good day, Mr. Forbes," Frederick said. "Was your ride splendid? Was this carriage more polite to your backside than the one yesterday? Perhaps more cushion on the seats."

"It was delightful, as always, with you at the reins." Kenneth took an exaggerated breath, keeping his head down. "This carriage is rougher than I like, but I suppose I should be grateful in our current circumstance. Wait here, Fredrick. I will return soon."

"As you wish."

"Also, be wary of the fallen women from Delilah's nearby, and do *not* let them near the carriage. They enjoy lifting you of your valuables and replacing them with things best left unspoken."

"Yes, and sir, do you think you should carry your cane around? It is a symbol of status."

Kenneth looked it over. He leaned on it and walked as if he had a limp. "Voilà."

Frederick nodded, returned to his seat, and tightened his coat as the wind blustered. Kenneth crossed the market, ensuring to keep his gaze hidden from those who looked too closely. His black cape and buttoned tweed jacket blended in with the townspeople of the district as he limped around them.

Kenneth perused the marketplace, the savory spice of baked apple dumplings filling his nostrils, reminding him of his childhood. He quickened his pace, passing several streetlights until he arrived at a condemned brick house. The cobblestone path turned to dirt and collected on Kenneth's black boots. He searched the alleyway, confused and aimless, recognizing no one as he pushed his hair back.

She was nowhere in sight.

Kenneth walked into the run-down street, turning to a merchant nearby. Stocked meat, fruit, and vegetables from the vendor's stand filled the air with a stale odor, causing him to step back. A young girl, with golden-brown hair ran up to the store. A man stood from behind the produce, wiping his hands clean with a dirtied rag.

"Mr. Porter!" she said, hopping in her spot.

"Little one, how can I help?" Mr. Porter asked.

"Sir, I need bananas and apples." The young girl held out her hand with two silver coins.

Mr. Porter lowered his head and let out a sigh. "We've been through this. You don't have enough."

"No, no. I have more." The girl searched her trousers, unable to turn up more coin.

The merchant looked and frowned. "Honey, perhaps next week."

The girl pulled her pockets inside out. "But my ma needs it. We have no more blossoms."

"I'm sorry, but I can't help. Perhaps find more flowers to sell."

"But they aren't growing. The harvest is ending."

Kenneth watched and eyed the vendor.

"I'm sorry, darling, but you must go. I have work to do. The harvest has taken most of my produce… Here, but you need to leave now."

The merchant handed her an apple and patted her along the way.

She glanced at her hand with the few pieces of coin and wiped her wet cheek. She pushed the silver into her pocket and scurried across the road.

Kenneth eyed the merchant, who tilted his head and shrugged. As his chest grew heavy, Kenneth tightened his grip on the cane. He stared at the youngling, who sat on the corner of an alleyway across the street.

Kenneth crossed the roadway, paying no attention to the carriages going by, jumping out of their way when they rattled by. "Little one, come here."

The girl stood with her head low, her hair sticking to her cheek from the tears, the apple in her hand.

"Now, now, child, it's all right." Kenneth pulled out a handkerchief and wiped her face dry. "That's better. You are too young to be crying. What is your name?"

The girl wiped the end of her nose. "Kathryn."

"Kathryn, that apple will not feed you and your ma, will it?"

She shook her head.

"I thought not." Kenneth pulled out a cloth bag from under his jacket and waved it in front of the girl, who studied the red satchel with a golden string.

"What's in there?" she said, her eyes red and wide.

"Take it."

Kathryn took the pouch, her arms dropping from the weight. She struggled to hold it as Kenneth untied the smooth rope. The girl looked inside at enough coin to secure an apartment or small business.

She peered at him. "Are you trying to get me in trouble?"

"No." Kenneth patted her arm. "I want you to cross this street, your head held high, and buy that stand from the merchant. You don't need society telling you what you can and can't have, and you should never have to accept handouts."

"But—"

"I believe in you. Wait until tonight, tomorrow, or later this season, that's fine, but you must eventually, and do not give it to your mother. This belongs to you, my dear. You took what you deserved, and I think it should stay yours, don't you?"

She nodded her head with a smile.

"Excellent. Now, I need your help."

"Okay."

"There used to be a young girl who lived in that alleyway." Kenneth pointed behind him. "She isn't there anymore. Do you know what became of her?"

"Oh, yes. Abbey. She's nice. She lives that way with her brother. Behind the boarding house."

Kenneth looked over the girl's shoulder, his gaze low. "Her brother?"

Kathryn hugged Kenneth around the waist, and he patted her on the head. She sprinted down the lane, stumbling as the weight of the bag shifted in her hand.

Kenneth wandered the boulevard, checking each alley, all lined with brick walls and flaming barrels. Looking into another, he spotted a young girl sitting with a blanket on her lap against a boarding house. He wasn't sure if it was her he searched for, though. He stepped between the brick houses, and she turned, her brown hair with a tint of red.

A young man slept at her side, next to stacked wooden crates. The shadows grew dark as the light faded on the horizon, and Kenneth could finally look up since his arrival. He stretched his neck and walked to her, the girl staring with wide eyes.

"Kenneth?" she asked, her voice rising an octave.

"Greetings, Sister." Kenneth stood over Abbey, resting on his cane.

Abbey rose to her feet and squeezed him, and he held her with one arm. "What are you doing here? It's been so long."

She smelled of burned wood and rags, and her oily hair rubbed off against his jacket. Kenneth sniffled and pulled himself away, holding her chin with his fingers. She leaned into his palm, her warmth unexpected in the evening chill of the night and her cheek soft despite how dirty she was.

He nodded to her, and she followed, walking into the deep alleyways between brick buildings. The sky grew darker by the moment, and the only light illuminated from the gaslights near the back doors of the restaurants.

"Kenneth, where have you been?" she asked, her gaze shifting between him and the ground. She wrapped her scarf tighter, pulled out a brush, and combed the ends of her hair.

"My apologies, Abbey. Life has been rather eccentric as of late, and I'm needed by the aristocrats. You understand." Kenneth wiped the front of his jacket.

"Yes, but it doesn't make me miss your visits any less."

"Well, I have tried to visit, but you moved. You didn't leave me a letter."

Kenneth glanced to her, and even under her circumstances, she stood tall with poise. She was ragged but carried youthfulness and tenderness, something Kenneth envied. Her eyes were an exquisite brown, like that of an aristocrat's dining table. Despite the muck on her cheeks and her tattered clothes, she shared a sharp, alluring chin similar to Kenneth's. She held her gaze high and did not slouch or linger as so many desperate men and women did in South Hills.

"I know. You missed my birthday. I thought you would come."

"You don't believe I could've forgotten, do you, Sister? Sixteen years young. Almost ten years younger than I, a month after my own to the day. To think, if you were in the North Hills, you would have your revealing to high society on the next full moon. The elegance we could share walking hand in hand, as brother and sister, to the aristocrats of Well's Peake would be marvelous."

Abbey swallowed hard and looked away, running the small brush through her hair again. "Yes, but positive moments are happening in the South Hills too. A delightful man is fixing the boarding houses down the street for the frost season to come. His name is Buford, no Bernard. He's tall and showed up a few weeks ago."

Kenneth and Abbey rounded the alley to another with more endless brick walls. "Mr. Griffin, no doubt. Always the entrepreneur when the occasion arises. He enjoys being in every corner of the districts."

"Yes, he's most kind." Abbey walked with hesitation, putting the brush away and rubbing her fingertips together. "He will ask for help, and he gives some of us supplies to deliver to those who are worse off."

Kenneth slowed his pace, pressing his lips together. "Did you receive these accommodations as well? Or was it all given to others?"

"No. Some need it more."

Kenneth rolled his eyes. "Why do you take care of others when you require help yourself?"

"Because they deserve it more, of course. There's something beautiful about helping them."

Kenneth looked to the sky, the hills of the forest, and the clouds blocked by the ridges of antique buildings. "Nothing is alluring within these brick walls."

Abbey rubbed dirt off her cheek, pulling on the end of her scarf.

Kenneth paused at an old chair and dusted it off. He placed his handkerchief down on the seat without tipping. Abbey looked around and sat in the middle of the dirty alley.

"You need to stop brushing and pulling your hair, or you'll take out all the oils. You won't be beautiful with damaged ends."

Abbey let go of her hair, resting her hands in her lap and peering away.

Kenneth eyed her, wondering what thoughts filled her head. How could she be so oblivious to her own gifts, her potential to be as grand as she dreamed or as influential as him? The Maker blessed Abbey with accommodations most never would have, yet she rested in the dirt, day and night, watching the aristocrats she wished to be. All she had to do was assert herself. Kenneth refused to do it for her, and if that meant leaving her in the dirt, he would.

"Am I still beautiful?" Abbey looked at Kenneth with interlocked fingers. "Like the paintings of the aristocrats you described to me?"

Kenneth rested his cane across his lap and his elbows, batting a kind smile to her. "You are impeccable and, despite your circumstances, still stunning. With a rinse, a cut, and a pat of powder, you would not believe who stood in the mirror's reflection."

Abbey blushed, and she held her cheek. "It's been a while since I've been able to wash my hair or see my reflection. I'm scared it won't be like it used to be."

"If you desire to be elegant, then why are you so persistent in staying here? There is nothing here for you, and in the rolling hills, your future is waiting while you sit here, broken and homeless."

Abbey pulled on her jaw. "There is more here than you see."

"Brick and dirt at the backsides of the buildings, where they throw their scraps and trash. Did I miss something?"

"I was referring to people and helping them."

"But it doesn't keep you beautiful." Kenneth waved his hand. "You grow hungry, you become ill, and your body pays the price. Don't you want to be where you can pamper yourself and live your life to the fullest?"

Abbey rubbed her arm. "It's not like you're helping me. Do you understand how hard it is to find the first step you're always telling me to take?"

"I don't help you because you don't push yourself. You sit here in the muck, almost as if you enjoy it. Your beauty fades in the slums. You dream of walking by my side, yet you refuse to take from society what is yours."

He didn't understand and couldn't figure her out. He had taught her how to take every opportunity, and she sat there, content with her lifestyle, what used to be his life.

Kenneth held his hand to the bottom of her hair, letting it sit in his palm. "You could wash it again. You could wear gowns and jewelry and gawk at buildings of stone and marble. No more brick, Abbey. You only need to take from others what you deserve."

Abbey rubbed her neck and pulled her knees to her chest, rocking back and forth. "I could—I love that you're succeeding, though. Just like Mother and Father always wanted. Maker bless their souls."

Kenneth's brow furrowed, and he could feel his fingers throbbing. He turned his head, and it cracked, letting out the stress that had built in his spine. "Oh, let's not forget Father and what he wanted for us."

"He only wished what was best for—"

"Him. He needed what was best for him." Kenneth stood, his cane falling to the dirt and stone.

Abbey pressed her soft lips together, and her eyes grew wide, losing all posture. She set her forehead on her knees and rocked back and forth, Kenneth unable to find her gaze.

"What's this about you having a brother?" he asked, glaring at her. "Is that the man sleeping next to you?"

Abbey looked to Kenneth, his scowl pressing and unflinching. "What do you mean? He was just sleeping there."

"I was told you have a brother. Have you mentioned me, Sister?" Kenneth checked over his shoulder, the dark alley barren.

"No, of course not. I haven't mentioned you to no one."

"To anyone?"

"No."

"So you aren't staying with someone who is claiming to be your brother?"

"No. No one."

Kenneth tapped his fingers on his hips and pulled in his bottom lip, biting the end to the point of aching. His hands went still, and his temples throbbed, blood boiling in his veins. Perhaps she was using his name, telling people about him. What other reason could there be for her to receive Bernard's consideration?

Abbey lifted her head. "I've seen—"

"What?" Kenneth jerked his attention to her.

"I… just wanted to say I saw a lot of work at your manor."

Kenneth let out a deep breath, moving his sharp jaw back and forth, the night darkening and the few gaslights filling the alley. "Um, yes. I have a young inventor, Aleksandar Scott, who is renovating. He has an underappreciated talent for art in a new medium. His progress in the past few weeks has been monumental, though, and I believe he is discovering that appetite."

"Wow, Kenneth, you deserve it." Abbey pulled her frayed coat tight.

"You're damn right I do." Kenneth bit his words, rubbing his lips together. "I deserve much more than that."

"Sure. Yes."

Abbey's hands shook, and tears ran down her cheeks, her hand holding the other as it flinched. Kenneth looked at her with a light head, his breath heavy. He dropped his arms, his maroon jacket fluttering behind him, and he wrapped his arm around her.

"Sister, no, please stop; we are all right. We're all right. You have no reason to cry." Kenneth held her tight, not worried about the dirt rubbing onto his jacket or the smell of burned rags. "Remember, you can rise to the top like me. All you have to do is decide—"

"I don't want to!" Abbey shoved Kenneth back.

Kenneth rested on his knees, his eyes narrow and stern, arms dropped at his sides.

"We grew up on these streets," she said, her words heavy between sobs. "This is where Mother and Father were, and you abandoned us. If they were here with us, why would I want to walk your fancy halls?"

Kenneth stood to his feet, brushing his pants free of dirt. "Mother and Father convinced us we needed to stay put because they were greedy and cared only for themselves. I didn't abandon you. You just refused to take what was yours."

Abbey walked across the alley, kicking a metal can at its bottom, which echoed in the alleyway. "They wished what was best, and you screwed that up."

"I won't apologize for taking what I was owed and what was mine. You had every opportunity as well, but you let it go."

"There was no coin left after you took it."

Kenneth shook his head with a snarky smile and snatched his cane from the ground. He looked away from Abbey and to the brick wall across from them.

He froze and stared at it, clenching his teeth: the red grain, the coarse grooves, and the crooked alignment from the work of the prideless. The brick wall he stared at for years as he lay in the dirt and trash.

He slept against it, cried against it, and ate against it.

Never again would he sit there staring at the brick prison that surrounded his childhood. From the backs of venues to the crowds who walked the streets, he sat in the city's shadows where no one could see him.

With a shake of his head and a snarl, he returned his gaze to her, her eyes red and wet lines through the dirt on her face.

"All you had to do was try, Abbey," he said. "Reach out and take your share of the fortune with a golden rope. That is on you, and now you have to find your own if you want to be at my side. Stay here; ignore what you deserve. You know what, Sister, I can't stand coming to this hole in the city because of you. You don't want life to change. You need it to remain as is. Nothing is charming between these facades. Just sadness and those whose lives will be bare and forgotten. I won't let that happen to me."

Abbey wiped the last tear from her face, dirt rubbing on the back of her hand. "Then why come down here at all?"

Kenneth swung his cane and held it to her, his breath showing in the air, the smoothness of the cane tight in his slipping grip. "Because I thought there was hope for you, but I see you'll never change. Look at me. I'm the man on the hill for the city of Well's Peake to embrace."

"Who determines what we deserve? You, who took what we all deserved. How could you steal what belonged to your own family?"

Abbey swatted Kenneth's cane out of her face.

"The coin I took belonged to me, and I also took what I was owed for the suffering our parents forced us to live in. Taking what's yours is nothing to be ashamed of."

Abbey pointed to him. "Maybe you come to see me not to make me miserable but because you want to hide from your fancy hill. Maybe guilt *has* found you. Does Kenneth Forbes miss his sister and want her close again? Did you realize everything you dreamed of up there is what you feared when you were here?"

Abbey stepped closer, and Kenneth looked away, his eyes bloodshot and a vein pulsing in his temple.

"Kenneth... you fear what you did," she said. "To leave us on the streets, more broken than we already were. Mother and Father aren't here anymore to give the forgiveness you seek."

Kenneth jerked aside, his jacket tails hitting his sister. He paced the alley of brick walls and stood next to the trash bins, eyeing them. He grabbed his cane and smashed the top in, steel ringing in his ear. With each swing of the cane, the dent grew deeper, his grip tightening as the force of his hits shook through his arms.

Kenneth's hat fell off, and his hair fell over his eyes. Abbey turned to him as he stood in a single gaslight, his hair hiding half his face.

He picked up his hat and rushed away. Abbey left in the dark alleyway, brick buildings standing tall around her and gaslights shimmering in the harvest air.

Her hands shook, and her lip trembled as she glanced to the sky, unable to see the stars or clouds. She wanted to sob. The urge was in her chest, but she held her waist and wandered through the shadows in silence.

She was close to her shelter, but every step took all the strength she could muster. As she walked into her alleyway of a home, she looked at the sleeping man near the crates.

Abbey wandered over, lifted her blanket, and lay behind him, hugging him as she pushed her face against his back. The wool of his coat was scratchy against her cheeks, but she ignored it as tears soaked the man's jacket.

The man awoke and rolled over, breaking her embrace and his finding hers. With her eyes shut, his breath against hers, the day finally felt comforting and familiar, if only for a moment.

She opened her eyes to Hugh, who looked back, his head on a flat pillow, his kind gaze on her.

"Abbey, what's wrong?" he asked.

Abbey tried to speak with a quivering lip but found no words, lost in her sobs. She pressed her face into his chest, and his arms tightened around her until she fell into a deep sleep between the red brick buildings.

CHAPTER TWENTY-ONE

A lantern lit the room from overwhelming darkness, burning red with shallow traces of orange inside a small metal chute. The smoke vented through a flue as black curtains absorbed any light from creeping into the darkroom.

A cloth-covered bench rested in the middle while a web of strings dangled from the walls, like a spider's den in the morning's dew. Pictures dried from the solution they had steeped in, shifting as Abel walked by.

Abel stood at the table, using a set of rubber tongs to pull out a soaked photograph as metallic fumes filled his nostrils. He carried it to a small tray, solution dripping on the wood paneling and staining the toes of his brown shoes. He rinsed the paper in haste and repeated the process, clipping it on a thread.

In the picture was a crowd of fairgoers gathered at the World's Palace. Shadows shimmered on the photo, and Abel's smile gleamed in the candlelight.

The curtain shifted, and Ferdie poked her head in, making sure no outside light crept in. "Abel?"

"Yes, Ferdie?" Abel studied the photos.

She stepped in, hands in her pockets, sporting her typical suspenders and striped shirt. "I have this horrid assumption you're taking me up on my offer. Your article on Mr. Scott's robbery was boring material."

"You wouldn't be as sharp as I thought if you didn't."

Ferdie nodded and pushed back her hair. "Be straight with me. This Black Harvest theory, do you believe it? Or are you just trying to find your big break?"

"I do, and I expect many others to as well."

Ferdie placed her hand on Abel's shoulder and turned him around, staring at him.

"Ferd—"

"Ab—"

They both paused and studied each other with unflinching gazes.

"I don't think you should publish this," she said. "I know I told you I would print it, and I'll keep my word, but this story, this conspiracy… people want to forget the Black Harvest."

"Did you need anything else?" Abel glanced at his photographs, putting his hands on his hips.

"I'm saying this as your friend, not your editor. If I told you I'd never ask you to drink my bourbon again, would you not do this?"

Abel chuckled. "Tempting, but I have the evidence needed for my article. You'll see, I promise."

"What evidence?"

"I want to surprise you. I promise it'll be worth the wait." Abel smiled and set his hand on her shoulder.

Ferdie let out a long sigh and rubbed her forehead. "Even with proof, this story is dangerous, and I'm afraid of what will become of you. You will set in motion events we have yet to fathom."

"Significant stories thrive when they are most difficult to discuss, and if it was that serious, wouldn't you stop it?"

"Not these stories. These are the ones you don't put out there. I will see for myself before final proof." Ferdie waved his hand away. "I understand why you're doing this, but you don't have to."

"I do. It's the only way she'll take me wholeheartedly."

"That's the problem. We all know you're a talented writer, but she knows the dangers that come with being the reporter you are, especially after Redwood. Maybe she'd return if you let this go. I don't blame her for distancing herself."

"Once she sees the significance of my article, she'll realize she was wrong to leave me. My work will bring to light the corruption of the aristocratic class. That'll be worth the risk." Abel pointed to his photographs.

"I'm begging you not to run this. If what you say is true, then let the Peake do their job and give them the evidence. Blow out your candle, go home, and enjoy your life."

Abel stepped back and looked at the photos, rubbing his thumb on his index finger. He wouldn't forget them. They were right there, waiting for their unveiling to Well's Peake, Belagrad, and the entire Northern Region. Ferdie couldn't admit it, but she did believe the dark beginnings of the Black Harvest, or else she wouldn't let him publish.

Abel's breath steadied, chatting his teeth. "In two days, everything will change, I promise. The worst will be over, and the Peake will bring to light the corruption that should've never happened. *Well's Peake Commons* will be known as the press who brought justice to those who suffered. When better than at the World's Fair."

Ferdie crossed her arms and stepped to the entrance. She reached for the drape and sighed. "I want to open this curtain and let in the light so that these photos disappear forever."

"Too bad you're a woman of your word and a journalist who knows the importance of this story."

Ferdie bit the bottom of her lip and walked out.

Abel listened to her footsteps as they faded away. The staircase door echoed down the hall, and he knew he was alone in the late night. His own breath mirrored the cracking of the wood wick candle, and he turned and bumped into his table stand, solution wetting the underside of his button-up. Some photos were coming in crystal clear, while many others remained blurry, still transitioning to their final state.

Abel walked through the heavy curtains, pulling them tight as he slid through the narrow opening into his office. He shut the darkroom door with a deep grin across his face, looking to his dog resting beside the couch.

She perked up with her tongue hanging out, her black and brown fur accented in the light. Her eyes widened, and she followed his every move with an enthusiastic tilt of her head.

Oh, Ferdie. It will be okay. Do not fear the truth.

Abel looked at the clock hanging above the mantel.

Midnight.

He wandered to the windows and looked to the cloudy night, rubbing the bottom of his chin, the stubble smooth to the touch.

Moonlight peeked through the clouds, lost in the city's foggy streets. The smell of cedar-scented candles filled the office, masking the solution mixture from his darkroom and shirt.

He sat at his desk, which faced a large window to the horizon of Well's Peake.

How could his passion scare her off? What he did was for society's betterment. To show them the truth.

Abel shook his head and ran his fingertips along the grain of the desk, pulling himself from his drowsy state. He paused, noticing a letter with his name on it on the counter. He broke the seal and pulled out a card with Ferdie's handwriting.

Make the right choice for us both.

Abel ripped the note in half, crumpled the paper, and flung it over his head, missing the trash bin.

Oh, darn.

The dog leaped from beside the couch, bumping into Abel's leg along the way, and snatched the ball in her mouth, whipping it back and forth.

"I wondered if you had fallen asleep."

The dog played with the paper in her paws, tongue hanging out the side, panting as if she ran for an hour.

"Yes, you're a good pup. Aren't you, Nellie?" Abel said, smiling as the dog rolled over on the rug.

Abel wadded another sheet and tossed it, and Nellie zipped across the office, running as fast as her little legs could carry her. She chewed the ball as soon as she reached it. She faced the other way; her eyes focused on the crushed paper.

Abel smiled and turned to his desk, tapping his hands on the edge.

He collected a stack of papers and set them on the end of the table. "There we go. Now, where should we begin?"

Abel took one last page and wrinkled it up, tossing it to his beloved pet. The ball landed next to Nellie, but she ignored the paper and looked away. Abel sighed and forced a smile.

"Good night, baby girl."

Turning to the headlines, he jotted down his thoughts and ran his finger along them, reading in silence. He listed several, crossed some out, and scribbled over a few. Abel pulled out a new sheet and set it in front of him, dipping a pen in the inkwell.

Inventors and their inventions are the keys to society's future. It is by their hands the road we will follow, but what happens when their hands lay a path that leads to a place we never wished to travel? What happens when we discover the people who designed that road are those of the aristocratic elite?

The pen in his grip was alluring and lifted his adrenaline. He re-dipped the tip, making sure each word was bold, reflecting his professionalism. His head swayed, and he created his masterpiece.

"You'll receive the king's treatment, Nellie. My passion will be our ascent into the halls of the aristocrats, the ones worthy of the title."

Nellie continued facing the wall with quick breaths, never looking back.

When the road leads to terror, to the Black Harvest, we must ask, how did we end up here? While we draw our paths from others, we are still in the carriage of society and deserve to know what has led us to where we now stand.

Abel bobbed his head like a child in the candlelight, amused with himself. He lifted the sheet and reread what he wrote. He smacked his lips, and as he held his pen, several drops of ink fell onto the paper, staining the corner.

"No-no-no."

Abel soaked the ink up with a cloth, but it was too late. He pulled on his slick hair, a spot of ink rubbing across the top of his forehead. Crunching up the paper, he tossed it at his dog. She crawled over, held it in her paws, and never glanced back.

The greatest story ever printed will not have stains on the original.

Abel pulled another piece of paper and rewrote what he had composed. With caution, he dipped the pen in ink and held his hand underneath as he reached his starting point.

Events have occurred that the masses are not aware of, but the aristocrats in high society have hidden. We have blamed the Black Harvest on the innocent, on inventors, while the wicked walk the marble halls of the aristocratic elite.

Abel wrote, but a sharp pain filled his right arm, cramping his hand. He set the pen down and wiggled his fingers, the ache passing as quickly as it arrived.

Come now, Abel.

With a sigh, he wrote, and the words flowed as smooth as glass, but he felt a sharpness in his arm, and it throbbed worse than before, his grip weakening. Abel rubbed his upper arm once more, stretching it high. Either from developing photos all day or the stress of sleep deprivation, he couldn't tell, but he would not let his moment pass him by. As the pain faded again, he noticed more ink had fallen onto the paper.

"Fate has a sick sense of humor," he said.

Abel crinkled the paper but froze, stunned as ink dripped down his finger. With much hesitation, he opened the sheet and looked at the smears.

The ink was not black but red.

Abel let the parchment slide from his hand and onto the desk, his palms covered in crimson. He squinted at it and saw that it was not ink.

It was blood.

Abel thrashed to his feet, his hips knocking the table into the window, splicing a small corner with a crack. The dog glanced over her shoulder.

Abel watched his arm as his shirt turned bloody. The dull pain returned, and he checked his shirt, noticing it was sliced and red dripped down his fingers to the wood floor. He held his hand to the cut, gagging as he pulled his palm back, covered in blood.

He gasped, but the air was thick and dry, and with clenched fists, blood oozed within his grip. His lungs felt like they were on fire, spreading through his chest. His heart pounded, and he became lightheaded as the office spun. Coughing as the room grew hazy, Abel's back burned, and he turned to smoke billowing out of his darkroom.

"My Maker," Abel said.

A tube lay underneath the black drapes; the door cracked open. He unclenched his fists, running blindly into the darkroom. Abel struggled to look around, the smoke blurring the room and the fumes from the solution burning his eyes. All he could see was the threads collapsing and the photos falling.

Abel tried to speak, but the smoke engulfed him, forcing him back into his office, stumbling over his own feet. Abel coughed and hacked, his lungs raw, phlegm dripping to the floor. With the back of his hand, Abel rubbed his eyes clear, smearing blood over his face, and found himself staring at a masked man with a knife in his hand.

Abel dropped to his knees as his head grew lighter, breathing in desperate pants to the point of hyperventilating. The man wore a mask curved like ocean ripples and the moon's crest, blue with silver beads.

"Has that arm served you well, Mr. Hawthorne?" the man asked.

Abel dropped to his palms, looking at the mask with drifting eyes.

"Like the words and stories you write to the people of Well's Peake, know they will *burn* with you."

Abel tried to stand but failed, his hands shaking and his throat raw.

The masked man raised his right hand, revealing a small version of the Red Breath on his wrist, connected to several tubes that wrapped around his waist. He clenched the valve, and fire spewed out of the nozzle, the pressure blowing papers around the room.

Nellie scampered to her paws, fleeing into the hallway.

The fire engulfed Abel in burning agony, and he howled throughout the office. His scream escaped the flames and smoke, tearing into the night as the heat tightened around him. Abel found the strength to get to his feet and threw himself at the masked man. The fire grew into a fury, Abel's clothes searing into his limbs.

Abel charged, but the masked man stepped aside, and Abel blindly ran into the window, smashing through the glass. Abel reached for anything, but he found nothing as he fell two stories to the cobblestone road.

The moonlight glimmered off the smashed glass and floating pieces of burned paper. Abel lay lifeless, aflame as his story around him burned to ash.

The masked man leaned out the shattered window, looking at Abel, who burned on the street curb. Blinking, he disappeared into the Commons, leaving only death in the late hour of the harvest night.

CHAPTER TWENTY-TWO

The moon peeked over the dark hilltops, the dim glow visible on the opposite horizon. The shadows were long in the river valleys, and Well's Peake was at its most peaceful state.

Nicoli walked down the cobblestone street, his shoes patting against the gloomy path, and turned to the Well's Peake Commons. Constables in blue jackets with gold embroidery and bronze buttons lining the front stood in a circle, surrounding a roped-off crime scene.

Nicoli glanced at a shattered window on the second story; paper stuck on the broken edges. Smoke caressed the rim of the ceiling as burned flakes of newspapers fell like black snow, filling the air with a charred musk. Chief Constable Dekker and Lydia May searched the walkway and gutters, handing off pieces of office debris to other constables.

Nicoli walked between the patrolmen and women, eyeing the covered body with curiosity. He kneeled and lifted the blanket, his hand clenching the rough fabric in his grip. His eyes widened, and his mouth went dry as his heart pounded in his chest, like horses' hooves against cold brick. He looked at a woman in purple, blood seeping out of the corner of her lips.

Her eyes were open, staring into the black abyss of the night, and Nicoli fought the urge to cry as his bottom lip quivered. Whispers filled his ears, but he couldn't make out the words as a dull memory blurred his thoughts.

Mallory, my dearest darling.

The thick blanket fell from Nicoli's hands. Lydia covered the body, and Nicoli shut his eyes. He focused on his breath in the cold air, the bitterness of the night bearing against his scarfed neck.

Lydia kneeled beside him and wiped his face before he could cry with the back of his sleeve.

"Nicoli?" Lydia whispered. "What did you see?"

Nicoli opened his eyes, focusing on his breathing, the world dark around him. Lydia's lavender perfume lingered around him, and it was calming and familiar, bringing Nicoli something to focus on. A branch to hold on to in dark memories.

Lydia put her hand on his shoulder. "It isn't her; I promise. It's Hawthorne."

Nicoli met her gaze, the bags under her eyes accented by the shadows of the oil lamps. He nodded, and Lydia lifted the blanket. She was right. There was no woman with bloody cheeks staring into the black abyss. It was Abel who lay on the cobblestone with no signs of life, his body burned. His mind had lied to him.

Nicoli stood and went to run his fingers through his hair but hesitated. There was ash in his palm, and he wiped it off on his pant leg, fighting the urge to push his hair back.

"Mr. Hawthorne's reputation for crossing the line may have been his undoing," Nicoli said.

Lydia eyed the other constables. "You don't have to be here."

Nicoli bit his tongue. "Your killer is growing more violent. Bolder. Reminds me of ours."

Nicoli inspected the road, constables searching every stone.

"We've found nothing on the street," Lydia said. "I was waiting for you to examine his office before we let anyone else in."

"Thank you. What do we know?" Nicoli kneeled and looked around the blanket.

"Murdered early this morning. The nearest residential building is a few streets away, so no one heard the glass break. Well, that we're aware of. A drunk couple stumbled across him."

"Did anyone disturb the body?"

"No. Undisturbed, from our knowledge."

"Good news for once."

"Dekker made sure they locked the office down until you arrived."

"Let's get going."

Nicoli and Lydia walked up the curved steps of the Well's Peake Commons, passing four constables who guarded the entrance, hands folded.

"No one is to disturb us," Lydia said, pausing next to the guard. "Dekker only."

"Yes, madam," the constable said.

The two entered a tiled hallway, lamps lighting the main lobby. The building smelled of ink and paper, with the musk of burned wood in the air. Metal glimmered as they stepped into the central corridor that loomed up the commons, branching off onto different floors and rooms.

Lydia glared at Nicoli as they trampled up the staircase, grabbing his arm, holding him back.

Nicoli didn't care what she said next. He welcomed her touch, for it was something he missed every day he was away from her. It pulled him from his vendetta, his tunnel vision of his killer. He turned to her, their eyes meeting, hers still hazel with a tint of violet.

"Say it," he said.

Lydia loosened her grip. "I can't tell you to stop because I know you won't, but have you ever thought about doing something for yourself? Instead of following bread trails the rest of your life and giving us what you promised?"

Nicoli stayed silent. She still cared. She still wanted him to stop his broken pursuit, the addiction he could not ignore. Relief consumed him, and he swallowed hard.

"You know I want that for us," he said. "But is it right for me to leave her memory behind?"

Lydia let go of his arm. "Nicoli, you wouldn't be forgetting her. She'll always be here, and that won't change." She put her palm on his chest. "You can move on and not forget. I loved her too, and I would never forget her, but it is possible."

"You think the killer remembers her? Gave her a second thought? I will not be like him."

"You know it's not the same."

"Maybe not."

Lydia pulled him close, holding his arms in hers. Nicoli wanted to say something, but her embrace was all he desired. Nicoli lowered his head and slipped his hands into hers, gentle and uncalloused. Her touch was soft, and he felt a warmth he hadn't in so long.

Nicoli slid his palms around her waist and pulled her close. She wrapped her arms around his shoulders, and he felt her breath against his. He wanted her. Everything about her was what he needed, but he couldn't. Not until he settled the past and put his late wife to rest.

"I want this, Nicoli," she said. "Every night before I go to sleep and when I wake in the morning. I need you to meet your daughter."

The pit in Nicoli's stomach returned, and he stepped back, holding Lydia's hands in his. "I hope you realize, every day, I dream of tucking her into bed. I wish to tell her stories of fables and happy thoughts. I will one night, I promise."

Lydia squeezed his hands. "When you do, I need to be there."

"You will."

Nicoli didn't want to let go of her touch, tender between his fingers. "We need to move on. Before someone sees."

Lydia shook her head, her breath heavy.

Nicoli kissed her on the forehead, and she arched into him, her body firm against his. She put her hand on his cheek with a faint smile.

Nicoli let her go, and they continued up the steps, entering the hallway of the second floor.

They walked into Abel's office and inspected the shattered window, scorch marks across the floorboards. The ruthlessness of destruction was like nothing Nicoli had experienced, and nothing appeared stolen or left behind, just blind chaos. Nicoli opened the darkroom drape to a can of ash with traces of burned photographs.

Lydia looked over Nicoli's shoulder.

"Be careful," she said. "The fumes might still be toxic."

Nicoli let the charred curtain go and wandered to the window, where glass rested on the sill, the night wind blowing a few pieces to the street. A few papers sat on the edge, and he lifted the edges, inspecting the photos.

Nothing...

Lydia walked to the center of the office. "What do you think?"

"It's too clean."

Footsteps echoed in the hallway, and Ferdie walked into the doorway, her hands on her hips, sporting her striped button-up and suspenders.

Lydia walked towards her. "Excuse me, this office—"

"This is my building, and I can stand wherever I please. Nicoli, what the hell is going on? Why is my friend on the corner of the street?" Ferdie stood tall, but Nicoli could hear the shake in her voice, the pitch of fear and loss, and possibly the slur of too much to drink.

"I don't have answers yet." Nicoli walked across the office.

"You don't have answers, or you don't care to share?" Ferdie strode in, sniffling.

"Ferdinand, I'm trying to piece things together."

"Well, how about you start with me and ask me what I know?"

Nicoli looked at Lydia and nodded. He waved Ferdie in, and she stepped to the desk counter, burned papers at the tips of her shoes, shaking her head.

"So, what do you know?" Nicoli asked, pulling out a notepad.

"I'll tell you what I know when you tell me what's important."

"As charming as ever," Lydia said.

"I have to agree, Ferdinand," Nicoli said. "Would you prefer if I told you I don't have a clue at the moment what to ask?"

"It's Ferdie, Nicoli. Mess it up again, and I walk."

Nicoli rubbed his forehead.

Ferdie sighed, kicking the bottom of the desk. "No, I'm sorry... this is my fault. I let Abel get too ambitious. I should've reeled him in when I had the chance. I never thought he would be so bold to go forward with his story. He must have upset someone."

"How so?" Nicoli asked.

Ferdie eyed Lydia and rubbed her thumbs down her suspenders. "Abel has been turning stones the past few years. He discovered this profound passion for fantastic tales, theories that upset the aristocrats. We all know what Abel had become."

"As in?" Nicoli ran his palm through his hair.

Ferdie pressed her lips together. "It started with the penny dreadfuls, but one day he discovered something, something that provided proof of a dangerous story. Now, most were outlandish. The living dead, vampires, the electric man, monsters of all kinds, but it's the stories within our world that were the scariest." Ferdie looked to the bookcase; the bottom burned and ready to collapse. She pulled a thin book from the top shelf, dusting off the soot. "Here. He has several copies floating about. It's one story I never let him publish, but I feel he shared it with a few."

Ferdie handed Nicoli the paper, and he checked the title.

The Black Harvest Returns.

Black trees and decayed wheat fields covered the book's cover in black and white, dreary like the early bloom season. Nicoli eyed Ferdie with a low stare, flipping through the pages.

"I let him write these things under an old pen name, not wanting to ruin his reputation, yet he found a way. Regardless, he took this one to heart when certain aristocrats in Redwood caught wind that it was being read in certain circles, and it was put to a stop. Without pause, Abel dived into this outlandish theory and found something, proof he planned on putting in the paper by week's end."

"He told you nothing?" Nicoli asked.

"No. He was a stubborn idiot with an inclination for flair. He had his flaws, I saw that, but he had good intentions when the moment arrived."

Nicoli closed the book and handed it to Lydia. "You think his digging into the Black Harvest led to his murder?"

"This was one story I believed he would never go through with. How else would you explain the coincidence?"

Ferdie looked at both of them, Nicoli holding her gaze.

"So it has to do with the Black Harvest?" Ferdie put her hands on her hips. "What else aren't you telling me?"

Dekker walked into the office, his stride calm and unnerved, his steps gentle across the scene.

"If this isn't a mess." Dekker inspected the room, looking at Ferdie. "Did I interrupt something?"

"Yes," Ferdie said. "Would you be inclined to tell me what the Black Harvest has to do with Abel's death?"

Dekker raised a brow, and Nicoli held his gaze.

"May I have a moment with them, Ferdie?" Dekker asked. "So I can give you a straight answer?"

Ferdie crossed her arms, pushing her tongue against her cheek. "You have ten minutes before I consider tomorrow's headline." With light steps, Ferdie left the office, and the door slammed down the hallway.

Dekker rubbed his stubbled chin. "I see we have let information slip."

Lydia walked forward. "She gave us certain info we needed, sir. Anyone could've pieced it together collectively with how specific it was."

"Thank you, Constable May, but I insist Mr. Lucas answer these questions. He's more than capable."

"Yes, sir." Lydia sat up and quickly walked to the hallway, guarding the entrance.

"Lydia is right." Nicoli turned. "Ferdie would've assumed it all."

"Detective, I don't care that someone pieced it together; I care that it was the editor of Well's Peake's biggest news press who did. She can make this investigation more difficult than getting you permission to walk these streets." Dekker waved his finger, dropping it as he rubbed the tip of his thumb. "For now, forget the details, for fear of someone listening, but tell me, does this sincerely concern the Black Harvest?"

Nicoli nodded, the light of the lantern catching his eye. "Possibly. Raymond O'Connell's field of study was the Black Harvest."

Dekker raised his eyebrows. "Well, that's unfortunate. I want complete silence from here on out, understood? I don't know how far behind we are with this murderer, but I prefer not to move backward in the matter."

Nicoli stepped to the edge of the window, peering past the broken glass to the dark street, where constables walked between dancing lanterns.

"Do we have any suspects?" Dekker asked.

"Nothing concrete, sir," Lydia said, not looking into the office.

"Well, there is one." Nicoli walked to Dekker, his scarf flicking from the outside wind.

"Who?" Dekker asked.

"Aleksandar Scott."

Lydia looked over her shoulder, and Dekker raised his posture.

"From the robbery?" Dekker asked, hands behind his back.

"Yes," Nicoli said. "I'm uncertain how many people you've informed about these murders, but Mr. Scott is my first. I mentioned to him an elemental killer, and here we are. Death by fire, not long after his own unfortunate predicament. An excellent cover or a marvelous coincidence. Just something to consider. I don't believe Ferdinand wished this upon Mr. Hawthorne, despite his nature, but I'm sure we'll have more insight by the end of this."

Nicoli looked to Lydia and Dekker, both staring at him. He could only imagine what was going through their minds. Only his thoughts mattered, and something wasn't right. Scenes, even when incomprehensible, had a dark familiarity. However, the office lacked what Nicoli needed to see. He eyed the floor, the desk, burned papers, the blackened darkroom—it was as if someone had painted a picture for him, the scene guiding him around the room.

It had his killer's signature.

His eyes lingered on the window again.

"Are you fond of heights?" Dekker asked. "Nicoli?"

Nicoli stared at the small pile of notes stuck to a glass shard in the corner. "Maybe."

Nicoli kneeled and pulled the paper off, reading each one over, the papers making no logical sense. Underneath was a minuscule patch of frayed fabric. He eyed it over, knowing the texture was fine and uncommon.

"Nicoli?" Dekker asked.

"I'm not sure."

Nicoli walked to Dekker, holding the fabric in his hand. "May I?"

"I expect a report and the cloth once you're finished," Dekker said.

"Of course. It doesn't appear to belong to Mr. Hawthorne's attire, but I will make sure. As instructed, no more press."

Nicoli wandered out of the room, and Lydia followed him down the stairs and back onto the street. He assumed Dekker would want to inspect the room, and he was more than welcome. There was nothing to be found.

"Nicoli." Lydia tilted her head.

Nicoli glanced at her, not moving his head.

"Don't push yourself over the edge. Promise me because I can't bring you back like before."

Nicoli turned to her, her eyes shimmering in the streetlight.

"Lydia, I promise."

She nodded and put her arms behind her. "Thank you."

He wanted to take her hand, walk away from the murder, and into the woodlands to live a life of peace in the rolling hills with her and their daughter.

Lydia stepped off the curb, and Nicoli looked around, pulled from his dream. He caught the dog out of the corner of his eye, next to the tree, staring at him with a piece of parchment in her paws. She rolled over, her gaze never breaking his. Nicoli strolled to the hound and petted her.

He turned back to Lydia, her head tilted.

"Make sure she gets a proper home," he said.

A constable walked to the blanket and uncovered Abel. Nicoli paused, his eyes wide, his fingertips tingling as his mind raced. A glimmer from the dead man's attire caught his eye.

"Nicoli?" Lydia reached for him.

Nicoli stood and rushed to the body. He shifted the cover, and the man's pocket glimmered again in the gaslight. A white envelope with a silver edge, untouched by the fire, stuck out from the vest.

How did he miss it? Did someone put it in after the fact?

Nicoli pulled the envelope out, walking back to Lydia as he flicked the cloth remnants away.

"What is that?" Lydia leaned over his shoulder.

He broke the seal on the letter and removed a thick piece of paper.

Listen to her or continue your painful pursuit into the dark of the forest, grasping for branches above your reach. You still have a choice.

Lydia looked to Nicoli, who stared at the card with a grin on his cheeks. His eyes glimmered in the dim light, and his fingers had never been so still, his desire so distinct.

"That could've been for Abel," she said.

Breathing in as much air as he could, Nicoli exhaled with a sharp chuckle.

"Not likely."

CHAPTER TWENTY-THREE

Aleksandar gripped the news press in his hand as he sat on a bench, the morning wind blowing through the World's Fair gardens, leaves brushing against his shoulders. His breathing was shallow; whether from the harvest season or the emptiness he felt in his stomach, he couldn't tell.

A headline stretched across every news press from South Hills to Downton. His eyes focused on each word, his cold fingertips on the thin paper.

The Death of a Reporter.

Two days ago, Abel Hawthorne, renowned journalist of the Well's Peake Commons, was burned alive on the streets of Well's Peake.

Aleksandar looked at the photo underneath, Abel posing in front of his house, the last photo to be taken of him alive. In the second photo below the headline, the Well's Peake Commons loomed with a broken window. Aleksandar couldn't tell much, but one thing was certain.

Torch marks reached from the inside of the office, like fingers pulling on a blanket. His fingers shook, and he struggled to get full breaths.

What if it was my invention?

Closing his eyes, he focused on nothing but the noise of the World's

Fair around him, the wind keeping him from his thoughts.

It started to drizzle, and Aleksandar faced the sky, raindrops soft against his cheek.

"Mr. Scott?"

Aleksandar turned to a woman's voice, Vida leaning towards him with fine brown hair caressing the top of her shoulders.

"Miss Harvey," Aleksandar said, staring at the thinning crowd as the shower grew heavy. "You're out in the rain?"

"Oh, this isn't quite enough to make me melt. I think the better question is, why are you sitting outside in such weather? I know we were to meet, but you could catch a cold."

"I'll be honest, Miss Harvey, the thought never crossed my mind."

Vida laughed with a rosy grin.

Aleksandar stood, taking a deep breath. "Would you care for a stroll?"

"In the rain?"

"Indeed."

"I would enjoy that," Vida said, her smile growing.

Water dripped off Aleksandar's jacket.

Vida was the distraction he needed from thoughts of guilt and of his invention that may have been used in Abel Hawthorne's death. He didn't want to ruin her day, and he hoped she found his company welcoming, not awkward or off-putting.

Aleksandar offered Vida his arm, angling his elbow. She slid hers through his, and they walked along the pavement, the trimmed green hedges of the gardens outlining their path. The rain grew heavy, and many scurried under shelter and umbrellas, but Aleksandar looked to Vida, who chuckled, and they kept walking.

～

"Mr. Scott?"

Aleksandar jerked his head, his gaze meeting Vida's, who looked at him with stern eyes, a coy smile breaking the tension.

"My apologies," Aleksandar said, looking at the rain that soaked into his jacket, the weight growing on his shoulders.

"Always off inside that mind of yours, I see." Vida elbowed him, and he teetered, her arm pulling him back in place.

Aleksandar nodded. "I'm sorry. What did you ask?"

"I asked what you have been doing, since you have not attended the fair."

"I felt staying home would be best. That and working at Kenneth's. Something just doesn't seem right. I'm not comfortable with my work anymore for some reason."

Vida's brow lifted. "Oh, that's quite a shame. I heard your presentation at the last exhibition was fascinating."

Aleksandar focused on the rain, which seemed to grow warmer by the minute. While he could not count the rainfall, he sensed each drop. It relieved him of his own thoughts but did not soothe him like snowflakes in the frost season.

Vida's pull on his arm brought him back to the present, and they came to a bench and sat, the tree behind them far enough away to not shelter them from the harvest shower.

"How have you been since the robbery?" Vida lowered her head, her arm shifting down Aleksandar's. "I apologize. I shouldn't pry."

"No, you're okay." Aleksandar noticed his leg bouncing up and down and stopped. "I don't know what to say. After the robbery, all I do is let my mind slip when my thoughts are overwhelming. It's shocking when one day you have a dream to follow, and in the moment it takes a leaf to fall from the tree to the ground, it's gone. What does someone do after that? How do they find their way back? It makes me wonder if my days as an inventor are ending."

Vida looked at the gardens, letting out a confident sigh. "We are tougher than we would like to believe in these moments, Mr. Scott. You may not be in the same spot you were, but at this moment, it's all about standing up and finding your motivation."

Aleksandar pressed on his pant leg. "Is it that obvious? You just push down the feelings and search ahead?"

"In moments of loss, hope for what you still have. A certain inner strength that you give yourself."

Aleksandar folded his hand, and a cardinal wandered across the sidewalk, its red feathers wet.

Aleksandar pulled a package of bread from his jacket and fed the bird. It whipped its beak, crumbs flinging over both his pant legs and Vida's dress.

Aleksandar glanced, and she held a stern smile.

"Mr. Scott. I'm not keen on cleaning up other people's messes. I won't have to clean up after you, will I?"

Aleksandar let out a laugh. He looked into the gentle rain as it collected on his cheeks, his brown hair heavy, to the point water dripped down his neck.

The gardens glowed as the sunlight cascaded through a thin cloud break, glistening off the red-and-orange leaves that would soon fall as the harvest bloomed.

"Miss Harvey, this is the calmest I've been in a long while," Aleksandar said. "I'll have to let Mr. Griffin know how uplifting you are, even when I'm determined not to be."

"He knows that, but I appreciate hearing it all the same."

With a small chirp, the bird leaped into the air and disappeared into the hedges. Aleksandar let his mind go blank, soothed by the rain.

"I'm a nurse, in case you were going to ask," Vida said, brushing against him. "I come to the World's Fair to see fancy medical equipment and learn about new advances in medicine."

Aleksandar's cheeks turned red. "I'm sorry, Miss Harvey. I should've—"

"Please, just Vida, and I only tease. A bit of humor is a wonderful cure, from what I've experienced." Vida straightened her back on the edge of the bench. "Remember, Aleksandar, despite how bad some days are; good days are soon to come."

"Is it that simple? To stand and go again?" Aleksandar pushed on his pants, water seeping from the thick threads.

"That depends on the person. Some would let tragedy ruin them and sulk. There's nothing wrong with recovery, and you must heal, but you don't have to stay there."

Aleksandar licked his lips and rubbed his hands. "I have been sulking all day. There's something on my mind, and I can't shake it."

"You're more than welcome to share."

He took a deep breath. "Did you see the news press today?"

"I did."

Aleksandar pulled out the wet paper. "There are scorch marks above the broken window. What if my invention was used to kill Mr. Hawthorne?"

Vida looked over, her gaze still. "Aleksandar, that fire could have started in a hundred different ways. We want to think the worst, but it rarely is."

Aleksandar nodded. "Did I tell you how insightful you are? Or do you know?"

"Oh, I'm more than aware, but I can't take much of the credit. My mum was the one who groomed me to the woman I am today."

The rain picked up, and the cold broke the lining of Aleksandar's jacket.

Vida stood and held her arms out, her brown hair shifting, like waves on a beach. Aleksandar rose with her, and they looked at the gardens, lush in red and orange. Fountains and stone pillars accented the curved pathways that led to the World's Palace.

"Aleksandar?" Vida said.

"Yes?"

Vida looked to him, her eyes unflinching in the rain. "The good and the bad are only consequences of one's actions. People suffer, and others are gifted. There's nothing you can do, and best intentions don't always succeed. You only need to focus on what you have and press on. I see it in your eyes, how you looked at that newspaper. You believe it was your invention that burned the Commons. If it did, that's not your fault."

Aleksandar stood there and wiped the water out of the top of his hair, covering the tear that dripped down his face. "I think I can press on."

"Good. Now go dry off before you catch a cold. Be sure to be here tomorrow at eleven so we can continue our conversation in better weather. And if you cry tomorrow, I will pretend it's still raining."

Aleksandar gawked at her, his fingertips tingling and his chest a little tighter than before.

Vida pretended to tip an invisible hat and walked down the path. With poised posture and her dress soaked, she strode as if there was no rain and the sun gleamed on her best day.

～

Aleksandar stepped into his workshop with no shoes, his clothes soaked from his day without an umbrella. He set his jacket on the workbench with a plop, water dripping to the floor. He pushed his hair back in damp clumps, water rolling down his neck.

Shae took a few uneven steps towards him, too lazy to carry her own weight, but looked up, tilting her head in her odd but usual manner. She stood for a moment, then leaped into the air, flying around the workshop, the wind rippling against her feathers.

Aleksandar had returned the benches to their upright position, despite the cracked siding and chipped edges. The lack of inventions left the shop desolate and hollow, like when he first moved to Well's Peake with nothing to his name.

Shae hooted at Aleksandar, and he walked to the puzzle wall, opened his secret room, and stepped inside. Each step on the cold floorboards was like ice on his wet skin. He grabbed the wool blanket, his fingertips drying on the fabric, and yanked it away.

His eyes lit up as the blanket caressed the floor, and everything he needed for his future, for her future, was in front of him.

I'm sorry I hesitated. I doubted your vision.

Thinking back to the frosted forest under the stars and his friend's warm fingers against his, Aleksandar still couldn't believe at their tender age she studied to change the world. He would now do it for her and make her proud.

Remember… I remember, love.

Aleksandar felt a bump at his ankle and looked to Shae at his feet, holding a crumpled brown wrapper, rolled up twice with twine. Aleksandar smirked and reached to her for the treat, Shae nipping at him as he took the package away. Pulling out the last two pieces of gingerbread, Aleksandar crushed them and tossed them to the floor.

Shae hopped around the small crumbs, devouring the bigger chunks with a delighted hunger. She paused and stared at him, hooting defensively.

"Don't be picky, now," Aleksandar said.

Shae hooted and scrambled into the barren workshop. She pulled on Aleksandar's jacket, which was on the floor, and nudged through the pocket, looking for more bread. She pulled out the dry news press, with Natalia and Abel on the front, dragging it across the floorboards in tiny determination.

Shae cocked her head, gazing at Natalia before her attention turned to Abel. She blinked twice, dropped her head, and let out a hoot.

CHAPTER TWENTY-FOUR

S anded smooth, a thousand passing guests could rub their hands along the mantel and never find a splinter in Kenneth's manor. Crafted by renowned architects, his home rested on the top of a hill overlooking Well's Peake.

His estate was perfected so the city could enjoy his dramatic flair for culture and architecture whenever they looked to the horizon.

Aleksandar lifted rubber hosing above the archway, above the back patio, humming with the wind of the harvest afternoon. He strapped himself into a leather harness connected to a crane, one small enough to fit against the side of Kenneth's manor. With a belt in hand, he strapped the tubing to the arch and pulled out a nail coated in a gold finish. He lined up the end and hammered it into place.

Despite the chill of the air, Aleksandar wiped the sweat from his brow, looking to the view that was Kenneth's back balcony. He found it hard to believe Kenneth walked his property and pointed out specific trees he wanted to be cut down. All to make sure the estate was balanced and every eyeline led to his home, clear of random shrubs. His manor had carved symmetrical decals on the porches and a redwood exterior with pale blue glass.

Beyond the estate, Well's Peake lowered and rose in the rolling hills to the forest that faded into the horizon. He couldn't hear the sounds of the city, but he could see tiny people if he squinted. The smokestacks from the southern side of town were barely visible through the rising vapor.

Kenneth watched from the balcony as Aleksandar pulled two straps from his belt and wrapped the piping. He reinforced the tube with several more nails and a brass bracket.

Aleksandar hammered on the brace, and a tiny shadow from above caught his eye. He glanced, seeing nothing there. He shrugged, returning to his work, but the figure reappeared in his peripheral. His eyes shifted, careful not to startle the blur. After a pause, a salamander popped over the ridge. It scaled along the tube and disappeared.

Aleksandar pocketed the hammer in his belt. "Mr. Forbes, I do say, your salamander still spooks me."

Kenneth laughed. "You grow comfortable with him. I once hosted dozens of the beautiful creatures, all from the same family, but they passed away over the years. There are only two left. One prefers its cage inside, and that one is a free spirit."

Aleksandar grinned, sliding across the banister. A sudden pain echoed through his elbow, hitting the valve from his oversized Red Breath. He massaged his arm, his shirt thin and greasy, and lifted the end of the tube above him, sealing it shut with a locking brace and a metal clasp on both sides.

Kenneth plopped into an elegant cushioned chair. He pulled up a cup of tea and sipped it. "These are magnificent, Aleksandar. Your alterations are gorgeous, and you have outdone yourself. I'm not sure you appreciate what you've accomplished. This is the beginning of a new era. Just imagine... Aleksandar Scott, the Father of the Elemental Renaissance."

Aleksandar smiled, tucking his elbows into his sides. "There's more to this modern age than inventions and architecture, Mr. Forbes. They say medicine has advanced more this decade than in the last century. I hear we could prevent another Black Harvest if it came to it."

"I did not know you were a man of medicine."

"Not me, but a friend of mine. She's in the field."

"Oh, do I sense a potential love interest?"

Aleksandar had never given it a thought. Vida only saw him when he was at his lowest, not an alluring image for courtship.

"No," Aleksandar said. "Not that I am aware of."

"You don't know if she is interested?"

"No, I… You see, Mr. Griffin sent her my way to help me out of my slump. I'm not sure how to describe it. I've been meeting her at the World's Fair these past few weeks, and she's been guiding me with what direction I want to go in life."

Kenneth sipped his tea. "Well, that sounds fabulous, nonetheless. Did you hear about the new relay system, allowing us to send messages to each other over dozens of kilometers between cities? Stagecoaches have become sturdier than ever, although they can be abusive to my backside. I've even heard about these, um, two-wheeled contraptions. They use gears, and we ride them on roads for pleasure? I must find one."

"I believe they call it a tandem. Or a bicycle. I can't remember." Aleksandar hammered a hose in place.

"Not to worry. You may not be aware, as most would not, but at the moment, I'm working with another inventor on what we suspect will be the greatest invention in modern transportation. The Steamrail." Kenneth waved his hand. "Natalia Arlen is the one who envisioned it. With my investment and the means of Fritz and Co, we are to create something glamorous."

Despite the six-meter drop to the balcony floor, Aleksandar was quite calm until Natalia's name reached his ears. Like getting punched in the stomach, an unnerving feeling shot through his gut and into his temples. He rubbed the side of his head, hoping for relief, not wanting to feel the guilt he had for putting her on hold. He swallowed hard, happy his work was finished.

"I'm done with this section," he said.

"Fantastic. Now come down. You have exerted yourself enough today. Will you be able to finish midday tomorrow?"

"That shouldn't be an issue." Aleksandar wiped his hands.

"Most marvelous."

Aleksandar grabbed the wire connecting him to the house and pulled, bringing himself to a ladder along the red ridge. With a release on his hip, he unhooked himself and climbed to the patio, hanging his belt on a hook.

"Are you a fan of new fashion?" Aleksandar asked.

"I am and have not found a hat that captures my figure."

"I remember you telling me that."

Aleksandar stepped to the beam under the spout, the faint shadow of the house giving him a break from the overhead sun. An installed control lever rested next to a stone pillar. Its handle was gold plated, with black sapphires lining the shaft—everything to Kenneth's request.

Aleksandar pushed the lever, and gears clanked under the floorboards. A fire billowed from the spout, flashing into the gray sky, dim against the pine and hemlock trees around Kenneth's estate. Aleksandar pulled the bar back, and the flame snuffed out.

Kenneth set his tea on the saucer. "I thought you said it wouldn't be ready until tomorrow?"

"It won't. I wanted to make sure I properly sealed the tubes and ensured the spouts worked. I will finish the calibrations in the morning. Care for a demonstration?"

"Oh, would I."

Kenneth rushed to Aleksandar's side with long strides. Aleksandar paused, noticing a fair-looking woman in the window. She looked out with a smile, her gaze gentle and sweet.

"The security brace should never be removed," Aleksandar said. "Each gear is a higher intensity. The seventh gear is for maintenance. Remember, with your schedule, I have not fine-tuned the invention yet."

"Hm."

"Mr. Forbes, like I said before, I don't know all the risks yet. A small-scale model expanded to a full-fledged model in the few weeks you have allowed me restricts how thorough I prefer to be. I see it working fine in fifth gear, but anything higher is too risky and dangerous. That is why I installed the guard."

"Aleksandar, there are moments we must leap off the hillside. I trust your judgment and have no doubt you will see me to the end. Just let me know when you're ready to push it further."

"There would be no need. It'll be bright enough for the entire town."

"As I said, I'll follow your lead."

"Okay."

Aleksandar forced a grin and walked back to his workbench, stained to match the color of Kenneth's house, with all the tools he would ever require. Another compliment of working with Kenneth Forbes.

Kenneth's footsteps grew closer behind Aleksandar, and he turned to the wealthy aristocrat.

"Aleksandar, I would like to say something. I know I have created this image and have thrust you into it, but know I am simple at heart. I'm a collector of the finest art. Some people gather paintings or marble statues, but they are only paying attention to the surface of what these pieces represent. I collect for those who do not respect the deeper value of culture. I preserve art for the breeding ground of the renaissance to come."

Kenneth held his arms wide, walking to the edge of the balcony and resting his hands on the edge.

"I want to make the difference that Well's Peake deserves," Kenneth said. "By finding and showing what is glorious about the era we are in. To bring that escapism to a period where we still suffer from the Black Harvest. The morale of the city is at stake, my friend."

Aleksandar walked to the railing and leaned on his forearms, folding his hands. "I can understand that. I wish to do the same with inventing, to create something that could turn the tide that has been pushed onto us."

"And you should." Kenneth patted Aleksandar's shoulder. "People make the mistake of not believing in creative encouragement. Look at Tesla in the North. He works on capturing the ferocity of lightning, harnessing it, using it to power our homes. He plans to put that vitality into bulbs the size of our palms. We're history in the making. It sets the world's beauty in something to be embraced and experienced for the next hundred years. Society craves escapism. It connects us to a higher calling above the redundancy of daily living. Tell me, Aleksandar, do you remember everyday moments or the accomplishments of more?"

"The latter."

"Precisely. Now answer me this, do you distrust your work here?"

Aleksandar looked up, turning his head to Kenneth. "I—no. Maybe a little. It's not what I expected, but I'm okay with what I've done."

Kenneth patted him again. "I sensed something was strange. If you don't doubt your inventing, is it your reasoning?"

Where was Kenneth going with this? It was as if he reached into Aleksandar's mind and knew what he couldn't piece together himself. He thought he hid it well, but it must not have been the case.

Aleksandar nodded.

"Ah, I was curious," Kenneth said. "This may not be what you foresaw yourself doing, but that does not mean you aren't doing well. Have you considered that, by association, other aristocrats will swarm to you, throwing coin at your feet, looking for you to do what you have done for me? With their investment, you can afford your dream."

"If you don't mind me asking, do you ever wonder if what you do is worth it? If the path you're on is worth staying away?"

"I'd never leave behind what I have. I'm blessed, and my investments have paid off handsomely. To start anew would be tedious, and I honestly see no other path to follow."

Aleksandar looked to the harvest trees, red-and-auburn leaves stretching until the hills blurred on the horizon as Well's Peake rested in the valley. It was no wonder Kenneth had such monumental ambitions with a view like his.

"So tell me, why wander the path you do?" Kenneth asked. "If not for the beauty or the spirit of the renaissance, what keeps the fire of your passion alive?"

Aleksandar arched his back as it tensed and closed his eyes. "A friend."

"Oh, how exciting!" Kenneth walked to his chair and plopped in it again, grabbing his tea. "I'd be most satisfied if you indulged me."

"It's not a story I have told for years."

"Please do not tease me with suspense, Mr. Scott."

Aleksandar rubbed his arm and took a seat next to Kenneth across a table stand. "When I was young, my childhood friend was my biggest inspiration in the world. I never knew what I wanted. I was shy and indecisive, but she was everything I wished to be. Her memory means everything to me."

"Where is she now?"

Aleksandar's chin trembled, and he held back his desire to want to walk away, to go inward where his feelings were only his own. "She passed as so many did when we were young. She was twelve. Because of her, I do what I do. I dedicated my life's work to her."

Kenneth rubbed the side of his chair, his vibrant demeanor calmer. "Aleksandar, I am sorry. I know the feeling. My family also passed when I was a child. If I may ask, what was her name?"

Aleksandar met his gaze. "Her name?"

"Yes. What was this incredible young lady's name who has changed your life forever?"

Aleksandar hadn't said her name in so long and never heard it throughout his stay in the city. Would it sound the same? Would he cry, or would a rush of relief come over him?

Aleksandar bit his lip. "Her name—"

"Hello!"

The woman from behind the window strolled onto the cedar balcony, smiling at Aleksandar and Kenneth.

Kenneth stood and stepped forward. "That passion we were talking about, Aleksandar, this is mine. This wonderful lady, my wife, has been so kind to let me be her husband. Good afternoon, my darling. How are you today?"

"I am splendid, my love," she said.

Aleksandar nodded in respect and wiped his right eye as the couple separated and looked towards him. He did not realize how vibrant her brown eyes were behind the window and how golden her hair was.

"With great pleasure, let me introduce my wife. Amia, this is the young inventor, Aleksandar Scott," Kenneth said.

"My spouse has yet to stop talking about you and your work, Aleksandar," Amia said.

"Pleased to meet you, Mrs. Forbes," Aleksandar said with a smile. "I didn't think I'd be so interesting to Mr. Forbes."

"Please, call me Amia. Pardon my lack of attendance these past weeks. My husband has me running errands morning and night for the gala this weekend. I hoped to make it home before you left, and well, here we are."

Aleksandar looked at Amia, and she carried a gentle calm, her hair feathering down in delicate layers like rose petals, and her eyes were rich like caramel.

Kenneth held her tight, showing her off as if she was his greatest source of happiness. She radiated kindness and subtlety. She was everything Kenneth did not seem.

"Indeed, we are," Aleksandar said.

Amia turned to Kenneth. "May I find you a glass of iced tea? Aleksandar?"

"Honey, you don't have to," Kenneth said.

"No, no. I can. You two are working. It's my pleasure."

"Thank you." Kenneth kissed her on the cheek.

Amia smiled and made her way back into the house. Aleksandar paused with his mouth open because of her calm and sincere nature. He could not help but wonder how Kenneth's personality attracted such a tender woman.

"Thank you!" Aleksandar shouted as he leaned towards the door, ensuring she heard him.

"Passion, Aleksandar, beauty—these are the things that will propel us forward," Kenneth said. "You need to recognize the importance of knowing where your passion is and what drives your motivation. The uncertainty of the two will not lead you anywhere."

"It's hard to look to the future after what happened. I'm too busy worrying one day I might be up against my past."

"We all do, but that doesn't mean we can't be optimistic about what's to come."

Aleksandar rubbed his neck, peering to the Red Breath. "Mr. Forbes, do you not have tea already?"

"Yes, but when the love of my life offers to bring me a gift, I'll never say no." Kenneth grabbed his tea and tossed it off the balcony, the cup breaking against the roots of the tree.

Aleksandar chuckled as Kenneth shrugged his shoulders, laughing.

"You see, Aleksandar, I put you on such a tight schedule because I'd love to present your invention at the upcoming gala."

"I assumed there was a reason for my work."

"You are a clever one. Don't let anyone else tell you otherwise." Kenneth waved his finger, putting his arm around Aleksandar.

"I try not to."

"So, I'd like for you to come this weekend."

Aleksandar turned to Kenneth. "Me? Oh no. I would not fit in well."

"You have created the main attraction. You deserve to be here for its revealing."

"I'm charmed for the invitation—"

"I've returned!" Amia walked out the door holding two glasses of cold tea. She handed one to Kenneth and the other to Aleksandar, Kenneth taking a quick sip.

Aleksandar held his drink. "Mr. Forbes—"

"My love, Aleksandar here has been officially invited to our gala, and guess what? He has cold feet."

"Nonsense," she said. "I don't see Mr. Scott here being the shy sort." Amia walked into the house and returned with an invitation, handing it to Aleksandar.

"Mrs. Forbes—"

"Aleksandar, you haven't opened your invitation yet," she said.

Aleksandar tried to put a word in, but he let out a deep breath. He took a sip of his tea and paused. It was immaculate, smoother than any beverage he had ever drunk, with a hint of orange and lemon complementing the robust taste.

"We cold press the leaves," Amia said. "It gives you that smooth texture you're experiencing now."

Setting the tea down, Aleksandar licked his lips and opened the invitation, pulling out the card. They lined it with a gold ribbon, and it showed red lettering on cream paper, scented with cinnamon and berries.

"You should have no second thoughts, Aleksandar," Amia said. "When the man on the hill invites you to the Harvest Gala, we only allow you to accept. We expect you at six."

"I don't have—"

"We will have your measurements before you leave, and your suit will arrive the morning of."

Hesitant, Aleksandar nodded. "I will be there."

"Ah, reason at last. I could not have done it without you, darling," Kenneth said.

"Just remember, Aleksandar, it's plus one," Amia said. "We await to see a woman on your arm when you arrive. If not, we'll place someone there ourselves." A minor scuffle came from within the manor, Amia looking over her shoulder. "Excuse me once more. Entertain yourselves while I find order with the servants."

Amia darted into the house, waving her hands. Aleksandar smiled and turned to Kenneth, who shared the same grin.

"She seems like an amazing woman," Aleksandar said.

"You are not wrong. She deserves all my kindness. I am aware of my self-absorption and selfishness, but I assure you, I'm fully aware of all that I do. Amia sees me at my best and my worst. That alone means I owe her my finest."

"That was quite poetic, Mr. Forbes."

"Thank you. I am a man of culture."

"Indeed," Aleksandar said. "Well, since we are in the giving mood, I brought you something as well. As a token of thanks for helping me through these past few weeks."

"Oh, I'm rather excited."

Aleksandar walked to the bench and picked up a leather box, carrying it to the table stand. He set it down, unlatched the locks, and removed the lid. Kenneth peeked over Aleksandar's shoulder, his hands cupped in front of his chest.

"Mr. Scott?"

Aleksandar pulled out a top hat sporting a curved, sharp brim. The black felt was pristine with a red ribbon at the base, a red feather tucked into the band. Aleksandar held it to Kenneth, who looked with childlike eyes.

Kenneth grabbed the hat with the utmost care, holding his breath. "For all that is desirable... Aleksandar, where did you discover this exquisite piece?"

"You have mentioned finding the proper hat since I have arrived. So, I made it, wondering if this might be it."

Kenneth glanced at him. "Do not play with me."

"It's true; I crafted it. I take you like?"

Kenneth lifted the hat and set it on his head, watching himself in the glass's reflection. "I have never seen such an amazing piece. Aleksandar, your talent continues to amaze me. You follow the path of an inventor, but I feel you're destined for greater endeavors. I can't thank you enough. When I walk into the gala, high society will focus not on me but on the image you have created."

Kenneth picked up their tea and handed Aleksandar his.

"To the future that guides us to places we could only dream of." Kenneth tapped his glass against the young inventor's.

Aleksandar took a sip as Kenneth walked into the house. He lifted his invitation and could feel his dimples as he stared at the red lettering.

Maybe this is the path...

Aleksandar turned to the vast harvest bloom and sipped his tea under the falling sun, knowing the weekend would bring a night for all to remember.

CHAPTER TWENTY-FIVE

Aleksandar slicked his hair to the side with his collar open, tie dangling around his neck as he dressed in the light of the sunset outside his window. He angled his face in the mirror of his washroom, making sure his image was proper, wanting to impress society.

While unsure of how the aristocrats would react to him, he smiled and wondered whether they would be fascinated by his invention or look to it as the judges did during the exhibition. Either way, his stomach was light, and he felt the warmth in his cheeks.

Shae sat on the windowsill, hooting at the busy street, as she glanced between the fairgoers and her owner.

Aleksandar buttoned his collar, pulled his tie tight, and exhaled into the mirror, a gift from Kenneth, fogging it up. The suit Mr. Forbes prepared for him was beyond stunning. The tailoring was perfect and snug, and he found it impressive that they adjusted it so quickly. A gray vest with white circular stitching was low cut and sharp, giving Aleksandar a sophisticated presence. If not for a leaning tie, he was flawless.

Maybe I shouldn't go. I could just stay here.

Shae hooted.

"I know, I'm going to the gala. So, what do you think of my suit? Rather dapper?"

Shae hopped to the sink and stared, tilting her head as Aleksandar spun in a circle.

"I'll take that as a compliment."

A muffled knock echoed from the living room, and Aleksandar pressed the shoulders of his cotton jacket.

"Oh, Shae. I'm not sure about this."

Another knock came from downstairs. Aleksandar blew out the candle and hurried out of the washroom, rushing to the living room. With a turn of the handle, he opened the door, Vida standing outside.

"Good evening, Mr. Scott," she said with rosy cheeks.

Vida stood in the city lanterns, the sun dipping over the rooftops, dressed to impress. Elbow-length white gloves covered her hands as she held an umbrella. The dress was thick silk, and she sported a corset and a silver necklace. Lined with pale blue lace, the dress hung like rain in the late night, shy of touching the ground.

"Good evening. You look stunning, Miss Harvey." A gust of wind blew Aleksandar's hair to the side, and he pushed his hand against it, wondering if it still looked okay.

"Thank you. It was my mother's." Vida blushed.

"She had great taste."

"Now, now, Mr. Scott. No need to seduce me. You'll run out of compliments for other women tonight."

Aleksandar tugged on his collar and cleared his throat.

"I believe our escort has arrived," she said, turning to the street.

Aleksandar looked over Vida's shoulder, and a gentleman with a high-rise hat and black attire stood with a gracious smile, his hands folded behind his back. His primed gray mustache formed to a point on each side, and his ruby scarf breezed across his beard that hung down his chest.

He posed next to a carriage with a single red-haired horse.

"I see Mr. Forbes favors you," Vida said.

"You have no idea."

Aleksandar grabbed his winter coat with a grin and threw it on, wrapping his scarf around his neck. As he buttoned his jacket, Shae wandered from the living room and tilted her head.

"I'll be back soon, little one," he said.

Shae plopped on her side and stared aimlessly.

"Now, now."

Aleksandar locked the door, and they walked to the carriage.

"Good evening," the chauffeur said. "My name is Edwin. I see we are ready for a night of beauty and splendor."

"We are," Vida said.

"Excellent." Edwin held out his hand, and Vida took it, guiding her into her seat. He turned to Aleksandar. "Sir."

Aleksandar climbed inside and sat. Vida looking at him with a smile.

The carriage swayed as Edwin mounted his seat, and with a snap of the reins, the horse trotted off, the city passing them by.

"I'm so excited, Aleksandar." Vida lay back. "I've never attended a party such as this."

"As am I. Thank you for coming. Mrs. Forbes insisted I bring someone, and I believe she meant it," Aleksandar said.

"Oh, so you brought me for her sake?" Vida asked, raising an eyebrow.

"No, that's not what—"

Vida put her arm on his. "Aleksandar, relax. I was only teasing. I'm in a delightful mood."

Aleksandar smiled and looked out the window, the city passing him by the block. Buildings of apartments and homes turned to ones of parliament, then to North Hills, and the homes for Well's Peake's aristocrats.

"I've been here once, with a doctor on call," Vida said. "Never did I realize how delightful it was during the night."

"Neither did I. I'm sorry again for taking so long to ask about you becoming a doctor. Have there been any changes?"

"It has proven to be more difficult than I appreciate, but then again, I do enjoy a challenge."

"What makes it so difficult?"

"Well, sadly, there are several *individuals* on the medical board who have yet to trust a woman's judgment. My physician has the utmost faith in me and has even written a letter of reference, but most academies don't take women as students. There are separate schools for nurses and assistants, but I want more."

"I'm sorry to hear that. I assume you've reached out to most institutes?"

"All, but they are realizing I'm quite persistent, and it's a shame they are as well. I understand your struggle of wanting to follow your dream and finding few ways of getting there. That's for certain."

Aleksandar took a deep breath and looked at Vida, who glanced back with a smirk.

"And yet, you're still smiling," Aleksandar said.

"Yes. I've been rejected, and it'll happen again before I succeed, so there's no point in not smiling. I'm optimistic and resilient. Hope is something we have to give ourselves, and I'm most hopeful. That, and I'm excited for tonight."

Her grin was genuine and gave Aleksandar hope, hope he didn't think he could find within himself but glad to have found in her.

"Aleksandar, look," Vida said, her face against the glass, fog forming on the edges.

Aleksandar peered out, his eyes widening. He had seen Kenneth's estate during the day, but he never expected the wonder in front of him.

Mr. Forbes' house glimmered on the hill, trees lined at the bottom of the house as if he lived above the treetops. Orange light glowed from the two-story windows near the back balcony.

"I think we can expect many surprises tonight," Vida said.

Aleksandar turned to her as his breathing thinned and his fingers tingled. He folded his hands together, preparing to embrace the evening to come.

Stars trickled on the horizon opposite the maroon sunset that washed waves of light into the hills. The sun shone on Kenneth's home as Aleksandar and Vida arrived, the carriage rattling on the brick road.

Edwin led them past dozens of carriages and people working their way to the manor, to the roundabout at the front steps. The horses were the finest the city offered, and each stood sleek and ideal, postured for their dignified owners with hair as elegant as wine.

"Mr. Scott and Miss Harvey," Edwin said. "I welcome you to this year's Harvest Gala, hosted by the Man on the Hill himself, Kenneth Forbes."

Edwin pulled the reins, and the horses halted at the house's entrance. He dismounted and held his hand out, helping Vida to the pathway. Aleksandar followed, and the gentleman bowed to them.

"I am at your service for the evening. Let the valet know when you are ready to depart, and I will deliver you home."

"Thank you," Aleksandar said.

"I'll hold on to your jackets for now."

Aleksandar and Vida handed their coats to the driver. He placed them inside, mounted the carriage, and took off down the road.

Vida turned to Aleksandar. "Shall we?"

"I think we shall."

Aleksandar held out his arm, Vida interlocking hers with his, and they walked up the steps into Kenneth's manor.

An archway laced with gems rested through the tall mahogany doors. Candles and lanterns lit the manor, flickering off the red molding of the house in serene bliss. Dresses of autumn colors and suits from the finest tailors captured everything Aleksandar visioned high society to be.

Vida stepped forward. "Aleksandar, are you seeing?"

"I am."

"We by far—I can't think of something clever right now."

Aleksandar blinked, trying to take in the estate's architecture, remodeled from when he last visited Kenneth. The aroma of cinnamon and pine filled the halls, and he could taste vanilla with how thick it was in the air. He reached out and touched the base of a golden stand with a dozen candles lit on top, wax dripping down the sticks. It had a pleasant warmth that lingered on his fingers.

Several aristocrats looked at him, eyeing him longer than he liked. Many carried the utmost posture, bringing to his attention his shoulders were not as far back.

"What in the bloody hell is an inventor like me doing here?" he said.

"Making appearances, of course," Vida said. "You might have forgotten, but you built tonight's main attraction." Vida elbowed him and grinned.

Aleksandar looked around, finding his gaze on Vida. "I was being rhetorical. You don't—"

"Now is not the night for thinking. Let's enjoy ourselves."

Aleksandar looked at the mansion. "No, no. I think I'll be going back."

Vida pulled him closer and steered him along. "You will not leave me with these people, Mr. Scott. If you do, may the Maker help you."

A butler stepped forward and waved Aleksandar and Vida into the living room, his buttons and shoulder straps glimmering in the light.

The ceiling towered above them, mimicking a spider web, as red lines layered throughout the glass. Large maroon-and-white drapes stretched across the wood rafters, like the inside of a circus tent. A butler with ruby gloves and a golden jacket walked by, carrying a charcuterie tray, spices of pepper and cumin lingering in the air. Another held glasses of eggnog with a cinnamon stick hanging on the edge.

Vida tugged on Aleksandar's elbow. "Where do we go? I'm getting a little overwhelmed."

Aleksandar pointed to a larger room, and they strode into the grand ballroom. The ceiling was lit with chandeliers, sending glimpses of light around as candles kissed the crystals. Windows with pillars between them rose a few stories high, towering over hundreds of people. A monumental staircase that split in two merged in the middle, laced with white cobblestone and slivers of silver.

Bernard stood in the center, his beard vibrant and his laugh echoing above many conversations.

"Oh, look, Bernard," Vida said.

"Should we say hello?" Aleksandar asked.

"I'm sure he'll find us by night's end. Best to let him make his rounds."

It was exquisite. Kenneth transformed his house for a party that would define a generation.

Aleksandar could sense how tense he was and rolled his shoulders, looking for a drink. A redwood bar lined the other side of the room, surrounded by dozens of people drinking, eating, and laughing.

"Wow," she said. "I know you said it was beautiful, but I did not expect this."

"Similar to the company beside me."

Vida laughed, patting his arm. "Like I said, Mr. Scott. Save your charm for the other ladies."

Aleksandar looked away, blushing.

Vida chuckled, and she let go, making her way for the bar. "I will grab the first drinks."

"Wouldn't you prefer I got them?" Aleksandar said, stretching out his hand.

"I'm more than capable."

"Okay then. I'll see if I can find Mr. Forbes."

Vida eased into the swarm of guests, and Aleksandar stayed, the air thinner without her. Everyone was chatting or eating, and he stood there like a groomed child, unsure of what to do. With a deep breath, he stepped into the crowd, soaking in the grand excitement he'd never felt before. He embraced the vigorousness and invincibility as the thrill overtook every nerve in his body.

Aleksandar hummed and folded his palms together, looking around the ballroom. He found a set of eyes on him and paused, swallowing hard. Between the heads of many, Natalia locked gazes with him.

Aleksandar froze, his hands slipping apart, and nodded, unsure of what to do. Natalia smiled and strolled through the crowd, making her way to his side. He wanted to walk away but fought his instincts. As nervous as he was about the past, he wanted to talk to her.

What do I say... what should I?

"Hello, Miss Arlen," Aleksandar said.

"Mr. Scott, it's good to see you again. How are you this lovely evening?" Natalia sported a blue-and-gold jacket, a vest complementing it. The thread was so bright, it seemed to glow in the candlelight, and her curled hair rested on her slender shoulders.

"I'm doing well, thank you."

"You seem a bit overwhelmed."

Aleksandar nodded. "Yes, I rather am. I've never been to a gala before, let alone one of this prestige."

"Depending on the host, they can be quite amazing. Mr. Forbes is not known for his subtlety, so it should be exciting, no less."

"I can only imagine. What about yourself? Are things going well?" Aleksandar rubbed his arm.

"They are. I hope you've found your footing over the past few weeks. After what happened, some would have struggled with such a quick recovery."

"I'm not sure I alone am responsible. Someone is watching after me."

"Oh, an angel?"

Aleksandar smiled. "Perhaps, but a friend."

"Is that so? I brought one myself tonight, but even I can lose the mountain of a man in this crowd," Natalia said, searching for her colleague. "Would your friend happen to be a woman?"

Aleksandar smirked in slight embarrassment. "She is. She is just a friend, though, and loves to remind me."

"Well, nothing wrong with that either." Natalia chuckled as a butler walked by with a tray of eggnog. She grabbed two glasses and handed one to Aleksandar. "Mr. Scott, how about a toast? To good fortunes and this delectable nog."

Aleksandar held his glass, and Natalia tapped them together. Aleksandar took a sip, delighted by the taste of cream and spices. The cinnamon was perfect, simmering into the creamy drink. He blinked, spinning the glass in his hand.

"I've tried, and no words can describe it," Natalia said, her smile wide. "Well, you must return to your friend. I don't wish to hold you any longer. It was nice seeing you, Mr. Scott."

Natalia nodded and stepped away.

The pit in Aleksandar's gut returned. "No, wait. I've been wanting to talk to you about an invention I've been thinking about."

Natalia turned around. "An inventor's trait, no doubt."

Aleksandar gave a brief laugh. "Yes. So, I had an idea. Many still believe the Black Harvest affects the farmland."

"Yes."

"Well, in areas close to the city, farmers are fine. However, farmers in more remote regions are still getting sick. Well, why is that? I think it's because the fields need to be cleansed. There's a technique called revegetation, where you take a blended mixture of certain plants and till them into the fields, essentially making them fertile again."

Natalia rubbed her cheek. "Okay, I think I'm with you."

"This is a natural phenomenon in nature, but the Black Harvest was man-made, so maybe we need to take responsibility. In the Day and Night Pass, I knew a farmer, Masanobu, who traveled the Southern Plains and collected exotic plants, roots, and seeds. He created a mixture that fertilized his lands in less than a year."

Natalia held her glass against her waist, pushing her tongue against her cheek. "So, where do we come in?"

"The mixture is combined with water and needs to be sprayed over the lands, and after the frost and bloom season, it should be safe, in theory. This mixture is very heavy, and we need a device that can propel the mixture across the lands. If people were to do it without a machine, they risk the Black."

Natalia tapped her glass. "How do you know so much about this?"

"My grandfather was a farmer back home."

"I see, and you assume the Lunarwheel is the solution?"

"Yes, or at least part of it. We will need a delivery mechanism, which I'm basing off my surface tension theory, but it is the main apparatus."

Natalia sipped her drink and rubbed her chin.

I knew it. Aleksandar held his tongue, realizing how outlandish he must have sounded. Why did he say it like that? He rubbed his neck, his knees weak.

"Well, Mr. Scott, the Lunarwheel is a little less than functional. We could work on the core idea, but your proposal depends on my invention.

If we solve it, progression rights prevent you from claiming success."

"I understand that, but your wheel is the key to a lot of problems. It could help people, and that means more to me than putting my name on it."

Natalia tapped the glass with her fingers. "I can appreciate what you're trying to do. You'll need to iron that idea out, but we might have something."

Aleksandar pulled on his arm. "I should also have never turned my back on your proposal. I may have wasted important days, and you were gracious enough—"

Natalia held up her palm. "Mr. Scott, you don't have to explain your actions to me. All is forgiven. You did what you needed, and I can respect that because the reality is, every now and then, our dreams require sacrifice."

Aleksandar nodded. He wasn't sure if it was in her eyes or her pleasant and calming tone, but he believed her. She sounded sincere and held no resentment. The pit in his stomach lessened, and his back did not seem as tense.

"So, would you like to try again?" Aleksandar asked, holding out his hand.

Natalia looked at his gesture. "I would not pass up this opportunity for a second." She shook his hand with a pleasant grip. "We have only months to prepare. How about we start tomorrow at nine?"

Aleksandar's let out a deep breath. "Yes, I'd like that."

"Do you still have my address?"

"I do."

"Then nine it is. I am excited to see what we can do."

"Thank you. I won't let you down again."

"I don't think you will." Natalia's eyes glimmered, like a crystal lake at sunrise. She rubbed her cheek, trying to hold back a smile.

Aleksandar exhaled and glanced at the surrounding people. At last, a weight lifted from his shoulders, and he could move forward in the way he wanted.

Vida was nowhere in sight, and Aleksandar realized he'd moved from where he was, so she perhaps lost him. Turning back to Natalia, she made eye contact with a man hidden within the crowd. Aleksandar leaned towards her to see Mr. Lucas peering in their direction.

"Pardon me, Aleksandar, but has Mr. Lucas been watching us long?" she asked.

"I'm not sure. What are you thinking?"

"I think we should invite him to our conversation."

"Invite him?"

Natalia put her two fingers on her forehead and lifted them as if she were taking off a hat. Mr. Lucas's vest was dark as night, with slivers of thin white stripes stitched up and down. His jacket was a darker shade of gray, a sterling chain connected from the lower middle button to a notepad that stuck out of his inner pocket.

Mr. Lucas rubbed his fingers through his hair and straightened his back, moving towards the inventors.

Why is the detective here?

Aleksandar crossed his arms but then dropped his hands, not sure how to stand, wondering if anyone noticed his indecisiveness.

"Hello, Mr. Lucas. How are you this evening?" Natalia said.

"I am well. I apologize if my wandering eyes upset you."

"Others may not take too kindly to such prodding."

"Most days, you'd be right, but this is the Harvest Gala, and these folks crave to be envied. Then again, I understand you two do not attend such occasions often either." Mr. Lucas moved out of the way of a dancing couple. "Mr. Scott, I see you're doing well despite recent circumstances."

"Yes, Mr. Lucas. I am."

"Please, call me Nicoli," he said.

"What brings you to the gala this evening?" Natalia folded her hands behind her back. "It'd be a shame to work during such a festive occasion."

"I'm here on behalf of Chief Constable Dekker. He did not seem interested in coming and thought I should take his place."

"A blessing or a curse?" Natalia pressed her lips with a chuckle.

"I think he hoped I would find this little tea party miserable."

Aleksandar coughed. "It's more than a small party."

"Indeed, it is. Well, I apologize; I must be going."

"Nicoli, wait," Aleksandar said. "Has there been any news on my inventions or who robbed me?"

Nicoli removed his hands from his pocket. "Not yet. There's not much evidence, and we've yet to discover any of your work."

Aleksandar nodded.

"Don't worry. If anything turns up, I will inform you."

"Thank you."

Aleksandar spun to Natalia as she stared at Nicoli as if he were a piece of art or something she did not understand.

"Nicoli," Natalia said. "You are one of Redwood's most famous private detectives, but I hear you're known as the man who catches killers. Why would someone of your prestige be interested in Mr. Scott's turmoil? Or what makes us so interesting tonight?"

Nicoli stared at the inventors. "I see my reputation precedes me, and that came not from blind luck or natural skill. I'm a thorough individual and follow up on any potential outcomes. It prevents mistakes and helps me in my search for all evidence before drawing a conclusion."

"Well, if that's the case, it's in our best interest you attain what you need."

"I hope you did not take it offensively. People are most relaxed when they don't think they're being watched. Only then do I have a clear impression of one's character."

"I'm not sure anyone can say anything with that sort of certainty."

"Perhaps you're right."

"Are you watching because we are of interest?"

A suspect?

Aleksandar tried to stay calm, but his chest grew tense, and the sweat on his arms stuck to his shirt. Why would Natalia ask something so bold?

"How could we be suspects?" Aleksandar asked.

Nicoli eyed the young inventor, running his finger down the chain on his jacket. "Like I said. I look at every angle. I'm sorry, I try not to reveal too much of my investigation while it's ongoing." Nicoli ran his hand through his hair. "Maybe you two could explain something to me. Word is spreading that inventors are going missing and turning up in disturbing ways, which I'm sure you both were aware. Mr. Hawthorne wasn't an inventor, so if this murderer is the same person, why would he change who he is targeting?"

His night of getting away from the world, from his problems, had faded. Aleksandar knew who he was, but the possibility of his work causing Abel's death made his stomach churn. He closed his eyes and thought to Vida and her words, finding some peace.

Aleksandar's hands shook, and he could feel the warmth in his cheeks. "Mr. Lucas, I understand you're doing your job, but I came here hoping to get away from this. I want to enjoy my evening without you being so rude to spy on us. Now that we know you're here, maybe you could go elsewhere."

Nicoli stood with stern eyes. "I apologize once again and will leave you to your party. I should have known better than to upset the guest of honor."

Natalia rubbed her chin. "If you need aid with your investigation, we'd be more than willing to help. If this concerns all inventors, we could provide insight."

Nicoli eyed the two, a smirk forming across his face. "I'll keep that in mind. Good evening."

"To you as well."

Mr. Lucas nodded and walked into the next room.

Natalia covered her mouth, letting out a slurred laugh. "Mr. Scott, that was a rather bold confrontation. How did it feel?"

Aleksandar cracked a smile. "That felt great."

Natalia raised her glass. "I would hope. Well's Peake is full of aggressive characters, and you will need a backbone. I hope the rest of your evening is well. How about you come over tomorrow when you're rested? Ten, eleven, that's up to you. I will sit on my back balcony and wait for the knock on my door."

"That sounds—"

Cymbals crashed and echoed throughout the grand ballroom. Aleksandar flinched and turned to the staircase as people screamed and jumped, a glass shattering somewhere on the floor and ropes dropping from the chandeliers.

Acrobats appeared from a secret door on the staircase and glided down the ropes in red-and-orange outfits. The beating of drums and melodies of wind instruments caressed the room, like a magician's show. An ensemble of musicians marched down the steps in superb fashion, kicking their legs and swaying between each other. Another rope dropped between the others, Kenneth standing at the helm.

He tapped his cane and removed his top hat, bowing to his audience with poise. The crowd erupted into cheers as Aleksandar gawked and Natalia applauded.

Kenneth leaped, hooked the handle onto the ropes, and glided overhead. Men and women gaped in fear, and as Kenneth soared over the staircase, he let go with a backflip and landed on his feet.

Between the roars and the cheers, Aleksandar clapped, shaken with the host's grand entrance.

Kenneth raised his hands in the air, and the music broke into a crescendo, the musicians performing at a marvelous level of musicianship. Kenneth kicked his feet in tempo, and in a final fanfare, the players hit their last note, and the room echoed to silence.

Aleksandar could hear the ruffling of someone's jacket, and the audience cheered again, raising their glasses into the air.

Kenneth skipped to the edge of the upper step and smiled. "Welcome, my dear ladies and the elegant gentlemen on their arms. Thank you for attending my lovely estate for an evening of significant pleasure and enjoyment."

The ballroom clapped again, and Kenneth silenced them with a wave of his hand.

"Tonight is to be a night of grandeur, revelation, and... unexpected relations," he said, his voice clear across the room. "I hope everyone is enjoying themselves, yes? All in due thanks to my lovely wife, the curator of this year's Harvest Gala. Amia, where are you, my love?"

The crowd looked around for his beloved. Amia stood from behind the bar and walked through the applauding room. She rushed to her husband, waving, and he grabbed her by the waist, pulling her in for a long kiss. Many cheered and laughed as some scoffed at their public affection.

"My love, Amia, you are my inspiration and my everything." Kenneth held both of her hands, looking only at her. "No matter the occasion or the struggle, you've been by my side. You are the most remarkable person I've ever met, and I cannot express enough my appreciation and gratitude. Amia Forbes!"

Kenneth lifted their arms together, and Aleksandar clapped as so many did.

"Tonight's gala is to one's own inspiration. For me, that inspiration is passion. The World's Fair has taken hold of our beloved city, and we could not be more grateful for such an opportunity. We deserve it, without a doubt. I want everyone to look to the inventors of this town and thank them for their dedication in making Well's Peake the city it once was. For without their incentive and inventions, we would not be where we stand today. Yes, some associate the Black Harvest and their resentment towards inventors, but those who are to blame are in the past. This is the present. Life is about not focusing on the breaths we take, but the moments that draw our breath away."

Kenneth leaned against the railing between the two staircases.

"But do not idolize them. Look to what they invent. Reach for that encouragement and make it your own, so we may do great things, for none of us are incapable of being inspired. Like grand deeds to those in need, inspiring others is contagious, and if we inspire one person a day, then we are making said improvement."

Kenneth looked into the crowd, pausing.

"I am provoked, as of late, to reach higher myself. Several weeks ago, I stumbled across a young inventor who created something I had never seen. While the judges did not see, I did with opportunity. Technology that is to complement art and culture."

Aleksandar tried to hold his smile, but his cheeks hurt from the strain of staying calm. His hands grew restless, and he folded them across his chest.

"He denied the offer at first," Kenneth said. "But we came to an agreement, and he delivered what I deserved. What he created is what I define as the first cultured piece of elemental technology: the Red Breath. Aleksandar Scott, I know you are here. Please, come up."

He stood still, stunned and gaping like a fool.

Natalia nudged him forward. "Here he is!"

Aleksandar glanced at her, and she nodded, winking at him.

The crowd cheered, and they guided Aleksandar as he stumbled on his own feet. He picked up the pace, and their encouraging pushes turned to applause and praise. He paced with slow steps up the stairs and held up his hand, not completely waving. The entire room focused on him, and he felt as if he would faint.

Kenneth grabbed Aleksandar's arm and yanked him between himself and Amia. Kenneth lifted their hands high, and the crowd roared, Aleksandar feeling the vibrations of their clapping and voices in his chest, like thunder in the valley.

"It's been almost thirty years since the Black Harvest took its deadly hold over the lands," Kenneth said. "This created a generational gap the younger members of our society had to fill. While the few remaining elders guide us, this town belongs to the young and to the inventors."

Kenneth put his palm on Aleksandar's shoulder.

"This young inventor is Aleksandar Scott, and know he will be the father of what will become... the Elemental Renaissance!"

Aleksandar arched his back, his chest vibrating from the crowd. He offered a humble wave as his body shook from his own adrenaline.

Kenneth leaned into Aleksandar. "I think the moment has arrived to show them what you have created."

Kenneth grabbed his wife's hand and tapped Aleksandar on the shoulder, and they headed down the stairs. He hurried them along as the musicians burst into another fanfare. Aleksandar scurried onto the back patio, and the crowd followed. Kenneth stepped onto the banister, and Amia waved him to come to the floor. He pretended to lean over the railing, holding his leg as if he hurt it. She smiled, and he bent over and kissed her.

Kenneth turned to Aleksandar. "Make me proud."

"What do you mean?"

"My boy, show them what you have created."

Aleksandar couldn't believe what was happening, his chest tingling and a smile etched into his face. He looked to the handle on the other side of the balcony as several aristocrats encouraged him over. Each step he took, they watched, envying his presence, waiting for his reveal. Never had he embraced such infamy, such exhilaration, as hundreds applauded for him, the young inventor.

Aleksandar walked to the controls, grabbed the lever with a firm grip, and looked back. Kenneth nodded.

Aleksandar pulled the lever, and the patio shook as gears shuffled below the floorboards, the hissing of gas rushing through the tubes. Several guests jumped back and into the ballroom.

There was a moment of silence, and Aleksandar stared, his heart knocking in his chest.

Why isn't—

A fire erupted from the spouts and into the harvest night, brightening the clouds in the sky. The flames were so bright the crowd covered their eyes before looking in wonder and awe. Kenneth waved Aleksandar over, and he sprinted to his side, jumping onto the banister with his hands raised. Kenneth nodded to the audience, and Aleksandar smiled above them.

Every eye was on his invention as the heat filled the air, the blazes catching Well's Peake's attention.

"Mr. Scott," Kenneth said. "Despite the hardships and the setbacks, you did this. You captured the very spirit and soul of this great city. What you feel right now is what you deserve."

The joy and success of doing something that meant more, in front of the crowd in such a majestic setting of grandeur, flourished within him. Aleksandar closed his eyes, a serene bliss overcoming him. The warmth against his skin, the echoes of their cheers, and his body trembling from pure euphoria... he finally stood in the position he craved.

After years of struggle and dedication, he created the difference he needed to make, the difference she would have made.

CHAPTER TWENTY-SIX

The clatter of applause faded as Kenneth, Aleksandar, and Amia dismounted from the banister, swarmed by the ecstatic crowd. Vida stared through the open pillars as she waited beside the polished bar.

Despite the midnight air that lingered from outside, the vast amount of people made the ballroom hot and uncomfortable as Vida's dress stuck to her.

Vida pulled her silk glove tight as she found herself fascinated by the artwork on the ceiling. It was lavish in its curvature designs, the pillars arching to the top, to a round window where she could see the stars above the flames of Aleksandar's invention.

"Excuse me, miss?"

Vida turned, glancing to those near her, realizing a fellow in a gray suit and teal bow tie looked to her with a drink in hand.

"Me?" She pointed to herself.

"Yes," he said. "If you're waiting in line, there's an opening there. Most are on the balcony."

"Oh. Why, thank you."

Vida wandered through the thinned crowd, reaching the mahogany bar and tapping her fingers on the railing. The bartender held up his finger with a smile, and Vida nodded.

The man in a bow tie walked up to her, his red hair slicked backward, his jacket capturing her attention. Several metal-handled tools protruded out of his top pocket.

"Thank you." Vida extended her hand. "Miss Harvey."

The gentleman returned the gesture. "The pleasure is mine, Miss Harvey. My name is Mr. Gray."

"As in Orson Gray?"

"An excellent assumption. I know my family is well known in Well's Peake, but why assume I'm Orson and not one of my brothers?"

Everyone had heard of Orson Gray. With a beard like a dark sunrise, it covered his childish chin, leaving him with a dignified face. Even with a nose too large for his face, it did nothing to diminish his professional and alluring presence.

"If I were to judge you from your attire and orange hair, I'd say you are the renowned physician," Vida said. "Your family's work in the Black Harvest and after has saved countless lives. Hard not to hear of such things."

"An impressive sense for detail, Miss Harvey. What is your profession?" Mr. Gray asked.

"I'm a nurse."

"Ah, so you recognized the tools in my pocket?"

"That might've helped," Vida smirked. "I guess I will need to call you Doctor."

"If you prefer."

Dr. Gray sipped on his drink, and the bartender moved over to Vida, pardoning himself into the conversation.

"What may I serve you, madam?" the man asked, his eyes low and easy.

"Yes, may I have two orders of champagne, please," Vida said.

"Any specific vineyard?"

"Um, something sweet, not served often, but still delicious."

"Right away, and your name?"

"Miss Vida Harvey."

The bartender picked up the glasses for Vida, setting them on the counter. He grabbed a bottle and a small sword, sliced the cork off in dramatic fashion, and poured the wine. He swirled the bottom and pushed them to her, holding his hands out for her to take.

"Two glasses, Miss Harvey? Is it not the man's delight to grab the first round?" Dr. Gray asked.

"Why do you assume that?" Vida said, raising her eyebrows.

"Mr. Forbes's bartender is known for his memory. That's how he builds his connections. That fellow, Simeon, wouldn't have forgotten your name, leading me to assume it's not the first, unless you're grabbing the second round, then I'd be making a fool of myself."

Vida held her drink higher. "I see you have a taste for detail as well."

"If not, many prominent families wouldn't have attended this evening."

Vida lifted the glass to her lips, enjoying the sweet, sharp flavor. Dr. Gray eyed her, tilting his head as she set the drink down with observing eyes.

Vida looked for Aleksandar, who stood on the balcony.

"Any other abilities?" the doctor asked.

"Just a simple nurse. I imagine it's nothing compared to your abilities."

"Oh, I'm not sure about that. I'm not one to save lives like most in my family. You could say I am an… artist in my craft. Most of my work is cosmetic, but there's some nobility when my skills become necessary. I help those who look in a mirror and don't want to feel dreadful about themselves. You'll see a lot of my work here, and if you can't tell, then I performed my purpose with precision."

Vida eyed him with a stern gaze and peered to the ballroom, her corset pulling against her ribs. She checked the faces of aristocrats but saw nothing unnatural. Some nobles were without arms, but nothing uncommon, no other scars in sight.

"Miss Harvey, I have an eye for many practices," Dr. Gray said. "The way you lifted the glass, how you drank from it, how you set it down, it tells me you have an impairment. If my prognosis is correct, you have a scar on the inside crest of your palm, lining your thumb."

The conversations, the musicians' ballad, all dimmed to silence in Vida's ears. She held her gaze to the mirror behind the bar, focusing on her reflection. She held her hand still as she glanced at her glove, finding no bulge or sign of what was underneath. The cooling sensation of the drink on her fingertips was the only comfort as his eyes weighed on her.

Vida took another drink and ignored his observation.

"One of my more recent studies, Miss Harvey, is scar revision," Dr. Gray said. "Because of the dangers and cost of the procedure, I have limited clientele, often to those few who can afford it. However, as my team and I improve, we hope to bring it to more than just the aristocratic elite, but those affected by the Black Harvest and victims of the unfortunate. While my focus is facial reconstruction, the restrictions of scars are similar. Yours seems moderate, possible flare-ups over a consistent affliction, perhaps. How have you continued in a profession such as yours, where they would not indulge you because of your hand?"

Vida refused to make eye contact with him. She stared into the mirror, making sure she did not give him the satisfaction to any degree. "That sounds like an intriguing field."

Dr. Gray stretched his arms, his shoulders cracking as he stood astutely. "Pardon me, miss. I do forget myself. My passion can lead me to overindulge in my craft." He rubbed his fingers. "Tell me, though, was I wrong in my assessment?"

"I am sorry, Dr. Gray, but you are mistaken," Vida said, her mouth dry.

"Of course. My apologies," the doctor said.

Aleksandar stood as aristocrats tapped him on the shoulders, hugging him and smothering him with their affection. With the pull of a lever, he had become the most interesting gentleman in Well's Peake. He held his hands up in appreciation, trying to walk into the crowd, but Kenneth pulled him close.

"Mr. Scott, let me introduce you to Sir Malcolm, famous adventurer of fabled lands and distant oceans," Kenneth said, turning Aleksandar to an older man. "This is the man who planted his family crest on the top of the Amundsen Peak with nothing more than his grit and revered machismo."

Sir Malcolm shook Aleksandar's hand. "My lad, you are quite the entrepreneur yourself, in your own profession, that is."

"Yes, Amundsen Peak? I've never heard of it. Is it in the Northern Forests?" Aleksandar said.

Sir Malcolm tilted his head, his brows reaching for his receding hairline. "Surely, you have heard. It's *thee* mountain of the Eastern Mountains. All wish to reach its summit and stake claim to the infamous title."

"Excuse me, but I'm not familiar." Aleksandar rubbed the bottom of his jacket.

Sir Malcolm stared and broke into a forced laugh. "Oh, that's all right, my boy, but enough about me, what about you? This incredible talent must have stemmed from studying under an esteemed inventor. Did you study under Johannes, Szalinski, or perhaps Hargreaves? Do tell."

"I never... had a mentor either." Aleksandar rubbed his neck.

"Oh." Sir Malcolm leaned back, rubbing his graying goatee. "Did you go to secondary?"

"I did, yes." Aleksandar's palms grew sweaty.

"There we are, at last. You must have gone to Lexford or Grantham for sure. My parents were professors at both."

Aleksandar stood rigid but moved his head. "I... went to Blackwell."

Sir Malcolm tapped his silver cane on the floor and nodded. "Oh. Well, Kenneth, you have another intellectual here. That's for sure."

Kenneth waved his palm in Aleksandar's direction. "Sir Malcolm, Aleksandar here is not used to our... prerogative state. Give him a little while, and he'll warm up."

"Right. Mr. Scott, good day." Sir Malcolm nodded and turned away.

"Yes, you too, sir." Aleksandar extended his hand but pulled it back when Sir Malcolm did not notice, walking away as he mumbled under his breath.

Kenneth glanced at him with wide eyes. "Nervous, my young inventor?"

"Maybe. I should go fetch myself a drink."

"Why in such a hurry, Aleksandar? There are many prominent families I *must* present you to," Kenneth said with a grin.

"I'm sorry, Mr. Forbes. I want to check in with my friend. She's waiting for me and was kind enough to say yes to my invitation."

"But, Aleksandar."

Amia stepped forward, placing her hand on her husband's chest. "Aleksandar, I am with you. We pressured you into bringing a nice young lady, and she is much more important than the stuffy men my husband has in mind for you. He can introduce you another night."

"Not so fast, love," Kenneth said. "Aleksandar may return to her on one condition. I want to know who she is."

Aleksandar searched the crowd for Vida amongst the faces. She was still at the bar, conversing with a gray-suited gentleman, taking a sip of her drink.

Aleksandar pointed, hoping not to draw too much attention to himself. "Miss Harvey is the woman conversing with the man at the bar, setting down her drink."

Kenneth and Amia looked and smiled, whispering to each other.

"She is beautiful," Amia said. "I'd return to her this minute. The good doctor is quite the charmer."

"I will return right away then. Thank you again for everything. I didn't realize what would come from all this when you invited me."

"It was the least I could do," Kenneth said. "Now go before I change my mind. Oh, wait!"

Kenneth reached into his pocket and pulled out a red bag with a golden cord. He held it to Aleksandar, who took it with a smile.

"A few gifts for your hard work." Kenneth smiled.

Aleksandar opened the bag, and inside was enough coin to support himself for a year and a pocket watch with a red tint. He smiled, feeling a rush of warmth through his chest. "Thank you, Mr. Forbes."

"You deserve it."

Amia held her hand out, and Aleksandar took it. She pulled him close enough to whisper in his ear. "Be sure to fix your tie, Aleksandar. A woman loves a sharp-dressed man."

Aleksandar looked to her, her lavender perfume at the perfect balance. "Thank you, Mrs. Forbes. I'll do so."

Aleksandar shifted through the crowd as if he were dancing, trying not to hit anyone as several conversed about the spouts of fire, waving with praise towards the young inventor. He moved back to the bar, where Vida stood looking in the mirror.

"Of course. My apologies," the doctor said.

"Just remember your manners," Vida said.

"Hello, Miss Harvey," Aleksandar said. "I'm sorry to keep you waiting. Kenneth was insistent—"

"Aleksandar! If you drink it fast enough, you might savor the flavor before it gets too warm." Vida picked up his champagne by the rim and handed it to him.

Aleksandar grabbed the glass and took a sip, rich in berries with a zest not common in northern drinks.

"Mr. Scott, meet Dr. Gray." Vida motioned to the doctor. "He's an esteemed physician in the Heron Province. Most sociable."

"Thank you for the introduction, Miss Harvey, but it's unnecessary," Dr. Gray said.

Aleksandar and Dr. Gray shook hands, and Aleksandar pressed his lips, thrown off by the man's sturdy handshake.

"Ah, Mr. Forbes's guest of the evening." Dr. Gray opened his palms.

"Yes, sir," Aleksandar said, shaking the sensation into his fingers.

"Quite the impressive addition you've built. You must be proud."

"I am, thank you. Although I'm not used to this type of attention." Aleksandar's mind flashed back to Amia, uneasy. He touched his chest and remembered. "Pardon me, but may I step away for a moment? I should fix my tie."

Vida set her glass down and put her palm on his arm. "I suppose. I will be waiting."

"Be right back." Aleksandar took off.

Aleksandar made his way through the crowd, under the staircase, and into a hallway with red carpet and white molding. He spotted a mirror, put his drink on an oak credenza, and attempted to straighten his tie. He struggled with the silk, untying it as he fought to retie it.

As his back tensed, he sighed and stretched his neck, squinting as the candlelight kissed his cheek.

"May I help you?"

Aleksandar turned to a stunning voice. A woman with a soft smile and braided brown hair that rested over one shoulder looked to him with eyes rich, like fresh amber.

"Um, yes. I think I might need it," Aleksandar said.

Walking up without the slightest hesitation, she grabbed his tie and wrapped it tightly through the loop as if the motion was second nature.

"Just remember, the rabbit runs around the tree twice before she returns home."

Just remember.

Alexander's thoughts faded, and he did not catch the rest of what she said, fascinated with her pleasant voice. It was as if part of her soul flowed around her words, like honey in the bloom season. Aleksandar found himself lost, looking dumbfounded as she stared back with her soft smile. She was close enough to where her vanilla perfume lingered, as exquisite as when he walked into Kenneth's home.

"Thank you," he said. "I appreciate it."

"My pleasure."

Aleksandar tried to speak, but he only chuckled, and she tilted her head with a smirk.

"My, ugh, my name is Aleksandar Scott." He blurted out.

"It is nice to meet you, Aleksandar Scott. I'm Ellie Fritz." She grabbed the tie again and angled it. "That's better. You're set to go."

"Thank you." Aleksandar couldn't help but make a bashful grin.

Ellie returned the smile and held her finger up. "You're the inventor?"

"I am. I'm afraid I don't know who you are."

"That's okay. My brothers are my invitation. You may have heard of them. They run Fritz and Co."

"The gear company? They create all the gears."

"They do."

"That's incredible. I use their parts in my inventions."

"I hear that often. Yes, they were smart and took over our father's business while I was off walking a different path."

"Oh, what road was that?"

"I was a traveler."

Aleksandar hesitated, the rumors he heard as a kid popping into his thoughts, that travelers were smelly, lived off the land and dirt, never wishing to step foot in a city. Ellie didn't seem like any of those things. "I'm sorry, I didn't mean to hesitate."

"It's okay. Unexpected, I know, and not very ladylike of me to be mentioning at the Harvest Gala, but I couldn't help myself. Living a nomadic lifestyle was peaceful. Not exactly one to fit in with the people here tonight, though. I took after my mother and wandered the Eastern Mountains. After a few years, I realized I had more of my father's blood in me, so I came home. Here I am."

"Do travelers come back often?"

"Not all, but most. It's not as taboo as everyone thinks. You essentially sleep in the woods for months on end and travel roads like those before you. You learn some handy life skills, though. Want to see?" Ellie stepped forward, a few inches from Aleksandar, and he gulped. "Watch this."

Ellie held her clenched palm in the air, holding a wallet. Aleksandar laughed and checked his pocket, his smile going blank.

His stomach fluttered, and his heart raced.

Ellie smiled and handed him his wallet. "Sleight of hand. Useful for more than picking wallets."

"I'll have to remember to check my pocket before I leave."

"I would. You never know."

They both laughed, and Aleksandar watched her pull on her braid.

"You don't seem like the others here," Aleksandar said.

"Neither do you. Is that a bad thing?"

"No, it's refreshing, to be honest. Many here are too sophisticated for me. Do you plan on leaving soon?"

"I didn't plan on it. Did you have something in mind?"

"Well, it seems like both of us realized we aren't quite at the same standing as the rest here."

"I would agree."

"And if you didn't have any other plans, maybe you would like to join me?"

"Oh? Would we stand in the corner and watch the fancy people?"

Aleksandar laughed. "Perhaps a dance. I'm not very good, but I can try."

Ellie leaned in with an open smile as white as snow. "Mr. Scott, do you fancy me?"

Aleksandar let out a nervous laugh. "I, uh, did not expect you to ask that. Yes, I do. How about I introduce you to a friend of mine? She came with me but was insistent I find someone else—"

"I'd love to. Lead the way."

Ellie held out her arm, and Aleksandar paused.

She leaned in. "I was mimicking what you should be doing."

Aleksandar's smile grew as he stuck out his elbow, and Ellie slipped her arm into his, and they returned to the gala.

Vida strutted around the ballroom, taking an interest in anything that wasn't Dr. Gray. In the vases of polished marble, the statues of horses that were elegant yet simple, or the over-indulged drinker whose wife kept waving off others, saying he was fine.

The lights of hundreds of candles caught her eye as they shone in glittering perfection, their glow enough to illuminate the ballroom. Vida looked past several people to Aleksandar, who walked towards her with a woman on his arm.

"Miss Harvey, I hope I didn't keep you waiting," Aleksandar said. "I met someone when I went to fix my tie."

"Ah, so you took my advice." Vida smirked.

"Vida Harvey, this is Ellie Fritz."

Ellie extended her hand, and Vida returned the gesture.

"A pleasure, Miss Harvey," Ellie said.

Her soft voice captured Vida's attention, as beautiful as it was to watch the candles' flames shift in the wind.

"As to you," Vida said. "I'm glad Mr. Scott found a charming young lady to talk to."

"He was subtle. Perhaps nervous and obvious, but subtle nonetheless."

"Well, that sounds like Mr. Scott."

The ladies laughed, and Aleksandar blushed, staring at both of them.

"Wait a second. Are you the sister of the Fritz brothers?" Vida asked.

"That's right."

"That is amazing. I never knew who their sister was."

"Most don't. I wasn't in the picture when they took over. So, I feel I've overstepped tonight. How do you two know each other?"

Aleksandar stepped in. "Miss Harvey is a friend of mine. I invited her for helping me out these past few weeks after some hard situations."

"Well, isn't that sweet? Miss Harvey here seems like a charming girl. I'm surprised you have not asked her to dance. She is your date, after all," Ellie said.

Vida smiled and let out a girlish laugh. "Mr. Scott is sweet but just a friend."

"I'm kind of excited to hear that."

"If Aleksandar asked you to dance, then please do. There is plenty for me to occupy myself with, and worst case, my escort home is available."

"Are you sure?" Aleksandar asked.

"Yes. I'm busy keeping Dr. Gray off my arm anyway. My hands are full." Vida took a large swig of wine and smiled, bringing a smile to Ellie's and Aleksandar's faces.

"If you insist. If you leave, let me know so I can walk you out."

"That I will. Now shoo and have fun. It was a pleasure to meet you, Miss Fritz. I feel I'll be seeing you again."

"The same, Miss Harvey." Ellie smiled.

Aleksandar extended his elbow, and Ellie slipped her hand in, chatting as they walked away. Stepping onto the dance floor, Ellie looked to his feet, and they danced, Aleksandar stumbling over himself.

Vida chuckled. "Best of luck, Mr. Scott."

She turned around, spotting Dr. Gray heading in her direction with a refill of champagne. She gulped the rest of her drink and strolled away, setting the glass on a butler's tray. Her hand caught the edge, and her glove ripped at the seam. She paused and covered her palm, looking to see if anyone noticed.

"Madam, my apologizes," the butler said, reaching out.

"That's all right," she said. "If we speak of it no more, I would appreciate it."

The butler stopped, his brow high, and Vida paced out of the ballroom. She hurried through the hallway and onto Kenneth's front steps.

A few nobles wandered about, but it was quiet, music muffled by the house's walls. Vida, relieved to be invisible again, preferred the trees and stars than to stand alone in a crowd of those who did not see her.

A couple held each other tight, laughing under their visible breath as they strolled behind her, heading to a carriage. Vida walked down the stairs and across the brick path, making her way to the front of the archway as the hemlocks grew thick against the road.

She strained her face to keep a smile and pulled off her glove, her scarred hand illuminated under the moonlight. She rubbed her fingers and her thumb, looking for any comfort or relief, finding no pain in it.

"Miss Harvey, you ran—"

"Goodness, Dr. Gray." Vida crossed her arms, hiding her exposed hand.

Dr. Gray paused. "I did not mean to frighten you. I wanted to apologize if I offended you earlier because I know I have an unpleasant habit of rambling and forgetting myself."

"No, you did not. I'm sorry. You just surprised me, is all." Vida held her hand, the doctor looking at it. "You're staring."

"May I see?"

"No."

Dr. Gray looked away, putting his palms in his pocket. "How about an offer instead?"

"I said no."

"You let me examine your hand—"

"What did I just say?" Vida's pulse raced, feeling it throb in her hand.

"I'll make sure your recommendation letter gets to the right people."

Vida stared, swallowing hard. "You know about my letters?"

"I'm on the board. You are a persistent one, and I can appreciate that."

"Why would you want to help me?"

"If it makes you feel better, I'm doing this for my own curiosity."

Vida tilted her head. "You think you could persuade them to approve my application?"

"I do. Is it worth the exchange for me to examine your hand?"

Vida stared at the man, her blood boiling, her temples throbbing. His suave was working, and she didn't want to let him have that satisfaction.

With a deep exhale, she stuck out her hand, and Dr. Gray pulled out a pair of glasses, looking at it with precision. His hands were soft, and he ran his finger along her palm, across the scar that had been there for years.

"A burn, correct?" he asked.

"Yes."

"No work done. Natural healing. Amazing how little it has affected your movement, but you can feel the tension." Dr. Gray pulled on her fingers, squeezed her wrist, and let go. "Thank you."

Vida folded her arms, and Dr. Gray tucked his glasses away. He nodded, slid his hands in his pockets, and walked up the road.

"Where are you going?" she asked.

"Back to the gala. Be sure to submit your application in the morning at Blackwell. Have a pleasant evening, Miss Harvey."

Vida let out a deep breath into the air, seeing it in the chilly night, noticing the goosebumps on her arm. She slipped the torn glove over her hand.

Just like that? Not another word?

With a nod of her head, she looked down the line of horses and carriages. She spotted the red-haired horse and Edwin with his gray mustache looking her way, brushing the horse's coat. With a smile, she walked to the gentleman.

"Miss Harvey, did you enjoy your evening?" Edwin asked.

"I did, thank you. I'm sorry to leave you out here."

"Oh, that's all right. I enjoy the horse's company. I grew up on the ranch myself."

"You must tell me more. Perhaps we can take the long road home?"

"As you wish, Miss Harvey. I hear the park is exquisite with the World's Fair at its back. Shall we?"

Edwin held out his arm, and Vida took it and let him guide her into the carriage, the horse neighing as she sat. He stepped up to his seat, and with a snap of the reins, the mare trotted off, leading them into the late night under the stars.

∾

Aleksandar and Ellie danced around the ballroom, the chandelier lighting their way between the aristocrats and servers. Violas and cellos sang through the air, and Kenneth and Amia nodded to him as they passed, Aleksandar unable to hide his smile with Ellie in his arms.

"You are a quick learner," Ellie said.

"Thank you," Aleksandar said. "I'd like to think so."

"Or maybe you have an excellent teacher." Ellie smiled, locking eyes with him.

"Indeed. I think it might be the latter."

They twirled across the dance floor, and the ensemble played their last note with flair. Aleksandar clapped with the rest, noticing Ellie glancing in his direction. While he thought his invention was what he wanted most, little did he expect what fate had for him.

The orchestra started a ballad, many putting their instruments on their lap, leaving only a few playing.

Ellie held up her arms, and Aleksandar mirrored her, and they shifted in a slow circle.

"She was charming, Mr. Scott," Ellie said.

"Miss Harvey? Yes. She has a good heart and amazing advice."

"That's always good. After our dance, I will have to introduce you to my brothers before I return you to her." Ellie moved to the side, avoiding Aleksandar's feet. "Have you danced much?"

"Maybe not to this caliber."

"Follow with your shoulders forward, so they think you're leading."

Ellie broke her pose and pulled Aleksandar towards her. He glanced over as a couple watched him with judgmental glares, snickering under their breath.

"Am I looking to impress someone?" Aleksandar asked.

"Well, that's up to you. If you don't mind me leading and looking like you don't, then you can follow and enjoy yourself."

Aleksandar adjusted his weak pose, straightened his back, and pressed his palm on her hip, her dress smooth against his fingertips.

Ellie peeked over her shoulder, eyeing her brothers, who spoke with Bernard and other prominent figures.

Aleksandar noticed and looked at her. "Are you close with your brothers?"

"Not exactly. I don't care too often about what they think anymore. They insist I follow the path of an aristocratic woman. While I have no issues with the lifestyle, it's not what I want. I prefer things to happen naturally and for people to follow their own paths. Like meeting you tonight, at the Harvest Gala, the most prestigious event of the year. We wouldn't be at Kenneth Forbes's estate on any other night, would we?"

"Do I look like I don't belong?"

"You do, and they enjoy your ruggedness because you are the guest of honor, but it's your mannerisms that give you away. Makes me think you're a little more in tune with yourself and not into whatever image these people fake."

Aleksandar grinned, and Ellie smiled.

"I'm not being proper, am I?" she asked.

"I would call it being honest. I prefer it."

Aleksandar could not help himself. His hand on her hip, her vanilla perfume, her down-to-earth outlook on life, it was captivating.

"I feel you have something to say," she said.

Aleksandar patted his lips. "No, I just am enjoying myself. I haven't, well, tried to court anyone for a while. You seem to have many attractive traits from the fifteen minutes I've known you."

Ellie let out a loud laugh before covering her mouth to contain herself, and Aleksandar couldn't hold back his smile as he looked at several couples watching them.

"That was bold, Mr. Scott, but amusing," she said. "I think you are rather handsome myself."

"If we are being bold, I got an idea," Aleksandar said.

"Oh?"

Aleksandar held on to her hand and led her onto the balcony, to the control arm for the Red Breath. Several people watched them, and he nodded to her, excited for her to see.

"You want me to?" Ellie asked.

"I do. You don't think they would mind, right?" he asked.

"Um, didn't you invent it?"

"You have a point. Let's make this a night to remember, Miss Fritz."

Ellie grabbed Aleksandar's hand and placed it under hers on the lever.

"Together?"

"Together."

Aleksandar and Ellie pulled the lever, and fire erupted into the late harvest air. The warmth hit his face, but it paled compared to what he felt towards her.

The flames, the applauding crowd, and the starry night, but the only thing he could focus on was Ellie's hand on his and her brown eyes looking into his.

CHAPTER TWENTY-SEVEN

The crisp night set on the empty streets of the South Hills, thinning as the temperature dropped to a bitter degree. Hugh took a hard breath, his lungs aching, the air as sharp as ice. It nicked his bare skin that his ragged clothes did not cover.

The chill remained, interrupted by bursts of fire from Kenneth's manor on the horizon, the red light glowing against the few clouds above the city rooftops. Shadows were long, and the gaslights on the street did not reach far into the alley.

The flames reflected in Hugh's eyes, and he swore he felt the heat once or twice, but he knew it was most likely his or Abbey's breath. He looked at her as she watched the red burst, her eyes unflinching, her fingertips white on her jacket. Hugh grabbed their last blanket, and he slid across the dirty ground, wrapping it tightly around them.

The icy air grew warmer as they gripped the corners near their feet and clutched them in hand. The blanket reeked of burned coal from the nearby factory and was stained black on the edges.

"Must be some party," Hugh mumbled.

"He's not known for his subtlety." Abbey looked away.

Hugh clenched his jaw, his teeth chattering. "How'd Kenneth end up there, you know?"

"Hugh, I don't want to talk about it."

"I wasn't asking. Just saying."

"It's fine."

Hugh leaned back and kept quiet, having never opened his mouth. The mention of her brother's name robbed her of her smile.

"Tomorrow we should make our way towards the factories," Hugh said. "Perhaps we can find a spot by the boiler shed like last year."

"I'm sure we could, but it might not be this cold the next few weeks. It will be hard getting used to the stink again." Abbey's breath shook.

She wasn't wrong. It took Hugh weeks to clean the smell out of his clothes last year, the taste of coal lingering on his tongue even longer. It reached the point where he could not walk outside South Hills without people gawking, covering their noses with handkerchiefs.

"Maybe there's a place further elsewhere." He rubbed his fingers along the frayed cotton of his jacket.

Abbey never glanced from Kenneth's mansion. Her nose was red, and her lips were to the point of cracking. "We were happy once."

Hugh paused, facing her.

Abbey pulled on the blanket. "Our childhood was hard, but we had each other. Mother, Father, they always looked after us and did what they could. It wasn't until Kenneth got older that things changed. He got greedy, thought he deserved more."

"Abbey, you don't have to."

She shook her head, pulling on her bottom lip.

"I never noticed because I didn't want to," she said. "But Kenneth grew too curious. Every year on his age day, Mother and Father bought him a ticket to see the circus. He was in love with the acrobats. One night after watching the show, he stayed after and convinced someone to teach him. He practiced for hours and talked about how he loved being part of something bigger, thinking he deserved more."

Abbey paused, and Hugh felt her shaking, more than she was without the thicker blanket. He tightened his arm around her, hoping if it was the cold, she would grow warmer.

"Every year, Kenneth asked for a second ticket, and he was okay with not getting another for a while, but one night when he was fourteen, he changed. He turned mad, and his curiosity got the better of him. He disobeyed our parents and searched their bedroom. Kenneth found a purse with enough money in it to feed the family for months. He threw it at Father, called him a liar, a thief. Father only saved because he was in and out of jobs, but Kenneth didn't care. He wanted what he deserved. He took the family fortune."

Hugh's mouth grew dry, and he swallowed. "He sounds—"

"Don't get me wrong, he has his flaws, but he could also be kind. He was always protective of me. He watched over me as long as I can remember." Abbey turned to Hugh. "You can't say anything."

"I won't."

"You promise? I remember you mentioned that one inventor built those things on his house. If you ever run into him, you have to keep my secret."

"I promise, I wouldn't tell him."

Abbey sniffled, and Hugh stared into the night. He could feel her gaze on him.

"I'm sorry," she said. "At least I see my brother."

Hugh held his side under the blanket, the warmth of his belly against his arm. "There are other types of family, Abbey. You have more than just him."

"Hugh, you know I don't."

"Not like that. I mean… family can be more than blood. Nothing could replace your parents and brother, but they change. I see you as my sister. There are a few who adore you for helping them at the boarding house too. I'm sure they think the same. Do you not see me like a brother?"

"I do. I guess I just never said it out loud."

A dog trotted down the alley and stopped, sniffing their feet, licking the edge of the blanket. He barked, Hugh lurched at him, and the animal rushed off.

"My brother makes me think I'm enabling them," Abbey said, "by not letting them learn to take care of themselves, but he doesn't understand. We never had help, and I don't want others to suffer the same."

Bells rang in the distance, and horses' hooves tapped on the cobblestone as they strode by the alleyway.

"You can't let him in your head. You're a good person, and it's easy for others to make us feel less than them, but nothing is black and white."

Abbey leaned on his shoulder. "I wish you were this confident every day."

Hugh coughed, his throat dry.

"May I ask you something else?" Abbey rolled her shoulders.

"Yeah."

"Do you think there's a point? I can change a few lives now, but in the grand scheme of things, is it worth it?"

Hugh sniffled as his nose dripped and his cheeks grew numb. "Yes. Many don't live the life they wish, but you're making it better. Even for a day, it means something. Some can't stand up for themselves, and they need someone else to help, and that isn't their fault. Society has forced us here."

"Kenneth says after they die, what difference will it make?"

"To them, everything."

The two sat in the frigid air, another surge of fire soaring above the rooftops. A thick breeze burst throughout the alleyway, leaves blowing across the ground. Hugh leaned closer to Abbey, tired of the bitter temperatures and the ache in his chest. He rubbed his knuckles on his chin, feeling the wear of living on the streets for so long: the divots and dry skin, the throbs in his hardened bones.

"You know you are, right?" she said.

Hugh arched his back as Abbey looked over, never sitting up. "What?"

"You're the brother I never had. You make me feel as if I mean something to someone. I wished he'd see that."

"Maybe you should stop thinking about him."

"Why would you say that?" Abbey sat up, the blanket stretching apart, the breeze rushing inside.

"Kenneth doesn't seem to care, and he hurts you. Perhaps we can move on with our lives."

Abbey's face scrunched, and she stared at the brick wall, a light fluttering from the side of the street.

Hugh looked away, stretching his eyes wide as they stiffened. "I hate seeing you sad after he comes around."

"You just need me to be your sister because you don't have a family anymore. You're jealous."

Hugh stood up and tucked his fingertips under his armpit, Abbey pulling the blanket tight.

"What if I am?" he said. "Why is it fair you give him your love for him to throw it back in your face? I'd sleep on the street for the rest of my life if it meant seeing my family one last night. For my sister to hug me again and tell me about the places she read about in books, or my parents to tell me they loved me. All Kenneth does is come here to satisfy himself, leaving you behind."

Abbey gazed into her lap, shaking her head. "Will you come back under the blanket? It's cold."

"You sure you want me to?"

"Stop being mean." Abbey looked up, biting her last word.

He stared at her, and she faced away, closing her eyes. Hugh shook his head, the breeze chilling him to the bone.

Abbey was all he had in Well's Peake, and without her, he'd have no one to smile or talk to in the empty nights in South Hills.

"You told me once, we all make mistakes," Abbey said. "We shouldn't give up on someone who's lost their way because that's when they need it the most."

"You think he's in trouble, up there, at the high table?" Hugh asked.

"Yes, from himself. I'm afraid of what will happen to him."

"He seems to do all right."

"He's not okay. That's why he puts on the mask for those prissy people. We don't always have to move on or stay in the past, Hugh."

Hugh sat in front of her, and she hugged him with the blanket.

"I'm your family too, you know." Hugh buried his face in her shoulder.

"I know, Hugh. I know."

A scraping of feet echoed throughout the alley, Hugh flinching as he watched a man and woman paused in the gaslight's shadow. Abbey pulled back, and Hugh stood, hoping to seem taller than he was. The fellow motioned the girl to stay, and he wandered between the buildings with slow steps. Hugh's eyes widened, and he looked to a wooden table leg lying next to his foot.

"Mr. Evans?"

Hugh's gaze went blank as if he'd seen a ghost. The woman whispered something he couldn't hear, and Hugh balled his hands into fists as the shadows rippled across the man.

"It *is* you."

Hugh squinted as the man stepped into the light. Mr. Scott.

"Miss Fritz," Aleksandar said.

Miss Fritz hurried to Aleksandar's side, standing behind his shoulder. "Who is it?"

Abbey looked to the couple, tightening the blanket.

"Mr. Scott? What are you doing here?" Hugh unrolled his fists, slipping them back under his arms.

"I was escorting Miss Fritz home to the high end of the Industrial District. What are you doing in South Hills at this late hour?" Aleksandar glanced to Abbey.

"Ugh, I was helping a friend."

"Why didn't you bring her to your flat?"

Hugh wanted to give every excuse in the book but found none. Like a harvest tree with no leaves, it exposed him to the world.

Miss Fritz eyed the two, putting her hand on Aleksandar's arm. "Aleksandar, I don't think he had that choice."

Aleksandar looked at Hugh. His mouth gaped open. "I'm sorry. I knew you struggled, but I never knew. You never said anything."

"It wouldn't have mattered."

"It would've. There was something that I could've done."

"There wasn't." Hugh pressed his lips, the one side splitting.

"How long have you lived on the streets?"

Hugh had nothing to say. The chill on his neck, his dry, cracked lips… He only needed some warmth and to be alone. The nights were rough, but he'd survived this long without help.

Miss Fritz leaned towards Aleksandar. "Is there anything you can do?"

"Hugh," Aleksandar said. "How about you stay with me this evening? For a few evenings? No one deserves to be outside in this weather."

"You owe me nothing," Hugh said.

"What if he did?" Miss Fritz said.

Hugh looked to Abbey, curled up in the blanket on the ground.

"What if Mr. Scott offered you an apprenticeship?" Miss Fritz said.

Aleksandar folded his arms. "Yes. As a master, I'd be obligated to offer you shelter. I have a spare room with a cot you can sleep on. It's not fancy, but it's inside."

Hugh's eyes shimmered, a small warmth within him fighting the crisp air.

"I thought you couldn't teach me?" Hugh asked.

"A lot has changed over the past weeks, and I have found my footing. I'm picking up some things I left behind. I can tutor you again if you wish."

"If I take your offer, you'd make me come live with you?"

Aleksandar tilted his head. "You don't have to, but I wouldn't want you to be on the streets either."

Hugh stepped beside Abbey. "I won't leave her here. We've made it this far because of each other, and that can't change."

Miss Fritz covered her mouth, pulling her coat taut.

Aleksandar looked at Abbey, who glanced at him. "What is your name?"

"Abbey." She pulled her blanket tighter.

Hugh wondered as Aleksandar reached into his pocket. He pulled out Kenneth's gift and put the watch in his jacket, along with some coin.

Aleksandar crouched and held the bag to Abbey as she kept her arms beneath the blanket, eyeing him. Her hand slipped out and touched the coin, pulling back. Aleksandar pushed it into her palm and closed her fingers around it. Abbey shook her head.

"There's enough here for you to stay at the Ocean's Hotel in Bedston. It's close to my flat. You could stay there for months."

"No, no, I can't." Abbey tried to push the pouch away.

"This is a gift. Please take it." Aleksandar let go, leaving Abbey to hold it between her fingers.

Abbey shook, whether from the frost or Aleksandar's gesture, Hugh couldn't tell. He wished he knew what Abbey was thinking, but with the money in her hand, he was unsure, knowing she was used to little.

"I can teach you." Aleksandar stood to Hugh. "I hope you know; I never thought little of you. After the robbery, I wasn't mentally there and needed to recover."

Hugh looked to Aleksandar and kneeled beside Abbey. Her breath hit his, and he pulled her blanket tight.

"Hugh, this is your dream," Abbey said. "It hurt you when you lost this chance, but it's here again. Do it for me."

"You said you didn't want to leave the past behind," Hugh said.

"No, but I'm not going to stop us from our future. Please do this, and if you do, I promise I'll go to the hotel. You can walk me there."

Hugh looked at the ground, the cobblestone riddled with dirt. Abbey did not deserve to have her life moved because of him and his childish dream. He knew it was too late to be an inventor, so why ruin her dreams? She was too busy doing everything for everyone else; the least he could do was what she wanted.

Abbey stood, grabbing Hugh's arms and wrapping them around her. She removed her scarf and slipped it around his neck, patting him on the chest.

Hugh held Abbey as she placed her cheek against his chest. He closed his eyes for a moment and opened them to Aleksandar with Miss Fritz at his side. With a shivering breath, he nodded to the young inventor.

∼

The snowy night grew into a frozen one, the cobblestone turning white as frost settled. Aleksandar paced down the sidewalk, crouched with his arm around Ellie on the quiet street.

Brick and marble apartment buildings lined the road, iron fences separating them from the trees bristling in the wind, leaves drifting at their feet. Despite his throbbing fingertips, having Ellie in his arms, his warmth against hers made up for it all.

"I disagree, Mr. Scott," Ellie said.

"I can't accept that." Aleksandar sniffled.

"And why not?"

"Because jasmine tea is best."

"It's too strong."

"That's because you're letting it steep too long."

"You should try plum, and then we can have this creative discussion. I'm not a fan of fruity teas, but this brew kept warm with a single candle underneath will make you a believer." Ellie leaned into him.

Aleksandar chuckled. "Just when I thought we were hitting it off. I could use a cup of tea right now."

"Looks like this could be the end."

Aleksandar knew she was joking, but he didn't want her to in the slightest. She was cunning and sweet, down to earth, and her voice was tender and smooth. The joke hurt more than it should.

"That was a generous thing you did for Mr. Evans and his friend," Ellie said. "What was her name again?"

"Abbey, I believe," Aleksandar said.

"Still, it was nice. They seem very close. Extended family is important to me, and while mine was here in Well's Peake, I had another on the roads. I could see their bond."

"I'm bothered he said nothing to me. In the least, I should have noticed."

"You can't blame yourself for not knowing, and you shouldn't be upset. Surely, there are things you don't tell people when you first meet them."

"Of course, but—"

"Exactly. Did you ever find Miss Harvey before we left?"

"No. I waited at the bar for her and searched the entire house. The carriage was gone, so I assume she went home. Hopefully, she made it back safely."

"She looked more than capable. I wouldn't worry."

They crossed the street, passing a lantern lighter.

"Mr. Scott, there was no need to escort me. I've walked these streets by my lonesome before, and I appear to be holding off the cold better than you." Ellie grabbed her wool scarf and tightened it around her.

"I assumed, but I enjoy your company. I'm also trying to build up my courage to ask for another night on the town."

Ellie slowed her pace and stopped in front of a large townhouse, and smiled, nodding her head to the household. "This is me."

Aleksandar held her gloved hands. Her cheeks were rosy, but he'd like to think it was because she felt the same way he did, and her smile was tight-lipped but cute. She looked elegant, even though her braid was stuffed under her hat, stiff from the cold. Even in the late night, he did not shiver, as a sense of calm flooded him with warmth.

He laughed, not sure how long he had stood there, Ellie batting him an eye.

"It's too warm out here for me," Ellie said.

Aleksandar swallowed, and he leaned in. Ellie mimicked him but stopped as she held his wallet. They both smiled, and she rushed in, kissing him on the cheek. Aleksandar grabbed his wallet, and Ellie glanced down, blushing.

"Will you call on me again?" she asked.

"I would like that," Aleksandar said.

"As would I. Don't wait too long."

"I won't. Good night, Miss Fritz."

"As to you, Mr. Scott."

Not wanting to leave, Aleksandar stepped away, but she did not let go, holding him back. Aleksandar looked over his shoulder, and they stared at each other, her smile vivid and white.

Ellie walked away and up the steps, entering her home. Aleksandar watched as she peeked through the door window, laughing when caught.

He took a deep breath and rubbed his hands together, turning onto the street. Breathing in the frosty air, he coughed in the cold. He strolled down the sidewalk and paused, putting his hand in his back pocket, his wallet still in place.

I wish it wasn't there.

With a tune in his head, Aleksandar hummed as his scarf brushed against his jacket, not ready for the night to end.

∾

The door opened, and Shae perked up, noticing her master come in with another. She stood straight until she spotted Hugh in the doorway, looking around the flat with a small bag over his shoulder. She arched her wings as Hugh closed the door, attempting a cute but defensive stance.

The house air was warmer compared to the outside, even without a fire burning. Hugh rubbed his fingertips as they tingled from the change in temperature.

"Did your friend make it to the hotel okay?" Aleksandar asked.

"Yes, thank you. I'll see her in the morning." Hugh pulled off his ragged scarf.

"There's a spare hook on the rack. You can hang your things there, and there's a room for you upstairs. It's a little cluttered, but the cot is decent."

Hugh looked to Shae as she patted towards him with large steps. She tilted her head and hissed, wings spread. Aleksandar grabbed the brace next to the door and fitted it onto his arm.

"Come here, girl," Aleksandar said.

"You have an owl?" Hugh asked.

Shae flew off the ground and landed on the guard.

"I do. Shae, this is our guest. You will not bite, or scratch, or hiss, or anything else you think is amusing. Is that understood?"

Shae looked at Hugh and twisted her head upside down.

"You should be fine, Mr. Evans. Let me show you to your room."

Aleksandar grabbed a lantern, and Shae flew off. He led Hugh up the stairs to the first bedroom on the right. They walked through the door to a cot and two stacked bookcases filled with slanted books, random pieces of metal, and an old birdcage.

"I hope this is okay." Aleksandar set the lantern on the nightstand.

Hugh walked to the center of the bedroom, looking at the bed.

"Thank you, Mr. Scott."

"You're welcome. Well, I'll let you make yourself at home. Would you care for some tea?"

"Thanks."

"I'll put on the kettle. Come down when you're ready."

Hugh stood there as Aleksandar left the room, his footsteps creaking on the staircase. Closing the door, Hugh stepped to the cot, set his bag on the floor, and sat on the edge. He rubbed his hands on the blanket, the wool warm against his fingertips. The feathers in the bedding underneath were soft, unlike any bed he could remember.

His skin wasn't aching from the bitter frost, and he couldn't see his breath in the air.

Wallpaper surrounded him, not brick or stone, and the floor was clean, not cluttered with trash and dirt. His thoughts lingered on Abbey, and Hugh lifted the scarf around his neck and held it against his face.

He looked at the lantern's flame with a simple, teary-eyed smile, wishing she was at his side.

CHAPTER TWENTY-EIGHT

Maple trees rocked in the gentle wind along the cobblestone street, painting it red, orange, and auburn with leaves. Aleksandar brushed through the foliage, carrying a leather tube over his shoulder, his hair rippling back as he paced up the walkway.

The cool morning warmed as the sun rose over the horizon, not as bitter as the previous night. Aleksandar did not remember the chill or the gala, only Ellie. While he wanted to think about her, he knew he had to focus on his opportunity with Natalia.

Aleksandar breathed in the clear air, unlike that which stunk near his home, lingering in from the South Hills. Instead, it smelled like bakeries who just removed pumpkin rolls and fresh lemon bread from the oven, leaving the windows open for a passerby to enjoy.

Aleksandar pulled out a piece of paper with Natalia's address.

4691 Old Makepeace Lane.

He looked to a mailbox at the end of a stone driveway with 'forty-six ninety-one' written on the side. The front garden was well maintained, with colorful maidenhair ferns, groomed hedges, and the forest blocking the house. A grand iron fence with spikes surrounded the estate.

Aleksandar strolled the hand-carved path, redwood trees rising around him. A green lawn with leaves pushed back to the forest roots came into view as the road widened. A white brick home with a tint of blue stood two stories high. Four pillars rose from the raised porch to the second-story archway with a smoking chimney built on the side.

Aleksandar walked up the steps and grabbed the bronze knocker, tapping it. Someone shuffled within but fell silent.

Aleksandar rocked back and forth and lifted his hand, ready to knock again, clearing his throat. He reached, but Natalia opened the door and stood in the entryway with a blue vest with silver stitching. Her sleeves were snow white, rolled perfectly to her elbows, her tie loose under her popped collar and black hair.

"Mr. Scott. Please, come in." Natalia stepped aside.

"Thank you. Good morning." Aleksandar unbuttoned his coat as he walked into the living room.

"There's a rack on the left for your scarf and jacket. You'll be more than comfortable inside."

"My goodness, it's so warm in here. Is this your work?"

"It is a system I invented because I'm always cold. I used my chimney, a pipe that transfers heat effectively, and lined it through the floors. With ingenuity and the proper materials, it has become one of my pride and joys. Too expensive to put in all homes, though."

"That's ingenious." Aleksandar pulled off his coat, setting the leather tube against the wall.

Natalia smiled as the young inventor hung his belongings on the hook. Aleksandar's tweed vest matched his lighter-shaded pants, and he hoped his sophistication matched that of his host.

"May I bring you a cup of tea or a glass of water?" Natalia asked.

"Either would be delightful. Thank you." Aleksandar picked up the leather tube.

"I just finished heating a kettle. Follow me."

Natalia headed into the kitchen as Aleksandar followed through the living room, which was well lit with the morning light through the broad windows.

"That is quite the exquisite vest, Mr. Scott," Natalia said. "Was that recently tailored?"

"Indeed. I thought it appropriate, considering I'd be working with an esteemed inventor. It was finished this morning."

"Well, when you see him next, be sure to tell him his stitch work is robust."

"Actually, that would be me. I did the alterations."

Natalia smiled. "Most impressive, Mr. Scott."

Connecting from the floor to the ceiling was a wet stone, baroque and rough. Water flowed from a chute in the beam, rippling in waves and foam, splashing against small rocks at the bottom. Dark rugs covered the pine floor, making him feel like he was standing in the forest.

Someone coughed, and Aleksandar jerked around to see Natalia leaning out of the kitchen.

"I seem to have lost you along the way," she said.

Aleksandar walked to her. "Your house is incredible, Miss Arlen. How did you move this water stone into the living room?"

"Very carefully. If the house impresses you, wait until you see what's off the back balcony."

Natalia handed Aleksandar his tea, and they walked out the kitchen and onto the redwood deck. The forest dipped into a valley that extended to the rolling hills with only trees in sight. Aleksandar leaned on the railing, a thunderous roar drawing him to the cliff next to the house.

Wow.

A gushing waterfall poured out of the rocks into the river at the bottom of the ravine. Mist wandered through the air, filling Aleksandar's nostrils with a woodsy aroma, his skin getting damp.

It was amazing, more than he could have imagined. The ingenuity of Natalia's home and the inspiration from nature made Aleksandar envious to be away from the carriages on cobblestones and the crowd of the World's Fair. He paused and listened to the roar of the falls, smelling the clean breeze from the forest.

"Where did you discover such a place?" Aleksandar said.

"I built it. The waterfall and formations were already here. I just needed to figure a way of digging into the rock, and I accomplished that with compressed air by using a waterwheel." Natalia batted a smile. "This is one of my greatest inspirations: the weight, the elegance, the force. If we made decisions with those qualities with every step, Well's Peake would be transformed. If only we were unrestricted like nature."

Aleksandar let the mist brush against his clean-shaven chin, a welcome change from the smog of the city. He remembered his tea and took a sip, blueberries from the harvest.

Natalia walked to the edge. "So, Aleksandar, tell me why you invent."

"For others. Some never get their chance to follow an inventor's dream, so I do it for them. Do you believe we'd be better off with no restrictions?"

Natalia ran her palm on the railing. "I don't have that answer, but what I do know is our only restraint is nature itself. Hesitation comes with being human, and that can be a strength and a weakness. I would love to see a future with no limits, where we excel to no ends."

Aleksandar walked away from the mist, sipping his tea. "Is this a test?"

There was something different about Natalia. She was inquisitive, looking to him as if he were a painting to be studied and debated. Her pale-moon eyes relaxed, and her smile softened.

Natalia tilted her head. "Is that inappropriate of me? We are two minds of the same kind, yet we think differently. I'm not per se testing you as much as I wish to learn about your philosophy on inventing. Would you say humanity can reach too far?"

Aleksandar rubbed the lip of the teacup. "Yes. Humanity's grasp has exceeded itself in the past. Imagine what would happen if we interfered with the laws of nature. To manipulate those laws, some people fear we will break them."

"Yet, you work with the elements?"

"I don't think I'm bending what would crack."

"Nature would not let us if we tried."

"So, what happens when we invent something that does more damage than the Black Harvest? When do we take responsibility before the next tragedy?"

Natalia rubbed her hands together. "You ask the good questions, Mr.

Scott. We could spend days on this balcony speculating, but how about we move downstairs to the workshop and ponder the near future instead?"

"Your house goes into the rock?"

Natalia batted her eyes and waved for Aleksandar to follow.

Natalia walked inside and opened a door to a grand staircase leading below. A ramp followed the steps, and walls shifted from wood paneling to hand-cut stone.

Aleksandar walked through the bottom archway, and light reflected off the waterfall outside, cascading through the windows with the morning's rays. A dome window faced the forest, two stories high, revealing the workshop to the hills of Well's Peake.

A stage made of the finest oak rose a meter above the floor, ready for someone to perform. The border was orange, stamped with floral designs, and accented with white pinstripes and blue paneling.

Aleksandar inspected the walls, covered in gadgets, some silver, some copper, some large and small, wandering through the workshop.

"It's so cool down here." Aleksandar looked at a circular ball with a pressure gauge on top. "Where did this one come from?"

Natalia set her drink on the desk and pondered the arched mechanism. She reached for her jacket but rubbed the edge of her vest instead. She closed her eyes for a moment.

Aleksandar batted his glance back and forth.

"To be honest, I don't remember," she said. "This wall is the embodiment of success and failure. I'm figuring this one didn't meet the mark a long while ago."

Aleksandar turned around, taking in the room, and set his tea on a sanded workbench. "This is a beautiful workshop."

Natalia folded her hands behind her. "Do not worry, Mr. Scott. Once you reach my age, you'll have a workshop similar to my own. It would surprise you what you will collect over your career."

"I've never been so motivated in my life." Aleksandar walked to the stage and rubbed his hand on the banister. The railing sanded to perfection; not a single bump or ripple touched his fingertips.

"Go ahead," Natalia said.

"Are you sure?"

"With certainty. Please."

Aleksandar shuffled up the steps and stood in the middle, the floor solid beneath him. The waterfall reflected ripples of light onto the massive dome window that looked out towards the untouched forest.

"I used that platform to showcase my work when I was younger." Natalia looked up at the inventor.

"You have showcases here?" Aleksandar asked.

"It's a rare occasion now, but in my prime, yes. While I do find some comfort in my older days, it just isn't the same. There's little sport in inventing anymore."

Aleksandar stepped down from the stage. "Why do you say that?"

"People are losing track of what's most important. You should not follow others but strive to create your own path. The ideal of individualism is forgotten in a city in which it should radiate. Inventors follow the Industrial Revolution, but there's more to consider."

"You don't regret being an inventor, do you?"

Natalia folded her arms and rubbed her cheek. "No. Everything that has happened has brought me to this moment, even if there are memories I'd like to change. I can't alter my past, but we can change your future, Mr. Scott." Natalia smacked her lips. "Now, I think we've had enough philosophy for today. How about we look into your idea?"

"Indeed." Aleksandar pulled the leather tube off his back and popped the cap off. He slid out a roll of schematics and laid it on the bench, Natalia setting weights on the corners.

"So, what are your thoughts?" Aleksandar asked. "I know my proposal needed refinement last night, but essentially, this is a glorified water hose. To do what I want requires a massive amount of pressure, which the Lunarwheel could offer. Do you think it is a design worth pursuing?"

"I would like to hear your opinion first," Natalia said.

Aleksandar opened his mouth, rubbing his thumbs on his fingers. "I uh… think it has the potential to change the farming community. The fact of the matter is, the fields are either barren or don't produce what they used to, and they need revived for the harvest."

"Sounds noble" Natalia chuckled and pointed to the wall covered in hoses, braces, nuts, and bolts. Everything Aleksandar would ever need for his designs.

"Look around and grab what we need. I'll clean the workbench off," she said.

"Okay. Do you have any battery cells?"

Natalia looked at the schematic, undisturbed.

Aleksandar waited, but she never answered. He searched the workshop, examining everything he considered useful. Each case was organized and dust-free, just as if he'd gone to the local store. Several trophies, blue and silver, rested next to little inventions in glass cases on the top shelf.

"I can assume these devices are off-limits?" Aleksandar said, pulling hoses and battery cells from the shelf.

"You would be correct. Those are my most prized possessions," Natalia said.

"Okay. Where does the Lunarwheel stand?"

Natalia stepped to the glass apparatus and put her hand on top. "It will cycle, but I cannot stabilize it. I have the weight of the waterfall to fuel it, but I don't know how I could accomplish the same with battery cells. They would drain too quickly."

Aleksandar looked at his schematic. "The Steam Engine wouldn't be enough to power my invention, and using it to feed the Lunarwheel would be counterproductive. Perhaps we should get the Lunarwheel working. Without that, my idea would be impossible."

"We should do both. I have a scaled-down version of the Lunarwheel, but anything larger I have yet to stabilize. It sounds like you need some significant power. If we had Tesla's electricity, imagine what we could do."

"I know little of his trade. Just that Belagrad is transforming because of his and Alva's energy race."

Natalia ran her hand across the schematic, and Aleksandar paused, setting another battery on the table.

"Is everything all right?" he asked.

"Are you sure you're okay with this collaboration? You would receive little credit, and I have no desire to insult you."

Aleksandar put down the supplies, running his hand through his hair. "I remember a man, Farnsworth, I believe, and he was a pioneer in the early Industrial Revolution. He lost the rights, despite being the original creator, but he didn't care. His only concern was that his ideas had changed humanity for the better. I think I could live with that if people chose not to acknowledge me."

Natalia's gaze lingered on him. "Well, if that's the case, you have my full support. Shall we?" She waved her hand to the bench.

Aleksandar nodded, and the two looked over the schematic, the sun high in the clouds. They laid out several pieces of tubing, metal, nuts, and bolts. They moved around each other as if they'd been working together for years. They thought of the same issues, went for the same tools, and studied the device in the same manner. It had been years since he experienced such a connection, such teamwork, thinking back to his childhood friend. They were seamless in their organization and construction.

The sun shifted from the highest point in the sky to the treetops on the farthest hill. The engine was completely stripped to a hollow glass shell and slowly put back together. It unfolded from Aleksandar's fingers as he hummed the evening away. He lost the day to his trade, overwhelmed by his drive and relentless motivation, feeling like a kid working on his own ideas once again.

Aleksandar wiped his upper lip, the musk of grease from his fingers lingering, and sat in his chair, his back tight.

"So, Miss Arlen," Aleksandar said, "did you think about Mr. Lucas after last night?"

"I did, although I would rather deny it. It seems we have stumbled into the middle of something bigger. Mr. Lucas appears to be a relentless fellow, and I would be disappointed if our paths did not cross in the future. A killer of inventors makes me doubt our profession."

"It is scary. I wonder if that's who robbed me. If so, why didn't he kill me like the rest, and what if he breaks in again?"

Natalia walked to the window and stared out, the orange glow fading as the blue moonlight filled the workshop. "I would watch your back and be careful when you travel. We all should. You can stay the night in my guest room if you are comfortable with it. While I don't like it, I understand why they would want to keep quiet. Panic in the streets would not make their investigation easy, but it's as if he wants us to spread the information he has given. He is digging."

"Do you think it could be an inventor committing these murders?"

"It is the logical choice. They must be proficient with the elements. I don't know anyone knowledgeable enough, and someone that skilled should be famous. Instead, they hide in the shadows."

"Unless he's kept his work secret." Aleksandar stood up, putting his hands on his waist. "If they were skilled, how did they remain unnoticed so long?"

Natalia turned. "I assume this man never craved attention. Not in the way most would. His intentions for madness were planted in his beginning, and there's no better moment to strike than during the World's Fair."

Aleksandar pulled a few pipes and couplings together and bolted them into place, securing the seal between them. "We can't keep this information to ourselves. Others are in danger, and they deserve to know."

"Absolutely not, but we should be smart about who we tell. The more information we possess, the more responsible we need to be."

Never had Aleksandar believed he would find himself in such a position, all because of his need to invent. His fingers were as icy as frost, and he felt heavy as if he woke from a deep sleep.

Aleksandar grabbed another handful of piping and set it on the workbench with a clatter of iron and brass. He tightened couplings and hoses, lining a cord to a control handle. Natalia pushed two pipes together in a dramatic fashion, her eyebrows high in the air.

"Shall we begin?" Natalia said.

Aleksandar smirked and turned to the schematics with Natalia, inventing into the late moonlight.

~

I feel guilt for the way I acted at Kenneth's gala. I was concerned, envying Aleksandar's work and newfound success, figuring he rejected my offer for the financial opportunity with Mr. Forbes. Perhaps I feared that without him, I could not find my peace as an inventor. However, I understand he had to do what was best for him. After spending the day inventing with him, I have seen his good nature.

Natalia wrote at her desk, the candle flame dancing near her journal. The waterfall shimmered in the late harvest night, sparkles glimmering throughout the shop. The device she and Aleksandar created rested on the table, far from finished but holding much promise.

With her elbow on the armrest, palm rubbing her cheek, Natalia sat with deep bags under her pale blue eyes. She stared, glancing at the little trinkets that made her workshop her own. Her eyelids grew heavy, and she dozed off for a moment, jerking awake.

I did not give him the credit he deserved when we first met. He was the answer to my stale ingenuity, but I did not realize his potential. As our partnership moves forward, I can only wonder what he will teach me and in what manner I could advise him. Interesting, knowledgeable, but young, he brings fresh life to an inventor's work. A spark that has been missing from me... a spark. An idea.

Natalia leaned back in her leather chair, wondering about the possibilities.

I struggle to remember, but it has been a long while since I've known such a desire to create something new. When I mentored my last apprentice is when I last felt this incredible sensation. She differed greatly from Aleksandar. While he thinks the sky only goes so high, she did not. She believed there were no limits to humanity's grasp, and that was her most admirable trait.

I wonder if there is a fine balance, like light and dark, like waves crashing on a sandy beach. Can an idea be too much? Could I ever envision something that pushes boundaries too far, and what is the harm in writing such concepts? I wonder how my younger self decided on such things with such conviction.

She closed her journal, but instead of tying it shut, she unraveled the string more, opening a smaller set of pages in the center of the front cover.

Natalia patted her cheeks with wide eyes and wrote her ideas. Great, new ideas.

CHAPTER TWENTY-NINE

The hotel room was quiet, lit by lanterns around the room. A bed rested against the white wallpaper and orange drapes, the top blanket and a pillow missing. Abbey lay on the floor, between the windowsill and bed, blanket underneath her and the pillow behind her back.

She rocked back and forth, her eyes lingering across the ceiling. Her satchel sat at the foot of the armchair, still packed. Rubbing her knees with her fingers, she sniffled, the pine scent overwhelming her in the room. She pulled on her hair, clots of dirt in the strands, the tips split on the ends.

Abbey stood and wandered across the room, picked up a book off the table, and rubbed her finger along the stitched spine. Abbey turned up her nose and looked away from the window with resentment.

She shuffled to the washroom and ran her fingers on the brass doorknob. It rattled as she turned it and walked in, her reflection in the oval mirror.

Pulling a towel off the counter, she dampened it in the water basin and leaned in, looking at herself with rich brown eyes, not used to seeing such a clear reflection of herself. She wiped her cheek, and the towel browned on the end. She lowered her hands and looked at the patch of skin, clean and rosy, smiling with cracked lips.

It had been so long since she saw her face, let alone without dirt and grime. To be back when her family sat with her every day, comforting her, walking with her through the parks. Listening to the birds and little critters as they snacked on acorns and scurried up the trees.

Abbey held her breath and exhaled deeply. With another dip of the towel, she wiped off the other side of her face, her chin, her forehead, not able to clean fast enough. She rushed, and with each dab, the water turned brown with dirt floating on the surface. Abbey patted herself dry and rubbed her fingers down her cheek with a tear next to her smile.

She dropped the towel to the floor and pulled her hair back, mud flakes falling onto the counter.

Knock, knock.

Abbey jerked around, pulling her hands to her chest, wide-eyed. She crept behind the wall, looking at the doorknob.

Knock, knock, knock.

"Abbey, are you there? It's Hugh."

Abbey tiptoed across the carpet and looked through the peephole to Hugh with a hand in his pocket. She unlocked the door with trembling fingers and opened it, Hugh staring at her.

"What?" she said.

"Your face. You washed it."

"Yes."

Hugh stepped into the hotel room, and Abbey looked out, then locked the door behind her.

She watched as Hugh looked around the place, eyeing her bed on the floor.

"Are you still not sleeping?" Hugh asked.

Abbey walked over, picked up the blanket and pillow, and set it on the mattress. "It's nothing. I just... the cotton is too soft, and I can't fall asleep."

Hugh nodded, slipping his jacket off. "I struggle too." He hung his coat on the hanger and searched the pocket, pulling out a small blue bottle.

"What's that?"

"Shampoo. Since they don't have any here for free, I thought you'd appreciate it."

Hugh handed her the gift, and she looked at it with a closed grin. The label had a picture of a woman with flowing hair looking over her shoulder.

Abbey put her palm on his hand and rushed to the washroom. She grabbed another bowl of water and pulled the cap off the shampoo, the aroma of lavender and mint sweet in the air. She glanced in the mirror with a smirk, Hugh standing in the door frame with a clean face and well-groomed.

Abbey's smile dimmed, and she set the bottle down, her chest tightening. A heavy dread filled her stomach, and she felt nauseous.

"What's wrong?" Hugh asked.

Abbey's voice cracked. "I shouldn't be here. Or doing this."

"Why not?"

"This isn't where I belong. What if my brother finds me here or realizes I'm not in South Hills anymore? He wouldn't like it—"

Hugh hugged her from behind. "Hey, now. Abbey, it's okay, it's all right. You're here because of me. You don't need to worry."

Abbey shivered in his arms, his warmth comforting as the pit in her stomach lessened. Her fingertips stopped shaking, and she looked in the mirror, unable to stop watching herself.

"What if—"

"No," Hugh said. "Mr. Scott is helping me, and you were just part of it. After getting to know him the past few weeks, I believe he's a good person."

"Then why do I feel guilty? I want to belong somewhere that isn't there."

Hugh turned Abbey around and wrapped his arms around her. "Abbey, you're allowed to be happy and not have to worry about these things."

Abbey waved her arms in the air, catching herself in the mirror and looking away. "How do you take his help?"

Hugh grabbed her hands and held them to his chest.

"How do you accept his kindness?" she asked. "Isn't it pitiful?"

"No, that's your brother talking. There's nothing wrong with accepting help from others. It's just tough because we're usually the ones helping."

Abbey opened her mouth but fell silent. He was right. Why was it okay for them to take support from her, but not her from Kenneth or Mr. Scott? Why did Kenneth's voice echo through her thoughts, like a clock ticking in the hallway at night?

Hugh looked down. "What has your brother said about helping others?"

"He says when someone is being kind, they are just taking pity. That's why our parents never helped us because we shouldn't be pitied. I want to belong somewhere, Hugh."

Abbey turned away, looking into the dark corner of the washroom to the brick surface.

Hugh tucked his hands in his pockets as the air grew stale. He shuffled out of the room and cracked the window, sitting across from the empty chair.

Abbey glared at the wall, the familiar breeze brushing against her, almost refreshing. She walked to the armchair and sat.

"If Kenneth finds me here, do you think he'd hurt me?" Abbey held her stomach, goosebumps on her arms.

"This isn't about him," Hugh said. "This is about you."

Hugh walked into the washroom, grabbed the shampoo, and handed it to her.

"What?" Abbey took the bottle.

"You are okay to use this. It's your favorite scent, and you deserve it.'

"What about the homeless I left behind? Some needed me, and I could help them. What if I used Mr. Scott's money for that instead? He'd be okay with that, right?"

"Abbey, no. That coin is for you."

"I can't stay here forever. I shouldn't even be here now. Helping others gives me a purpose."

Hugh stood and crossed his arms, his beard moving as he shook his head.

"What aren't you telling me?" Abbey walked to him, and she lifted his face.

He choked up. "I don't want to lose you, Abbey. You're the best thing to happen to me in a long while, and you filled the hole my family left behind. I'm afraid if I try to be an inventor, it could take me away from you."

"You can invent and stay near me."

"Can I? You wish to help others, but what if we can't be close and grow apart?"

"Don't say those things. We are better than that. I could help in other places near your inventing."

"But you won't leave the area you live in now."

Abbey's hands slid from his face. She closed the window, stepped into the washroom, and stared into the mirror.

"He wouldn't care," Hugh said.

"That's not true. Kenneth may not show it, but he cares, in his own way."

"Abbey, look at how he treats you, how he left you on the street. Why would any brother do that? I'd take you with me, but he leaves you in the shadows."

"Shut up, Hugh. What would you know? You haven't seen your family in years and wouldn't understand what family does for each other. You attached yourself to me because you have no one else. If you found another, you'd walk off with them and not think twice."

Hugh let out a deep breath, closing his eyes. "Why would you say that?"

"Because everyone does. Kenneth used to visit me every week before he married Amia. I understand my place and what I can do. He'll see me."

"See what? You? And when he does and wants you to come, will you leave? Forget those you want to help and me?"

Abbey set her hand on the counter and rubbed her forehead, still clean but rough.

"It sounds like you are doing it for yourself," Hugh said. "For a brother that'll never treat you as a sister. Just look back to what he did to your parents."

Abbey slammed her fists on the counter. "You don't talk about him that way. I remember what he did, and only I can hate him for it. Forget it. I can't be here. Maybe you should figure it out too. Always trying to leave South Hills, even though you're forever stuck there."

Hugh pushed his tongue into his cheek.

Abbey breathed heavily, her shoulders going up and down, unable to catch her breath. "Hugh…"

He turned around and wandered to the bed, plopping onto the edge with his palms folded. Abbey shook her head.

Stupid girl.

Hugh folded his arms together and looked into his lap.

She rubbed her hands together and walked to him, sitting at his side. "Hugh, I didn't mean it. Ugh, I'm sorry. I was just upset." She put her hand on his arm, and he did not move. "Say something, please."

Hugh looked up at the ceiling, the lantern flicking against his face. "What happens if I do lose myself?"

"No, of course you won't. Some people don't know redemption because they have never had to recover like we have, which makes it harder to forget. I'm sorry for what I said."

Abbey leaned on Hugh, and he rested his head on hers. She held him tight to the point she felt his quick heartbeat.

"I have an idea," she said. "I'll help others from here. Kenneth can see me during the day if he comes looking, and you keep learning to be an inventor."

Abbey reached and wiped Hugh's tears away.

"Will that work?" she asked.

Hugh paused, his eyes closed. "Can you do something for me?"

"What's that?"

"Try the bed again. It gets easier, I promise."

Abbey nodded. "Okay, and would you do something? For me, that is."

Abbey walked into the bathroom, grabbed a towel, and dipped it into the water basin. She opened the shampoo and looked back to Hugh.

Hugh dried off his cheek and forced a small smile. "Okay."

CHAPTER THIRTY

Water, crystalline and shapeless, ran through Amia's blonde hair, like waves on a beach. Kenneth scooped more and held it above her as she rested on a cushion in the tub, pouring it over her head.

The water caressed her face, running down her neck and across her breasts, the soap foaming as she opened her eyes.

Red drapes made of silk hung in spirals throughout the marble washroom, swaying in the gentle wind from the open window. Cinnamon filled the air, and Kenneth took a heavy breath, invigorated with its spice.

Amia pushed the water out of her hair with her palms, pulling it behind her ears as it ran down her collarbones. She smiled as Kenneth washed her shoulder that was missing an arm, shifting his hand under her breast and holding it in his palm like a peach.

Amia leaned closer to him and kissed him on the lips.

"Love, there's no need," Amia said, reaching for the cup Kenneth held out of reach.

"You're right. I don't, but I will anyway." He kissed her again, her lips soft on his.

Amia slipped into the tub, and Kenneth stood, sporting a white nightshirt with knee-length trousers. His clothes waved in his steps like a ballet dancer on their best night, and his long hair unraveled, brushed glossy straight. He couldn't keep his amber eyes off his wife as she washed her legs.

"You are *so* beautiful, my love. I have not forgotten to tell you enough, have I?" Kenneth stepped to the vanity, looking at Amia's reflection.

"You could tell me more. I wouldn't mind." She blushed.

Kenneth smiled as he sorted through the drawers. "I'd be lost without your beauty, all beauty in the world. I pity those who look the wrong way, missing out on what's stunning."

"It is everywhere, my love. Those who don't see just aren't looking."

Kenneth paused, his hands folded, watching the dozens of lit candles around the room. "Do you wonder if beauty fades over the years?"

"Of course not."

Kenneth sighed. "Thank goodness. If they robbed the world of your charm, I'm not sure what would become of me."

Amia leaned on the end of the tub, her head towards Kenneth, the light shimmering against her face. "Did you think I was beautiful when we met?"

Kenneth spun around on the stool. "I knew you were."

"Even with—" Amia looked to where her arm should be, her eyelids lowering, her words fading away.

Kenneth rushed across the room, kneeling next to her. He caressed her chin with his fingertips, soft and delicate, and pulled her in for a deep kiss, breathing hard before he leaned back. "Yes, without doubt."

Amia smiled, and Kenneth stood, walking to the vanity. He reached into a small drawer along the mirror, pulling out a white leather box. He clasped it in his hand and returned to Amia.

"Did you need something from the vanity?" Amia shifted in the tub.

Kenneth raised his finger with a grin and opened the ring box. Amia's eyes lit up like emeralds, looking at a ruby ring.

Her smile made everything worth it. Kenneth's lungs grew heavy as Amia tried to catch her breath. His world, his love, she was his anchor in life. When the days seemed long, or the sun set too soon, she put the stars in the sky.

Amia pulled herself to the side of the tub, and Kenneth slipped the ring over her finger, next to her wedding band.

"Mrs. Forbes, will you marry me?" he asked.

Amia covered her mouth, looking at her gift. "Again?"

"Yes." Kenneth smiled. "Once more, and then again."

Amia stared into her lover's eyes and put her arm around him, soaking the upper part of his shirt as she kissed him, her naked body against him. Kenneth held her as close as he could.

"You have done so much for me," Kenneth said. "The least I can do is ask you this."

Amia slid into the tub. "Do you remember everything you've told me you deserved?"

Kenneth sat in the chair next to her. "It's not that long of a list, is it?"

"Somewhat, but you mentioned there was one thing you didn't deserve." Amia moved closer.

"Yes."

"Well, I'm tired of you having doubts. I want you to believe it."

Kenneth rubbed his pant leg. "Don't I?"

"You aren't always right, my love. None of us are. I know you want people to recognize your worth, but you only need me to see you, and I do."

Kenneth looked away as Amia grabbed his hand. "But I don't see myself as perfect enough. If I am *good* enough."

"I choose you nonetheless. We all have our faults, but that doesn't make us unworthy of love. Now say it."

Kenneth opened his mouth but hesitated. The words were there, resting in his thoughts, but they would not come out as his throat dried.

"Tell me, love. It is true." Amia stared.

"I... deserve you." Kenneth paused, making sure he believed it.

"You have always deserved me," Amia said with a passionate smile. "And if you have any doubts, I will change them. I will keep you away from your old life, and if it's that important, I'll make sure the families see your worth."

"You would do that?"

"Of course. Here's what I think. That day will come when Well's Peake is reminded of the cultural beauty you present, and when that moment comes, we leave."

"Leave?" Kenneth tilted his head.

"Yes. We retire and live our lives in the country."

"But won't that undo everything we're trying to do?"

"No. It cements your place in history. It pushes what a man represents like a painting in the Grand Hall of the Peake. When you are on top, to stay there, you do something that writes your name in the book."

Kenneth thought about it and smiled.

"We can take care of each other and the family we may have," Amia said.

"I think I could, but I'm not sure."

"You aren't your parents."

"I know, but I can't help but feel sorry for them some nights."

"That's okay, but the past is simply that. To live the life you want, you must move on. It's a shame your sister passed so soon. She seemed like a positive influence for you."

"Yes, she was."

Kenneth set his palm on Amia's and kissed her again. They looked at each other and grinned, cheeks blushing.

"I'm going to turn on the Red Breath. I want Well's Peake to know marvelous things are coming," Kenneth said.

Amia stood, grabbed his waist, and pulled him close, putting his hand on her thigh. "Be quick about it. I'll be ready for you when you return."

Kenneth kissed her and strolled out of the washroom, hearing his wife splash into the tub. He walked through his bedroom, down the stairs, and onto the redwood balcony. Kenneth pushed his wet hair back before resting his elbows on the railing. The breeze nipped at the dampness in his shirt, the sky cloudy.

A salamander ran along the beam beside him and looked at him, flicking its tongue. Kenneth petted the salamander with the backside of his finger and lifted him, allowing him to crawl around his hand as he walked to the controls. He pulled it, and the flames kissed Kenneth's cheek in the chill air.

With a raised chin, Kenneth realized the flares were smaller than what he remembered.

That's not right.

Leaning back, he waited a moment, hoping to see them grow larger, but they dwindled. With a puzzled look, he paced to the controls and shut it off. He yanked the lever again, and the fire was dimmer yet. He frowned at the machine and rolled his shoulders, pushing out the stress.

Kenneth examined the security brace and tugged on it. Unable to move it, he made his way into the manor, returning with several wrenches.

Nothing personal, Aleksandar.

Kenneth tried a few sizes and found a wrench that fit the bolts. He unhinged the lock, bolt by bolt until it fell apart around the base.

Kenneth paused for a second, shrugged, and pulled the lever as far as it would go. The fire erupted into the air, brighter, more violent and twisted. Kenneth walked to the balcony railing, setting the salamander on the ledge. His pet scurried off into the house as Kenneth eyed the flames dominating the sky, lighting the clouds.

He smiled with his chin held high. "Beautiful."

Kenneth made his way inside but glanced at the growing flames. A smell of burning wood and metal filled his nostrils. With a small cough, Kenneth watched as smoke rose from the machine, something it had never done before. A scalding heat surrounded him, and sweat dripped down his forehead.

He glanced to the control and listened as the gears vibrated under his feet. Kenneth's skin started to burn, and a spout shrieked on the side, Kenneth holding his breath.

Heat barraged from above and battered against the windows, the glass shattering, falling at his toes. The banners on the beams lit up and fell as the frayed ends burned to ash.

Kenneth shook and gasped, coughing as if the air was being ripped from his lungs. He tried to move, but his feet felt like cement, and he coughed until his body listened to his mind. He propelled towards the doors but halted as the heat pounded against him. Kenneth backed up, unable to duck underneath the flames.

A spout creaked, and metal snapped and collapsed, the structure smashing into the timber beams, shaking under his feet. It erupted in a fiery explosion as cinders and ash filled the air.

The machine exploded, and Kenneth tumbled to the rail, snapping it, hanging off the back. Barely catching a grip, he pulled himself up and searched for any sign of his wife.

Kenneth cupped his hands. "Amia! Get out!"

The fire slithered through the house, lighting everything aflame faster than any he had seen. He ran to the edge closest to the manor and looked out to the drop. With no hesitation, he climbed and jumped.

As the air cooled around him, his foot bent under the weight of his fall, causing him to slip down the hill in the wet grass.

Pain surged through his leg, and Kenneth panted as he rolled back and forth. As the injury dulled, he looked to the town, wondering how many were watching the disaster.

Wood splintered and fell to the hillside underneath the balcony support. Kenneth stood to his feet and climbed the slope with a limp, his foot heavily bruised and his manor burning beside him. He reached the top of the hill and ran to a window. The fire consumed half his home, engulfing everything he owned.

The ballroom was in a blaze, Kenneth thinking Amia couldn't have escaped before it took hold of the house. He glanced to the front door, which was also blocked. She had to be upstairs still; there was no other way. If she was on the outside balcony of their room, she would be trapped.

Kenneth grabbed a potted fern next to the sill and smashed it through the living room window. Kenneth jumped in, cutting his palm on the window shards, finding the fiery red and black chaos blinding him as he struggled through smoke and flames. The furniture on one side remained intact, but the burned interior kept spreading.

Kenneth brushed past the fire that licked the fibers of his shirt. He fought his way through the vapor but slipped on some loose planks. He tried to grab anything but fell, smacking his head off the floor.

Kenneth's vision blurred, and he stared into the rug, a ringing in his ears. The smoke felt like faceless fingers wrapping around his throat, attempting to suffocate him, a dry musk filling his mouth and lungs. He struggled to crawl to the bottom of the staircase, refusing to give up. Kenneth gagged and spat onto the charred steps, his lungs burning.

Flames engulfed the ballroom, glass shattering beside him, forcing Kenneth to bow beneath its prestigious power. He crawled up the stairs to the third floor, barely avoiding a painful death, and found enough air away from the fire and lifted himself to his feet.

"Amia!" Kenneth coughed. "Amia!"

With a stumble down the hallway, Kenneth put as little pressure on his ankle as he could, blood trickling down his forehead, dripping into his eye.

He found the door to his bedroom closed and pushed on it, trying to open it with no success. He rammed his shoulder into it, and it cracked. Kenneth stepped back and lunged into it, the door breaking off the hinges. He coughed with temporary relief, discovering the room filled with little smoke and no fire, but the wallpaper peeled as the heat fought to break in.

Kenneth ran into the washroom. "Amia!"

She wasn't there. She was nowhere.

The tub rested undisturbed, the red curtains untouched by the surrounding turmoil. Kenneth searched the bathroom and bedroom, finding no trace of his wife.

A curtain swung from the ceiling against his face, his hair catching fire. Kenneth rushed out of the room, patting his head as it burned underneath his palms. It stopped, but not before burning close to his scalp.

He ran out of the hallway to the overhang of the ballroom, fearing the worst.

The steps to the stairwell were charred, and one side collapsed, leaving a gap between the third floor.

Kenneth sucked a mouthful of air into his lungs. "Amia!"

"Kenneth!"

His heart dropped.

"Amia! Where are you?" Kenneth looked in all directions, unable to spot her.

"Kenneth!"

Amia's scream was one of fear, which emptied Kenneth's dying hopes.

Kenneth took a deep breath and sprinted off the edge, jumping into the toxic air. He hoped to catch the rail as the smoke and cinders tore at his eyes. He found the handrail of the burning staircase, but the flames burned his hand and forced him to let go.

Kenneth rolled down a flight of steps before breaking through the railing and falling one story down. Kenneth slammed into the hardwood and knocked the wind out of his lungs.

Blood oozed out of his eye like a red tear as he held his head with both hands. The roaring fire surrounded him. Between the blazes and the smoke, he could not see into the house. He could only look at his injured salamander crawling across the floor, slowing to a struggled pace.

His manor, his wife, and his life burned around him, unrecognizable from its former grandeur. Rolling to his side, not sure what he was doing, Kenneth picked up the nearby salamander and placed it on his chest, not wanting to leave his pet behind. He attempted to drag himself across the floor, but hope faded in his lack of strength.

Embers and cinders flew around him, burning into his skin and shirt. The sound of smoldering wood drowned out his moans of pain and agony, and glass shattered nearby.

Kenneth let out a roar that was deafened by chaos.

He stopped and looked once more at the injured salamander that had fallen off his chest, crawling beside him.

Kenneth closed his eyes as a picture of himself and Amia fell to the floor, flames burning the corners. A wooden beam above rippled in a devouring sea of fire and fell next to Kenneth's side, the heat beating against him. The painful destruction grew silent as agony left his body, allowing him one last moment of inner peace.

Everything went quiet. The roar of the wildfire, the breaking of glass, the aroma of ashes, tranquility had—

"Kenneth!"

Amia's voice echoed through Kenneth's ears. His eyes jerked wide, and his mouth opened in dread.

"Amia!"

CHAPTER THIRTY-ONE

The fire crackled and popped in the fireplace, embers drifting at Aleksandar's loafers while smoke lingered up the chimney. He pulled his feet from the warmth, straightening his back as he rocked in the wooden chair.

Despite the cramped conditions of the living room, Shae mastered the space in which she lived, flying in and out of sharp corners and shallow heights. She gripped in her talons a weaved basket with small pieces of baked bread—a sweet, yeasty smell in the air.

Hugh walked down the stairs as the kettle whistled and steam blew out of the spout. He quickened his pace and pulled it off, pouring two cups of water. He slipped some tea bags in and handed one to Aleksandar.

Aleksandar rocked in his chair with a dull squeak when he leaned forward. "Thank you. Mum always said there wasn't a thing a spot of tea couldn't fix."

Hugh sat in the faded armchair, resting back into the cushions, Shae soaring overtop. She dropped the basket into Hugh's lap, and he flinched, nearly spilling his hot drink.

He set the basket on the coffee table and took a slice of bread. "I've never seen an animal move like that."

"She's not ordinary, that's for sure." Aleksandar grabbed some bread and ripped it apart, soft and warm to the touch. "When I was young, my family lived in the outskirts of town. During the frost seasons, whiteouts were common, and one night while I was sleeping, a snowstorm blew a tree branch through my window. I jumped from my bed, snow and glass resting on the floorboards. In the leaves was a nest with a tiny Shae inside."

Aleksandar rocked backward in his chair, enjoying his tea. Hugh listened without comment. Shae landed on the post next to him, nipping chopped beef out of a narrow bowl. Aleksandar rubbed the back of his hand down her neck, but she ignored him as she ate.

"My parents didn't want me to keep her. Said owls were nocturnal and mean, but she is more... judgmental than anything. I couldn't let her go. We put her in a tree outside the house, but she kept coming to the window. When my father realized I was feeding her, she was already part of the family."

Hugh sat there and took a sip, the steam running up his face.

Aleksandar watched with chai spice tingling on his tongue. He wasn't sure what was wrong with Hugh. He had said little over the past few weeks, just listening as if he was waiting for something to happen.

Hugh was picking up his lessons well, but he was always quiet. He had few questions, and when he did speak, it was short. Their progress was good, but Hugh had not shown a desire to create anything from what Aleksandar taught him. Maybe because he struggled to think of an idea or did not realize he could up to that point. He had created the base of something but had gone nowhere with it.

Aleksandar tapped the porcelain rim of his cup. The room was quiet and dim, the fire their only source of light, with the faint blue of the outside moon shining inside. The shadows danced across the bookshelves as the flame wisped in the fireplace.

Aleksandar reached over and lifted the frame of Hugh's invention off the coffee table, examining it in his hands. "So, Hugh. We have gone over a lot of basics, so I'm curious. What would you prefer to learn now?"

"What choices are there?" Hugh shuffled in his brown button-up.

"Well, there are lots." Aleksandar rubbed his neck. "We can begin with elemental principles or industrial. I'm more knowledgeable with the elements, but I have some industrial wit."

"I don't know. I'm not much of an inventor as you can see."

"I'm not sure that's true. You struggle to create, but you seem to excel in improving on what is."

"I don't know. I'll only know what you teach me and be what you make me." Hugh set down his tea.

"I don't agree with that. I'm not interested in making you a personal project. You should want to enjoy it and do what you choose."

Hugh leaned forward, facing his palms towards the fire. "You hardly knew me when you brought me in and let me stay here. Why would you do that?"

Aleksandar tilted his head, and Shae looked around. "Isn't it proper practice to do so?"

"It's kind, but most wouldn't. Up here, I guess you would be okay, but if you did that in South Hills, you'd be robbed blind."

"Well, there's not much to take anymore. If you find something, let me know."

Hugh smiled through his shaggy beard and rubbed his hands together, his cheeks rosy from the heat. "During the frost, I sit at a different fire every other night, looking for warmth. I never thought sitting at this fire would feel strange. When I was a kid, I loved standing on the street, when gaslights became more common. I'd run into the street and down the middle. Just something about it. When I came to Well's Peake, being on the streets didn't feel the same."

Aleksandar's chest tightened, and he swallowed his tea. He leaned forward, setting Hugh's invention down, and folded his hands.

Shae flew to the window and smacked her wings against it, pushing her face up against the glass.

"Hey, be a little more delicate," Aleksandar said to Shae.

Hugh grabbed a piece of bread from the basket and took a few bites.

Aleksandar sat there, waiting for Hugh to say anything else, but he stared into the fire, never looking away.

"I remember you mentioned you had a sister at one point." Aleksandar picked up his teacup and saucer.

Hugh sighed and scratched at his short, untamed beard. "Yes, I did. She's no longer with us." Hugh coughed.

"I'm sorry. I didn't mean to bring it up."

"Don't be. It's okay. I do have good memories of her, though."

"Could I hear one?"

"She always wanted to train horses. One day we came along a group of travelers, and she couldn't help but ask. Oh, can I ride? Can I ride? She had never ridden before. Their leader, Joshua, hopped down and handed her the reins. It was a smaller pony, but I was... they scared me, but she got on before he could assist. He taught her how to guide the animal. She did just that, and the pony trotted down the road. She smiled and looked back at me, see... well, she should've been the one watching. She rode *right* into the bushes."

Hugh laughed and wiped tears from his cheek.

Aleksandar chuckled, sipping on his tea.

"Sorry. You didn't ask for a book," Hugh said.

"It's all right. I enjoy a good story."

"We were on the streets by then. Laughs were hard to find some days."

"How did you end up in Well's Peake?"

"After her passing, I had no family left. The riots in Granville grew too much after they cut rations, and the fields were still broken from the Black Harvest. Not long after, I found my way to Well's Peake. I met Abbey, and she's been my best friend ever since. She looks out for me every day, just like my sister did. I looked up to her. She's more confident than me."

Aleksandar sat back in his chair, stopping it from rocking any further. He remained quiet as Hugh faced away from the flame to the city outside the window. The fire crackled as the log split, and embers lingered into ash, the aroma of pine filling the air.

Hugh swallowed and sat back in his chair, grabbing another piece of bread. He exhaled through his nose, closing his eyes.

"I'm sorry, I've asked too much." Aleksandar spun his cup between his fingers, tapping his foot against the cotton floor rug.

"It's fine." Hugh took a bite of bread and turned to Aleksandar. "Who do you look up to?"

His childhood friend flooded Aleksandar's thoughts like she always did. She was everything he ever looked up to, strived to achieve. He wanted to keep her close to his heart, but she'd faded over the years the less he spoke of her. It was always nice to hear her name out loud, knowing she was not forgotten.

Aleksandar rocked forward in his chair. "I owe you that."

Hugh leaned back.

"I had a good friend when I was young," Aleksandar said. "A better friend than I ever was. She wanted a lot out of life, and I always wondered how someone so young had dreams like her. I can't even imagine what she'd be dreaming of if she were here today, and I know I could never reach her level. If she were here, she'd clock me in the arm for thinking such a thing."

Hugh blinked and glanced out the window, Shae looking with her wings perched.

Aleksandar's palms grew sweaty, and he took a sip of tea. "Years ago, we hiked into the woods, late at night, on our way to see a magician." Aleksandar paused.

Hugh stood and stared outside.

"Hugh?" Aleksandar said, taking a sip.

"Mr. Scott." Hugh coughed. "Something's wrong."

Aleksandar leaned forward and looked beyond the glass, a crimson haze glaring over it.

He rose with the tea in hand and walked to the living room window, looking to a night sky of red clouds. Flames loomed in the far distance, smoke billowing into the air.

Aleksandar's legs weakened, and he could hear his heartbeat in his ears. He watched as the blaze loomed over a mansion, burning beneath the smoke.

Swallowing the remnants of tea in his mouth, he gasped for air and looked to the horizon, the sky as bright as dawn.

CHAPTER THIRTY-TWO

The flames feasted on the scraps and burning remnants of Kenneth's manor. The fire raged at the remaining part of the house, the roof in the middle of the ballroom. The shadows waved across a blanket of ash that covered his past life.

A salamander dragged itself through the soot, collecting it the further it crawled. He pulled and crept, looking for an escape from the surrounding death, making his way through the cinders.

As embers drifted above him, the salamander found a small slit in the flooring and inched through, falling onto a pile of charred money and jewels. He tried to crawl further but succumbed to his injuries, next to the leg of a man who lay half-buried in his splendor.

Kenneth could not hear the chaos above as the wind rushed by his ears. He jolted awake, eyes wide and bloodshot. He coughed, his lungs tightening under his shallow breath. With the back of his sleeve, he wiped his mouth off, feeling the wood flakes on his chapped lips.

The flames shimmered on his face, causing him to turn away, trying to focus his vision. Fresh from the gash on his forehead, blood flowed around his eye and down his cheek, dripping onto the money. Looking around to determine where he was, Kenneth found the strength to pull himself up, stumbling onto his knees. He peered through the slit of metal resting over him, staring at the blurry outside world.

"Amia?" Kenneth said, his voice low and soft. It seemed like minutes passed as he waited for a response that wasn't the wind against the fire or the embers crackling.

The scent of charred wood filled his nose, and soot settled on his tongue in wet clumps. Kenneth reached above and pressed on the metal lid. His hand sizzled, and his skin burned.

Ah!

Kenneth ripped his palm away, collapsing into the cash and rolling around as his hand stung like a thousand hot needles. He opened his grip, and his wrist shook as he watched the skin blister, blood seared in several spots. With clenched teeth, he ran his fingers through his hair, catching it on melted strands.

Kenneth grabbed some burned cash, shook his head, and pressed his cracked lips together. With the money between his palm and the singeing steel, he pushed with much resistance. Kenneth struggled hard, and it still did not shift. With each grunt, he thrust harder and harder.

Open, you bitch!

Kenneth squatted the best he could with his weak ankle and shoved the lid open, climbing into what used to be his living room.

Loose debris and wood splinters fell off his back. The lid slammed against the ground behind him, ash floating in the air. His white shirt was torn, burned, and black. His one ear was clogged, blood dried below his eye, and sweat beaded on his skin.

Kenneth coughed at the immense amount of dust, the fire still raging on the outer walls of the home.

Where is everyone... Why did they not come to my rescue?

As he stood looking, the air above his head emptied, blurring his vision for several seconds. The end of his life lay at his feet, and he'd lost everything he ever deserved.

"Amia?"

Kenneth's soft voice showed no sign of hope as ash fell from above, drifting along the remaining leaves in the nearby maple trees. He limped across the floor, searching for his beloved, pushing piles of cinders that did not seem hot. He found a handle and pulled hard, money still protecting his good hand, the other cradled in his chest—another safe room, with more paper bills and priceless artifacts.

No signs of Amia.

Rushing away, he searched the ground, passing burned wood and embers. He tripped on a covered beam and fell onto a dying fire. Kenneth rolled out of it and patted his singed clothing as the pain surged throughout his lower back. He pulled on his shirt, the melted fibers peeling off his abdomen.

"Ah!"

His chest swelled, and his head pounded as if someone kicked him in the temple. The soot warmed his backside, but he'd never felt so cold, so empty in his stomach. Kenneth pushed himself up and grabbed another cover. The lid collapsed in, leaving only the handle in Kenneth's hand.

Nothing but ash was left.

After two more busted compartments, tears dripped through the black tar on Kenneth's face, his eyes still in the dim moonlight, his nose dripping.

He looked back to his original compartment and spotted something near the lid. He swallowed hard, ignoring the fresh ember that burned against his calf. With each step, his soul darkened. He had missed what was right next to him all along. He saw parts of scorched fabric, like a robe he had given his wife only a week ago.

Moans of sorrow emerged from his lungs, taking his breath.

"No... no, no, no." Kenneth rushed through the pain and dropped beside her.

Ash ended where his wife's charred remains began.

My love.

Kenneth touched her remaining hair, the other side of her face blackened, untouched by flames. Her arm lay where the lid edge was, indented by the weight that was on it.

Why didn't you get in with me?

"Amia, it's over. The fire is over. You can come to, my love."

Kenneth pleaded, losing his words in his broken sobs.

"Amia, come to. You're okay. You're okay... please. Honey, wake up. Wake up! I deserve you. You said that to me. I deserve you. Don't leave me. Please don't leave me."

Kenneth lifted her and held her to his chest, his burned hair dangling over their faces. Tears ran down his cheeks, into the blood on his face, red drops collecting on his chin. He sobbed, and his body trembled.

My love. My sweet Amia.

His mouth gaped open, and he looked at the smoke looming above him. Kenneth let out a roar like wolves on the new moon.

The moon dimmed against the fire's shadows, darkness covering Kenneth's face. The breeze was hot until he no longer felt it, the silence of the night growing numb around him. Kenneth sat there, lost to Well's Peake.

"Mr. Forbes? Mr. Forbes!"

Kenneth didn't move as a constable walked onto the pile of ash and fire, carrying a lantern. The constable inspected him as Kenneth kept his focus on his wife.

"Mr. Forbes? You're alive," the constable said. He crouched, looking at Kenneth as he raised the light near his face. "Mr. Forbes?"

Kenneth did not look, lost with a quivering lip to Amia's lifeless gaze.

"Mr. Forbes, we must find you a doctor. You're injured."

Kenneth kept his eyes on his wife.

"Mr. Forbes, my name is Constable Salek. I'm sorry I was not here sooner."

The constable reached towards him, placing his palm on Kenneth's shoulder. Kenneth looked to him with a hazed stare, lost in his thoughts.

"Mr. Forbes?"

"Do not touch me!" Kenneth smacked the man's hand away.

Salek stepped back, holding the lantern between them. With quivering lips, Kenneth kissed his wife on the forehead. He sat on the ground for several minutes, letting his mind fade in and out. He rubbed her cheek once more and set her in the ash, laying her arm over her stomach.

Kenneth stood, his arms and head low. "Take me away from here."

"Of course, Mr. Forbes." Constable Salek extended his elbow.

Kenneth took the man's gesture, and they walked across embers with slow-moving steps, Kenneth struggling without his shoes. He dropped to his knees, hunching over.

His sobs echoed through his chest. "I can't leave her here."

"Mr. Forbes, I know this is hard to hear, but we need to get you to a doctor and inform others if they haven't noticed. We will come back for her."

"What, why wouldn't they have noticed?" Kenneth lifted his face.

"Until I was near, I didn't realize you weren't using your new machine, that this was an actual fire. We must alert the Peake because I'm uncertain anyone else is coming."

Kenneth clenched his fists. "No."

"If it helps, carry this lamp. Hold on to something."

With his sleeve, Kenneth wiped his eyes, grabbing the constable's wrist. He pulled himself up, and Salek handed him the lantern.

"Are you sure?" Kenneth asked.

"Of course." Salek propped Kenneth on his arm.

Kenneth limped for a moment before letting go of the gentleman's elbow, wanting to walk on his own. The constable followed, holding his hands out in support. They made their way across the ruin, Kenneth stopping at the door frame of the house, looking at his wife.

"We will come back for her. I promise," Salek said. "You are lucky to be in one piece, Mr. Forbes. She didn't deserve to die here, but you're lucky to be alive."

Kenneth coughed, biting his cracked lip. "Okay."

Salek placed his hand on Kenneth's shoulder, and it stung on his tender wounds. Kenneth's hands ached, and his ankle throbbed into his leg. His breath was raspy, and thoughts were as dull as a smothered fire.

Amia, the love of his life, was gone. There was nothing left of his life. People would pity him, give him handouts, and be sorry for his tragedy.

They would pity him... if they knew he was alive.

Kenneth's eyes widened, his pupils flaring. He eyed the man and whipped the lantern, shattering it across Salek's temple, glass slicing into his skin. Kenneth lost his footing, and they both fell into the ash. Salek lay unconscious, a splintered piece of wood sticking out of his leg. Kenneth screamed as he glanced to his house, gritting his teeth.

He grabbed Salek and ripped off his uniform, removing all trace he was a constable.

Salek regained consciousness and struggled, pushing the man away. "Mr. Forbes, what are you—"

"It's what I deserve, is it? I deserve to be alive? Well, tell me. Tell me!"

"Mr. Forbes—"

Kenneth got in Salek's face. "I'll tell you what I deserved. Her. She deserved anything but this."

Kenneth grabbed the back of Salek's shirt, lifted him, and slammed the man's head against the floor. Kenneth seized the constable again and dragged him through the soot.

"Mr. Forbes?" Salek slipped in and out of unconsciousness.

Kenneth pulled Salek as fast as his sprained ankle would let him, ash collecting on the man's collar, cinders searing into his shirt. His gaze widened to a burning stake in Kenneth's path.

Kenneth lifted Salek and tossed him onto the stake, the wood ripping through the man's chest. The constable's breath erupted into gasps and wheezes that escaped his punctured lungs. He lay limp, staring wide-eyed.

Kenneth's bloodshot eyes stared with deep bags.

He kicked the board, snapping it in two. The impaled constable fell to his side, only to lie still, life having left his body. Kenneth grabbed a smothered beam with a flame on the end, lifted it, and dropped it across the constable, pinning him further into the chaos.

Kenneth's scowl faded to a pained frown, tears flowing down his cheeks. He picked up the half-broken lantern and lifted it to his chin.

"This is not what I deserved." Kenneth dropped the lantern on Salek, lighting his body on fire, shadows fading from his face.

With a blank stare, Kenneth grabbed the constable's belongings and walked to his wife, tears dripping off his cheeks. He kneeled and held her, kissing her on the forehead, her cinnamon perfume no longer there.

With the hill behind him, high above the peak, Kenneth limped into the forest, and disappeared into the cold, late night as ashes filled the air.

CHAPTER THIRTY-THREE

The sun, red and gracious, radiated through thick clouds on Well's Peake's horizon. Harvest trees were barren, with only a few leaves resting on their branches, the rest collecting on the weathered roots. The leaves crunched under Aleksandar's footsteps as he walked the cobblestone path leading to Kenneth's house. Natalia trailed at his side in her navy-blue jacket; her hair pulled into a messy bun. Only a few charred beams supported the remaining frame of the manor, the rest under mounds of hot coals and ash.

Aleksandar clenched his shaking hand, focusing on his broken breath as he neared the destruction. He paused on the front steps, the same place he was a weekend ago. Then, a night of grandeur, but now, a place of death and suffering. It was all gone. Kenneth and Amia were nowhere in sight, and Aleksandar's heart sank as he looked to the constables that investigated the property.

Nicoli and Lydia searched the premises with several others, Owen standing on the mangled balcony. Aleksandar made eye contact with Owen, who stared back at him, holding his hand to the morning light.

Lydia May patted Nicoli on the shoulder, and they looked towards Aleksandar. Owen stepped forward, and Nicoli waved him to stay in place, Owen never taking his eyes off Aleksandar. Constables searched the debris,

Nicoli wrote in his journal, and Lydia shuffled through the ash.

"You have nothing to be nervous about." Natalia checked the estate. "Best to be calm and collected until we have answers."

"I'm afraid I already do."

Aleksandar waited, his chest tightening and thoughts stumbling. The red drapes, the candles, the marble pillars, all crumbled and destroyed. What if it was his invention that burned down the house? It had to be— first Abel, and now the Forbeses.

Lydia reached the steps, and Aleksandar folded his arms, pulling on the wool of his brown jacket. The manor smelled like scorched leather and was so thick that Aleksandar tasted the ash on his tongue. Nausea settled in his stomach, causing him to shudder.

"Mr. Scott," Lydia said. "Thank you for coming. Miss Arlen, we were not expecting you."

"I asked her to come," Aleksandar said, swallowing hard, touching his hat. "I don't see Mr. Forbes. Is he in the hospital? Where is he?"

Lydia eyed Natalia for a moment and shifted to Aleksandar, clearing her throat. "Mr. Forbes and his wife did not survive. We found them this morning."

Aleksandar shut his eyes.

Even with his hands under his arms, they shook, and the thought of Kenneth and Amia burning alive flashed through his mind. Their pain, the suffering. He didn't want to cry but felt the pressure behind his eyes. He'd expected the worst, but nothing prepared him for the truth.

Aleksandar opened his eyes to Lydia on the bottom step.

"Mr. Scott, I have a few questions regarding the invention you installed for Mr. Forbes," she said.

"I understand."

"Would you prefer to do this alone?"

"Miss Arlen can stay. That's fine."

Lydia pulled out a notepad and pencil. "Where were you last night?"

"I was home."

"Is there anyone who can confirm that?"

"Yes. Hugh Evans. He lives in my spare bedroom."

"Were there any issues with your invention before you installed it in the house?"

Aleksandar tapped his elbow. "No, none."

"Are you sure?"

"Yes. There's always a risk, but I did a lot of work ensuring it was as safe as possible."

"Could it have been safer?"

"Yes... maybe."

Lydia caught up on her notes, and Aleksandar looked to Natalia, her hands folded behind her.

Aleksandar peered up, Nicoli standing at the top of the steps. "Constable May, I'm going to borrow him for the moment. Mr. Scott, please come with me."

Aleksandar shook his head, stepping up the staircase to what was the grand hallway. Nicoli led him through a cleared path, and Aleksandar could not help but linger, looking to the sky where the ceiling should have been. There was little that still shined or carried pristine, for everything was black. What used to be a chair sat lopsided, missing an armrest and most of its cushion. The wall was half torn; one side of a picture frame stuck out from the debris.

Aleksandar stepped onto the remaining balcony, where a small section that was supported enough near his invention stood, the rest collapsed into the front yard. Owen stared at him with his fine mustache and dirty hands, leaning on his good leg. Nicoli walked around them both, standing next to the dismantled control lever.

"Aleksandar," Owen said.

"Owen, I didn't expect you to be here."

"Nicoli asked for a second opinion. I figured it was the least I could do."

Aleksandar's back tensed as a breeze from the hillside blew against his face, the aroma of pine needles mixed with a smoky residue. He pulled on the brim of his hat, his hair shifting.

"Could you explain what this is?" Owen gestured to the melted brace.

Aleksandar studied the mechanism, Owen having cleared most of the debris away. With his brow furrowed, he squatted and held his hands to the mount.

"What is it?" Owen asked as Nicoli looked over their shoulders.

"This isn't right. I installed a security clamp to ensure Mr. Forbes didn't overrun the machine. I even warned him."

"And the problem is?" Nicoli asked, stepping beside the inventors.

"The guard has been removed. You can tell the control lever is in the highest setting. Mr. Forbes knew not to remove the brace. He must have tried to turn it off, but maybe the valve stuck open."

"So this has happened before?" Nicoli stepped around the lever.

Aleksandar stood. "At my exhibition. My earlier invention had a minor issue, but I fixed it. I know I did."

Nicoli ran his fingers through his hair. "Mr. Forbes was impulsive, but not foolish. Would he know how to remove it?"

"Someone removed the brace before the fire. It's not there. There's no way it would've melted."

Nicoli glanced at Owen, and he nodded.

"Did it… take long?" Aleksandar asked.

"With the fuel used with your invention, no," Nicoli said. "It burned faster than anything we've ever seen. We had no chance of putting it out. It's a shame we didn't realize it was an actual fire until it was too late."

Aleksandar had nothing to say. His invention replayed in his head, and a sense of self-loathing overcame him. He thought of every brace, bolt, and calculation, knowing he triple-checked his work. The Red Breath could be dangerous, but he installed the guard for a reason.

What if it was my fault? What if I caused Kenneth's death? Did I miss something crucial in my design?

"Mr. Scott, come with me, please." Nicoli headed off, waving his palm.

Aleksandar stepped forward, but Owen held him back by the shoulder. He turned, looking with a broken gaze.

"I warned you," Owen said.

Aleksandar smacked Owen's hand away. The two stared at each other, and Aleksandar turned away. He followed Nicoli through the remnants of Kenneth's mansion, feeling the grime at his feet. Marble, stained black, rested beside him, and the floor creaked under his footsteps. His leg busted through the floorboard, and he caught himself before falling over, pulling his foot out. Several constables watched him with stern gazes. Aleksandar's pant leg turned gray, and he felt splinters in his shoe.

They wandered down the steps, Natalia and Lydia looking their way. Lydia held a notebook and pencil to the esteemed inventor.

Nicoli guided Aleksandar to a small tent with a table of evidence and two beige blankets covering a few cots. Bloodstains mixed with ash marks stained the one, the other black from head to toe.

Aleksandar froze, and his heart raced, struggling to catch a full breath.

"Mr. Scott," Nicoli said. "Mr. O'Connell assured me you worked for Kenneth for weeks leading to the gala. Mr. and Mrs. Forbes have no next of kin, so perhaps you could help identify the remains."

"Me?" Aleksandar asked, his voice cracking.

"Yes. Is that a problem?"

"I don't know if I can." Aleksandar swallowed hard.

"You saw him more than anyone else these past few weeks. I think you owe him that."

Aleksandar looked at the covered bodies and nodded.

"Thank you." Nicoli bent over, grabbed the corners, and pulled the sheet back to a bloodied, blackened figure.

Aleksandar closed his eyes, a tear dripping down to his chin, and pulled his arm tight against his side.

Mrs. Forbes lay there, half of her body burned like a charred piece of wood, half of her face still intact, and with only one arm. The stink of ash and flesh filled Aleksandar's nostrils, and he gagged, holding his hand to his nose.

"Who is this?" Nicoli said, losing his gaze on the remains.

Aleksandar cleared his throat. "That's... I think Mrs. Forbes."

Nicoli nodded and covered the corpse. He moved to the next and removed the blanket, smudging more black over it and knocking a few leaves to the ground. The man was unrecognizable, burned, with a hole in his stomach. Aleksandar knew the eyes were missing, and the limbs were shriveled like a dead plant.

Aleksandar choked on his words and bent over, his hands on his knees, trying not to throw up.

"Is that?" Aleksandar shivered, a chill brushing against his neck.

"We are unsure. Are there any features that belong to Mr. Forbes?"

Aleksandar stood, leaning towards the body but never taking a step closer. "No, I can't tell. I'm sorry."

"Mr. Scott—"

"I don't know. Who else would it be?"

Nicoli left the remains uncovered. "We can only assume."

Aleksandar glanced away, looking to the leaves and the bushes unscathed from the fire. His heart sank deeper into his chest as his breath escaped, leaving an empty, tingling feeling that spread to his fingertips and toes.

"It took a while to pull them out," Nicoli said. "Other than ashes, we found very little. Quite the gruesome scene. Is there anything you can tell us, Mr. Scott? We have many questions with few answers."

"I don't have them." Aleksandar turned around.

Nicoli crossed his arms. "Mr. Scott, what are the chances your invention cost the Forbeses their lives?"

"I—I... could you cover the bodies, please?"

"Something happened here, Mr. Scott, and I believe you have information you're not sharing. You need to come clean before this gets worse."

Nicoli returned to the carnage, and Aleksandar stood stunned, holding his hand up, his fingers aching and shaking.

Natalia walked to the young inventor, Lydia following.

"Miss Arlen," Lydia said. "Before you go, I need your signature for your statement."

"Of course."

Lydia handed Natalia the notebook, and she signed the bottom of the page and gave it back. Lydia looked at the ink.

"You have excellent writing, Miss Arlen. Did you study at the William James Academy?"

"I did not, but I tutored there for several seasons, and the calligraphy teacher was a friend."

"I recognized her work. Thank you." Lydia turned to Aleksandar. "Mr. Scott, I'll need to finish questioning you before you leave, but I will give you a moment."

"Could you please cover that body?" Aleksandar crossed his arms.

Lydia nodded as much as the brace allowed her and covered the corpse, walking to Kenneth's manor.

Aleksandar could not pull his eyes from the ash and cinders, knowing Kenneth's body was pulled from them. "This is my fault—what have I done?"

"We don't know what happened," Natalia said. "You can't blame—"

"What's left to see? What am I supposed to think?" Aleksandar bit his words.

Natalia turned her back to the constables and the investigator. "Listen. You must not create a scene in front of people like Nicoli Lucas. They want to pressure you for information, to make a mistake even though you aren't guilty. You need to wait for them to finish their investigation."

"This is my wrongdoing."

"Is it? Did you come over here and burn down Kenneth's house? No. Your invention may be involved, but you did not intend for this."

"But I gave him the opportunity. Owen was right. Just because we can invent something doesn't mean we should."

"You're not responsible for how other people use your invention. You built it for a purpose, and Mr. Forbes abused that. His mistake does not define you, but how you respond to it does."

Aleksandar rubbed his neck and walked away, wandering to a scorched bookcase that had collapsed into the ferns around the house's foundation. He spotted a charred book in the ashes, lifted it, and turned the pages. The corners had burned off, but the cover was intact with remnants of gold embroidery. He set the book on the shelf, his hands black, and spotted something familiar.

He bent down and pulled out a burned top hat, the one he made for Kenneth Forbes.

"Aleksandar." Natalia stepped closer.

Aleksandar mumbled and set the hat back down.

Natalia stood close, her breath on Aleksandar's ear. "If you act irrational, you'll only make them more suspicious. Your robbery, and then this. They will pressure you, and you should not give them a reason to think you're guilty."

Aleksandar stood wide-eyed, breathing deep. He looked to Nicoli, Lydia, and the other constables searching the scene. Owen stared at him, his gaze unrelenting.

Are they thinking that? That I'm responsible for Kenneth's death?

Wiping his eyes, Aleksandar turned to Natalia. "I can't let this happen again. I just can't."

"You need to find something to focus on, something good."

Aleksandar sighed.

"You could try to channel these feelings into our work and still focus on the exhibition."

Aleksandar turned around. "The exhibition? Isn't this bigger than that? My invention, indirectly, has killed people. I have to fix my mistake."

"That is part of our profession. While we have our own reasons for inventing, we are inventors nonetheless. Without the investment and the good graces of the public, we have no means of making the change you wish to create. We can move on, despite what has happened, but you must keep pushing if you feel the need to focus. Without that exhibition, you might not have a chance to make that change."

A sudden rush of coldness spread through Aleksandar's chest as he let out a deep breath, losing his focus on Natalia.

"This is your chance to build something with meaning," Natalia said. "To prevent *this* from happening again."

Aleksandar pulled on his hat, shifting in his spot. He did not want to nod. "Okay."

"Okay?" Natalia tilted her head.

"Yes, okay."

Natalia put her hand on Aleksandar's shoulder. "I know it's hard to hear right now, but let me look out for you."

"I'll trust you." Aleksandar swallowed hard.

"Your faith will not be misplaced. There's one last thing, Aleksandar, that I think you should consider. It might be best if you refrain from the World's Fair for a few weeks. The city will grow unpredictable after this disaster. The press will be relentless, and you don't need that burden. Inventors already have a tarnished reputation, and the danger surrounding us grows."

"Indeed," Aleksandar said.

"That is only my insight."

Aleksandar turned, and Lydia walked down the steps. "Mr. Scott, would now be all right to ask some questions?"

Aleksandar nodded.

"I'll leave you to it," Natalia said. "I will be at the road's end."

Natalia tilted her head to Lydia and made her way down the path, Lydia staring in her direction.

"Mr. Scott," Lydia said.

"Yes?" Aleksandar pulled his scarf tighter as the wind picked it up.

"If I were you, I'd refrain from leaving Well's Peake for a while. Just until we settle this affair."

Aleksandar looked to the constable with jaded eyes, knowing something in Well's Peake was not how it appeared.

As the morning faded to midday, Aleksandar returned to his home, his feet sore and chafing. His steps were all that radiated in his ears as he wandered the city streets. Neither the wisping of wind nor the rattling of carriages distracted him.

He opened the door and looked to Shae with her eyes half shut, resting near the fireplace. She let out a soft hoot and closed them again.

The young inventor hung up his coat and hat, wrapping them around the hook. Lost in thought, he walked to the kitchen, grabbed a slice of bread, and ripped off a piece. Shae opened one eye, and he tossed her a bite, Shae snatching it in her beak.

Aleksandar chewed and paused with alarmed eyes. He missed it, walked right by it, but at the bottom of his door rested an envelope sealed in red wax. He dropped the bread next to Shae, rushing through the living room.

With the letter, he hurried into the kitchen. Shae hissed as he dashed by, and she flew to a post, wings perched, her talons scratching into the wood. Aleksandar ripped the seal and opened the note, sweat dripping down the back of his neck.

Aleksandar unfolded the message, holding his breath as his eyes met the words.

Mr. Scott,

Legacy can be so easily burned. You, of all people, have experienced this. For that, I am sorry. Darkness spreads like wildfire through the streets of Well's Peake, and I fear more will suffer. You are in danger and under suspicion from Dekker and his men. Someone is using Kenneth's death to cover something up that is much larger in comparison. Take caution, Mr. Scott. What will soon happen is unpredictable.

Aleksandar glared at the note, lost in the words before him. He bit his lip until it cracked and threw the letter to the floor. His vision blurred as he clenched his hands, the veins in his arms protruding and his knuckles white.

He swiped the pots and pans from their racks and slammed the ledge with his fists until the counter rattled under his fury. He sobbed in deep gasps, and his teacup rolled off, shattering on the tile. Aleksandar slid down the cupboard to the floor, the shadows lingering over him. He covered his face as he sobbed, his hands pressed against his eyes.

Aleksandar's vision clouded as he glared into the living, but he could still make out Hugh, who stood on the staircase, watching in silence.

CHAPTER THIRTY-FOUR

K enneth scaled the hillside, his feet slipping on the leaves beneath
him, reaching for Well's Peake's highest point in the dark
moonlight. He looked over his shoulder to the rolling hills, his
manor resting in shambles near the bottom of the slope.

He grabbed mossy trunks and cracked branches, pulling himself up
with one hand and holding the constable's jacket on his shoulders with the
other. Kenneth slipped, skidding into the roots of a tree, and flopped onto
his back to the moonbeam above him. Tears dripped through the dried ash
on his cheeks, leaving wet lines in the dirt.

It was quiet. Well's Peake was far enough away for the trotting of horses
and the hourly bells to be nonexistent. The trees were no longer green,
growing bare in the harvest. Leaves turned to a crisp auburn and collected
on the ground, bustling against each other as the wind blew downhill. The
harvest season settled on the city, with the frost soon to come.

Kenneth stared into the sky, his expression blank, like the husk of a
man he was. Thunder rolled in the valleys, growing louder by the second.
He felt the vibrations in the leaves resting against his back. Scattered
raindrops pattered against his face, the cool sensation nothing compared
to the chill he embraced the night before.

His burned hand peeled, and his arm twitched, a shiver causing his hair to stand on end. Kenneth rolled onto a massive rock that stuck up from the ground, overhanging the hillside. He looked down on the city, feeling no emotion when he glanced to the streets lit by gaslights from the World's Palace.

Kenneth's fingers were white as he clenched the jacket, and his feet ached from the constable's boots, which were tight on him.

Amia.

Kenneth tried to piece a thought together, but the realization of his loss shattered him, splitting his soul in two.

Amia rushed through his mind in fragments. Her tender smile, her soft touch, and her cinnamon perfume. He could sense her warmth against him but knew it was only his breath as he exhaled.

Kenneth breathed heavily, and a grimace etched into his face. He raised his hand and smacked it off the stone, biting the pain that surged through his burned palm, welcoming any sign that he was still alive.

A crack shot from the woods, but Kenneth ignored it, hoping death was searching for him. Guilt washed over him as he thought of the constable he killed. At first, he wanted to live, only without the pity of the city. Now, he wished he would've jumped into the fire and ended it there, but if Salek saw, the city would hear of his madness.

He forced himself up but dropped to his knees, almost falling over the edge of the overhang. Uncaring, he slumped to his side, resting his head in the dirt.

Did I… not deserve any of it? Did I not deserve her?

The crack in the woods grew louder, but Kenneth refused to look. Someone or something stepped behind him, but he thought nothing of it, wondering if a bear or wolf was to be his end. He was not nervous, not afraid. Kenneth stood, his bones aching, and turned to find himself face-to-face with the masked man lingering under the shadows of branches.

"Mr. Forbes, you survived." The masked man eyed him. "Death has not found you yet."

Kenneth glanced to the man's hand, his red cane firm in the stranger's grip. He brought his sunken gaze to the mask, the eyes behind it lost to darkness. "Has it not?"

The man stepped to the overhang. "Tell me, Kenneth, what is a day of life worth to you?"

The masked man remained still, and silent, longer than Kenneth preferred. Kenneth dropped to one knee, his muscles sore and unable to hold his weight. His knuckles rested on the stone. "What is worth living if something has consumed your life?"

"Have you truly lost everything? You have suffered greatly, yet here you are. You still have the will, passion. Perhaps your desire to put beauty in the world remains."

"There's no beauty left in this wretched curse we call a city."

The masked man turned to Kenneth, narrow slits haunting, the blue-and-silver beaded design reflecting the glimmer of the moon.

"Your sense of what is beautiful can manifest from days past. The beauty I speak of is not what most consider... elegant."

Kenneth snarled, the dried blood cracking on his cheek and flaking onto his burned linen shirt. He glared as the masked man stepped towards him, pressing the cane against his shirt. The woodsy scent of a burning fire filled his nostrils, and the dry bite of dehydration clamored on his tongue.

"Who do—"

The masked man lifted his leg and kicked Kenneth in the chest, his ribs surging with pain. The world flipped upside down, and Kenneth fell from the overhang, the air bustling around him. He landed with a thud, feeling the sticks snap against his spine.

Kenneth rolled uncontrollably down the steep hill, smacking his arm off a tree. His shoulder caught a bush, ripping the jacket from his shoulders. Flailing to grab hold of anything, Kenneth skidded to a halt, his face buried in leaves.

Blood dripped off his brow and into his eye, and dirt rested on his cheek. Kenneth rolled over, and the rain grew heavy, every drop stinging his wounds. He pulled his hand down his forehead, blood smearing over his cheekbones.

The masked man walked to him, eyes blacker than night.

"Are you *truly* dead, Mr. Forbes?" the man asked.

Kenneth stared, and a grin formed on his face. He chuckled, and it grew into laughter, his chest aching, knowing it was bruised over. "I wish I was."

"So something has awakened?"

Kenneth blinked, his laugh fading to an empty gaze, his hands spread across the ground.

"I see the storm that stirs within you," the masked man said. "Would you want your wife to lie—"

"No!" Kenneth slammed his fist with furrowed brows. "You will not speak of her."

"So you are still in there. When you have nothing, after everything has burned, you find yourself a sapling, ready to grow into a great oak. To find your purpose."

"I will lie here in the dirt and wait for my last breath. As I pass, I'll think of Amia."

The masked man pointed the cane at Kenneth. "Would you embrace death knowing your wife's killer is alive?"

Kenneth's lip quivered, and he pushed himself off the ground. "What did you say?"

The masked man stared, unflinching.

"Hey! I'm talking to you." Kenneth raised his hand. "Why did you say that?"

"Because what happened to you was intentional."

Kenneth looked down the hill, Amia running through his mind, bathing in the tub with a smile, unbeknownst of what her fate was to come.

She couldn't have been… who?

"How would you know?" Kenneth asked.

"You may have been foolish in removing that brace, but you would have perished regardless. Your machine was sabotaged."

"How do you know?"

"I saw it."

"Why would you have seen this happen?"

"Because I was at your manor, to kill you myself."

Kenneth lowered his hand, his eyes bloodshot and gaze fatigued. "So it's you murdering inventors? Did you decide to step it up to aristocrats and make it worth your while?"

"My reasons for killing are my own."

"You didn't tell me who killed my wife."

"Do not worry. I will. I am a lot of things, Mr. Forbes, but—"

"Who killed her?" Kenneth scowled, spitting in the air.

The masked man glanced at Kenneth. "You have yet to listen to my proposal. I need for you to spread the beauty of a different kind."

"Enlighten me, and while you're at it, how about you tell me who you are and take off that mask."

The masked man tossed the cane onto the ground. Kenneth picked it up and straightened his back, looking at the bronzed handle and red oak. The only item intact from his stolen life.

Kenneth's grip on the cane tightened, and he swung it with all his might. The masked man dodged it, grabbed the cane, and yanked it from his hand. Kenneth lost his footing and fell onto his face.

The masked man grabbed him by the waist and tossed him, Kenneth slipping further down the hill.

Kenneth lay with a drifting gaze, leaves covering his body. Blood seeped from his cheek, and the cane rolled next to him. He grasped it and closed his eyes, waiting for death to take him.

Amia…

The masked man jumped from the high ground and landed near Kenneth's head.

Kenneth focused on the earth against his nose, overwhelmed by the musky smell of pine needles. He dragged his hand, dirt collecting under his fingernails and blood dripping off his face.

Make it stop, Amia. None of this can be real.

"Now tell me, what is a day of life worth to you?" The masked man pulled out a red metal mask, sitting on the ground.

Kenneth looked through the empty eye slits, the darkness behind them.

"Mr. Forbes, if you take this and spread the beauty of my choosing, you will right the wrongdoing to your wife."

"And what beauty is that?"

"The kind that rests in your soul, at this very moment."

"And if I say no? Would you kill me now?"

"If you wish. It makes no difference in what's to come."

Gashes and fresh scrapes mangled Kenneth's face. He smirked, blood dripping down his stubbled chin. What did it matter how Kenneth got revenge? In the end, he would give justice to Amia. This masked man did not matter. He meant nothing, and Kenneth was going to make sure everyone would remember the Forbes name.

"Now, would you kindly?" Kenneth gritted his teeth. "I want a name."

The masked man looked to the city and back, rain collecting on his mask. "His name... is Aleksandar Scott."

~

Bright lights and rowdy people filled the smoky bar, clapping along to the jazz band on the corner stage. The sun faded behind the hills hours ago, and the patrons gorged themselves with the town's finest cocktails and whiskey.

Simeon, with skin as rich as caramel and eyes dark like chocolate, smiled at a woman in a red dress sitting next to a candle. He blushed and poured a drink, another bartender coming from the kitchen. She washed her hands in a basin under the bar and dried them against the towel on her waist.

The band, dressed in white suits, played with a robust melody that brought everyone's foot to a tap, the pianist swaying in delight.

Simeon walked to his coworker, leaning in under the blaring music. "I'm going to step out to catch a smoke."

"See you soon. You might have a better memory, but let me show them how to pour a proper drink."

She elbowed Simeon in the side, and he waved his hand. The bartender snatched a bottle, nearly dropping it as she tossed it in the air. The crowd laughed and cheered as she grabbed glasses, sliding them across the counter with a smile.

Simeon walked down the line, smiled at the woman in the red dress, and exited out the bar door. He passed through the kitchen and out into the alleyway behind the restaurant. Silence and a moment's rest awaited him after hours of drinks and empty conversations. He pulled out a cigarette and lit a match, lighting the end. He sucked in and blew out, resting his forearms on the patio railing.

Relief soothed his headache, and he stretched his neck and rubbed his shoulder. He leaned further across the rail, bringing the tobacco to his lips.

Simeon took another puff, coughing in the bitter air, his lungs stinging. He wandered down the steps and paused, a glimmer in the shadows catching his eye.

"Simeon."

Simeon jumped back, his heart beating as Kenneth emerged against the brick wall with a burned top hat resting on his head. He pulled his scarf down, revealing his blistering face with dried cuts and gashes, and his one hand was bandaged.

"Mr. Forbes?" Simeon coughed on the cigarette smoke. "You're... I thought you were dead."

"I was, but now I have returned." Kenneth walked towards the bartender, his hair frayed and charred at the tips hanging over his cheek.

"Why are you hiding? Well's Peake has done nothing but speak of your tragedy."

"Please, wait. I need your help. Mystery shrouds my attempted murder, and you have the answers I deserve. We must keep this quiet before the city learns of my existence."

Simeon stared at Kenneth from head to toe. Ragged and cheeks taut, he looked as if he had not eaten in days. "Murder? What would I know?"

"The night of my gala, just before my speech, a woman sat at the end of the bar conversing with Dr. Gray."

Simeon glanced down the alleyway as a carriage rattled by. "Yes... what about her?"

"I need her name."

"What does—"

"Her name!" Kenneth flexed.

Simeon backed up, dropping his cigarette. "Miss Harvey. Vida Harvey. What did she do to you?"

"Nothing, but she knows someone who did, and I, for the life of me, can't remember where he lives."

Kenneth rolled his wrist, and the Red Breath slipped from under his cuff, glimmering in the gaslight. Light glared off a small tank on Kenneth's back, catching Simeon's eye.

Simeon inched towards the door. "Mr. Forbes, you need a doctor. To alert the authorities."

He swallowed his rising terror as Kenneth blocked his way.

"Do not fear, my friend," Kenneth said, his words hollow. "Everything will be all right."

Kenneth raised his hand to Simeon, and with a sudden click, air sucked into the gauntlet.

Fire screeched off Kenneth's hands and swarmed the alley, engulfing Simeon in the scorching heat. His tears evaporated, and his screams echoed throughout the alleyway. He flailed to the ground with his clothes ablaze.

Simeon thrashed on the cobblestone, his flesh burning off his bones, as Kenneth stood over him with an empty gaze.

CHAPTER THIRTY-FIVE

Snowflakes fell in a gentle breeze through iced branches gleaming under the twilight. Snow crunched under Aleksandar's boot as he looked through the hazy forest amid a whiteout.

He squinted as the crisp wind kissed his cheeks, searching for his friend but finding nothing except pine trees and cold rocks. Someone giggled, and he scrambled around a tree, seeing no one in sight. His blue scarf brushed against his wool coat, and the tip of his nose was red. He rushed to the edge of the forest, lifting his feet higher to avoid any covered roots, and looked into a meadow of unharvested wheat. A magician's tent rested at the foot of the hill.

A little girl kneeled in the snow up to her waistline and stared at the blue-and-white canvas as a shadow rested over her.

Aleksandar closed his cold lips and walked to her. She reached up and grabbed his hand, pulling him beside her with a pearly smile and braided brown hair.

She sat there, her eyes drifting to him. "Alek…"

He shifted to her, breathing easy and calm.

"Always remember that promise for me. Please?" A tear slid down her cheek.

The snow lifted off the ground in a thunderous wind, sweeping the meadow. Blinded, Aleksandar reached for the girl, only to find her impression left in the wheat. He closed his eyes as he started to suffocate, the air ripped from his lungs. His chest tightened, and a blinding light blurred his vision.

"Aleksandar!"

∾

Aleksandar jarred awake, flexing his arms against his hips. He shook with shallow breaths and sweat running down his forehead. A fire crackled in the fireplace, the woodsy aroma filling his nostrils, and it was dark outside the windows, clouds hiding the stars.

"Aleksandar?"

As the headache set in, he looked to Ellie kneeling beside him against the old sofa, her hand on his. Hugh stood behind her with raised eyebrows. Aleksandar sat up on the cushion, stretching his neck from the ache of propping his head too high.

"Miss Fritz," Aleksandar said. "How are—you're here?"

"Why good evening to you too, Mr. Scott." Ellie batted a coy smile.

"I'm sorry, I didn't mean it like that," he said with a groggy voice. "I just wondered how you are here."

"Mr. Evans showed me the way after stumbling across him. When I looked at the World's Fair, you weren't there. I haven't seen you since the gala and was concerned after what had happened with Mr. Forbes last week."

"That's sweet of you, thank you."

Aleksandar lost himself in her rich, inviting eyes. He had forgotten how soothing her voice was. She kneeled there in her green shirt knitted with brown trim, embroidered with flowers on the sleeves. It fit her well. She seemed so innocent, her presence captivating.

Aleksandar smirked, and Ellie smiled back, blushing.

"I'll make some tea." Hugh walked into the kitchen.

"I love tea," she said with enthusiasm. "And books, which I see this house has plenty of."

Her demeanor was sincere, and Aleksandar could sit all day listening to her.

"Did you know, Mr. Scott, that anxiety and fear cause nightmares?" she said.

Aleksandar pushed his tongue on the roof of his mouth. "It didn't start as a nightmare."

"They never do. Actually, that's a lie." She paused. "I guess there have been some terrifying ones from the beginning."

Aleksandar put his feet on the floor, and Ellie sat next to him, looking to the dim fire. She batted him a glance, and he chuckled.

"It's nice to see you again," he said.

Ellie held her smile. "Likewise. I've been hoping to learn more about you. My brothers' partners are all business and society, and I hoped for anything but."

"We could discuss nightmares?" Aleksandar rubbed his pant leg.

"Oh, do you enjoy scary things?"

"Not particularly, but it seems you do."

"It depends. Hugh seemed frightened when I asked where you were."

Hugh paused in the door frame, balancing three cups of tea in his hands, looking at them both. "Usually, when someone shouts out my name, I need to go the other way."

"And you tried." Ellie laughed.

Hugh set the drinks on the coffee table and eased into the rocking chair. Aleksandar grabbed his cup. The robust aroma of lemon and bergamot mixed with the fire's musk filled his nostrils.

Ellie leaned back, watching the log pop in the fireplace, rolled her neck, and relaxed into the head cushion. Aleksandar smirked, intrigued by her uncanny manner.

"So, Mr. Scott," Ellie said. "I'm interested in this nightmare of yours."

"Oh, it's not much of anything."

"You don't expect it has something to do with what's happened?"

Aleksandar rested his hands in his lap, holding his teacup, the warmth lingering on his fingertips. "I know it does, but all I ever had was good intentions, and we've seen those outcomes."

Hugh watched Aleksandar as if hanging on his every word, and Ellie looked to him, patiently waiting for Aleksandar to continue. From the moment he presented the Red Breath at the World's Fair, his life had gotten worse. Each event had only battered his mind worse, making his inner thoughts loud and rampant. His throat felt thick, and he sighed.

"I am…" Aleksandar said. "Guilty. I know people say it's not my fault, but I feel responsible for what happened. I can't stop asking myself, why do bad things happen to those with good intentions? At this point, even if I created a positive difference, would people accept it? I wish I could take it all back."

Aleksandar set his drink down and grabbed Hugh's project off the table, fumbling it in his hands.

Ellie laid her hand on his arm.

"It's not your fault," Hugh said. "Things just happen, and that's all. Good or bad, I don't think we can change what will happen. Have to move on and keep pushing."

Ellie's touch on Aleksandar's arm was comforting, and he forced a smile.

"A man of few words," Ellie said. "But great ones. Your past won't define you. If we had let the Black Harvest mark us, we wouldn't be where we are today."

Aleksandar stood and walked to a three-legged stool next to the chimney. He grabbed the fire poker from beside the hearth and shifted the coals away from the floor. "I think I could, but part of me wonders if I should follow a different path."

Ellie sipped on her tea, looking into the cup. "Do you remember when I told you I was a traveler?"

"Yes."

"Well, I left that lifestyle for a reason. After many years of traveling, it came to a rather unpleasant end. We settled in the east for a few weeks outside Oakvale. The people there weren't fond of us, and at first, they only scowled and ordered us to leave, but we stayed. We weren't hurting anybody, just looking for a place to rest."

Aleksandar watched, leaning in.

"Our camp was downriver, and one day they opened the dam. It wasn't some massive flood, but it washed away our supplies, waking us in the late hour. We all survived, but after more attacks and my friends' injuries, we grew divided. Some wanted to go home, but I didn't. I worked so hard to leave my past life behind that being on the road was all I cared about."

Ellie pulled on her braid.

"My dismay about my life before I became a traveler trapped me into watching friend after friend leave until only a few of us were left. I grew lonely and realized there was nothing left for me. After that, I found my way home to my brothers. I tried so hard to stay away from my past so it wouldn't define me, but instead, it did just that. Being able to accept coming home freed me of being trapped by my past."

Aleksandar bit his lip. "I'm sorry."

"I had a choice to make. Let my past define me or not, and I choose the latter."

Ellie pushed her hair back and tapped the side of her cup. Aleksandar rubbed his hands, and Hugh set his tea down, his mouth open as if he was trying to say something.

"As a kid," Hugh said, "my sister was my best friend. We did everything together, our parents were kind, we had a home, and everyone was happy. My parents owned a lot of land for the harvests, but they were no longer fertile. Our parents rushed to do something, but an aristocrat conned them out of the deeds and left us broke."

Ellie looked up from her glass, and Aleksandar's eyes were wide.

"We were on the streets after that. My father died because he gave his food to us, and my mum passed in less pleasant ways. We had nowhere to go, so we ran to the countryside and ended up in Granville. Soon after, the city broke into riots, I lost my sister, and I was all that was left. I want to move on, but I haven't yet, I know that. Not sure you can overnight, but each day gets easier."

Aleksandar looked out the window, his chest heavy and tight.

"Thank you for sharing, Hugh," Ellie said. "I wouldn't expect anyone to forget their past after all that."

Hugh nodded and pulled on his scarf, holding it over the bottom half of his face.

Aleksandar remained quiet and pondered their stories, looking for the moral of them. He swallowed hard, trying to keep his mouth from drying out. "How do you just push forward?"

"I said goodbye to my friends even when I didn't want to," Ellie said. "I moved on and hoped to find some land in the city to raise horses. That is my dream, always was."

Aleksandar put a log into the fireplace and sat next to Ellie, and they all sipped tea in silence as minutes passed. The fire crackled, the flames grew, and the bark smoked into the chimney.

Aleksandar closed his eyes, thinking of his past and future, wondering what may be in store for him.

"I'm sorry to hear your stories. I didn't have that growing up, and until a month ago, life was normal. There was little choice with everything that's happened, and I think I'm ready to make a difference."

Knock, knock, knock.

"I'll get it," Hugh said.

Ellie put her hand on Aleksandar's arm. "You can make that change. Maybe a walk later tonight would be insightful."

"I would like that. Will you come with me?"

"As much as I'd enjoy that, you need this walk alone to clear your head."

Aleksandar folded his hands. "I hope you'll join me another night at least."

"Of course."

"Mr. Scott," Hugh said.

Aleksandar looked over his shoulder to Hugh holding the door handle, Nicoli in front of the flat. Aleksandar stood as he rubbed his arm, an empty feeling filling his stomach.

"Hello, Mr. Scott," the detective said, the gaslight behind him.

Aleksandar wandered to the door and nodded to Hugh. He closed it and stepped outside, the wind cutting through the fabric of his sweater vest. He folded his arms to keep himself warm.

"We could've spoken inside," Nicoli said, running his hand through his hair.

"That's okay." Aleksandar chattered his teeth. His mind raced to Kenneth's fire, fearing the worst. "What can I do for you this late?"

"I wanted to chat without the Peake over our shoulders."

"And why would you want that?"

"Whenever I see you, it's always after some tragedy. I wanted to apologize for my methods the other day. I realize it was a bit extreme."

Aleksandar paused with unflinching eyes. "Extreme? You showed me a dead body that had been burned to nothing."

Nicoli rubbed his upper lip. "I had no intention of coming here to upset you. You weren't at the World's Fair the past few days, and I tried to avoid disturbing you at home. Why haven't you attended?"

Aleksandar held his gaze, shaking his head. "I thought it wise for me to stay away from the public. I know I'm a suspect, and some won't take kindly to that."

"Yes, but if it's any consolation, I don't think you're the one we're looking for."

"You do."

"Actually, I don't. It's nothing personal, but you lack the fortitude to be the killer in these recent murders."

"Recent? As in…"

Nicoli looked down the street. A couple walked across the road. "Several nights ago, he burned a bartender alive in a back alley, followed by a tailor in North Hills. Two days ago, a doctor from Redwood at the local academy. Someone is using your invention, that I am sure."

"You're certain?"

"So much that the Peake is referring to this killer as the Phoenix."

Aleksandar rubbed his right arm and closed his eyes for a second. He breathed in, pausing as he grew lightheaded. He looked away from the investigator, and chills ran through his limbs to his toes.

Nicoli pulled a schematic book out of his bag. Aleksandar's pupils dilated.

"This is the reason I stopped by." Nicoli handed Aleksandar the workbook. "We found it in the forest behind your house."

"How long have you had this?" Aleksandar looked into the book, blank pages in the back, and the rest ripped from the binding.

"A week. Shortly after Mr. Forbes's death."

Aleksandar glared at the man. "And you're just giving this to me?"

"As I said, I searched the World's Fair, but you were not there."

"Is there anything else, Detective? If not, please go."

Nicoli pursed his lips and tipped his hat, walking down the street.

Aleksandar stared until Nicoli rounded the corner. He walked into the house, Hugh and Ellie looking at him from the living room.

"What happened out there?" Ellie asked.

"I uh... need just a minute. I'll be right back."

Aleksandar marched to the staircase and stepped down into the workshop. His head throbbed, and his headache turned into a migraine. Shae slept on a post, struggling to open her eyes as Aleksandar set the book on the counter. He flipped through the empty pages, searching in the shadows.

Please be here.

Aleksandar slipped his fingernail into the seam of the book. He pulled, and the binding opened with a sticky snap, revealing pages of hidden notes and drawings of a circular machine with metal beams arched over a round disk.

Aleksandar cuffed his hand over his mouth and looked to his secret room, his breath shaking through his fingers.

CHAPTER THIRTY-SIX

Aleksandar walked with his hands in his pockets alongside the World's Palace, the glass towering above him. Gaslights illuminated the gardens and fountains as clouds hid the stars.

The fair crowd had thinned, but a few still strolled the pathways, looking to the statues of the distinguished men and women who built Well's Peake. In the center of the fountain rested a statue of an angel with water flowing down its marble wings as exotic and vibrant fish swam underneath. The air carried a floral aroma from the rows of tulips, roses, and lavender planted along a large pool. A cobblestone road with hedges lined the sidewalks next to the hedge maze.

Aleksandar rounded the pathway, looking for the closest place to sit. He pulled his scarf tight, and his breath lingered in front of his face, his cheeks growing red. A woman in a purple dress sat on a bench, rubbing her hand. He leaned over, recognizing her gloves.

"Miss Harvey?"

Vida turned with wide eyes, straightening her back. "Mr. Scott. My goodness, what are you doing here so late?"

"I was out for a stroll, looking to clear my thoughts. What are you doing at the World's Fair?"

"There was a seminar for alternative medicine called morphine. It puts people to into a lucid state when painful surgeries are needed. It ended a few hours ago, but I enjoy the gardens at night. Please sit."

Aleksandar pulled his hands from his pockets and sat, the wood cool on his backside.

Vida touched her chin. "I'm sorry, by the way."

Aleksandar glanced at her with his brow raised. "Sorry? Whatever for?"

"After Kenneth's gala, I left without telling you, and then after what happened to him, Maker bless his soul, I never came to check on you. I worried I'd be bothersome, but that might've been selfish of me."

"You don't need to apologize. I'd say I'm not in a normal situation."

Vida nodded, pulling on her bottom lip. "Is that why you're out walking?"

Aleksandar leaned forward, his hands on the bench's seat. "I'm looking for… a sign, I guess. I need to do something, but it has been so random, and happening outside of my control. I just wish I could erase this scar."

Vida smirked. "I know about scars, and let's just say we don't have to let them define us. Doesn't mean they don't get to us."

Aleksandar's thoughts wandered. He felt fatigued as if he had been walking for days. What was he to do? His mind was his own worst enemy, and he exhausted endless scenarios, every emotion.

"Have you gotten out much?" Vida asked.

Aleksandar lifted his head. "Not really. I go to Miss Arlen's house to invent, and then there's food and the necessities. I was a homebody before, so I'm used to it."

"True, but not wandering after so long could drive anyone mad."

"Indeed. How are things in the nursing world?"

Vida licked her lips and turned to him with a grin. "Well, after applying to academies from Belagrad to the Southern Plains—"

Aleksandar sat tall. "And?"

Vida pulled out a letter with a broken seal, holding it in front of her.

"Vida, that's amazing. Where were you accepted? When?"

"Blackwell. Of all places."

"I thought they denied you?"

"They did, but someone came through. Do you remember Dr. Gray from the gala? He's on the board and spoke to the right people." Vida held her head back, pulled out a purple handkerchief, and dabbed her eyes. "Excuse me."

"Are you all right?" Aleksandar asked, not knowing what to do.

"It's fine. I just never thought this would happen to me. I'm sorry. You've been through tragedy, and here I am."

"No, no, this is good news. I could use more of it."

Vida wiped her cheeks and bit her lower lip. "I want to show you something, Mr. Scott. I sit here and tell you that scars don't define your past, but mine has haunted me for so long."

Aleksandar nodded. "What do you mean?"

Vida took a deep breath and rubbed her palm between her fingers. Closing her eyes, she grabbed the end of the glove and rolled it to her fingertips. Aleksandar watched, glancing between her and her hand. There was a scar that ran up her wrist and wrapped around the thumb.

"This," Vida said. "It could've ruined everything I wanted in life. I am my own worst enemy, as we always are. I never thought I'd receive a chance, but now, I can pursue my passion."

"Well, I guess we will see what Dr. Harvey can accomplish."

Vida chuckled.

"The Harvest Festival is not far away," Aleksandar said. "We should go to celebrate and watch the firelights."

"I would like that."

Aleksandar watched Vida stare into the gardens with a grin, taking deep breaths. He looked to red-and-blue flowers, the stars glimmering above them. With the World's Palace behind him and hanging gaslights lining the cobblestone paths, Aleksandar felt a moment of peace, the first in a long while.

He closed his eyes and listened to the faraway conversations, the wind bustling against the trees and hedges, the water dripping into the fountain. His scarf was tight, and the inside of his jacket held in the heat. He thought to a childhood friend, thinking of the snow and the magician's tent.

Aleksandar blinked, catching Vida's smile fade as she focused down the cobblestone path. Aleksandar squinted and turned to a figure in the distance walking with heavy steps, an iron tank on his back. The man wore a burned top hat with a red metal mask, making his way between the green bushes and colored flowers, dead leaves at his heels.

Vida stood. "Who is that?"

Aleksandar rose, his heart beating against his rib cage, his mouth drying out. He grabbed Vida's arm with his clammy hands, and the smell of burned wood permeated the air.

Fairgoers stumbled away as the sinister figure reached the glory of the World's Palace.

Aleksandar pulled Vida back as the Phoenix lowered his head, eyes full of darkness. The masked man lifted his fists, gauntlets on his wrists, and Aleksandar held his breath.

My invention!

The machine hissed, and fire erupted from the tips.

Aleksandar grabbed Vida's waist and pulled her into the fountain, submerging them both under the surface. The world became muffled as blazes roared over the edge and blistered against the top of the water. Steam billowed around the angelic statue, scorching the side of it. Aleksandar kicked and swam with Vida under his arm, choking.

Vida flailed and broke from his grip, pushing off the bottom. She broke through the chilling surface and hacked up water. Aleksandar followed her, gasping for air, looking to the chaos. The Phoenix hopped on the rim and sprinted with a limp. He shot a wave of fire towards Vida, and she leaped over the far railing, slammed onto the path, and groaned as she grabbed her shoulder.

The Phoenix waved streams of flames as Aleksandar pulled himself to the pathway. He ducked, and the flares rippled against the glass behind him, innocent bystanders screaming.

A constable stormed from the Palace, a baton in hand. "That's enough!"

He dashed for the Phoenix, who jumped to the pavement, hunched over like a creature stalking its meal. The killer unleashed a firestorm upon the constable, who dropped to his knees, screaming. Smoke rose from his body as he plopped next to the fountain, burned alive.

Aleksandar ran around the statue, but the Phoenix caught up. Vida lunged from behind a fern and tackled the man, and they fell to the ground, Vida smacking her head off the pavement. She stood, stumbling to run away, but the Phoenix grabbed her by the waist and lifted her above him as his gauntlets ignited, catching her dress ablaze.

He slammed her into the cobblestone with a thud, hitting the top of her spine, where she lay unconscious.

Seeing Vida's skirt on fire, Aleksandar stopped and splashed water on her, unable to put out the flames. The Phoenix jumped onto the fountain's railing and looked at Aleksandar. His gauntlet hissed, and Aleksandar dove into the fountain, water rushing into his lungs, burning like a hot iron.

"What will you do when your air runs out, Mr. Scott!"

Aleksandar's chest felt as though it were on fire, and his body shivered. He pulled himself across the bottom, making sure he did not rise to the surface or get caught in underwater plants. He watched the blistering light in the reflection.

Aleksandar smacked his head on the edge and slid out of the water, the Phoenix shooting the wrong way, blinded by his own madness. With his clothes soaked and shoes heavy, Aleksandar took off into the icy breeze.

Several constables emerged from the World's Palace and tried to stop the Phoenix, to no avail, finding themselves set ablaze. A fair patron sneaked around, stomped out the fire on Vida's dress, and tried to drag her away from the chaos.

"Over here, over here!" Aleksandar shouted, his hands cuffed over his mouth.

The Phoenix spun to Aleksandar's call and jumped from the fountain. He pointed his gauntlet at Vida and the bystander attempting to rescue her.

"I wouldn't if I were you," the Phoenix said. "I implore you to come here, or I'll burn the flesh from her bones."

Aleksandar froze, trying to think, but no ideas popped into his head. The voice behind the red mask was feral, like an animal's growl haunting him.

"Now!"

Aleksandar realized his distraction failed. He started with a single step as the Phoenix held his arm to Vida without a flinch.

Constables flooded from around the World's Palace with batons drawn. "Protect the people!"

The Phoenix twisted and pulled the handle in his palms. Flames erupted towards Vida, but a constable blocked the path, his clothing searing against his skin. The others headed for the Phoenix, but he sprinted for Aleksandar.

Frozen in fear, Aleksandar watched the man light the bushes on fire as he neared him. The Phoenix barreled down, and Aleksandar found himself stuck as if someone cemented his shoes to the ground.

Run!

Aleksandar flinched and took off. The footsteps behind him grew louder with every second. Despite the weaving and turning at the crossways, Aleksandar could not gain a lead. The man was swift and unrelenting.

Aleksandar rushed into a hedge maze, hoping to lose the killer; however, the layout was not much of a puzzle. They built it with long hallways of hedges, marble pillars, and iron fencing, leaving long rows for the madman to see down.

"You were lucky, but now you'll never escape!" the man said.

Fires raged, and the landscape billowed into smoke, a musky haze filling the air. Aleksandar glanced over his shoulder. The Phoenix was missing.

He paused, not sure if he had lost him or worse. Aleksandar looked to a thinner hedge and tried to slip through. He got stuck, the branches cutting his skin through the cotton of his coat, his cheek bleeding. A snap came from behind, and he grabbed the nearby fence and pulled himself through the thicket despite the pain.

Aleksandar paused and listened between the crackling of burning hedges, the screams of the crowd, and shadows lingering in the haze.

The Phoenix lurched around the corner, and Aleksandar was too slow to run off, the gap closing between the two. His attacker barreled through the vapor and slammed Aleksandar into the hedge, the sharp edges slashing into his skin. The man in the red mask slid to a halt with a weak breath, eyeing the young inventor.

Trapped, Aleksandar struggled to pull himself from the thicket, only wedging himself deeper. He could feel the blood inside his jacket as the Phoenix stepped away, chuckling.

"Oh, this is well deserved," the Phoenix said.

"Why are you doing this?" Aleksandar reached for anything to grab hold of.

The Phoenix held out his gauntlet and lit the hedges around Aleksandar on fire. The branches burned and wilted as the heat and embers drifted into Aleksandar's coat, his hair falling over his face.

"Why?" Aleksandar struggled.

"Please, be quiet. There's no reason to tell you shit."

The flames ignited a vine, and it fell on Aleksandar's arm, searing into his forearm.

"Ah!" Aleksandar screamed, the pain stinging and his nerves shaking.

Through unbridled fury, Aleksandar found the strength to push off the weakened hedge, ripping his jacket. The Phoenix snarled and grabbed Aleksandar, pinning him against a marble pillar. His gauntlet erupted in a blaze, and he swung at Aleksandar, who caught the man's wrist and directed the machine aside.

Aleksandar held the killer's strength, keeping the nozzle away from him, but he grew weak. The Phoenix kneed him in the groin, pushing the gauntlet forward. The flames sizzled against Aleksandar's forearm and incinerated the fabric from his arm.

Ahhh!

Aleksandar dropped, and the Phoenix fell headfirst into the pillar. Aleksandar collapsed to the ground and rubbed his cheeks, still warm from the heat of the fire. He lay on his back; his shoulders arched as the Phoenix held a gauntlet to him.

"Where did you find those?" Aleksandar stared down the nozzle of the Red Breath.

The Phoenix ignored his question, raising the other hand to Aleksandar's face.

"You deserve to suffer, you bitch." The Phoenix pulled the triggers.

A glimmer of metal flashed in the corner of Aleksandar's eye, and a mechanical leg slammed into the ground behind the madman. The limb lashed out and knocked the Phoenix off his feet, sending him rolling against the cobblestone.

Aleksandar looked up to Lydia, wielding Owen's Limbs of Life and towering over him like a spider.

The Phoenix stood and raced for Aleksandar.

Lydia struck him again, and the killer flew through a hedge, lying flat on the other side of the pavement, branches and leaves around him. Aleksandar slumped against the pillar, holding his arm as he watched her break through the shrubbery.

The Phoenix jumped to his feet but was no match for the eight-legged invention. The constable nailed him again from behind, knocking him towards the end of the maze. He stumbled up and rushed into the shadowed forest behind the World's Palace.

He lit everything on fire in his path, blocking their pursuit. Lydia tried to step over the flames, but the Phoenix fired back, causing her to waver.

Aleksandar crawled and peered through the broken hedges, but the man disappeared into the thicket behind smoke and fire. Lydia made her way to the arched entrance and looked out, squinting up the hillside. Her head sagged to the side, and she held it up with her hand, securing a loose metal bracket on her neck.

Several constables ran through the maze, coming to her aid.

"Find him before he escapes!" She pointed at the hill.

Aleksandar watched as the constables stormed off and disappeared into the dark forest, towards the beast that fled his hunt.

CHAPTER THIRTY-SEVEN

In the darkness, a sharp ringing filled Vida's ears. She pressed her palms against her head, trying to silence the noise. Her temples pulsated as a stinging pain rippled down her neck.

She looked left, knowing her eyes were open, her fingers trembling. Pulling on her eyelids to make sure they were not closed, she sobbed, and tears ran down her cheek. Vida lifted her hands, looking for anything to grab hold of but finding only air.

"Help, help!" Vida's voice shook.

The blanket on top of her was heavy, but someone slipped between her arms, embracing her whole.

"It's Aleksandar," he said. "You're okay. We're safe now."

"Why can't I see? What's happening?" Choking on her words, Vida blinked, the room still dark.

She clutched Aleksandar as curtains became clearer behind him. A doctor walked in with a candle in hand, showing Vida that her vision may still be there.

"Miss Harvey, it's Dr. Doyle." He set the light on a stand. "Is this candle too bright? I've been taking precautions."

"No, is something wrong with my eyes?"

"You took a serious blow to the spine, young one. Thankfully, nothing was broken, and you appear to be fine, despite the bruising. Your eyes have a white discoloration, so I wanted to be careful and not cause further damage."

"How long have I been out?"

Vida hung on to the back of Aleksandar's shirt, feeling his bandaged arm against her chest, trying not to put pressure on it. The walls were dim, and there were glimmers of light off the metal instruments. She looked to the hospital garden, which lay out of the window.

Her breathing grew heavier, and nausea filled her.

"Vida, it's okay," Aleksandar said, trying to pull away.

She gripped him harder, not letting him stray far.

"I'm not leaving you. I promise," he said.

The doctor set his hand on Vida's shoulder. "Everything is all right, my dear."

Vida did not want to let go of Aleksandar. His warmth was the only thing comforting her, keeping her from unraveling at the seams. She loosened her grip, and Aleksandar straightened his back, sitting on the edge, and held on to her hand.

"What happened?" Vida coughed, wiping her cheeks.

Dr. Doyle sat on the other side of the bed. "Do you not remember?"

Her shoulders tightened, and she got the cold sweats. "I can't... the man, in the red mask. He was walking towards us."

"And then what?"

"He... attacked us. I was in the water. Did I pass out?"

"No," Aleksandar said. "You tackled him, and he threw you to the ground. He knocked you out."

"Why did he attack me?"

"I don't know. I think he was after me."

Vida tried to sit up, but she slumped. She wanted to run away, every nerve in her body telling her to, but she was too weak. Her head spun, and she thought of the red metal mask, the killer's eyes reflecting in the shadows.

Dr. Doyle grabbed Vida's arm. "Please, you must relax. I don't want you getting worked up, in case there—"

"Someone tried to kill us! Why?" Vida raised her voice.

"Vida."

Vida squinted, the world spinning around her. She squeezed Aleksandar's hand and bit her lip, trying to control her sobbing. "Is there something wrong with my vision?"

The doctor stood, tapping his fingers together, letting a moment pass as her breathing leveled out. "Miss Harvey, I don't have the answers yet. I hope you understand I'd be the first to tell you if there was damage to your sight."

Dr. Doyle leaned over, looking into her eyes with a scope, a faded haze resting over them.

A nurse walked in with a basin of water. "You sent for me, Doctor."

"Yes, if you would tidy Miss Harvey up." Dr. Doyle put his palm on hers. "I'm going to step out for a moment and borrow your friend. You won't be alone, I promise."

With every touch, Vida flinched, her body thinking it was the hand of someone unkind. She wanted to stand, to be home in her bed or the bath with her favorite soap, but her mind lingered on the attack. The blistering warmth of the fire on her skin and the water as it flooded her lungs.

The doctor looked at Aleksandar, nodding to the hallway.

Aleksandar straightened the blanket over Vida and leaned in. "We'll be right back."

"Please don't leave me," Vida muttered the last word.

Aleksandar followed the doctor out, who watched Vida through the curtain. They stood near a massive window facing a stone building with pillars, gaslights illuminating the World's Fair.

"She is my best nurse." Doyle kept his voice low, looking over his shoulder. "I can't believe she's awake. She took significant stress to the brain, and I feared this man may have injured her spine."

"What's happening to her? With her vision?" Aleksandar asked.

Dr. Doyle held his finger over his lips, glancing to Vida. "I don't know. Trauma to the head is tricky. She appears fine on the outside, but on the inside, there could be damage. I believe it damaged something behind the eyes, leading to her hazed vision. I'd prefer she rest before I pry too much on symptoms."

Aleksandar sighed and looked at Vida as she clenched her white cotton blankets, bringing them close to her face. She stared out the window and held still. The nurse dabbed her forehead, wiping dirt away.

"How bad will it be?" Aleksandar asked.

"These next days should answer more questions. Sadly, all we can do is wait. I'm sure she'll appreciate your visits."

Aleksandar nodded, looking at his clothes, ripped and bloodied. "I wish I could help more."

"The Peakeland Yard has everything under control that we can't. They have posted constables throughout the clinic, and I believe they have an escort waiting for you."

"Thank you."

"And you? How's that arm treating you?" Dr. Doyle yawned in the late night.

Aleksandar touched his bandages. "Stiff, but they said I'll be okay. My jacket took most of the damage, but there's a burn along my forearm. The cuts and bruises are small."

"The doctors are masters of scars in this clinic. Thankfully, someone was on call before it became a serious issue."

"Indeed."

Doyle walked to the curtain. "Now go home and sleep."

"I promised her I wouldn't leave her alone."

"She won't be. I'll stay here overnight and watch her personally."

"Are you sure?"

The doctor grabbed Aleksandar's arm and checked the bandages. "Miss Harvey is not the only one who needs to heal. This *will* leave a physical scar, but also one up here." Dr. Doyle pointed to his head.

"I don't think mine matters much compared to hers."

"You have both suffered. While her injuries are great, that does not mean we should ignore yours. Look after yourself, and if you need someone to talk to, we're here."

"Thank you, Doctor."

"Of course. Remember to change those bandages. If not, you'll find an infection."

"I can do that. I'll come in before I head home."

Doyle nodded, and they both walked in through the curtain.

Vida looked beyond the window and stared, her eyes glazed over like frosted glass. Aleksandar watched as she bit her trembling lip, knowing on the inside she was shattered.

Aleksandar stepped onto the street of Well's Peake, the bags under his eyelids dark and heavy. His hair was tangled and covered in broken leaf fragments. Eyes hazel and bloodshot, he stared at the moon that crept through the clouds.

The air was crisp, and although he was fatigued, his mind had never been clearer. He knew what he had to do because none of it was going to stop until he put an end to it, and he could not wait any longer.

He tucked his hands in his pockets, shielding them from the cold. Owen walked down the street with two constables and his invention attached to their backs.

Owen stepped close with his cane. "Are you okay?"

"As well as anyone could be. What are you doing here?"

"Glad to hear. They inclined me to retrofit more constables as an escort for you. You have become quite the priority to certain people. I figured it best I be here to supervise my own invention."

Aleksandar covered a yawn. "Makes sense. I didn't see you offering your invention for this."

"This is an exception."

Aleksandar nodded. "Do you know if anyone else was hurt?"

Owen glanced over, then looked away.

Aleksandar rubbed his temple as pressure filled his chest.

"You're right. This was my fault."

Owen stared into the distance and bit his lip, putting his weight on the cane. "No, it's not. That doesn't matter, though." Owen put his hand on Aleksandar's shoulder, letting out a deep breath.

"Let's get you home."

~

Kenneth pushed hard, finding himself at the ridge of the hill, his muscles fatigued and cramping. Taking off his mask, he dropped it on a moss-covered stump. He could see the dim lanterns bouncing between the trees down the mountain, like lost bugs looking for a resting place in the night.

Kenneth spat blood from his mouth, the metallic musk from his mask lingering on his face. Sticks and leaves cracked downhill, but the Peakeland Yard would never find him.

As smoke billowed from the gardens, showing everyone that Well's Peake was no longer safe, Kenneth stood with a sharp smile, snickering in the lunar light.

CHAPTER THIRTY-EIGHT

S it down!" Chief Constable Dekker pounded his fist off the desk and plopped into his seat.

Nicoli sat across from him, sporting his typical gray jacket and silver vest, pushing his palm through his hair.

When Lydia arrived that night and informed him Dekker wanted to meet, he knew he had to pick up his pace before they threw him out of the city.

"You've heard what's happened?" Dekker asked. His finger on his chin, still in a black jacket and nightshirt.

"Yes, sir, the fountain attack."

"I'm not sure what pisses me off more. The possibility you've made progress and not informed me, or that you don't have any answers, and someone is making us look like a pack of twits. How come after you showed up, my city went to shit tenfold?"

"I fear the killer knows I'm here, and that has agitated him."

"And why would he care that *you're* here, Nicoli?"

"I found evidence. A note in Abel Hawthorne's jacket."

"What did it say?" Dekker pulled on the end of his nose.

Nicoli wanted to reach for his pocket, the paper having never left it, but he hesitated. He knew Dekker would deport him to Redwood if he had any suspicion Nicoli was making matters worse.

"It said, listen to her, you still have a choice."

Dekker's hand flopped onto the desk, papers ruffling from the hit. Tapping on the edge of his worn chair, he straightened his back. "That could be directed towards anyone."

"The killer left it for someone, and I think I'm that person."

"Perhaps he likes the thrill. Maybe it survived the fire on Abel's body. A third was still intact." Dekker folded his hands. "Obviously, he enjoys making a spectacle with how he leaves his victims. What about Aleksandar Scott? First, a robbery, which had no relevance to our case, yet you investigated. Then several deaths by fire, and now an attack on his life at the World's Fair. Any progress on that lead?"

"He could be innocent, and his invention a coincidence. You may not want to hear this, but we might have a second killer."

"Impossible."

Nicoli shifted in his seat. "These past few murders, and this attack on the entire World's Fair, feels off. I don't believe it's the same killer. These are different types of attacks."

Dekker stood, leaning over his desk. "Nicoli, I want this lunatic off the street, and I pray we don't have a second madman out there. This Peake is in chaos, the city is on high alert, and I need answers. Several aristocrats even paid me a visit. If he and the council revoke my position, you will never step foot in this city again, and that prevents us from stopping these scumbags."

Nicoli chattered his teeth, his leg bouncing on the floor. Did Dekker think he knew pressure, the true stress of dealing with actual monsters on the streets? Each day was another tragedy to Nicoli. In his career, he saw what people did with his own eyes, not from the files Dekker had on his desk.

"Is there something I can do? Regarding the fountain attack that is?" Nicoli asked.

"No. The Peake took care of it, but I need you to detain this Phoenix. My goodness, what a name. Give me progress, Nicoli, before I find someone who does. Any word on that fabric sample?"

He nodded. "Understood, and none."

Dekker sighed and turned to the window. The city lights were bright, and the roads were busy in the late night, carriages rattling and people talking on the street.

"What happened, Nicoli?" Dekker asked. "When I was young, murderers and thieves were simple. Tragic, but at least familiar. My father would be broken if he saw the level of madness we find these days. Who thinks of killing so horrifically, let alone does it?"

Nicoli rubbed his hand. "The world is changing, and so are those in it. Every day we're pushed a little further, and when people break, they snap harder, farther than before. Your father told me that."

Dekker lowered his eyes and closed them. "I want who's responsible for the fair attack in cuffs. The aristocrats demand results, and I need to give answers."

Nicoli stood and ran his hand through his hair. "It'll be done."

"I hope so. If half the stories my dad told me about you are true, then we need your skills now."

Dekker turned back to the window with his hands on his hips.

Nicoli pushed his tongue into his cheek and headed out of the office, several constables glancing his way.

He kept his head low and walked down the hallway alongside the offices, the musky smell of stale air filling his nose. He rounded the corner, entered the staircase, and climbed to the rooftop where the fresh, night breeze greeted him.

Lydia sat on the raised edge of the roof, leaning back on a brick pillar overlooking the World's Palace. She glanced at him, and he could not help but smile as a warmth filled his chest. He leaned on the railing, admiring her in uniform, golden buttons in rows of two, and her black hair slicked behind her ear.

"Do you remember when we'd sit on the roof in Redwood for hours watching the city sleep?" Lydia glanced over the horizon.

"Yes. A while ago."

"Doesn't feel that long to me. I thought things used to be peaceful when my mind was clear."

"It'd be darker if not for you and what you do for the Peake."

"I only do it because of what we've suffered."

He felt weak in the knees. "Lydia—"

"Lydia, what? Nicoli, I'm tired of not talking about what happened."

"There's no point. It's in the past, and we can't change it."

"But I don't want to keep mourning by myself. It hurts to listen to our child ask me where her father is or why she has no one to grow up with."

"Lydia, I—"

A constable opened the door, looking at them near the edge.

"Come back later," Lydia said.

The man paused. "But I—"

"Find your own rooftop." Lydia pointed to the staircase.

The constable lifted his brow and walked back into the station.

Nicoli's stomach tingled, and he tapped his foot off the roof. "Why can't we—"

Lydia glared at him, her eyes more violet than usual, shimmering in the light that cascaded from the World's Fair. Even when she was upset with him, he wanted her embrace. He could not let his feelings block his way, not until he settled their past.

"I understand why you want to stay away, but we have done that long enough," she said. "What happens if we never find him?"

Nicoli stood up, snarling in her direction. "Why would you say that?"

"Because you've been doing this for years, and I'm ready to raise our daughter together."

Nicoli crossed his arms and looked to his feet, his thoughts growing out of control.

"You aren't there yet, but you're slipping," Lydia said. "I can't keep picking you up. I know you're in pain, but we need to move on from Mallory."

Nicoli rubbed his hand along his hair. He imagined it was Mallory's touch, soft and gentle. As he lay in bed, she would press behind him, wrap her arm over him, and every morning run her fingers through his hair. No matter how terrible life was, she could bring him the happiness he searched for since he was young.

"Nicoli?"

He snapped out of his daze, Lydia only a few inches from his face. Her breath was warm as the night nipped at his cheeks, her voice drowning out the hum of the wind.

"Don't keep going there," she said. "I know it's comforting, but you're stuck in the past, and there's a future that I'd love for you to be a part of."

Nicoli grabbed her hands and lifted them to his lips, kissing them. "I can't as long as he's out there, knowing he might exist. What would happen if I lost you? If we lost Rosaline?"

Lydia paused, a faint smile spreading across her face.

"That's not funny," he said.

"I know. I just don't remember when you last said her name."

They looked to each other, pausing as each other's breath rest on the other.

Lydia leaned in, and she kissed him with soft lips, sweet like blueberries. It had been so long since he felt her warmth in his hands. As the night sky covered them, the moon glowed over the city, and they put their foreheads together.

"They did not give us a normal life, Nicoli. We both loved and lost Mallory, but if I can carry on, you can too."

"It's not that easy."

Lydia stepped back, exhaling through her nose. "It can be. We both know whose fault it is."

"I'm not doing this." Nicoli shook his head.

"You know."

"No."

Nicoli lowered his gaze, able to see the one tear that dropped down her cheek.

"It's my fault," she said.

"Stop it."

"Nicoli, accept it. I got her killed. If anyone should be guilty, it should be me." Lydia looked into the horizon. "Did she ever tell you why she left me before she found you?"

Nicoli lifted his eyes to hers, his throat getting dry. "Lydia."

"I knew she wanted to leave. We had it hard enough being who we are, but what ruined it was my inability to let go. When she told me, I begged and pleaded with her to stay, but she believed I was going to get myself killed… and she paid the price."

"Lydia, stop."

"I can never forgive myself, and I don't want anyone to, but after Rosaline was born… I knew for our child to have a normal life, she needed a mother, and me pounding the concrete every night would not work. She needed someone who came home every night and tucked her into bed. She wants her father as well."

Nicoli pulled on his collar, looking to the city. He wanted to reach out, to hold her close and tell her he would let it go, but he could not lie to her.

"We're in danger, always have been," she said.

He looked up, eyes wide. "What do you mean?"

"My killer, your killer, he knows you're here, and…"

"Lydia, what do you know?"

She rubbed the side of her neck. "I believe I'm being followed."

Nicoli went stiff, and he froze in place. "How long?"

"I'm not sure."

"Is it him?"

"You're missing the point. Whether or not you want to. The exact thing you said you were protecting us from is happening."

Nicoli stepped in closer. "If someone is following you, I'll follow them, and if it's him, maybe this is our chance to end it."

Lydia tightened her lips. "This is what I mean. You'd rather chase this man than be with your loved ones. I can't promise Rosaline and I are always going to wait for you. I tell her you'll come home for now, but one day I might have to say otherwise, or she'll stop asking. This is the point before you slip. Before you become someone you aren't."

"So you just want me to forget Mallory?" Nicoli waved his palm.

"Of course not. I think of her every night, but I couldn't let go, and I lost her. If you don't let go… you'll lose us."

Lydia leaned in, putting her hand on his cheek, rubbing her fingers back through his hair. She looked to him as she always did, with love. He kissed her, holding her tight.

"Will you come home with me tomorrow night?" she asked. "To meet your daughter so we can be a family?"

Nicoli sobbed, and his eyes glazed over with tears. He nodded, his voice too shaken to speak, and embraced Lydia in his arms.

CHAPTER THIRTY-NINE

The moonlight beamed through the window, dancing with the candle's flame as Ellie brushed on the white canvas and followed the line.

Her hand was light and precise, and with every curve, she tilted her head, glancing to the housetops from the attic, without a cloud in the sky.

With a yawn, she rolled her shoulders, stretched her neck, and leaned back in her chair, propping her feet on the windowsill. The room wasn't dusty or unkept with collapsing boxes from years of neglect, but it was clean, free of a dry musk, with covered couches, a painting, and a chandelier hanging in the middle.

Her brother's footsteps were soft but grew louder as Jonah walked into the room, pondering Ellie's picture.

"Ah yes, the Maker blessed you with Mother's creativity as well." Jonah plopped in the seat next to Ellie. "Not bad for a pikey."

Ellie looked away. "That's not nice, Jonah. There are a few words for the aristocrats you might find offensive."

"No, thank you, p—"

Ellie kicked Jonah in the arm, almost knocking him off the couch. He turned to her with a stern stare.

"I told you." Ellie glanced out the window, the cool breeze brushing against her green nightgown, soft against her arms.

"Very ladylike. Father would be impressed."

"Can I help you? Do you have a reason to be up here, or are you just looking to upset me?"

"Yes, I did, before you damn near knocked me over. I'm curious where you've been the past few days. You haven't been getting in until late."

"I didn't realize I had to check in."

"A lot is happening in Well's Peake with the fair and murderers. When you didn't come into the office, we worried something was wrong."

Ellie stood with a dramatic exhale. She pulled a stool to the windowsill and turned the canvas, looking away from Jonah.

"Would you like to tell me where you've been sneaking off to?" he asked.

"Perhaps I was soul searching."

"You spent enough of your life in the Northern Forests to figure that out. Wasn't that the whole point, to calm your inner chaos?"

"Now that I'm in Well's Peake, I have *new* thoughts, and I do my best thinking at night."

Jonah stood and leaned against the wall, looking at her painting. "Anything I can help with?"

Ellie brushed the edge of the canvas, the white-and-blue colors blending in arches. She took another deep breath and pressed her tongue into her cheek, the aroma of berries lingering off her braided hair from her recent bathing.

Jonah never could leave her alone. Dennis was difficult, and Theodore was always on some righteous cause, but at least they kept to themselves. Jonah felt the need to involve himself in every part of her life, and Ellie did not miss it. His thumb had been on her since she returned, and she was not used to anything but freedom in the open lands.

She looked up, Jonah waiting for her answer.

"It's difficult being here," Ellie said. "You're right. I thought I figured out what I wanted. I came back, searched for it, and it's not what I imagined. Out there, you can expect animals to be feral and remember which berries are delicious, but it's hard to understand people in the city. They are unpredictable. I hoped things would've changed being a little older."

"You know it doesn't work like that," Jonah said. "The World's Fair is here, and it has brought all kinds to Well's Peake."

"And I prepared, but it would've been nice if there were some adjustments." Ellie dabbed her brush in blue paint, some flicking on her gown. "I'm happy with myself, I know me, but I'm interested in finding another I can be happy with."

"You must learn to live on your own first."

"I have, but that doesn't mean I wouldn't enjoy *sharing* my life."

Jonah huffed and picked up the easel, setting it aside. Ellie dropped the brush on the floor and slapped her sides. She knew where the conversation was going, which was why she didn't mention Aleksandar directly, not that Jonah would pick up the hint to drop it.

Jonah sat on the sill, glancing to the street.

"What happened between us?" he asked. "We used to be close, tell each other everything, then one day you left. You hardly wrote; you never visited. It was hard on the family."

"It was only fair. You boys did what you wanted. Why couldn't I?"

"Because a traveler is not—"

"A what?" Ellie stared.

Jonah sighed. "Never mind."

Ellie crossed her arms with a rigid posture. "I didn't leave carelessly. The first person I asked was Mum, and she approved. She wasn't fond of the idea, but she understood it was right for me."

"And Father?" Jonah looked down, playing with his fingernails.

"You know Dad. He'd rather spend the day at the factory than come home for dinner. I hated going there to see him."

"He loved his office, but you must understand the company wouldn't be what it is today without his dedication."

Ellie crossed her arms. "Why value hard work like that? While he put his commitment into the shop, we saw little in our family. That's a reason I left."

He stood, holding up his hands. "Because Dad worked?"

"Because it didn't seem like family mattered much to him. Can you remember when he'd stay at the office for a week's end, and we would hardly see him?"

"He did it for us."

Ellie pointed her finger in his face. "I did not want some famous metal building. I wanted Father to come home and play with me, teach me, and tell me it was okay when I got embarrassed or made mistakes."

Jonah chattered his teeth, looking elsewhere with his hands in his pockets.

"I promise you, when I find my family, they will always be first," she said. "Just like Mum did for us. If anything happened to my child, I'd be there, no matter how far away or hidden they were to me."

Ellie paused, her finger in the air, Jonah looking at her with a forced gaze. Her breath was heavy, and she felt the warmth in her cheeks. She walked to the center of the room and crossed her arms.

I thought I moved on from this...

Even after death, her father still had a way of upsetting her. She did not hate him, she loved him and longed to hug him again, but it would not make up for lost memories.

Ellie turned around, her brother staring out the window.

"I'm sorry," she said. "I guess I still haven't let go."

Jonah looked over his shoulder. "Ellie, many opportunities are happening around us, and we need to be forward thinking. I'm up here because I wanted to talk about Aleksandar, who I think is a danger to you."

"What's wrong with Aleksandar?"

Jonah walked to the center of the room, hands on his hips. "I imagine that's where you've been spending the late hours."

"If it makes you feel better, there has been no—"

Jonah shook his hand. "Don't need to hear it."

"I've been helping him through a hard season."

"And that's kind of you, but you're putting a lot of effort into a man who is opposite of the life you want. You want stability, and you think you'll find it in him? He's being investigated for murder. The allegations and path behind him concern us. How are we to know if he's putting you at risk?"

"We? As in Teddy and Dennis, too?"

"We're concerned."

"I am fully appreciative of *my* situation and your concern, but don't you think I considered that? What am I doing spending days with a man who's lost everything or could be a killer in disguise? Of course, I thought of breaking ties. Just because I don't tell you something doesn't make me oblivious. We all have Father's intellect."

"Which is why you'd be excellent at the factories. You are smarter than Dennis and me combined, and you rival Theodore at his best. Use that as your stability. We're to establish the deal of a century, and Fritz and Co will flourish into the rail industry and leave behind the gears and bolts. True titans of industry. Wouldn't that be exciting to be a part of?"

Ellie rubbed her hands together. "Now, tell me, are you asking me not to see Aleksandar because you're worried about me or because of the company's reputation?"

Jonah paused. "Whether or not you like it, you're a Fritz, and your legacy is attached to Father's business. Your association with Mr. Scott is going to ruin your influence, and when you choose to be part of this family, it'll be too late."

Ellie smacked Jonah in the shoulder, her lip curling. "You ass. I see what this is."

"Oh, do you? What happens when you decide you don't want to be with him and move on, like you always do? What about Mr. Scott? You give him someone to lean on, and if things worsen, you choose to run? Is it wrong to worry about my sister and the company all at once?"

Ellie knocked down her easel. "How about you piss off?"

"Once again, very ladylike."

"Don't you act all noble. I'm aware of everything you told me. I considered you and our brothers, and while I don't know what to do, you don't get to stand there and pretend you're doing this for me. You're doing it for the family, just like Dad used to say. You're worried about the company, and that's all it ever is, all it ever will be, hence, why I left. Once Mum passed, no one cared about me. It was all Fritz and Co. You, Teddy, and Dennis. When Dad's health failed, you followed in his steps and were gone when she was sick. Even after Mum told me to travel, I didn't. Not until her funeral did I leave. Why should I give myself for the *family* now?"

Jonah stood there, tongue in cheek.

"How long did it take before my brothers noticed I was even gone?"

He swallowed hard. "Too long."

"I didn't leave you. You left me."

Jonah nodded, his eyes closed. He picked up Ellie's painting, put it on the easel, and walked to the door.

"What happened wasn't right, but that was then, and this is now," he said. "You have a choice to make. To either help the family, Aleksandar, or maybe yourself. You won't choose us, which is fine, but at the least figure out what you want."

Jonah wandered into the shadows and down the stairs, his steps fading into the night. She looked outside, the moon covered by clouds and the candle flickering in the growing breeze.

Ellie picked up her brush off the floor and set it at the bottom of the canvas. Pulling on her brown hair, she stared at the brushed arches, unable to figure out what mattered most.

CHAPTER FORTY

The streets were bustling with fairgoers, and carriages rattled over the bridge that connected the Cultural District to the World's Fair. The sun hid behind the clouds, the city resting under an even light on a cool harvest day.

Natalia walked down the street in her blue vest with her white collar popped. Her jacket hung loose on her shoulders, and she stared aimlessly ahead, bumping into people walking past her, her arms not swinging with her steps. Her gaze shifted from one empty spot to another without a thought running through her head.

The aroma of fresh apple pie and the whistling of street vendors did not pull her from her trance. With calm eyes and her chestnut hair pulled back in a loose bun, she watched, searching into the unknown.

Natalia bumped into a woman with a news press tucked under her arm, her hat snug over her brow.

"Watch it!"

Natalia let the words drift off, like a leaf in the winter wind.

"Miss Arlen?"

Natalia pressed on, rounding the street corner as her cheeks reddened in the breeze. The faces of others meant nothing to her, each passing as if invisible.

"Hey!"

Natalia stopped, someone grabbing her arm.

"Miss Arlen, what's the matter with you?"

Natalia turned to a woman with auburn hair in a pinstriped shirt and vest, walking around like it was warm out, her jacket over her shoulder.

"Do I know you?" Natalia asked.

The woman stood with a tilted head. "Miss Arlen, it's Ferdie, from the *Well's Peake Commons*. I've done countless interviews with you. The Commons are right across the street." She pointed.

Natalia glanced to the building, scorch marks still on the side. "You know who I am?"

Ferdie let go of her, looking with stern green eyes, no one else paying attention to the women standing in the middle of the sidewalk. "What's the matter with you—do you not remember me?"

Natalia glanced at her palms, turning them towards her. "I don't remember anyone."

Ferdie rubbed her forehead, heavy bags under her eyes. "So Abel was right. Of course he was."

"Abel?"

"Abel Hawthorne. You don't remember him? You two weren't the best of acquaintances."

Natalia shook her head without a smile, no expression.

Ferdie looked across the block, and Natalia followed her gaze, looking to the pubs, galleries, and gift shops.

"Let's sit you down for a drink," Ferdie said. "Maybe that will settle you out."

"That sounds nice."

Ferdie slipped her arm through Natalia's. "Come on, before you make a bloody fool of yourself."

They crossed the road, and a man yelled at Ferdie for being in front of him, but she ignored it. Through a pair of golden doors, they stepped into a bustling pub. It was not fancy like those in North Hills or run-down as in the southern districts. The bar was light brown, the liquor cabinets a darker shade, and the floor was black-and-white wood paneling.

Ferdie led them both to a booth and looked over her shoulder as they sat in the shadows.

"Where are we?" Natalia asked.

Ferdie glanced back, taking a deep breath. "We're at Fiennes, the finest pub on the World's Hotel block. It might do you good to get away from those fancy places you call pubs and enjoy a real one."

Ferdie waved her fingers at the bartender. "The usual, Francis. Please."

"Two bourbons it is."

"Make it three. One for her." Ferdie looked to Natalia, who stared. "What?"

"I thought we were at Fiennes?"

"We are."

"But you called him Francis?"

"Well, that's his name."

"Then why is it called Fiennes?"

"His name is Francis Fiennes. My goodness, you're a mess."

Natalia rubbed her hand, and Ferdie sighed, rolling her eyes.

The bartender set the drinks down, eyeing them both and not leaving.

"Can I help you?" Ferdie asked.

"You normally come alone. Who's your friend?"

"Francis, go do your job before that creepy owner of yours with the mustache evicts you and puts a nicer pub in his strip."

"Yeah, yeah."

Francis walked off, and Natalia tried to say something, but she had no desire. All she gathered was a woman dragged her off the street, set a glass in front of her, and claimed to know what she did not.

"I'm sorry for being short," Ferdie said. "I haven't been myself." Ferdie took a sip, tapping the glass edge with her finger. "Wait. Abel used to tell me. Oh dammit, what was it? A book. You have a blue journal on you that you look to when you have an episode. Did you check your pockets?"

Natalia patted her legs, then her jacket, and reached inside, pulling out the journal. She looked to Ferdie with parted lips. "Just like you said."

"Open it. What does it say?"

"It says I have memory issues. That I'll lose my place in the world, and some moments are longer than others, but to trust only in the words of my own writing. That it will be okay."

Ferdie glanced at the journal.

"Do you know who I am?" Natalia asked.

Ferdie lifted the crystal glass and took a sip of her drink. "You are Natalia Arlen, a very prestigious inventor."

"Well's Peake?" Natalia nodded. "I remember the city."

"That's good."

"What sort of person am I?"

Ferdie leaned back. "Personally, I know little about you, but from what I remember, you're kind, smart, and have a weird habit of being over the top. I guess we all have our moments. People see you and know you've accomplished some incredible things."

Natalia pulled on her hair. She smelled the bourbon, the scent of vanilla and caramel luring her in. She sipped on it, licking her lips at the end. "Have I done things that aren't incredible?"

Ferdie tapped her fingers on the edge of the table. "Now your professional life, I know well. You have been successful in every endeavor, except one."

"What happened?"

Ferdie took another sip. "Miss Arlen, I'm not sure this is a story you want to hear."

"Please. I imagine most don't learn about themselves from a stranger."

Ferdie lifted her brows. "Well, you still sound like you." Ferdie swallowed a large gulp. "It was at Oakvale. You were revealing the Lunarwheel. Do you remember that?"

"No."

"It's a machine you thought would surpass the steam engine. You believed it would be more powerful than its predecessor by a hundredfold."

"Did I fail?"

Ferdie rubbed the bottom of her fist on the table, glancing around. "Everything seemed to go as planned. Your presentation was flawless as it always is. You were optimistic, but something was wrong. Your machine shattered into the crowd. It injured many people, but no one there was seriously hurt."

Natalia watched with her eyes attentive, never flinching from Ferdie.

"Well," Ferdie said, "there were repercussions upriver. Your engine was attached to a turbine up at the dam, and the sudden force caused the dam to fracture and flood the park. Your husband was in that park." Ferdie took a deep breath. "He never came out."

Natalia stared down, her breath heavy. "I remember his face, but not that I killed him."

"No, no, you didn't kill him. It was an accident." Ferdie reached across the table. "You must remember him since you still wear your ring."

Natalia pulled up her hand, a rose gold band snug on her finger. "And people don't hate me?"

"No, they don't. Many girls look to you for inspiration. I still looked up to you after it happened."

Natalia leaned back, slouching over.

Silence grew between the two, Ferdie chattering her teeth and looking deep into her glass. "You might not remember, but Abel used to drag you into situations you didn't deserve to be part of. For what it's worth, I'm sorry for what he did."

"I can't recall, but thank you. Hopefully, I remember when this passes. What am I to do?"

"I don't know. Is there anything else in your journal? Is there an entry from today?"

Natalia flipped through the pages, looking up. "Yes, from this morning. Aleksandar... who's Aleksandar?"

"Another inventor you work with."

"A handsome name. I wrote, Aleksandar is becoming overwhelmed, and I worry he will lose sight of what we are trying to accomplish. His motivation, his desire to overcome obstacles grows, but I haven't seen what we reach for. He is nothing like when I met him. The drive, the passion he once had in his eyes was inspiring."

Natalia flipped the page.

"He will do great things, and I'm unsure if he sees that yet. The first step is always the hardest, but once he finds his path, he'll become the inventor he needs to be."

"It seems you hold him in high regard." Ferdie sipped her bourbon, her words beginning to slur.

Natalia turned the page. "His legacy could be the very thing I strive for myself. However, I can no longer accept what I once held dear. This battle of understanding who I am and why I grow conflicted with my legacy is tiring. To be me, or the person they expect I am... Can I be two different people with the legacy I fought for, for so long?" Natalia stopped and closed her eyes. "It's blurry, but I'm remembering that I wrote this."

"That's good progress."

Natalia rubbed her arm. Her mind was no longer blank but fuzzy with pieces that did not connect. Memories grew with every word, but she understood so little about who she was.

"What do you figure?" Natalia grabbed her drink.

"Of what?" Ferdie looked into her lap.

"The person I am. Who I want to be?"

"I'm not sure I can answer that. You know how I feel and how others see you, but only you understand you. You ask whether you need to be the person we see or the person you want to be, but you're going about it the wrong way."

"How so?" Natalia sipped on her drink.

"You need to ask yourself, who are you now? Who is Natalia Arlen?"

A headache set in, but Natalia could feel herself getting closer to her old memories. Ferdie no longer seemed like a stranger, and the World's Fair echoed through her mind.

She checked her pocket and found a pen, holding it above the journal. She glanced to Ferdie, who finished her drink, and signaled the bartender for another two glasses, Natalia's still half full.

"So what do you think?" Ferdie licked her lips.

Natalia turned the page to the last entry and wrote.

Who am I now?

CHAPTER FORTY-ONE

Aleksandar's eyes darted across the street, gaslights breaking up the darkness in the early evening. The pathways grew less crowded as he walked from the World's Fair, but he felt someone's gaze lingering on his shoulder.

Aleksandar first felt the eyes linger in his direction several blocks ago when he was looking through the glass of a tailor shop, admiring the new vests. He knew it was not smart to be out with a killer on his tail, but what if he was waiting at his house, knowing where he lived? To risk Hugh, and what of Ellie? Did the Phoenix follow her as well, standing by to capture her? Or for her to lead him to the young inventor?

Aleksandar's thoughts ran rampant as he paced his way around the intersection, trying to shake whoever followed him. Another shadow flashed in the corner of his eye, and he sprinted across the road, almost hit by a carriage. He propped himself on the building's foundation, searching, but no one followed him.

I swear.

Leaning against the coarse brick, Aleksandar focused on his breathing, the air showing in the chill, noticing the temperature despite the sweat on his neck. He loosened his scarf and eyed the street. A man stepped out of a butcher shop and pulled in his sign, closing up for the night. The library next door was filled with books and fairgoers, and beside that, Westley and Co Smithing.

Through the window, swords, knives, batons, and more rested on shelves, and Aleksandar could not take his eyes off them. He peeked around the corner once more, didn't spot anyone suspicious, and crossed the cobblestone street.

A bell dinged on the door, and inside were two customers looking over brass and gold weapons. Aleksandar rubbed his hands together and flinched as the bell chimed again. A fella with a thin mustache, holding his son's hand, strolled past him towards the back of the store.

"May I help you?"

Aleksandar turned to the counter, facing a man with a stout face and plump cheeks, looking at him with raised eyebrows.

"Me?" Aleksandar pointed at himself.

"Yes, you. Would you come over here?"

Aleksandar walked to the glass displays, shelves full of handheld weapons.

"My name is William Westley, but call me Westley." The man spoke deeply. "Were you searching for a particular item?"

"Um, no. I saw your shop across the road and considered I'd buy something. Maybe a baton?"

"A baton?"

"Yes. Do you not have batons?"

"We do, but not much use for a baton unless you are a collector. They are not great for conversation pieces on the coffee table either, and usually the Peake are the only ones interested. Why do you need it?"

Aleksandar glanced around the smithing shop, no one looking his way. "For protection."

"Against what?"

Aleksandar put his palms on the counter. "Just in case. Something could happen."

"Perhaps. The folk who come in here checking on batons are looking to break someone's knees. Enough to intimidate, but not to kill. Are you looking to hurt someone?"

"No, no. I thought—"

"You thought wrong." Westley walked down the counter with a swaying step. "If you're searching for defense, you'll want to try out one of these."

Aleksandar waited as Westley pulled a few weapons from the shelf and walked back with slow steps. He set a bronze sword on the wood counter, still in its scabbard, and a dagger with elegant scrollwork lining the sheath.

"We have more formidable protection, but you strike me as a fella who has little experience with hand-to-hand, so let's start with the basics."

Aleksandar leaned over the counter.

Westley picked up the dagger and withdrew it, the gray-and-black blade singing from its cover. "Don't let the patina fool you. It is perfect in every way—an excellent short knife with an edge that could filet a fish. My brother forged it, and he is an authenticated master. This blade would be proper in close quarters but not very useful mid-range."

Westley held out the blade, and Aleksandar grabbed it, the leather comfortable in his grip. It was light and flowed through the air.

"I wrapped the handle myself. I developed a technique that ensures it never slips and never unravels. If it does, you come to me."

The man lifted his palm, and Aleksandar handed it back.

"Next is a favorite of mine, the Belagradian Saber. While thinner than most, it has an edge unlike any others, and it's strong like stone." Westley raised the blade and pulled it out, glimmering in the candlelight. "She is polished, so it could catch your attacker's eye, but if you learn how to use it, they won't have the opportunity to stop its slash."

Aleksandar took the sword, seeing the balance in his grip. He waved it around. "This seems nice."

"It is," Westley said, putting the scabbard overtop. "A little more pricey and harder to conceal if you don't want people knowing you have a weapon. We no longer carry firearms for obvious reasons, so these two would be your best options. Although we have brass knuckles, you don't look like much of a fighter."

Aleksandar shook his head.

"Now, before we continue, I must ask again. Do you intend to harm someone?" Westley set his hands on the counter.

Aleksandar looked with shocked eyes. "No, I'm not."

Westley stared with an unblinking gaze. "Just standard procedure. You aren't the type."

"What does that mean?"

"It's nothing personal, but you haven't held a blade in your life. Your palms are calloused, but not like a fighter. You carry yourself like a young pup and don't understand how to wave a weapon, so I must ask. Why do you need to defend yourself?"

The man was subtle, stern, and grounded. He did not speak with an attitude or demeaning manner, and Aleksandar could sense his authenticity.

"Because someone attacked me, and I'm scared they'll kill me if they come back and I have nothing."

Westley pushed his tongue into his cheek, nodding slowly. "I see. That's a tiring fear looming over you. I could sell you a weapon, but unless you know how to handle it, it'll do you no good. I guess with it at your hip; it might boost your confidence, which helps. In this case, I suggest the smaller blade. Easy to conceal, and the element of surprise is something you can pick up with ease. Just don't waste it."

Aleksandar grabbed the dagger, his lips parting.

"Can you afford the price?" Westley said.

"Yes, I have the coin."

"That's not what I'm asking. I mean, could you afford the price of the blade if that moment ever came?"

Aleksandar rubbed his finger along the knife, tightness sitting in his chest. He'd never thought about it. He wanted to defend himself, but what if that meant harming another, to kill? The heavy weight sank in his stomach, and he closed his eyes.

"Does anyone know before that moment?" Aleksandar swallowed hard.

Westley nodded. "No. If there's one thing you might have compared to most who enter my shop, it's insight. This blade is yours to buy. However, I want you to reflect on something."

"What's that?"

"Your problem. It will not go away if you wait for it. Consider facing it head-on and solving it before it solves you. You can't always let things happen to you when you need to make them happen yourself."

Aleksandar swallowed and rubbed his fingers, thinking to how he had not made a move since the beginning of the World's Fair.

∼

The marble pillar was still scorched, and someone had trimmed out the damaged hedges around it. They sculpted them to match the allure of the World's Palace, which glimmered in the thousands of gaslights lining the paths and roads.

Aleksandar stepped over the freshly laid dirt and faced the arched entrance of the maze. It opened to the forest where the Phoenix escaped, disappearing into the night as constables chased at his heels. They could not catch him, but Aleksandar knew he was what the killer wanted. He would not run.

Why did the Phoenix hunt him? What were his reasons?

I'm tired of waiting.

Aleksandar checked his side, the blade strapped to the inside of his hip. He walked under the arch and into the forest. The gaslights faded as he furthered his stride, and the aroma of pine and hemlock trees lingered. He knew any thought would hinder his determination, so he pushed on.

Through the branches that flicked against his face, he stumbled on the ground, unable to see his steps. Leaves crunched under his feet, no matter how quiet he tried to be, and sweat soaked into his shirt, his tweed jacket keeping in the heat.

The moon peered through the empty trees above, and Aleksandar looked back to Well's Peake below him. The World's Palace radiated in the night.

I can do this. I remember. I'll always remember.

He trudged up the hillside, slipping on loose dirt and foliage. His feet ached, and his face grew tender from the branches smacking him against his cheek. He would not quit. The answers he deserved would be his, and he would stop the Phoenix from hurting anyone else.

Aleksandar lost his footing and slipped down the hill, catching a branch. Blood rested on his cheek, and dirt covered his face. He tried to pull himself up, but the roots gave way, and he slid further down the hillside, the rocks and leaves collecting underneath him. He slowed to a stop, next to a log and a small ravine.

Aleksandar rolled onto his back and checked for the blade, which was no longer on his hip.

"Ugh, dammit."

He put his palm against his cheek, pulling off blood and dirt, and with his jacket sleeve, he wiped it clean. Blood ran down his chin as he rested his arms on his knees, holding his head.

He thought to his childhood friend and looked into the sky.

∽

A young girl with blue eyes and a leather satchel on her back raced up the squeaky staircase, under the wall lanterns, and rushed into Aleksandar's room at the top of the steps.

"Ah!"

Aleksandar fell off his stool, and the girl closed the door.

"What is it?" He lifted himself off the floor, picking up the screwdriver he dropped.

The girl pulled a book from her backpack. "Alek, I found it. The book!"

He looked it over. It was the same, only the spine wasn't falling apart and the cover not faded. It was blue with spirals across the top, and the title was as clear as day.

The Magician.

"You found it?" He peered up with wide eyes.

"Yes!"

She felt the warmth in her cheeks, and despite running from the hilltop, she was not out of breath.

"Where did you find this?" he asked. "I thought they made only a few when our parents were kids?"

"It was in a shop."

"Did you—"

The girl nodded. "Yes. I finally could read the ending. This one has all the pages."

She grabbed his hand, and they sat on the floor, looking at each other. Opening the book in her lap, she turned to the last page and showed him a picture of a machine, the musk of a new book against her.

It was round, like a sphere, with four arms that arched over top. It looked like it was spinning and glowing.

Aleksandar picked up the book from her hands and eyed the drawing. "It's beautiful. How does the story end?"

"It doesn't."

Aleksandar glanced at her. "What do you mean?"

"There's no ending. It starts with a new story. A new book."

"Did you find the new one?"

"No, but listen. I know what I want to do now. I found my dream."

Aleksandar closed the book and rubbed his hand along the cover. It was soft, and the stitching of the title was smooth to the touch. "What is it?"

"In the story, the magician is an inventor. She doesn't have any magic, but she makes it look like she does. Someone asked her what she wanted to do, and she said to make a machine to change the world. Make it a better place."

"What did she want to create?"

"She didn't know. She kept inventing and making machines, changing the world, but she never thought she made the one that truly mattered. In the end, she realized it wasn't about changing the world around her, but her own."

"I don't understand."

"Maybe it's something we won't until we are older, but that's what my dream is. To create a machine and make a change in the world."

"We are already nine. How old do we need to be?"

The girl lay on her back, looking at the ceiling. The planks had been steamed and bent into circular puzzle pieces, like the bottom of a rocky stream. Aleksandar sat beside her, and they both stared as the patterns flickered with shadows from the lantern on the workbench.

The girl held her book tight and smiled. "Perhaps when we are ten, we'll know."

≈

Aleksandar opened his eyes, the forest shifting in the wind around him.

"I shouldn't be the one down here, you know. I'm sorry I've made a mess of your dream, but I thought I was doing the best I could. I knew I could never be the inventor you strived to be, but I didn't think I would create such tragedy."

Aleksandar stood and sat on the fallen tree, looking to the moon, his eyelids heavy with fatigue.

I'll be lucky if I make it down this hill alive.

Aleksandar's breath slowed, and he sniffled, feeling his eyes water.

Aleksandar wiped his face before any tears could fall and glanced to Well's Peake, the city as radiant as ever.

"I know, I know." He sighed. "When I get there, I hope you're looking because I'm going to make the difference you wanted. I'll fix the land and make the harvest bountiful again."

Aleksandar stood and looked up the hill, darkness lingering on the peak. He turned to the World's Fair and pushed his lips together, rubbing his chin with the back of his hand.

With careful steps, he worked his way down the slope, the light of the city growing bright ahead of him.

I promise I'll always remember.

CHAPTER FORTY-TWO

Nicoli stood in front of the brick villa, the sun setting behind its golden roof. A family crest etched in stone rested between the top windows in the shape of a flower.

He rubbed his arms until they turned red, and his mouth dried from swallowing too much, waiting outside the oak door. The bronze knocker was there, waiting for him to knock.

What if she's scared of me? Or mad that I wasn't around?

He wanted to walk away, knowing he grew closer to capturing the man who took Mallory from him, but behind the entrance was a woman who loved him and a daughter who longed to see him, whom he'd never met.

Nicoli turned to the street and stepped down to the stone pathway. The gaslights were lit, shining off the dewy ferns against the iron fence surrounding the home, smelling like roses in the late harvest season. Lydia always made sure a flower was in the room, one that left an aroma that captivated him, especially vanilla orchids.

He took a heavy breath and turned to the villa, stepping to the door. He grabbed the cold handle and knocked.

A woman in a butler's outfit, with brown, wavy hair that curved no lower than her chin, stood in the doorway, one arm behind her.

"Hello, Mr. Lucas," she said.

"It's good to see you, Monty. You look well."

"To you as well, and I hope so. I'm still slightly younger than you and Miss May." She smiled. "Please, come in."

Nicoli walked in, Monty closing the door, and looked at the redwood flooring that stretched in every direction, accented by white crown molding. Large carpets filled the hallways and living room, and paintings of landscapes and gardens lined the walls between thick, hanging curtains.

"I see she still loves the family heritage." Nicoli handed his coat to her.

"Of course. The day this house doesn't radiate like a garden is when we must worry. I'm excited you're here. Miss May is as well. I will fetch her."

"Thank you, Monty."

She walked down the corridor, and Nicoli wandered into the living room. He rubbed his elbows again and ran his hand through his hair until his scalp grew tender. He sat, but his legs were restless, and he got back up to pace around the couch.

Wood carvings of animals rested on the mantels, and floral teacups sat in the cabinets. A bookcase stood between the windows, and Nicoli walked to it. He removed a book, and it smelled like a flower.

I expect nothing less.

Her footsteps were soft, and Nicoli turned to Lydia standing in the lantern's light. She had a dark blue jacket that split at her waist into tails behind her, and her black hair was pulled into a loose bun. With a grin, she walked to him, holding her arms.

Nicoli looked around her to no sign of his daughter.

"She's in the other room with Monty," Lydia said. "I wasn't sure if you'd come. To meet our little rose."

"Neither was I." Nicoli licked his lips.

Lydia ran her fingers down his silver vest, smoothing out a stray wrinkle. She straightened his gray tie and put her palms on his chest. "You were always so handsome."

"I didn't want to scare her off."

"You won't. She's been waiting for so long."

Nicoli lowered his head.

Lydia grabbed his hands. "What's wrong?"

"Nerves, I guess."

"That's okay." Lydia hugged him, and he held tight. "I would too. You'll do great."

"What if she acts… differently than we hope?"

"Then we work on it. It may not turn out how we want, but we have to start somewhere." Lydia kissed him on the forehead. "I'm proud of you." She took a deep breath and nodded. "I'll be right back."

Lydia stepped into the hallway, and Nicoli tugged the bottom of his vest, his fingers fidgeting. He ran both of his hands through his hair, massaging his head, a little lightheaded.

What will she look like? Will she have my smile or her mother's? It would be a sin if she didn't have her mom's wit and charm.

Nicoli faced the window, away from the hallway outside the living room. He could see the lantern's reflection in the glass and the outline of the corridor. The flame danced and popped as seconds felt like minutes.

Lydia walked into the light.

Nicoli gasped, and everything went silent. He held his hands tight, trying to stop the shakes.

"Rosaline, could you come here, honey?"

Nicoli covered his mouth, his breath quivering. His eyes pooled up as little footsteps grew louder.

A child's reflection appeared in the glass, and she stood next to Lydia's leg with a doll in her hand.

"Mummy, who's that man?"

Nicoli hesitated but turned around to a young girl with a purple ribbon, her blond hair to her shoulders.

She has my blue eyes.

Rosaline tucked behind Lydia, who kneeled beside her.

"Rosaline, this is your father."

Her eyes opened like a flower in bloom, her lips parting, looking to her mother. "Mine?"

Lydia nodded, and the small girl turned.

Nicoli dropped to a knee. "Hello, Rosaline."

Rosaline paused, her lower lip sticking out. Nicoli rubbed his palms together as she took a step towards him and waited in silence.

His pulse quickened as she stared at him, holding a warm gaze.

She raced across the floor, dropping the doll, and hugged him as tight as her little arms could. Nicoli welcomed her embrace, running his hand through her hair. He set his cheek on hers, tears collecting on his chin.

"Daddy!"

She giggled as she cried and looked up at him, her face getting red. He wiped her cheeks off and put his fingers on her tender face.

"I missed you." She leaned into his chest, and he could not stop sobbing, unable to hold her enough.

"I missed you, too. You're so big."

"Mum says I'll grow bigger."

Nicoli's voice shook with his words. "That you will. Your mum's a clever woman."

"Yeah." Rosaline put her face against his, smelling like roses. "Oh, Daddy."

He looked to Lydia, who held her hand over her tears, and she hurried to them. Nicoli pulled her tight, putting his forehead against hers. As she kissed him with wet cheeks, everything he craved for years was in his grasp. He tried to look at Rosaline, but his eyes were too blurry, and he could only make out her soft smile.

Nicoli picked her up as she wrapped her arms around his shoulders, kissing him on the cheek. He pulled Lydia in by the waist, unable to have her close enough.

"Are you going to tuck me into bed?" Rosaline whispered in his ear.

Nicoli leaned back and nodded, struggling to say anything. Lydia looked into his eyes, hers reddening, and she ran her hand through his hair. She nodded with pursed lips.

"I'm sorry," he said.

"No," Lydia said. "You're here now, and that's all that matters."

Nicoli buried his face into Lydia's chest, she and Rosaline holding tight, and he embraced his family.

~

Nicoli held Rosaline in his arms as she slept on his shoulder, shifting gently in her dreams. He played with her hair, unable to hold back a smile as he thought of all the future moments with her.

Lydia watched as she leaned against the wall in a long nightgown.

"You can take her to bed when you're ready," Lydia said, keeping her voice low.

Nicoli nodded and lowered his head, taking in a deep breath. "She's the most precious thing."

"She is. There's a little of your stubbornness in her."

Nicoli chuckled. "It's useful on occasion." His eyes drifted out the window to the trees in the wind.

"What are you thinking?" she asked.

Everything. From the moment he saw Rosaline, his mind had not stopped racing.

"How could I have gone so long and not realized what I've missed?"

"Nicoli, I don't want an apology. I don't need one. You did what you thought was best for this family, and I can respect that. While we can't relive those lost years, we'll make up for it. I love you, and you being here is what matters most."

Nicoli leaned towards her and kissed her on the lips, losing himself to her. She and Rosaline were all he needed.

Sweet Rosaline.

Nicoli touched Lydia's cheek. "I'd like to tuck her into bed."

Lydia put her hand on his, and a grin stretched across her face.

Nicoli carried their daughter up the steps and down the red-and-white hallway. Lydia opened the bedroom door, and they walked in, toys scattered across the floor.

"She likes the dolls?" Nicoli asked.

"I love my dolls," Rosaline mumbled, still half asleep.

Nicoli chuckled, and he lifted her blanket as Lydia watched from the door frame. He laid her in bed and tucked her in, kissing her on the cheek.

"Daddy?" she said.

"Yes?"

"Will you be here in the morning?"

Nicoli nodded, sniffling. "I'll be here."

Rosaline brushed her face on her pillow. "Thank you."

Nicoli covered his mouth with his fist, holding back the sobs. "I love you too, little one."

He rubbed her cheek as she drifted back to sleep, her breath slowing down. Nicoli stood and walked to the hallway. Lydia wiped her eyes dry.

"Lydia?" he asked.

"I've waited for this moment, for so long."

"I'm done."

Lydia turned to him, eyes wide. "What do you mean?"

"I'm done chasing him. I don't want to waste another second of my life without you and Rosaline."

Lydia closed the door, and Nicoli stepped out. She put her hands on his face. "You don't—"

"I know, but I'm ready to be Rosaline's father. To share the lives you've wanted for too long."

Lydia stared with parted lips, and Nicoli pulled her close, wrapping his palms around her waist, pulling her against him. He leaned in and kissed her, her tender lips the taste of peaches.

Just how he remembered.

Hand in hand, Lydia led him through the hallway with the lantern glimmering off the brown-and-white molding. They walked into the bedroom, and she hung the light on the hook. She stepped backward as Nicoli stayed close, feeling her breath on his. He kissed her, a heat rising inside him.

He reached for her neck brace, and she caught his wrist, both never looking away, eyes locked. Slowly, he leaned in, and she pushed herself against his embrace, her hand falling from his. Nicoli grabbed the clamp and unhooked it. Lydia let the weight of her head rest in his hand, and he set the brace on the drawer.

Nicoli supported her onto the bed, resting her head on the pillow. He lay between her legs, and she pulled him tight, kissing him, their touch never leaving each other.

He rubbed her thigh and unbuttoned her nightgown, opening it across the blankets as she slid her hands under his shirt and untucked it, her warm fingers soft on his hips and chest.

His shirt slipped from his shoulders, and she looked at him with a smile. He grabbed her breasts and pressed himself against her, holding her tight. Her heartbeat pulsed against his, and her breath lingered on his neck.

She was his everything, and he could not embrace her enough, feeling the warmth between her hips against him.

Nicoli lifted his head, and Lydia looked back with glimmering eyes. "I—"

"Never let me go again." Lydia looked deep into his eyes.

"I won't."

Nicoli leaned in and kissed her, holding in his arms the one person who reminded him he was not alone.

CHAPTER FORTY-THREE

Kids ran down the street laughing, pushing each other across the cobblestone. One stumbled and scraped his knee, only to rise and run in Abbey's direction.

She watched from the steps of the boarding house with cold cheeks, smelling the lavender and mint from her hair. The afternoons were darker as the harvest neared its end, with the frost season on the horizon.

The little boy ran to his sister further down the path and hugged her. Kids from the other group blocked their way, circling the siblings, and an older boy grabbed the brother and pinned him in a headlock. Others shoved his sister until she tripped back, hitting her head off the sidewalk.

Abbey stood and rushed to her while the children laughed and stared.

"Leave her alone." Abbey separated them, reaching for the little girl. "Don't you have someplace to be?"

"No, you city creeper. No one cares about us, and you just pretend."

The boys patted the other on the arm, cheering him on.

Abbey pulled a piece of paper from her coin bag and passed it to the kid. "Go there. You'll find a cot to sleep on and food to eat if you make yourself useful."

The boy put it in his mouth, chewed it, and spit it to the side. "We don't need your help."

Abbey slapped him across the face, everyone watching in silence.

The boy gasped and ran off with the children. The brother helped his sister up, and she picked up the paper, wiping it off on her dirt-stained shirt.

"Is there food there?" she asked.

"Yes," Abbey said. "They take care of those who lend a helping hand."

"What do we do?" a boy asked.

"You'll work around the boarding houses and clean. Those who can use a hammer could help fix the inside. The houses a few streets down are being worked on."

The kids scrunched together and looked at the address.

"Thank you." The sister pulled her hand from her forehead, blood in her palm.

"Are you okay?" Abbey asked.

The girl shook her head and sniffled. Abbey lifted the girl's chin, seeing a slight cut in her hairline.

"You know what, I have bandages and live just down the lane. Want to come?"

The girl nodded. "Thank you."

Abbey picked her up, the brother following her. The street was rather quiet for the afternoon, and Abbey glanced over her shoulder, finding her nerves on end. She had a pit in her stomach, feeling as if she was not alone.

Abbey walked to the edge of the alleyway and saw her belongings on the ground, her satchel scattered. She set the girl down and held her hand to the children.

With careful steps, she looked around and pulled out some wraps and gauze, walking backward.

"Do you know how to use these?" Abbey asked.

"Yes?" the girl said, her voice unsure.

"Go home or to that address. Just look after yourself."

"Okay. Thank you."

The brother and sister took off. Abbey never took her eye off the shadows that lingered in the alleyway, and she grabbed a wooden rod off a cinder block, gripping it in both hands.

"I don't care who's out there, but show yourself."

Abbey stood as the chill whipped between the brick buildings. She swallowed hard as a man stepped out with bandages on his arms and leg.

"Who are you?" Abbey yelled, holding the rod out.

A scarf covered the man's face, and his hair was pulled into a tangled ponytail. He was frail and squinted in the light.

It can't be. He's dead.

Kenneth leaned against the stone foundation of the building. Forcing a smile, he lowered the scarf from his mouth.

Abbey hyperventilated and walked to him. He extended his scarred hand as she looked with fearful eyes.

"Kenneth?" Abbey hugged him slowly, pulling him close, feeling his rib cage against her. "The news press said you were dead. I thought—"

"It's okay, Abbey. I apologize for not coming sooner."

She leaned back. "Kenneth, I saw your house on fire."

"You didn't tell anyone I was your brother, did you?" Kenneth stood in her face.

"No, no. I've never said who you are."

"You're positive?"

"Yes. Kenneth, what *is* going on?"

Abbey backed up, unable to catch a full breath. Something was wrong. His voice was feral, and his eyes empty.

Kenneth slouched. "Little sister, I need your help. Someone is out to murder me, and they almost succeeded. If anyone knew we were related, you'd be in great danger."

"Who would do this?"

"It's uncertain, but I have a hunch. You must stay quiet until I do what I must."

"With what?"

"Do you still have the key I gave you years ago? I lost mine in the fire."

"I do." Abbey paused, Kenneth watching her with unflinching eyes.

"Abbey?"

"Yes. Of course." She walked to the wall and stuck her finger underneath a loose brick, removing it. "Kenneth, we need to take you to a hospital. Look at you."

"No!" Kenneth snatched the key and shoved her back.

Abbey fell to the ground, the bag of coin falling off her waist. Kenneth checked the key, and she swiped the money under her blanket, holding her breath. He turned around before she could hide the thread that tightened it shut, trying to look calm.

Kenneth paused. "I've lost everything, Abbey. When I rose from what should have been my grave, all I wanted was to find the man responsible for my wife's death. I needed him to suffer." Kenneth looked to the rooftops. "But as the nights pass, I think of Amia and how I don't want to feel this pain anymore. To be gifted a new beginning is what I deserve."

Abbey stepped towards him and in front of her blanket. "Can't the Peake help, though? I thought I lost you. Your last worry should be this key."

"That's my business and no one else's, and if you think about going to the Peake, you'll need the doctor, Sister."

Abbey swallowed hard and put her hand on his arm. Kenneth flinched at her touch. Like a wounded animal, he looked at her with wide eyes, waiting for her next move. *What happened to him?* The question ran through her mind, thinking about how sweet he was as a child.

Abbey grabbed his hand, looking at him. His knuckles were blistered, and his dry hands cracked. She stepped in and hugged him slowly. Kenneth fought at first, but his shoulders loosened, and he rested on her shoulder like a child to his mother.

Kenneth sobbed, and they kneeled to the ground. Abbey ran her palm along his matted hair, patting his bony back.

"I don't know what you're trying to do, Kenneth, but you can leave that path. You can stay with me."

Kenneth leaned away and rested on his heels. "What do you mean?"

"You could stay here. Marvelous things are happening. The South Hills are being fixed. This building will be a boarding house for the homeless. All thanks to Mr. Griffin."

Kenneth grabbed her wrists, and she froze as he lifted himself to his feet. He pushed her back and pinned her against the brick wall.

"Why did I bother coming here to visit you? You have no appreciation of what it is like to lose everything. To be denied what you deserved. You had nothing, so you never had to suffer. What I require now is to take what I deserve."

"Kenneth, you need help. You're going mad; you're sick."

"Sister, you need to trust people some days. You know me, so have faith. The harsh reality of Well's Peake is upon us, and I'll figure this out for both of us. Maybe we'll... What's that smell?"

Kenneth squeezed her cheeks one-handed, muffling her voice. His scarred hand twitched, Abbey gasping as she grabbed his wrist. She shut her eyes and tried not to fight it. The pain was worse when she struggled. He pulled her face close, the veins popping in his neck, and the scars on his face stretched.

Kenneth bit his words. "Have you been taking handouts, Sister? You think me dead and then go wash your hair? You shampooed your hair! Who washed it? Who knows about me?"

"No one, I swear! I found it in the trash. I collected water one night and used it. You have to believe me."

Abbey's mouth opened in a silent moan, his fingernails digging into her skin as she attempted to hold still. Kenneth looked to the street and let go. Abbey dropped to her knees, her palms on the dirty stone. Kenneth lifted her and hugged her as she cried against his chest, her arms down by her side.

"Hush, hush," he said. "That was unkind of me, but you must understand. I am reborn. I will grow into something beautiful and find a glorious path." Kenneth held her still as he glanced to where his manor used to be. "I know what I must do, but you stay here and do what you do best. Keep my secrets."

Kenneth yanked on her hair, and she stumbled to the side, tripping on the blanket. The coin bag was in sight.

Kenneth lifted the scarf over his face. "Tell no one. If you see a man with a blue mask, know I'm dead, and you'll soon follow."

He disappeared around the corner without a glance.

Abbey cried in silence, shattered and battered. She touched her sore face, red from where Kenneth's fingers clenched her skin. Covering the bag under the blanket, she wept into her lap, numb to the icy air.

She did not know how long she lay folded over, but she fell asleep, her mind slipping to Hugh and memories of happier days.

CHAPTER FORTY-FOUR

Bernard walked down the grand hallway, light cascading through the two-story windows against aged wood and paintings. The rooftops glowed in the morning ambiance, the halls illuminated as if from the heavens.

His stomach was uneasy, but his smile was large and chin high as he reached the door. Ellie sat on the chair beside the entrance.

"Miss Fritz, a pleasure to see you again," Bernard said.

Ellie stood with her hands behind her back. "Hello, Mr. Griffin. I hope you've been well."

"I have. When I received word of your brothers' reconsideration of my proposal, I couldn't have been happier."

"I'm sure. They are inside, along with Mr. O'Connell, but I wanted to catch you beforehand. I brought you something."

Ellie reached behind the chair and pulled out a wrapped piece of canvas with a golden ribbon. She rubbed her hand along the side and held it out.

Bernard took it from her, his grin larger than before. "What is this?"

"A gift for being so kind. You appear to be a positive influence in Well's Peake and appreciate art, so I hope this inspires you to reach higher than my brothers. It reminded me of your painting, and I thought it would make a nice gift."

Bernard smiled and opened his present. There was an abstract drawing of a metal tower on the city horizon. Three legs curved into the clouds. The canvas was smooth and smelled sweet, but there was a dented corner.

"Sorry about the edge. It may have found its way across the attic at one point."

"A painting and a story. Great art is not made without emotion." Bernard looked it over and smiled. "I love it. What shall we call it?"

"I was thinking, *La Dame Du Peake.*"

"The Lady of the Peake? Perfect."

Ellie bowed. "Best not keep them waiting. I wish you well."

"Will you not be attending today?"

"My brothers and I are not on the best of terms."

"Please, I insist. You lighten the room."

"I should go."

"I can't accept your gift if you don't."

Ellie scoffed with a smile. "Mr. Griffin, that hardly seems fair."

Bernard tilted his head, and Ellie let out a small breath.

"Fine," she said. "Follow me, but you've been warned."

Bernard chuckled, and Ellie led him into the World's Grand Hall. The windows stood tall, the sun radiating on the two oak tables in the middle. The chandelier glistened, crafted of polished crystals, and red banners hung low, woven from the finest silk and cotton.

Dennis, Theodore, and Jonah sat at the center table of the colossal room, Owen resting on his cane across from them.

"Mr. Griffin, a pleasure." Theodore stood, his brothers following suit. "I see you have convinced my sister to join us."

"I did, indeed." Bernard shook each of the brothers' hands and patted Owen on the shoulder.

"I hope the morning has treated you well," Jonah said.

"It has, thank you. Miss Fritz was most kind."

"She can be, yes."

Bernard glanced to Ellie as she batted an eye at Jonah, pouring glasses of water.

"Should we move right to business?" Theodore asked.

"That's fine with me." Bernard sat and propped his bear-like arms on the edge of the table, folding his fingers over each other. "It surprised me to hear of your reconsideration."

"The climate of Well's Peake has changed, and we now see the benefits of your proposal. Just some details to iron out."

"Of course." Bernard rubbed the bracelet on his wrist.

"After the World's Fair incident, we need a deterrent from the greatest risk, ourselves. Your vision could help guide the upcoming revolution."

Bernard leaned back and smiled. "I'm glad to hear. As an inventor at the forefront of this new era, Owen is here to show support for the league and to answer any questions you have from an inventor's perspective. He has been teaching constables at the Peake about elemental and industrial inventions to help deter any attacks from this killer. He also has been talking with numerous inventors who would stand to support the league."

Owen leaned forward. "A lesson I learned from my father is I cannot partake in unnecessary risks, but I must not stand by either. I want to play my part, as should you. Hopefully, my words and influence carry the weight of Bernard's validity."

"They do," Theodore said. "As we are all aware, Kenneth Forbes has passed, and his death has left uncertainties in our future. We don't wish to abuse the situation, but we have a company to consider, and we've given more than what we have received."

"I assume you wish to discuss the Steamrail?" Bernard said.

"Yes. The rail is the key to the future, to expansion, to meet Belagrad at its doorstep. Ourselves and Mr. Forbes both had a stake, as you did. We held twenty-four percent to his twenty-five, and his rights have passed to us in accordance with the Financial Rights Provision."

Dennis slid a folder across the table. Bernard pulled out his pince-nez, put them on the tip of his nose, and browsed the new proposal.

Ellie set a tray of water on the table and handed them out, the glass ringing in front of Bernard.

Jonah leaned forward. "As you can see—"

"I see fine, thank you." Bernard took off his glasses.

"In exchange for our funding—"

"You want production rights of my factories?" Bernard folded his hands, looking up.

"Not all. Just in South Hills for five years."

"Why would you need mine? They are not fitted for rail construction."

"We explained the details in the latter pages, but for year one, we'll install the machinery needed for production. We'll utilize the factories for the remaining contract, and then we give them back to you. You can then sell off the equipment or use it for your own. Either way, you'll have the ability to run them as is, or as we designed. A gift from us."

"You'd have to shut down for a year for refitting, leaving many workers jobless. They do not have the experience to implement new equipment."

"Sadly, that's something we cannot work around, but once finished, we'll be able to rehire them and more. More jobs, more factories, and transportation of materials will increase fiftyfold. The market shall open, the city will flourish, which only means continuous funding to your league."

"Many could not survive a year homeless," Owen said. "You could live with that?"

Bernard looked to Ellie, who stared at her brothers with troubled eyes.

"No, so we conceived a solution," Theodore said. "As a token of principle, we felt Bernard would be interested in a restoration operation. It would start with the protection and security of those who lose their jobs. After that, you build it into what you wish. By funding it, you show us your good faith, for the coin we'll invest tenfold, and you, as always, can be a beacon to the city."

Bernard sat back. He knew the Fritz brothers would force a delicate deal, but the idea of uplifting so many lives with little transition made his stomach weak.

Owen stared at him, his hand in a fist on the table. "Bernard?"

"I'd make the accommodations, but now you worry me by controlling the market. You risk running other companies out of business, and that's not a quick process. Livelihoods will dwindle before they sell what they've known their entire life."

"And we will buy them, refurbish them, and secure the workers." Dennis waved his hands like it was obvious. "We plan to settle with them before they reach such a stage."

"And what of the current conditions of your factories?" Bernard asked. "I hear they are less than ideal. Do you intend to give mine the same treatment?"

"All locations meet regulations," Dennis said.

Jonah leaned in. "While that is true, Bernard is not wrong in his assessment. Some do lack the luxury of our competitors."

Bernard sipped on his water. "If so, I want signed guarantees that Fritz and Co will be lifted to a higher standard within the year. Along with an advocate assigned to oversee the changes."

"As if we'd let an outsider rummage through our factories," Dennis said. "Is that why you brought Mr. O'Connell? He would not be kind to us."

"For good reason." Owen tapped his cane.

"I had another in mind," Bernard said. "I'm thinking of someone you trust. Perhaps Miss Fritz would be up to the challenge."

The men looked at Ellie, whose eyes were wide and mouth open. "Absolutely not."

"What better person?" Bernard rubbed the palms of his burly hands. "She is family and appears to have the sensitive touch needed."

"I *don't* think so," Jonah said. "We love our sister, but she lacks the desire to involve herself in our company. She has told us herself."

"She does not belong at Fritz and Co." Dennis leaned against the chair and crossed his arms.

"I like it," Theodore said.

Dennis and Jonah glanced at him with confused stares.

"You can't be serious," Jonah said.

"Of course he's not." Dennis stood. "She's spent the last three years traveling the roads, hugging animals, and kissing trees. She's just a pikey."

Jonah glared at Dennis, who shrugged his shoulders.

Ellie looked at Bernard. "You know what, I'll do it."

The brothers turned to her, and Theodore grabbed the folder. He skipped to the amendments section and wrote. He held the pen to Ellie as she walked over and signed the bottom. Bernard followed, and Theodore slid it across the table.

Dennis shoved the proposal away. "I don't think so."

Jonah pulled the file in front of him and shook his head. "Dammit."

"You know we shouldn't be signing that." Dennis glared at his brother.

Jonah hastily wrote his signature on the page and pushed it to Dennis. "Now you have to."

Dennis stared as Jonah held the pen. He snatched it and leaned in his chair. He wrote his name without looking and stood, walking out of the room. Ellie sat and smirked, pulling on her braid.

Theodore slid the folder to Bernard. "With that settled, we have two remaining conditions."

"Let's start small," Bernard said.

"So the Harvest Festival was Mr. Forbes's idea. We were also in on the Financial Rights, as we were looking to reveal the Steamrail. After the attack at the World's Palace, we have doubts."

"That festival is a beacon of Well's Peake," Bernard said. "If you cancel, you'll break the city's spirit, and no matter how suave you think I am, I could not convince the aristocrats otherwise."

"We agree, and it's more beneficial for us to see this through. We still want to present our work and advances. However, we lack the protection needed."

"I thought the Peake would handle security."

"Yes, but containing and protecting a few hundred thousand people is no simple task. They need an edge, an advantage to take action if needed. While a smaller detail, Owen is the one to decide."

"For what?" Owen said.

"We want usage rights to your Limbs of Life to support the Harvest Festival. We can manufacture them quickly—temporary rights for that occasion only. I have spoken with Chief Constable Dekker, and he wishes the same after seeing the attack with Constable May. After the event, we gift them to you, free of charge. The moment they abuse your machine, you revoke the rights, even while being trained."

Bernard turned to Owen, who sat with a pressed gaze. "I would have complete control? I say no more, and they follow my command?"

"Yes."

Owen rubbed the side of his head with his cane. "Then… I would be willing."

"Just like that? I thought it'd be more challenging to persuade you."

"Any other day, perhaps."

Theodore patted the counter. "Well, the rights agreement is with the chief, and you can finish with him. Our signatures are already there, effective upon yours and Dekker's."

"I will stop by later today."

"Thank you," Theodore said. "Now, there is one last stipulation we wish to discuss."

Bernard did not want to hear any more, for he knew what they wished to discuss. He saw the page in the proposal and refused to read what they asked of him. He sought to the Grand Hall and envisioned his dream. He could fill it one day with those who supported his vision—a world where they could protect themselves without overreaching or ruining the balance of nature itself.

"Mr. Griffin?" Theodore lifted his brow.

Bernard looked to Owen, who watched with a curious gaze, and to Ellie, with wide eyes.

"Yes, proceed."

Theodore opened the folder to the end pages. "I think it's come to where we must discuss Natalia Arlen."

CHAPTER FORTY-FIVE

That was everything I could tell them. From what I remembered. It didn't seem like they believed me."

Aleksandar sat on the sofa in the small living cubby of his workshop, holding a warm cup of tea at his fingertips. Gazing at the paneled ceiling, he thought of what happened to him, distracted by Ellie beside him. She set her drink on the coffee table, pulled her feet beside her, and rested her hand on his knee.

Aleksandar picked up his hat and sewed the brim to the centerpiece as the afternoon sun filled the room.

Shae trotted over and eyed Ellie, tilting her head until it touched the ground, and Hugh walked through the workshop with a few brackets and laid them on the workbench, sitting on the stool. He shifted springs and gears around, his tongue sticking out in concentration. A spring popped up and hit the ceiling, and Aleksandar flinched, almost dropping his hat as the piece chimed in front of him. Ellie turned to Hugh, catching Shae's stare.

Hugh looked at the tip of his finger. "Sorry."

"If it's any comfort, it beats my record." Aleksandar smiled, catching Shae's determined stare.

Ellie shifted her head, mimicking the owl. "Does she not like me?"

"It may seem weird, but that's a good sign. She shows her affection by staring at you for hours on end before cuddling against you every moment of the day."

"Oh, good. I love making new friends."

Aleksandar turned to Hugh. "Can I see that?"

Hugh held out the device. Aleksandar picked up the spring off the floor and pressed it into position, securing the latch. He looked it over as he handed it back.

"What is it?" Aleksandar asked.

Hugh grabbed a small piece of bread from a plate on the counter and set it in a tin cup at the end of the mechanism. He clicked his tongue, and Shae turned around, watching him crank the lever. Hugh pushed another button, and the food ejected across the room. Shae leaped into the air and caught it in her beak, swallowing it before she landed on the bench.

"Um, a pet toy for lazy people?" Hugh shrugged.

Aleksandar shook his head. "Hugh, you missed what I asked?"

Hugh glanced at the invention. His eyes widened, and he tried to hide his bashful smile. "Thank you."

"No need to thank me. You did the work." Aleksandar stood and patted Hugh's back.

"I didn't think I'd be able."

"Some days we think that. Just have to find a way."

Aleksandar walked to Ellie and sat, leaning his head on her shoulder.

"What's on your mind?" she asked.

"Everything. I can't keep waiting for the next thing to happen."

"True, but you shouldn't go out chasing what can't be found either. You need to be ready when he comes back." Ellie bit her lip. "Can you fight?"

"Fight? Like with my fists?" Aleksandar turned, chuckling.

"I'm serious. Don't laugh." Ellie nudged him.

"Who could show me?" Aleksandar asked.

"I can fight."

"You can?"

"Yes."

"Would you teach me?" Aleksandar sipped on his tea and stood, waving his hands at Ellie.

"You're okay with a girl beating up on you?" Ellie crossed her legs, her cheeks rosy.

"If you can fight, why does it matter?"

"I guess it doesn't. It would offend others."

"Most are idiots," Hugh said. "Where did you learn?"

"It was the morning after a new moon years ago. I know, rather specific, but we met up with another group of travelers. Highway thieves had robbed them, leaving them with little, but they were more or less in one piece. They knew how to fight."

"Was it that dangerous out there?" Aleksandar leaned on the armrest.

"Some days. You had your thieves, wildlife, occasional fight with commoners when you went into towns. I think Well's Peake gives it a run for its money. Anyway, there was this older woman with them, Lee. You'd never meet a more stubborn person in your life. For a traveler, she was strict on the rules, but we convinced her to train our group. Never had an issue with thieves again."

Ellie leaned back in her seat. "It seems so long ago. I wish I could connect with my brothers like I did with them, but they just don't make it easy. With my family on the road, we connected like that. Same interests, same wants in life. Here, my brothers want to be *titans* of industry, but I can't help but see the suffering and hollowness of the factories." Ellie looked to Aleksandar. "What about you?"

"What about me?" Aleksandar straightened himself.

"We're always telling you stories. I think we deserve one of yours. I want to know why you became an inventor. What drives you to do what you do?" Ellie put her hands in her lap.

Hugh paused and set his invention on the counter, looking over without turning his head too much.

Aleksandar rubbed his forehead, his chest growing light. He found his seat next to Ellie, who looked at him with a charming smile.

Rubbing his chin, he leaned back. "Few people have heard that story."

"Perhaps I can be the next. With Hugh, of course."

Hugh glanced with a confused stare.

Aleksandar scratched his face, rubbing his arm.

"Oh, come on. Please tell me." Ellie nudged him.

Shae hopped to her post, joining the group.

"You too, huh?" Aleksandar petted the owl with the back of his hand.

Aleksandar coughed, a thickness growing in his throat. He rubbed his knee until he felt a tender hand hold his still. Ellie was the only thing that brought him comfort from his tragedy. Her constant kindness, the lasting gazes, the warmth of her fingers between his, and the sound of her lovely voice.

Aleksandar inhaled, the tightness loosening in his chest.

"When I was young, my parents took me to see a magician. This show had everything: the elephants, the wands, the hats. I loved the hats. At that age, you want the magic to last forever. In the finale, she performed this trick using a machine. I thought it was just glass and water, but when she waved her hand, it came to life. It was no trick; it had to be something else. Something magical."

Ellie watched in silence, and Hugh moved from the stool and sat in the chair across from them.

"My best friend, she had this book with a picture in it. Never knew what it did, but the magician's machine reminded me of the one from her story, and that book meant everything to her. So one night, I knew I had to show her. We snuck out, made our way through the forest with the snow at our waist, and if not for the moonlight, we would've been lost. It was a miracle we didn't freeze.

"We slipped into the magician's tent and watched the machine, overwhelmed by its power. It still hummed as if it had a soul. We sat there for hours, and she told me everything about that book. I didn't care that I'd heard it before. Her passion was nice to hear."

Aleksandar chuckled.

"An older lady with a rose gold cane showed up, a hat covering her snow-white hair, and watched over our shoulders. She smiled when I spotted her and told us we needed to leave. On the way home, I couldn't keep up. My friend ran so fast, dragging me through the snow, just to get home and look at the drawings in the book. It was weeks before she talked about anything else. She'd even come over late some days, convincing my parents to let her stay, and we'd spend the night talking about every detail."

Aleksandar rubbed his cheek.

"She was so passionate about what she wanted to do, to change the world, to make it a better place by fixing the lands of the Black Harvest, and I thought I was meant to follow her steps. She is why I invent."

Ellie glanced to Hugh and back to Aleksandar, smiling. "Did she ever make that change?"

Aleksandar closed his eyes and shook his head. "No. She died before she ever got that chance. That's why I do it. Because she never did."

Hugh lowered his head, and Shae hooted.

Ellie leaned against Aleksandar. "Thank you for sharing. I can see how meaningful that evening was to you."

Aleksandar pictured his friend's face, smiling on that cold evening, the snowflakes brushing up against her cheek. His stomach grew uneasy, and he opened his eyes, looking to his hands clenching his pant legs. He batted an eye and stood. "Well, that's enough of that. How about we begin instead."

"With what?" Ellie tilted her head.

Aleksandar grabbed Ellie's tea and set it down, pulling her to her feet. "You can teach me how to fight."

"Oh, can I? Are you ready for that?"

Hugh held his palm to his face and squeezed past them, making his way to the workbench to focus on his project. Aleksandar locked eyes with Ellie.

"You think you got what it takes?" she asked.

"I hope—"

Ellie threw a right hook, hitting him in the arm. Aleksandar stumbled, tripping on the corner of the bench.

Ellie winked at him. "I assumed you were ready." She moved the coffee table against the wall, giving them plenty of space on the old carpet.

"That's dirty." Aleksandar pushed himself up, oddly holding his fists.

"Hold on, what is that?" Ellie covered her mouth with a grin.

"What? I'm going to fight you."

Ellie walked to Aleksandar and repositioned his arms into a fighting stance. Aleksandar blushed as she moved her hands along his arms.

"This doesn't seem right," he said.

"That's because you're used to city fighting. All show and no sport. If you wish to defend yourself in real life, you need to know how to rumble like a proper gent. Muscle memory will kick in, but now for the basics." Ellie held her hands up in a dramatic pose. "I want you to dodge this."

"Which way?"

Ellie jabbed, and Aleksandar shifted, her knuckles skimming the top of his shoulder.

"I pulled my punch," she said.

"I figured."

"As long as you do. Your turn. Mimic me."

"What if I hit you or you can't—"

Ellie raised her brows. "Aleksandar."

"Right."

"I'm waiting," she said.

Aleksandar threw a punch, and she shifted sideways with little effort.

"Again."

With another jab, he felt the muscles in his back that he never used. He rolled his shoulders.

"Again."

With each strike, Aleksandar became more sure of himself, but his form seemed weak. He wiped the sweat from his brow, wondering. Ellie seemed to enjoy every attack, moving on the carpet like a dancer. She watched, anticipating more. One after another, Aleksandar threw his fists at her until his arms were sore and his back ached.

"Again."

Aleksandar held his hands against his chest.

"Keep going. To be fast, train fast."

Aleksandar punched again.

"Again."

"Ellie."

"You can do it."

Aleksandar slowed, his feet tender from the constant circling, the workshop seeming to spin. His breath was heavy, and she didn't have a bead of sweat on her. Aleksandar opened his hands, stretching his fingers.

Ellie dropped her arms.

"Sorry," Aleksandar said. "I might have rushed into this. Just a—"

Ellie took a step forward. "Do you fancy Miss Harvey?"

He froze, shifting his ear to her. "Do I what?"

"Do you look to Miss Harvey in that certain way?"

Aleksandar rubbed the side of his arm, confused. "I... enjoy her company, but not—"

Ellie walked up to Aleksandar, grabbed him by the collar, and kissed him on the lips. She tasted sweet as vanilla, and Aleksandar lost himself in her embrace, closing his eyes.

She pulled away, but Aleksandar knew she was near, her breath still on his cheek. His gaze opened to her while she blushed, eyeing him back. He pulled her close and pressed his lips against hers as she cupped his face, giggling in the moment.

Hugh cringed, and in a single sweep, he scooped up his invention and hurried up the stairwell.

Aleksandar looked to her, lost, holding her close.

"Better," she said. "You need to take charge more often and stop backing down. Don't let things happen around you when you should make them happen yourself."

"We're talking about boxing, right?"

Ellie tilted her head. "In a way."

"It might mean little, but I've wanted to kiss you much more. I wasn't sure what you thought of me with everything that's happening."

Ellie brushed his hair aside. "It is a lot, but I couldn't keep to myself any longer."

They blushed.

Ellie stepped back. "Now that you understand bold, I want—"

Aleksandar swung at her, and she grabbed his wrist, stopping him in his tracks.

Aleksandar paused. "I'm so sorry."

Ellie smiled and punched him in the gut, Aleksandar clenching his gut.

Aleksandar held up his hand. "My goodness. This seems cruel."

"Is little Mr. Scott a whiner?"

Aleksandar peered up, smirking. "I see how it is." Aleksandar lifted his hands as she shoved him, circling him.

"Best put that foot behind the other, or else you'll trip."

Aleksandar looked down, and Ellie jabbed him in the shoulder. He backed up and dodged a second strike, locking eyes with her.

"That's better," she said. "Focus on me. I'm the threat."

"Is this how your teacher was?"

"Oh, no. She would have knocked you out just to prove a point."

"No, thank you. Honestly, though, the chances of me getting near him are slim. Now that I'm thinking, how's this going to help?"

"They say if you're close enough, hand-to-hand is best."

"What I need—" Aleksandar paused, hands still. "I focused on a water invention, but what if—"

"If you what?" Ellie punched him, and he didn't flinch.

Aleksandar stopped, his eyes looking up into his head.

"What is it?" Ellie asked.

Aleksandar licked the bottom of his lip and rushed to a workbench, knocking over one of Shae's posts, and she hissed at him. He moved scrap metal around until he found a pencil and pulled paper from the desk, drawing long lines across it.

Aleksandar sensed Ellie behind him, but his thoughts flowed from his fingertips, finding themselves on the parchment. He knocked over a cup of tea, the corners soaking up the liquid, but he paid no attention. After several minutes, Aleksandar held the pencil still and set it on the table.

"What is it?" Ellie looked, setting her cheek on his shoulder.

"I have an idea."

CHAPTER FORTY-SIX

Vida sat on the edge of the hospital bed, looking out the window into the courtyard. Her vision was hazy, and she squinted in the gloomy afternoon, watching a squirrel scurry up a leafless tree.

She stood, her knees stiff under her weight. Her head throbbed with each step, and she tried to keep her balance, but nothing compared to the pounding headaches from days before. She looked into a basin, her face rippling in the water. Her eyes were cloudy, like fog in the moonlight. She splashed her face and rubbed her temples.

A tear dropped into the bowl, and Vida took a deep breath, trying to compose herself. The door creaked behind her.

Vida did not turn from her reflection. "I spent so long hiding my scars, but how is someone to disguise this?"

"Miss Harvey?"

Vida turned to a woman with a metal neck brace. "I'm sorry, I thought you were the nurse."

"That's all right. How are you this morning?"

"Better. Thank you for asking." Vida walked to the bed and sat.

"My name is Constable Lydia May."

"Constable? I didn't think they allowed women at the Peakeland Yard."

"Uncommon, but not unheard of. I'm here to talk about you, though."

Lydia held her hand to the chair. "May I?"

Vida nodded, and Lydia sat beside the window, pulling out a notepad and pencil from her jacket.

"Miss Harvey, I'm here on behalf of the Peakeland Yard. I was hoping to hear your story myself."

"Others have been here." Vida folded her hands in her lap.

"I'm working with an established investigator, and he is most thorough in his work. We believe there are details the others did not ask about that we might find relevant."

Vida turned away, not wanting to relive the experience again. Her breathing grew heavy, but she straightened her back and tried to relax. She lay down, resting her head on the pillow.

"Most of that night is blank," Vida said. "I remember someone walking towards me with a mask of red metal. Aleksandar pulled me into the water, and we were attacked. After that, I woke in the hospital, unable to see. My vision is hazy depending on the hour."

"You believe it's a man?" Lydia asked.

"I don't know. Whoever it was covered their face, they had long hair, but that's all I noticed."

"Did you hear your attacker speak?"

"I can't remember."

Lydia nodded. "Has your eyesight returned?"

"It's fuzzy, but the doctor told me he's optimistic. I can see most things, but everything is in a haze. In a weird way, I can see details better up close."

"I'm glad to hear you're improving. You said Mr. Scott dragged you into the water fountain. Why did he do that?"

"He was protecting me."

"Was he?"

"Why else would he do it?"

"I need to know if he was trying to help or harm."

"To help, of course. We were attacked together."

Constable May wrote on the notepad faster than most ever could.

Vida sighed and rubbed the bridge of her nose. "Every night I go to sleep, I see the fountain and sense the cold water. When I wake, the world feels darker."

Vida turned to Lydia, who sat with attentive eyes. She looked at the brace attached to her neck, wondering what had happened, wondering how long it took for Lydia to grow used to the stares of those who noticed her affliction.

Does it bother her still?

Vida leaned up. "I don't mean to be forward, but do you mind if I ask about your..."

Lydia closed her book and rubbed the cover. "Just an old injury."

"Does it bother you when you're in public?"

"It did for a while. Then I realized it shouldn't. It's part of who I am, and there's no changing it. My grandfather would say, what you can't cure, you must endure. So one day, I accepted it. It didn't happen overnight, but the stares did not bring me down as they did. Their opinions were none of my business."

Vida rubbed her arm. "I've always worried about my scars. If society would think I was a freak."

Lydia nodded. "I know those thoughts, but they pass. I loved someone very special who showed me, despite my injury, that they loved me back. You should surround yourself with those people. They'll help lessen the burden to where you can carry it on your own. And if it's any consolation, even with them hazy, you're a lovely young woman."

Vida grinned, not having smiled in days. Her thoughts drifted from the attack, and she thought to happier memories. She paused and looked around. "What day is it?"

"It's Thursday. Does it seem like it?"

Vida looked at the ceiling. "No."

"Are you feeling okay? Do you need anything? I have several questions and prefer you to be comfortable."

Vida bit her lip, and Lydia watched her, resting her hands on her lap.

"Is something wrong?" Lydia asked.

Vida looked up and sighed. "I know this is not orthodox, but I was wondering if you could help me with something."

"What would that be?"

Vida reached to her belongings on the chair next to the bed and pulled out her acceptance letter, handing it to Lydia, who read it and looked up with beady eyes.

Vida pressed her lips. "Would you be so kind to cover for me? I have worked years to get accepted into a school, and to miss my first class would break me."

Lydia took a deep breath. "How far away is it?"

"Just around the block."

Lydia tapped the end of the letter and stood. "Oh, let the Maker watch over us. Grab your things."

Vida sat up with a grin.

～

Constable May walked down the hallway with a glass and pitcher of water, nodding to several nurses.

Dr. Doyle walked the other way, signaling Lydia. "Constable May, is everything all right?"

"Dr. Doyle, yes. Our questioning might take a while, so I wanted to ensure Miss Harvey was comfortable."

"I appreciate that. Your colleagues do not carry the same sensitive touch. Please do not push her. She has much healing to undergo."

"I'll keep my questions short."

"Thank you. I'll be sure to check up on her later."

Lydia headed down the hallway as Dr. Doyle took his leave. Lydia looked through the glass with a raised brow. She opened the door, and as she expected, Vida was nowhere to be found.

～

Dozens of well-dressed students wearing tailored vests and dresses strolled across the pavement outside the university. Some carried books while others walked, elbows locked in conversation. Vida relished it in awe, enjoying the wind against her face, free from the staleness of the hospital.

Through the fallen leaves, the buildings rose around her in gray stone, orange banners hanging between the pillars and staircases. Brick pathways lined the courtyard with a tree in the center, taller than the buildings under its canopy.

With a headache and weak legs, Vida tried to enjoy herself, forgetting her condition. She jolted hard to the side, head filling with nausea, and her eyes hazed over. She stood still, concentrating on her breathing, and after a moment of uncertainty, she walked across the pavement and into a smaller stone building that read, *Ragnos Of Medicine.*

Vida noticed several people walking into a larger room. Unsure of which classroom was hers, she looked to her schedule. She glanced through the glass and recognized the gentleman next to the professor's desk, Dr. Gray.

She confirmed the classroom number and wandered in, eyes darting in her direction. She peered at Dr. Gray, and he motioned her to take her seat.

A fellow with a tight collar and muttonchops walked into the room, checking his pocket watch. He closed the door softly and set his suitcase on the desk, turning to the chalkboard. He wrote Professor Garret.

Vida kept her head down since no other girls were in the class and hoped her eyes were not cloudy.

She focused hard, but the desks and the students drifted away from her. The room circled her as the faces blurred to oval shapes. Everything meshed together, covered in white static. She grabbed her hand and pulled at her old scar through the glove. She blinked, and the classroom returned to normal.

The man walked to the middle of the classroom.

"Hello. My name is Professor Garret, and I'll be your mentor for the next six months. We have selected you from a thousand of the finest young men in Well's Peake. This is where the foundation for your career as practicing doctors will begin. From this moment, you must weigh everything into factor because people will look to you to perform miracles."

Professor Garret stepped into the middle aisle.

"There will be days you make hard choices, choices that could end or save lives. I do not wish to dissuade you, for this is a noble cause, but you must understand the mental expectations of holding life in your hands. I'm proud of you who have pursued good in this world. The Maker knows we have seen enough of the contrary."

Professor Garret walked down the aisles, looking over his students, a notebook firmly in his grasp. With glasses on the tip of his nose, Vida could see the red marks where they usually sat.

She tried not to keep eye contact long, but he paused beside her, studying his notebook.

"I apologize, miss. The nursing classroom is one down the hall," he said.

Vida glanced at Dr. Gray, and he motioned her to stay calm.

"They accepted me into the program." Vida lifted her head, finding the class's attention.

"That would be odd. Our university does not accept women for higher doctoring."

"They did a week ago."

He looked into his notepad, running his finger down the page. He took off his glasses and tapped them on the edge. "Vida Harvey?"

"Yes, sir." Vida rubbed her fingers.

"This is unexpected." Professor Garret turned. "Mr. Cunningham?"

A man in the front stood.

"Just so you all know, Mr. Cunningham will assist me this season. I'd appreciate it if you showed him the same respect. Mr. Cunningham, could you please check with the headmaster on Vida Harvey's acceptance?"

"Right away, sir," Mr. Cunningham said with a bow.

"Thank you."

Mr. Cunningham exited the room, and Professor Garret looked at Vida. "Who were your references?"

"I've worked with Dr. Doyle for several seasons."

"Good man. Who else?" He crossed his hands.

Dr. Gray stood. "I am. I was fortunate enough to meet Miss Harvey one night, and she displayed the insight a doctor needs."

"Well, with referrals such as those, I see a convincing argument. You may stay until your confirmation is approved or disapproved. I have no objections to a woman in my class. However, I can tell some disagree."

Several men nodded their heads, and one pointed to the exit as Vida looked over her shoulder. She sensed the pressure growing behind her eyes and rubbed her temple as Professor Garret walked to the front of the class.

"For those who believe in these ideals, I acknowledge your naivety and arrogance. If you intend to practice, your judgments end here. You will encounter many situations and people in your years to come, and it would surprise you how many women are forced to pick up the bandages in moments of turmoil. I know several that would make you look like toddlers with cherry-glazed gauze. Those who served in the Harvest saved many prominent bloodlines, a few here today."

The classroom fell quiet, and Vida held back a smile.

"Anyone who feels they lack the self-discipline to do so, please leave now. For if I discover this later, you will never step foot in the halls of another academy."

The room remained silent.

"Fantastic," Professor Garret said. "Let us begin."

He opened a door within the wall and pulled out a stretcher with a blanket covering a body. He pushed it into the aisle as a rancid stench filled the air, several burying their noses and groaning.

"Get used to the smells," he said. "This is elementary compared to the Black Harvest."

Vida looked on, ignoring the few glares from her classmates.

"Underneath this blanket rests a man recently passed." The professor folded his hands. "Dr. Gray knows the man's cause of death, and only him. I'm sure you've all heard of his influence, considering your interest in the field, so I'll skip the pleasantries. He will share his expertise at the end of class. Until then, I'd like volunteers to come and inspect. We're interested in your theories, and for your peace of mind, the body is safe to examine."

Professor Garret removed the sheet, revealing the corpse, which had not yet decayed. Vida looked as a student rushed to the body, leaving no chance for anyone to beat him to the first test. The dead man had dry lips and was skinnier than most healthy adults.

"I ask you not to touch," the professor said, "Mr.?"

"Mr. Dublin," he said, shaking his head. "Would it be Black Harvest?"

"It would not. If he passed from Black Harvest, we would not be safe. I mentioned he was earlier. Every detail, no matter how simple, needs to be taken into consideration. Whether someone was to mention a random drink of water to a minor cut walking down the street, consider it important. Next?"

Vida moved to stand, but another student beat her to the test. She sat and watched as several others guessed. From influenza to measles, Dr. Gray shook his head no. They were rushing, trying to look good, but none were taking the moment to examine the body. One after another, they all failed.

Professor Garret waved his palm. "I think that is plenty."

Vida held her hand up but pulled it down.

"Valiant efforts, but know you must study to remain in this class. Judging just from the looks of this man, I would say he passed from cholera. Most likely, he drank from an unclean source of water, contracting the disease, which caused everything from brain problems to muscle spasms and digestive issues."

Vida raised her hand.

The professor wrote on the chalkboard.

Dr. Gray coughed. "Professor."

"Yes?"

"You have another volunteer."

He faced the class. "Miss Harvey?"

"Sir, if you would be okay with it, I would like to step up," she said.

"Why is that?"

"I think it's something else. May I?"

The professor glanced at Dr. Gray and tapped his glasses. "Please do."

"Thank you."

Vida stood, the weight of the classroom on her shoulders.

"This is insulting. This woman—"

"Enough!" The professor slammed his palm on his desk, and the room fell silent. A student looked on, pulling on the end of his jacket. "Young man, you're dismissed from this program and any class I have any association with. Take those who share your beliefs with you."

The student stood awkwardly as everyone waited for him to leave. He muttered, but Professor Garret held his finger in the air and pointed to the door. The student bit his lip and left the room.

The professor nodded to Miss Harvey.

"Thank you." Vida smiled until her cheeks hurt and examined the body. The chapped lips and convulsed muscles spoke to her more than anything. She inspected every detail, from the discoloration of his jaw to his strained limbs. The more she noticed, the more her head throbbed. She gripped the edge as her hand flinched and steadied herself.

"If it's too much, please sit," the professor said.

"Tetanus," Vida said.

"Excuse me?"

"He died from tetanus. If he had cholera, the innards would've rotted out, but they're still there from what I can see. I don't think this man was getting any fluids. His lips are cracked, and his throat is swollen. Also, his muscles are convulsed. All of which leads to contorted limbs. If you look at his ankle, there is a cut on the backside, which is where he might have contracted it."

Professor Garret looked at Dr. Gray, who had a massive smile on his face. "Miss Harvey, tell me more?"

"Yes. Tetanus is a newer condition that Dr. Doyle has recently discovered in the area. Also known as lockjaw, an infection. As metal rusts, it becomes riddled with bacteria. When people scratch themselves, depending on the severity, they could contract the infection. This man could've survived if he'd found a doctor. I assume he was homeless, and it was noticed too late."

Vida turned to the class, several staring, others writing in their notebooks. The professor crossed his arms and pushed his glasses further up his nose, and Mr. Cunningham returned to the room.

"Mr. Cunningham," the professor said. "What did you discover?"

"There's no mistake. They accepted Miss Harvey into the doctoring program," he said.

"Indeed, no mistake at all." Dr. Gray clapped his hands.

Everyone turned their attention to the surgeon, who walked to the center, covering up the body.

"It was no mistake," Dr. Gray said. "She pointed out a condition without touching the body. Shows what we can determine through observation."

Professor Garret raised his eyebrows. "Very good, Miss Harvey. Your skills are most impressive. It's with great sadness; I must dismiss you."

Vida's head flared in pain. It spread into her chest, fingers, toes. She felt her eyes hazing over and steadied herself on the table as the professor's words shattered her spirit.

The room gasped, then passed in silence, leaving Vida standing wide-eyed.

"But why?" she asked.

Professor Garret held his palm up, silencing them. "Let's have a hard discussion. Show of hands, how many of you were taught women lacked the skill to be doctors?"

Almost everyone in the class raised their hand.

"And you believe this?"

They lowered their arms.

"Now I have liars in my classroom, or maybe you've reconsidered and are striving to fix your flaws. If that's the case, I commend you. For those who think I based my decision on Miss Harvey being a woman, pay attention."

Professor Garret walked up to her. Her stomach ached, and she grew lightheaded as her legs felt like they would give way.

"Miss Harvey, I have no doubt you think the worst of me, but believe me when I say you have the talent I'd want if I ever needed medical treatment. However, I'm dismissing you because of this."

Professor Garret reached down and touched her hand. Vida's lips trembled as she looked across the room.

"You could save lives with these hands, but you could also end them. I noticed the slightest flinch when I first stood by you, when you gripped the table, and when you rubbed your temple. My fear is when it matters most; what will happen when your nerves take over?"

Vida swallowed, trying to fight the tears.

Professor Garret pursed his lips. "I'm so sorry."

His words fell on deaf ears. Vida's eyes widened, and she could tell they were hazing to where everyone would notice. She covered her face and rushed out of the room, passing Dr. Gray's outreached hand.

The hallway was long, and she sprinted along the tiled floors, her footsteps echoing, hollow. She stumbled as she flew through the university doors, running down the pavement as her limbs burned. She rounded the corner until she faced the massive oak that overshadowed the academy, rain falling from the sky.

Her lungs felt like they were collapsing, and she clenched her chest, losing her balance as she dropped to her knees. The world blurred and spun as she leaned against the bark of the tree, gripping it with her fingertips.

She caught her blurry reflection in the small pond next to the roots. She looked back at herself with frosted eyes, and a tear fell from her cheek into the water.

Vida shut her eyes and held on to the tree, sobbing, begging the world to stop being so cruel.

CHAPTER FORTY-SEVEN

Clouds drifted in the afternoon sky, the sun dim and the wind brushing through the pine. In a blue shirt, Natalia raked the leaves and needles in her yard, looking at the orange-and-red forest valley. She rolled her shoulders and rubbed her cheek, loosening her jaw from the tightness of the cooling weather. A squirrel ran across the grass and zipped into her leaf pile. She kneeled, and the creature popped its head out with a nut in its paws.

He sprinted into the forest, through the fence, and scurried up a tree trunk. Natalia turned to creaking metal, Bernard standing at the back gate.

"Bernard, did I forget you were coming by? Come in." Natalia leaned on the rake, and Bernard let himself in.

"No, no. I'm here unannounced. I hope I'm not disturbing you."

"Of course not, and thank you. I was just taking a break from the work Mr. Scott and I have been doing. Would you care for a drink? I made some delicious iced lemonade."

"Iced? Yes, please."

"I'll be right back. Take a seat."

Natalia set down the rake and stepped up the redwood deck and into the kitchen. She grabbed a few glasses from the cabinet, poured the lemonade, and put in some ice from the icebox. She walked outside,

Bernard resting in a chair under the tree in the center yard.

Thick pine trees lined the lawn with an iron fence near the roots. The garden was empty, the grass covered in leaves.

Natalia made her way to the patio and set the glasses on the table, sitting across from Bernard.

"Here is my mother's finest lemonade." Natalia lifted her glass, chilly against her fingertips. "You have not had perfection until you've tried this."

Bernard held the drink up, looking at the cubes. "Where did you find an icebox? Doesn't it last only a few days?"

"It does, but I have another in my workshop, and since it's under the stone of the waterfall, the temperature always keeps it cooled."

Bernard took a sip, and his eyes widened. "Now, this is delicious."

Natalia lifted her eyebrows, and they laughed.

Bernard leaned back, holding the glass between both hands. "I remember when you built this house. Some believed you mad, keeping to these rocks for those few years."

"It was rather simple in design, just hard work. I found a few books on stone crafting, and here we are."

"The fact that you wanted to build into the hillside, next to a waterfall, was quite daring. It is a shame most will never see its beauty in full, with your workshop below and this view of the valley."

"Not anymore, at least. That's okay. I enjoy my personal space."

Bernard chuckled.

"So, what brings you here, Bernard? You rarely drop by unannounced." Natalia brushed her hair behind her ear, the wind blowing it across her face.

Bernard looked into the glass. He took another sip, set it on the table, and played with his bronze bracelet. "They've forced me into a difficult position."

Natalia straightened her back. She guessed but did not want to consider the possibilities, hoping it was a dilemma only Bernard found serious.

"As you know, I've been meeting with several prominent figures and families to raise funding for the World's League. The latest and largest being Fritz and Co."

Natalia bit her lip, feeling her chest tighten. "Ah, and the only connection involving me is the Steamrail."

Bernard tapped his fingers. "Yes."

Natalia folded her hands in her lap. "Do they want my rights?"

"No, but they might as well ask. They want mine as well as my word that you won't put in a claim against them. If you do, that I will defend them." Bernard rubbed his forehead.

Natalia swallowed hard. "Have you signed?"

"Not yet."

"Why not?"

Bernard stroked his beard. "I didn't see it as such a simple matter. This affects you and your future too. You gave me the two percent to be the breaker in these conditions, not to use it against you. The Fritz brothers didn't like Mr. Forbes's vision and can now pursue their own. They want to thrive as Belagrad does, and they are using their investment position as leverage to jumpstart the rail industry."

"They are your rights, Bernard. You can do with them as you wish. I knew the possibilities and the consequences. Mine still belong to me."

"It's not kind of me to give up your legacy for my vision."

Natalia sucked in her check and crossed her legs. She wanted to be upset with him, to curse out the Fritz brothers, but she did not have the urge. Something was calming about being removed, not having a choice, and letting the decisions fall to others.

"Listen to me." Natalia leaned in. "You know, and I hate to admit it, but my memory is not what it was. All I ever wanted was to move on from my past and protect the future. It's rather poetic, securing my legacy as my memories grow foggy. As the days fade, I'm only reminded of my failure through my journal. Perhaps I should let my failures go."

Bernard stood and crossed his arms, looking at the waterfall behind the house.

Natalia leaned back. "Do you remember the talk we had a few years ago? We said we were the people who'd do what's necessary to guide the future."

"We weren't supposed to be detrimental to each other." Bernard rubbed the side of his head. "There's more than just this. I'm aware of something that I have not disclosed to you."

"What's that?"

Bernard bit his lip. "You're being investigated by association with Aleksandar Scott."

"That's only logical. It's in their best interest. But since I'm considered a suspect, and I have named you my successor, you'll be given my rights. Which will transfer to Fritz and Co, assuming they demanded your ownership and not the two percent we assigned you."

"Yes. You could lose everything until they restore your rights after the investigation."

"I lose every way."

"Does it not anger you? The position they have put you and me in?"

Natalia pulled her shirt taunt. "Sign the pledge."

Bernard turned with his hands on his hips. "And give them the majority?"

"Like I said, maybe I should let my legacy be."

Bernard shook his head again, pacing in a circle. "If there was any other way."

"Where's the paperwork?"

Bernard paused. "In my coat."

Natalia pulled a pen from her pocket and set it down. "Take out the proposal and sign it. You agree, something is coming to Well's Peake, something bigger than us, and we need to rush ahead of it. This is the path for the World's League and its future."

Bernard hesitated and removed the paper from his pocket, holding it in his hand as it ruffled in the wind. "I don't like this. We can't predict how it will end."

"It'll all end as it should." Natalia glanced at the pen, wiping a tear from her eye before it fell.

Bernard grabbed the pen with reluctance. "Tell me something."

"About what?"

"Are you upset about this? In any way?"

Natalia rubbed the back of her neck and sipped on the sweet lemonade. "Who wouldn't be?"

~

Natalia watched out the window of her study as Bernard disappeared down the path to the main road. She pulled the journal out of her jacket and sat at her desk, pulling herself close as she picked up a pen.

Today was one of those days a memory returned to me. When Bernard looked at me, he could see my defeat. He wanted me to be more dismayed as the wind brushed against my face, to tell him not to do it, but I would not give him permission. His vision is import-ant, and I know a necessary part of the future, even at my expense.

His disappointment reminded me of my apprentice from years past. We were on grand strides, looking to change the world as she believed we would. However, after my failure at Oakvale, I lacked the drive to mold her. She noticed and was saddened by my lack of passion. I tried, but I could not lift myself from the ache that came after the death of my husband.

She would hold the Spark to me, but I was not gifted with the motivation or the ideas we needed. She grew upset, and I felt nothing. Her parents caught on, and they threatened to pull her apprenticeship and find another mentor. That also did not faze me.

Life was moving on without me, and I saw no future. Like I don't now.

As much as I hate feeling hollow, this memory has returned… perhaps I have found my legacy in rebuilding my past. If only I knew what triggers I needed to rebuild my mind and no longer depend on my journals.

Natalia closed the journal and turned in her chair, the fireplace behind her. She looked at the bookcase's edge, stood, and pushed her desk against the shelf, hopping on the end. Natalia pulled the molding away to a blue book inside the frame. She took it out and blew the dust off, a woodsy aroma lingering in the air.

A note in her husband's writing was sealed to the cover in wax.

Do not read until you remember what's within.

Did it matter anymore? It was where her life would grow simple, and she would live out the rest of her days, people unaware of what she pursued.

Natalia looked at the spine, rubbing her fingers down the aged fibers. She put her finger on the cover and opened it, the pages crisp. Before she could read, she closed her eyes and shut it.

Why can't I look?

A tear fell down her cheek, and she wiped it away, setting the book back in the cubby. She sealed it and lowered herself to the floor.

She wanted to read it, to remember her past, knowing it lay in the pages, but her husband's note had to have purpose. Why did she have to remember before reading it? She had to know before she opened the cover again.

Pulling her knees to her chest, Natalia held herself, feeling the emptiness of lost memories.

CHAPTER FORTY-EIGHT

Orange-and-red leaves collected on the ground as night consumed the day. The glowing sunset faded into a blue haze that hung over the town and forests of Well's Peake.

Kenneth listened to the wind blow around him, leaves scraping against the stone. He wondered if someone passed by; they would question if he was dying in peace. His face had healed from the fire, but his body was thin from starvation, his skin tight against his cheekbones.

He stared at the horizon with bloodshot eyes, the sunset bringing him a sense of calm. A sour taste formed in his mouth as he peered at his mask, wanting to hide, longing for days without heartache. He pulled a satchel against the stone of the overhang and removed a stick with little meat left on it. He nibbled off the end, the beef dry and tough, and it caused his stomach to ache and his chest to tingle.

Kenneth stood, blood rushing within and his vision blurring as he steadied himself, holding his hands out for balance. He collapsed to one knee, his legs too weak from sitting on them all evening. He continued to glare at the sunset, the frigid wind blowing tears off his cheek before they could reach his jawline. After the shine hurt his eyes, he looked to the rim of the overhang, his mind wandering to dark places.

Kenneth bit the end of his lip and stumbled, the tip of his boots over the edge. He whispered under his breath so quietly he could not hear himself.

His wife, sister, parents, and the life that abandoned him were all he could think about. The balance of his existence hanging on end. He shifted, feeling his stomach grow lighter as the wind drifted through his matted hair.

The leaves rustled, and footsteps approached, but he did not care. He leaned towards the edge, waiting for the breeze to do what he could not.

Kenneth did not turn around, knowing only one person visited him.

Kenneth lowered his head. "Fate has taken away every beautiful aspect of my life, yet it spared me?"

"You only cause yourself pain by being here. Well's Peake has carried on, and maybe it's come to where you must consider the same."

"I failed to kill Aleksandar. It will now be impossible to get close to him with the Peake on high alert. I will never succeed now. What's the point of suffering on this hill as I waste away?"

The masked man walked beside him, and Kenneth could see him out of the corner of his eye.

"On the other side, you will discover what you've lost," the masked man said. "You'll find what was once beautiful."

The air grew dry, and the moonlight dimmed behind darkening clouds, leaves rustling across the stone ledge.

Kenneth looked over his shoulder. "Do you think the afterlife is lovely? After the things I've done?"

"Yes. All aspects that are ugly are transformed. You'll change for the better. You are looking to me for approval, but that is a choice you must make for yourself."

Kenneth looked to the ledge, knowing the fall may not be high enough. If he landed just right, it could end his suffering, but land wrong, and he might survive.

The masked man stepped forward, pausing. "You deserve this."

Kenneth's eyes opened wide. His breath grew deep, and his lip curled. A gust of wind shook the leaves from the branches, a wall of red and orange drifting through the surrounding forest.

Kenneth turned around, his face pale. "So life is meaningless until it ends? No one is beautiful until they die?"

The masked man moved to the center of the rock. "Not compared to what we'll become."

"So if I killed you, you'd become beautiful?" Kenneth asked. "Wouldn't everyone be better off dead if such a place existed?"

"Perhaps."

Adrenaline rushed through Kenneth's body, and he felt the strength return to his limbs.

Kenneth tightened his grip around the levers on the gauntlets stuffed in his cuff, and his eyes narrowed. "So you are telling me, until she died, Amia was not beautiful? That her only purpose was to die?"

"That's not what I said."

Kenneth turned and lowered his arms. *How dare he speak of Amia that way. She did not deserve to die so young and beautiful. What if other people thought the same? Crooked in their minds, not knowing what was best for them? They should pay for that. I can make them pay. I will make the masked man pay.*

"And what of me?" Kenneth said. "You say Well's Peake has moved on, but have they? Do they not search for me, haunted by my name? For a moment, I thought fate stole my life, but what if you have given me the means to show them beauty? A new purpose. When they see horror, would they turn to what's beautiful in their lives?"

"Anything you do now belongs to the Phoenix, not Kenneth Forbes. You may stand, but Kenneth Forbes is dead. No one will speak of the man on the hill. Not like they once did."

Kenneth grimaced and pushed his tongue against the inside of his taut cheek.

"I... will do as I please. Kenneth listened to the lies you spun, but the Phoenix listens only to me. Me!" Kenneth hissed. "How dare you stand there thinking you are better than I. You wanted me to jump, didn't you? Is that your perversion? To torture those until they are no more. Without that mask, who are you?"

"Do not think I am careless with your design." The masked man rolled his shoulders. "You need to stop and think."

Kenneth waited for more, but none came. A soft wind brushed against his face, the oak and pine strong in the air. The masked man stared with black and empty eyes.

"You can leave now. This is my hill, and you are no longer welcome."

The masked man stood still. Kenneth watched, waiting for his next move. The cold steel in his grip, the tightness of his skin. He felt every sensation in the breeze. He would not—

The masked man yanked out two whips and cracked them through the air, binding Kenneth's wrists. He pulled Kenneth to the ground, his face scraping against the stone. Kenneth shuffled to his knees and sprinted forward, his hands stretched, unleashing a deadly burst of fire. The masked man rolled through the leaves, losing control and finding himself in the thicket.

Kenneth unbound himself and released a fiery fury, ensuring the forest trapped his attacker. The masked man dodged the blast and waved his arm, a whip wrapping around Kenneth's leg. He yanked Kenneth's knee from underneath and brought him to the forest floor.

The spray from his gauntlet lit the ground on fire. Kenneth shot at the whip, burning the end attached to his ankle. The masked man raced forward, heaving his whips back and forth in an attempt to snag Kenneth once more, the tips shredding through the leaves. He tossed them into the air as chaos ensued between the two. Kenneth dodged the attacks and threw blasts of fire, evading his enemy.

Kenneth created a massive wall of flames and directed it towards the masked man, who took cover behind a tree, nearly encased in death. He trudged around the tree and burned the bark away.

The fire raged up the trunk, the bark splintering, leaving only a black scar.

Kenneth squeezed the levers in his hand until his fingernails dug into his palm. The heat beat against his knuckles, and his lips dried as he squinted in the light. He held as long as he could, letting go as his hands trembled in the heat.

The tree was scorched and burned at its roots, leaves drifting in the air. Kenneth stumbled to the tree, his fists out, looking for a dead man, but he found none.

A stick cracked, and Kenneth turned towards the masked man. A whip clasped around his throat and ripped into his skin. Kenneth grabbed his neck as blood trickled between the leather braids, his hair falling over his face.

The masked man yanked Kenneth to his back, dragging him across the ground as he struggled to breathe. Kenneth reached over and burned the lash once again. He loosened his chokehold and pushed himself to his feet—the masked man rushing for him.

Kenneth gasped, succumbing to the lack of air as he fell to his knees. The masked man paused, and Kenneth locked eyes with him, his chest tight.

"Do you not find it wise to run in the other direction?" Kenneth asked.

The masked man jumped and swung his whips, and Kenneth shot flames into the air, blocking the charred tips from reaching their target. Kenneth rushed through the fire and grabbed the masked man by the waist, pummeling him into the dirt, a whip bouncing away.

The masked man broke free and dodged Kenneth's fury. Kenneth threw the roars of fire in every direction, driving the masked man to move to his will, around the trees in the forest moonlight.

The masked man snapped his whip, only to catch nothing. Kenneth shot a wave of fire, forcing the masked man out of cover and singeing his back. The masked man crawled onto the overhang, trapped, smothering the flames on his shoulders.

Kenneth fired at his opponent. The fireball hit the masked man as he fell onto the edge, his head dangling in the air.

The masked man lay there, breathing heavily.

Kenneth stood over him with a wicked smile. "You made yourself to be higher than me. As if you were significant in this world. You are nothing special."

The masked man held on to the ledge, trying not to fall.

Kenneth glanced at his mask on the ground and picked it up. He slipped it over his head, the cool metal soothing against his blistered face. "Now, let's see who's under the mask."

With a deep breath, Kenneth reached out to the masked man, who lay on the peak of the rock, breathing hard.

Kenneth grabbed the top of the mask with his fingertips, but the man snatched Kenneth's wrist and swiped for his feet, but Kenneth leaped back. The masked man stood, trying to flee, but Kenneth blocked his way and lifted his foot. He struck the masked man in the chest. He kicked again, and the masked man stumbled over the edge.

The masked man fell through the air, and his mask slipped off, down the slope. Kenneth watched, and in a breathless moment, he heard his body slam, snapping through the thicket until hitting the roots of a tree.

Kenneth watched as the body lay lifeless, wrapped around the tree trunk. He pulled off his metal mask, his bloodshot eyes wide and unflinching.

"Finally, what you deserved."

Kenneth took a deep breath and made his way down the hill, skidding on loose leaves and hidden rocks. He shifted down the slope and paused, looking up to the overhang he threw the masked man from.

Skid marks from where the man landed and slid into the tree were clear in the shadows, but no one rested at the bottom of the trunk.

Kenneth glanced around and clenched his teeth in the harvest night, knowing he was not the only monster in the forest.

CHAPTER FORTY-NINE

Aleksandar walked up the steps of the World's Palace, the crowds filling the Sky Canopy in the morning light. The pillars, crafted to look like trees, branched into the upper floor of the hall.

Paths rested between the leaves of real oak and those of stone. Aleksandar moved in line and handed his ticket to a gentleman in a ruby vest. The man stamped it, gave it back, and Aleksandar walked through the gate, free to roam as he pleased.

He walked to the banister, shaped like branches, and set his hands over the end. Thousands of people explored underneath, the fair growing grand in its last days leading up to the Harvest Festival. Through the glass, the gardens were radiant in the morning, old oaks lingering over ponds and pathways.

Rubbing his fingertips, Aleksandar closed his eyes and listened to the surrounding crowds. The Lunarwheel, the Phoenix, and, most of all, Ellie shifted through his mind. He thought of what he would give to walk through the fair with no worries. To be free of the burdens on his shoulders.

"Mr. Scott?"

Aleksandar glanced over his shoulder, pulling on his tweed jacket. "Yes?"

"You may not recognize me, but I'm one of Ellie's brothers, Jonah."

He stood with his hands at his side, wearing a coat with two lines of buttons along the front.

"I remember, we met at the gala—this is a coincidence; I am meeting your sister soon. We have tickets for the canopy walk."

Jonah shook Aleksandar's hand. "I heard. She had quite the skip to her step this morning. This is not very formal of me, but I was wondering if I could have a moment, before Ellie gets here."

Aleksandar swallowed hard. "I suppose so."

"Excellent." Jonah walked to the edge of the balcony and rested in a chair. Aleksandar sat across from him. The man's cologne overbearing, rich like pine.

"This might be rather awkward, so I'll cut to the chase," Jonah said. "I can't help but wonder about your relationship with my sister."

Aleksandar folded his arms. "What about it?"

"With her traveling the countryside the past few years, I know her understanding of relationships is not like our own in the city." Jonah crossed his legs. "She is quick to move into things, and with everything happening, I can only wonder what you have in mind for her. Have you given it much thought?"

Aleksandar pulled on his cuff. "I have. She means a lot to me and has been very supportive."

"Exactly my point." Jonah waved his finger. "You're going through a rough patch, to say the least, and it concerns me. I worry for my sister's well-being. She is strong-willed, but she doesn't understand the danger that follows you."

"She's more than capable."

"Simply a persona. She is not as confident as she'd like us to believe."

Jonah stood and leaned on the railing, leaving Aleksandar at the table. Aleksandar eyed him and pressed his lips, standing and following him.

"She means a lot to me," Aleksandar said. "As I'm sure she does to you. I wouldn't put her in danger."

Jonah looked over his shoulder. "I don't doubt your intentions and that you believe in what you say, but is your relationship what's best for her?"

Aleksandar's chest tightened. "You don't think I'm a good option?"

"Perhaps, if the situation were different, but you were attacked by a madman, robbed, and involved in the death of Kenneth Forbes. Some think you a killer. Any of which is a risk to Ellie. If something happened to her, it would haunt you forever, would it not?"

Aleksandar glanced away.

"We need to be realistic, Mr. Scott." Jonah pulled a leaf off the tree. "What can you offer my sister?"

Aleksandar looked back. "What's that supposed to mean?"

Jonah rubbed his hand. "Mr. Scott, we live in a world where influence is important, and you have very little. That's not something that matters to me, but what happens if you and Ellie ended up together? You would struggle to give her the life she has now, that she did in childhood. What happens when you can't provide?"

"You don't know her the way you think."

"Don't I? Tell me, what success have you had as an inventor? We see the failure that is your Red Breath, and I've neither heard nor seen anything that shows you could take care of her. Will she have to wait for you to find your path?"

Aleksandar tried to fight the words, to push them out of his mind, but they ate at him.

"From what we've gathered," Jonah said, "you lack the proper motivation."

Aleksandar clenched the end of his jacket, pressing his arms against his sides.

"I've seen none." Jonah shook his head. "Maybe if you believed in yourself or found a real purpose, you would find the path that suited you best, where you could discover success. Nonetheless, it is irrelevant. My point is, you need to ask yourself whether my sister's best interests lie with you. You are a danger to her and have no means to provide. You are a smart lad, and I know you see reason."

Jonah rested on the railing and looked to the fair and gardens through the glass. Aleksandar looked out, fighting the pressure behind his eyes.

"She is starting life again, within the family," Jonah said. "She has a future, and you put that at risk. Please enjoy your day together, and at night's end, you know what you must do."

Aleksandar watched him with an unflinching stare.

Jonah turned back, tilting his head. "I'm sure you care little for me, but I will only say it once. If you're thinking of telling her, don't. She *would* lash out at me and only hold on to you out of spite. That's not the relationship you wish for, I'm sure."

Aleksandar lowered his gaze.

"Do it for the family." Jonah patted Aleksandar's shoulder. "Let her go."

Jonah walked towards the staircase, putting on his hat, and slipped his hands in his pockets.

A sinking feeling filled Aleksandar's stomach, and he bit his lip. Every nerve in his body burned to the point that he might combust. Jonah's words lingered in his thoughts, a part of him considering them. What *if* Ellie deserved better? What if he was putting her in danger?

Aleksandar focused on the man, his eyes narrow. "Mr. Fritz."

Jonah paused and turned.

Aleksandar took a step forward, lifting his head. "I'm going to prove you wrong."

Jonah sighed, and his shoulders sank. "We'll see." With a nod of his hat, Jonah walked away and stepped down the stairs.

Aleksandar breathed heavily, feeling as if he had not taken a breath in an hour. He wandered to the rail and looked to the fair below, moving as it did.

A sharp whistle rang out, and Aleksandar looked up. Ellie was waving from the crowd, smiling as she him blew a kiss. Aleksandar caught it in his hand and pushed it onto his cheek.

CHAPTER FIFTY

Natalia's workshop was crystal clear as the morning shined through the dome window. Aleksandar laid hoses across a cluttered workbench, securing them to the wood with braces.

He attached the cords into the Lunarwheel, hands wrinkled from working in the water. He shivered and struggled with the wet metal smell. With every piece, he grew closer to completion, and Natalia sketched the schematic behind him.

Natalia shook her hand and stretched her neck, popping her white collar high. She loosened her blue tie and charted the design in her notebook, her detail meticulous. She wrote as Aleksandar finished his adjustments with the wheel.

"Do you feel the excitement, Aleksandar?" she asked. "Imagine what could change once the Lunarwheel is finished. If this becomes the marvel it deserves to be; the future could cascade upon us. Energy, transportation, life as it is could evolve in a season."

Aleksandar pulled his hand from behind the machine and closed a porthole to the wheel. "I do, I wonder—"

The engine burst alive, water vibrating, spiraling within the glass. Natalia's eyes widened, and she stepped towards Aleksandar, who watched with a grin.

He clenched his fists. "Natalia, did we?"

The water beneath the cords rippled, creating small waves that pulled together, splashing before rising to a point and peaking in the middle. It collected and grew thicker as it lifted into the air in a shimmering arch. The engine glowed, pushing the morning light from the workshop with rays like ocean ripples.

Aleksandar took a step back, licking his lips. The Lunarwheel blasted the water backward with incredible force, splintering the glass. It cracked down the sides, and the machine's supports shrieked.

Aleksandar flinched. "Natalia, turn it off!"

Natalia was near the wall, severing the batteries. "It has to power down!"

Natalia pushed Aleksandar behind the blast door, and the wheel split. Water exploded across the room, and a shock wave shook the workshop. Natalia lost her balance and flew into the stage, smacking her ribs off the edge. Aleksandar ducked against the barrier as water seeped through the floorboards.

He held his arm and shook his head, looking at Natalia as she struggled to push herself off the floor. "Natalia, are you okay?"

Aleksandar stood, his body throbbing, and helped her to her feet. She clenched her side in pain, holding her waist.

"How bad is it?" he asked.

Natalia grabbed the ends of her shirt and lifted it, the skin over her ribcage red and irritated. She touched her side and winced. "Ugh, I don't think they're broken."

"You can't be serious. Are you—"

Natalia held up her hand and lowered her shirt, closing her eyes as she rested on the stage end. Aleksandar stepped back, holding his arm, glancing to the Lunarwheel.

Another failure...

Natalia slowly stepped to the workbench and grabbed the schematics, and they crumbled through her hands to the floor. Shaking her head, she crossed her arms and rubbed her cheek.

Aleksandar slid onto the wet floor, blood seeping through his shirt.

"Where does it drain to?" Aleksandar asked.

Natalia walked around and looked at him. "When I last flooded the workshop, I installed more drains between the floorboards. Aleksandar, your arm?"

"Clever." Aleksandar pulled his hand away, staring at a small tear. He opened the hole to a minor cut. "It's not bad."

Natalia reached out, but Aleksandar wandered to the dome window, looking at the valley.

He clenched his jaw, the stress in his neck aching down his spine. They were getting nowhere with the Lunarwheel, and with the Harvest Festival arriving, he wished he had not taken the challenge.

"How does anyone build on such a scale so quickly? How am I, of all people, supposed to make something to stop a killer that can light a single hedge and risk burning half the city to the ground?" Aleksandar grabbed the gloves from his pocket and whipped them at the invention. "I gave a madman the power of fire in his hands. If this isn't exceeding humanity's grasp, I don't know what is."

Natalia looked at the bags under Aleksandar's eyes. Acne riddled his face, and his lips were dry from the lack of hydration.

"Aleksandar, you're pushing yourself to a breaking point. We don't make these things overnight, despite some stories told." Natalia held her chest.

Aleksandar shook his head. "I know, I know. It's not my fault."

"It isn't. You doubting yourself will take you nowhere."

Aleksandar moved to the chair and sat in the shadows of the workshop. "Have you realized we're building yet another invention that could bring disaster? How do we justify such a thing?"

"As inventors, we must realize others can misuse our inventions. Technology is not what's bad, but how people use it."

Natalia took a step forward, but Aleksandar held up his hand. His arms tensed, and he flared his nostrils. He picked up a dented brace off the floor and snapped it in half. He tossed the piece and walked to the machine, tossing several more into a bin and repairing what he could. Natalia walked over and grabbed Aleksandar by the arm.

Aleksandar looked down, closing his eyes. She pulled him close and hugged him softly, and he rested his head on her shoulder. Her embrace made him want to cry, but he couldn't as he held back.

"Breathe, Aleksandar, breathe. Now and then, you have to take a break. Anyone would crack from the weight on your shoulders."

Aleksandar stepped back. "Why does this feel like my last chance?"

"It isn't. Maybe mine, but not yours. Our last chances are the first for the next generation. We are to pass on our knowledge and legacies. That's how people change the future. I'm going to teach you that. I promise."

Aleksandar looked into her pale blue eyes. She did not flinch; she did not hesitate. Her words were heavy, and he believed them the more she spoke.

"You should take a break," she said. "Spend a night with friends, loved ones. If you keep pushing, you are going to make mistakes."

Natalia grabbed two pieces of the Lunarwheel and handed one to Aleksandar, holding on to the other.

"This is going to hurt." Natalia hurled the glass across the workshop, and it shattered against the black stone wall. She held her side, laughing through the pain.

Aleksandar smiled and threw the piece, glass breaking on impact.

Aleksandar stepped away and rubbed his temples for relief. "How did you do it?"

"Do what?"

"How did you recover after Oakvale?"

"I'm not sure I have." Natalia rubbed her cheek and sat. "It was not so easy. There were many facets to my failure at Oakvale. I still struggle to this day, while others have forgotten. You find your way and accept your past. It's difficult, and it can take a while, but that's okay."

Aleksandar sat, nodding his head.

"I wish I could remember more," she said. "It happened so fast. I've told few this, but while it was my invention, it was not my fault the town flooded." Natalia rocked her leg and set her arms across her waist. "I should have stopped it when I had the chance. The Lunarwheel was to change the world, but it only changed mine. When the engine failed, and the pressure rose, it created only a bomb."

Aleksandar leaned forward, his forearms on his knees.

"When it exploded, we were lucky. There were some injuries, but thankfully no one near it died. However, the explosion damaged the dam. Part of it collapsed and flooded the park… it destroyed their fields and crops, and the city never recovered from the Black Harvest, so they were left destroyed. It didn't matter that they controlled my machine; it was mine. I thought of that mistake for years, feeling responsible for it. What if I'd never waived the rights? What if I didn't allow someone to use the Lunarwheel?"

Aleksandar saw his struggles in her. She experienced the same, but she sat there as a confident and esteemed inventor.

Natalia played with her fingers. "I lost part of myself that day. I had trouble finishing anything, finding the passion I once held dear." Natalia forced a smile and chuckled. "Of course, Mr. Griffin was there. He swooped into the aftermath and restored the fields as quickly as my machine destroyed them. He saved me from a load of heartache. If we had waited on the company who sponsored me, the town would've died."

Aleksandar rubbed his hands together.

"I see a lot of myself in you, Aleksandar," she said. "The trials, the choices. It takes a toll, but you learn to be resilient. You don't stand up to that turmoil right away, but it comes with encouragement and when you look to better things."

Aleksandar lifted his head.

Natalia looked at him with confident eyes. "You ask me these questions, but know I don't have all the answers. Even after all these years."

Aleksandar stood, pacing around with his hands on his hips. "You still don't think humanity has a limit?"

"That limit is what we set on ourselves. The Maker gave us the world to use. We are meant to do just that."

"That doesn't mean destroying it and ourselves in the process. You said it yourself. I'm pushing too hard."

Natalia stood. "Humanity is progressive by nature, and we must maintain that progress. It's how we better ourselves, how we give meaning in life."

"At the expense of humanity, though? Accidents are one thing, but we are creating machines that could shake the earth. We are going to violate the natural law of things. I created a monster with one machine. What happens if we unleash something that could calm nature in ways we can't see yet?"

"I understand your concern, but progression comes from those who are willing to push beyond humanity's grasp. That's how we've made it this far. There is good, and there is bad, but we are still here."

Aleksandar looked at the shattered machine and sighed.

Natalia stepped to his side. "Aleksandar, you've given me hope that I've lacked for years, and I have no intentions of losing it again. You may not know it, but one day we'll stand side by side in this world, when we least expect it, on a bridge that connects us all. At that moment, we'll do great things, and it will all be worth it."

Aleksandar turned to her. "How do you keep pushing? What pushes you so far?"

Natalia looked up. "Curiosity. I've always wanted to see what comes next."

"I feel as if I've lost mine." Aleksandar reached into his pocket, pulling out an envelope with a broken red seal. "I'm afraid, Natalia. Because of this."

Natalia batted a glance.

"I should show you something." Aleksandar handed the letter to Natalia.

Mr. Scott,

The moment we fear is upon us. While we can hold no one at fault, I suspect darkness will take hold of this city in the coming nights, and we all will experience its wrath. You must protect yourself and those closest to you because as night falls, the monster reveals itself.

Natalia looked at Aleksandar as she handed it back. "Well, that was rather disturbing. Who sent this?"

"I don't know. Someone has been sending me letters, looking out for me, but who? Why me? From the Phoenix, to being a murder suspect, to my own failures… why am I so important?"

"I cannot say, Aleksandar, but this attack was not random. He attacked you with a vengeance, from what you've told me. Why did he tempt you when he was so quick to kill others? It sounds personal."

Aleksandar walked to the window.

"If he comes back, I must be ready. I must." He rubbed his forehead, searching for relief from his migraine.

Natalia stepped to the rack and picked up Aleksandar's jacket, handing it to him.

"You will be, but tonight, go. Spend the evening with someone who means something to you."

Aleksandar looked at the coat and grabbed it. "Okay. What about the workshop? I made a mess of things."

"Leave it to me. Go, and I don't want to see you until morning."

Aleksandar nodded and chuckled. He went to speak, but Natalia shook her head.

"There's no need to say more." Natalia rubbed his shoulder. "Have a good evening. We will discover our best motivations by dawn and figure this out."

Aleksandar smiled and walked into the stairwell, Natalia smirking. His steps faded until the door shut at the top of the stairs.

Natalia turned and sighed, smiling at the carnage. She grabbed a broom and swept the glass and metal fragments to the center of the room. She paused, her gaze going blank, drifting around the workshop. Natalia looked over her shoulder, sensing a gaze on her back, and put her hand against her ribs. Searching the shop, she wondered, and let her mind rest with some restraint, not seeing anything.

She swept again, humming under her breath.

Across the room, a large spruce closet next to cluttered racks remained closed with a small slit in the middle, allowing a sliver of light to shine through. A light that glimmered off a blue mask as the door opened to the disaster that was Natalia's workshop.

CHAPTER FIFTY-ONE

A raging fire roared, and smoke filled Natalia's nose. She tried to prop her eyes open, but a bright light blinded her from an intense heat that dried her lips and slammed against her face. She rested against a wall, her legs on a stone floor.

She rolled and slumped into a pile of wood shavings. Her wrist jarred back, cuffed to a pipe. As her sight adjusted, she found herself inside a burning warehouse.

Flames kissed the glass ceiling, the heat warping it black. Over the violent crackling of fire, she couldn't hear the glass breaking, and the shock came as it shattered. Natalia quickly tried to cover her face as shards rained through the air, feeling a few tear through her jacket. She opened her eyes and gasped.

The Steamrail, her engine, was engulfed in a blistering fire, the metal shrieking in the intense heat.

Natalia glanced at her cuffed hand. A letter dangled on her wrist.

Read Me.

Natalia's breath shuddered. She looked at her invention, her lungs aching from the smoke. She struggled to open the note with sweaty hands and wiped her brow from the splinters and ash. An ember landed on her cheek.

Ahh!

Natalia swiped it off and kicked the pipe, her foot tingling from the hard surface. She opened the letter. The black smoke emitting from the fire greatly obstructed her vision; she could barely make out the words.

If you can't remember your own legacy, no one should.

Natalia's breathing grew heavy, and the air thinned. A beam broke from the rafters and smashed into the ground, embers soaring high. She tugged on the cuffs, but they wouldn't bend as her hands slipped with sweat. She kicked the pipe with her heel, but it only shook from the force of her foot.

Sweat soaked into her jacket, and her skin stung as the heat grew hotter. A barrel exploded alongside the Steamrail, and she ducked as shrapnel surrounded her.

Natalia grabbed the cuff with her free hand, propped her feet against the wall, and pulled with all her might, lifting herself off the ground, he ribs stinging in pain. The chain snapped, and she dropped onto her back, knocking the air out of her lungs.

Natalia clenched her chest, wheezing, and patted her jacket. Her notebook was missing. She turned her head along the floor. The book was under a burning panel where she woke. She crawled over and patted out the flames. It was burned across the spine, and several pages fell out from the bottom. She stuck the remains into her pocket and stood, her knees weak.

A metal beam broke from the ceiling and slammed into the ground, Natalia covering her ears as the steel rang sharply, the concrete cracking like ice.

Squinting through the smoke, she stumbled to a sliding door and yanked on it. It stopped, a chain wrapped tight on the outside handle. She turned around as the fire grew closer, and the heat blistered against her face. She stuck her head out, taking in as much clean air as she could. With one hand still cuffed, she pulled herself through, splinters ripping into her shirt. She fell to her side, struggling to move.

An explosion sent a shock wave from the building, and Natalia struggled to her feet, limping into the dark, burning night.

～

"I didn't mean it that way. I was only saying." Aleksandar rubbed his forehead, blushing.

"Yes, you did. You can't even deny it." Ellie bumped into him.

He laughed, and she pulled him close as they locked elbows. They strolled through the park, leaves stretching along the gardens and collecting in the river flowing through the middle. The moon was high with only a few clouds hiding the stars.

Ellie tapped his forearm, and Aleksandar looked at her with a grin.

"Just accept it, Aleksandar. You are a jerk," she said.

"I never meant it."

"Yes, of course. How do inventors say it, an observation?"

"Why are you so bent on ruining our evening?"

"I was making it more creative. You're the one who finds insults hilarious."

Aleksandar stared at her, shaking his head. "I could walk myself home if you like."

Ellie pulled him tight against her side, strolling between luscious trees that reached for the sky.

Leaves fell in a graceful dance through the gentle wind, and silence descended amongst the park.

Natalia was right.

Aleksandar needed this night out, and with Ellie, his troubles faded. Her breath against him, her tender touch on his arm, and her soothing voice made everything peaceful again.

Aleksandar and Ellie walked over the bridge, passing above the river with golden-orange leaves flowing in the current. The trees were old and tall, hiding the city horizon, hiding Aleksandar from his struggles.

He turned to Ellie, who rested her head on his shoulder. "What are you thinking about?"

"Is there something on my mind?" she asked.

"I'm not sure. You seem quiet tonight."

Ellie straightened her neck. "I thought maybe it was just me. You do too."

"A little, I guess." Aleksandar tightened his jacket, and they paused on the bridge.

"You first." Ellie slid her hands around his waist and hugged him as the wind nicked at her scarf.

Aleksandar took a deep breath. "I just want the struggle to be gone, I want you to stay, and my life to be normal again. It baffles me how much is outside our control. Makes me wonder if we should step back and make sure we're on the right path."

Ellie lifted her head. "You're talking about inventing, right?"

"Of course. You know what, I'm sorry. We're out to stay away from problems, not focus on them."

Ellie stared at him as his hair blew ever so gently. She did not blink as much, and her stare was stiff.

"Are you okay?" he asked.

Ellie chuckled, and she bit her lip. Aleksandar gazed into her eyes and pulled her tight, placing his lips on hers. They were soft and warm. They stepped apart, and Aleksandar had a pit in his stomach.

"What's wrong?" he asked.

Ellie sniffled and looked over the bridge to the water. "I just... I thought you were breaking up with me. When you talked about stepping back, I expected—"

"No, no." Aleksandar hugged her, feeling her bury her face in his chest. "I was talking about inventing, I swear. You've been the most amazing person to me since we met. I know things aren't normal right now, but I wouldn't let go unless you told me to. The idea of missing you is something I don't want to feel."

Ellie leaned back with glistening eyes. She put her hands on his cheeks and kissed him, holding his lips to hers.

"I know how that feels," she said. "Missing what matters most, that is."

"How so?"

Ellie grabbed his hand, and they walked to the ledge, leaning over the river.

"One thing I miss most from traveling is running through the fields in the late evening. With the moon shining bright and the silence of the night, I felt peace. Every moment I'm with you, I feel that, and to know I can't have either scares me."

Aleksandar wrapped his arm around her. "I won't take that away from you."

Ellie leaned on his shoulder, and Aleksandar felt the deep exhale as she snuggled her cheek against him.

"Thank you," she said.

They rested in silence as the water moved beneath them.

"Do you have a memory like that?" Ellie rubbed his arm.

Aleksandar rocked on his arms. "There's one from when I was little. I used to run through the forest and the snowy hills in the Day and Night Pass. There was a small valley close to my house that overlooked a meadow of wheat, and I'd go out every night my parents allowed. I would climb, run through the fields, and it was nice."

"It sounds peaceful."

Aleksandar licked his lips. "I wish she was still alive. She could've put an end to it by now."

Ellie grabbed Aleksandar's hand and kissed the back of it. "I'm sure she's very proud of you."

"There's a part of me that wishes she'd tell me to move on and follow my own dream, but until she does, I must follow this path." Aleksandar turned to Ellie. "I'm sorry you entered my life when so much is going on. You need someone stable and who can provide for you."

Ellie stood, tilting her head. "Did one of my brothers talk to you? Those are their words. Oh, they won't like me tonight."

Aleksandar nodded. "Jonah did."

"While they've been on my case about you, I've thought late into the night about this. I want to be with you."

Aleksandar looked up, trying to keep his eyes from watering.

Ellie glanced into the sky, then back to him and held his hands, pulling them to her lips. She kissed his knuckles and smiled. "If I'm walking home, I want you with me."

Aleksandar bit his lip. "And I will."

Ellie lifted her hand, Aleksandar's wallet in her grip. He chuckled and leaned in, kissing her. Ellie opened his jacket and slid the wallet into his inner pocket.

"It will be safer there." She patted his chest.

"Indeed."

Ellie looked into the sky, raising her eyebrows.

"What is it?" Aleksandar glanced over her shoulder.

Ellie stepped forward, and Aleksandar squinted at the horizon. Clouds rose into the air. The moonlight caressed the smoke as a red tint glowed underneath.

Ellie stopped, gasping. "Is that—"

Aleksandar grabbed Ellie's hand and paused. He swallowed hard. "We need to go."

∾

Smoke billowed over Well's Peake, fire raging behind rooftops, a crimson glow lighting the sky as ash fell like snow.

Constables raced through the streets on horse and foot, heading towards the disaster. Chaos overwhelmed the city, and people barred their windows, rushing inside their homes and panicking on the walkways.

The air grew thick as Aleksandar and Ellie made their way into town, the streets darkening. Explosions rang through the alleyways, and Aleksandar's heart skipped with every boom. He pulled Ellie close as a group of people rampaged by them, rushing away from the red glow.

"Can you see?" Ellie said, still wrapped in Aleksandar's arm.

"No, but it's coming from over there."

"That's near Fritz and Co!"

Ellie rushed off.

"Ellie!" Aleksandar chased after her, her speed quick and nimble.

Constables ran alongside them, and Aleksandar noticed Owen's invention on the backs of a few. He heard the metal striking the cobblestone behind them as they sprinted by.

Aleksandar and Ellie ran into the Industrial District, Fritz and Co Towers in the middle of the circle. A warehouse burned behind it, surrounded by the forest, which was ablaze, stretching into the hillside. Men cut at the bases of trees with saws, and several with Owen's invention stabbed at the trees, guiding them in the chaos.

"Fire!"

A building exploded, and brick and wood fragments soared into the woods. Aleksandar grabbed Ellie by the waist and spun her away as splinters flew into the sky, small pieces of wood falling around them.

"What are they doing?" Ellie found her footing. "They are destroying Fritz buildings."

"It's a firebreak," Aleksandar said. "They are trying to stop the blaze before it spreads into the city."

Timber cracked, and Aleksandar looked to a tall redwood as it leaned down the center of the street.

"We have to go!" Aleksandar grabbed Ellie's hand, and they sprinted towards the alleyway.

The tree fell, its branches breaking on the rooftops, leaves whipping around. They ducked into the alley as the wood hit the cobblestone like thunder. The ground shook beneath their feet, and Aleksandar dropped into the dirt.

Ellie helped him up, and they looked to the chaos as several constables lay near the fallen tree, unmoving. Aleksandar scrambled to a man, who gazed up with a lifeless stare. Aleksandar's fingers trembled, and Ellie put her hand on his forearm as the heat of the fire bared down on them.

"Hey!" a man shouted. "Get out of there! You'll be crushed!"

Aleksandar looked to the constable, who rushed in their direction.

"You two need to leave. It's not safe here," he said.

"My brothers!" Ellie grabbed his shoulder. "Have you seen the Fritz brothers? Do you know if they're safe?"

"Yes, they've been evacuated. My men took care of it." He caught his breath and wiped the blood from an open gash in his forehead, dripping down his ash-ridden face.

"What happened?" Aleksandar looked at another dead constable.

"There's not a moment to talk. Let's get you out of here. Water is not stopping this fire, and we can't slow the spread."

Aleksandar looked at the flames licking off the tips of the forest. "Wait, I might be able to help."

"Doubt it. Now let's go."

"Listen to him." Ellie faced the constable. "This is Aleksandar Scott. He is an elemental inventor. He can help."

The constable looked over his shoulder and sighed. "How? Why?"

"Does water make it worse?"

"Yes."

"Then it's not regular fire. There's a chemical in it. Baking soda will stop it."

"Are you mad?"

"Listen to me. This isn't a natural fire. My solution is being used."

The constable stared at them, wiping his forehead, blood on the back of his hand. "Fine. I'm taking you to the others."

"Others?"

"Yes. Let's go."

The constable rushed alongside the tree; the road cracked underneath, and Aleksandar followed with Ellie.

Behind Fritz Towers, several men talked under a tent against a table as fire engulfed the hill across the street, flames spitting back at those who tossed water into the chaos.

Owen stood with his Limbs of Life, pulling three constables from the carnage, his jacket singed on the ends.

Aleksandar turned to Natalia, also wearing Owen's invention, pushing debris into the fire to create a distance between the blaze and the city.

Aleksandar cupped his hands around his mouth. "Natalia!"

She peered over her shoulder and walked towards them, lowering to her feet, the metal legs closing against her back.

"Aleksandar!" Natalia rushed to his side. "In the Maker's name, what are you doing here?"

"Natalia, what happened?" Aleksandar asked. "Why are you here?"

"We don't know, and that's a story for later. The fire started in the warehouse and worked itself up the hill. Before we knew it, the town erupted into a panic. Owen arrived, and we suited up. We're able to spare the district, but the forest is burning, and if it loops around, it could hit the World's Palace."

"Natalia, I don't think this is a normal fire. My solution is in that fire, which is why water isn't working."

"That could explain why it spread so fast. We are trying to break a line, but it's proving to be difficult."

"You need to find a way to get baking soda. It should stop all this. I'm sure there's a factory in this district that mass produces it. Their stocks must be full."

Natalia smiled and patted him on the shoulder. "I take back what I said earlier. I'm glad I bumped into you tonight."

A large snap echoed from the forest, and they turned. A massive tree fell sideways. It slammed into the roots, and another cracked. A constable burst from the broken thicket as death loomed over him.

Natalia sprung to life with the limbs and crawled over at an incredible speed. As if she had mastered the invention.

Owen sprinted and stabbed the left legs into the ground, using the other four to catch the tree as it nearly crushed him. The constable tripped and rushed over the debris, making his way onto the cobblestone. A pressurized cylinder exploded on the backside of Owen's invention, and he leaped to the side as the tree demolished the right legs, pinning him to the forest floor. Owen struggled to unhook himself, the fire burning close.

Aleksandar sprinted off, but Ellie held him back.

"No, look!" she pointed.

Natalia vaulted over the log and cut the straps holding Owen to the machine. He stood and limped out of the forest, Natalia behind him.

Owen coughed, black phlegm dripping down his chin. He wiped his face, and Natalia lowered to her feet, talking to him. Owen's eyes widened, glaring at Aleksandar.

"Mr. O'Connell, wait! He has a plan." Natalia reached for Owen, but he rushed to Aleksandar.

"Where were you tonight?" he asked.

Natalia pushed them apart. Owen tried to move around, but Natalia refused to let him through, leaving Aleksandar holding his hand in front of Ellie.

"You have something to say?" Ellie pointed in Owen's direction. "Aleksandar wants to help."

"If I discover you're behind any of this, I will ensure they strip you of your rights forever. The people of Well's Peake don't deserve this. This was your machine, wasn't it?"

"Owen, you need to find baking soda," Aleksandar said. "It could stop this fire."

"Why do you say that?"

"I believe my solution is in the fire."

Owen stared and licked his lips, covered in dirt. He headed off towards the small tent, speaking with several of the members, who looked in Aleksandar's direction. Owen smacked the table and walked to another set of his invention. Buckling himself in, he pulled the strap tight and stormed off into the district.

A large group of constables arrived on the street, with Lydia May and Chief Constable Dekker at the helm.

Aleksandar swallowed hard and turned to Natalia, the men staring. "You believe me, right? Natalia, I did not do this."

"I know, but the situation is bad. You wanted to help, and you have, but you need to leave. I sense some here are not happy with your presence."

"We could go to your house. We could get the Lunarwheel to work. I know we can. It'd have the power to quench the fire, even with my solution in it."

"Even if we could, there's not a big enough source of water here to use it. Aleksandar, you must step back and go."

Several men from the tent walked towards them.

Aleksandar looked at the group of people. "Who are they?"

"They're the owners of the factories here."

"You!" A burly man with a thick beard to his chest clenched his fist. "Are you Scott?"

Aleksandar froze. "Yes—"

The bearded man swung and cracked Aleksandar across the jaw. He twisted around and landed on his knees. Ellie jumped forward and punched him in the nose, the man losing his balance. Another backhanded her along the chin.

"Don't you—" Aleksandar stood and tackled the other man. He punched, but his hits did little.

The man grabbed Aleksandar around the waist and tossed him aside. Several aristocrats shifted over him. They kicked him in the gut, and Aleksandar covered his face, unable to get to his feet.

A boot hit his jaw, while another hit his shoulder. He covered his face as he felt the bruises form over his body, blood trickling down his face.

Lydia and her men stepped in and forced the owners back.

"That's enough!" Lydia pointed, waving her hand.

The owners glanced at each other, the biggest stepping forward. "You're going to protect him? This madman?"

"Unless you have proof he started this fire, you all best stand down."

"Who else could it be? Scott has been involved with everything since the beginning. If the Peake will not serve justice, we will."

"You will do no such thing."

The burly man rolled his knuckles and swung his arm. A constable stopped it, and another cracked his baton against his chest.

A fight broke out between the constables and the factory owners. Aleksandar crawled to his feet in the chaos. Punches were met with batons, and the constables quickly overpowered the owners.

Aleksandar helped Ellie to her feet, her cheek already starting to swell. "Ellie, are you okay?"

"Where is he? I'll show him."

Aleksandar grabbed her waist, pulling her back.

Lydia walked to them. "You need to leave now. Where can you go that's safe?"

"Leave?" Aleksandar asked. "They'll only think I'm guilty."

"We'll handle that. Is there somewhere safe you can go?"

A man broke through the line, but Natalia smacked him with a metal leg. He arched over, clenching his gut.

Lydia put her hand on Aleksandar's shoulder. "Where?"

Aleksandar blinked. "Um, my parents' place. In the Day and Night Pass."

"Good, now we must go."

Aleksandar shook his head. "No, I can't just leave."

Ellie stepped close. "We need to. There's a carriage we can use."

"Your friend is right," Lydia said. "I'll escort you."

Aleksandar turned to Natalia, noticing several cuts and scrapes on her face. Blood stained her clothes and marred her skin, some dried, some fresh. One of her wrists was bruised and cut.

"Are you okay?" Aleksandar asked.

"A story for when we meet next."

Aleksandar nodded. "Thank you, Natalia. For—"

"Thank me if you are still alive after the week's end. Now, go."

Ellie pulled on Aleksandar. He hesitated, but they rushed away from the blaze, Lydia guiding them through the street. The heat faded, but the ash grew heavy. Aleksandar watched Owen and factory workers arrive with horses and carriages with brown bags in the back.

Baking soda.

Aleksandar held Ellie's hand, and they sprinted down the street, Lydia watching over them like an angel. He looked at Ellie. A speck of blood dripped on her cheek.

~

Aleksandar sat on the cushioned seat, the carriage rattling as it sped out of the city. The driver snapped the reins, and Ellie peered out the window with him.

The fire burned brightly but dimmed near the Industrial District, the baking soda hopefully at work.

Failure filled Aleksandar's thoughts, blinding him to any hope. He looked to Ellie and bit his shaking lip as they fled over the rolling hills, leaving Well's Peake behind in its destruction.

CHAPTER FIFTY-TWO

Light squeezed through the coarse fibers that tugged tight, leaving a burning sensation on Nicoli's face. Dried blood stuck on his cheek and forehead, ripping as the burlap sack over his skin shifted in his captor's grip.

With his hands tied and mouth gagged, he stopped struggling. The bindings cut into his wrists, and he needed to save his strength for a moment of opportunity. If his kidnapper spared him this long, there was a reason.

Lavender and jasmine filled his nostrils between the musk of burlap as if he were walking through a garden in the bloom season.

Someone sat him in a chair and bound him to the back, tightening a rope against his chest. Nicoli felt his nose poking through the fibers that left an unbearable itch that he could not scratch.

The air grew thinner as thoughts invaded his mind with every passing second, remembering being near the fire, looking amongst the death and destruction. Before he could turn around, his face hit the dirt, and the light vanished.

His temples ached as he looked through the frayed darkness. The dried blood on his swollen cheek peeled off as the bag shifted.

Someone ripped the burlap off, taking the scabs with it and allowing the wound to bleed down Nicoli's cheek like red tears.

Nicoli squinted. Weak, faint, and sedated. Too relaxed.

As his vision cleared and adjusted to the light, he looked at the masked man, who stared back with a scraped mask and tattered clothing. However, his stature and posture could not be more straight and self-assured. Nicoli glared at the blue-and-silver mask, curved like the ridge of the moon. The mask that haunted his dreams since he could last remember.

The masked man stepped forward. "Is this everything you ever wanted?"

Drool dripped down Nicoli's chin, his eyes never leaving his captor, his breathing heavy.

"Fate is ironic as it keeps bringing us together." The masked man tilted his head. "I understand the anger you hold towards me, but we can be civilized."

Nicoli slumped to the side, looking to the white oak room, his thoughts running rampant. The masked man paced around, blood dripping on the edge of the mask.

"The world has evolved, Mr. Lucas, and will continue to expand over the next generation. In the field of medicine, with a new creation, I was able to subdue you into a medicated state, allowing me to bring you here without worry of you knowing where we were or how we got here."

Nicoli found the strength to glance at the masked man, his eyes black behind the mask. He tried to shake, judging how tight the bindings were. There was no shaking from them, but he didn't care. All that mattered was the man in the blue mask.

"You've looked for me since I can last remember," the masked man said. "What is it like being so close?"

Despite the drugs in his system, nausea in his stomach, and fatigue in his arms, Nicoli leaned forward, the seat creaking, his breath deep. He jerked up and tried to stand, but he fell, and the feet of the chair slammed on the floor.

"Do not scuff my floor." The masked man lifted a silver case on the table, unclasping the locks. "Do not worry for your strength. It will return."

Nicoli slumped forward, his back straining from the uncomfortable position, his spine aching. He clenched his fists and flexed the ropes tight on his chest, adrenaline building in his veins. He wanted to rip the man apart, serve justice.

The masked man hesitated.

Nicoli gritted his teeth, growling through the pain. His head dropped, losing the strength.

The masked man opened the case. "I brought you here, Mr. Lucas, because I trust you and what you do. I hope you will learn to trust me."

Nicoli looked up, his eyes watering.

"You see, we are dealing with delicate matters. I appreciate knowing I can depend on you for the purpose I wish to give you. I expect you to do what's right." The masked man shifted several mechanical devices around. "I've heard that you catch serial killers. I know where to find one. Your past with murderers whose minds are broken echoes on the streets. Your dark history. This knowledge assures me you'll capture the Phoenix with ease."

Nicoli gritted his teeth, focused on the masked man.

The masked man nodded and stood, walking behind Nicoli with a cord in his hand. "I admire your resilience, Mr. Lucas. A respectable trait."

A shock seared up Nicoli's spine. He threw his head back and screamed, his nerves stinging, his muscles tensing. A buzzing filled his ears, and he smelled the burned fibers of his jacket.

The pain stopped, and the man walked around Nicoli. In his hand he held a metal rod with two prongs on the end.

Nicoli tried to kick away with his feet, but they were too weak. His hands shook, and he had a metallic taste in his mouth. He stared forward with bulging eyes, breathing heavily through his nose.

"I am not the beast you believe I am. I hate to tell you because I know it will bring you pain, but I am not the monster you're looking for."

Nicoli scowled and closed his eyes, feeling himself drift, his limbs weak under the restraints. He swallowed and sniffled, tears stinging in the open cut on his cheek.

The masked man stepped to the table and lifted a larger version of the machine. He connected the electrode into the handle and pushed the device against Nicoli's chest, the cold metal against his shirt.

The masked man pressed the button. Electricity surged between the peaks, surging into Nicoli's chest. He screamed and shook, falling over with the chair on his back. Nicoli's head hit the floor, and he faded in and out of consciousness.

The masked man walked to the table and wrote several things in his journal. "Society will not balance itself, and occasionally, we must meet extremes with an opposing force just as extreme." His voice cracked for a second, softer than before.

Nicoli bit his lip, trying not to pass out, mumbling his words.

"I need you to capture the Phoenix. I prefer you not to be conflicted, so here's what I will do. You'll be sedated and returned to Well's Peake. There you can hunt the Phoenix with your chin held high, knowing you didn't let me walk away. I will gift you this invention."

The masked man lifted Nicoli back up.

Nicoli mumbled.

"You finally wish to say something?" The masked man paused. "Please do. I'm not one to overshadow a conversation."

Nicoli rolled his shoulders, and with all his remaining strength, he lifted his head and licked his lips. "You exist."

The masked man turned his head, blinking behind his mask. "How does it feel, after so long, to know you're not crazy?"

Nicoli furrowed his brow. "You do exist, but you no longer matter to me. Someone will stop you someday, but it will not be me."

The masked man picked up a rod off the table, gripping it and connecting it to a backpack of metalwork and conductors. He held it up in the air and turned it on. A static hum filled the room as blue streaks reflected in Nicoli's eyes.

The masked man looked over his shoulder. "Catch the Phoenix, and I'll no longer haunt your memories. I will remove the mask and turn myself in for my crimes when the moment comes. You don't have to believe me. What you believe and what happens are two different things. Do you accept my offer?"

Nicoli attempted to stand but slumped back into the chair. Taking a minute to think, he looked up with pursed lips.

"We always have a choice. Remember that." The masked man grabbed a syringe, sticking it in Nicoli's arm.

Nicoli flexed, blood oozing out of his forearm.

"When you wake, you will have everything you need."

The masked man injected the contents of the syringe, and Nicoli felt it flow through his blood like warm water. His eyes grew heavy, and hands weak.

An unnatural warmth filled his veins, spreading like fire in a hayfield. Nicoli stared at the man with his blue mask, watching as his eyes shut, his world growing black and empty.

CHAPTER FIFTY-THREE

Rocks and snow stuck to the carriage wheels as they moved across the road that curved up the hillside, separating the mountains and harvest plains. Aleksandar looked from behind the curtain, his breath fogging the glass.

The oak trees rose and grew thick as the driver steered around the pass where spruce pines riddled the land and lavish fields of crops lined the sides of the trail, row by row. The cabbie tugged on the horses' reins, leading the mares onto another road facing the frosted mountains. Along the ridge, houses spread far apart, resting in the upcoming season that had yet to touch Well's Peake.

Ellie held the orange shades, gazing with wide eyes at the vast fields set between the clustered forests. "Oh, how I've missed the hills and peaks."

She sat back, pulling the blanket over her lap and tucking the corners under her leg. Aleksandar pulled on his jacket with cold fingertips. He looked to Shae dozing off in her cage.

He shook his head. "Must be nice."

"Does it always snow so soon in the pass?" Ellie snuggled close.

"Some years, but not this early. Some haven't even harvested the last of their crops."

Aleksandar wrapped his arm around her and looked at her cheek, bruised along the jaw.

"How bad is it?" she asked.

"It's there. Does it hurt?"

"It is tender, but okay." Ellie held her gaze. "Thank you."

"For what?"

"Fighting for me. Few would have."

Aleksandar kissed her on the forehead and leaned on her shoulder, exhausted from the little sleep in the night. "What did your brothers say when you took the horses?"

"I didn't ask."

Aleksandar smirked. "Do you think it was a bad idea to leave?"

"Maybe, but what's done is done. Let's enjoy these next few days with your parents, who I am excited to meet."

"Oh, it will be interesting, indeed."

Relaxing as the carriage pulled them across the stony pass, Aleksandar and Ellie watched the rows of frosted crops and houses drift by as they traveled into the hillside.

Aleksandar leaned in his seat as the forest thickened around the road and branches shaded the trail, red-and-orange leaves still on the branches. A tree with several spiral trunks split into three canopies, overlooking a white house with blue shutters. Aleksandar tapped on the driver's window.

Ellie sat up.

"We're here."

The carriage rolled to a stop, and the cabbie dismounted, snow crunching under his feet as he brushed flakes off his jacket.

Aleksandar smiled as he stepped out and helped Ellie out of her seat, looking to his childhood home. He pulled out Shae's cage and opened the door. She flapped her wings and rushed out, flying to the branch above the house, hooting.

An older man looked out of the house's cedar-trimmed windows, smiling ear to ear with aged dimples and full head of gray hair, he waved at Aleksandar and stepped outside in a light sweater. "Samantha, come look who's here, with a pretty lady, no less."

"It's not Aleksandar, is it?" Samantha's voice rang from inside.

Samantha moved to the window with a grin. She walked onto the porch with a coat hung over her shoulders. "Oh, my goodness, she is adorable."

"Now, don't scare her off."

"Daniel, please, it is you who likes an entrance."

"That hurts my feelings."

"We can hear you," Aleksandar said.

The two stared and laughed as Daniel put his arm around Samantha's waist, holding her tight. She brushed off Daniel's shoulder and turned with soft movements, steady for her age.

Aleksandar glanced at Ellie, and she looked down, blushing.

The cabbie walked to his side. "Mr. Scott, I am to return to the Peake. Constable May will inform us when it's safe to retrieve you. You're to stay here, is that understood?"

"Yes, thank you. I have no plans of leaving."

The cabbie nodded and pulled two luggage bags from the back and carried them to the porch.

"Aleksandar!" Samantha said. "You didn't mention you were coming. I can only assume this is Ellie."

Daniel tilted his head. "Ellie? How do you know her?"

"Darling, did you not read Aleksandar's letter?"

"I thought so."

Aleksandar leaned into Ellie and whispered. "I'm so sorry."

Ellie smiled. "You wrote about me?"

Aleksandar smiled, and he took her arm. The cabbie walked past, mounted the carriage, and snapped the reins, heading back down the hillside.

Aleksandar let out a deep breath. "Ellie, this is my mother, Samantha, and my father, Daniel. Mr. and Mrs. Scott."

"It is a pleasure to meet you both," Ellie said.

"To you as well. I'm Samantha," she said.

"You can call me Mr. Scott." Daniel leaned with a hunch.

Samantha tapped her husband against the chest. "Daniel! She can call you anything she wants now."

Ellie covered her mouth, hiding her smile.

Daniel chuckled and waved his hand. "Come in, come in. It's too chilly for outside conversation."

"Thank you," Ellie said.

Daniel rushed into the house, and Samantha guided Ellie inside. Aleksandar stood behind as his parents focused on her, leaving him on the porch by himself. He shook his head. "Ah, to be expected. Come on, little one!"

Shae pressed her face against the glass from inside the house and hooted. Aleksandar raised his brow and walked inside his childhood home.

Around the table, they enjoyed a meal of fire-baked potatoes, tea, and aged steak seasoned with an old rub, a recipe passed throughout his family for generations.

Shae ate out of her bowl next to Samantha's feet, looking up with ruffled feathers.

Aleksandar bit into his steamed, honey-glazed carrots and cabbage as seasoning filled the dining room, and melted butter dripped over the edge of his steak, soaking into the potatoes.

Samantha, covered in a blanket, took a slice of bread and turned to Aleksandar. "I didn't realize it was so severe or that it involved you. We heard rumors about this killer, but details fade in these parts. Without a paper, we're not well informed and didn't know inventors were missing either. Why didn't you tell us?"

"I hate to worry you." Aleksandar bit into a carrot.

"Why don't you get a news press?" Ellie asked.

"It's nonsense," Daniel said. "Little truth anymore. We'd rather be uninformed than misinformed in this house."

Samantha shivered, and Daniel reached over, pulling his wife's blanket tighter around her.

"Are you warm enough, Mum? I can fetch another." Aleksandar stood.

"Oh, sit down," Samantha said. "Don't worry about me. This snow is just early, and your father takes every chance to comfort me." Samantha looked for a smile.

"Okay." Aleksandar rubbed his forehead.

Ellie batted him a grin, and he took a sip of tea. Daniel, with his elbows on the table, held up his broad chin, glancing at Samantha, who winked.

Aleksandar set his drink down, spinning the cup in his fingers, zoning out to the world.

Samantha tilted her head. "Three, two, one."

"Right now?" Aleksandar pulled his arm back.

"Always. Tell me what's on that mind."

Aleksandar bit his lip. "I'm just... lost. I've put myself at risk, Ellie in danger. Look at where I am now."

Daniel reached over and patted Aleksandar's wrist. "You're home; that's where."

Aleksandar nodded, taking a deep breath. "Everything is changing, and my invention is being used for chaos. Change seems to ruin what is."

Daniel sipped his coffee, having finished a cup of tea already. "Change is the only certainty, Son. Some for better, some for worse. The only reason it's not good is because people abuse and take for granted what they've received. Your intention was for the best, and those with wicked minds abused it. Their will is their way, but you need to move forward, and you will."

The gravity of his father's voice carried much weight and comfort.

"I never thought of the consequences. Well, some, but not all." Aleksandar rubbed his fingers on the oak table. "If I knew all this would happen, I never would have become an inventor."

Ellie reached up and held his hand, holding tight. Aleksandar focused on the warmth of her tender hand between his fingertips.

Samantha held the warm tea and gave her son a sympathetic smile. "We make mistakes, dear. We always will. No matter how many years we're on this earth. I know you, and you won't make it again."

A dog trotted in with a wagging tail, lifting her nose to the table with a lick of her chops, white ears drooping against a brown coat. Shae stepped over and tilted her head, the dog licking her feathers as its ears flopped against her cheeks.

"Oh, hello, Cub," Aleksandar said. The dog brushed his leg, and he rubbed the dog's back as it looked to the table. "I know. It's been almost a year since you've seen me."

Aleksandar threw a small piece of beef at Cub, who picked it up and rushed away.

"You'll have to fetch that. She likes to take food and hide it around the house." Daniel leaned back.

"Oh." Aleksandar smiled and looked at his dad, who stared. "Right now?"

"You seem to be finished eating. Best before she stuffs steak in my slippers again. Between that and your mother's—"

Samantha coughed, and Daniel stopped as she gave him a deadpan stare. Aleksandar smirked and stood, heading towards the living room.

"Don't worry," Ellie said. "I can help your mum clear the table."

"You sure?" Aleksandar paused.

"Best of luck with Cub."

Aleksandar batted his eyes and walked away, rubbing her shoulder as she caressed his hand.

Samantha waited to make sure her son had wandered off. "Do you mind if I ask you something, Ellie?"

"Of course," Ellie said.

"Hold on now." Daniel stood. "I'll move out of your way."

Daniel pushed on his lower back, straightening his gentle and thick stature, and walked out of the room.

Ellie watched. "I didn't offend him, did I?"

"You're fine." Samantha petted Shae, who wandered away to the door frame. "He's not one for other people's business. He'll bug me later. I'm sure he's most interested in what you have to say about our boy."

Ellie smiled. "You have a beautiful home."

"You're too kind. So how are you, my dear? Are you comfortable? I see that mark is quite blue on your chin."

"I'm fine, thank you. You've been very kind."

"Good. I'm curious about how Aleksandar is doing. Growing up, he could be so hard on himself. He doesn't ask for help often. He had no one who shared his interests for so long, and he didn't fit in as much as I would've hoped. Many said his dreams had no meaning, but he was smarter than that."

"He's doing okay, for what it is. In his situation, anyone would feel the way he does. I didn't realize he was on his own so much."

"Did he tell us everything?"

"More or less."

"Good. He wasn't at first. He did have a very kind friend, a sharp young lass, but she passed when she was young."

"It's a shame so many suffered from the Black Harvest."

Samantha glanced up but looked away.

"I'm sorry. Did I say something wrong?" Ellie asked.

"No, no. Aleksandar never told you how she died?"

"I guess not. I assumed it was the Black Harvest."

"No. She—maybe I best let Aleksandar tell the story."

Samantha took a deep breath and forced a smile.

Ellie felt the room still. "That's all right. I'm sure he'll open up when he's ready. Um, what did Mr. Scott think? With Aleksandar not following his footsteps as a farmer?"

"He wouldn't love his boy any less. Daniel encouraged Aleksandar to find his own way in life. Farming is rough on the body, and the back pain when you're older is horrid. He wanted him to be happy on whichever path he chose."

"Everything I've seen him do has been for good reason. He doesn't realize that despite what's happening, doing the right thing matters most. It's never a means to an end."

Ellie looked away and pursed her lips. She turned back to Samantha, smiling at her.

Ellie leaned forward. "May I ask you something?"

"Of course."

"I don't know if this is awkward, but I need someone to talk with. I'm scared, unsure, and I'd like to tell Aleksandar about it, but I worry he'd push me away if I told him it worried me." Ellie took a deep breath, holding her hand from shaking.

"Do you have doubts about him, being with him?"

"I did, but I want to be with him. It's just what's happening is terrifying."

"I understand," Samantha said. "I think you should talk with him. He can handle more than you might realize. He was never one to push people away when something gets hard."

"I had this image when I moved back to the city about things I wanted, still want, but I wish to be with your son more, despite what's happening."

Ellie nodded and looked to Shae, who cuddled against her leg.

"You learn to lean on each other when the days are tough. You'll pick the other up when they're down." Samantha reached across the table and put her hand on Ellie's.

Ellie pulled in her bottom lip. "You remind me of my mother. Caring and insightful. You would have gotten along."

"I wish I could've met her. I think you know what you want. You just have to commit. Not to make him sweeter than he appears, but my Aleksandar will do the same for you. You seem like an incredible young lady. I pray he never loses you. Know he would always remember you."

Ellie looked with a gorgeous smile, feeling a sense of relief.

~

Aleksandar played with Cub upstairs, resting next to his old bed. His room was the same as when he moved out, glowing in the lantern's light that he set on the windowsill.

He stood and skimmed over the books his grandfather gave him, rubbing his fingers along the spines. From woodworking to plowing, everything a man ever needed to raise a family in the fields rested in front of him. His workbench sat between the hand-carved shelves, made of agarwood. Its stain had worn, but the quality was beautiful. Aleksandar remembered the late nights and long days of endless studying.

As the sun faded on the horizon, hidden behind the thicket, he nudged Cub around. Footsteps grew louder in the hallway, and Aleksandar turned to his father in the door frame.

"Can I come in?" he asked.

"Of course. This was your room before mine." Aleksandar played with a wrench.

"It still is." Daniel winked.

His father walked to the bed and sat, resting his arm on the frame and letting out a sigh. "You never enjoyed asking for help, but I could tell when you needed it."

"The downside of wearing my feelings on my sleeve."

"You don't as much as you think." Daniel rubbed his aged cheek and took a deep breath.

Aleksandar looked down at Cub lying on the rug, panting. "I don't know what to do, Dad. I've never seen a fire like that. It was terrifying. To be seen as the end of the World's Fair because of my invention. This dream wasn't supposed to lead to this."

Aleksandar clenched his jaw.

"You did what you thought best," Daniel said. "You wanted to help people, to bring a dream to life. Don't let the consequences blind you to your true intentions. Guilt will mask the good nature of your actions and personality. You'll make it right. It's who you are."

Aleksandar sat next to his father, resting his arms on his knees. "I can only doubt anymore on whether I should keep pushing. I don't want to disappoint her."

Daniel straightened his back. "I know you're trying to do right by her and that you care for her memory, but Alek, you cannot live your life for hers. If you do, you'll never enjoy your own, and you have good around you."

"Why can't I? She lost hers and had so much to give when I didn't. I owe her the dream she had for the world. She was the true inventor."

Daniel stood and walked to the shelf. He lifted a leather box off the top and wiped the dust with the back of his hand.

Aleksandar turned and looked. "What's that?"

"A special someone gave this to me one day. It was meant for you." Daniel sat on the bed, removed the lid, and pulled out a bowler hat.

Aleksandar stepped forward. "It can't be."

"It is her hat. I took it to that fancy joint in the Peake when I visited last year for some repair stitching, and they said there was none like it. She gave this to me all those years ago. She said I should give it to you, but only when absolutely needed. I'd say now is that moment."

"I've tried for so long to recreate this, but I could never remember the shape."

Aleksandar wanted to reach out and set it on his head like she did when they were kids. Her friendship, her love, was something he wanted to feel worthy of again, but he turned away. "I've failed her and everything she was meant to be."

"Son, listen to me. I think it's come to where you need to do what's best for you. If your dreams are the same, believe it. You can invent for her memory, but if you don't want that for yourself as well, you'll never get there. If you put on this hat, wear it as she would have."

Aleksandar looked out the window at the glow of Well's Peake over the hills and frosty mountaintops.

Daniel held out the hat, and Aleksandar pushed his tongue against his cheek. His fingertips brushed against the brim with a teary smile, and he set it on top of his head.

A perfect fit.

"Everyone needs a good hat. I, we, are so proud of you," Daniel said. "We know you left to do good. Just remember that she's above and smiling on your deeds."

Aleksandar's father embraced him. The young inventor clung on, happy and confused, not letting go as the night closed upon them in peaceful bliss.

CHAPTER FIFTY-FOUR

Aleksandar pulled a piece of paper over the diagram on his desk, working in the moonlight. He drew a spear-shaped weapon, his eyes wide, unable to sleep.

He heard every pencil mark in the night's silence, taking him back to his childhood. From sneaking around in the night to tinkering on inventions, the late hours were comforting and nostalgic.

Aleksandar finished the sketch and clenched his fists with an exaggerated breath. The doorknob creaked, and he turned, Ellie waving from the hallway.

Aleksandar motioned for her to come in, looking into the dark hallway.

She closed the door and walked in with a white nightgown and sweater, crossing her arms in the cold as she tiptoed across the rug. "How's the tinkering?"

"Good, surprisingly. I didn't wake you, did I?"

"No, I haven't fallen asleep yet." She looked over the drawings on the workbench, her fingers touching the edges of the paper. "You remember we left Well's Peake to get away from inventions."

Aleksandar smirked. "Yeah. I think I might have something, so I had to write it down."

Ellie leaned against his back. "Did you ever keep your parents awake working into the night?"

"No. They're downstairs, across the house. I used to sleep in the room next to them, but I assumed they moved me for a reason."

Ellie paused, looking at the ceiling. The steamed planks bent into circular puzzle pieces like a meandering river.

"Wow. I've never seen wood crafted like that before."

"That was all my father. He thought a little inspiration as I fell asleep would be good for the soul."

Aleksandar turned and hugged her around the waist, resting his head against her chest. She ran her palm through his hair, and he closed his eyes, lost in her comfort. Her voice was so smooth, like that of a finely tuned instrument. Something he enjoyed every moment he was with her.

"What are you doing up?" Aleksandar looked at her.

Ellie bit her lip. "I wanted to talk to you about something." Ellie held out her hand, and Aleksandar glanced at it, his mouth drying out.

She touched his arm, rolling up his sleeve to the healing scar from the Phoenix attack. Aleksandar nodded, and she rubbed her fingers across it.

"Does it hurt?" Ellie met his gaze.

"It's still tender, but it seems to be healing."

He slid his fingers between hers, and she guided him over to the bed. She sat at the end and crossed her legs, and Aleksandar rested across from her, his hands on his knees.

"Is everything okay?" he asked.

Ellie pulled on the end of her sleeve. "Yes, there's something I want to say, and I should've said it already."

"Ellie, you—"

"No, please. I need to tell you this."

Aleksandar pulled on his fingers, a pit growing in his stomach.

Ellie took a deep breath. "When I returned to Well's Peake, I thought I knew what I wanted in life. As much as I loved nature, wandering the green horizons, I was missing something. I was missing someone."

Aleksandar tightened his lips as Ellie covered her mouth.

"All my family on the road had that special person to hold, and after watching them every night, I grew lonely. Traveling the Northern Forests for a few years shows you what's important. When I wondered what mattered most, I'd remember what my mum always told me. That no mother deserved to have their daughter grow up to sleep alone."

"Ellie—"

She held up her hand. "I'm almost done, I promise. There's no way for me to see everything I want in life, and I realized I'm okay with that. I thought I needed stability, and I do, just not through the house, career, and influence like my brothers force on me." Ellie ran her hand through her hair, which was down and curving from her braid earlier that evening.

Aleksandar wanted to reach out, but she held his hands tight. He blinked, trying to keep the water from building behind his eyes, unsure of what she was about to say, what she wished for.

Ellie slid closer, smiling. Her deep brown eyes gazing back at him. "I don't care where my path leads, Aleksandar, as long as I have someone there to go with."

Aleksandar pulled her hands to his mouth and kissed them. She sniffled and exhaled deeply.

"You told me you don't know where you're going or what you want out of life, and that's okay. I've made my choice, but I need you to tell me, even though you're lost—"

"Ellie…"

She paused, and Aleksandar found a smile.

"I'm certain about you," he said. "Not about a lot, but I am about you. You're one of the best things to ever happen to me. You've been at my side through all this. Yes, I worry for your safety, and I might be selfish for putting you at risk, but if you're okay with it, I want you as much as you want me."

A slow smile spread across Ellie's face, and she blushed. She wiped away a tear on her cheek. "You mean it?"

Aleksandar slid closer, their knees touching, and nodded. "Yes, but I don't know how this will end."

"None of us do. We haven't been given a normal hand. All I ask is that if the worst happens, you never pull away because the moment you do, we'll both be lost."

"Never."

Aleksandar put his palm on her cheek, and she rested into it, putting her hand on his. She wanted him. With all the risks he carried, she still chose him. He couldn't take his eyes off her: the loose hair on her shoulders, the red in her cheeks, her desire and support of him.

He chose her.

Aleksandar smiled, and she chuckled. Their smiles turned into a comforting gaze, and Aleksandar rubbed the inside of her palm. She unfolded her legs, and he slid between them, never looking away. He swallowed, and Ellie reached up and pushed her hand through his hair. Aleksandar leaned, and she rushed in, kissing him deeply. He pulled her against him, her warmth comforting him, passion in their embrace.

The moonlight from behind shimmered on her hair, and her eyes lit up like gems in the lantern's light. She tasted like vanilla, and her chest was as warm as a flame in the fireplace.

Aleksandar paused, gazing at her.

"It's okay," she said. "I know it's not common, but I want the same."

Aleksandar slipped off the bed and helped her remove her sweater. On her back, tattoos of flowers that mirrored that of a necklace caressed her shoulder blades. He looked up, Ellie blushing.

They lay down, and Aleksandar pulled the blanket over them, the soft cotton tightening around them.

For once in a long while, he felt loved, and she didn't feel alone. Two lost souls looking for someone to hold in an uncertain world found each other when they needed someone most.

Aleksandar and Ellie smiled, their breath against each other. He set his lips on hers, her hands gripping his waist, and they kissed as young lovers into the evening, lit by the gleam of the moon.

CHAPTER FIFTY-FIVE

Aleksandar sat on the stage edge in Natalia's workshop, the afternoon light beaming on his shoulders. Natalia rubbed the side of her cheek and rested her hand against her mouth in silence.

He waited for her to say something, but she only looked off into the distance, her gaze blank and unflinching. She bit her lip, wearing her blue vest with the white collar popped.

It had been three weeks since the fire, but it seemed like a year. So much had changed. When he arrived in the city the day before, constables flooded the streets, and Aleksandar kept his head low. No one confronted him per se, but he could feel the tension within the city.

The fire destroyed several warehouses, a shipyard, and scorched part of the forest on the outskirts. Thank goodness they were able to put it out because it would take a torrential downpour or the might of the Lunarwheel to quench a fire infused with his chemical solution.

"Natalia?" Aleksandar leaned her way.

She reached into her jacket and pulled out a burned book, flipping through the front of the journal.

"Natalia?"

She blinked, looked to Aleksandar, and let out a hard breath. "I think you'll need a portable battery. The only ones I'm aware of are in Belagrad.

There's mine, but it's rather heavy and outdated."

Aleksandar hopped off the stage, straightening his cuffs. "Is there any way of making it smaller or putting it inside?"

Natalia's eyes opened, and she looked over with tight lips. "Tesla has been trying that for years. What makes you assume I could do it?"

"Because you're the great Natalia Arlen."

Natalia smiled, her cheeks growing red. "Flattering, Aleksandar, but electricity is nothing to play with unless you know how it works. I'm sure you've hit a wrench off the top of your battery and felt what happens."

Aleksandar made a fist, rubbing his hand. "Yeah."

"Will this fire spear work as designed? The chances are slim to none, and it doesn't put out the flame as the Lunarwheel could. Maybe you should focus on that."

Natalia walked to the bench and hunched over, holding herself. Aleksandar held out his arms, but she raised her hand, her wrist still red and healing.

"It's okay. I'll be all right." Natalia rubbed her side, her eyes heavy.

"How bad is it?"

"Not as rough as it seems. When I took that hit to the ribs, it left its mark, and being tied up didn't help either."

"Did they discover who put you in that warehouse?"

"No, despite their efforts. Constable May is determined to find whoever was responsible, but it's been several weeks. What could they find now? Many people are upset about the Steamrail's destruction, and they are pressuring the Peake for answers." Natalia closed her eyes and shook her head.

"I'm sorry you had to go through that," Aleksandar said. "The Steamrail seemed like it would've changed everything."

"Perhaps, but nothing will sting like the failure of the Lunarwheel." Natalia stood straight. "Were you able to talk with the Peake?"

Aleksandar ran his hand through his hair. "It doesn't look good. Constable May told me to keep a low profile because many of the industrial aristocrats want my head. They think it was me who started that fire. Have you heard anything on any murders? They wouldn't give me any information."

"I was at the World's Fair, and inventors are on edge. We haven't heard of anyone missing as of late, but some are pulling out and leaving the city."

Aleksandar held his hands on the back of his head. "If not for Ellie and the Harvest Festival, I would go mad. Natalia, I have to wear my scarf high just to walk through the city. I even found a flyer on the ground demanding I stand trial. The World's Fair was supposed to be a positive change for inventors after the Black Harvest. All I've done is tarnish what we are trying to do."

His world and his dreams were crumbling with every breath, and Aleksandar had no way of knowing what was to come. The Lunarwheel seemed to be the answer to all. A device to stop another fire. A device to stop the killer and clear his name, restoring a positive reputation to inventors throughout the region.

Natalia grabbed his shoulder, and Aleksandar pulled himself from his thought.

Aleksandar glanced at Natalia, and she forced a smile.

"What's wrong?" he asked.

Natalia folded her hands. "I have doubts about the Lunarwheel."

"I know, but we're getting close. We'll get there."

"My passion for the Lunarwheel is drifting. Some days I wish for a different path."

"You can't mean that. With everything going on, the murders, the fire, the aristocrats wanting to beat me on the street, this is one of the only good things in my life." Aleksandar pulled up a chair and sat across from Natalia.

"I have spent many years trying to make up for my mistake, to redeem what I lost that day. It's come to where I hardly remember the loss and can no longer see the dream, or why I cared so much to leave a spotless legacy. Maybe some dreams need to be let go."

Aleksandar leaned back, tapping his thumb on his finger. He didn't know what to say. All he ever chased was one dream, and to see Natalia's dilemma with giving up hers made him wonder if everything he worked for would be forgotten as well. His life, his career, everything started coming together, and he thought it would continue with Natalia as his mentor.

Natalia stood and stepped to the window, tapping on the glass. "I know you think I might be mad, but when you grow older, you see things in a different light. Holding on to those dreams takes a lot out of you."

Aleksandar looked at the wool blanket covering Natalia's invention. "Just like that? You could leave everything behind?"

"I had a wonderful career. Not perfect, but greater than most dreams."

Aleksandar stood and paced around the room, lavender masking the watery musk. "I've figured out where I'm going, and I thought we were going to build something that would change the world and keep changing it."

"You will, and I could watch as you do. I'm not sure I can alter my past, but I can change your future."

Natalia walked onto the stage. She held out her hand, Aleksandar looking at her arm with a lifted brow.

"Amuse me for a moment."

Aleksandar reached out, and she pulled him onto the stage. He glanced around the workshop, benches on both sides and shelves with books and machines as high as the ceiling reached. He stared through the dome window to the valley of pine arching into the hills, stretching as far as he could see.

"What am I looking at?" he asked.

"I struggle to remember, but I recall standing on my first stage, to a crowd of none. It was nothing but empty chairs. As the years went on, the crowds grew larger and looked with awe, but as they grew, I saw even less."

Aleksandar glanced over his shoulder, Natalia looking to a clear spot in the workshop.

"All were one of many faces I would forget. When I presented my Steam Engine at the World's Fair, the crowd felt as empty as this room. That's when I realized I had no desire for other inventions, so I forced myself to work on the Lunarwheel. I hoped to find that passion, but I see now that it might be okay to let go because I found my peace."

Natalia let out a long breath and smiled, rubbing the underside of her cheek.

Aleksandar sensed her relief as if a weight lifted off her shoulders from a struggle that held her down for years. There was something in her smile that didn't seem like happiness, as if part of her wanted to feel content.

"I'm sorry, Natalia, but I don't believe you."

She turned to him with a tilted stare.

"I haven't had the strongest conviction," he said. "But you've supported me since the beginning, so now, I'll do the same for you."

Aleksandar jumped from the stage with a thud and grabbed the coarse blanket. He yanked it off, the Lunarwheel humming in a low state, the water circling on the bottom. "You don't have to give up your dream just yet."

Natalia pushed her tongue to the top of her mouth. She stared into the machine, and Aleksandar paused with her, looking at the wheel himself. It was peaceful, the soft glow of light pushing against the afternoon sunlight.

He picked up a valve, and Natalia crossed her hands, holding her healing wrist.

"Do you think it's worth it? To push just a little longer?" Natalia asked, her voice low.

Aleksandar walked to the stage. "I do, and so do you. You're tired of struggling, and I could never empathize with that, being so young. However, I understand not wanting to give up on a dream that means everything to you."

Aleksandar jumped onto the stage and held the metal valve to Natalia, looking her in the eye. "So, what do you say? Let's finish one last invention, and we can watch from that stage as any inventor should."

Natalia looked at the valve, then to the ceiling with a serious smile on her face. She grabbed it, rubbing her thumb over the handle.

Aleksandar nodded. "We will share the same legacy. Your moment is coming, and after tonight, everything we do must lead to that."

CHAPTER FIFTY-SIX

Nicoli walked down the pavement with a brown bag of groceries in hand, the wind blustering his scarf against his neck. His cheeks were red as he rounded the corner, looking for the warmth of Lydia's embrace.

He had forgotten what it was like to have a normal day, where he thought about dinner with his loved ones and learned about Rosaline's hobbies and stories. The night before, she was cute enough to cuddle next to him, trying to read the first few pages of her book. When she couldn't find the words, she shrugged and tossed it on the floor.

While they read, Lydia watched, curled up in her chair with a book in hand. She looked at Nicoli as if everything was right in life. With her hair straight behind her neck, she was as beautiful as ever, looking on with tender eyes.

The wind blew again, and Nicoli shook himself from his memories, crossing the intersection to the gate outside Lydia's house. He pulled out his key and held it to the door but froze, his hands going cold.

It was cracked open.

His gut hardened, and he bit his lip, resting his hands on his head. Setting the groceries on the step, he grabbed the baton at his hip and peeked through the window, unable to see anyone.

Please, no.

He pushed the door open, without a creak, and tiptoed inside the house. He looked up the stairs to a few lanterns hanging but no sign of Lydia, Rosaline, or Monty. Firewood burning lingered from the living room, crackling in the dead silence.

"I'm back." Nicoli looked around. "They had what we needed."

"Nicoli."

His heart dropped at Lydia's voice. She sounded out of breath and fatigued, and her voice trembled.

Nicoli held the baton forward and eased his way through the hallway into the living room. Lydia sat in her chair, upright with her hair down to the side. Her cheek was swollen, and her lip bloodied. She looked to him with pursed lips and cold eyes.

"Lydia."

Nicoli walked further in to see the masked man standing behind her with the electric weapon extended, a static hum in the air.

"You son of a bitch." Nicoli paused with a furrowed brow, his feet wide apart.

The masked man shook his head, waving his thumb above the button on the weapon's handle. "Hello, Nicoli. We've been waiting."

Lydia eyed him, breathing heavily.

"Let's be civil now." The masked man nodded. "If you would kindly sit across from Lydia May."

Nicoli's eyes searched the room.

"No need to worry." The masked man stepped to Lydia's other shoulder. "Your dearest Rosaline, and Monty, is it, are out on errands."

Nicoli glanced at Lydia, who nodded.

"Now, would you kindly."

Nicoli could feel the blood pulsing through his neck, his heart beating in his ears. He lowered his baton and sat across from Lydia.

"And the baton. Toss it near the doorway."

Nicoli tossed his weapon and leaned back, making sure his hands were visible. He looked to Lydia, feeling the water build in his eyes, her gaze never leaving him. "Are you all right?"

"I'm okay."

"We were catching up while we waited," the man said. "It surprised me when Lydia knew about your kidnapping. I thought you would have kept it a secret."

"What do you want? We haven't pursued you," Lydia said. "You left us alone for this long, and when we finally move on, you come back."

The masked man walked between the two, never pointing his device away from Lydia. "I've returned because I asked Nicoli to capture the Phoenix, and yet he roams free."

Nicoli wanted to strangle the man. Every word made him want to kill. He looked to the coffee table, but there was nothing to attack within reach.

"When I suggested capturing the Phoenix, that was more than an offer."

"Catch him yourself." Nicoli bit his words.

"I insist on you. Was my return gesture not worth it?"

Nicoli closed his eyes, trying to find his center, to keep it together so he could save Lydia.

"Nicoli, I need you to stay focused." The masked man pushed the button, and arcs of lightning rippled between the metal prongs. Lydia flinched, and the man grabbed her wrist, holding her still.

Nicoli stood, and the masked man batted his empty gaze. "Sit!"

Lydia shook, Nicoli seeing the violet in her eyes. He stepped back, and the masked man pulled his hand away.

"That's better. Now keep going, a little further."

Nicoli sat, his jaw flexed so hard, his teeth ached.

"To be clear," the masked man said. "If you try anything, I'll jam this into her neck, and it will kill her. Do you understand?"

Nicoli glared at the mask.

"Nicoli!"

"Yes."

"Good. Finally, some mutual ground. I'm going to make this simple. You and your family will never be safe from me if you do not capture the Phoenix."

"I don't know where he is."

"Find him. That's what you do, what you've done since our paths crossed." The man looked at Lydia. "Do you remember when we crossed paths, Lydia? On the night we were to dance in the moonlight?"

Lydia's eyes narrowed, and she clenched the fabric of the chair.

The masked man strolled behind her. "A mother's fury, a lover's vengeance. Lydia, your ability to remain still in this moment is admirable."

Lydia stared at Nicoli and then closed her eyes.

"Why haven't you crawled back into the shadows where you belong?" Nicoli asked.

"You're a monster," she said. "That's all you'll ever be."

"You two think so low of me. You believe I choose to do what I do. To see the heartache that's fallen on you is my burden, and to know I've done the same to others pains me. Would any sane person wish to commit such evil if not for proper reason?"

Lydia turned her head. "Yet you do it anyway."

"What I do is not my choice. The actions I follow and the words I weave are for you. For everyone. You do not realize the storm that lurks across the rolling hills. If you did, you might understand."

Nicoli swallowed hard. "What you do is butcher the innocent."

"No." The masked man waved his finger. "I kill because it's demanded. I must sacrifice who I was as a person for what will save us in the end."

"You are a *murderer*."

"To some, yes." The masked man rolled his shoulders. "Do you still blame me for Mallory's death?"

Nicoli glanced at Lydia, who lowered her head, tears dripping off the tip of her nose, holding a hand over her face.

"Can you not shut the fuck up!" Nicoli waved his hand.

"It was supposed to be Lydia," the masked man said. "Lydia knew she was to die. Were you aware of that, Nicoli?"

Nicoli paused, his nostrils flaring, and tried not to look away. From the corner of his eye, he saw a reflection in the window.

Monty.

He couldn't make out where she was, but she was there. He swore it.

The masked man waved the weapon over Lydia. "You are refreshingly open with each other. I envy that. There is one question that begs me to ask, though. Why was Mallory there when it should've been you, Lydia?"

Nicoli paused, his hands ready to throw his weight into the air, but he loosened his grip. He never knew either and promised he would never ask why.

Lydia looked up, her eyes red, never wiping away the tears on her cheeks.

Nicoli wanted to reach out, to console her, but the masked man was too close. He did not have the edge.

"Lydia, why was she there? From what I understand, you two were lovers from years past, and when your secret love failed, you two never saw each other again. Never wrote, never spoke. So why, out of all nights, did she decide to visit you after so long?"

Lydia sobbed and lifted her head.

The masked man walked around the chair, bending over. "Tell me why her life had to end."

Nicoli couldn't help her. "Stop. It's me you want. I'll do as you ask, but for the Maker's sake, leave her be."

"Because I asked her to," Lydia mumbled under her breath.

Nicoli froze, his lips parting.

"Why would you call on her?" The masked man tilted his head. "Why did Mallory agree to see you that night?"

Lydia held the back of her hand over her mouth. "Because I told her what I was doing, and I needed to tell her I would always love her, just once more. That I was sorry for not putting her first over my investigations. I thought I was going to die."

"Lydia." Nicoli reached out.

The masked man pressed the trigger, and Nicoli did not move an inch further.

"I didn't think she was showing up, so I left. You weren't supposed to be at the house."

The masked man unpressed the button and moved around her.

"Why did you do it? If you knew it wasn't me, why did you kill her?" Lydia buried her cheeks in her palms, trying not to sob.

The masked man lowered his arm. "There was no choice left."

"I was the one working the case. Why did you not leave her alone?"

"Because... she saw my face."

Lydia looked up, tears falling from her chin.

Nicoli froze, with an ache in his chest that could have swallowed him whole. His love, broken in front of him, and he was powerless to comfort her, to end the pain she carried for so long.

"If she breathed a word of who I was, this world would fall into chaos," the masked man said. "You *think* the destruction of the Phoenix is devastating; then you lack the foresight to see we are on course to another Black Harvest."

Nicoli stood, and the masked man lifted his head.

"Nicoli, I'm trying to be cordial. Please sit."

Nicoli waved his hand. "Let my family go."

"Sit."

"Leave her be."

"Sit!"

Nicoli's eyes glanced to the side, despite his instincts, knowing he messed up. Monty leaped over the couch with his baton, and the masked man jerked away, thrusting the device into her chest. The electricity singed a black mark in her vest, and she collapsed onto the carpet, unconscious.

Nicoli and Lydia bolted up and grabbed the masked man's arms. Nicoli dropped his weight, and the weapon fell to the floor.

The masked man slipped out of their grip and elbowed Nicoli across the face. Nicoli fell and broke through the coffee table, glass shattering around him. Lydia grabbed the baton and swung, striking the masked man in the forearm. Without losing a second, the masked man grabbed her brace and yanked it, snapping the supports.

Lydia's head slumped, and she collapsed onto the carpet. She grabbed her neck and looked at Nicoli, who stood with the electric device in his hand.

The masked man looked with a low gaze, his hands out. "Nicoli."

"This ends tonight."

Nicoli pressed the button and thrust the machine. The masked man dodged the attack, kicked Nicoli's arm away, and grabbed him by the throat. He head-butted Nicoli, silver flakes shimmering off the mask. The man threw him over the couch, into the molding of the fireplace. Nicoli crashed to the floor, his ears ringing and throat sore.

The masked man rushed out of the living room, and a door slammed down the hallway.

The world blurred and refocused. Nicoli reached out, trying to find anything to hang on to. His neck ached, but he found the bottom of the sofa. He pulled himself along the carpet, burning the underside of his arms as Monty lay on the ground, unflinching.

"Monty?" Nicoli held his hand to her nose. She was still breathing.

Thank the Maker.

He peered up, and Lydia lay across the broken coffee table, tears streaming from the corner of her eye. Nicoli pushed himself to his knees and crawled to her. He lay next to her and wrapped his arms around her as she sobbed in his chest, shaking under his grip.

"It's okay. We're okay now." Nicoli kissed her forehead, his hand on the back of her head.

"Monty?"

"She's alive."

Lydia could not stop trembling, "I'm sorry. Everything is my fault, Nicoli. This all started—"

"Lydia, it's okay. Shh."

He was holding her as tight as he could, the carpet at their side, and it was still not enough to make her feel safe.

"What are we to do?" Lydia asked.

With tears in his eyes, he squinted as his chin and cheeks tightened, looking down the hallway. "We're going to catch that son of a bitch."

CHAPTER FIFTY-SEVEN

Hugh walked down the street with Abbey, who kicked rocks across the pavement with a cheery smile while he looked to the rooftops on the windy evening. Gaslights lined the roads, and with everyone at the World's Fair for its last days, their walk was more or less peaceful.

Hugh bumped into Abbey, and she smirked, nudging him back.

"I miss our walks." Hugh tucked his hands into his pockets.

"Me too, but you are a busy boy with all that inventing."

"I don't mean to be. You—"

"Oh, stop. I was joking. I wouldn't have it any other way. After your apprenticeship, perhaps, you can bring those talents to the district."

"I'd like that. I've made little progress, but Mr. Scott seems happy. We could figure it out."

"That, or maybe we do something else."

Hugh looked to Abbey as her gaze lingered on the walkway. "What do you mean?"

Abbey bobbed her head, hesitating. "Do you remember when we'd talk of moving elsewhere? About Allura? I always loved the mountaintops."

"Here and there. I didn't think you wanted to leave."

"The homeless are everywhere. It'll never end, but we can make things better. We should go where we wish. It doesn't matter if we do it here or there. I know it's a lot to ask, with Mr. Scott being your new family, but would you want to try somewhere else?"

Hugh looked around, the scarf hanging off his neck. "You're my family."

Abbey looked up, her eyes narrow.

"You know that, right?"

"I do. I just struggle with Kenneth. To see you as my brother makes me feel guilty. I was afraid you'd be mad at me."

"Of course I wouldn't." Hugh grabbed Abbey's hand, and they paused on the sidewalk. "What if we left soon?"

"What about your inventing?"

"I might understand enough to start on my own. I can always write to Mr. Scott. There is a lot going on, and he said it might be safer if I don't go back to see him for a little bit. Maybe one day we could find a home with windows that aren't broken. Eat and bathe with a roof over our heads."

Abbey smiled and shook her head. "I thought this moment would be different."

Hugh looked down the street. "What do you say?"

Abbey rubbed her shoulder and smirked. "I, ugh, yes, why not, but take this first." Abbey handed Hugh some coin. "We will need some food. Grab enough."

His chest seemed light, and Hugh played with his scraggly beard. "Okay. I'll meet you in the alleyway, and we can make plans to leave. Just think, by the end of the weekend, we could be looking back to the city before we head out into the forest."

Abbey leaned in and hugged him. "I didn't think I would be this excited."

Her hair still smelled like mint, soft against Hugh's cheek. Abbey nodded, and she headed off, leaving Hugh on the street.

With a deep breath, he walked several blocks to the market circle, which was crowded compared to when the fair wasn't in town. Vendors of all kinds were lively with their trades on display.

Hugh popped his brown collar to where his eyes met the rim and eyed the crowd. With the wind nipping at his scraggly beard, he pushed his wavy hair, slicking it in place.

A few gentlemen walked by with a side glance towards Hugh. He bit his fingernail and removed a hat from his jacket, slipping it over his head, the ends fraying and dangling on the back. The sounds of shoppers and vendors filled his ears, and he rocked sideways, pulling on his ripped cuff.

Yes, I think I'm ready to go.

He paused next to a woman in a violet shirt with blonde hair in a loose bun, perusing trinkets.

She walked towards him, glancing in his direction. Hugh straightened his back, trying not to get in her way.

"They are lovely, aren't they?" the woman asked.

Hugh did not look. "Yes."

"And they say you can't find something good in South Hills. More to this side of the city than most want to give credit."

"Oakvale has nice clothes too."

"I've never been. Is it nice out there?"

Hugh closed his eyes and lowered his gaze. "It was."

Hugh forced a smile and walked away to the center of the market.

Let's get the food before I get second thoughts.

He shook his head and turned around, bumping into a man whose scarf covered his face with a low-brim cap. Hugh banged his hand off something hard and glanced at a metal spout on the man's wrist.

Hugh paused and stared at the oddly dressed man, who forced himself through the crowd, making his way through the alleys of South Hills.

Abbey sat on the stoop ledge of a boarding house with her feet tucked in, holding herself from sliding onto the cobblestone. The wind blew in the cloudy evening, the lamps shimmering in the hard gusts. She pulled her jacket tight, holes in the elbows where a small chill put goosebumps on her arms.

She wrote a note on a piece of splintered wood resting on her lap, careful not to mess up. Doubt clouded her thoughts, and she could not help but wonder if she could leave. With the single bag she would pack, she glanced to the building, thinking she would miss it once they left for Allura.

Someone coughed, and Abbey looked to a hand waving her over at the end of the alleyway. She tucked the note into her jacket pocket and hopped to the sidewalk, inching her way to the alley, making sure she stayed on the street. Abbey peeked into the shadows. No gaslights in the darkness.

"You must be dumb if you think I'd fall for that." Abbey stayed away.

"Abbey, it's me."

Her eyes opened, waiting for someone to walk out. "Brother?"

"Be quiet. Yes, come here."

Against her instincts, Abbey walked to the edge of the alley. Kenneth stepped away from the wall, his face dirtied and his clothes tattered. Abbey shook, and she ran up and hugged him. He cringed, arching his back in her embrace.

"Kenneth, where have you been? I heard rumors of a madman on the streets. He attacked the World's Fair and killed people. Was he coming for you?"

Kenneth rested his weight on her, and she attempted to hold him, feeling the bones of his rib cage. He was thin and his stature weak.

Abbey helped him onto the ground, and he sank against the brick, the top hat propping up his neck. She rushed to her bag, pulled out a small piece of bread, and handed it to him. Kenneth then devoured it like a starving animal.

Abbey sat next to him, picking up his cane and setting it in her lap. "Kenneth, you need help. Have you seen yourself?"

"No." He held his stomach. "I will not go to the Peake. They would have me killed."

"Then let me put you in one of the boarding houses. There's a nurse and food."

Kenneth paused, glaring at her. "I do not want their help." Kenneth threw what was left of his bread at Abbey. She picked it up and knocked off the dirt, placing it back into her bag.

With heavy breaths, the veins on Kenneth's neck popped. His cheeks were taut against his face as he tensed his jaw, and his breathing faded into sobs. He closed his eyes, tears falling onto his cheeks.

Abbey felt a lump in her throat, and her chest tightened as she slid closer to her brother. She wrapped her arms around him, holding him close.

He cried against her shoulder. "I don't know what I'm doing, Abbey. I thought I needed to do this, but who knows what I deserve anymore. I've been lost for weeks."

"Kenneth, you're scaring me. Is that killer who attacked the fair the one looking for you?"

"No. I was not the one in danger."

"Then who was?"

Kenneth shoved his sister and leaned back. "It does not matter."

Abbey stood with Kenneth's cane in hand. "Kenneth, I'm tired of this, of not knowing what's going on. Why can't you tell me anything? What's so bloody important you have to stay here? If this murderer doesn't kill you, you're going to starve to death. Die in some alley like Mum and Pop."

Kenneth's eyes lit up. The first sign of life. He scowled and bit his lip until it bled. "I will not succumb as they did. Tell me, Sister, what out there's worth anything?"

"How about you stop questioning me and trust me for once?"

Kenneth froze as Abbey stood, realizing how quiet everything got. There were noises in the distance, but between her brother, even he held his breath.

"What if I told you we could leave tonight, so this monster couldn't follow you?" she said. "We go somewhere you can be safe, where we are a family again? I don't want to lose what's left of mine. Please, you need to come with me."

Kenneth pulled down his scarf. "You're right." Kenneth stood and grasped her arm, dragging her along the dirt.

"Kenneth, now wait." Abbey pried his hand off and smacked him away.

"What are you doing?" Kenneth asked. "We can go. We have to go."

"We can't just leave. Well, we can, but there's someone else coming."

"No, now. We can't take the risk."

"Kenneth!"

Kenneth grabbed her arms, squeezing to where it hurt. "We have to leave. We've waited too long as is because I refused to listen."

Abbey stared into his bloodshot eyes. He wasn't thinking. His gaze was low with dark circles, and while a husk of a man, his conviction kept his grip strong. Kenneth let her go and snatched the cane from her grasp.

"Kenneth?" Abbey stepped back.

"I want what you've said. To leave. We stay off the main roads, using only the alleys until we reach the forest. There are horses and a carriage I kept near the old stables outside the city."

Kenneth gripped her hand and ran off.

"Kenneth, I have to grab my stuff."

"Well, hurry!"

Abbey rushed to her cubby and grabbed her bag. She paused and dropped to her knees, removing the note. Everything was happening too fast. Her heart pounded, and her fingers shook. Abbey glanced over her shoulder, Kenneth looking up and down the alley. Pulling a pencil out, she wrote on the letter, trying to be quick but legible. She could feel Kenneth's gaze behind her, waiting.

"Abbey!"

"Coming." Abbey pulled the brick from the boarding house and stuffed it in the wall.

She grabbed her bag from the dirt and lifted her head, jerking to a stop with Kenneth in her face.

"What are you doing?" he asked.

Abbey tightened her grip around her bag, shifting in front of the crates. "I was collecting my things, making sure I left nothing."

Kenneth gazed to the street, and Abbey turned.

"What's wrong?" she asked.

"Nothing. Now, let's go."

Kenneth took off, and Abbey followed. She slung her pack over her shoulder and glanced to the brick, hoping by some miracle Hugh found it and her apology would be enough.

CHAPTER FIFTY-EIGHT

Abbey struggled to keep up with Kenneth's pace, the sweat dripping down her back, despite the bitter air of the harvest evening. She paced through the shadows of Well's Peake, making her way towards the city's edge.

Abbey walked to the end of the alley to a dirt road that led into the rolling fields and forest. The moon radiated through the leafless trees, lighting their path.

"We're almost there." Kenneth searched the outskirts.

He waved Abbey to follow, and they hid beside the stone wall surrounding the South Hills, passing a new stable and heading to the old. Abbey looked over her shoulder, wishing for a sign to turn around, back to her cubby, where life was familiar and comforting, despite her circumstances. It was happening too fast, but she couldn't fight Kenneth.

He was in control.

Abbey pulled her bag tight against her back and ducked as a constable patrolled the streets. Kenneth stared at her, covering his lips with his finger. She was cautious of each step until they reached the stable where a carriage rested on the side and a few horses pattered inside.

She wanted to be happy, find a new home, and help other people, but her stomach was upset and hollow.

"We must hurry," Kenneth said. "It is only a matter of—"

"Kenneth, can't we stop and take a minute to think. I want to go, but you're acting like a madman. Look at you—what has happened?"

Kenneth waved the lantern. "Abbey, not right now. I'm in danger."

"And me because you refuse to tell me what's going on."

Kenneth put his satchel in the carriage's trunk. He grabbed Abbey's handbag, but she resisted as he struggled to remove it. The strap broke as he tried to take it off and stumbled backward. Kenneth glared at Abbey and stuffed the pack into the chest. It didn't fit. He shoved and pushed on it until his bag popped open and a top hat with a red metal mask attached fell out onto the ground.

Kenneth paused as Abbey's gaze locked on it. She stepped to the hat, pulling it out of the gravel, pebbles falling off.

Kenneth held out his hand. "Abbey."

"I knew I had a bad feeling. They said the man who attacked the fair was wearing a red mask." Her eyes darted to him, the metal cool on her fingertips.

Kenneth walked to her, trying to take it from her grip. "Abbey, give it here."

Abbey's fingers trembled, and her stomach knotted so quick, she almost threw up. *He couldn't be, but he could? Was Kenneth the killer? Would he kill me for knowing?* Abbey covered her mouth, trying not to faint.

"What is this?" she said. "Are you the Phoenix? Why would you bring it if you wanted to leave and change?"

"Can we talk later? If we're spotted, we'll have bigger issues."

Kenneth yanked the mask from her hand and stood there.

Tears rolled down her cheeks, but she did not sob. Her shaking hands steadied, to the point where Abbey's mind fogged over. "So, it's you. You're the danger to everyone else. Not the other way around."

Kenneth put the hat in the trunk and closed the lid; Abbey's satchel pinched on the end.

Abbey clenched her fists and pursed her lips, not wanting to move, her blood boiling towards her brother. "Do you remember when we were young? When you joined the acrobat show to make coin for the family?"

"Yes." Kenneth pulled a horse from the stable. "Abbey, we—"

"I know Mum and Dad didn't like you helping, but I did, Kenneth. I was proud to be your sister. How did you become... this?"

Kenneth glanced at her, guiding the horse to the front of the carriage. "Was? You're not anymore?"

"Don't you dare turn this on me!"

Kenneth clutched her mouth, looking around. "Listen here."

Abbey grabbed his neck and shoved him away. "Do you realize how scary this is?"

"There's no need to worry, Sister. Once we leave, we'll be safe. Free of this city. It's what we deserve."

"You killed innocent people. Why? Why did they deserve what you did to them?" Abbey gripped his arm and pulled up his sleeve to three nozzles on his wrist.

Kenneth froze, stunned in place. He yanked his hand aside and leaned against the stable, licking his dry lips. Abbey walked to him, the moon catching his sharp jaw.

"I'm sorry," he said. "You weren't supposed to know."

"You think I wouldn't figure it out?" Abbey folded her arms, a ringing in her ears. "I guess not. You never imagined I would when you stole the family fortune, so why now—leaving us on the streets. We never took the chance you did because we had nothing to take us there. You had all the coin you needed to start a life we all dreamed of, but you damned us to die on the street."

Kenneth rubbed the bridge of his nose.

"Those people have done nothing to you. What happened to you and Amia is awful, but what you're doing will not bring her back."

"She should be leaving with us. Amia was all that was elegant in this world, and she's gone. She's gone." Kenneth's shoulders lifted high, his breathing heavy, his lip quivering. His words slowed and grew painful.

Abbey wanted to hurt him, expose him for who he was, but he was still her brother. He was nothing more than a broken man.

"Do you think she'd want you to give up on what's still beautiful?" she asked. "What about those people who died in the forest fire?"

"Abbey, I didn't start that fire. I chased people down, but I didn't start it."

"You didn't?"

"No. I never touched it. I know when this forest deserves to burn. If only I could recall where he lived. One night I was there, but my mind—I can't remember."

"Where who lived? And if you didn't start it, who did?"

Kenneth raised his wrist, rubbing the gauntlet. His silence did not reassure Abbey in the least.

"The person who created that hell is the man we're running from," Kenneth said.

Abbey stepped slowly towards him, and Kenneth watched, his hands shaking in front of him. She rolled his sleeve up and looked at the device. "Can't you just leave it? If you can do that, leave the mask behind, I'll go with you." Abbey forced a smile. "Kenneth."

Kenneth held on to the machine, and Abbey felt him shake in her grip, trying to hold back his sobs. He closed his eyes, and his breath quivered.

"Brother, let us move on with our lives," Abbey said.

Kenneth's gaze dropped, and he cried, coughing, keeping himself away from Abbey as she loosened the gauntlet.

"I miss her so much." He held his hand over his face, and tears flowed down his cheeks as Abbey set one Red Breathe in the dirt.

Abbey wrapped her arms around him, and he put his face on her shoulder, holding her tight. Her hands tingled, and she tried not to cry, but it grew more difficult by the second. Her brother, a broken man, held her as if he had nothing left in the world.

They cried together, keeping each other warm in the icy breeze. Kenneth stepped back and untightened the straps from the other gauntlet, sliding it down his wrist. The valve snagged his cuff, and a burst of fire shot at her and the trunk.

Abbey leaped back, her arm catching ablaze, looking to the fire with wide eyes. Kenneth put out the flames on her jacket and ran to the carriage, opening the trunk and patting the fire out of the bags. Their contents spilled onto the ground, and his gaze lingered on the silver coins in the dirt.

Abbey's heart dropped. She gasped for air, screaming in her mind as her fingertips turned cold. Kenneth's face grew pale, and she gulped, the muscles in her throat twitching.

"Kenneth?" Abbey tried to move but held her hands at her sides, picking at the bottom of her jacket.

He kneeled and picked up the coins. "Where did you steal these?" He pulled a money purse out of the dirt, and his nostrils flared. "Were you taking handouts, Sister? Wait, this is my bag. The one I gave to…"

"Kenneth, I haven't spent that coin. It's for others."

Kenneth glared at her and gritted his teeth. "Tell me where, Sister. I want to hear you say it."

Abbey gulped. "I didn't use any—"

"Tell me!" Kenneth stood, his finger pointed at her.

Abbey shoved his hand away. "You spoke to Mother and Father that way, but I won't take it. The only reason you got what *you* deserved is because I allowed you to steal what was mine. I gave you what you needed to make your mark because I cared more about our family!"

"Liar!" Kenneth smacked her across the cheek.

Kenneth grabbed her by the throat, covering her mouth with his other hand. The gauntlet dangled off his wrist as he slammed her against the stable, knocking the air from her lungs.

Abbey could smell the fuel from the Red Breath. Kenneth's hands reeked of it. She waited for him to let go, but he didn't, and the little air she had was almost gone.

Abbey kicked him in the groin, and his grip weakened. She pulled on the gauntlet, and it ignited.

Fire erupted, and Kenneth jumped back while Abbey grabbed a piece of wood from against the stable, smacking her brother in the neck. The horse inside jolted up, neighing at the heat, and the other rushed into the forest.

Kenneth stood with a snarl, his neck red and bleeding.

"Kenneth, fight it. Don't do this."

"You're just like the rest of them. You were only thinking of yourself when you took from me."

"Listen to yourself!"

Kenneth lunged with his arms raised, and Abbey swung the board, smacking him across the face. She stumbled as the wood split, and Kenneth arched his back, blood dripping down his cheekbones.

He leaped for her, and she rushed into the stable, looking for anything she could use but finding nothing to defend herself. Fire erupted through the broken boards, and the horse kicked the wall, creating a hole large enough for him to rush out.

Abbey followed the animal out, and Kenneth rammed her into the carriage. She felt her ribs crack and fell face-first into the dirt.

He stood over her, and she grabbed his wrist, ripping off the gauntlet. Kenneth pulled her up by the collar and punched her in the jaw as she collapsed onto the ground. Blood dripped from her cheek to the gravel and brick.

Kenneth lifted her and flung her against the stable, where she fell again. He smacked her against the boards, over and over, until they split, her arm pinned between them.

Cinders from the burning stable drifted in the steady breeze, brushing in the air and burning against her cheek.

With each hit, her shoulder and face grew numb, the pain fading while growing all the same. Her vision grew hazy as the blood and dust clouded her eyes. She grabbed his forearms, but even in his frail state, he was too strong and threw her off.

Abbey closed her hand, the dirt digging into her fingernails as her brother slipped the other gauntlet onto his wrist, connecting the hose from under his cuff. He kicked her in the stomach, causing her to arch underneath him. Holding his foot on top of her, he pressed her into the dirt, blood soaking into her collar.

"You had me fooled you were serious, Sister," Kenneth said. "I thought you wanted to be a family."

"I don't anymore." Abbey pushed his boot off and rolled onto her back, looking up to the blurred sky, the stars glimmering between broken clouds.

"You never cared for me," he said.

"I have nothing left to say, Brother. You don't deserve my attention. You don't deserve redemption, and you don't deserve the peace you think you should have." Abbey pulled herself against the ruined stable, her eyes slowly closing.

Kenneth grabbed her by the throat and lifted her to his height, her feet kicking under her. The alleyway was silent except for Abbey's hard breaths, and tears fell down her cheeks.

"Kenneth?" Abbey said.

"What, little sister? A touch louder for me."

"You never deserved her."

Kenneth's smirk faded into a snarl. He let her go, and she dropped into the dirt.

Abbey looked up, her teeth chattering, and Kenneth tightened the gauntlet on his wrist. He lifted his hand and smiled.

A firestorm erupted into the air, engulfing her in a bright fury. Abbey tried to cover her face, but the fire consumed and blinded her. She struggled to cry, to yell for help, but it was too late.

Kenneth lowered his arm as the flames spread across Abbey's body, trapping her. She did not scream as she flailed to put herself out, falling into the dirt.

Kenneth smiled as he watched with wide eyes.

There was a scuffle behind him, and he turned to the sound of gravel crunching, spotting Hugh standing still outside the alley. Hugh's eyes filled with tears, and Kenneth took a step towards him, his grin slithering up his cheekbones.

He pulled the scarf over his mouth, his black, bloodshot glare over the fabric. Kenneth sprinted off, and Hugh ran into the alley with a serial killer at his heels.

CHAPTER FIFTY-NINE

Aleksandar sat in his chair, bouncing his foot off the ground as he looked to the sunset outside the living room window. Ellie straightened the cushions on the couch, eyeing him as he rubbed his palms.

"If you keep rubbing your hands like that, they'll dry out," she said.

Aleksandar held on to the arms of the chair and sighed. "What if she doesn't show?"

"Then she doesn't, but she will. Don't worry."

Shae soared through the room, landing on the post beside Aleksandar, tilting her head upside down with brown beady eyes. Ellie picked up the owl guard and clicked her tongue. Shae lurched into the air and landed on her shoulder.

"Aleksandar, when did you last dust?" Ellie asked.

He stood. "I'd like to tell you, but I'm not sure I remember."

"Oh—well, don't move too much then."

Aleksandar paused, cracked a smile, and finished lining the coffee table to the rug. "Where did you find her, anyway?"

"On the streets as I was buying yesterday's supper. She was sitting on a bench, bundled up close with a lantern."

Shae took off from Ellie's shoulder, snuggling into the couch cushions.

Aleksandar shook his head. "I wish she'd come around more often. After what happened at the fair, she's been so distant, and we never had a chance to talk. I showed up at the hospital one day, and she was always with a nurse, and then she wasn't there at all."

"I can understand. After being attacked by some madman, maybe she needed to collect her thoughts."

Ellie hugged Aleksandar and smiled. He kissed her, Ellie putting her hands on his cheek. They put their foreheads together, and Aleksandar couldn't help but blush. He waited for so long to feel such a connection, and Ellie treated him the way he always wanted.

"Thank you." He nudged against her.

"For what?"

"For being here."

Ellie kissed him.

"I'll take a peek outside," Aleksandar said.

Ellie held his hand until it slipped out from the distance. Looking out the window, Aleksandar glanced up the street, his hazel eyes blinking from the brightness. People strolled down the sidewalk, but none looked like Vida. He pulled the curtain further and noticed someone walking the other way.

Aleksandar opened the door, the cool wind breezing in. "Vida?"

She stopped in her tracks, facing the other way.

"Miss Harvey? Did you forget where I lived?" Aleksandar stepped into the street, wondering if it was not her, but she turned around, pale.

"Aleksandar, my apologies. I thought it was further down," Vida said.

Aleksandar paused as Vida's eyes darted down the road.

"Please, come in; it's cold," he said.

Vida found a smile, and Aleksandar waved her into the house.

Ellie stepped forward. "Miss Harvey, it's good to see you again."

"Yes, Ellie, you too."

"I can hang up your coat." Aleksandar held out his hand, and Vida handed him her jacket. Aleksandar hung it up for her, hoping she felt welcomed and safe.

Vida sported a purple dress with her usual gloves, folding her hands.

Ellie leaned against Aleksandar.

"You two seem to pair nicely." Vida batted a smile.

Ellie blushed. "We have, yes. Would you like to sit? Something to drink?"

"That would be nice."

Aleksandar nodded and stepped into the kitchen. The teapot was still warm. He licked his lips and steadied his hand as he poured tea into the cups.

Get it together. It's fine. She seems okay.

He didn't think he would be so nervous but couldn't push the guilt out of his stomach. Was she walking away from the house? Did she want to distance herself for fear of being near him?

Aleksandar lifted the tray, the aroma of jasmine lingering, and walked into the living room. Vida sat on the couch across from Ellie, and he set the plate on the table, noticing Shae staring at Vida with a tilted gaze.

"Thank you," Ellie said.

"Is she bothering you?" Aleksandar asked.

Vida sipped on her drink, and Shae bobbed her head back and forth. "No. She is adorable."

"She can be. If that changes, let me know."

Shae batted Aleksandar a stare, and he sat, Vida taking a few sips as Aleksandar glanced at Ellie.

Ellie crossed her legs. "How is the nursing going, Vida? Aleksandar told me it's a big dream of yours."

Vida looked up from her teacup awkwardly. "It is… challenging. More steps back than forward at the moment, but I'm thinking that might turn around soon."

"That's good to hear." Aleksandar sipped his tea; the jasmine blended perfectly. "You mentioned you got accepted at Blackwell, right? How did that go?"

Vida sighed as she set down her cup. She gulped as if she was trying to speak, but nothing came out. She attempted to take deep breaths, but her eyes glazed over.

Ellie put her hand on Aleksandar's, and he shifted over to the couch.

"Vida… are you okay?"

She wiped a tear off her cheek, and she pulled out a letter, handing it to Aleksandar. He glanced at Ellie and opened it.

Dear Miss Harvey,

I hope you remember me from the Harvest Gala and your class with Professor Garret. My apologies for your early expulsion from the university. Please accept this as an apology. I have taken notice of your dedicated skill and outstanding performance. I belong to the board of a smaller but more open academy on the outskirts of Well's Peake in Downton, accepting all people. The details are in the envelope. Your hand does need to be discussed, but you have safe options. Eagerly awaiting your reply.

—Dr. Gray

Aleksandar looked at Vida, not wanting to make her eyes obvious. "They expelled you?"

Vida nodded with a frosted gaze, wiping her cheeks.

"But it sounds like you have another opportunity. That's good, right?"

Vida pulled on her glove and nodded.

Aleksandar glanced to Ellie, who shrugged and tilted her stare towards Vida.

"Vida?" He chattered his teeth. "I know a lot has happened to you. The attack, the university. I wish—"

"I am so sorry."

Aleksandar paused, his mouth gaping open. "No—Vida, you don't have to be sorry. For anything."

"Bernard asked me to help you, but I can't. Not with everything that's happened. It may not seem like a big deal, but Bernard and you were counting on me, and I failed. I thought we could be friends and encourage each other, but what's happening... is terrifying."

"It's not your fault. I should be the one apologizing. You have a lot going on, and my mess fell on you."

Vida tightened her lips. "I tried, Aleksandar, but I can't walk down the street and not wonder if he's behind me. To be a doctor means everything to me, and I don't feel safe even when I'm practicing. Now that I have two scars."

Aleksandar's mind raced, trying to put the pieces together. Was she talking about her eyes and her hand? His thoughts froze as his chest stiffened. He opened his mouth, but no words came out.

Vida grabbed her glove, took a deep breath, and unrolled it. She held out her hand and shook her head. "Remember this? My mother left me this years ago. When I was younger, I nearly died in a house fire, except my mum came back for me. She pulled me out, threw me onto the deck. I tried to pull her up, but I was too weak, too little, and my lungs burned from the smoke. I held on as long as I could, even as my hand burned, but I couldn't hold on forever."

Aleksandar and Ellie sat in silence as Vida straightened her back to proper posture.

"I only have one thing left from my mother," Vida said. "You can't see it now, but I flinch on occasion. I want to be a doctor, but I can't with this scar, but if I remove it, I lose what's left of her. Do you want to know what's sad? I still write her letters, even though she'll never receive them. My way of keeping her memory alive. Maybe it's just denial."

Shae stepped to Vida and brushed against her leg. Aleksandar held her hand between his as she held back. "Vida, I'm sorry. I didn't understand how deep your scar went."

Aleksandar rolled up his sleeve and showed her the mark Kenneth left him. The burn stretched down his arm. She stood, and Aleksandar did the same. She touched his arm and closed her eyes.

"I wish you didn't have this—I shouldn't have come here." Vida walked away, heading for the door to grab her jacket.

Aleksandar tried to stop her. "Vida, wait. I don't understand."

Vida turned around, unrolling her glove. "I know. Aleksandar, I wish I could have been the friend you wanted me to be, but our friendship won't work. I'm sorry for not giving you answers, but I'm lost in what I am doing, and what to do. I need to be alone. One day I'll be composed enough to sit and talk about this. Don't think I have something against you because you as a person are wonderful."

She slipped on her jacket and stepped towards Aleksandar, and he stared at her. He wanted to help her, to hug her, cry with her, anything to make her feel better.

Vida leaned in and placed a kiss on his cheek. "She's a sweet girl. Be kind to her."

Vida opened the door and walked outside. Aleksandar glanced to Ellie, who watched as well. She placed her hands around Aleksandar's chest from behind, attempting to comfort him as he stood in the frame, the wind of the evening brushing against his face.

Vida headed off into the soothing sun, wiping her cheek dry.

Punching and blocking, Aleksandar sparred with Ellie, his mind wandering in the late night. She twisted around, kicking in the air. Aleksandar dodged the blow, but another nailed him in the gut. He attempted to regain his defensive posture, but Ellie landed several jabs into his shoulder before he stepped back.

"Okay, okay. You got the kicks in." Aleksandar took a deep breath.

"Sorry." Ellie laughed with little remorse.

"It's fine." Aleksandar rested in his chair and looked out the window.

Ellie walked over and rested on his lap, leaning against him. Aleksandar set his head on her, rubbing his cheek against her hair which smelled like vanilla.

"There's nothing we could've done," she said.

"I know. I just hate how we can't always help someone."

Aleksandar caressed her arm, and Ellie looked up to him. She kissed him, finding some comfort.

As his chest rose and lowered, Aleksandar stared at the front door. He chattered his teeth, wanting to walk through it and fix what he didn't know how. He needed to fix it, and he needed to soon.

"Hey."

Aleksandar broke out of his trance to Ellie, gazing at him. "Yeah?"

"You've done nothing wrong."

Aleksandar nodded.

"Things will get better, in—"

The door burst open, busting off its hinges and slamming against the wall. Aleksandar and Ellie jumped to their feet, and Hugh fell to the floor, holding his stomach in pain, the light shining on him from the fireplace. Shae hissed, and Hugh looked up at them with terrified eyes, his cheek cut and his forehead covered in dirt.

"Hugh!" Aleksandar ran to his friend, rolling him onto his back as Ellie stood over them. "See if you can close the door."

Ellie lifted it and closed it the best she could, and Aleksandar tried to calm Hugh down.

"Ken—" Hugh gasped for air.

"Hugh, what happened?" Aleksandar held Hugh's jacket sleeve, the ends singed by fire.

Out of breath and nearly unconscious from exhaustion, Hugh peered up. "Kenneth. Kenneth Forbes is alive."

Aleksandar stared at Hugh, baffled. Hugh gripped Aleksandar's forearm, pulling him closer as he glared with strained eyes.

"The Phoenix," Hugh stuttered. "Kenneth Forbes is the Phoenix."

Aleksandar clenched his jaw, and his face flushed white, holding onto his apprentice in absolute terror.

CHAPTER SIXTY

Aleksandar and Ellie walked down the steps into the workshop, moonlight billowing from the windows. Aleksandar covered his mouth with a clenched fist.

"It can't be true, can it?" Ellie held her arms out.

"I'm not sure, but you saw him. Hugh's convinced it was."

"Well, he hasn't given you any reason not to trust him. Maybe he saw what he did."

Aleksandar walked around with his hands on his hips. "Was he still sleeping when you checked on him?"

"Yes. He told me he has been running since last night and how he escaped by hiding all day, unsure if it was safe. His feet are blistered, he's dehydrated, and he drifted off mid-sentence."

Kenneth is alive?

In a way, it lifted his guilt, knowing he didn't kill him, but that meant Kenneth attacked him at the fair. A knot in his stomach grew, and his breath was heavy.

"What do you want to do?" Ellie asked.

Aleksandar rubbed his arm. "I'm not sure. We should go to the Peakeland Yard, but I don't know if Hugh would."

"If what he said is true, we need him to report it."

Aleksandar leaned back and chattered his teeth, the stress tightening his back. Ellie wrapped her arms around him from behind, and his breath quivered as her vanilla perfume calmed him.

"What if he is alive, Ellie? I thought I killed him. Was Amia my fault?"

Ellie stepped backward and grabbed his shoulders. "Aleksandar, it's not your fault. What happened was an accident, and you mustn't beat yourself up anymore. If Mr. Forbes is the Phoenix, something beyond you happened."

Aleksandar nodded and kissed her on the forehead. "Okay. I know I can't change the past. I promise I'll start thinking forward."

"We're going to figure this out together." Ellie squeezed his hands.

"I think I—"

A rumble echoed upstairs, and Aleksandar glanced up. He rushed up the steps into an empty living room, the front door still in the frame. He hurried to the second floor as fast as his feet would go, his shoe clipping the top step. Aleksandar dashed into the guest bedroom to find Hugh in the lantern's light, picking up his invention off the floor. He shoved what little he had into his bag, Shae watching from the tall shelf on the bookcase.

"Hugh, are you all right?" Aleksandar asked, Ellie standing in the hallway.

Hugh mumbled and carelessly packed his belongings, knocking his scarf to the floor.

Aleksandar inched closer. "What are you doing?"

"I'm not safe in Well's Peake. I have to leave. He'll be looking for me." Hugh's voice was faint, shaking.

Hugh tried to steady his hands as he hurried, throwing little trinkets into his bag, with deep bags under his wide eyes.

Aleksandar walked over and turned Hugh around by the shoulders. "Hugh, many things are about to happen, and you can't leave. Not now. We need your help to stop Kenneth, and you need to come to the Peakeland Yard with us and tell them what you saw."

Hugh pushed Aleksandar back, his jaw shaking and his hands in the air. "I'm sorry. He'd expect that and try to kill me there. There's nothing left for me."

"What about your training? What about Abbey?"

"She isn't here anymore!" Hugh gasped and bit the end of his knuckle, closing his eyes. "She isn't here anymore. We're all meant to move on at some point. This is mine."

The strain of Hugh's stare, his monotone voice, and the fatigue in how he moved, looking as if he could pass out at any moment onto the hardwood floor, unnerved Aleksandar. He eyed the burned coat and the frayed fibers across Hugh's back, seeing how close The Phoenix came to killing him.

Hugh packed his belongings in a disorderly way as tears soaked the collar of his burned jacket. He paused when he saw the scarf on the rug, his grip still on the bag handle.

Abbey's scarf.

Hugh frowned and closed his eyes. "Something wasn't right, Mr. Scott. He bumped into me, and I knew. I tailed him, and she followed him for some reason."

"Who?" Aleksandar stepped forward.

"Abbey." Hugh held himself. "She was like a sister to me. He killed her, Mr. Scott. He burned her alive."

His soft sobs grew louder, and he groaned. Ellie walked around Aleksandar, who stood stunned, and hugged Hugh. He leaned on her, his hands at his sides.

"How could he do that to her?" Hugh dropped to his knees, Ellie making sure he did not fall. "His own sister, she didn't deserve that."

Hugh lifted the scarf off the floor and held it against his chest. It was dirty and riddled with stains, but the stitching read:

For those lost in the cold at night, wear this to bring the warmth of summer's light.

Hugh sniffed the scarf and covered his face. Aleksandar kneeled next to him and placed his hand on Hugh's shoulder, looking at Ellie, whose eyes watered.

Hugh stood between them and pushed more into his bag.

"Hugh, you can't go," Aleksandar said. "We need you. You're the only one who has seen him, and if you leave, who knows who'd believe us?"

Hugh ignored Aleksandar and strapped his satchel tight.

"I know you wish to finish your training, and I don't think you would want to leave knowing Abbey's killer is free. It's hard fighting past the fear. I let it overwhelm me, and the people closest to me have gotten hurt. I understand your suffering. The Peakeland Yard could protect us if they knew Kenneth needed found."

Hugh stopped and hung his head, finally looking at Aleksandar. "Mr. Scott, I'm not like you. When life goes wrong, I find a safer place. Society doesn't listen to those in the shadows. I have to change who I am and move on."

"But you're wrong, Hugh. You don't have to change. You can stay here and grow. There's a difference between the two. If you change, does that mean you'll leave behind what's most important? You're scared, but we'll fight through this."

Hugh stared, holding his packed satchel to his chest. He held it tight, his fingers gripping onto the old leather.

"Abbey was my sister. She was everything to me, and now that she's gone, there's no one to care for me as she did."

"We can, Hugh. We'll look after you."

Hugh closed his eyes and swallowed hard. Aleksandar watched as his words carried no weight. Hugh wasn't thinking, fear scattering his thoughts, and he was too tired to understand.

Hugh turned his head. "What would you have me do?"

"He saw your face, but he probably doesn't know who you are, right?" Aleksandar asked. "Were you sure it was Kenneth?"

"It has to be. From what I overheard and what Abbey told me, it was him."

"Then we need you, Hugh. Please stay and come to the Peake with us. At least stay the night and rest. You can't go out this tired."

Hugh stood there looking at his bag, the scarf sticking out of the end. "I won't leave, but I won't go to the Peake."

Aleksandar lowered his head. "Well, that's a start."

"I shouldn't be here, though."

Aleksandar's shoulders dropped, and he nodded.

"I could help on that front," Ellie said. "My brothers have safe houses throughout the city in case something were to happen. They're never used."

"In South Hills?" Hugh asked.

"Some. I'm sure I can make the arrangements."

Aleksandar reached into Hugh's bag and pulled out the scarf. He held out the scarf, and Hugh took it in his hands.

Hugh nodded and wiped his cheek. He pressed his exhausted face against the scarf and wrapped it around his neck, his eyes heavy, shifting as if he were going to fall asleep on himself.

Ellie held Aleksandar's arm, and Aleksandar hoped Hugh would find the truth in his words. In a way, he understood Hugh had to leave, to discover his own path, to protect himself, but he didn't want him to go.

Hugh secured his bag and let his hands rest on the top as he took a deep breath. He flung his belongings on his back, looking at Aleksandar. "What if I never see you again, Mr. Scott?"

Aleksandar stuttered, lifting his head. "You will. There's much for us to do."

Hugh walked over and hugged Aleksandar with one arm, holding his bag with the other. Aleksandar had a sinking feeling, knowing it would not be easy. Knowing the worst was yet to come.

CHAPTER SIXTY-ONE

Aleksandar stood in the forest while snow fell in gentle flakes to a glow in the valley hidden below. He shivered in the night as the storm grew worse and clouded his vision.

His tongue was dry, and he swallowed hard, the wind blistering against his face as his fingertips turned white. Her screams faded, and he fell on his side, the roots landing against his ribs. The moonlight vanished, and darkness blinded him, leaving him alone and shaking.

Aleksandar.

The voice echoed around him, but the whistling of the wind in his ears kept him wondering where it came from. He reached out to nothing and found no warmth, no comfort, crouched like a scared child.

Aleksandar!

Aleksandar blinked and flinched, jerking up from the couch in his workshop, his chest shaking under his breath. Ellie stood over him with her hand on his shoulder. He gazed at her with a knot in his stomach, his bottom lip shaking.

"She's dead." Aleksandar's voice cracked, his hands trembling.

"Hey now, you're all right. You're okay." Ellie kneeled next to him and wrapped her arms around him.

She brushed her palm against his cheek, and he felt her cool touch and realized he was sweating through his shirt.

"How long was I sleeping?" Aleksandar rested his head on the cushion.

"I'm not sure. I just got here." Ellie rubbed her fingers through his hair.

"Is Hugh settled?"

"I took care of him last night and checked on him this morning. Still skittish, but better rested."

"Good. That's at least one good thing."

Ellie looked away, Aleksandar watching her troubled gaze.

"What's wrong?" he asked.

She did not turn for a moment but let out a slow breath, holding up a letter with a broken red seal. "When did this arrive?"

Aleksandar sighed. "This afternoon, of all days. Did you look at it?"

"No."

"I'd like you to. I need help."

Ellie nodded and read the message.

Mr. Scott,

I believe we are entering the endgame of what is to come. Tomorrow is the Harvest Festival, and I fear the World's Fair is in danger. The Phoenix searches for you, and I suspect he will attend. We are at a crossroads. You put people at risk by attending, but the result could remain the same regardless. We need him to show his face, and the city is ready to capture him, but without you, he may not reveal himself. What is being asked of you is difficult, but I hope you see my reasoning. May the Maker hold us in the palm of her hand.

Ellie set the note on the tea table. Shae hopped from the chair, pressing her beak against it.

"I'm not sure what to think." Aleksandar leaned up, Ellie sitting next to him, holding him in her arms. "If I try to draw him out, I put Well's Peake at risk, and I don't want that."

"Have you considered the person sending these is trying to mislead you?"

"Yes. I thought about taking this letter to the Peakeland Yard, but what if someone there is dirty? They already see me as a suspect. Either way, I lose. If I stay, go, or if I alert the constables. I just want to make the right decision."

The moonlight beamed through the bottom windows, bouncing off the wood floor and across the benches. His shirt was unbuttoned, and his hair shaggy to one side, but Ellie held him as if none of it mattered.

Aleksandar looked past her into his secret room, his invention covered in heavy wool blankets. "This could be real. A genuine chance to stop what I created. The odds are not in my favor, but I have to try."

"But maybe it's a trap."

Aleksandar swallowed hard, flexing his jaw. "If only we had the Lunarwheel. That could stop him. Stop a fire from breaking out."

Aleksandar grabbed her hand and set her palm on his cheek, closing his eyes, losing himself in her embrace. It wasn't just her touch or the soothing nature of her voice, but her confidence, her care for him that brought him peace.

His eyelids grew heavy from inventing all day, and he drifted.

"Aleksandar?"

He looked at her as he rested on her shoulder. "Yes?"

"Why did you say she's dead?"

Aleksandar gulped and leaned up in the cushions. His hands grew clammy, and his thoughts lingered on his childhood friend. He reached over and held Ellie's hand. "Because she is."

"Your friend?"

Aleksandar nodded. "I'm sorry I haven't told you the whole story yet."

"If you want, you can share with me. I've wanted to know why you remember her so dearly."

Aleksandar closed his eyes and focused on the warmth of her touch, settling his thoughts. "I told you the story of the traveling magician, right? How I took my friend to the magic show to show her the machine from her book. Ironically, it was called *The Magician*."

"Yes."

"That book made her who she was. To be an innovator, someone who changes history in an instant. A dream not everyone has or keeps. A year later, the show returned to the valley. She waited for months, and I wanted to take her badly, and of course, I did."

Aleksandar's throat grew dry, and his breathing grew shallow. His eyes watered, nodding his head back and forth. Ellie's touch tightened, and he looked to her.

"On the way there," he said. "We were caught in a blizzard, one like we had not seen in years. The snow was soft but thick, and with the strong wind, we couldn't see the path. She wanted to turn around, but I believed I could get her there, knowing the hillside. I was wrong. We kept moving, but the storm grew thicker, and we were lost. We huddled under a tree, hoping to wait it out, but we realized we'd freeze by morning.

"I led us over the hill, but I took us too far. On the backside was a ravine with an iced ridge. It held me just fine, but I must have cracked it when I crossed. She followed, and I noticed too late... she fell through. I couldn't see... I lost her, Ellie. I lost my best friend."

The pain in his chest swelled, and his words faded. He leaned forward, holding Ellie close, wishing he could hold her tighter. He sobbed and grabbed the side of Ellie's shirt, tears soaking into the fabric.

"Aleksandar."

"It's my fault. She died because I made the wrong choice. I wanted her dream to come true. For the best of her to shine, but I stole that from her."

Ellie cupped his face and lifted his chin, his eyes red and puffy. "You didn't mean for it to happen. You can't blame yourself."

"Well, I do. Everything I do is for her, to give the world her dream. A dream she deserved to show Well's Peake. And look how I ruined it."

Aleksandar's workshop darkened again. The sting of the frost lingered on his palm, and he remembered every sharp gust of air from the forest. From that night, his life changed forever. He wanted to close his eyes and wait for the pain to disappear, but it never did. The constant ache of his guilt grew every day he did not make the change he promised her.

Ellie leaned back, a tear on her cheek. "Aleksandar, you make her proud every day. You try, you struggle, but you have not once given up, even when you thought you would. The difference she wanted doesn't happen right away. I'm certain that you will succeed."

Aleksandar grabbed Ellie's hands and kissed them. "I have to. Like what the magician did for my friend, you do for me. You give me the hope I didn't see. With her vision and you here now, that's all I needed to be motivated. I wrecked so much, but I'm going to change that."

Ellie smiled, and Aleksandar kissed her, wrapping his arms around her waist, never wanting a moment to separate them from one other.

He leaned back in her arms and stared at her, wiping off his wet cheeks.

"Do not ask me what I think you're going to," she said.

"I won't. There's so much uncertainty in my life, but you're not part of that. I don't want you going anywhere, but tomorrow night, I need you to stay home, so I know you're safe."

"So you aren't going to the Peakeland Yard?"

"I'm not sure they'll believe me, so I'll do this myself."

Ellie held him close, putting her cheek on his chest. "Okay, but listen to me. I am yours to hold. You must be smart, and if you do this, understand I want you back at my side. Don't do this if you don't think you're able."

"I wouldn't have made it this far without you. To wonder where I would've been—"

"Stop." Ellie put her finger over his mouth. "There's no point in wondering because you have me. That's what matters."

"What if what I have to do requires me to reach too high?"

"Then I will hold you down. Hold you close."

Aleksandar bit his lip, tears rolling onto his cheeks. He reached to wipe them, but Ellie stopped him.

"Some tears dry on their own," she said. "But with me, I'll make sure yours don't."

Aleksandar smiled and kissed her again, lost in her embrace. As the evening grew late, they held each other in the workshop, Shae resting on the chair nearby. The night coming was unknown, and Aleksandar was unsure of the right decision, but he had little choice.

No more sitting by. Now was his moment.

Ellie looked at him. "So how will you stop him?"

Aleksandar raised his finger. "With this."

He walked into his secret room and came out carrying a thin oak case. He set the box on the bench, opened it, and pulled out a staff with two pointed prongs on each side.

Ellie walked to the edge of the doorway. "When did you work on this?"

"This is the idea I had while we were at my parents' house. Enough was happening without bringing this up."

Aleksandar pressed a button in the middle, and the staff extended in both directions. The handle was mahogany, with brass supports running along the shaft, metal extensions near the ends. He walked to the bare side of the shop and stood, holding it in his hand. He opened the center and pushed a charged battery inside the machine.

"Could you turn the valve at the end of that table?" Aleksandar asked.

Ellie looked to where Aleksandar had pointed. The control arm leading to the Red Breath, which was aimed at him. "Isn't that—"

"Yes."

"Won't that burn you?"

"In theory, no."

Ellie rubbed her braid, swallowed hard, and grabbed the lever, holding it firm.

"Wait, wait."

Ellie jerked away, and Aleksandar ran to her. He pulled her close by the waist and kissed her, her lips soft against his.

Aleksandar leaned back, his breath still on hers. "Just in case."

"That's not very reassuring," Ellie said.

He paced to his spot and inhaled deeply, nodding to her with the staff in hand, bracing himself.

"Aleksandar, I don't think this is a good idea. What if it doesn't work?"

He paused and lowered his shoulders. "It will. I wouldn't ask you to trust me like this if I didn't believe in it."

Ellie swallowed hard. "You sure?"

He nodded, staring into the invention. His heartbeat pulsed through his arms, the sweat dripping down his brow.

Everything around him seemed to slow, knowing his life could end at any moment. His device may not have enough power to reflect or guide the flame away from him, and if it did, he didn't know for how long. It was his only countermeasure to repel the Red Breath. His only hope.

Ellie bit her lip and pulled the lever. Fire burst from the nozzle in a roar. The redness in Aleksandar's eyes became bright and hot, blinding him in the heat. He raised the staff and whipped it into the flames.

Ellie covered her mouth and watched as Aleksandar disappeared, like a magician, in a raging inferno.

CHAPTER SIXTY-TWO

The sunset faded on the horizon of Well's Peake, and the stars shone against thousands of gaslights in the Harvest Festival, Lydia standing beneath them.

She walked the midway path where red, blue, and purple flames lit the crowds of fairgoers, illuminating the gardens and festivities of the World's Palace. Fireworks exploded in the air, drawing the attention of the youngest toddlers to the oldest of grandparents. Merry people of all kinds flocked to the carnival booths and games inside the tents of orange-and-white stripes.

The highlight was the carousel. Lines stretched as long as Lydia could see, all waiting to witness the first mechanical marvel. Chairs and horses spun around, people attempting to cut in line of those who waited hours.

Food and treats from all over the world filled the fair with smells of the exotic and creative, bringing thirst and hunger to everyone. Lydia stopped and grabbed a dish of fried batter with cinnamon on top.

She walked to the west entrance, her neck brace hidden behind her tall jacket, and eyed the crowd with caution. A patrol building lay near the gate, and she stood across from it, resting against a tree, waiting in the shadows.

Fairgoers flooded into the festival, but she focused, knowing someone could hide in the midst that shouldn't be. Constables patrolled the guardhouse with Limbs of Life strapped on their backs, casually looking around, lost more in their conversations than their duty.

Lydia tilted her head as Owen appeared with his cane, leaning on the other side of the tree.

"Constable May," he said.

"Good evening, Owen. I see you donated your invention to the Peake."

"Sadly, but I trained them well, I assure you. If only—"

"Their skills as constables were as adequate."

"Yes. I did not want to say it."

"That's all right. I have a few trusted men at each entrance while many loosely play the part."

Owen nodded, glancing at the crowd. "I'm sorry to hear about the attack the other night. I'm glad everyone is okay."

"Thankfully, my daughter did not see what happened. The butler saw through the window and stashed her in a safe house out back."

"Thank the Maker. And it was the Phoenix who attacked? Where is Inspector Lucas this evening? I would assume he'd be here."

"The *chief* believes it is, and Nicoli is. We thought it best he kept a low profile, considering his reputation."

"Agreed."

"What about yourself, Owen? Why are you here?"

"I brought my daughter. Bernard stole her away for a few games while I grabbed something to eat. I saw you walking through the crowd and wanted to say hello."

Lydia shifted in the shadows, her eyes batting back and forth. "I hope she enjoys herself."

Owen peeked around the trunk of the tree, his jaw tight. "Lydia, should I not have brought my daughter here?"

She swallowed hard and took a deep breath. "I'll be honest, Owen, none of us should be here."

Aleksandar walked under the arch that stretched over the cobblestone road, looking to the sign that hung across the midway. People cascaded around him and through the entrance, bumping shoulders to the point he lost his balance.

He skimmed the fair and took a deep breath, his senses overwhelmed. From the perfume and cologne to the sounds of bells and laughter, he was taking it all in, thinking everything was a danger. He did not sleep enough the night before, which worsened his rampant imagination.

He walked in, the street vendors pushing carts up and down the paths. Someone offered Aleksandar a drink, but he waved his hand.

"No, thank you."

Not knowing what to search for, Aleksandar waited to see if anyone approached him. The Phoenix knew who he was and was most likely hiding in the crowd, waiting for his moment to strike. It would not be long before someone discovered him, his home, or worse, Ellie. Aleksandar was on the underside of the hand being dealt, and he couldn't wait for disaster anymore.

Aleksandar felt as if he was suffocating, but he rolled his shoulders and walked through the gardens in front of the World's Palace, which stood tall, like a crystal in the moonlight.

What if this is an ambush?

The Phoenix may not show, knowing the risk was too great. *He wouldn't want to be caught, would he? Or was his passion for revenge so immense that it no longer mattered?* So many outcomes spun through Aleksandar's head, exhausting him.

After walking by several exhibits, Aleksandar paused, his heart sinking in his chest. His eyes lingered through the crowd to a woman in a purple corset, looking into the sky.

Vida.

A firework launched behind the tree line, and she smiled as it exploded into hundreds of meandering light streaks across the horizon. Aleksandar quickened his pace to reach her side. If the Phoenix attacked and hurt Vida again, she would never forgive him. He could never forgive himself. To tell her what was happening would scare her off, most likely forever.

His temples throbbed as he hurried along the path, Vida turning in his direction.

"Vida?" he said.

"Hello, Aleksandar. I didn't expect to see you here."

"I wasn't planning on it at first." Aleksandar looked over his shoulder, his back sweating.

"Me neither. I decided I needed to enjoy the fair while it was still in the city. It will not last forever."

Aleksandar nodded, trying to find words, but it took every ounce of self-control not to look like he was panicking on the inside. Vida seemed okay, and he didn't want to frighten her, hearing the shyness in her voice.

They both went to speak but paused, Vida chuckling. "Aleksandar, I'm sorry for the other night. I was not pleasant. You deserved answers and some respect."

A bell chimed beside him, and he flinched.

Get ahold of yourself. Take a moment. Breathe.

Aleksandar closed his eyes and let the reckless thoughts fade away. Had it been a second or a minute that passed, he did not know, but a hollow sense of calm fell over him. His head grew steady, and his back loosened.

"Aleksandar, is something wrong?" Vida asked, her gaze widening. "You're acting strange."

Aleksandar paused and stared at her, forcing a smile. "Yes. Sorry. I didn't expect this much noise, and I still get headaches. I think I'll be all right."

"Okay. Maybe you'd like to join me? I was thinking of getting some hot cider. I heard it was quite soothing."

"That'd be great. I hear there are dumplings next to the midland bridge."

"That sounds excellent."

Aleksandar nodded and held out his arm, Vida slipping hers in his. It took every muscle in his body to keep away the shakes. He eyed the crowd, as if someone was watching them.

∾

Lydia tailed Aleksandar and Vida as they strolled through the fair, keeping her distance to where she was afraid she would lose them. She rushed closer, pausing at a hat stand, and paid the vendor. She took a fedora and pulled it tight over her head.

∼

Hours passed, and a chill filled the air as the crowd thinned, but only a little. Aleksandar grabbed the end of his scarf and wrapped it around his neck, popping his brown collar up.

Vida sat beside him on a bench against the tree line, wiping crumbs from her lips. Aleksandar took a bite of apple cobbler, cinnamon coating his tongue in a perfect balance of powdered sugar. He licked his lips, the smell of fried batter still on his tray.

"Much better than the dumplings I mentioned." Aleksandar patted his mouth with a napkin.

"I'd have to agree."

They sat as the night grew late with no sign of slowing. Aleksandar looked to Vida, and she smiled, her cheeks rosy.

"I'm glad we could catch up and enjoy each other's company," she said.

"Me too. I missed when we could sit on a bench and discuss whatever came to mind."

Vida grabbed Aleksandar's tray and tossed it into the trash bin. She leaned back, looking at the crowd. "Do you remember that letter I showed you? A few nights ago?"

"From the doctor?"

"Yes. Well, he has officially accepted me into Downton. It's small and not the most credited, but they are open to the possibility of a female doctor. However, that depends on after we discuss my hand."

Aleksandar turned and rested his elbow on the back of the bench. "How does that make you feel?"

Vida looked at her palm and pulled on the glove. "That scar has been a big part of my life, and to erase it makes me nervous. I've seen it for so long; I wouldn't know what to think if it wasn't there. That or maybe the surgery could go wrong... then everything could be ruined."

"I'm not the greatest at this, but I remember something my mum used to say. We have to make the hardest choices at the most emotional moments, and we don't always have a choice. We're pushed into those moments, and we have to make the best of them."

Vida laughed and covered her mouth with the back of her hand.

Aleksandar blushed and straightened up. "Was it that bad?"

"No, no." Vida smiled at him. "The message was beautiful. With a little more finesse, you could be my replacement."

Aleksandar grinned and looked away. "I doubt that. I'm not suave in the slightest."

"Oh, don't lie to me, Mr. Scott. Miss Fritz seems infatuated with you."

Aleksandar hoped so. Ellie walked into his life when he least expected it, and he wouldn't change a thing if it meant not meeting her. He lifted his head, and his smile faded. His eyes grew wide as he locked stares with a woman in a fedora and a neck brace.

He didn't want to make his gaze obvious and alarm Vida, but he was unable to look away from the constable.

Lydia May.

∼

Lydia drifted elsewhere, not wanting to spook Aleksandar more than she already had. There was no doubt he saw her. She thought she was smart, but she got too close.

What would he think? Did he connect the wrong pieces? She paced around the game tent, glancing at Aleksandar, who still looked her way.

Her cover was blown.

She had to tell him before he became too obvious and scared off the Phoenix. It was the only option.

Lydia stepped onto the midway, but she paused as a black shadow entered the corner of her eye. A thousand people surrounded her, but one caught her attention in a way she found suspicious.

Something was wrong.

She shifted towards a man in a cape who disappeared through a tent. She scratched her face and looked in Aleksandar's direction, who was still on the bench. Whether he was looking at her, she was unsure.

Lydia closed her eyes, knowing she had a choice to make, a risk either way. She stepped towards Aleksandar and Vida, but the man with the cape snuck behind a row of tall oaks and hedges, heading near the fireworks display.

The pit in her stomach was too much, and she broke cover, assuming she spooked Aleksandar. She rushed through the tree line, hoping the shadow was only her imagination gone wild.

~

Aleksandar's eyes shifted along the horizon; his jaw clenched so tight his teeth hurt. It was Lydia, and she was watching him. *What was happening?*

He turned to Vida, who fidgeted with her gloves. "Aleksandar. I need you to be honest with me. You were strange earlier, and you're scaring me now. Why are you here alone instead of with Ellie? Why do you seem to be afraid?"

A thickness grew in his throat, his words dry and rough. "Vida—"

She leaned back.

Aleksandar clenched his hands, unable to break his gaze with her. She swallowed hard, her bottom lip trembling.

"Aleksandar?" she asked. "Why are you here?"

~

Lydia made her way around the corner leading into the fireworks display, where dozens of pyros set up the next strand of fireworks. Several bystanders walked down the narrow path.

She searched the horizon, pulling herself through the crowd, looking for the cape. Between the suits and jackets, the bells and whistles, she spotted a suspicious person near a covered carriage behind the barrier.

He snuck under the rope to a line of carriages, and she watched the man dig through the lights. He threw some to the side, hooking several primer cords to wicks on the end.

Lydia tiptoed forward, squinting in the wind gust, trying to see the clear picture. Sweat dripped from under the fedora, and she stopped at the tree line. He turned around. Her neck throbbed from the stress, and her face flushed white.

It was Kenneth Forbes.

～

Aleksandar reached for Vida's hand, but she slapped it away, standing with her back towards the crowd.

He stood and held his hands out. "Vida, I can explain."

"Aleksandar!"

Several bystanders paused and inched closer; some focused on Aleksandar. He did not move further, afraid he would attract more attention.

"Vida, do you trust me?" Aleksandar asked.

"What are you doing here?"

"This looks bad, I know—"

"Mr. Scott." Vida rubbed her hand. "Tell me now."

The words were there, but he couldn't speak. He stepped forward, but two disgruntled fairgoers closed in.

Aleksandar's palms sweat as his heartbeat echoed in his ears.

～

Lydia sprinted through the fair, making her way to the guardhouse, her body sore from running into so many people. She tore off her hat and cloak, revealing her uniform.

Her neck brace seemed looser than she liked, but she couldn't stop to fix it. The crowd glared at her as she rounded the midway to Owen and a group of constables on patrol bearing Limbs of Life on their backs.

Owen walked towards her. Lydia slowed to a halt, hunched over, breathing so hard she wheezed.

"Lydia May?" Owen rushed to her, another constable at his side. "What's the matter?"

"Owen. Kenneth Forbes is alive."

Owen's eyes widened, and he glanced at the officer. "That's not possible."

Lydia pulled herself up. "Listen, I just saw Kenneth Forbes near the fireworks exhibit. Ready the patrol."

"*Thee* Kenneth Forbes?" the constable asked.

"I can't stand here and explain! Assemble the patrol. Come on!"

The men obeyed, and Lydia took off, constables at her heels, the heft of the legs slowing them down. The crowd parted with the squad in full force, and they arrived at the fireworks display, making their way past the barriers and meeting opposition from those preparing their work.

"What is the meaning of this?" The head pyro stepped forward with dark gloves burned on the fingertips.

"Constable Lydia May." She held up her badge. "A suspect was sifting through the carriage behind you, and we have reason to believe he is dangerous. Was anything taken or tampered with?"

"We are preparing—"

Lydia grabbed the man by the collar, pulling him close enough to see the sweat on his brow. "This is not a spectacle. Show us now."

She let the guy go, and he wiped his untamed mustache. He jogged to the carriage, and Lydia followed. She waved to the constables to search the fair, glancing over as the man investigated. Not wanting to delay the inevitable, she walked towards the fairgoers that gathered and watched.

"We need your help!" Lydia held up her hands. "Have any of you seen a frail gentleman in a black cape? He was wearing a red scarf wrapped tight around his face. He would've been acting suspiciously."

The crowd, aimless and inattentive, showed no response. Lydia shook her head and looked back to the pyro, who waved another to the second carriage. The air thickened, and Lydia saw a haze filling the air. The people grew uneasy as she paced over the grass.

"Anyone!"

"I did!" an older woman said.

Lydia spun to her near the end of the crowd. She ran over as the woman spoke with a broken dialect.

"I saw the fella carrying all those firelights. He was to drop the lot."

"Where did he go?" Lydia got closer.

The woman pointed to the midway.

Lydia's heart sank as she turned to the constables. "Dark cape. He appears frail. You know who we're looking for. Find him!"

The officers fanned through the crowd at alarming rates. People scurried out of their way, fearful of the inventions on their backs, several panicking.

Lydia rushed to the carriage, where the pyro shook his head. "What is it?"

The man brushed his mustache. "Someone took the primer cords."

"What could someone do with those?"

The man gulped, sweat dripping down his brow.

Aleksandar tried to hold Vida's hand, but a man pushed him back.

"Excuse me," the fairgoer said. "But I don't think she wants you touching her. We know who you are, Mr. Scott."

Aleksandar ignored him and stared at Vida. "I'm here because of the Phoenix. I was going to tell you, but—"

Vida reached out, and the other patron steadied her. Her eyes glazed over, and her legs buckled under her weight. Several more held her up as a few grabbed hold of Aleksandar. He tensed his arms, trying to break free, but they gripped him tightly.

"No, stop, listen to me! I think we're in danger. The Phoenix is here. I know it!"

~

Lydia ran her hand through her hair, hearing a slight commotion from the midway. She jumped onto a bench and looked to see Aleksandar being held back by several people through the tree line.

The pyro searched through the supplies and dozens of fireworks again. He paused, a hissing noise capturing his attention. He stepped back and kneeled beside the carriage. Lydia turned to the man, who pulled the tarp away from the bottom to find a lit wick burning across the grass.

The man turned his head, and Lydia saw the blood rush from his face.

The carriage exploded in a massive fireball, and the force blew Lydia off the bench, throwing her into a tree. She looked up, only to find a bright flame cascading around her.

~

The ground shook, and the crowd turned to the explosion, flames rising into the night. Aleksandar broke free, a red glow kissing his cheek.

Hundreds of people shrieked in terror and dismay as smoke filled the air, many rushing away from the incident. A sharp whistle roared through the chaos, and a firework exploded in the sky above them. Several more followed, bursting lower and lower as the dying sparks fell into the crowds, one lighting a tent ablaze. Aleksandar stepped closer and watched as dozens of fireworks ignited in the tree line.

"Run!"

Fireworks soared into the crowd, hitting fairgoers, tents, and carnival games. They exploded, and the shock waves echoed through the midway. Aleksandar rushed for Vida as red-and-orange light trails sparked against his arm. A thick fog filled the air, the lights flaring as Aleksandar lost sight of where he was.

A firework landed next to him, and he leaped towards Vida, shielding her. It exploded, and Aleksandar's ears rang as hundreds of mini-explosions danced at their feet. He could feel the heat against his face.

Screams and whistles echoed louder than thunder in the valley, and the fire spread, tents on fire, smoke rising in the sky. People ran in complete horror, fleeing for their lives as constables lifted themselves into the air with the Limbs of Life and attempted to guide them to safety.

Another wave of fireworks soared, bursting beneath their legs and causing several to collapse.

"Aleksandar!" Vida dropped to her knees and reached her hand out, and Aleksandar helped her up.

They scurried between the crowd, pushed side to side, unable to see the people next to him. A large man barreled through, knocking Aleksandar to the ground.

He was trampled by a dozen patrons, and he covered his face as he was kicked in the head.

Vida lifted him, almost knocked over, and they headed towards a booth that erupted like a bomb, splinters of wood showering them.

Aleksandar and Vida pushed through the fairgoers, finding no room within the panic, preventing them from knowing where they were. The smoke was tinted red as the fire raged, and cinders and ash fell through the night air, collecting on their shoulders. As a little room opened, Aleksandar turned and froze, his nightmare becoming his reality.

As the crowd separated, a man with a burned top hat and black cape walked calmly through as fireworks exploded around him, people crawling by his feet. The fire flickered against the Phoenix's red metal mask, cinders batting against it.

He roamed the walkway with demonic delight, the flames and smoke encasing him. He grabbed the rim of his hat and nodded in respect.

The Phoenix aimed his hand down and fired, igniting a wick. The cord singed the ground.

"We need to leave!" Adrenaline pumped through Aleksandar's body, and he ran faster than ever before, even with Vida at his side.

Dozens of fireworks erupted beside the killer, shooting off in every direction in cluttered destruction. Carnival stands exploded, Aleksandar's feet shaking beneath him. The explosives hit the ground around him and mushroomed into red-and-orange blasts, blinding him from where he was running. He wiped away an ember from his face, his cheeks stinging.

The concussion deafened Aleksandar, causing him to cover his ears. Vida tried to keep up with his pace. There was a whistle, and a firework struck her in the back, sparks searing her dress black. She fell to the ground, and Aleksandar stopped, seeing the burn marks on her neck.

Aleksandar turned to the Phoenix, who ran at him in rage. He lifted his gauntlets, and Vida screamed with wide eyes.

This ends now.

Aleksandar reached under his jacket and pulled out the staff, the ends extending into the air. He held it defensively, and the Phoenix unleashed an inferno, flames erupting around them.

Aleksandar waved his invention and cut into the flames, feeling the weight of power split at the ends of the staff. The fire changed direction, shifting as Aleksandar guided it with his machine. He stood unharmed, sparing his and Vida's lives.

Aleksandar cast the attack back at the Phoenix, and the killer rolled to his side.

The Phoenix held his arms up, breathing heavily. "How?"

He shot random bursts of flames like punches, and Aleksandar redirected them, protecting Vida at all costs.

"Vida, run!" Aleksandar shouted, coughing on the air, sweat dripping along his brow in the intense heat.

She hesitated, but sprinted into the smoke, lost in the haze. The Phoenix fired, and Aleksandar lunged to the side, hoping the madman would follow.

"Is this what you envisioned, Aleksandar? Such beauty and grace. You will not escape. Not again!"

The Phoenix chased Aleksandar through the ashes and flames. The fireworks had died to nothing, leaving the fair ablaze and in chaos.

As embers filled the sky, the wind blew hot cinders near Aleksandar's eyes, obstructing his vision. He ran into a woman with a round hat, and she fell into the nearby fire. Aleksandar pulled her out and pushed her behind a tent. He ducked as fire hit the ground where he stood, knowing his speed had faded. Pushing himself up, he found his feet and rushed through the smoke with his invention in hand.

Aleksandar's legs felt weak, and he knew he was slowing down. He couldn't outrun the madman, and his strength would fade before the Red Breath ran out of fuel. He turned and held his staff, the fire splitting around him, and he could feel the force and weight in his control. His feet slipped back on the gravel.

Blocking several hits, Aleksandar jumped to the side and rushed into a storage shack. A constable soared over the hedge line, but the Phoenix grabbed him by the throat, stuck a nozzle to his face, and burned him alive.

The killer dropped the man and pulled a primer cord from under his jacket. He lit the end and tossed it into the building. Aleksandar gulped as it landed beside him.

He picked up a steel lid as the bomb went off.

The force blew Aleksandar off his feet, throwing him through the planks of the tent and dropping him on his back.

It knocked the wind from his lungs, and Aleksandar arched his spine, a small piece of wood in his shoulder blade.

The Phoenix threw massive waves of fire. Aleksandar barely stood, pushing and pulling the attack apart, protecting himself while twisting and manipulating the energy in an arc around him. He was running out of strength; the weight of moving the flames with his staff was too heavy to hold.

He wasn't strong enough.

Aleksandar flung the fire with the rest of his might and darted between two burning tents, into the hedges, and to the gardens behind the World's Palace. He heard the madman's footsteps on his tail as twigs snapped behind him and the leaves crunched under his feet.

The destruction raged, and the darkness hid him away.

~

Kenneth raced after Aleksandar, jumping and dodging low-hanging branches. The path grew dark, and the shadows danced as embers and ash drifted between the tree trunks.

He chased with fury, breathing heavy, ready to catch his prey. Smacking his mask against unseen sticks, Kenneth ducked and followed the shadows, his feet pounding against the dirt. Once he heard only his own footsteps, he slowed to a stop and looked at the empty forest, seeing only twigs and trees with no sign of anyone else.

Even as the smoke thinned further from the festival, Kenneth realized he stood alone in the night. He glanced over his shoulder to the midway, which burned against the glass of the World's Palace, people screaming and fleeing the carnage.

Kenneth looked to the woods, dropped to his knees, and pulled off his hat, the mask attached to the rim.

"Ah!" Kenneth cried out.

Veins protruded from his neck, and sweat dripped down his jaw and chest as the rage in his muscles caused his shoulders to ache. Kenneth leaned back with his face to the night sky, resting in his defeat as the destruction continued behind him.

"Is this not my path? Am I not allowed to give him what he deserves?"

Kenneth screamed loud, his vocal cords cracking and his throat left tender.

He leaned forward, his cheeks red from the heat, and made fists out of his blistered hands, his knuckles tender and chapped. His hair lay over his stare, and he watched the ash floating around him.

Kenneth blinked and peered up at a man in a gray jacket, his head wrapped in a high scarf, so only his eyes were visible.

"And who—"

The man whipped out a metal rod with two prongs, and lightning sparked from the center, erupting into the air. It hit Kenneth's chest, and he convulsed, falling into the leaves. He clenched his body, his nerves stinging as if they were on fire, and the man held the weapon above him.

"Kenneth Forbes, by rights of the Peakeland Yard, you're to be detained for murders of the innocent and crimes against society. Do you submit?"

"Is that you, Nicoli?" he asked with a growl.

Nicoli squeezed the handle, and sparks flared off the ends, static humming in the air.

As the sting left his fingertips, Kenneth swiped Nicoli's feet and knocked his enemy to the ground. Nicoli jumped up and swung, flinging electricity into the dirt. Kenneth scurried between the trees and dodged the attacks, feeling the nerves in his body regulate.

Nicoli attacked again, and Kenneth barely dodged it, realizing Nicoli was quick, if not quicker.

He had to be smart.

Kenneth jumped between several redwoods and tucked himself into a divot, holding his breath. Nicoli whipped the weapon, and electricity pierced the bark. The wood scorched, and splinters blew off by the hundreds. Black scars marred the tree as leaves shifted away from the roots.

Kenneth smiled as his wait paid off. "Fool."

He whipped around the tree and squeezed the nozzles, setting the air aflame. Nicoli lost grip of the electric rod, his hands weak from the heat.

Kenneth trudged forward, and Nicoli tripped onto the ground, looking up to the madman. Kenneth leveled his fists and scorched the earth, holding the fire long and bright, ensuring the kill was his. It wouldn't be long before someone saw him on the hill, so he had to finish quickly.

Satisfied, he let go of the valve, and burned dirt was all that remained, but a dead man did not lie at his feet. Nicoli leaped from behind with the electric rod and rammed it into Kenneth's rib cage.

Lightning surged from the invention into his muscles, which tensed and twitched. His veins stuck out from his neck, and he gritted his teeth. Kenneth jerked his arms and knocked Nicoli's hands away. Nicoli jabbed again, and Kenneth smacked it aside, feeling his strength weaken, knowing he barely blocked the attacks.

The third blow struck Kenneth's chest, and the stinging pain surged through his limbs to the tips of his fingers. Losing his strength to push back, Kenneth collapsed to the ground into a pile of leaves, several floating over his body.

Nicoli held the rod true and looked down at his murderer, pulling his scarf down, pausing at the sight of Kenneth at his feet. His eyes widened, and his shoulders raised with his heavy breaths.

"I wish it wasn't you."

CHAPTER SIXTY-THREE

The plume of smoke over the Harvest Festival blurred as the night cooled and fires faded over the blackened midway, ashes covering the ground in a lingering haze.

A makeshift hospital was erected in front of the World's Palace, and they transported the injured inside, as all available doctors attended those with burns and wounds. Groans and crying echoed through the crackling flames, but most remained silent as the wind pushed the musk of death over warm embers.

Bernard searched the wreckage of a burned festival tent, looking to aid anyone in need, and constables shifted around him, tending to the injured. The smoke was still thick and pungent on his tongue. The glow of lanterns glistened in the haze.

"Help—"

Bernard paused, the faint mumble nearly lost in the cries and moans of other people.

"Hello?" Bernard closed his eyes, focusing on the surrounding sounds.

"Please."

Bernard turned to a woman stuck under a pile of collapsed crates trapped in the carnage. Bernard rushed over and lifted the boxes, making sure they did not fall back on top of her. Her arm was bleeding as she stared with a broken gaze and weak breath.

"Hang in there," Bernard said. "It's okay. It's over."

"Help me, sir."

"There are doctors nearby. May I move you?"

The woman nodded, and Bernard slid his arms under her knees and shoulders, carefully carrying her down the path. He walked into the tent and set her on one of the few cots, most of the injured on the ground.

Vida brushed by Bernard with a dirtied apron, her neck black on the backside. She helped a man onto the ground, propping his head.

Bernard rushed to her. "Vida."

She glanced over her shoulder. "Bernard. Thank goodness you're okay." She hugged him. "Were you here?"

"I was. Listen, I just set that woman over there, and she's bleeding out. She needs stitched up."

Vida turned. "You shouldn't have moved her."

"She didn't look good. I wasn't sure what to do."

"Follow me." Vida waved her hand, but Bernard stepped in her way.

"Vida, are you okay? Have you seen your neck?"

"I'm fine. It's not a burn, just soot or whatever comes from a firework. I'll be all right, I promise."

Bernard nodded and followed her to the woman. "Can you help her?"

Vida paused, looked her over, and swallowed hard. "I can't. She should wait for one of the other doctors."

"You can't?"

Vida held her hand. "I can't stitch. I mean, yes, I could, but I shouldn't."

"Vida, we don't know how much longer she has."

"If I mess up, I could hit a vein, and she'd bleed out."

"If you do nothing, she *will* bleed out."

A young child rushed into the tent. "Mum! Mum!"

He leaned next to the woman, and Vida stepped back. The mom had little energy and struggled to touch the boy's cheek.

"Mummy, are you okay?" he asked with his lower lip out. He turned to Vida, who stared at him with cloudy eyes. "Please help my mum."

Bernard set his hand on Vida's shoulder. "Vida."

"I can't."

"You must."

Vida breathed heavily and tightened her lips. She peered at her hand, her glove covered in blood, and pulled it off, focusing on her scar. It did not shake, and she let out a short, controlled breath. With a nod, she rushed to the supply station and grabbed a needle and thread. She leaned over the lady, and Bernard pulled the boy back.

Vida looked over the woman's arm, rubbing her forehead. The cut was not deep, but her wound was bleeding out. She could tell her eyes had glazed over but could see the point perfectly.

Vida held the needle as the woman looked on with a fading gaze, took a long breath and pushed the tip through the woman's skin. Despite her fear and the empty pit in her stomach, she ignored the tingling nerves and did not flinch. With each pass, doubt faded, and her grip was steady and calm in the procedure.

Bernard kneeled next to the boy as they looked at his mother, who cringed, gritting her teeth. Vida tied off the stitch, unable to look away from her work, her hands still steady. It was finished, and the arm was no longer bleeding.

"You did it," Bernard said.

The boy rested his head on his mother's lap, and she turned to Vida, rubbing her fingers through her son's hair. "Thank you."

"I hope I got it done before it was too late." Vida put some gauze against the wound and wrapped it with linen. "They will have blood to give you soon from what I'm told."

The mom nodded and rested her eyelids.

The boy grabbed Vida's arm. "Did you save my mum?"

"I believe so." Vida found a small smile.

The boy looked at Bernard. "She looks like an angel."

"Who?" Bernard asked.

"Her." The boy pointed to Vida, who stood speechless, tears building in her milky eyes.

Vida walked to the edge of the tent, covering her mouth, hushing her sobs. Bernard followed and pulled her close, squeezing the side of her arm. "Your mother is smiling. I'm sure of it."

"I hope."

A group of constables paced into the makeshift hospital with Owen and Nicoli at the front, pulling a stretcher with Lydia on top.

Bernard rushed out. "What happened?"

Owen waved them inside. "Mr. Griffin, we got him."

"Who?"

"The Phoenix. Nicoli captured him, and he's being transferred as we speak. Chief Constable Dekker is at the helm."

Vida let out a sigh of relief, her chest loosening and shoulders lowering.

Owen looked around, leaning on his cane. "I wasn't one hundred percent sure, Bernard, but you now have my full loyalty. I believe we desperately need your league more than we know."

Bernard nodded. "Now more than ever."

"People will recognize this could've been avoided," Owen said. "The Peake has already expressed their support."

Vida stepped forward, her hand in front of her. "Has anyone seen Aleksandar Scott?"

Owen glanced over his shoulder. "No. I don't believe we have."

Aleksandar sat in the dark, hiding in the shadows of the World's Palace. He breathed deeply with his eyes closed, his cheeks smothered with ash, streaks of tears creating lines down his face.

He rocked forward, his teeth chattering in the chill night, holding his knees against his chest. Not knowing how long it had been, he stayed silent, with the faint crackling of the Harvest Festival on the other side of the glass building.

Aleksandar pushed himself up and peeked around the edge, accepting the Phoenix did not know where he was. He watched his every step as he tried to stay quiet. He stepped into the light, the staff compressed on his back, and held his arm close as he made his way to the path, walking to the midway with a bloody arm.

The groans of injured people and doctors grew louder, and the smell of charred wood and burned fabric lingered. His skin was tight from the heat of the fire, leaving his lips chapped. With bloodshot eyes, he stared at the destruction the Phoenix left in his path.

The carnage he influenced and brought to Well's Peake.

Aleksandar searched the fair. His hands shook, and he thought he was going to fall to his knees, but he steadied himself, his mind racing to Vida. He picked up his pace in the faded smoke and passed several people crying next to bodies that lay lifeless on the ground.

His heart seemed to beat louder as he found a tent with doctors and nurses caring for the injured. As his thoughts blurred, his focus returned as they laid several bodies beside his feet. He stumbled as they set a boy on the ground, his arms limp at his sides. With empty eyes, he stared at nothing, absent from the world.

A tear ran down Aleksandar's cheek, and he looked away, smearing the ash on his face. He turned and looked through the crowd, noticing Nicoli resting near Lydia. The investigator rose and walked across the midway.

Aleksandar remained still, waiting to be arrested.

Nicoli stepped close and eyed the lane, letting out a deep breath. "Are you okay, Mr. Scott?"

No words came to mind, and he shook his head.

"We got him."

Aleksandar jerked around. "The Phoenix? You caught Kenneth Forbes?"

Nicoli batted an eye and lowered his voice. "I wouldn't let people know you had that information. They'd assume you had a part in this. From here on out, tell no one."

Aleksandar eyed the investigator as questions filled his mind. "Why—"

"Not here. Know while I doubted, Lydia did not, and her words were not misplaced."

Aleksandar turned. "She wrote those notes?"

Nicoli didn't answer his question. "All you should understand is, if not for you, more could've died tonight. You saved lives, Mr. Scott. You made a difference, and we stopped him. That is what's important, and we must remember that."

"But it came at a cost."

"That happens, sadly."

"What I did wasn't worth it."

"But you don't have to live in fear anymore. Something would have happened eventually."

"That's not true. He wouldn't have attacked if I just stayed home."

"For some reason, I don't believe that. He had grown brash and desperate. Find comfort that he's behind bars and will be transported soon. Well's Peake will see what you did here tonight."

Nicoli's words did little to comfort him. All Aleksandar could do was stare and let his mind accept whatever was said. He felt the weight of all the deaths on his shoulders. Someone's mother, father, son, or daughter would not be going home that night.

"Am I to be detained?" he asked.

"No. Many saw what you did. Most are not demanding an arrest as they once did."

"When will he be taken away? He's still a risk."

"He'll be removed by the end of the weekend. With the Harvest Exhibition before week's end, we want this city in good spirits."

A constable walked over. "Mr. Lucas, Constable May asked for you and Mr. Scott."

Nicoli nodded, and they followed the patrolman into the tent, a lantern's flame lighting the space.

Lydia lay on a stretcher, staring aimlessly. Her neck brace was broken, and her clothes singed from fire. Someone had wiped her face clean, small patches of scabs riddling her face. Her eyes batted towards Aleksandar, and Nicoli waved the other constable away.

"Mr. Scott. You survived." She gulped hard.

"Are you okay?" Aleksandar asked.

"I'm told I will be, but it hurts like hell." Lydia coughed up red mucus, and Nicoli wiped her mouth clean.

"You need to rest." Nicoli rubbed her forehead.

Lydia glanced over, and Aleksandar turned, Vida rushing to him.

"You're alive." Vida embraced him.

Aleksandar held her tight, not expecting to find her alive. A sense of dread lifted from his shoulders, goosebumps shifting up his arms. He tried not to cry. She didn't let go, and he felt her silent sobs in his chest.

"Vida, I'm so sorry. I tried so hard to tell you, but I wasn't sure he would show up."

Vida stepped back, sobbing. She stared at him and slapped him across the face. Aleksandar stumbled backward, but she grabbed hold of him and pulled him close again, crying in quiet anxiety with pale eyes of bliss.

Aleksandar looked to Lydia, who returned her gaze to the top of the tent. He glanced to Nicoli. "You saw him? For sure?"

Nicoli glared at him but nodded.

Aleksandar bit his lip, tasting the dirt, smelling the burned fibers of Vida's dress.

"Aleksandar." Lydia let her head roll to the side. "You can rest tonight."

Aleksandar looked to Nicoli, who shook his head no, but he leaned towards Lydia anyway. "Why did you send me the notes? Why not just tell me?"

"Intuition. Something wasn't lining up." Lydia grimaced. "To think I would have escorted you out if I saw you show up. What a mistake that would've been."

Nicoli waved a nurse down. "You need a proper hospital. I want someone else to look at you there."

Lydia nodded, and several shifted to her and picked up her stretcher. As they carried her away, Aleksandar tried to hold his tongue as Nicoli told him to, but he couldn't. Something clicked and felt wrong.

Aleksandar's chest surged, and he lifted his head. He let go of Vida and cupped her face. "I'll be right back."

Aleksandar rushed to the stretcher, but Nicoli blocked him from Lydia.

"I need to ask her something," Aleksandar said.

"She needs to rest. We'll talk later."

Nicoli turned away, but Aleksandar grabbed his jacket, stepping closer.

"You best unhand me," Nicoli said.

"Listen to me, please. Lydia said she wouldn't have let me in. Why would she say that if in the fourth letter she asked me to come? It makes little sense."

Nicoli's eyes widened, and he glanced at Lydia. He studied Aleksandar and leaned in. "Fourth letter? She only wrote three."

Aleksandar stood still as Vida walked to his side and held his arm. The doctors and nurses carried Lydia away, disappearing into the swarm of injured people, and although Nicoli hesitated, he rushed back to her side.

Aleksandar pressed his lips together, his hands trembling. His mind replayed the chaos, but he prayed the long night would not rise with the morning, knowing someone else may still be watching.

CHAPTER SIXTY-FOUR

Ahand caressed Aleksandar's shoulder, and he opened his eyes to the sunset outside Natalia's workshop. He rubbed the bridge of his nose and leaned back in the creaky chair. Natalia stood beside him with two cups of tea in her hands.

Aleksandar struggled not to dose off, stretching his face muscles. She set his cup on the workbench, the Lunarwheel in front of him, and walked to the dome window, staring into the forest valley.

The smell of fruit and a campfire filled Aleksandar's nostrils, and he closed his eyes with the potent aroma.

"How long have I been sleeping?" Aleksandar lifted the teacup and held it to his nose.

"A few hours. Perhaps a little more." Natalia walked back and sat in the chair next to him. "That's called Lapsang Souchong. A robust blend I found in the Eastern Mountains."

Aleksandar sipped his tea, thinking if a campfire had a delicious flavor, that was it. "My goodness. That's—"

"Different. It grows on you after a while."

Aleksandar took another drink and set down the cup. "You should have woken me sooner."

"You have worked endlessly the past three days, and before that, you fought off the madman himself. You needed some rest. We are not the machines you know, and with everything you've been through, you deserved it."

"We only have a few days left. It doesn't look like we're going to make it."

Natalia crossed her legs, bouncing the one on top. "There will be another exhibition, Aleksandar. Maybe not for a week or another month, but it'll come. This isn't the end."

To be so close, knowing defeat was possible, ached in Aleksandar's chest. The mental fatigue was setting in, and the exhaustion was overbearing. He didn't want to accept his failed invention after so much struggle.

"Has there been word from the Peakeland Yard?" Natalia asked. "What about Miss Fritz?"

Aleksandar set his cup to the side and worked on the Lunarwheel, opening the front plate and calibrating the internal gears. "Little. They gave me a pat on the back and told me I am no longer a suspect. That I helped saved lives, but I still get looks from people. Ellie has been with her brothers. According to her, if she wasn't handling the fallout, the brothers would throw away a third of their factories."

"That's good."

"I don't believe it."

"Why is that?"

"Something feels off. What happened at that festival was my fault."

Natalia lifted a pot off a nearby bench and poured tea into her blue cup. She refilled Aleksandar's as he lost himself in his work.

"Did you ever hear about the condition where people are incapable of sleeping?" Natalia asked. "They're always in a daze, which makes daily tasks difficult to focus on. They live as if going through the motions, their mind unable to settle on anything."

"Do you think that of me?"

"Of course not. You're just pushing yourself too hard, is all, but seeing you work so diligently brought it to mind. Rather saddening, if you ask me. To be handed all hours of the day yet be unable to make the most of them. Instead, we sleep, but we create marvels. My point is, you need to relax your mind."

"That is something. I know someone who could provide more information if you're interested."

"Please do. I was born with an unnatural curiosity. Books were my teachers, and I feel I could never have enough."

Aleksandar paused and glanced over, nodding his head. His thoughts faded, and he had no words. He enjoyed listening while he worked, and it helped him focus.

He tinkered as Natalia watched him, hoping for another marvel. The young inventor took a sip of tea, looking to keep his mind busy.

Natalia tapped the counter, studying the crystal-like glass of the machine. "If you were to finish it, have your thoughts changed? Do you think humanity would be ready?"

"I figured we're the ones that need to be prepared. If we are, we have a chance. The future will come whether or not we want it. As Bernard said, we just need to guide it."

"The day this engine becomes what I dream, I'll have made my last mark, and you will have created your first. You'll soon be able to close this chapter and begin another."

"I'm looking forward to the next, but I think I'll hold the page until it turns." Aleksandar paused and straightened his back, staring at the machine.

"What's wrong?" Natalia held up her cup.

"Something's missing, Natalia. It makes little sense." Aleksandar stood up and took his drink to the dome window, the light fading on the horizon.

"We will figure it out. I promise."

"No, I mean, not with the Lunarwheel, but with Kenneth. Him being the Phoenix makes no sense."

Natalia sipped her tea and rubbed the side of her cheek. "Why do you think that?"

"I don't know yet." Aleksandar put one hand on his head and paced alongside the stage. "With how people are acting, something's off. Every piece is being thrown around like that damn machine. If only it stuck together—"

Aleksandar glanced at the machine, lifting his chin in the sunlight.

Natalia uncrossed her legs. "What?"

Aleksandar rushed to the workbench and set down his drink. He opened a brown box and took out several pre-built pieces. He put them inside the Lunarwheel and joined them with rods and braces, connecting them to wires.

Natalia set down her tea and watched over his shoulder, pulling out her journal to write everything down.

It was right there. His own concept, to amplify the surface tension of a liquid. Control. It was clear. Aleksandar closed the plate on the front and flipped the switch.

Natalia reached out. "Aleksandar, don't rush—"

The Lunarwheel erupted to life with a fine-tuned hum, like a violist's bow on a string. Both inventors stepped back, watching as the machine glowed, the humming low and dense. The teacups rattled on the workbench, along with loose metal nearby.

Aleksandar's hazel eyes inspected the engine as it developed more into a caged beast. His heartbeat raced, and adrenaline pulled him from his weary state, waiting for disaster. He was ready to run behind the shield, expecting the flooding water to soak his shoes, but then silence. The kind you find in the forest after nature falls asleep in a rainstorm with stars above.

The room glowed with a pure, soothing aura, light filling them with a gentle calm as the humming of the engine rang throughout his ears in a beautiful pitch.

Aleksandar and Natalia stood for several moments, unflinching. He stepped forward, and Natalia grabbed his arm. He moved to the panel and flipped many switches, and the humming grew louder, the water twirling inside the device.

Despite Natalia's stare of disapproval, Aleksandar placed his palm on the glass. It was warm, and his skin rippled like waves in a cove. The power surged through him, and he smiled, his teeth gleaming in the night, and turned to Natalia with enthusiastic eyes.

She put her journal into her vest pocket, pushed her hair behind her shoulders, and examined the switches.

Aleksandar studied his reflection in the glass and pulled on his arm, lost in the light.

"It was right there." Natalia held her cheek as it grew rosy. "Every day, it stared us in the face."

Aleksandar looked at the teacups and lifted them, the liquid leaning to the side closest to the machine as if it was being pulled to the source. He handed Natalia her cup, and they turned to each other. Natalia nodded, and Aleksandar smiled, running his hand through his hair. She held up her cup, and he pressed his against hers, toasting with their drinks.

Aleksandar let out a long sigh, his stomach fluttering. "We did it."

"No, you did."

"You must have figured it out at some point. I only recreated it."

"It's both of ours. You captured my biggest disappointment and turned it into what will be your greatest achievement." Natalia pressed her lips together and smiled.

Aleksandar glanced over his shoulder at the last arch of the sun through the pine trees. He could make the difference she always desired. A warmth filled his chest, and he wanted to cry, but all he could do was blush and smile.

Aleksandar looked at the engine and into his cup, the liquid shifting to the side.

He glanced at the machine and tossed the tea at it. The liquid slowed in the air, gravitating towards the source and sticking to its side.

Natalia's mouth opened, and she walked to the Lunarwheel. "Our hand has reached beyond humanity, Aleksandar. Let's be sure to guide it. With Tesla's electricity, we will make this portable and do what we both hoped for."

"So this is it?" Aleksandar asked.

"It is," Natalia said.

"What do you want to do with it first?"

Natalia smiled, her teeth gleaming. "Do you remember the Steamrail that was destroyed?"

"Yes?"

"How does the Lunar Rail sound? From Redwood to Belagrad, the city of light."

"I guess this is where we change history."

"This is where."

Aleksandar felt the energy throbbing against his chest. Looking with an enriched gaze, he admired the device, but his smile faded, and his mind wandered.

"Aleksandar?" Natalia asked.

He licked his lips. "I'm fine. I just hope this is a new chapter, Natalia."

She put her hand on his shoulder. "You did well. Within days your past struggles will pass. You should consider something else, though. What will *you* do after that?"

"What do you mean?"

"Well, you'll have fulfilled your vision of creating something good in the world for your friend. Don't you think you should do something for yourself?"

He nodded. "The other night, when you mentioned moving on, it got me thinking. To move away would be nice. I'd prefer a more simple life, a less dangerous one. I'd make hats."

"Hats?"

"Yeah. Everyone needs a good hat."

Natalia smiled and nodded.

They both looked at the machine, the blue glow glistening through the room, water droplets forming on the outside.

Natalia set her hand on the glass, the light glowing between her fingers. "There's a part of me that thinks you and I will do this until the end of our days."

CHAPTER SIXTY-FIVE

Brittle leaves brushed against Vida's shoes as she stood in the courtyard of Downton University. She gazed down the brick walkway in the cloudy afternoon, the grass trimmed with a tint of blue.

The buildings, made of red sandstone, rose several stories high with a trail that split in two, wrapping around a central tower that connected into the grand halls. Vida smiled as she walked down the path. Pine and fir trees surrounded the courtyard, their sharp aroma filling the air. A fountain with a statue of an angel rested in the center, wrapped in white brick. Vida paused and looked, losing herself in the pearl eyes.

Just like the one at the World's Fair, water flowed down the wings, the cool mist brushing against her cheeks. Pushing her hair back, she hesitated, holding her gloved hands in front of her. She bit her lip and pulled the glove off her scarred hand.

Vida dipped her fingers into the icy water and embraced the chill that ran up her arm, the breeze cooler than before. Pulling her hand out, she stared, realizing how her thumb curved towards her finger. Not by much, but enough.

Vida studied the white statue, listening to the droplets fall into the fountain, finding a sense of calm.

Nurses and doctors paced by her, and Vida looked down the path, quick to follow them into the grand hall.

The hallways were cut from stone and tall planks of redwood. It smelled like the forest, a rich musk lingering through the glamorous halls. There was noise echoing down the hallway, and she walked to the end, discovering cots and curtains for the many injured who recovered there.

Doctors and nurses checked on patients, reminding her of the night at the Harvest Festival, only less chaotic and controlled. She stepped forward, walking at the edge of the beds, rubbing her forearm. Several rested on their pillows, all bandaged. While most slept, a few played cards on the blankets or conversed with the person next to them.

"Miss Harvey?"

Vida turned to Lydia lying in a bed further from everyone else. Nicoli stood near the headrest, and a little girl sat in Lydia's arms as the sun beamed through the narrow windows.

"Constable May." Vida stepped closer. "I see the university has been a big support over the past week?"

"Yes. With the hospitals full, the headmaster was sympathetic. A rather bold gesture."

"It was kind. Few would be so willing."

"Indeed. Miss Harvey, you might remember Mr. Lucas."

Nicoli nodded.

"What about me?" The girl glanced up with blushed cheeks.

Lydia smiled and held her tight. "This little one is Rosaline, my daughter."

Vida leaned and waved. "Hello, Rosaline. You must be so proud of your mother."

"She's the nicest." Rosaline turned to Nicoli. "Right, Dad?"

Vida eyed Nicoli, and he smirked.

"Maybe it's best we give Mum some rest, honey," Nicoli said.

"Ah, no. Just a wee longer."

Nicoli looked at Lydia. "I need to prepare for tonight. We should go."

Lydia grabbed his hand. "He assured me the Peake would be there. Be safe."

Nicoli rubbed Rosaline's back. "Give Mum lovings."

Rosaline put her head on Lydia's stomach, and Lydia hugged her the best she could, wincing.

"Good day, Miss Harvey." Nicoli lifted Rosaline in his arms, and they walked off, the little girl waving at Vida.

Vida returned the gesture and looked at Lydia. "Are you okay?"

"As well as could be. Please, sit if you're not in a hurry." Lydia eyed the bottom of the cot.

Vida sat, looking at the bandages on Lydia's collar. "Will you be left with a scar?"

"No. My neck needs a few weeks to heal, but I'll be all right. I was lucky once again."

"Glad to hear."

Vida nodded, gazing around the room, inspired by so many being treated and attended to.

"It was you in the bed when I last saw you. How did that class ever work out?"

Vida chuckled. "Not well, to be honest. You should have kept me there."

"Oh, I'm sorry."

"Don't be. It helped me in a lot of ways. It was tough, but I learned a lot about myself. What you tried telling me weeks ago, that is. I walked in here, and no one is staring. I'm not sure why I thought they would."

"What appears big to us doesn't always to another." Lydia rubbed her neck.

"I know, I shouldn't complain. Mine is nothing compared to the stares you mentioned."

"Doesn't make yours any less."

Vida folded her arms across her lap, looking at her hand. "The night of the Harvest Festival, I had to—accept people seeing my scar, me knowing the severity of the situation. Their lives were literally at my fingertips, and when I realized how selfish I was, I knew no matter what, others needed me more. I swore an oath to them. I'm here for a consult about getting rid of my scar because, with it, I can't fulfill my promise."

Lydia smiled. "I understand that feeling."

Vida rubbed the back of her hand. "I suppose I should let you rest."

"Thank you, Miss Harvey. It was nice chatting, and I wish you the best."

Lydia pushed herself up, so her back wasn't as bent, pulled her neck to the side, and took a deep breath.

Vida stood. "Let me help you." Vida grabbed Lydia's waist and lifted her, positioning her at a slight angle and fluffing her pillows behind her shoulders.

"That's better, thank you." Lydia closed her eyes for a moment.

"Of course." Vida stood and started to walk away.

"Miss Harvey?"

"Yes?"

"My passion as a constable is everything to me, along with being a mother. I grew up in it through my father, so it means a lot, but if I had a chance to cure my injury knowing I'd risk never serving again, I'd take it. Not from desperation, but because I wish to play with my daughter. Do you see what I mean?"

Vida smiled towards the window into the hedge garden. "I do."

Lydia reached up and grabbed Vida's hand. Her hands were calloused but tender to the touch. Whether it was the attacks or the denial at Blackwell, Vida had a sense of surety, knowing the future was open and possibilities were happening. It comforted her, knowing her moment had arrived.

"Get some rest." Vida stood.

Lydia nodded, leaned backed, and looked to the gardens.

Vida smiled and walked past the foot of the cots, into the grand hallway that towered into arches above her and extended to the end of the university.

As she climbed the circular steps to the third floor, she couldn't help but think to her mother. It wasn't a matter of whether she would be proud of Vida, but knowing she was. The doubt faded from her mind, and Vida paused outside a closed door.

She lifted her arm, staring at the scar, knowing the moment she walked through that opening, her life was going to change. Whether the best or the worst was to come, she would know. Vida bit the corner of her lip and rubbed her fingers around her thumb, feeling the tense nerve underneath.

She closed her hand and knocked.

Footsteps shuffled inside, and a shadow lingered at the crack beneath the wood frame. Dr. Gray opened the door. His desk sat in front of the curved window, overlooking the Downton Courtyard. He looked to Vida, finding a smile.

Vida held her chin high with glimmering eyes. "Hello, Dr. Gray."

"Miss Harvey, I've been expecting you."

CHAPTER SIXTY-SIX

Fire reflected in Natalia's eyes as she watched the flames caressing the logs in the fireplace. The night was young, and the wind gusted against the window of her study.

She leaned her head back with a smile and sipped on blueberry tea, the sweetness lingering on her lips. The warm cup was soothing against her fingertips as a draft of air touched her.

Natalia turned in her chair and set down her drink, lifting her pen. She dipped it in the inkwell and opened her journal.

We have finally finished it. I cannot believe what I wished for so long has transpired. It's rather interesting knowing what we desire lies there for weeks, months, and once we discover it, it all seems so simple.

Maybe tunnel vision does come with age, blinding us from fresh perspectives, from the spark that inspired us into who we are today. Aleksandar is an incredible inventor who has yet to blossom, but he is becoming what we need him to be. Despite his inexperience and setbacks, he has shown great fortitude and returned stronger. While he may fail once more, I have faith he will recover, but there will be a day where he does not break, a moment none will forget.

Natalia paused, holding the pen over the paper. She looked up, and her smile faded. She rubbed the edges of the journal, the ripples of the pages soft on her fingertips.

While I ponder the success I share with Aleksandar, I cannot help but feel guilt for my old apprentice and the failure we shared. She was so sharp, cunning, and determined. I failed her in the months after the revealing of the Lunarwheel, yet she stood by my side for so long, even when she wanted to leave.

It is returning to me… I remember the day it all ended, growing tired of my weak composition and inability to stand on my own feet. I was determined to be the inventor society recognized before the Oakvale Exhibition. It was the only way I could live with myself.

When her thoughts became destructive, with ideas that were groundbreaking and transforming, she followed a different path, a darker path. Her work grew manipulative, and I feared I started that journey in my absence. I knew she had to be stopped. She lacked control, and her ambitions were, as Aleksandar would say, beyond humanity's grip.

If I had not saddened her enough, when the day came, I took the Spark back and relinquished my role as master. I crushed her. It was hard on her with her parents' passing and my failure as a mentor. I realized she was devastated and broken, but I was in no position to be the positive influence she needed. I left her in good care, but I worry they weren't successful in guiding her to a happier future.

That was the last I saw of her. She is but a distant memory now, but even I can feel the pain she experienced. When the thoughts are not there, and my mind fades, I pray she has done well and has recovered. She deserved the world.

Natalia took a deep breath.

It makes me think I did more wrong throughout my years than good. What did I accomplish? The preparation I strived for is nonexistent, and with the World's Fair, I stand as one in a crowd of thousands. My moment of redemption has come, a path so many should follow, so we may embrace the day that Well's Peake shines again in the golden harvest.

I want to shine again, so it may be a day I never forget. A day I may stand beside

Aleksandar and know I discovered my purpose.

Natalia dipped her pen in ink.

I'm ready to recover, to move forward, and stand before the city so they may see me for who I truly am.

CHAPTER SIXTY-SEVEN

Kenneth stared at the brick wall with bloodshot eyes, trapped in his cell. Iron bars rested against his spine, and his mind focused on the wall that reminded him of his childhood.

That bloody brick.

He dragged his cot towards the red surface but was yanked back, a chain on the leg of the bed. He flexed his jaw and sat on the edge, picking at the brick with his fingernails.

Abbey rested in his thoughts, and he paused, looking at his cracked hands, dried blood spots in the folds on his palms and knuckles.

She did not deserve what I gave her… No, she did.

His eyes were crimson with deep veins, strained from the lack of sleep. His face was tight as the bones pressed against his skin. He licked the saltiness off his cracked lips, inhaling the cold musk of the room. As the days passed, he refused to eat and looked like a deranged animal from an old forest.

There were two vacant cages between him and the office, and lanterns hung on the walls. The cobblestone floor was clean as if the cells were never used.

Growing more uncomfortable in his detainment, he sighed louder and picked at the brick until his finger turned bloody.

"This is cruel. I might have spent my wealth fixing places such as this if I knew they existed."

Kenneth looked over his shoulder and scowled, receiving no attention. He stepped to the locked gate and tapped his finger against the metal, the bar ringing in the hallway.

"*Why* am I still here?" he shouted, staring down the cells.

Kenneth kicked the hinges, stubbing his toe, his nerve stinging. He glanced up, and Nicoli stood in the lantern's light, walking down the corridor with slow steps.

Kenneth eyed the man like an animal about to strike and thrust his bloody hand through the cell, Nicoli just out of reach. "I have complaints about this so-called prison of yours. We aren't at the Peakeland Yard. Why?"

Nicoli ran his fingers through his hair, his gaze never flinching. "Mr. Forbes, I warned you, if I had to come back here, I'd muzzle you. I suggest you go to sleep or eat. You will receive answers in the morning."

"Get on with it, you putz. No one deserves to sit in this hellhole. How about we wait in that cozy little office of yours?"

"You'll regret not cherishing this place while you had the chance."

"I'm not being sent somewhere uglier, am I?"

"You're on your way to Redwood."

Kenneth's face flushed white, and his grin vanished. "Oh."

Nicoli remained expressionless.

Kenneth raised his brows. "Do you smile, Mr. Lucas? I can't help but notice you seem disappointed that you have me. Am I not enough? Not who you're looking for, perhaps?"

Nicoli pressed his lips together, not giving Kenneth the satisfaction.

Kenneth stepped back and wiped his dripping finger on his burned jacket. "I almost had him, you know. Mr. Scott. I thought I deserved to kill him, but for reasons unbeknownst to me, he keeps getting away."

Nicoli eyed the man and chattered his teeth. "Is there any part of Kenneth Forbes alive in there?"

Kenneth lowered his gaze and stared at the cobblestone. He did not feel himself, as the man on the hill that society knew, the husband Amia loved. He looked at his blistered hands and swallowed hard, sitting on the edge of the cot.

"Do you wonder when people die if they are lifted to paradise?" Kenneth rubbed his hand.

"That depends on the person. If you are talking about yourself, I would worry."

"No. My wife. She was an exquisite soul and deserved more than what she received. All to save me. She should've been the one to walk out of the flames."

"You don't seek paradise?"

"No. I fear that for he who has destroyed his life and the lives of many, redemption would not be offered."

"Maybe at one point, but I can't tell you if you seek forgiveness now, that you'd be forgiven."

"As long as Amia sees the eternal light. Her sacrifice for this husk of a man warrants it." Kenneth looked to himself.

Nicoli paused and stepped closer to the cell. "So let me ask you. Did you remove the brace from the invention on your house?"

Kenneth nodded. "Yes."

"Did you burn your manor down on purpose?"

Kenneth leaped to the bars, showing his teeth. Nicoli stepped back, out of harm's reach.

"How dare you assume I would hurt my wife. It is Aleksandar Scott who's responsible for her death."

Nicoli's eyes widened. "Why would you say that?"

"Because it was his invention that destroyed my home. Why do you think I've been after him?"

"You were the one who removed the safety mechanism."

"He sabotaged it! Him alone."

Nicoli tilted his head. "You suspect he did it on purpose?"

"I know he did. There was a witness."

"Who?"

Kenneth held his gaze, his eyes strained and heavy. "You know."

Nicoli angled his head. "What do I know, Mr. Forbes?"

"I heard rumors, but I didn't connect the two. The attack on your life. It was him, I guarantee it. The masked man."

"He told you Aleksandar Scott was looking to kill you?"

Kenneth's grin stretched across his face, his cheeks tight. "Why am I here?"

"You believed him?"

"Why am I not at the Peake?"

"Has he been the one pulling your strings? Did you go mental, and that's why he wanted you stopped?"

"He did *not* control me." Kenneth licked his lips. "I am the Phoenix, and I know no master, but you do. Did he give you that nifty invention to capture me? Do you answer his calls?"

Nicoli stared. "No, but he will mine."

"He's not as tough as he portrays. His talk of the seasons is empty. What makes you think he'll come here?"

Nicoli held his composure and walked away.

Kenneth grabbed the bars and pushed his cheek against the raw iron. "You play a dangerous game, Nicoli. You don't believe you can capture him yourself, do you?"

"Who says I'm alone."

Kenneth pulled himself tight against the cell, watching with inflamed eyes as the inspector walked into the other room. He blew air out of his nose and remained quiet, eyeing the cobblestone floor.

~

Nicoli closed the door, locked it, walked to the window behind a bare desk, and peeked out behind dusty curtains. He looked for any sign of constables, impressed he could not spot one, knowing they hid in the shadows.

He pulled the curtain back and glanced at the bottom drawer of the cabinet, his weapon ready to capture the man who murdered his wife, who nearly killed Lydia and Monty. The killer who'd haunted his life for years, intruding on his soul. Nicoli's thoughts drifted to Lydia, picturing her on that cot, not knowing if she would fully recover. Running his fingers along his face, he turned around and paused.

In the shadows, the masked man stood in the corner, his hands behind him. He leaned off the wall, remaining where he was.

Nicoli rolled his shoulders, staring at the blank, empty eyes.

"You looked surprised," the masked man said.

"I'm not. I assumed you'd double-cross me after I captured him."

"But you did it, anyway."

Nicoli cracked his fingers. "You gave me little choice."

"I gave you years to decide. I could have let you live the life you choose, but you are responsible for where you now stand. Why didn't you just move on after Redwood? The pain could have ended, if not lessened as the seasons passed."

Nicoli stepped towards his desk, rubbing his thumbs against his fingertips.

"I admire your passion," the masked man said. "Know I am sorry. Mallory was in the wrong place at the wrong moment."

Nicoli clenched his fists. "You think yourself clever?"

The masked man paused. "Thank you for the compliment."

"It wasn't one. You can't even fathom you are deranged."

The masked man blinked. "I am curious. Tell me."

"Your problem is you believe yourself wise. Knowledge is a curse to people like you because you lack the ability to balance what you know and how to handle it. You start small, but once you do things over and over, you grow mad and learn how to influence the situation. Manipulate people's nature against them. You stop doing it on purpose, and it becomes an instinct until you realize you're the monster."

"Why are you telling me this?"

Nicoli furrowed his eyebrows. "While you stand there and try to influence me, you are too blind to see you've been manipulated by yourself. I'm not afraid of you, but *you* should be."

Nicoli's breath grew heavy, and a sob escaped his lips.

The masked man glanced at Nicoli. "We already—"

Nicoli whipped the drawer open and reached in, finding it empty. He bit his lip and slammed his palms against the desk. The masked man stepped forward with the electric rod in his grip, standing tall. Nicoli stepped around the cabinet, and the hair on his arm rose as static filled the air.

"Even with it, you have lost." Nicoli never flinched.

The masked man lifted his fist and opened his fingers. Three constable badges rattled off the floor.

No.

"Your constables of the Peake were no match. Did you expect more than a few? The Peake lacked the same faith in my existence."

It will not end like this.

Nicoli lurched for the masked man, who dodged his strike, and the room erupted with electricity. Light flashed against the walls, nearly blinding Nicoli. The masked man swung the weapon, and the surge missed, hitting the desk. Splinters exploded from the top, showering the room.

Nicoli pulled a nightstick from behind a shelf and struck the man across the mask, cracking it down the middle. The electric rod bounced onto the carpet.

The masked man thrust his hand forward, grabbing Nicoli's throat and pinning him against the wall. He punched Nicoli in the face, hitting his cheekbone with each strike. Nicoli's face grew bloody, and the masked man threw him to the floor.

The masked man realigned his mask and stomped on Nicoli's back, shouting as loud as he could. Nicoli pushed himself up, but the masked man kicked him in the stomach, knocking the air from his lungs.

Nicoli looked past the carpet fibers as the masked man picked up the electric rod, the power humming off the prongs. He tried to roll over but was too weak.

The masked man lifted the weapon and thrust it into Nicoli's back.

~

Kenneth held his face against the bars, watching the light surge through the cracks in the frame, the sound of electricity buzzing from the office.

The door creaked open, and the masked man walked in with a box in his grip. Kenneth dropped his hands and stepped back against the brick wall, claustrophobia settling over him. Pieces of rusted iron clung to his skin, the bar imprints visible across his taut face.

"Ah," Kenneth said. "If only he ended you for me."

The masked man faced him, standing silent and still.

"Be quick about it. I grow tired of knowing if I deserve life or death."

"I am here to release you," the masked man said.

Kenneth tilted his head, smiling. "I'd appreciate that, but tell me something. Why go through the endless trouble just to free me?"

"I have no desire to, so make no mistake; I'm not doing this because I wish. You are playing a role in events yet to come."

The masked man stared, and Kenneth's eyes narrowed, a pit in his stomach growing, waiting for the killer to be done with him. The man set the box on the ground, unhooked the lid, and set the Red Breath on the cobblestone.

Kenneth pushed his tongue against his cheek. "You know what I intend to do." Kenneth rubbed his hand against the brick, each bump on his fingertips. "And what of Mr. Lucas?"

"He is no longer a concern."

Kenneth noticed the blood dripping from under the man's mask.

"What will you do once I'm freed?" Kenneth asked.

"Worry about yourself. You will do your part, and then you are to flee to the hills and never return. They left nothing for you in Well's Peake."

"After tonight, I'll have no reason to stay." Kenneth stepped forward, but the masked man did not move. "Is there something else you wish to say, dear creator?"

"Know everything you've done is because it was written."

Kenneth lifted his eyebrow.

"I'm surprised you have yet to go straight to Mr. Scott's home. Have you forgotten where he lives?"

Kenneth snarled, and the masked man nodded.

"You will find your possessions in this box, along with his address."

The two stared at each other.

"Yes, Kenneth. I know you have been there before when you robbed Aleksandar. Did the madness cloud your memory?"

The masked man walked away without a second glance, and Kenneth rushed to the bars. He tried to slip on the gantlets and gear, straining for the weapons. They were almost out of reach, but he wrapped his finger around the glove and pulled it through the opening.

"You could not have known I was there!"

The masked man disappeared into the office, and Kenneth listened to the body dragging across the floor, a door closing moments later.

Kenneth lay on the cobblestone, pausing as he looked to the ceiling. Amia flashed through his mind, and he rubbed his hands together.

He secured the machine to his arms and held his fists to the cell hinges. Fire screeched from the gauntlets and encased his chamber as he laughed in furious delight.

CHAPTER SIXTY-EIGHT

Moonlight cascaded through the leafless branches of Well's Peake, the forest slowly shifting in the frigid harvest air. The masked man walked out of an alley and into the park, taking a path less traveled.

A high collar hid most of his face, and he shifted off the pathway, wandering into the woods. There was no cobblestone, just dead leaves and broken branches on a narrow dirt trail alongside the river.

The rushing sound of water grew loud, and the breeze cooled as he stepped beside the stream. His eyes looked to the moon as the city slept comfortably. He stood, embracing the quiet moment, the calm before the chaos.

The masked man lifted his hand and rubbed his fingers along his face, feeling the crack down the center of his mask. He reached around, untied the back, and pulled it off, the breeze against his skin. As the mask rested in his fingertips, he rubbed his thumb across the cheek, making sure not to drop it.

With a deep breath, he tossed it into the river, and the water filled the crack and eye slits.

He watched as the mask floated along the ripples, disappearing into the shadows of the twilight.

~

Aleksandar rolled in his sheets as they tightened around him, sticking to him as he sweated despite the harvest cold. His eyelids twitched, and his hands gripped the blanket, pulling it close to his chest.

His eyes jarred open, and he breathed heavy, Shae glancing back to him with a wide gaze. He sat up, his hair sticking up on the side, and wiped his cheek with his hand. His head slumped as he drifted to sleep, but he jerked awake and looked out the window to the moon behind few clouds.

Aleksandar closed his hands, attempting to stop the shakes. His dreams were growing vivid, and he was feeling the exhaustion. He bit his lip and reached out to Shae, petting her feathers.

"It's okay, little one. We're okay."

Aleksandar set his feet on the frigid floor, a shiver running up his legs.

"I don't think we're going to sleep much tonight. Want to go for a walk?"

Shae perked up and rocked back and forth. Aleksandar smiled and stood, walking to the closet. He slipped on a sweater and his pants and walked out of the bedroom. Pausing in the hallway, he looked into his empty guest room, nodding as he strolled downstairs. Shae followed, and Aleksandar put on his coat, wrapping a scarf tight around his face. He set his bowler hat on his head and pulled the brim to his eyebrow, wandering into the frosty night.

The wind blew, and Aleksandar's cheeks grew red. A crisp chill at his skin pulled him from his tired state. Shae soared ahead as pines reached over the cobblestone road, swooping low, staying at Aleksandar's side in complete control.

Flakes of snow danced in the air, far enough apart to blend in with the last of the falling leaves.

"I don't understand, Shae. You'd think I would sleep through the night now. I wish Ellie wasn't so busy with her brothers' cleanup."

Aleksandar walked into the park and paused on the bridge, looking to the river. The current was strong, splashing against the white stone. He shuffled down and around and rested on the bench, the bitter steel doing little to keep him warm. The mist was thick enough to settle like cold water in his mouth.

Shae landed on a wet rock and stuck her beak into the water, fluffing her feathers. The rushing sounds of the river patted against the rocks where shards of ice formed. Shae leaped and landed on the railing with a light thud, cuddling against Aleksandar with her wings tucked.

Aleksandar glanced at her. "What are you doing, love?"

Shae rubbed her head sideways, looking curiously into the distance. Aleksandar listened to the silence of the night, leaning back with his hands in his pockets.

It made little sense. It was over, he should be able to rest and feel as if he accomplished something, but he felt hollow. His friend's vision did not seem fulfilled, and an urge lurked inside him. It could be an unsatisfied desire to invent more or a pit of defeat. He wasn't sure.

Shae peeked her head up and rushed to the river's edge, nipping at the tiny fish. Aleksandar hummed, watching her bob back and forth. She snatched something from the water, flew back, and dropped it on the bench.

"Shae! It's all wet." Aleksandar slid away, pulling his hands from his pockets. His pants damp.

Shae pecked at the debris, and Aleksandar picked it up, flicking it off the tips of his fingers. He flipped it over, finding himself face to face with a mask, cracked down the center. It was blue with silver beads, like rain on a window.

Aleksandar brushed the mask with his thumb and lifted it to the moonlight. He swallowed hard and lost himself as he stared into the eye slits, catching something in the distance.

Aleksandar lowered his hand, his gaze fixated on a red glow that kissed the bottom of the clouds, a warmth filling the air. He glanced over his shoulder, looking to the other horizon, still blue under the moon.

Shae shifted back to the river, ignoring Aleksandar's quivering lip as he dropped the mask on the ground.

"Shae, let's go. Come on."

Gray plumes rose above the empty treetops, and Aleksandar's heart dropped, freezing in his spot. Barely visible at first, the smoke darkened, turning crimson in the sky.

"Shae, now!"

Aleksandar sprinted off onto the trail and into the park. He leaped off the path, running into the thicket to the hill that loomed ahead of him, full of old oaks that hid what was on the other side. He ignored the sticks that slapped against his face, nearly knocking his hat off.

Shae soared above him, and Aleksandar's heart pounded in his chest. His fingertips tingled from the freezing temperature.

Please be a dream. Wake up, Aleksandar.

Aleksandar tripped on the slippery slope and pulled himself up with the nearby hedges. He slipped again and used his hands to stay up, digging his fingernails into the dirt and broken leaves. He reached the top of the crest and slowed to a halt. Shae swooped in front of him, and his breath hovered in the air.

Aleksandar opened his eyes and watched in horror.

Flames consumed the North Hills and the forest behind the World's Fair, ash falling like snow on the hilly city.

Aleksandar swallowed hard as the heat brushed against his face. He sprinted into the valley as Well's Peake burned under the pale moonlight.

CHAPTER SIXTY-NINE

With a satchel on his back, Hugh wandered the city streets lit by gaslights and the moon's dim glow. His cold fingertips gripped the leather straps, and he kept his head down, shifting throughout Well's Peake.

Every shadow in the corner of his eye sent chills down his spine. He heard they captured the Phoenix, that Kenneth Forbes was behind bars, but he knew better than to think he was safe. The dark alleyways were his teachers, and to grow comfortable to any degree was a death sentence.

With a tug on the brim of his hat, he paced through South Hills, his gaze drifting to anyone who passed by.

Hugh rounded the street corner, and a couple ran into him. He stumbled, catching himself on the lamppost as they rushed across the cobblestone and disappeared around the block. Hugh squinted at them and shook his head, pulling his satchel back over his shoulder.

He walked down the path and paused at a stoop, eyeing the boarding house behind it. With a heavy sigh, he placed his hand on the ledge where Abbey used to sit, looking to the roads with dreams of helping people.

He sniffled and felt the chill spread through his body. His empty stare focused on nothing, and the dirty musk of the coal factories filled his nose and coated his tongue. It was familiar and comforting despite the scratchiness it left in his throat. With a moment of hesitation, he walked away and turned into the dark alleyway, stopping under the single gaslight that led into it.

He reached behind a trash bin and pulled out a lantern, grabbing a long stick with a burned end. He lifted it into the light, pulled down the flame, and lit his lantern. He walked into the alley, to the cubby where he and Abbey would sleep, talk, and survive.

Her blanket still lay in the dirt. Hugh picked it up from the ground and held the frayed fabric in his hands, pressing it against his forehead. Despite the smell, the shampoo still lingered.

Mint and lavender.

Hugh opened his satchel, stuffed her blanket inside, and sat on the wood crate next to the brick wall. He set the lantern down as his scarf whipped in the wind, tears blowing off his face.

She was always there for him, and the moment she needed him most, he wasn't. His lower lip pushed out, and he rubbed his pants, feeling the thread at his fingertips.

Abbey stepped in when he had no one and filled a hole that he never could himself. Despite the fights, long nights, and freezing frost, they always made it through.

Hugh covered his face with his hands and held in his sobs. With a quivering breath, he wiped his tears away, stood, and nodded.

It's okay, Hugh. I'm all right.

He hesitated, holding the lantern to the bricks. Hugh pulled one out, revealing Abbey's secret stash. He reached in and paused, finding a letter with his name on the front. With the lantern high, he looked into the hole, seeing nothing else.

The envelope had black smudges in a few spots. He peeked around and sat, opening the note.

My darling Hugh,

 The days have been uncertain, and I don't know where we'll be by the frost season or the seasons after that.

I understand why you hated that I held on to Kenneth and that hope of family, and I want you to know I'm working on letting that go. I don't know how you tell you this in person, so I wrote it down.

I'm excited to head to Allura with you and start a chapter where we can live with no worries. I hear the hills roll into the snowy crescent mountains, and I want to find more beauty in the world.

Part of me thinks you'll not want to leave because of your apprenticeship.

Whether you stay to be the inventor I know you'll become or find me in the beautiful cliffs in the Northern Forests, remember I love you. Be easy on yourself because no one has been easy on you. You're the brother I always wanted mine to be, and I never appreciated that. I could never forget you. Your smile and dreams will inspire me always

Forever your sister,

—Abbey

Hugh, Kenneth came back! He's alive and taking me, and I don't know how safe it will be. If you find this letter, please find me, protect me if you can. If it's too late… remember you were only ever my one true brother—

Hugh stared with a quivering lip, wiping his face as a tear dripped onto the paper.

"No, no."

He tried to wipe it off, but it soaked into the creases. As he held his hand over his mouth, he steadied himself from the pain, the loss. The tears stopped, but his heart ached, and he just wanted to lie down and sleep, hoping that when he woke, she would be there holding him.

Not wanting to read it again, he put the letter in the envelope and stuck it in his bag. He pulled the satchel over his shoulder and walked out of the alley, pausing on the street.

Hugh stared back, the lantern still lit in the cubby, like he would see every night before he returned to her. He closed his eyes and turned to the cobblestone road, promising himself he would never turn back.

A man rammed into Hugh's side, and he stumbled, falling onto the path. Hugh looked up, and the stranger never stopped, as if he had not hit anyone, fixated on his destination.

Hugh froze, his gaze wandering to the rooftops. A red glow shone behind them. Ash drifted from the sky like snow onto his hat, and Hugh pushed himself up and walked to the corner of the block with a hand on the satchel strap.

He lowered his head, focusing on the road in front of him, and looked to the forest on the south side of the city, leading into the rolling countryside.

More homeless people from the alleyways stepped into the street, and Hugh ignored them, holding his hand out as it filled with ash. A warmth spread through the district, and he swallowed hard, feeling the panic from the growing crowd. He faced the northern hills, then back to the countryside, and bit his lip, uncertain.

Hugh opened his eyes and looked at the burning hills on the horizon, angling himself towards them. He pulled the satchel straps tight, took a deep breath, and rushed onto the street, sprinting between the lanterns' light.

CHAPTER SEVENTY

E choes of explosions rippled through the hills and valleys of Well's Peake. Aleksandar sprinted between the shadows on the cobblestone street, Shae flying high in the red sky.

The air thickened as his heart pounded, ash falling around him like a blizzard but with rising warmth. Terrified bystanders gathered on the road, looking to the destruction on the horizon, but Aleksandar rushed past them without hesitation.

He rounded the corner as his feet throbbed but slowed to a stop, exposed in the road. He focused on his shallow breath, locking eyes with the Phoenix with hands at his sides, hunched over like a beast.

The sky was as bright as day, the fires roaring above the pines as smoke blacked out the stars and the moonlight.

A carriage rattled around the corner as the driver snapped the reins, and the Phoenix did not move. The horses missed him as leaves blew out from under their hooves. Aleksandar leaped onto the sidewalk, dodging the thundering wheels.

With a burned top hat and a crimson red jacket that caressed the ground, the Phoenix positioned himself, his wrists high and bloodshot eyes fixated on Aleksandar.

"Is it really you?" Aleksandar stepped into the street, Shae hovering.

The Phoenix flipped the mask up into his hat, Kenneth smiling with a sharp jaw. "At last. I have you with nothing else in my way. No Peake. No friends or allies. Just me and you. You could not fathom how deserving this is."

Kenneth's hair was loose under the brim of the top hat, strands lying over his face like bars around a cell.

Aleksandar squeezed his hands into fists, trying not to shake as he struggled to catch his breath. "Kenneth, I don't know what's happened, but you have to stop. Can't you see what you're doing?"

"You haven't figured it out, have you?" Kenneth pushed his hand through his matted hair, lifting the top hat.

Sweat beaded on Aleksandar's forehead. The musk of burning wood, brick, and fire lingered around him, and ash covered the street.

Kenneth found a crooked grin and pushed falling flakes away with his hand. "Tonight is the night, Aleksandar. Tonight it ends." Kenneth looked at the top hat, his reflection in the red metal. He snarled and whipped it across the street. "I no longer need the mask."

Aleksandar propelled forward, and Kenneth mimicked his actions. Fire filled the air, and Aleksandar tried to crouch beneath the heat, but the blaze drifted to the ground and forced him to the cobblestone. Kenneth fired again, and Aleksandar stumbled to his feet and fled, his hat falling off, and moved along the street side.

Aleksandar sprinted as fast as he could, unable to break Kenneth's pursuit, forcing him to hide behind a mailbox. He heard the metal creak in the heat, the fire wisping at his ankles, about to overwhelm the barrier.

Aleksandar tried to escape, but the flames trapped him.

"Goodbye, Mr. Scott."

Aleksandar bit his lip and embraced his fate, but death did not find him. The warmth faded, and the bright glow vanished. Aleksandar stood, seeing Kenneth clutching his face, looking away in anguish. Aleksandar sprinted and jumped onto the tank strapped to Kenneth's back, slamming him to the ground.

Aleksandar went to kick but froze, realizing Shae had her claws in

Kenneth's cheeks. He pulled her off and tossed her into the air.

"Fly! Go home!"

Shae flapped across the ground and soared towards the treetops.

Kenneth swiped Aleksandar's feet from under him. He stood and held his wrist in the air.

"Don't!"

Kenneth unleashed his rage, encasing Shae in fire. She screeched, soaring out of the sea of flames, her wing burning on the end. She fell out of the sky and disappeared behind the trees, her wail echoing in Aleksandar's ears.

He gasped as the veins throbbed in his arms, clenching his teeth at the monster before him.

Kenneth turned with slashes in his face, blood streaming through his demented smile. "That felt good." He lifted his gauntlet and fired.

Aleksandar leaped out of the way, booking it towards his house. A stinging heat grew against his back, and a fireball hit the side of his home, the brick popping in the heat. Aleksandar broke through the door and rushed across the house, skipping steps into the workshop, knocking over an end table.

He heard the scuffle behind him too late, and Kenneth slammed into his shoulder, knocking Aleksandar to the floor. He rolled away and crawled between the workbenches as Kenneth singed the tops, flares bursting above him, hitting gears and metal around the workshop.

The heat cascaded on Aleksandar, and his shirt was drenched in sweat. Smoke filled the workshop, and his lungs stung in the haze.

"How does it feel, Aleksandar? To know you'll burn to death in your home, as you intended me. It is what we deserve!"

Kenneth lifted his left hand, setting the ceiling ablaze. The flames spread, and the house creaked and splintered in the intense heat, beginning to engulf itself. He turned to Aleksandar, who held the fire spear in his palms, breathing heavily as sweat dripped down his neck, salty on his lips.

"I wish you the best of luck." Kenneth threw his fists forward, a spinning inferno soaring through the air.

Aleksandar twirled the blazes aside as the tips of the staff extended out, whipping it away in stunning arcs and circles. He sidestepped to the stairs and rushed up in a last-ditch effort.

He sprinted into the living room, but clouds of smoke and ash blinded him. His eyes became inflamed, and he coughed hard, heading for the door, but the fire was relentless. It was too hot to pass through, even as he whipped the chaos aside.

Aleksandar glanced over his shoulder, and Kenneth blocked the kitchen exit, blood drying to his cracking and slashed skin. The light reflected in Kenneth's eyes, and his hair was singed on the ends, clotted with ash and dirt.

Kenneth attacked, and with every swing, Aleksandar's arms tired, the weight of the flames heavy as they were repelled from the staff. His muscles burned, and he grew weak—his odds of escaping dwindled.

He lost the strength to push the fire, and he was forced upstairs. Though the ceiling was intact, the flooring buckled from the raging fire, embers floating as the smoke thickened. Aleksandar stayed low, choking in his escape.

He rushed into his bedroom and barred the door with his dresser, knocking heavy furniture over with a thud. The frame slammed from the other side, and Aleksandar watched the wall shake from Kenneth's barrages. Aleksandar panted and searched for an escape, the room not smokey.

"Aleksandar, if you hope to die in there, so be it!"

Flames erupted around the door, flowing through the crack underneath it. It burned, and the crisp noise of splintering wood filled Aleksandar's ears over the roar of his home burning. He held up his staff and waited for his last stand; as seconds passed like days, Kenneth struggling to break in.

"Was it worth it? Everything that you did?" Kenneth peered through a slit with bloodshot eyes.

The heat licked through the floor, and swollen walls snapped under the wallpaper. A window cracked, and Aleksandar stared at it.

An escape.

He rushed for it, but the enlarged wood would not budge. He grabbed a book from the shelf and smashed the frame away.

Kenneth beat on the door, almost through. "Aleksandar, you can't fight the seasons. You think you lived? All you did was wander, following another's dream. You need to be honest with yourself and accept your passion had no meaning."

Aleksandar paused with the book above him, glass in its pages, and let out a long breath.

"That's right. You heard me. You, your dream lacks purpose. Deserves no life. Explains why that loving friend of yours met her end so early."

While the house grew hot and Aleksandar could not keep the sweat out of his eyes, his blood boiled hotter. He turned and lowered his arms.

Kenneth bashed the door, and it fractured, leaving Aleksandar with only a second of decision. He looked to the window, knowing freedom was close, but Kenneth could escape, and if he did, no one would be safe. Aleksandar closed his eyes and thought to his friend. To Ellie, Vida, Hugh, and Natalia.

He pictured himself in the woods, the cool breeze against his back, snow lightly falling from the sky, with the moon shining brightly. If only—

Aleksandar opened his eyes and took a deep breath, the burning sensation of smoke in his throat. His fingers tensed around the staff, knowing his last moment had arrived. Sweat curved down his temples, and he rolled his neck. "Come on already!"

Kenneth busted through the door and stood in the charred frame. "Is this what you wanted? To think, my so-called creator almost robbed me of this glorious moment." Kenneth raised his arms in pride.

"Creator?" Aleksandar shook as he swallowed his breath.

Kenneth stepped to the side and fired in a ferocious stream, but Aleksandar guided it away, the bookshelf taking the carnage. They circled each other, waiting for the other to slip up in their deadly dance. Fire singed Aleksandar's clothes as his arms strained from the exhausting heat.

The floor weakened beneath his feet, and he watched his steps as floorboards cracked underneath their weight. Aleksandar stared at Kenneth, seeing his moment.

Aleksandar hit Kenneth across the face. Kenneth grabbed him and threw him through the weakened wall, and Aleksandar collapsed in the hallway, losing hold of the staff. He crawled to his feet, but Kenneth kicked him down and lit the air, pinning him to the ground.

"Rise, Aleksandar!"

Aleksandar swiped Kenneth's leg, bringing him to his side, the gauntlets going quiet. He stood, and Kenneth grabbed him again, throwing him back into the bedroom. Aleksandar snatched the staff and pushed himself up, watching with wide eyes.

Kenneth lurched towards Aleksandar, and before he could move, it was too late.

The board splintered under the weight of his foot, and his legs fell through. Kenneth leaped forward, looking to kill, but missed as Aleksandar slammed into the living room below. His knees buckled under the force of the fall, the beams from the ceiling smashing around him.

Aleksandar gasped for air between the smoke and the impact but found little. Hope faded, and he felt as if his soul was leaving his body.

A picture shattered on the floor, and Aleksandar shook, rolled onto his side, and looked up as the flames grazed near his sides.

Kenneth gazed at the young inventor with an enormous smirk and bent over, picking up the fire spear that was wedged between the floorboards. He waved it in his hands, flames attracted to the ends.

Looking up in defeat, Aleksandar accepted the peace he could muster.

He was not strong enough.

He could not win.

Not skilled enough to stop a man who had nothing to lose.

He grew lightheaded, feeling sick in his stomach.

Aleksandar struggled to his feet, the weight too heavy on his weakened knees, and stumbled as another beam cracked and swung from the rafters.

Aleksandar tried to move, but it slammed him in the back, throwing him through the air and against the wall. He fell to the floor, nearly unconscious.

He held his arm as the beam broke off and shattered through the living room floor. Aleksandar slid into the hole, falling into the pit of fire and smoke that was once his workshop.

Kenneth embraced his kill as the shadow of the young inventor was consumed by flames.

With blood in his bright smile, Kenneth lifted his chin as the floor shattered. Losing his balance, he spun the staff and fell into the destruction and beauty to which he belonged, pushing away the fire as he landed safely.

CHAPTER SEVENTY-ONE

Kenneth burst from the flames of Aleksandar's former home and waved the fire away with the staff. He stood with his hair over his face, under the black-and-red sky, his crimson jacket fluttering in the warm breeze.

He glanced behind him as the house collapsed on itself, feeling his pulse spike. Embers and ash filled the air as the town burned on the horizon, creating a false sunset in the late evening.

Kenneth brushed soot from his shoulder and noticed the owl lying still next to the roots of a tree. He smirked and tugged the inside of his jacket, then headed into the forest. He paused, his gaze lowering to a burned top hat resting in the tree line, the red metal mask staring at him.

Kenneth chuckled and took a deep breath, lifting his stare with a chapped grin and aiming his gauntlets.

Sticks and leaves cracked in the shadows, and Kenneth turned to the closest sounds. He glanced back to the house, and a man in a hooded cloak stood with a dark blue mask with thin lines of silver concealing his face.

Kenneth shook his head, smiling. "I think this town has enough masks."

The man stood silent. Still.

Kenneth's smile faded to uncertainty. "Who are *you?*"

He waited in silence, his patience fading as the masked man stared.

Kenneth squeezed his hands enough not to pull the valves open but ready to strike. His blistered arms stung from the heat, and his eyes were swollen, blood dripping down his dirty face.

"Are you the one who started the fire at Fritz and Co? Did you destroy the Steamrail?"

The man stared, unflinching.

Kenneth tapped his finger on the end of the gauntlet, and his neck grew stiff. "Who are you?"

The wind blew against the masked man's jacket. "You have served your purpose."

"Ah, I know that voice! I knew it. So you found a new face, my creator. I would burn the flesh from your bones just so you could never think to stand over me again, but I have done what I wished. I will go." Kenneth turned and walked towards the forest.

"I wouldn't rush. You'll want to hear the truth."

Kenneth paused and swallowed hard. "You have nothing left to tell me, and I gave Mr. Scott what he deserved. I am fulfilled."

"I'm giving you a choice and the truth. Once you've listened, you may walk away, live a free life elsewhere, but if you stay, I will kill you."

Kenneth turned around and gazed at the masked man, clenching his jaw as he licked the dry ash from his lips. His mind went back and forth, thinking of every scenario.

Kenneth tapped his fingers together, and his bloodshot eyes widened. His lip quivered as he glanced back to the house, his tongue in his cheek. For the first moment since the destruction of his old life, he thought of all the angles. "Did you… do this to me?"

"You caused great grief for many people, and I saw a perfect candidate for an elemental experiment. You reaped what you deserved."

Kenneth clenched his fists and stepped forward. "Did *you* take her away from me?"

"I was there that night, and I followed you to your secret stash after the robbery—quite the collection of memorabilia. Collected over the years, I'd say. It will belong to me once we're finished."

Kenneth looked back to the house, his shoulders rising as he sighed, tears forming in his eyes. He snarled, and his nostrils flared. He wiped the tears off his cheek. "It was you."

"You have a choice, Kenneth," the masked man said. "Walk away, enjoy what's left of your life. I am a man of my word."

Kenneth balled his fists as veins bulged under the blood on his neck.

"Leave."

Kenneth stepped forward, and his voice tore into the air. "Tell me who you are!"

The masked man stood there, eyes piercing the night. "I am no one. I have no beginning, and I have no end."

Kenneth glanced at the hat and red metal mask and slid the staff across his back, pulling up his scorched sleeves. The masked man shifted in his stance and whips unraveled to the ground. He turned a dial on the handles, and they hummed as water flowed to the tips.

He took her from me.

Kenneth lifted his arms and fired. Flames tore through the air, encasing the surrounding forest, leaves burning as they blew away like ocean waves. Kenneth rolled to his side, shooting in all directions, ensuring there was no escape for the masked man.

A ripple of steam sliced through the flames as a water whip slammed into the dirt beside him. Kenneth jumped as the lash cut near his ankles, another missing his arm.

The masked man leaped through the blaze, swinging the deadly weapons in a mastered grace. They ripped through the bark, splinters flying into the air, and Kenneth dodged the attacks, firing back.

The man masked ducked behind a tree as a fireball sizzled against the bark. His whips cut through the trunk like paper, and the tree split and fell through the pine and oak forest.

Limbs splintered off, the timber cracking through the canopies, and Kenneth jumped as the tree crashed and shook the ground between him and the masked man.

More limbs shattered around him, and a twisted branch smacked him across the face, blood gushing from his forehead.

The masked man climbed and stood on top of the fallen tree with empty eyes. Kenneth climbed up the side of the trunk and fired. The flames caught the downed canopy on fire, sprigs burning apart. The masked man jumped down, flinging his whips, nicking Kenneth along the thigh.

Kenneth patted his leg and ducked, narrowly missing another attack. He leaped off the log and fired. The masked man rolled and pressed a button on the handle, and a curved knife extended out the back.

He struck and sliced Kenneth's cheek in two.

Kenneth's skin dangled off his jagged jaw, his teeth and gums exposed, blood dripping from his lips. He cringed in pain, red filling the crevices of his mouth.

Kenneth let out a bloodcurdling shriek into the harvest night and snarled. He waved his hands, and a wall of fire surged through the forest. The masked man sprinted and jumped over fallen branches, trying not to trip as the flames grew close.

I have him!

Kenneth opened his left hand, but the gauntlet did not shut off. He tried the trigger again, but the valve stuck open. He could not pry it back, his hands burning too much from the heat.

No, no, no.

Kenneth growled, grabbed the hosing on the side, and yanked it apart. The fire caught the exposed liquid, and the tube exploded.

Kenneth flew into the dead leaves as his clothes burned into his exposed chest. The left tank hissed, and he unstrapped it. He crawled to his feet and jumped behind a tree.

The device exploded, and fire rained around him like hail. He raised his head, pushed off the roots, and fell into the dirt, dodging a water whip as it sliced into the bark.

Kenneth lifted his face from the forest floor, the loose skin stinging. His jacket had caught ablaze. He pulled out the staff and ripped off his cloak as the masked man closed in on him.

Kenneth lifted the burning fuel off the earth, whipping it between the trees with the staff in hand. As a circle of fire trapped the two together, Kenneth laughed through his pain, taking control of his arena.

They dodged each other's attacks, using the trees as shields, watching each other for their moment to strike.

The masked man turned the dial on the whips and snatched the end of the staff. He yanked it, and Kenneth hung on with a firm grip, stumbling.

Kenneth tugged and ripped the whip out of the masked man's hand, breaking the hose from under the cloak. Water dripped onto the ground.

Kenneth let go of the staff, and the masked man stumbled back. He rushed forward and, with his only gauntlet, fired.

The flames encased the masked man, who fell onto his back and rolled away to snuff out his shoulder.

Kenneth grabbed the staff from the dirt and swung full force. The flames collected into a sea of fire, and it surged towards the masked man. Kenneth smiled in delight as the heat barraged against his face.

Finally, the night ends.

Kenneth struggled to hold the staff, the weight of the elements weighing it down, but he found a smile, seeing the masked man fall behind the flare.

A whip surged through the top of the wave, and the water exploded off, clearing a gap as droplets sizzled in the air.

The masked man hit the ground again, blowing another hole in the flames, and rolled through the opening.

Kenneth watched as his heart rate quickened, his hands unable to move fast enough, his mind racing to Amia. As the water reached the tip of the whip, it sliced through his chest.

Kenneth fell into the downed tree and caught on the broken branches, blood covering his burned chest. His body shook, and he gasped.

The masked man stood tall over Kenneth, looking with unblinking eyes. "You could have walked away."

Abbey, Amia. Kenneth's mistakes echoed louder than the pain that surged through his nerves. His mind fused together again, finding a fragment of peace.

Kenneth tried to lift his gauntlet, choking on blood with a grimace.

Fire spewed from the nozzle, but his hand dropped into the dirt, the quick burst dying out before it could make it far.

The masked man stared at Kenneth's body hanging on the downed tree, blood soaking his clothes. Half his face was torn to shreds, the other dirty and burned.

The husk of a broken aristocrat.

The masked man grabbed Kenneth's legs and dragged him off the burning branches and to the tree line outside Aleksandar's house. He picked up the staff, nodded to Kenneth, and stepped into the forest as the shadows overcame him.

In the circle of fire, Kenneth rested in the leaves as ashes from the red sky covered his body, guiding him to the next world.

CHAPTER SEVENTY-TWO

Explosions riddled the city and shook its foundation at its roots. Natalia watched under the red night sky as the ground trembled beneath her feet, buildings demolished in the path of fire.

The destruction spread towards the World's Palace, leaving a trail of embers. Ash rained from above, covering everything in its wake.

The warm breeze blew her hair back as she paced alongside her home, opening two doors that led into her workshop. She rushed to the stable and grabbed her two horses, saddled them, and guided them to the house. They trotted and kicked, neighing in the commotion.

"It's okay, girls. I promise."

She scrambled across the shop and twisted three cranks on the workbench under the Lunarwheel, the sides falling to the floorboards. Underneath was a cart with wheels, and she pulled several levers, unlocking them from the floor. It took all her might, but the security clamps broke free. The wheels turned, and she steered it outside the house.

She connected a hook to the end and rotated a crank, pulling the device into the small carriage. Natalia attached it to a mounted swivel and hopped on top of the seat. With a snap of the reins, the horses pulled the buggy onto the cobblestone road and deeper into Well's Peake.

The mares were capable, and Natalia wanted to push them to their limits, but the machine rattled behind her. She bit her lip, not wanting to risk breaking it, her heart pounding. She wondered if it would crack on the way down.

Natalia neared the city and looked towards the red destruction. People raced for the hills, close to being trampled by her horses, fleeing the smoke that filled the streets with a toxic haze. Constables rushed in a fury, and injured fairgoers crowded the alleyways and lanes as she closed in on the World's Palace.

Another buggy flew from around the street, smacking against Natalia's. The reins slipped from her grip, and the brace to one of her horses snapped. Natalia's horse took off with the madman in the other carriage, lost in the smoke.

"It's okay, Lady. Keep pushing."

Lady grew tired with every corner they passed. She slowed as the crowds thickened, and Natalia lost valuable moments. After what seemed an eternity, she reached the World's Palace and its gardens, ash covering her shoulders. A group of constables scurried ahead, and Natalia pulled on the reins.

"Get out of there!" a man yelled.

Natalia turned, and an explosion rocked the nearby building. The force blew her to the side, and she dangled over the edge of the carriage. The horse bucked and broke from the clamp. Lady bolted off, and the leather straps hooked the endpin of the frame.

The buggy twisted around, and Natalia fell from her seat, smacking her head off the ground. The carriage lifted off two wheels.

Natalia tried to roll, but the carriage flopped on top of her. The frame was high enough not to break her leg, but it pinned her in the grass.

Natalia arched in pain and yelled, grabbing her thigh. She pushed and tugged, but she did not budge. She lay back and looked to the city, upside down, as ash fell on her face. It burned, and she exuded sweat as the heat grew hotter. The wind picked up, and the flames raged towards her.

She searched for constables, but no one was in sight.

Natalia pulled on her leg, trying to break free, but still no luck. She could feel the blood pressure build in her leg, the muscles starting to go numb. An explosion went off, and debris landed in the bushes near her and caught fire, feet from the canvas on the carriage.

Come on. Come on.

Her breath shivered, and the pressure built behind her eyes, her throat scratchy. The world spun as she inhaled the fumes of burned brick and wood, looking around with blurred vision. A shadow formed into that of a large man with a thick beard, and he raced towards her.

Bernard.

"Natalia! Bless the Maker; it's you." Bernard ran to the carriage, and with his burly hands and feet planted, lifted it. Natalia pulled herself free, and he helped her to her feet, unable to put all her pressure on it.

"Am I glad to see you." Natalia put pressure on her foot. It was not broken, but far from okay.

"Likewise." Bernard glanced to the fire raging a block away. He winced with a blistered face, and his beard was riddled with ash, splinters, and soot. Buttons were missing on his jacket, and the top flap hung loose. "What are you doing here?"

Natalia looked up.

"Is this the Lunarwheel?" he asked. "Is it working?"

"Yes, but the horses were spooked. We need to reach the river and fountains. Without a large source of water, we won't stand a chance."

"Well, let's move. The fire is mostly in the north, but it spreads towards the mid-districts. If it passes Central Square and hits the factories, we'll lose the city."

"Can you pull it over the ridge?"

He smirked. "Do you know who you're talking to?"

Bernard rubbed his hands and walked to the front of the carriage. He grabbed the hitch behind his back, lifted, and pulled, huffing as his boots pressed into the dirt. The buggy moved out of the damp grass. His massive arms flexed, the stitching of his jacket ripping, and the muscles in his neck tightened. Bernard hiked it over the ledge and to the cobblestone, sweat dripping down his brow.

Natalia smiled and looked around, swallowing as the fire devoured the city street.

"Get this thing ready!" Bernard tugged with rushed breaths, a vein popping out of his forehead.

Natalia hopped into the carriage and connected the tubes to the wheel. She focused on the calibrations as the floorboards shook, the shadows and flames towering over her. Bernard watched as the hedges beside them burned, and the pavement was scorched black, stone popping from the intense heat. He turned as Natalia leaped to the ground, careful not to put too much weight on her leg.

Bernard slipped on the ash, attempting to pull the Lunarwheel to the river that flowed into the ponds. He set the hitch down with a sigh, dropping to a knee. He wiped his brow, took a hard breath, and pulled the ash from his beard.

Natalia put her hand on his shoulder, looking to the World's Palace behind them, the windows splintering. "Bernard, I've never tested it to this scale. I don't know what could happen."

Bernard stood, eyeing the wildfire. "I'm not sure we have a choice."

"As long as you know."

"Could it kill us?"

Natalia shrugged, pursing her lips.

Bernard nodded. "So be it."

A gust of hot air blew, the warmth causing Natalia's clothes to stick to her sides. The glass split under the raging heat and shattered. Thousands of shards fell behind them. Natalia covered her face as a piece slashed her arm, and blood soaked through her sleeve. She pulled a handkerchief from her pocket and tied up the wound.

Natalia rushed to the back of the carriage and twisted the Lunarwheel on its mount. Grabbing the hoses, she carried them with Bernard's help and dropped the ends into the river. She stepped to the machine and planted her feet.

Natalia grabbed hold of the control handles. "Bernard, brace yourself. Things are about to feel a little off. When I say, pull the lever on the bottom."

Bernard lifted his brow. "What's that supposed to mean?"

Natalia held on to the Lunarwheel and flipped several latches.

"Natalia! What does that mean?"

Fire cut across the front lawns, cutting off their escape, and Natalia glanced over her shoulders, her eyes widening. She focused on her device. "This is it."

Bernard searched the gardens. *"Natalia!"*

"Back up!" Natalia checked the hoses and tightened a few clamps. "Get ready. I'll need you to push the buggy along if this holds."

"If?"

"Lever!"

Bernard yanked the handle.

The machine surged to life, a blue glow flaring across the gardens and glimmering off the marble and stone. The engine sucked water through the tubes and hummed loud until it felt like thunder echoing through the hills.

Natalia's neck tensed as vibrations rippled through her arms, the carriage creaking beneath her. Water jettisoned through the front plate and spiraled into the fire like a horizontal waterfall. It ripped into the hedges, destroying them but putting the flames out in an instant.

Bernard watched and wiped his forehead, pausing as sweat floated off his hand and into the air towards the machine.

"Natalia, look!"

Bernard pointed, and Natalia watched as a small funnel formed in the center, water traveling back into the device, only to be propelled out again.

It's working!

Natalia turned the machine on its mount, aiming towards the fire that surged before them. The stream sizzled on contact, evaporating in the smoldering heat. Bernard flung off his jacket, lifted the hitch, and pushed the carriage with all his might.

Natalia created an escape path and guided the Lunarwheel in all directions. The gardens ripped apart, but it pushed the fire back, the first sign of hope.

The World's Palace was protected, and Natalia turned her aim towards the city. She doused the streets and buildings in water, turning raging fires into puddles as Bernard directed her through. Stone and brick chipped, and glass shattered from the power of the Lunarwheel, blowing streetlamps out of the pavement.

Natalia and Bernard reached Central Square, where crowds of thousands fled the destruction, constables rushing to their aid. Flames arced along the river, consuming the city park, and Natalia saw that she stood between it and hundreds of helpless people.

The Lunarwheel roared, and the carriage wheels shattered under the intense weight. The machine tipped over, falling to the ground and flinging Natalia overtop and onto her back. She rolled over, clenching her chest, to see the corner of the engine cracked. The wheel shifted, blasting Natalia, pushing her across the cobblestone.

Bernard sprinted to her side and pulled her up. The machine roared louder, but it died in an instant, water sloshing to the ground. The hoses were still in the river, but the water drained from the tubes.

Natalia ran to the Lunarwheel, turned off the handle, and inspected the crack. It was deep but not leaking. She cupped her hands and looked into the glass, noticing the piece Aleksandar put in was dislodged.

She pulled out her book, but it was waterlogged. She flipped to the most recent pages, but the ink had bled together, and she was unable to read her notes.

"What's wrong?" Bernard rested his hands on his knees, looking like he was about to pass out.

"The wheel, a piece, is not connected. It's uncalibrated."

"Can you fix it?"

Natalia searched her thoughts, but no solution came to mind. "No, I can't remember how. My journal is ruined."

Bernard set his hand on her shoulder. "Natalia, forget that damn book. The answers are in there." He pointed to her head. "They must be."

"If I don't calibrate this right, it could malfunction, and nothing says that crack wouldn't shatter and rip us to shreds."

Bernard took a deep breath and looked at the fire that roared a block away. Natalia watched as venues were consumed, people screaming, unable to evacuate. Bernard tilted the machine up and looked at her as if she was the only one to save the city.

I don't have a choice.

Natalia opened the front plate and reached in, the water ice-cold. She pulled the calibrator out and tinkered with the freezing device, her fingertips numb after fiddling with it in her hands. She thought back, trying to remember, but the fog blurred Aleksandar's work.

Natalia leaned on her knees and closed her eyes, but the hum of the engine still echoed in her ears, distracting her as she pictured Aleksandar finishing the Lunarwheel. She thought of herself writing, looking down at her journal.

"Natalia."

She looked up, the heat of the fire covering her back, and knew it was now or never.

"Please tell me you have it." Bernard stood over her, ready to move on command.

Natalia shifted a few pieces of the calibrator and installed it, closing the panel and locking it. She crouched behind the engine, grabbed the handles, and nodded to Bernard. He shook his head and pulled the lever.

The Lunarwheel roared to life, louder than before and shuddering in Natalia's eardrums. The crack split further across the wheel, and she opened the valve, water gushing from the front piece into the fire. The crowds watched in horror.

Slowly, the device rose in her hands, and the light grew as it spun faster. Her footsteps were heavy, her arms fatigued, but she lifted the machine to her chest, the energy enabling her in some unknown way. She felt her body attracted to the device.

She tried to angle it but was losing her grip, the engine ready to slip from her palms. "Bernard!"

The water raged, and Bernard braced Natalia from behind as she nearly fell back from the Lunarwheel's power. Bernard cupped his hands around hers and lifted, groaning against the energy.

The fire broke into Central Square, and Natalia and Bernard turned. The water vortex appeared and destroyed everything in its path, quenching the flames from reaching further into the city. Natalia tried to shout, but she could not hear her own voice over the humming nature of the machine. She could sense Bernard's laughter in the face of fear and saw his arms rippling like deep waves.

Natalia's fingers tingled as she looked at the glass, splintering from the corner across the top. The pressure built in weak areas, glowing more intense in the growing cracks. She did not have long before she was ripped to shreds.

Natalia and Bernard fired at the blazes, and pockets of soaked debris emerged as they fought it back. Smoke rose into the air, and wet ash clung to their faces. Droplets of water hovered from the ground, floating towards the center of the vortex in a gravity-defying manner, collecting on the glass's surface.

Steam riddled the block while Natalia guided the never-ending spiral through the destruction, only to be cycled out in ways she could not explain.

Natalia pushed forward with Bernard's help, fighting the fire, stopping the monster in its tracks.

Water filled the cracks of the town, and the red sky dimmed as the moonlight shone through the clouds, the destruction fading below.

The glow of the machine grew to the point that it blinded her, and she hoped Bernard could still see their path. Natalia was soaked to the bone, her muscles heavy, and she prayed as the glass cracked down the handle, feeling the split in her palm.

After what felt like days, the wildfire shrank, retreating into the charred remains of the North Hills.

Well's Peake was no longer in danger.

Natalia blew out the last of the flames and reached for the control arm, but the weight of her hand was too much, and she couldn't reach it. Her heart pounded against her rib cage, and Bernard grabbed her wrist and pushed it forward. She wrapped her fingers around the handle and shut the Lunarwheel off.

It became heavy and slammed into the ground, the bottom shattering into hundreds of pieces, pulling Natalia over the top as Bernard dropped to his knees. She lay on her chest and gasped for air, her face numb against the cold cobblestone, covered in mud. She sprawled out and struggled not to pass out with fatigue, a slight smirk on her face.

Bernard looked around, admiring Well's Peake and looking up the main road to see the World's Palace standing in the distance. With parts of the city burned and the other buried in ash, only a few small fires remained. His lungs filled with laughter, and he stood, lifting Natalia on his arm.

Constables and fairgoers cheered, inching near them. Natalia struggled to open her eyes, to stay awake. People rushed around them, and they tapped her on the shoulder as Bernard held her up. She felt the water drip down her body, shivering as the chill air of the night returned.

Natalia glanced at the World's Palace and rubbed her cheek, blushing. A smile spread across her face in the moonlight as she fell asleep, knowing when it mattered most, she remembered.

CHAPTER SEVENTY-THREE

The injured and the dead flooded the Downton University courtyard from the night before. Lydia paced through the stone and wood-paneled halls, looking with reddened eyes at the early morning.

As they brought more people in for treatment, she searched, waiting to find Nicoli on a stretcher or to walk in pushing his hands through his hair. She could not sleep, and her neck was stiff, her chest tight.

Hours passed, and there was no sign of him. She waited at the arched entrance, biting her lip, hoping someone from the Peake would arrive. She pulled the fibers on the end of her uniform, kicking her toes into the grass next to the walkway.

The courtyard was full of doctors, nurses, and injured people. The sky was cloudy, but there was no rain despite the frosty chill that lingered in the air—only specks of ash blowing off the university roof.

Another carriage stopped next to the curb, and several constables climbed out. They rushed to the back and pulled three stretchers from within, carrying dead officers on them.

Lydia stepped forward, recognizing a patrolman. "Rupert, what the hell happened?"

"Constable May." Rupert saluted her. "These men lost their lives in the fire."

Lydia rubbed her neck as the other constables carried in the lifeless bodies. "Have you seen Detective Lucas? He was to report by morning, and there's been no word."

"No, ma'am."

"What about Dekker?"

"Dekker is supposed to be here. We had orders to brief him when we arrived."

Lydia tilted her head. "Did he tell you where?"

Rupert swallowed hard. "I must be going. The chief doesn't like to wait."

Rupert tried to walk away, but Lydia grabbed his arm.

"Rupert, where are those men coming from? We both see the fire did not kill them."

He dropped his head and batted his eyes at her. "Lydia—"

She squeezed tighter. "Where?"

"I don't have all the details."

Lydia let go. "I'm sorry, I shouldn't put you in this position. Just tell me where Dekker is."

He sighed. "Fourth floor. There's an office set up for him."

Lydia rushed off. If Rupert was trying to stop her, she did not hear it. The courtyard smelled of burned clothes and linen wrappings, and people groaned from the pain and aches. Lydia tried not to picture Nicoli out there alone, injured in some forgotten forest.

With a pained stare, she looked up at the central tower as she neared the university, her heartbeat rising. She skipped up the steps, reached the fourth floor, and turned into the office.

Dekker sat in his chair with a binder in his hands. "Lydia."

She took a deep breath and walked into the room, closing the door behind her. Her mouth was dry from lack of hydration. The morning sun shone through the green-tinted glass and reflected off the oak office, causing her to squint.

Lydia stood firm, and Dekker held his breath.

"Three men just arrived." Lydia stared. "Why did Rupert lie about their deaths?"

Dekker tapped the desk and rose from his chair. "Lydia—"

"Have you been here all morning? You knew I was here waiting for answers. You didn't come find me?"

"That's enough, Lydia. Let me explain."

The door creaked, and Rupert walked in. "Sir, my apologies."

"It's okay. Wait in the hallway."

Lydia glared at Rupert as he closed the office door. She turned back to Dekker. "Where's Nicoli?"

Dekker shook his head and crossed his hands. "To be honest, I don't know. We found our men outside the safe house but no trace of him. Kenneth Forbes was missing, but thankfully he has been found dead. We do know there was a struggle."

"Three? Is that all you sent?" Lydia waved her hand.

"I committed my best, and we can't just put up a perimeter throwing Kenneth's location on display. The city was ready to break into the Peake. If they discovered his whereabouts, they would have hung the man."

"You sent three men to guard someone who has killed hundreds, injured thousands."

"I did what I thought wise." Dekker pointed his finger.

"And look where that got us."

"Careful, Lydia. I understand what you're going through, but I'm still your chief."

"What about our plan? We told you he was real, that the masked man existed and would show. We discussed that, and you gave me your word. You said right to my face that you'd send the men needed to stop that madman. Dekker, you lied to me!"

He lowered his head and pulled on his bottom lip. "I'm sorry, but I didn't believe it. Nicoli's been chasing that shadow for years with no proof."

"But I'm the one who told you. We made the plan together. Did you not trust me?"

Dekker crossed his arms. "I am aware of your history with Nicoli. I see you believed it was real, but I think Nicoli convinced you to put faith in his lie."

"You son of a bitch. You lied to me, told me you understood the threat, that you would protect him!"

"And I did!" Dekker stood, his voice booming. "I have three dead constables. I have to go to their wives and tell them their husbands won't be coming home tonight, not because of one madman but another. Not including all we lost in the fire."

Lydia stared at him, uncaring of his words. "That's on you. I did my job and gave you everything you needed, and you made the wrong choice."

"We fail some days, Lydia. I'm not happy about it, but I can't change what happened. What I can do is launch a full investigation to capture this monster, find Nicoli, and seek justice for those lost."

Lydia stood, not considering his words, his false sympathy. If only she had been there, she could have protected Nicoli, saved him from his fate. She felt hollow and stared off into the courtyard, looking to the countless people who cried, slept, healed...

"Lydia?" Dekker stepped forward.

She stuck out her hand and reached to her chest, removing the badge from her lapel. Lydia held it in her palm, rubbing her thumb over the brass.

Dekker exhaled hard through his nose, his arms dropping. "I refuse your resignation."

"Take it." Lydia held out her hand. "Or I will drop it on the floor and let you pick it up on my way out."

Dekker let out a held breath, shaking his head. "I did what I thought was right. I'm sorry it was a mistake."

"You knew exactly what you were doing. Now take it. I no longer belong to the Peake. My watch is over."

Dekker sighed and put his hand under hers, and she placed her badge in his palm. "After all this, all the progress you made under your family's name, you're willing to throw it away?"

"I've lost much more than I've gained."

"If you leave here without this, you are no longer welcome at the Peake."

Lydia stared, turned without words, and walked out the door.

~

The masked man smashed the lock, and it sank into the leaves near the base of the stone cabin. He opened the gate, finding Kenneth's secret vault in the middle of the forest.

He lit the lanterns on the walls, and the shadows faded in the flames, revealing inventions, art, coin, and more. Kenneth riddled the shelves with trinkets of all values, and the masked man's eyes lingered over the collection.

Walking through the aisles, he examined the objects, grabbing everything he pleased, including Aleksandar's stolen inventions.

He stumbled across a small device and paused. He lifted it and pressed the button on the bronze handle. The tips sparked, spiraling with electricity.

Interesting.

He slipped the Spark into his pocket.

The masked man carried several bags and boxes to the carriage outside the cabin. He walked back in and kicked the shelves to the ground, glass and artwork shattering. Pouring fuel across the floorboards, he set the canister at his feet, grabbed a lantern off the wall, and slammed it into the shelf. The room ignited in flames.

As the horse led the carriage into the harvest night, the masked man glanced over his shoulder for one last look as the cabin burned to ash.

CHAPTER SEVENTY-FOUR

The World's Palace rested under the silver clouds, and a gentle snowfall drifted in the morning sky, covering the ground in white bliss. Leaves with frosted tips shifted at Natalia's shoes, her scarf brushing against her blue jacket.

She stood with her chestnut hair brushed behind her shoulders, staring at nine caskets, six in the back, and three in front, at the foot of a stage. The fountain with the burned angel rested behind them, and she struggled to pull her gaze from the palace's shadow, feeling hollow.

Seven women with matching blue scarves walked along the pathway, with violas under their arms. They sat, lifted their bows, and played a somber song.

Natalia took a heavy breath, sensing the thousands of people that stood behind her outside the roped-off stage. She eyed the three caskets up front, each with a plaque on the lid. On the left, it read *The People of the World's Fair*. On the right: *Constables of the Peake*. She put her hand on the middle casket, the wood raw on her fingertips. A bowler hat rested on top, and she closed her eyes as she read the name on the plaque.

Aleksandar Scott.

With a restless stance, she could not fathom his death, her stomach hardening as she shivered, trying to piece together what happened. He was taken from the future to come, unable to leave the mark he wanted, and she believed he was the one to change it all.

Natalia sniffled, pushing her tongue against her cheek.

"Miss Arlen?"

Natalia turned to a woman with a brown braid, eyes like amber. "Yes?"

"Hello. I'm not sure—"

"Ellie Fritz."

Ellie paused and nodded. "I am."

Natalia looked over Ellie's shoulder at a woman in a purple dress. "And you must be Vida Harvey."

Vida tilted her head. "You know us?"

"I do." Natalia glanced at the coffin. "Aleksandar spoke of you both. You were close friends from what I could gather. Ellie, you were something much more."

Ellie's shoulders raised, letting out a broken breath. Her eyes were puffy, certainly from crying all morning.

"I am sorry for your loss, both of you. Aleksandar was quite the young man, and I grew very fond of him, myself. I thought I had the hindsight to see when such tragedy grew close, but I was so wrong. When he needed me most, I wasn't there."

Natalia closed her eyes, the pressure building behind them, not wanting to embrace the pain of another apprentice lost to tragedy.

A hand slipped between her fingers, and Natalia turned, Ellie looking at her with tears on her cheeks. Ellie stepped closer, and Natalia's chest tightened. The warmth on her fingertips was comforting.

"Thank you." Natalia rubbed her chin.

Ellie pulled Vida near. "I hope he made the difference he always wanted."

"I believe he did."

Bernard, accompanied by Chief Constable Dekker, the Fritz brothers, Owen, and several prominent figures, walked up to Natalia.

"We are about to begin," Bernard said, his gaze low.

Natalia nodded, and Bernard stepped to the casket and set his palm on the end. With a deep sigh, he headed towards the stage, the rest following.

Natalia joined the end of the group and looked at Ellie until she broke their glance, sobbing as she looked at the coffins.

Vida held her from behind, both sniffling in the cold air.

With every step up the platform, Natalia felt the weight of the world falling on her shoulders. She took her seat on the end, beside Owen, and Bernard walked to the center podium. He raised his arms, and the crowd grew silent, the violas fading into a soft, slow song.

Natalia had never heard such silence, even in her own workshop. She cupped her hands to keep the chill off her fingertips and looked to Bernard, thinking about Aleksandar working in her shop.

Bernard pulled out a few pieces of paper and unfolded them on the stand. He removed his pince-nez and set them on the bridge of his nose.

"Citizens of Well's Peake and the World's Fair, thank you for gathering here today." Bernard eyed the masses and pulled on the end of his beard. "These past few days, we have suffered a tremendous loss of life, and spirits have been broken. A lot has transpired, and I believe it best to clear the air and inform you on the future of this still remarkable city, The City of the Golden Harvest."

Bernard looked out, the people quiet, listening to his every word.

"The Peakeland Yard confirmed the information I now share. There are still unanswered questions, but a full-scale investigation is underway to discover the truth. What we do know, to great dismay, is the person responsible for these crimes against society is Kenneth Forbes."

The crowd gasped, and Bernard held up his hand.

"I know this is shocking. Mr. Forbes somehow survived the fire that consumed his home, and for some reason, tragedy consumed him. He once stood as the man on the hill who flourished, bringing culture and growth to this city, but in his last days, he fell to madness and brought devastation to the innocent. He has since been found dead, so please do not fear for your lives. His terror has ended."

Natalia exhaled and closed her eyes.

"The Peake works diligently to provide further answers. With that, I wish to look to those who brought these terrifying nights to an end. For they reminded us there is always hope and that we will recover. We can cultivate and rebuild the spirit of Well's Peake, and I say we do it in memory of those who are no longer here."

Bernard paused and took a deep breath.

"At the foot of the podium lie nine caskets. The names of those fallen are to be inscribed and given their respective funerals. Six caskets, one for each district of Well's Peake. One for the citizens of the World's Fair who visited our city, and another for the noble men and women of the Peake. Their memories will not be forgotten."

The wind blew against Natalia's scarf, her blackberry perfume bringing her little comfort. The snow brushed against her cheeks, and she looked to the sky, wondering what could happen, what would. Her days as an inventor were to end and Aleksandar's to begin, but now nothing was on the horizon.

Bernard flipped his papers over. "The last belongs to one of the individuals responsible for the invention that saved Well's Peake from certain destruction. Aleksandar Scott.

"At one point, many believed Mr. Scott was responsible for the undoings of this city. We misjudged him and treated him unfairly, and now we can't apologize. He was humble and spirited. I will not forget Mr. Scott, and I hope none of you do either. The young inventor had great potential, looking to make a positive change in this city. I hope we can set a better example for the future."

Bernard waved his hand as an assistant carried an easel with a blanket over the top.

"The city would like to apologize, and in his legacy for the false allegations we carelessly pushed against him, we proclaim Aleksandar Scott, The Martyr of Well's Peake. We ask for forgiveness. We, the people and aristocrats of Well's Peake, dedicate to you, the beacon of what will become the coat of arms for the World's Fair."

Bernard gripped the blanket and pulled it off. Underneath was Ellie's painting of a bronze tower with three legs, reaching into the clouds on the city's horizon.

"I present to you, the *La Dame Du Peake*, the symbol of hope in the upcoming restoration. This city will rebuild, and we shall stand tall, aiming higher than the sky."

The crowd clapped, and Natalia joined them; however, she did not hear them, feeling numb. The heartache overwhelming her senses.

Bernard raised his arms. "At Aleksandar's side, another rose to the occasion. To be recognized as the Savior of Well's Peake, creator of the Lunarwheel, she stood at the gates of chaos and held her ground. Ladies and gentlemen, Natalia Arlen."

Bernard turned to Natalia and lifted his hand. She stood and walked beside him, looking at Ellie, who wiped tears from her eyes.

Natalia stepped forward, and Bernard shook her hand.

He pulled her close and hugged her. "I'm proud of you."

Natalia held his forearm. "Thank you."

Bernard waved her to the podium, and she stepped forward, lost in her thoughts. She glanced to Ellie and Vida, who held on to each other.

Natalia stood as thousands focused on her, wishing it was a different occasion. She reached inside her pocket for her journal and paused. Licking her lips, she tucked it back in. "I'm not sure I am worthy of such honor. While I had my hand in the matter, Aleksandar was the one who finished my invention. He took my flawed design and transformed it into what saved the city."

Natalia stuttered and rubbed her cheek, her mouth dry. "Pardon me. I grew very fond of Aleksandar over these past few months. He became a close friend, and reminded me of myself at his age. It is a shame I could not have known him better. Aleksandar lived and invented for another, who I think would be proud, and I think we should strive for the same. Our future is uncertain, but we must remember there is life after tragedy."

The crowd applauded, but whispers lingered and Natalia let out a frigid breath.

"We are like leaves in the moonlit forest. While we may fall in the harvest, we flourish through the seasons only to find ourselves as great pines, to one day stand tall and unflinching. Some moments in life shake not leaves but branches from the trees, but we'll make certain we guide the future to where such a tragedy will never be seen again."

The whispers amongst the people grew, several gasping loudly, splitting the crowd down the center.

Natalia looked to the darkening sky, the clouds graying and the snow growing heavy. "As someone once said, we will rise, finding ourselves floating, like an auburn leaf in the harvest wind."

The crowd gasped, and Ellie covered her mouth, her arms reaching out as tears fell along her cheeks. Natalia turned to the commotion, and her lips trembled. Her grip on the podium faded as all the tension in her body released at once. She walked around the podium with weak knees, every fairgoer turning to a man in the center.

Bernard stepped beside Natalia. "It can't be."

Natalia walked to the edge, her breath quivering with each step. Thoughts and memories flooded her mind.

Aleksandar stood hunched over in Ellie's grasp, his clothes bloody and scorched, his eyes bloodshot. His gaze dropped, and he stared at the coffin, his eyes widening as he read the casket with his name on it, the bowler hat resting on top.

Natalia stood tall in the icy wind, water building in her eyes. Snow fell on her shoulders, and her lips parted, thankful to see the young inventor alive in the morning's light.

EPILOGUE

Nicoli gasped for air, arching his stripped body, tied to a workbench with leather straps. He flexed his muscles, pulling his arms as far as possible, his veins popping out of his skin.

His back ached, and his nerves burned as if they were on fire from where the masked man electrocuted him in the spine. His eyes focused as he squinted under the bright lanterns, and his mouth tasted of blood. He could see beyond the light to a ceiling made of white oak, bookshelves lining the room, and a table with metal instruments on top.

Nicoli gazed past his chest, bound in place, and the masked man sat in a chair with his legs crossed, watching with empty eyes. He wore a tailored suit, glaring through his mask.

Nicoli laid his head back and let out a shivering breath. "You just can't leave me alone, can you?"

The masked man stood and walked beside Nicoli, eyeing him. "You brought this on yourself."

"Damn you to whatever hole you came from."

"I did not crawl out of some hole. The truth is much scarier than that. I was bred and cultivated in the very society you look to protect. If you knew where I was raised, maybe you would understand why I do what I do."

"Nothing could ever justify the pain you've caused."

"I fear you are right, but I must do it nonetheless. Not everyone believes in a means to an end, but we are not always given the choice. You had that opportunity, Nicoli, but instead, you could not resist your impulse, no more than I can control mine. You lacked control, manipulated yourself for so long to follow my shadow. I am sorry for the suffering you have endured."

Nicoli looked straight, eyeing the machines above him. They connected to wires and couplings and machines he had never seen before.

Lydia and Rosaline ran through his mind, and he closed his eyes. To be in a safe place, holding his daughter and knowing that she and Lydia were all he needed. The thought of her floral perfume comforting him. He clenched his fists, and he thought of Lydia running her hands through his hair, telling him she loved him.

Nicoli opened his eyes and thrashed around, his wrists cut in the restraints. Blood ran along his arms, and goosebumps stretched up his hips and onto his neck.

The masked man grabbed a rag and wiped his skin clean. "There is no use. You'll lose a hand before you break free. I suggest you relax for what is to come."

"Let me go!" Nicoli shouted.

The masked man walked to the table, and Nicoli pulled with all his might. His spine throbbed, and his feet curled over the edge.

It will not end like this.

The harness around his wrist broke, and he reached for the other. The masked man grabbed the electric rod and jammed it into Nicoli's chest, electricity surging from the tip into his rib cage. He clenched his jaw, and his muscles tightened.

Nicoli collapsed onto the table with a cloudy gaze, his breath showing in the air.

The masked man grabbed another strap and secured Nicoli's hand and head, slipping a pillow under the base of his neck. He picked up thin rolls of brass and copper wire and strung them across the table.

Nicoli looked up and closed his eyes, tears running down his cheeks.

The masked man paused and pulled out a cloth, wiping them away.

"There is no need to cry. I have no intention of killing you."

"Then what will you have of me?"

Without another word, the masked man picked up a bronze device with two prongs. He held it over Nicoli's face, pressed the button, and a spark shimmered on the end. Nicoli swallowed hard as the musk of heated metal filled his nostrils. The masked man carried the Spark to a machine and stuck the device in a socket. He turned it on and pulled a lever.

Static hummed from the wires, and a small jolt shot across the ceiling, Nicoli's hair standing on edge.

"It saddens me we have to resort to such extremes. I need another Kenneth Forbes, but one that is compliant. I know what you will do to protect others."

Nicoli did not look at the masked man again, pressing his lips together, focusing on his breathing.

In and out, full and controlled. Focus on the ceiling. The books. The leather strap. The table. The ceiling, the book, the strap, and the table.

The masked man snapped his fingers, but Nicoli did not flinch, his concentration turning to the metal probe that hummed above him, static flicking off the sides.

"I admire your dedication and determination, Nicoli, and that is why I have chosen you. I'm sure you remember Abel Hawthorne. He was investigating a story that would shake the fabric of our future. Something I need your help in ending. It's why I killed all those inventors to begin with."

Nicoli's eyes widened, and he glanced with disdain.

"The seasons are inevitable, and we must play our part. Accept that truth, accept your past, and you will be free before this is over."

Nicoli gritted his teeth. "You think you can control what's to come, to change what you fear? If so, you're more blind than the rest of us."

"This is why you failed. You let emotions like guilt and anger control you."

The masked man twisted the Spark, and a bluish glow filled the room, reflecting off the white ceiling.

Nicoli's breath grew heavy through his nose as he tried to calm himself, the chill of the bench spreading throughout his body.

White ceiling. Books. Leather strap.

The masked man grabbed a mouthguard and stuck it in Nicoli's mouth. He picked up a curved scalpel and pressed it against Nicoli's skin, dragging it along his arms. Nicoli flinched but held his stare as blood dripped around his arms.

The masked man set thin copper wire into his skin. He opened a door, pulled out a machine of electrodes, and locked it in place. Metal rods hung above him, and a vibration pulsed through the air, warming Nicoli's face.

Mallory. Lydia. Rosaline. Please forgive me.

The masked man grabbed the lever with a firm grip. "I hear you catch serial killers, Mr. Lucas. Let's see where we can find one."

The masked man flipped the lever.

An electric arc surged between the metal probes, jumping from one circuit to another and crackling on impact. Currents riddled the room as they danced off their conduits, shrieking into each other as static built within the machine.

Nicoli took a deep breath and closed his eyes.

Lightning pierced the air, sounding like thunder, and struck Nicoli's shoulder. His veins burned blue, and electricity rippled across his chest. The copper sizzling into his skin.

Lightning surged up his neck and spread across his face, blistering into the corner of his eyes. The workshop glistened, and then the world went dark.

THANK YOU FOR READING

Dear Reader,

I hope you've enjoyed getting to know the inventors and aristocrats of Well's Peake. The World's Fair Saga is just beginning, so if you'd like to follow along, I invite you to sign up for my Readers List on my website, where you'll receive notifications for promotions, giveaways, and more as new books in this saga are released.

I also hope you'll consider dropping an **honest review** on the book store of your choice. Thank you for being a part of this story and entering a world like none other.

Timothy Lyon Jr.

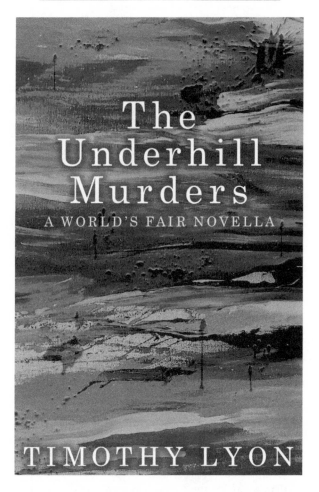

ACKNOWLEDGMENTS

Thank you. All of you. God, my parents, my friends, and more. I could say thank you until it had no meaning and still not have told you enough how much it means to have your support as I chase my dreams, when so many can not.

When I first started writing, I never thought it would consume my life like it has. I may work an extra twenty-five to forty hours a week, thinking and writing late into the night, but I wouldn't change it for the world. Yes, I had to sacrifice some things along the way, but I think all dreams require some. The life of an author can be disheartening occasionally, but it brings a sense of fulfillment I've never experienced. To share a story that many can enjoy and want to talk about is an indescribable feeling.

Thank you, Dad, for letting me live at home so that I could write this book. Mom, thank you for the support over the years. Without you two, I wouldn't be where I am today or have been able to bring this story to life.

I can't thank Alyssa Matesic, Lisa Gilliam, and Rachel Sappie enough for being such incredible editors. Many will never notice the hours and hard work that you all put into this book on every level. Knowing that each of you enjoyed the story kept me hopeful that others will love it as well. It was a joy to work with every one of you, and without your help, *Ashes* would not be the book it is today.

And Rachel, I need to give you special praise. You went above and beyond what a proofreader ever had to do, and I hope you know your talent and skill mean very much to me. I hope my appreciation matched your effort to push Ashes a step further in the right direction.

Thank you, Heather Busse and Jennifer Chase, for taking the time out of your busy lives to beta read *Ashes*. Your suggestions also brought the book to a level it would never have achieved without your involvement.

A special shoutout goes to Josh J., Tabatha R., Billy P., Chris C., Anthony S., Joey K., Forrest K., and Twig L. Some of you, I don't even talk to anymore, and you'll never see this dedication, but without you all, my path as a writer would never have happened. As far back as fifteen years ago, each of you played a pivotal role in sending me in the direction I now face, and I appreciate that. Thank you.

I need to thank my best friend Josh for always standing by my side. You have listened to me talk about my book more than anyone (as much as I've listened to you talk about cars and motorcycles). Thank you for being one of the most supportive people in my life. You have helped me grow into the person I am today. Even when you don't understand what I'm talking about, you've always made an effort to help and understand, and that's more than what most ever would.

I can't imagine the number of people I have bugged with questions like, "What do you think of this?" or "Can you look at this for me?". All of you who I may not even remember asking, thank you.

It took over a year to create the live-action trailer for the *Ashes* book release. It was not without the support of many talented individuals that brought it together after so many ups and very few downs. To all the actors and actresses (Alexis, Devyn, Hannah, Jason, Josh, Matt, Salysa, and Zach), thank you for taking the time out of your days to act in this trailer. For the hundreds of takes of running, getting hit, and looking dramatically into the camera… thank you.

Tabatha Roche, the time and amount of work you put into the visual effects of the book trailer are beyond what I could ever imagine. In one of the busiest times in your life, you kept your promise and helped me with this trailer, and you delivered. I hate that you live so far away, but know despite the distance, our friendship has never faded from our college days. Thank you for being so kind to me, and I hope one day I can return the favor. You're one of my best friends, and I'm so thankful to have met you and Bobby boy.

Patrick Trentini, you were last in a line of several composers that attempted to create what I envisioned as the musical score of the book trailer, and you pulled it off. You worked with my sometimes misdirected perfectionism and produced a piece of music that draws every reader into the trailer. Thank you for your amazing skills and time. I hope this is a piece you can be just as proud of and know I am forever grateful.

Matt, thank you for putting yourself at risk to help create the practical effects in this trailer. It would not have been the same without your talents.

I want to thank the Struthers Library Theatre, and Cynthia Morrison with the Greene Acres Estate for allowing us to film on location for the book trailer.

Kesara Bandara J.M, thank you for illustrating the map of Well's Peake at the beginning of the book. After seven years, seeing this city in front of me was a crazy experience. You put in a lot of work, and I'm sure, painstaking detail into this map, and I'll never forget it.

A special shoutout goes to Joe Garritano at Shadywood Designs Co. (ShadywoodDesignsCo.Etsy.com) for bringing the emblem on the front cover to life. What many don't know is Joe created the piece by hand, and then I photographed it and blended it into the final cover. Without his craftsmanship, the face of this book could have been much different.

Ashes was not a concept that came together all at once. My fascination with the movie, *The Prestige*, and *Hannibal*, the TV series, were two driving factors that created the basic concept for what would become *The World's Fair Saga*. That, with the thoughts of everyday life and creative discussions with people, led to what it you all read today.

And just in case I forgot someone in the previous or following paragraphs, know that I am sorry, that my memory is a little rough, and I can't remember the awesome people who brought this dream to life.

ACKNOWLEDGMENTS

Ashes would not have happened if not for the many who put their faith in me and donated towards the editing costs. Here is a list of some very special people.

A special thank you goes out to Kenan Raffalovich, who helped fund my passion from the very beginning, and with the remaster.

Amanda Nichole
Amy Morningstar
Andrew and Susan Jones
Angela
Bails
Brad and Allison Deeter
Calvert Pearson Insurance Group
Carrie and Jason Peterson
Chris and Erika Cole
Chris Colvin
Edgar and Nancy Burris
Emmie and Alan Buehler
Evalynn Hush and Bentley Andrew
Fred and Beverly Callahan
Hannah Banana
Heather Busse
Heather Lee
Jocelyn Courtney
John Morton
Justin and Margia Hansen
Katelyn Guzman
Katie Rose-Moody
Kris Bines
Kris Delcamp
Lance VanCise
Leslie B.

ACKNOWLEDGMENTS

Maddie Groover

Melissa Rae

Mindi Nobles

Nicole Cope

Queen Colleen

Rachel Buehler Shaffer

Rachel Sappie

Renee Massa

Robert McCoy

Sarah Buehler

Seneca Agens

Sticky Finga the Wandering Wizard and Rachel Bidwell

Taylor Klark

The Corse Family

The Schipani Family

Valerie Eaton

Yaris

Your Biggest Fan - KH

And all those who asked to remain anonymous

THE MASKED MAN

ABOUT THE AUTHOR

Timothy Lyon Jr. grew up in Northwestern Pennsylvania, where he dedicated many hours to his craft of storytelling. He specializes in creating period pieces full of vivid imagery and rich characters that will remain with readers long after the last page turns.

When Timothy is not writing, he enjoys drinking tea, listening to ska music, and testing his hibachi skills.

He is an upcoming author with many tales to share.

Follow on social media and join his mailing list to keep up to date with current projects, giveaways, and more.

timothylyonjr.com
facebook.com/TimothyLyonJr
instagram.com/timothylyonauthor

Photograph by Sarah Elizabeth Photography

CPSIA information can be obtained
at www.ICGtesting.com
Printed in the USA
BVHW030230171121
621838BV00005B/157